Barton-Sinkia, Ginette, 1975-
By the next pause

2018
33305242904567
sa   07/16/19

BY THE NEXT PAUSE

G. BARTON-SINKIA

By The Next Pause
Copyright © G. Barton-Sinkia, 2018
Published by G. Barton-Sinkia, First edition
www.gbartonsinkia.ca
Printed in the United States of America by Ingram Spark
Issued in print and electronic formats
ISBN 978-1-7752102-1-4 (ebook)
ISBN 978-1-7752102-2-1 (paperback)

All rights reserved. No part of this publication may be reproduced, distributed, or transmitted in any form or by any means, including photocopying, recording, or other electronic or mechanical methods, without the prior written permission of the publisher, except in the case of brief quotations embodied in critical reviews and certain other noncommercial uses permitted by copyright law. This is a work of fiction. Any resemblance of characters to persons either living or deceased is purely coincidental. For permission request, write to gbartonsinkia@gmail.ca.

The author wishes to thank Prof. Franz J. Vesely, Ph. D., from the Estate of Viktor Frankl for permission to reprint lines from *Man's Search for Meaning* by Viktor E. Frankl.

Nothing Even Matters
Words and Music by Lauryn Hill
Copyright (c) 1998 Sony/ATV Music Publishing LLC and Obverse Creation Music Inc.
All Rights Administered by Sony/ATV Music Publishing LLC, 424 Church Street, Suite 1200, Nashville, TN 37219
International Copyright Secured All Rights Reserved Reprinted by Permission of Hal Leonard LLC

Edited by Michael Kenyon
Cover Design by Ingrid Paulson
Book Design by E-Book Formatting Fairies
Author Photograph by Desiree Thomas

Library and Archives Canada Cataloguing in Publication:
Barton-Sinkia, Ginette, 1975-, author
By The Next Pause / G. Barton-Sinkia

*This book is dedicated to my husband and children.
I also dedicate it to my grandmother,
Gloria Mollison, who was my lifeline
and inspired me to live my dream.
I love and miss you, Gran.*

PART I

1

Simone's frozen body sat alone on the cold bench, watching a stray German Shepherd scavenge for food. The frost managed to crack some of the red-and-white beads that decorated the ends of her braids. She clutched her thermos full of hot Milo, wishing she wasn't out in the bitter cold so early. She would have preferred to stay snug in her bed, beneath her warm comforter, but according to her mother, it couldn't be helped. It was either be at the school early or not at all.

St. Augustine Elementary looked nothing like the bright, colourful buildings she had been used to in Mandeville. Her Jamaican primary school had beautiful murals on every side of the small building. Local artists had adorned the walls with majestic pictures of Marcus Garvey, Alexander Bustamante, and Bob Marley — Jamaica's national heroes.

She grimaced at the crumbling brick sidings — just old, rusty brick walls. No bright colours; not even art hung on the windows.

She thought of the stories of little kids in New York getting snatched from department stores along with their mothers' purses. It didn't matter that this was North York, Toronto, and not New York City; in her mind, the names were similar, so the cities must be the same too.

Finally, the early morning sun peeked through the frosty air.

As weeks went by, Simone slowly got used to being the first to arrive at school. She became braver, using the early hours to explore the spacious yard. Her favourite mornings were those when she would arrive just after a snowfall. She liked the way the grounds looked, blanketed by white, powdery snow, clean, pure and undisturbed by the hundreds of children who would soon appear.

If the mornings were warm enough, she would lie on the playing field as the snow continued to float down. She would stay perfectly still, allowing the snow to slowly cover her face. She would lie that way until she heard the distant sounds of children playing in the yard, then promptly get up and head back to her spot on the bench, sitting unnoticed until the first bell rang.

It was all she would remember about her first weeks in Canada — the cold, the snow, and the taste of winter. And the sadness. She was starting to forget Jamaica. She remembered the way her Aunt Marva's kitchen looked, and the smell of fresh mint and thyme, but she was starting to forget the names of the friends she'd had at her old primary school and the neighbours who used to greet her on her walk home. The only vivid day in Jamaica she held onto was the one that began with her tethered to her aunt's nightgown, crying out in fear when she looked over to see the old woman lying very still with her eyes wide open, and her lips purple and swollen.

Aunt Marva, or 'Auntie', had been the only constant in her life; the only family member she had left on the island. Simone had been sent to live with her shortly after she was born. She didn't hear much from her parents, with the exception of brief Christmas Eve phone calls from her mother who worked in Canada.

She rarely gave a thought to the fact that she didn't have

parents. It just became a normal part of her life. As far as she was concerned, Auntie was the only family she needed.

That terrible vivid morning, Simone had wrestled with the large safety pin her Auntie often used to secure their nightgowns together for fear that Simone would fall off the giant oak bed. She remembered tearing her nightgown as she finally unhooked herself from the woman's cold body, before frantically calling the telephone operator for help. She remembered sitting in the armchair as one of the constables ransacked the small house, stealing anything of value, before the coroner came to remove the body.

"Just between you and I," he said as he slipped her a $100 Jamaican bill.

She stayed with neighbours for a few weeks before being transferred to a foster home in Saint Ann. She was in the foster home for almost three months before her mother was finally located.

◄◄

"GOOD NEWS, SIMONE," the young social worker said gleefully. "Your mother is aware that your Auntie died and has sent for you! Isn't that wonderful? You're going to be living with your mummy in Canada."

"Is my mummy coming to get me?" Simone asked. Her eyes darted around the room. She wondered how she was going to travel to such a far-off place.

"No, sweetheart," sang the social worker. "You are going to take a plane ride to Toronto all by yourself. Isn't that exciting? Have you ever been on a plane before?"

"No."

"When I was your age, I always dreamt of going on a big plane and visiting far-off places," she said. "What a way! Your first plane ride!"

"Planes crash," Simone said. Her eyes drifted towards the morning paper on the desk, featuring a splashy headline of the Avianca plane crash in Spain.

"Oh no, my dear," said the social worker. She noticed her distraction and pulled the paper off her desk. "This plane is quite reliable. It's from Canada. They are very reliable people." She looked hard at the little girl. "Look, Simone, I'm not going to pretend that everything is going to be peachy-keen, but life is about making the best with what you got. You are lucky to have a mother, especially one who is living in Canada. Not a lot of children even have that much. She sounds like a lovely woman and...*and* she told me she has a good job in a big hospital in Toronto. Can you imagine? A black woman in 1984 working in a *big*-time job like that?"

She could tell that Simone was not all that impressed, looking down at her feet as teardrops stained her brown, leather loafers. She wished she could do something to ease the little girl's fears, so she opened the top drawer of her wooden desk and pulled out a pack of playing cards.

"Look here," she said, opening the fresh pack. "Do you play cards?"

"No, Miss."

Simone looked at the picture of the white sandy beach and crystal-blue ocean with *Jamaica - No Problem, Mon!* printed in bright red on the back of each card and picked one up. "This is pretty," she said. "Is this place in Jamaica?"

"Yes, my dear! It's a beach in Ocho Rios," the social worker said. "I'm going to ask you to do me a big favour. Can I count on you?"

Simone nodded as she flipped through the cards. This was a Jamaica she had never seen before.

"I'm going to give you my special deck of cards. Anytime you feel scared or lonely, I want you to play with them, and it will remind you of home. Maybe you can play with your mother. She probably knows a whole heap of card games."

"Do you know any games?" Simone asked.

"I know a few." She took the cards and started to shuffle them. "Have you ever heard of gin rummy?"

Simone shook her head.

"Well then! Let me show you." She lifted Simone's chin and smiled at her. "It's simple to learn."

A week later, Simone was strapped into her plane seat with her deck of cards and a plate of cheese and crackers. Her eyes grew large as the plane's engines rumbled through bouts of turbulence. Convinced the plane would crash, she mumbled a prayer her Auntie had often said during the heavy rainstorm season.

The flight crew took turns plying her with caramel drops and refilling her cup with root beer. She'd never had root beer before, but she liked the sweet, creamy taste. Midway through the flight, when the plane finally settled, she started to forget her fear of flying and played gin rummy with a few passengers near her. It didn't faze her when the plane shook through a heavy Canadian ice storm. She felt at ease. When the plane finally touched down, she excitedly applauded the pilot's safe landing along with the rest of the passengers.

Simone was the last to disembark, and all of the flight crew, even the pilot, hugged and kissed her. They commended her on how brave she was and filled her pockets with sweets. The most exciting part was talking to the pilot.

"A first-time flyer, eh!" he said. "I'm honoured to have piloted such a beautiful young lady." He pulled off one of the pins he had on his jacket. "Why don't you take this as a souvenir of your very first flight?"

"Thank you, *sah*. You are a good pilot."

"Well, thank you, precious." He pinned the gold-plated wings

7

on the lapel of her jacket. "Stay sweet," he said as he buttoned up her jacket for her. "It's cold outside, so keep warm."

As she walked down the corridor, she quickly looked back at the flight team waving at her and wanted to run back to them, wishing she could stay on the plane, eating caramel drops and drinking root beer forever.

Her eyes teared up as she suddenly felt her stomach turn into twists and knots.

▶▶

"MOM, THERE'S THAT GIRL AGAIN," said Nolan O'Shea as they walked up the path, which was nearly covered in fresh powdered snow.

"What's that?" Meghan O'Shea tucked away her auburn hair beneath her woolen hat. "Walk quickly, Nolan! I don't want to miss my bus. I can't be late for class again."

At the school gate, she knelt to tie the laces of Nolan's winter boots, glancing back to make sure her TTC bus hadn't arrived yet. She stood up and frowned at him before wiping away dried oatmeal that lingered on his cold pink cheek. She then straightened his knitted blue toque that sat on top of his curly brown hair. The young boy squirmed as his mother pushed strands of his hair beneath his winter hat. "Don't forget that your sister is picking you up after school," she said. "I'll be home late tonight, but there is bread and peanut butter for dinner, okay?"

Nolan gave her a look. She had already packed peanut butter and jelly for his lunch. He didn't want it again for dinner. She quickly kissed his cheek before walking back down the slippery walk. She barely caught her bus before it tore off, leaving him behind at the nearly empty school.

Nolan knew that his mother was excited about going back to college, but he hated it! He hated waking up so early to get to school and he didn't understand why his parents argued constantly about his mother getting a college degree. He'd cried when his father moved out because of it and spent most of the evenings home alone. His older sister, Dana, was only home long enough to unlock the front door of their duplex before heading out to be with her friends. "Don't fucking burn the house down," she would say. "And there's a dollar in it if you keep your mouth shut." But most of all he despised peanut-butter sandwiches for dinner. His mother never had time to go to the market anymore, and the only thing that seemed to be in full supply was peanut butter and jelly.

Nolan wished things would go back to the way they were before the fights and the tears and the broken dishes. He missed seeing his mother when he came home from school. He longed for the old Friday nights around the kitchen table with his father grinning and his mother firmly planted on his dad's lap. If his father was in a good mood, he would let Nolan sit with them very late as he told stories of growing up in Toronto when Canada was the greatest. Sometimes his parents would play cards and smoke cigarettes with the neighbours, his father animatedly entertaining everyone with one of his long tales.

Now Nolan was left wondering if things would get better before they got worse. The new setup between his mother and father had been teetering towards disaster for a while.

2

The first time Mike O'Shea decided to check up on his kids, he had stayed away for almost a month. He hoped the time away would prove to Meghan how difficult life was with him away from the home.

He took the afternoon off from work and got his curly ash-brown hair cut short the way she liked it, with a bit of a wave on top and closely shaven on the sides. He stood in front of the mirror and examined the shirt he wore and realized that his old red-checkered flannel shirt looked washed out against his medium build. He pulled out a button-down top she'd bought him for Christmas that matched his crystal-blue eyes and splashed on a little cologne against his rugged face. He hoped that she would admit she missed him and realize that she was needed at home instead of squandering her days in some college classroom.

When he arrived, the duplex was a complete mess. Clean laundry was scattered all over the couch and coffee table in the living room, the kitchen sink was piled high with dirty dishes, and a week's worth of garbage sat by the back door, flies hovering above. And Nolan was trying to light the gas stove pilot in an attempt to cook a can of SpaghettiOs. Point proven.

"Nolan, what the hell are you doing?" He snatched the matches from his son. "Where's your sister? She's supposed to be home with you."

"I dunno," he said, shrugging his shoulders.

"And why is this place such a goddamn mess?" He turned off the stove.

"Dad, don't get mad. It's my fault. Mom told me to have peanut butter sandwiches for dinner, but I wanted spaghetti. I'm sorry, Dad. Don't get mad."

Mike stood in the middle of the kitchen, fuming. He hated the fact that his family was slipping away from him. Things had all gone to hell. He'd known this would happen. The moment Meghan complained that she wanted to go back to school he had told her that the family would fall apart. He only wished that he had fought harder against it.

Last year the discussions had been civil enough, Meghan smiling and telling him the wonderful advantages of going back to school, hoping to sell him on having two incomes to rely on instead of his alone.

"Mikey, I could finish my degree in two years." She nuzzled next to him one night in bed. "There are so many businesses looking for bookkeepers."

"That's too long, Megs!" he said, sitting up. "That's two years of you being away from the kids. I'm already working two jobs. Plus, I'm trying to get us a house. I'm not wasting my money for you to sit in a goddamn classroom. I'm this close to getting enough for a down payment."

"You said that five years ago." She moved away from him. "I'm sick of being stuck at home! Nolan is in school all day. I can do this!"

"Keep your voice down, Megs. You're going to wake the kids."

"Don't fucking tell me to keep my voice down," she continued. "How much money do we really have saved, huh? The money you bring home barely covers the utilities. Forget the goddamn down payment for some fairytale house!"

"What have *we* saved?" Mike replied. "What money have *you* saved, Megs?"

"See, that's what I'm talking about! You work and bring in all the money and hold it over my head. I don't have a say on what happens to this family or even get the right to make decisions for myself because you fucking control everything."

"Calm down, Meghan. Please, I'm sorry!" he said, grabbing for her hand. "That's not what I meant. All I'm saying is that you need to be a little patient. Tommy is going to set me up in the new bar he bought. I'll get shifts on the weekend and weeknights if I have to. Just give it a little more time. Okay? Once I get us in our own house and I'm in a better place, financially, then we can talk more about you going back to school."

"No fucking way, Mike," she said, getting out of bed. She grabbed her pillow and headed for the door. "I don't need your permission to do this. By the end of the year, I'll be enrolled in my first class for the winter semester, with or without you."

Over the months, they continued to bicker over her plans, each discussion more contentious than the last. By the holidays, they were barely on speaking terms and their children spent a miserable Christmas watching their parents avoid each other.

The final straw was when Meghan withdrew money from their savings to pay for her tuition.

Nolan and Dana huddled in their room as their parents screamed at each other. Nolan sat on his bed, covering his ears tightly so he didn't have to hear the dishes being slammed against the wall. It was only when Dana ran into the kitchen, threatening to call the police, that they stopped arguing.

By the beginning of January Mike had moved out.

He had waited patiently for Meghan to see the light. He thought if she was forced to juggle everything on her own, something would give, and she would have to drop out of school. But this evening, when he found Nolan trying to cook his own dinner, he realized that the situation was in dire straits. It had become more than a clash of wills; the safety of his youngest was at stake. Mike didn't want to be proven right that badly.

When Meghan got home she was startled to find Mike in her kitchen washing dishes and Nolan sitting at the table crying as he ate his bowl of spaghetti. She placed her keys on the dining room table and noticed the duffle bag filled with Nolan's clothes.

"What the hell are you doing? Why is there a bag with Nolan's stuff?"

"I'm sorry, Megs, but enough is enough!" Mike said. "Do you know the fucking shit-storm I walked into here? The place is a fucking pigsty, and don't get me started about Nolan. When I came in he was about to burn the fucking place down trying to cook his own dinner...and where the hell is Dana?"

"I don't know where she is." Meghan sat down next to Nolan. "She's supposed to be here."

"Megs, something has to give," he said more calmly. "Nolan is only eight years old! He can't be home alone with no one watching him. You can't have these kids parenting themselves."

"I know."

"Until you get your priorities in order I'm taking Nolan with me," Mike said, hoping that would bring her to her senses.

"Okay," she replied.

"Okay?"

"Yes, take him. Dana is old enough to take care of herself and I need the break. I can't concentrate on school if I'm worried about Nolan."

"You're unbelievable." Mike laughed stiffly. "Un-fucking-believable."

"Stop, Mike. Nolie understands. He gets it." She turned to Nolan. "Right, sweetheart?"

Nolan looked up at his mother in disbelief. There were tears in her eyes.

"I need to concentrate on school," she said as she cupped his face in her hands. "And the only way I can do that is by letting your dad take you for a little while. Just until I get used to my new schedule."

"Is Dana coming too?" Nolan asked her.

Meghan looked up at her husband, who turned away from her. She then looked back at Nolan and smiled at him.

"No sweetie. Dana needs to stay here with me. Your daddy can't manage the both of you. Neither of us can manage the both of you properly on our own. But it will be okay, I promise! It won't be for long. Just until the summer."

Nolan started to cry. "Please, just make it like it was before," he whimpered. "Please, Mommy...please, Dad! I promise I'll be good."

Mike stood and watched. He didn't know what to say because he also wanted their old life back. He wanted to come home and for them to be the family they had been before everything got out of hand. Before the yelling and screaming. Before the love between them started to strain. He could feel the fallout as he watched Meghan hug and kiss Nolan, promising him that everything would change for the better.

3

Mike continued to work long hours. He was even more determined to save enough money for a house. He still hoped that having a home of their own would prove to Meghan that he was a man of his word and she would come back to him. For Nolan, though, nothing really changed when he moved in with his dad. All it meant was that, instead of coming home to his father in the evenings, he came home to the neighbour down the hall in the apartment building they lived in.

He still had to wake up early to meet his mother at the corner and they would both take the 7:00 am bus so that Meghan could drop him off at school before her classes. Each morning, he shrugged off her hug as he went into the school grounds, angry that he had to sit alone on the cold bench to wait for the rest of the students to arrive.

The only consolation was that he wasn't completely alone. He sat on the bench watching the new black girl with her big round almond eyes and funny accent, as she played in the snow. She was always there, and he often wondered if she ever went home at night. He would sit next to her school bag and thermos and watch her make snow angels in the field. He wanted to join her but was too shy.

She was in the other second-grade class and all he knew about her was that her name was Simone and she always wore colourful beads at the ends of her braids. He liked the way the plastic beads clicked against one another any time she turned her head. And the way they hung along her pretty light brown face, almost covering her left eye.

He noticed that she kept to herself most of the time. She didn't have any friends and spent most of recess sitting in a corner, reading a book. The few times she did speak, some of the older kids would tease her Jamaican accent. Her face would turn a shade of red and she would quickly retreat behind her book.

The first time he saw her outside of school was in the elevator of his building. He was coming home with his dad from a high school hockey game when Simone and her mother walked into the elevator. They all stood uncomfortably as the elevator slowly went up. Neither parent made eye contact or even politely acknowledged the other. Nolan noticed Simone's mother pulling her closer.

They all got out on the same floor and Simone's mother quickly rushed her down the hall. Their apartment was right next door.

"Isn't that a bitch?" said Mike. "I don't know what the hell she's so scared of. As if she has anything to steal."

"Shhh, Dad! They can hear you."

"I don't give a crap what they hear," Mike said loudly as their door slammed shut.

It made Nolan cringe when his father talked like that. He was glad it was his mother who took him to school. At least she kept her comments under her breath. His father always said exactly how he felt, loud enough for everyone to hear.

Mike's favourite topic of conversation was how St. Augustine had gone down the dumps over the years and how it wasn't the same when he had attended as a child. During his time, the school's student population had been primarily Irish and Scottish students. The most exotic student he had known was a francophone Métis student from Quebec whose family eventually moved to Winnipeg.

When Dana started at St. Augustine, Italians, Germans and students from almost every country in Eastern Europe were slowly diluting the pool. By the time Nolan had started junior kindergarten, children from all over the world over-populated the school. Students with parents from India, Colombia, El Salvador, Jamaica, and China were now the mainstays for most Willowdale schools.

"A complete mess," is what Mike said of St. Augustine's new makeup. "You have half the school speaking every other language like the goddamn Tower of Babylon and the other half speaking piss-poor English."

Nolan nodded mindlessly when his father went into one of his rants. None of what his father said mattered. It didn't bother him that some of his friends spoke a different language or what area of the world their families were from. As long as they played baseball as well as he did and had their own gloves, he didn't care.

He also didn't care that his best friend was a Jamaican Canadian boy named Kester Daniels — the class clown who constantly made other students laugh with his antics. The two boys had been inseparable since kindergarten, with Kester the short persuasive leader, and Nolan content with being his most loyal friend and sidekick.

Kester's family had emigrated from Jamaica but he and his three older siblings were born and raised in Toronto. While most children of immigrants struggled to be more Canadian, Kester had easily assimilated. His strong Canadian diction made Nolan's own accent sound foreign.

Kester was always setting the trend for the kids in their class. When most of the boys were excitedly awaiting the beginning of the NHL season, Kester quickly converted them into diehard basketball fans and had them trading Kareem Abdul-Jabbar sports cards. When "Pass the Dutchie" first played on the radio, he became so obsessed with the song that most of his classmates started humming it, and they were even repeating the dirty patois sayings he taught them during gym class.

During lunchtime, they often huddled together and swapped out their packed lunches. Kester loved Nolan's peanut butter and jam sandwiches, while Nolan loved the leftover dinners Kester brought from home.

"What the hell is this shit in your lunch box," Mike said, sniffing Kester's container of food as he cleared out Nolan's lunch pail one morning.

"It's not shit," Nolan said as he ate his oatmeal. "It's curry chicken and rice."

"Well, where did you get curry chicken and rice?" he asked as he tried to wash off the yellow sauce that stained his fingers.

"My friend's mother makes it for his lunch."

"Which friend?"

"My friend Kester. He's in my class."

"Are you stealing this kid's lunch?" Mike asked. "I won't tolerate that crap from you, Nolan."

"No...no, Dad! We trade lunches sometimes."

"Nolan, I make lunches for you and you alone. Not for some kid who eats this slop."

"Curry chicken," Nolan said as he stared down his father. "Not slop."

"Watch your tone." He poured Nolan some orange juice. "Why haven't I met this Kester kid? Where's he from?"

"He lives in Toronto," Nolan replied.

"I figured that, Nolan. Where's his family from?"

"Jamaica," Nolan mumbled.

"Jamaica, huh!" Mike said. "Since when did you start hanging out with Jamaicans?"

"Since always, Dad. There are a few kids in my class that are from there."

"Yeah, well, when I went to St. Augie, all there were was Irish and Scots and we barely got along," he railed. "Now the school is infested with niggers from Jamaica and every other piece of trash from around the world. A regular fucking shit pile."

Nolan sat at the kitchen table trying to block his father's morning rant about how great St. Augie was when he went there. How the school was practically brand-new and everyone wore crisp uniforms and had pride in themselves.

"Why haven't you brought this Kester over?"

"I don't know," he shrugged. "He lives too far, I guess."

"Where does he live?"

"I think he lives in the houses near the ice rink."

"Well, la-di-dah. Isn't that special. I live here all my life and have to scrape and scrimp for us to get a house and some kid from the Bahamas lives in a house on Bayview!"

"Jamaica, Dad…not Bahamas."

"Whatever, the point is it's a new world these days," he went on. "Guys like me work our asses off and some trash from Jamaica comes to Canada…probably on the government's dime and gets a bloody house."

Mike's morning rants usually ended with him complaining about how everyone was taking all his opportunities. If it wasn't Blacks, it was immigrants, women, Protestants, even the blind man down the hall was taking some opportunity that should have gone to him and would have if only the son-of-a-bitch wasn't blind.

Mike could never admit the real reason why he wasn't able to move up in life. He preferred to blame everyone else instead of accepting the fact that he'd cut his own opportunities short by dropping out of high school his senior year. After Meghan got pregnant with Dana, he had quit school, got married and worked odd jobs to provide for his family.

Meghan had managed to get her GED before giving birth to Dana, but Mike felt it was useless for him to do, since he wasn't planning to go to college. He couldn't understand why someone would spend time and money on school unless they were working towards being a doctor or a lawyer.

He spent the next five years working in construction until he finally landed a part-time job working as a building engineer for Ryerson University. When he decided that he wanted to own his own home, he started working for St. Augustine Church on the weekends as their facility manager, which was just a fancy word for church janitor.

Nolan sat at the breakfast table playing with his oatmeal as his father droned on about the meaning of hard work and not expecting handouts. Nolan was glad when he finally heard the buzzer. He got up quickly to grab his bag and meet his mother in the lobby.

"Go on now," said Mike. "Your mother won't let me hear the end of it if she misses her bus."

"Okay, Dad." Nolan shoved his lunch pail and Kester's curry chicken container in his school bag.

"Alright, buddy." Mike kissed the top of Nolan's head. "Have a great day at school. I hope this Kester boy likes jam sandwiches."

"He does," he said, heading out the door.

◀◀

SHE SAT WATCHING Simone slowly spoon out the leftover milk from her cereal bowl. She glanced at her watch.

"Simone! I don't have time for you to nurse your milk all day. Let's go! Let's go! Let's go!"

Simone quickly guzzled the rest of her milk by tipping the bowl to her mouth, spilling it on the dining table.

"Clean that up," her mother said, jumping back before any of the milk spilled on her black pleated skirt. "Hurry, nuh! I don't want to miss the bus. I'm not going to be late for work today."

"Yes, Ms. Pam," Simone said rushing to the sink to grab a kitchen towel to wipe up the spilt milk.

It irritated her every time Simone called her Ms. Pam. It was what the airline representative had used to introduce them: "Ms. Pam, I presume?" she had said as she held Simone's hand. "I believe this little one belongs to you."

Simone had looked her up and down. She had stuttered trying to call her Mummy and ended up saying Ms. Pam instead. Pam had hoped that after a while she would try Mama or even Mother but she ended up sticking with Ms. Pam. It bothered Pam. She was a young slender woman with light brown complexion and wavy black hair that fell past her shoulders. Her petite stature complimented her refined face and high cheekbones. Calling her "Ms. Pam" made her feel old.

Living with Simone wasn't easy from the beginning. Pam tried to connect with her but each failed attempt left a sour taste in her mouth and it didn't help that she found Simone's quirks annoying. The way she took forever to eat her meals, carefully chewing each bite a hundred times before swallowing, the long showers in the mornings that made her late for work.

At first, she held her tongue. After all, it was as much of an adjustment for Simone as it was for her. But patience wasn't Pam's strong suit. She had never lived with a child. Children were noisy and messy, and Pam was very particular about everything. The house was to be quiet and pristine and she wouldn't tolerate dishes left in the sink or clothes dropped on the floor. It didn't matter that Simone was seven years old—she was expected to keep the apartment neat and tidy.

When Simone finally cleaned up the spilt milk, Pam hurried them out of the apartment and down the eleven flights of stairs instead of waiting for the elevator. It was still pitch dark and freezing as she hustled them up the pathway towards the bus stop just as the bus pulled up. They sat in the back by the rear window. It started to rain again. She looked over at Simone and frowned. Her daughter hadn't brought the umbrella she had bought her.

"Here," she said passing Simone her own umbrella. "Don't lose it."

"Yes, Ms. Pam," Simone replied sleepily as she took the umbrella.

Pam looked at her watch and then out the window. The rain continued to drizzle. She hated leaving so early but it was the only way she could get Simone to school and herself to work on time. The only solace she had was that they weren't sitting in the freezing rain waiting for the next bus. In Jamaica, rain was refreshing and made everything greener and the air cleaner, but Toronto's freezing rain always left her miserable. In fact, Canadian winters often left her depressed. Some would find snow-capped rooftops beautiful, but she groaned, knowing that she had to wallow through the muddy slush.

"Snow is only a luxury for white people," she would grumble to herself any time she had to navigate an icy patch. She missed the warmth of Jamaica's early morning sunrise—that special time in the morning when it was cool enough to catch the mountain breeze but warm enough to feel the sun penetrate her skin. She missed the bright orchids and ackee trees that stood by her bedroom window. Now she was greeted with dreary grey days and wet snow that seeped through her boots. The irony wasn't lost on her that she had had to leave paradise to find peace. She only wished that the Canadian winters didn't serve as a constant reminder of the irony.

She couldn't afford to look back. In Jamaica, her ghosts haunted her and knew her by name. Back home she was that girl — that tragic girl. Here in Toronto, she was nobody. Just a young educated black woman with a good job as a hospital administrator. She was a newly minted Canadian citizen and Jamaica had to stay in the past where it belonged but all of that changed when her aunt died.

When the Canadian Child Welfare Agency contacted her about her aunt's death, every fibre in her body wanted to deny that she was Simone's mother. She didn't know the first thing about raising a child. She was barely an adult herself. She lived in a one-bedroom apartment with a girlfriend and slept on a twin mattress on the floor. She had just gotten a job at the hospital and had only a little money saved. She went to her parish priest in tears and told him she didn't know what to do and should she give Simone up for adoption?

Her priest eased her fears by putting her in touch with different government agencies that helped her and, by the time Simone arrived, Pam was on government assistance and had secured a small, subsidized, two-bedroom apartment in a safe neighbourhood. Being a single mother was never ideal, but in Toronto it was possible.

The Crescent View Apartment Complex wasn't a dream come true. It was a little farther away from her job, but it was fairly close to Simone's new school. The complex was bordered by the 401 highway and had four 15-story buildings arranged in a circle. In the centre of the circle was a huge courtyard that enclosed a children's park and an empty rusted outdoor swimming pool lined with mud and dead leaves. The greyish white buildings were weathered and worn from the cold harsh winters. Despite the newly refurbished lobby, the hallway's grey speckled carpets constantly looked filthy, with slush, salt, and mud embedded in their fibres. Each floor was dimly lit and had a musty mildew smell that competed with the strong scent of curry that seeped through the walls.

They lived on the 11th floor, overlooking the courtyard. Their apartment wasn't big and spacious but it was clean and large enough for the two of them. The only problem was the shared balcony. She didn't like the idea of sharing the space with anyone and hoped that the family living next door wouldn't be a complete pain in the ass.

As the bus pulled up to St. Augustine, Pam pulled the bell. She was grateful that the rain had stopped for the time being. They walked slowly up the hill towards the school, attempting to avoid the slippery patches of ice on the sidewalk.

"Excuse me, Miss!"

Pam looked up to see a pudgy woman in a heavy red down-filled coat rushing through the school's gate towards them.

"Is who this?" she asked Simone.

"The vice principal," Simone replied.

The woman slipped and slid towards them, her plump face red as she tried to catch her breath. "I'm sorry," she said, wheezing in the cold icy air, "but you cannot leave a student here before the school opens."

"Who are you?" Pam asked.

"I apologize," she said, pulling in her jacket against the wind. "I'm Mrs. Wilson, St. Augustine's vice principal."

"Yes, well, Mrs. Wilson, it is nice to meet you, but my bus is about to arrive." Pam handed Simone her school bag. "If I don't leave now I'll be late for work."

"Hold on!" Mrs. Wilson said. "It's 6:30 am in the morning. We don't officially open our gates until 8:00 am. You need to stay until then. It's not safe to leave this child alone."

"I appreciate your concern for Simone but, as I said, I am going to be late for work," Pam said as calmly as she could. "Simone has been instructed to sit on the bench until school starts. She has been doing that for the last two months. She will be fine."

"I'm sorry, Mrs..."

"Ms. Allen," Pam responded.

"Ms. Allen, I'm not sure if you are aware but it's against the law to leave minors by themselves. If you insist on leaving your daughter unattended I will have to get the authorities involved."

"A fool you take me?" Pam said. "Do you realize that I have to work and that the only way I can get Simone to school is to drop her off beforehand?"

"Maybe you can rearrange your work hours or have her father take her to school," Mrs. Wilson said, smiling stiffly. "Assuming that Simone's father is involved in her life."

Pam was stunned.

The vice principal continued to smile at the young mother. She knew the type. She saw it all the time. A young woman from the islands who probably wasn't married but had two or three kids from different men. These women came by the boatload, bringing in their bastard children, expecting a handout from hardworking taxpayers like herself. She was surprised this one actually had a job.

"You're here now," Pam said steadily, gritting her teeth. "Can't you let her stay with you this one time while I try to make arrangements with my employer?"

"I'm not here to be your child's babysitter. I suggest you sit tight until the gate officially opens."

Pam wanted to slap the smile off her face but couldn't afford to lose her temper. Without a word, she pulled Simone's hand and they walked back down the sidewalk.

"Where are you going?" Mrs. Wilson called out.

"I'm taking my daughter back home," she yelled back, dragging Simone down the sidewalk. "Simone is sick and won't be in school today."

"Typical," Mrs. Wilson uttered to herself.

Just then Nolan and his mother rushed past them towards the school gates.

"Not another one." Mrs. Wilson turned to Nolan's mother. "You Irish are just as bad as the Jamaicans."

▶

WHEN PAM GOT HOME, she called in sick and then pulled out the Yellow Pages, hoping to find a suitable daycare or sitter at the last minute, but all the places she called were either too far from the apartment or too expensive. She had almost nothing in her savings after moving into the apartment.

She had no idea what she was going to do. She thought about talking to her boss about adjusting her hours but quickly dismissed the idea. Part of her job was to start early in the morning to check in patients. As for today, she debated having Simone stay home by herself but didn't trust her alone in the apartment.

She was taking out the garbage that afternoon when she noticed the little boy next door about to walk into Mrs. Price's apartment across the hall. Mrs. Price was her Jamaican neighbour.

"You!" she said to Nolan. "I saw you this morning. You go to Simone's school?"

"Yes," he said, squirming.

He stood in the hallway, a little startled and frightened, worried that he was in trouble. Pam could tell that she was making him nervous and smiled at him. He relaxed and smiled back at her.

"Why are you going into Mrs. Price's apartment? Don't you live next door?"

"Yes, Ma'am," he replied. "She takes care of me after school."

"Nolan, is who you talk to?" asked Mrs. Price as she opened her door. "Lawd, Ms. Pam. Is yuh out here with Nolan?" She quickly ushered him in and instructed him to start his homework.

"I'm sorry, Mrs. Price," said Pam. "Mi didn't realize yuh were watching de boy."

"Yes, Mam. Him fadda give mi ah lickle money to watch him."

Pam clapped her hands for joy and hugged her.

Mrs. Price looked at her a little confused.

"Mrs. Price, how much you charge?"

When Pam returned to the apartment she was humming to

herself and grinning like a Cheshire cat. She had completely forgotten about nosey Mrs. Price.

Lineve Price hailed from Jamaica and had moved to Toronto in the 1960s with the first wave of immigrants from the island. After her husband died, she worked as a bank teller for almost fifteen years before arthritis forced her into early retirement. She had been living on disability in the complex for almost ten years by the time Pam and Simone arrived and she often babysat kids in the building to make extra money.

Pam had met Mrs. Price the first day they moved into their apartment. She had not unpacked a single box before the old woman came knocking on her door with a spice bun and a million questions. By the end of the visit, Mrs. Price had gone through Pam's entire family tree, remembering and calling out several of her family members that had died years before. She had grown up in St. Elizabeth, a neighbouring parish of Manchester, and had even gone to the same school as Pam's Aunt Marva.

"Yes, Mam! Mi know aal yuh people," she said smiling. "Lawd Jesus! What a small world! Whatever happened to your fadda? Last mi hear, he still living in Kingston."

"My father is no longer with us," Pam said. "He passed years ago."

"Yes...yes," Mrs. Price remembered before pausing. She looked up at Pam and stared at her before she started to make the connection. "Lawd Jesus! I remember you now...oh...yes...it's now mi remember."

Pam's face burnt hot as Mrs. Price looked at her with pity. She had hoped to leave her past behind, but it was clear now that, no matter how far she ran, she would never escape it.

The old woman picked up Pam's hand and patted it. Pam quickly withdrew it and moved away. Mrs. Price could see how uncomfortable Pam seemed and took her leave, saying she was right down the hall if she needed her.

Pam had been angry with herself for saying too much. Her

anxiety had bubbled up as she watched Simone playing with her deck of cards on one of the moving boxes. But now Mrs. Price had become her saving grace. She hated having to rely on anyone, but the school left her no choice. It would have to be Mrs. Price. She didn't have the time or patience to figure out something better.

When Pam came back into the apartment, with the garbage bag still in her hand, she was humming. Simone looked at her mother curiously.

"Mrs. Price is going to watch you in the mornings and after school," Pam announced.

"But you said you didn't want me talking to her," Simone said. "You said that I'm to stay away from her."

"Yes, well, that was before my meeting with your bitch of a principal," Pam muttered. "Don't repeat my bad words, but right now Mrs. Price is the best I can do. Just make sure you keep your mouth shut around her. Whatever happens in this apartment is none of her business. Her only business is to make sure you catch the school bus in the mornings and that you come straight home after. Do you hear me?"

Simone nodded at her mother. She was glad that Mrs. Price would be watching her. She didn't know the old woman very well but any time she saw her in the hallway she always had a warm smile on her face. She was also glad that she didn't have to wake up so early to go to school.

"Simone, go and take the garbage to the chute," Pam said, handing her the bag. "And don't hang about. Dinner is going to be ready soon."

Simone grabbed the garbage bag and headed out the door. Nolan was in the hallway with his father and he looked over and smiled at her. She smiled back at him. She liked Nolan. He was the only kid at school who didn't tease her about her accent.

"Hi, Nolan," she said.

"Hi, Simone," he replied. "How come you weren't at school today?"

"Mrs. Wilson wouldn't let my mother leave me at the school so early," she said. "We had to go back home."

"Yeah, I saw you guys," he said. "Mrs. Wilson let my mom leave me in the office. Why didn't you stay in the office like I did?"

Simone shrugged.

"I'm going to stay at Mrs. Price's before and after school now," she said.

They walked together down the hall to the garbage chute.

"I stay with Mrs. Price too," he said smiling at her. "Maybe we can sit together on the bus."

"Sure," Simone said.

They both turned when Nolan's father called after him.

"I have to go," Nolan said. "I'll see you tomorrow?"

"See you tomorrow," she said.

4

P am met him at a dance in Toronto. Her hair was freshly coiffed and she was wearing a lapis blue chiffon dress that flowed down to just above her knees. She smelled of the cocoa butter that she had lathered on her body to mask the lye relaxer she had applied earlier that morning. She hoped he wouldn't notice it as he spun her around the wooden gymnasium floor.

She didn't dare look up at him. She felt strangely shy, fearful that if she looked into his hazel eyes she would blush. Instead, she looked off to the side, concentrating on their locked hands, as they slowly danced to Patti LaBelle's "If Only You Knew". She focused on the beauty of their hands, the way his rich dark brown complexion complimented her creamy honey-coloured skin.

She could feel the tension inside her heighten as he pulled her closer. She was never usually this timid around a man. She had perfected building walls around herself to protect her from ever showing weakness but this man — he was different — he left her breathless.

It wasn't the first time she had laid eyes on him. She had noticed him the previous year, at one of the many Jamaican Canadian Association parties she attended. Back then, he had worn a purple silk shirt, unbuttoned, and was dripping with sweat with some girl on his arm.

But this time he had come alone and he was dancing with her.

The dance led to dinner the next weekend, a movie the following weekend and, before she knew it, four months had passed and she was his woman and finally felt like she could find happiness.

He was different from most of the island men she knew. He didn't live in the dance halls on the prowl. He was a simple man. A nice guy. Which was maybe why most women grew bored with him after the first date. He liked to spend quiet evenings in his basement apartment listening to music or out on the fields playing cricket. He had dreams. He wanted to be an investment banker. He took classes during the day, hoping to earn a degree in finance, and at night he drove a cab to pay for school.

Pam thought he was the perfect man. Someone she could centre her life on. A man she had chosen for herself. Someone who adored her, despite her moody disposition and quick temper. A man who looked at her with a glow in his eyes — a look meant only for her.

He never called her Pam. Her name was too beautiful to be shortened, he said. He always addressed her as Pamela. And, when he introduced her, it wasn't as his girlfriend, only as 'his future wife' or 'the mother of his six sons'. It tickled her that she had someone in her life who cherished her. It gave her a sense of relief that her life was coming together. But all of that quickly changed when the call from Kingston came, dragging her past back to the surface.

Pam had shared little information with Caleb about Simone. The most she revealed was that she had a child living in Jamaica. He never asked and she never divulged anything further, but now that Simone was coming to Canada she was a reality that Caleb had questions about; she could no longer be a name without a face.

"Why did you leave her in Jamaica?" he asked. "What about her father?"

"It's difficult to go into," she always replied. "Can we not talk about this now?"

When Simone arrived, Pam kept Caleb at bay. It wasn't that she didn't want him to meet Simone, but she wanted to get to know the girl first before any introductions were made — before any explanations were given.

"Not yet. Soon," she said, nestled in his arms as they lay in his bed. She had left Simone with Mrs. Price that Saturday evening in order to be with him.

"Pamela, I don't understand why you feel the need to wait so long. You're not the first woman I've dated with children."

"You don't understand," she said.

"No I don't," he said as he got up to get dressed. "It's like you have something to hide."

"I don't," she stammered.

"Get dressed," he said tossing her clothes at her. "If you don't want a relationship, then say so."

"When the raas did this become about us?"

"Pamela, she yuh pickney," he said. "She a part of you and when you don't want to introduce her to the man you claim to love, how it look? What's holding you back?"

Pam sat at the edge of his bed for a while, then she silently got dressed.

"Pamela, I love you and will love her, too," he said. His voice was soft. "I just want to meet her so we can stop all this sneaking around."

Reluctantly, she agreed to have Caleb meet Simone the next evening. She prepared Caleb's favourite — lasagna with Caesar salad; she dressed Simone in her best outfit and told her daughter that they were having a friend over for dinner.

The moment Simone met Caleb, she knew that this was her mother's mysterious boyfriend.

Caleb was so pleased. His eyes lit up when he saw the pretty girl with her hair braided in two, wearing a red-checkered dress. She had Pam's delicate features and dark brown eyes — the kind of questioning eyes that pierced into people.

He went all out to win Simone over. He complimented her dress and told her that she was pretty like her mother, but Simone barely gave him a smile. When he presented her with the doll he had bought her she quickly informed him that she didn't play with dolls anymore.

"Well then," he said. "What do you do for fun?"

"I read," she said, handing him back the gift. "You can have your doll back."

"Simone!" Pam barked. It was exactly what she had been afraid would happen. Simone was being politely rude to Caleb, showing the same indifference that she had shown her over the last few months. "I won't tolerate any facety behaviour from you," she said. "Pick up the doll and put it in your room."

"Yes, Ms. Pam." Simone went into her room and tossed the doll on the floor by her bed before coming back to the dinner table.

"Yes! Yes! Yes!" Caleb said gleefully as he cut into the bubbling hot lasagna. "Simone, did you know that your mother's lasagna is the best in the world?"

Simone sat there staring at him as he cut a piece for her. She looked at her full plate and wasn't sure how it would taste in her mouth. She had heard of lasagna, but it looked like someone had chewed up the food and spat it out. She took her fork and stabbed it, trying to separate the spinach from what looked like meat, but the gooey cheese made it impossible.

"Eat your food," Pam said curtly.

"Don't you like lasagna?" Caleb asked.

She shrugged and continued to play with her food.

"What's your favourite food?" he asked.

"Not this," she said.

Pam flashed her a look as if she was going to slap some manners into her, but Caleb grabbed Pam's hand and kissed it.

"Ms. Pam, can I be excused?" she asked. "I'm not hungry."

"Fine," she replied.

Simone carried her plate into the kitchen and threw out the lasagna. She grabbed a handful of cookies, stuffed them in the pocket of her dress, and headed back to her room.

"Well," Caleb said as he polished off his dinner. "She's an interesting girl."

"Now do you understand why I've been avoiding this meeting?" Pam said, glaring at him.

Throughout the evening, Pam was further embarrassed by how Simone was acting. The quiet and respectful little girl who had emerged from the plane had turned into a mouthy pretentious know-it-all. It irritated her how rude Simone was to Caleb, treating him like one of her schoolyard friends. But Caleb loved it. He was tickled by her smart remarks.

"Don't sweat it, Pamela," he said.

"Don't encourage her," Pam snapped.

Next morning, while Pam was washing the breakfast dishes, Simone sat at the table playing with a plate of scrambled eggs that Caleb had prepared for her. She complained that the eggs were too hot, and ten minutes later she sulked because the eggs were too cold and nasty to eat. Pam wanted to pull her from the table by her neck but Caleb merely laughed it off and poured her a bowl of cornflakes instead. After she finished her breakfast, Simone got up from the table, leaving her cereal bowl behind, and went back to her bedroom.

Pamela sucked her teeth and glared. "Not even a thank you." She picked up Simone's plastic bowl and tossed it in the sink.

"Come on, Pamela," Caleb teased, pulling her into his arms. "You have a bright one there."

"Don't do that," she said pulling away from him. "You wash

over her rudeness with a joke and what she really needs is a box across that smart mouth."

"Yes, there is some cheek in her, but rather a cheeky girl than some of these lazy children." He polished off the last piece of bacon. "And what more can you ask in a child? You say she keeps her room clean and does well in school…"

"Barely," Pam interrupted. "Her smart mouth is constantly getting her in trouble. Last week her teacher call me. She want me to miss half a day of work so I can hear her complain about Simone's bad attitude. You know, I don't think there is one adult that child shows any manners to."

"Well, I don't know about that," he grinned as he got up for more coffee. "She's starting to like me."

"Ya fool, ya," Pam said. She couldn't help laughing. "Which part of 'nasty eggs' tells you that she likes you?"

"Well she ate the bowl of cornflakes I poured her," he replied. "I call that progress."

▶

It wasn't that Simone hated Caleb. She just hated her mother more. Simone hadn't expected a huge reception when she arrived from Jamaica, but she had hoped for maybe a hug, a kiss on the cheek, and some sort of explanation as to why she had been abandoned all those years ago. Instead, all she received was a winter coat and a chilly "Welcome to Canada."

The weeks after were no better. Her mother was unbearable with her never-ending list of strict rules. No playing outside unless Pam was there to supervise. No playing in the hallway. No television during the week. No reading past bedtime. No leaving the lights on. Every day there was a new rule. There wasn't anything she was allowed to do.

In retaliation, she had decided to make Pam's life equally difficult. When Pam was busy and Simone had to answer the phone, she purposely wrote down the telephone number wrong. When her mother yelled a lot at her, Simone would unravel the hems of her skirts or pull off the middle button of a blouse and flush it down the toilet.

Most of what she did never fazed Pam. She knew her friends' telephone numbers by heart and had a cookie tin filled with extra buttons to replace the lost ones. What pushed Pam over the edge was the backchat. While Caleb enjoyed bantering with Simone, Pam cringed whenever Simone opened her mouth. She was always kissing her teeth at him, calling everything he did "stupid." She was not used to children speaking to adults that way and whipped Simone's behind whenever Caleb wasn't around.

Simone started to warm up to Caleb when he began sticking up for her. He was always running interference, trying to keep the peace between them.

And Caleb hated to see Simone always in trouble, so when Pam wasn't around he would try to talk to the little girl. "I know you can be a good girl," he would say, sneaking her some mints. "Promise that you'll listen to your mother."

Simone would only sigh and nod as she popped the candy in her mouth. She would agree to anything for candy.

But Caleb's attempts to mend their relationship only served as a band-aid to a deeper infliction. Something that candy couldn't mend.

▶

SIMONE SAT OUTSIDE HER CLASSROOM, listening to the mumblings between her teacher and Pam grow to a feverish pitch. She didn't know what was being said, but she could hear her mother yelling at Mrs. Zennewich in patois. It was the first time she had heard her mother speak in the Jamaican dialect. Patois was kitchen talk, usually reserved for other Jamaicans. Pam never spoke the dialect to strangers.

When Pam came out of the classroom, she grabbed Simone by the arm and stormed out of the school. They barely spoke on the way home. And when Simone asked her what had happened, Pam just ignored her and continued cussing to herself.

That night, Simone heard Caleb and Pam arguing. She had never heard them argue that much before and started to worry that her mother's meeting with her teacher had been more than a discussion about her attitude. She got out of bed and stood outside Pam's bedroom door. She could hear Caleb telling Pam that Simone was gifted and that her talents needed to be encouraged, not held back.

"Do you think they care how gifted and talented she is?" Pam said. "To them, she's a nehgah first and gifted last. She doesn't need to be told that she's special. She needs to work harder."

"How much harder do you expect her to work, Pamela?" he said. "You're already too hard on her."

"And I'm hard on her so that she can handle herself in the real world. In the real world, they will kick her arse more than I will."

"Do you hear yourself? Where's the war? She's a little girl who needs her mother to be on her side, not telling her that everything she does is wrong."

"Yeah, well."

"Pamela, if the whole world is out to kick her arse then shouldn't you be the one person that's there for her?"

"You know what!" Pam shouted. "Fi mi business how I parent that child. I don't need you telling me what to do!"

"I don't get it," he said. "You've had this anger towards her the moment she stepped off the plane. What's making you so bitter? Why you bother bring her to Toronto if you planned to be this miserable?"

"Do you think I wanted her here? She's my bloody cross to

bear. My constant reminder! You know nothing about what I had to deal with. What I still deal with!"

Silence.

"I'm not trying to upset you," he said softly. "I'm trying to help."

"Well, go be Donahue to someone else," she said. "I think it's best that you go home now."

He walked past Simone lurking in the shadows and slammed the front door. Simone quickly scurried to her room. She jumped into her bed and pulled the covers over her head and, as her mother's harsh words laid waste to her mind, she started to sob. She used her pillow to stifle her cries but her tears continued to fall steadily, barely leaving her room to breathe.

On her way to the bathroom, Pam walked past Simone's room and heard the muffled cries and stopped and listened. She didn't know what to say or how to comfort her daughter. She wanted to love the little girl. She was her own flesh and blood, yet she couldn't put into words why she felt nothing but resentment for her. Instead, Pam went on to the bathroom, then back to her bedroom and quietly closed the door behind her.

Simone woke at dawn with a dull feeling inside. She spent the morning in bed, refusing to get up even when Pam called for her. Eventually, the anger left and she fell back asleep, plotting her escape from her unfeeling mother.

When she finally awoke she felt her bed tilt. She slowly opened her eyes to see that it was raining outside her window. When she turned she saw Caleb smiling down at her.

"Well good afternoon, sleepyhead," he said. "Your mum said that you were not feeling well today."

Simone nodded.

"Your mother made some pepper-pot soup," he said. "It's in the kitchen whenever you're ready to eat something."

She nodded again.

"And I got you something." He pulled out a pink and green notebook. "This is for you."

Simone sat up. She looked at the notebook. It was beautiful, with soft cream-coloured lined sheets with gold edges.

"Do you like it?" he asked. "It has a lock and a key so that you can keep it private. You know…"

"A diary," she said as tears spilled down her cheek.

"Yes, a diary," he said, grinning.

"Thank you, Caleb," she said, wiping her tears with the back of her hand.

"Do you like it?" he asked again.

"Yes." She nodded. "I like it."

"Good. It's just for you. It is for you to write whatever you want, and when you fill it up I will get you another one."

She nodded before she wrapped her arms around his neck, giving him a big hug.

"Thank you," she whispered. "Thank you."

Caleb smiled at her and patted her shoulder before leaving her room. He walked back to the living room and found Pam in the kitchen washing dishes. His eyes softened when he thought about the argument they'd had the previous night. He had never seen Pam unravel like that before and realized that he had pushed a button that was out of bounds, even for him. He tried to reach out to her but she quickly pulled away. He loved her but knew that being there was making her more upset. He tried to kiss her, hoping that she would change her mind, but she left the kitchen instead and went into her bedroom, slamming the door.

5

Simone sat at her desk and watched the heavy snowfall through her classroom window. The flurries weren't big enough for a snow day but they were enough to force everyone indoors during recess. She started to calculate exactly how many snowstorms she had lived through since moving to Toronto — she guessed a million.

She pulled at the itchy woolen stockings she wore under her school kilt. The classroom was stifling hot with every radiator on full blast and the burning heat rash was spreading down her thighs making the day unbearable.

She fidgeted as Mrs. Zennewich continued with another math review lesson. It was boring. Simone had learned how to add and subtract two years ago and she also knew algebra, so it was a struggle to sit still while her classmates fumbled with a simple equation. It left her so antsy.

"Mrs. Zennewich, can I be excused?" Simone waved her hand in the air. "I need to use the toilet."

"Yes, Simone, you may use the *restroom*," she emphasized. "We are not vulgar animals in this class. Use the proper words."

"Yes, Miss," Simone said, rolling her eyes. "May I use the *restroom?*"

"Quickly," her teacher said, turning to help one of the students at the blackboard.

Simone walked towards the bathroom, trailing her index finger on top of the cork bar that ran the length of the hallway, peeping into classrooms. Each room featured their weekly artwork on the cork bar. She liked to look at them any time she went to the bathroom. This week her favourite was the third grade's stained glass windows, made from construction paper and colourful tissue paper. She stopped at the drinking fountain to taste the ice-cold water. She winced as she took a big gulp. The pipes were so cold that the water gushing into her mouth gave her a brain freeze.

As she strolled past the gymnasium, she heard footsteps behind her. She turned to see Sarah Jane Ryden. In every school, there was a Sarah Jane Ryden, the smart, pretty, blonde child whose main purpose in life was to make sure that everyone knew that she was smart, pretty, and blonde. Sarah Jane followed her into the bathroom.

"What are you doing, Simone?" she asked.

"What does it look like?"

"Well, why are you in *this* bathroom? There's one closer to our classroom."

Simone ignored Sarah Jane. She opened the stall door and found the toilet filled with shit and squinted her face and then quickly closed the door.

"You know, you should really flush the toilet," said Sarah Jane, using her foot to flush down the waste. "It's not a big deal."

"That's disgusting," said Simone. "It's not my shit to flush anyways."

"I'm going to tell," Sarah Jane said, shocked. "You're not supposed to swear."

"Swear?" replied Simone. "When did I swear?"

"You said the 'S' word. You are not supposed to say the 'S' word."

"You mean shit?" Simone laughed. "How else am I supposed to describe it? It's shit!"

"There! You said it again." Sarah Jane squealed, covering her ears. She quickly washed her hands and left the bathroom.

Simone smirked. She didn't understand some of the Canadian children at her school. They seemed to get bent out of shape over everything. The colder it got, the worse they acted.

She slowly made her way back to class. Mrs. Zennewich stood in the hallway waiting for her with a scowl on her face.

"What took you so long?" her teacher snapped.

"I was in the toil…" She sighed. " …restroom, Miss."

"Why did you go to the restroom all the way by the gym when there was a restroom right around the corner?" her teacher demanded.

"It was the closest one to the water fountain. I had to get a drink of water *and* use the restroom and I thought—"

"I don't care what you thought. You shouldn't have been in the gym restroom."

"But Miss, you never told me which restroom I could use. You never told me that I couldn't use *that* restroom."

"Well, I'm telling you now," Mrs. Zennewich said, folding her arms. "And since you also have a problem with flushing toilets, you will spend your lunch recess making sure that the gym washroom is clean."

Simone looked over at Sarah Jane, who was sitting in the front row smiling at her. Simone felt her entire face turning red when she noticed teachers from the other classrooms standing by their doorways, listening to the entire exchange.

"Did you hear me, Simone Allen?" her teacher asked loudly.

"Yes, Ma'am," she replied. "But just so I understand: I'm in trouble because I went to the gym restroom?"

"Yes! That's exactly it!" she replied in frustration. "Maybe the next time I give you permission to use the restroom you'll do as you're told instead of wandering the halls. Do I make myself clear?"

"Yes, Ma'am! Very clear," Simone said. "Does that mean Sarah Jane will be cleaning the gym restrooms with me during recess, since she was there, too?"

Mrs. Zennewich stood there dumbfounded as some of the teachers chuckled to themselves.

Simone smiled up at her teacher. "I mean, you just said that I didn't flush the toilet," she continued. "And the only person who would have told you that was Sarah Jane, right? I'm just wondering, since she was *also* wandering the halls and using the toilet by the gym."

Mrs. Zennewich's face quickly turned red. She looked over at Sarah Jane. She couldn't lie. The whole class had heard Sarah Jane tell her that Simone was fooling around in the gym washroom.

That afternoon Simone cheerfully cleaned the sticky floor of the washroom with a sponge and pail alongside Sarah Jane, who was steaming over having to crawl on her knees to pull up the dried tissue paper that stuck to the floor. Simone was happy to be in trouble if it meant wiping the smug look off that girl's face.

"You missed one," she said to Sarah Jane as she flushed the toilet with her foot. "You know, all you have to do is scrape the tissue with your fingernails. It's not a big deal."

▶

NOLAN SAT on Mrs. Price's guest bed trying to read *Frog and Toad Are Friends* for a book report that was due. He was struggling, about halfway through the book. He often did his homework in the spare bedroom while Mrs. Price and Simone watched "The Young and the Restless."

Mrs. Price lived in a small two-bedroom apartment on the

quietest end of the building, overlooking the highway. He liked her home. It always felt warm and had lots of oversized furniture. There was far more furniture than his father had in their sparse apartment. All they had was a kitchen table and the mattress they slept on. Mike was still "working things out" on that front, which meant another month with no television.

Nolan got bored with his book and put it aside while he got up to stretch. He studied the pictures on the bureau of Mrs. Price's many relatives. They were cluttered on top of the big mahogany dresser. Her relatives were dressed in suits and fancy dresses. All of them were black people, and none of them looked shiftless, as his father claimed.

He couldn't understand why his father constantly talked badly about Blacks, especially since he relied on Mrs. Price to care for him. The few black friends Nolan knew from school were a lot like him. Some, like his friend Kester, were even better off than him. Kester's father was a mechanic for the Toronto Transit Commission and his mother was a nurse. He had mentioned that to his father during one of his rants, but Mike still managed to find a way to discount it.

"Don't be fooled by the few exceptions," Mike said. "Most of them barely have it together. Look at your little girlfriend Simone."

"She's not my girlfriend," corrected Nolan.

"Ya, ya...okay. Look at your *friend* Simone," he continued. "Who knows where her father is?! It wouldn't surprise me if he's sitting in a jail like most of them."

"Or maybe her parents are divorced like you and Mom," Nolan interjected.

"That's not the same."

"How's that not the same?"

"Well, for one thing, your mother and I are not divorced. I doubt Simone's mother even married her father."

Nolan sat there and shrugged.

He hated how his father went on about Simone and her mother. He couldn't understand why he hated them without even knowing much about them. Nolan liked Pam. He thought she was pretty, and she was always nice to him. It embarrassed him the way his father talked down to her, especially when both parents picked him and Simone up from Mrs. Price's at the same time.

In the beginning, Pam and Mike just ignored each other, barely muttering a polite hello. The disdain they had for each other became clear when they started to make snide remarks as they waited for their children to get their belongings. It would be small little comments — innuendos from Mike about Blacks or sly remarks from Pam about the Irish. By the time they all headed back to their apartments, Pam would be cussing him out in patois. Nolan cringed every time they showed up together. It was one thing for his dad to argue with a stranger at the supermarket, but this was different — he went to school with Simone.

Tensions came to a head the week before Easter, when both parents ended up in the elevator at the same time. Pam was loaded down with groceries. Rather than make pleasant conversation, Mike started up with his sarcastic comments, grumbling about the smell of fresh curry wafting through the hallway.

"Why do you people keep making that curry crap?" he complained "It keeps stinking up the entire floor. I can barely breathe with that stuff lingering all day and night."

Oddly, it was the one thing they could agree on. Pam also hated that half of their neighbours were Punjabis from Delhi. She found the sharp smell of spices so nauseating that she would run into her apartment and slide open the balcony door in the dead of winter. But, even though she agreed with Mike, she couldn't let his comment slide.

"And which people are you referring to?" she replied angrily. "The people who feed your son because your lazy behind can't find a grocery store?"

"You just don't back down, do you?" he snapped back at her.

"And why should I?" she responded. "And why do you always have to comment on everything?"

"Come on," he started up again. "You can't tell me that smell doesn't get to you."

"That's not the point! You act like every issue in this world starts with black people. Have you even smelled curry coming from my apartment? You are so ignorant that you don't even see that most of the people in this building are Pakis."

"Well why don't you say something to them," he said, laughing. "Don't you people band together?"

"Do I look Indian to you?" she said. "Or do all of us look the same to you?"

"You said it," he laughed. "All *you* people look alike."

"Why do you hate black people so much, anyways?" she said. "I hear the crap you tell your pickney! I'm not deaf."

"I have nothing against black people, or anyone for that matter," he replied. "I'm just sick of you people coming to this country, taking away all our jobs and being ungrateful after people like me have been gracious enough to let you stay here in the first place!"

"Oh please! Your father was probably fresh off the boat from the potato fields," she snickered. "You should be happy that *your* people were sober enough to find the shore."

They went back and forth like that until Mrs. Price whipped open her front door and slammed it behind her so the children couldn't hear what she had to say.

"Uno keep uno voices down and stop all dis arguing," Mrs. Price hissed at them. "Yuh pickney dem a listen to this garbage and I know dey sick of it! Fi mi sick of the nasty way you talk to each other. So mi gwaana say this one more time for unuh hard a hearing! Either keep unuh comments to yuhself or di both a yuh need to find annadah sitter."

She then went back into her apartment, slamming the door and sliding the deadbolt shut.

Pam and Mike stood in the hallway, glaring. Each was itching to say something back to the other, but they held their tongues. They had never seen Mrs. Price so angry and knew she was serious about her threat.

"So do we ring the bell again to get our children?" asked Mike.

"I wouldn't test her," Pam replied. She headed to her apartment.

"Yeah, I guess." He watched her attempt to open her door with her groceries balanced in both hands. He sighed at her struggling. "You know it might be easier if you put your bags on the ground and then open the door," he said sarcastically. He walked up to her. "Here, let me help you."

"I don't need your help," she said stiffly, continuing to fumble with her keys. "I can manage all by myself, thank you!"

"Now come on." He grabbed her keys and opened the door for her. "I'm trying to be neighbourly."

As the door opened he glanced into Pam's apartment. It was nothing like the man-cave he shared with Nolan. Her home was nicely decorated and had an overstuffed white sofa flush against one pastel blue wall. He looked at the colourful African and Caribbean art around the room.

"Wow."

"Wow what!" she barked. "You think people like me can't own nice things? Or do you think that everything we own falls off a truck?"

"No...come on," he said, grabbing one of her bags. He walked into her kitchen. "I'm just impressed how nice your apartment is. If you saw my place you would think that I just moved in yesterday."

"Well, what can I say?" She looked at him impatiently. "Look, I hate to be rude, Nolan's father, but I have a lot of groceries to unpack and my ice cream is starting to melt."

"Mike," he said, handing her the grocery bag.

"Sorry?"

"My name is Mike O'Shea." He extended his hand to her. "Not Nolan's father."

"Okay, then," she said ushering him out the door. "Thank you for your help, Michael O'Shea, but I have things to do."

"It's Mike…" he said as she closed the door on him. "What a fucking bitch!"

▶

FOR WEEKS AFTER, Mike and Pam made every effort to avoid a fight for the sake of their children. Neither of them could afford to lose Mrs. Price as a sitter. But, in private, they remained cold towards each other, barely nodding as they passed in the hallways.

The winter does that to Torontonians. The end of the cold season brings many to their breaking point and, just when tensions start to boil over, the city finally sees a thaw with the onset of spring. Everyone's good spirits suddenly awaken from the dark winter slumber as the warmth of the sun filters through the city.

For Nolan and Simone, it meant no more snowsuits, heavy sweaters, or frozen fingers. It meant their days would be warmer and longer, giving them more time to play outside with the rest of the latchkey children in the building.

The buildings were filled with them, kids who streamed out of the yellow buses every day after school and had to take care of themselves until their parents came home. Most of them didn't have a Mrs. Price to watch over them. Parents had to work and often didn't come home until long after the school bell rang. The students who had mothers who greeted them didn't live in the complex. They lived on the other side of Bayview, where the streets were paved and had sidewalks.

The kids in the complex only had a key, a snack in the cupboard, and a telephone they sat by. Those children waited patiently by the phone for their parents to call and check in on them. The smarter kids used that time to finish their homework so they wouldn't have anything to do when their hour of freedom came. The others would sit, waiting with their shoes tightly laced, their jackets zipped up and a skipping rope or baseball glove in hand. Once the calls came in, all of the kids would head out the door in search of adventure. Most parents were aware of the ritual but turned a blind eye. They didn't have the time or resources to keep an eye on their children. They had to hope that their kids were savvy enough to keep themselves out of trouble.

Simone and Nolan took full advantage of their spring freedom. They would hop off the bus and race to the elevator. If they were the first in the elevator car they would press and press the 'door close' button before the other kids caught up with them. They lived on the 11th floor and couldn't afford to lose time — sharing a full elevator car with kids who lived below them meant stopping on almost every floor.

They would then run to Mrs. Price's apartment to finish their homework. Nolan always had homework to do. He wasn't as crafty as Simone, who got her work done during recess. She would end up helping him with his homework, but would cuss him any time he had a lot to complete.

"We're going to take out the garbage," they would yell to Mrs. Price, and then they would head out to play.

Mrs. Price was often too distracted by her programs to notice that they never had a garbage bag with them. When she did notice, she didn't mind. Children should play, she thought. And it was a welcome relief to have time alone to watch her soaps.

If the stars were properly aligned, Simone and Nolan would have two solid hours to play with the rest of the neighbourhood kids. They usually played hide-and-seek tag, or, if there were enough players, they would start a soccer game.

Simone started to make friends during this time. She became friendly with Yvette and Angie, two girls in her grade who lived in the complex and were also in the same class as Nolan. These girls had been best friends since kindergarten. Like Kester, they were Canadian-born West Indians. Yvette's parents were from Jamaica, while Angie's parents were Guyanese. Simone gravitated to them, since they were the only other black girls in the school, but she had little in common with them. They weren't anything like the girls she had known in Jamaica. When they spoke they sounded like white girls with their crisp Canadian accents. They barely understood Simone, who often lapsed into patois when she played with them. But she found them interesting. She had never met kids with island parents who were so Canadian. It wasn't just their accents—everything about them was the quintessential Canadian child; the pop music they listened to, the clothes they wore — there was nothing West Indian about Yvette and Angie.

The three of them often played jump rope if there wasn't a game of tag organized but, more often than not, Yvette and Angie got into squabbles. Most of the time the arguments resulted in the two girls storming off in opposite directions, leaving Simone holding the jump rope. Eventually, they would make up and all would be right with the world again but, on the occasions when they refused to speak to each other, Simone would go off and play with Nolan on the monkey bars.

Nolan loved the few hours of freedom he had after school, but he longed to play baseball at the park with the older kids. The park wasn't far from the complex, but it was twenty minutes by foot and Mike made it clear that he was not to go alone. Nolan envied the freedom some of the older kids had, especially Kester, whose parents let him go anywhere he wanted.

One afternoon, Kester came over to the complex to show off the new mountain bike he had inherited. It was a blue bike with old faded stickers all along the top and down the tube of his bike. It didn't look like much of a bike, but it was more than what most of the neighbourhood kids had.

"Where did you get that?" asked Nolan. "It's so cool."

"My cousin just had a birthday and got new wheels," gleamed Kester. "This is his old one but my dad says he's gonna paint it up nice this summer."

"Man, what I wouldn't do to get a bike like this," Nolan said. "I bet if I had one like yours it would only take five minutes to get to the park."

Simone too was watching Kester show off his new bike. She had joined the group just as Kester began bragging about it.

"Where did you steal that from, Kester? Mi know you didn't just get a bike just cause."

Simone didn't like Kester. She found him annoying, always clowning around, showing off. The feeling was mutual. Kester had been friends with Nolan since kindergarten and didn't understand why Simone was always hanging around them. They couldn't do anything without her know-it-all big mouth telling them what to do.

"Not that it's any of your business, nosey, but I got it from my cousin," he gloated.

"If it wasn't any of my business then why are you telling me?" said Simone. "Anyways!"

"Anyways nothing," he spat back. "Why are you here? My man Nolan and I are making plans that don't include you."

"What kind of plans?" asked Simone.

"Nothing really," answered Nolan. "I'm going to ride with Kester to the diamonds to play some baseball."

"Now?" asked Simone. "We have to get back to Mrs. Price before our parents get home and you know I can't go back upstairs without you. Mrs. Price will know that you're gone."

"Yo, relax, Star," said Kester as Nolan climbed on the back of his bike. "We'll be back quick!"

Simone stood there steaming. "I'm not going to cover for you, Nolan!" She watched Nolan and Kester take off down the street. "I mean it, Nolan!" she yelled as they rode away. "If you don't get back in time, I'm not covering."

When Kester and Nolan reached the diamond a full game was in progress. Nolan had never seen any of the kids before, but Kester seemed to be friendly with all of them. Most of the boys playing were older Black and Central American kids from the neighbouring schools. They joined the game in the third inning, with Kester on one team and Nolan joining the Salvadorian and Guatemalan kids on the other team. While many of them didn't speak much English, like Nolan they lived and breathed baseball. He instantly felt at home with them.

The game was intense, with all the boys arguing over every pitch. They only had one tennis ball to play with and used their knapsacks as makeshift bases. After the seventh inning, most of the kids left so they could get home before the streetlights came on. A few of the players walked with Nolan and Kester. Scott and Wes were brothers from Barbados who lived in Kester's neighbourhood.

"You guys playing this weekend?" Kester asked Scott.

"Yup," Scott replied. "We're gonna get out here early so we get first dibs Saturday morning."

"You in, Nolan?" asked Kester.

"Not sure." He hesitated. "My dad might be working on Saturday. He doesn't like me leaving the house alone while he's at work."

"Who works on a Saturday?" Wes asked.

"My dad does. He's a janitor at Ryerson University so sometimes he has to work weekends."

"Your dad is a janitor?" snickered Wes. "Does he push a mop and stuff?"

"Yeah...but he's also a bartender."

Both of the brothers laughed and shook their heads.

"What? There's nothing wrong with what my dad does for a living."

"Yo, slick, calm down!" Scott laughed as he threw the tennis ball in the air. "I just never heard of a white man work so many jobs. What is he, Jamaican?"

"No, he's Canadian," Nolan said. His eyes narrowed and his brow wrinkled with lines as the boys continued to chuckle. "Well, at least he works! What does your father do? Collect welfare?"

"Yo, our pops writes the welfare cheques," Wes said.

"Hey, Star, there's nothing wrong with what your dad does, *styll* I wouldn't start off telling people that he's a janitor," explained Scott. "Anything would be better than that. If it was me, I would be telling people that he's a bartender. No offence."

"I guess," mumbled Nolan as they passed underneath the highway.

It was bad enough that his dad constantly gave his opinion about everything and everybody, but now the shame of what he did for a living washed over him. His father wasn't a big shot, but he worked harder than most and Nolan wished he had the words to tell them that.

"Yo, Kester, this our street," Scott said. "See you at the diamonds on Saturday. We're bringing more equipment and this time we're playing the full innings."

"Ya sure," he responded. "Can Nolan come too?"

"Ya he can," Scott said. "Just bring your glove and an extra ball. You got a glove?"

"Ya I do," said Nolan, forcing a smile.

"Cool," replied Wes. "Later."

"Later," said Kester. He and Nolan hopped on the bike and rode fast up the street.

Simone had been waiting by the road, looking for Nolan, and now the sun was starting to come down. Most of the building kids had already gone in. She looked around anxiously. She sat on the stoop of the building's roundabout, angry that Nolan would ruin a good thing by going off with Kester. She knew that Mrs. Price was probably already wondering where they were and was probably going to pitch a fit.

As the streetlights came on, Simone debated whether she should go up without him.

"Serve him right if I went in without him," she mumbled to herself. "I told him this would happen. I knew they wouldn't get back in time."

What really bothered her was that Nolan had ditched her for Kester. Over the last few months, she and Nolan had become close friends. Living next door to each other meant sharing a balcony. Over the winter, when the days were warm, they would spend the weekends on the balcony doing their homework, playing cards, and listening to the radio. Back then, the only time she had to deal with annoying Kester was during recess, but now that the weather was nicer, Kester was always around.

"Don't you have a house to go to?" Simone would say to Kester as he sat at Mrs. Price's kitchen table eating cake. "You're always here!"

Mrs. Price would tell Simone to hush and leave him alone, as she cut Kester another slice of cake. Mrs. Price had a soft spot for 'Little Kester'. She knew his family from when she lived in Jamaica and she always made Kester feel welcome any time he came over. Simone, on the other hand, would sit on the chesterfield, scowling, as Nolan and Kester played checkers.

As the sun started to dip, she worried that something might have happened to them. She was convinced that Nolan had fallen off Kester's bike and was lying in a ditch bleeding to death. Just as she was imagining the ambulance hauling his lifeless body away, Nolan and Kester came riding up the driveway.

"What took you so long?" Simone yelled. "I thought your brains were splattered on the road."

"Chill, Simone, it's not even dark out and we're back," laughed Kester. "Catch you later, Nolan."

Simone glared at Kester as he rode off. As they walked back to the building, she continued to carry on at Nolan about leaving the grounds.

Nolan was still upset about the other kids laughing at his father and was starting to blow his fuse with Simone yapping in his ears.

"Shut up Simone! Just shut up!"

She quickly stopped talking. She looked at Nolan as they waited for the elevator. He continued to ignore her as he kicked at a piece of paper by the elevator door.

"What's your problem?" she asked.

He pressed the elevator button a bunch of times. "Nothing," he replied.

"Then why are you yelling at me," she shouted. "I'm not the one who is going to get us in trouble!"

"I'm just tired of you telling me what to do, okay!"

"Fine," she said, pursing her lips. "Next time don't expect me to cover for you."

"Who asked you to cover for me?"

When the elevator door opened, Mike stood in front of them with his face red and eyes bulging.

"Where the hell have you two been! Mrs. Price had to call me at work when she couldn't find you anywhere!"

"We...I lost track of time," stammered Nolan. "I'm sorry, Dad, I—"

"What do you mean you lost track of time, Nolan! Mrs. Price damn well almost called the cops to find you. What were you thinking?"

"I'm sorry, Mr. Mike," Simone said. Tears streamed down her face. "We were up the road and didn't realize how far we walked away. It was my fault."

Mike looked at Simone. He wanted to lash out at her too, but he knew she was lying for Nolan. When he'd driven up to the building he had seen her standing by the corner looking out for Nolan. He had watched her angrily pacing back and forth. He also knew that Simone feared her mother too much to leave the building grounds.

"Come on, the both of you," he said.

It was the longest elevator ride for Simone and Nolan. She was terrified of what her mother would do if she found out. When they got back to Mrs. Price's apartment, the door flew open, but Mrs. Price just looked relieved to see them safe and sound.

"God Almighty," she cried out. "Where the raas have you two been? Yuh have mi worry sick!"

"Mrs. Price, it's obvious these two have nothing constructive to do after school," Mike said, pushing Nolan into the apartment. "So, since you two can't be trusted, you'll both be given chores. I'm sure there are things you can do to help out around here. Mrs. Price, it looks like your kitchen can use a good sweep every day and your windows are due for a good wash. Don't you agree?"

The two children stood with their heads down, too scared to speak.

"Don't you agree," he repeated loudly.

"Yes, Dad," Nolan responded.

"Yes, Mr. Mike," Simone replied.

"Good," he said. "Mrs. Price, we'll see you tomorrow. Go get your stuff, Nolan."

"Yes, sir."

Nolan ran past Simone into the other room to get his book bag. He knew that she was only in trouble because of him and felt awful. When he came back with his bag, she was sitting on the chesterfield. He whispered her name. She looked up at him.

"I'm sorry," he mouthed before heading out the door with his father.

"Look, don't mention any of this to Simone's mother," Mike whispered to Mrs. Price in the hallway. "The last thing I need is to hear her blowing her top over this."

"You are a good man, Mr. Mike," she said as she grabbed his hand. "God Bless you."

He winked at the old lady and she quietly shut the door.

6

Mike was silent with Nolan for the next hour, waiting for some type of explanation. He'd known raising Nolan alone would be hard but he wasn't prepared for issues like this. He wished Meghan were around to handle this. She was always good with Nolan. She knew how to speak his language. He had never been home long enough to learn.

"So are you going to tell me where you were?" he asked.

Nolan opened the fridge, looking for a snack.

"I'm waiting."

"Nowhere," Nolan replied, sniffing the milk bag. "Kester and I had some time and went to the park to play baseball with some kids from the neighbourhood."

"Look, buddy, I know that I'm not able to take you to the park like your mom used to, but you can't just pick up and leave." He took the milk jug away from Nolan. "What am I paying Mrs. Price for if you're going to be running the streets like a hooligan?"

"I'm old enough to take care of myself."

"Oh, really?"

"I'm not some baby! Kester is my age and he gets to go wherever he wants." Mike laughed out loud. "It's not funny, Dad. I'm being serious."

"Okay! All right!" Mike said, pulling out a box of Kraft dinner from the cupboard and a package of frozen hot dogs from the freezer. "If you think you can handle being alone then let me see you cook dinner."

"What?"

"You heard me," said Mike. "I'm going to take a shower and when I come back I'm expecting dinner to be cooked and on the table. If you can cook dinner, then you can stay home by yourself."

Mike took his time showering, trying to hold in his laughter. He loved Nolan and knew that he was a good kid, but he had the O'Sheas' hard-headed nature.

Nolan did his best to figure out how to cook the mac and cheese. It looked so easy when his father did it, but he didn't know how hot the water had to be before pouring in the macaroni or how long to cook the pasta. He figured five minutes should do it. He guessed that hot dogs should be nuked in the microwave for around three minutes each.

When Mike came out he couldn't mask his horror when he saw the food on the table. He knew that he had to at least sit down and try the food, for Nolan's sake. He looked at the pieces of hot dog scattered on his plate and the barely cooked macaroni with chunks of powdered cheese stuck to the noodles, and his stomach groaned.

"I guess I should have mentioned that it had to be edible," he mumbled under his breath. "Let's eat before everything gets cold."

Nolan sat silently, looking at the mess. His eyes welled up with tears as he watched his father prepare to eat it. By the end of the meal, the most they had been able to digest were some of the exploded hot dogs. Everything else was deemed too dangerous to eat.

"Well," Mike said. "I guess I was wrong. If you want to stay home by yourself you are more than welcome to. I'm sure you will be okay making your own snacks and the occasional dinners. I'll talk to Mrs. Price first thing in the morning and let her know that you will no longer be going over to her place after school."

Nolan looked fearfully at his father. He didn't want to make dinner again and he did not want to starve to death. "It's okay, Dad," he mumbled, sulking.

"What's that?" Mike asked.

"I said it's okay," he said loudly. "It's probably better if I stayed with Mrs. Price...I mean...it's not so bad there."

Mike let out a hearty laugh and patted Nolan's mop of curls.

"Are you sure?" he asked. "Because if you are going to stay with Mrs. Price you have to follow the rules. No leaving the neighbourhood."

"Yes, sir," he replied. He hesitated. "Here's the thing, Dad, I want to play baseball with some of the kids in the other neighbourhoods. That's all. They usually play after school."

"I get that, Nols," he replied. "But you're too young to just go off on your own. Give it a few years and when I think you're responsible enough I'll be the first to let you go off as you please."

"You're just like Simone's mother. She doesn't let Simone go anywhere, and it's boring here. I hate having to be stuck here while everyone else gets to go out and do what they want."

"Well, maybe Simone's mother has a point," Mike said. "Kids these days get into too much trouble when they are left alone, and I hate to be the bearer of bad news but, until you get a little older, you are going to have to accept the way things are."

"Well, maybe if you and Mom didn't split up, I wouldn't have to go to Mrs. Price or live in this dump or have to stay indoors all the time."

"Whoa, where the hell did that come from? You don't know anything about what happened between your mother and me."

"I know a lot," Nolan yelled back. "You're the reason why everything is so bad! You're the one with all these rules that everyone has to follow. That's why everything is so bad. You never let Mom do anything. You never let any of us do anything. It's always your way."

Nolan got up from the table and went into his room, slamming the door.

Mike remained in his seat, surprised by his outburst. He hadn't spoken to Nolan about his split from Meghan because he had hoped that in time they would get back together, but hearing his son blame him felt like a kick to the gut.

Mike got up and cleared the table in an angry rush. In the kitchen, he found the disaster that Nolan had left behind. A sink piled high with every utensil he had used and powdered cheese all over the floor. He spent the next hour scouring the entire kitchen. After cleaning the mess, his eyes started to water from the strong smell of bleach and he went outside to get some fresh air and to stew over the fight.

"Bad day, huh," he heard from the other side of the balcony.

Pam had been sitting on her orange folding lawn chair, trying to get away from her own stresses. She hadn't planned on speaking to Mike, but she had overheard the argument through the thin walls. She pulled out a cigarette and lit it.

Mike glanced over at her and sighed. He leaned on the railing and looked up into the night sky. "How do you do it?" he asked her. "How did you go all these years without anyone backing you up?"

"Do what?" she asked, offering him a cigarette.

"Raise a kid on your own," he replied. He took the cigarette and lit it. "It shouldn't be this hard."

"Tell me about it," she said, blowing out smoke. "Unfortunately you're asking the wrong person."

"What do you mean?" he asked, taking a long drag.

"You have several years on me," she said. "I've only had a few months with Simone."

"Wait, I thought...I thought you've been a single mother all this time?"

"Well, you thought wrong," she said, exhaling deeply. "Simone has been living in Jamaica all of this time. She only came to live with me after my aunt passed."

"Wow!" he said. "I guess we're both in the same boat. Nolan's mom always handled everything. I'm just trying to figure all this out and it's harder than it looks."

They both silently looked over at the playground where a group of teenagers hung near the swings, passing a joint around. It had been a long time since either of them had had a chance to unwind and truly vent.

"This kid has no idea what I do to keep things running," Mike complained. "I work two jobs just to make ends meet and he throws a tantrum because I won't let him run the streets."

"I wish I could say that I don't know what you're going through, but Simone shows me little respect on a daily basis. I'm the one who keeps the lights on and puts food in her belly, yet I get the silent treatment."

Mike had not realized that Pam's relationship with Simone was so tumultuous. Simone always seemed so obedient. But knowing that he wasn't the only one drowning made him feel a little better. He pulled out a milk crate he had on his side of the balcony and flipped it over to sit on.

"Tonight Nolan attempted to make mac and cheese for dinner," he said, smirking. "The deal was if he made dinner he could watch himself after school."

"And how did that go?"

"Had to throw out a perfectly good pot."

They both laughed.

She passed him another cigarette. "Did he even read the instructions?"

"Doubt it."

"I guess we're a lot like these kids."

"How so?"

"Neither of us are doing a good job reading the instructions."

Mike chuckled. "I don't know about you but I didn't even get a manual with my kid, I think it got lost in the mail."

"Hell, if I got one I would have memorized every damn page," Pam said. "Better yet, I would pay top dollar for someone to teach me how to deal with Simone without strangling her little rude behind."

"You know, tomorrow night they're having a parenting class at the church," Mike said, putting out his cigarette. "I saw a flyer on St. Augustine's community board. They're holding free parenting classes every Wednesday night in the church basement."

"Backside!" Pam said, laughing. "They have just about everything in this country."

"We should go," Mike said. "I mean if you want to."

"You know what?" she said. "I'll go if you go."

The next evening when Mike arrived at the class only a few parents were there. He looked around for Pam but didn't see her. He felt awkward sitting between a young woman who was nursing her baby and two women speaking animatedly in Spanish, but just as the class was about to begin he saw Pam sneak into the room. She sat way in the back row, away from everybody.

"All right, everyone!" Mrs. Hanson, the church's coordinator, smiled as more people wandered in. "It looks like we have some stragglers. Why don't you all grab a chair and bring it to the front so we can make a circle."

The room started to buzz as everyone moved in closer to one another. Pam looked over at Mike and waved. He nodded at her. He was glad that she had come, but he still felt uneasy. He wished he wasn't the only man in the class and slouched in his seat, hoping the two hours would go by quickly.

Pam recognized only a few from their building; the others at the seminar were complete strangers and, she noticed, most were immigrants like her, presumably trying to grapple with raising a 'Canadian' child.

Mrs. Hanson went around the room greeting parents and

handing out little prayer cards; then the parents were asked to join in and recite the opening prayer.

"Dear God, give us the strength to raise our children right and the ability to see the good in them," they all said in unison. "Give us the strength to keep them safe and to keep our sanity through this plight we call parenthood. Amen."

After the prayer, Mrs. Hanson began the class by encouraging everyone to introduce themselves.

"Hello, my name is Clara and I have eighteen years to go," said the woman trying to calm down her fussy baby.

"Hi, Clara," said the group.

"Hello, my name is Margarite and I have four years to go," said the woman next to Pam.

"Hi, Margarite," said the group.

When it got to Pam she had no idea what to say. She looked around and felt a little tense. She didn't see the point of people knowing who she was. She looked over at Mike, but he seemed just as confused.

"Uhm...yes....hello," she stumbled. "My name is Pam."

Silence.

"Hello, Pam," smiled Mrs. Hanson. "How many years to go?"

"Years of what?" she asked, and the group laughed.

"Years left before these evil children turn nineteen and are officially adults," responded a black woman who sat next to Mike. "In other words, our freedom papers."

"Let's have Pam start over," Mrs. Hanson suggested. "Go on."

"Yes...well my name is Pam and I have twelve years to go," she said.

"Hi, Pam," said the group.

Other parents introduced themselves before it got to Mike.

"My name is Mike and I have eleven years to go, but you never know," he said smiling. "I'm still young."

Silence.

"Hi, Mike," said Mrs. Hanson.

"Wow, tough crowd," he whispered to himself as the remaining group members finished their introductions.

"Okay, everyone, tonight marks the new session and, as outlined in the agenda, we are going to talk about setting boundaries," Mrs. Hanson began. "Whether it's with your newborn or your teenager, boundaries are necessary in order to help your children grow into successful adults. The key is for you to establish the boundaries, and for your children to understand and respect those boundaries."

Pam grew excited over the topic. This was exactly what she needed to hear. But as she sat through the first hour, the only things discussed were Bible passages that showed examples of parents interacting with their children. She looked again at Mike, who was nodding off as Mrs. Hanson read the Prodigal Son parable.

"This is very good, everyone," Mrs. Hanson said. "Let's take a quick fifteen-minute break so we can stretch our legs."

Pam didn't know what to make of any of it. She looked at her watch and sighed when she realized that they still had another hour to go. She decided to escape and walked up to Mrs. Hanson, who was by the exit talking to one of the other mothers. Pam was going to politely apologize for having to leave, saying she had an emergency she needed to attend to, but as she waited she heard Mrs. Hanson berate another parent who was also attempting to leave early.

"Connie, in order to be the best parent for your children you have to put in the work," she said curtly. "Your Sharon has already been in trouble with her teacher twice this week and your boys are always in and out of detention. Do you really think you can afford to leave now?"

Pam sighed. There was no getting out of the seminar. Just as she was about to go back to her seat, someone grabbed her arm and pulled her into the dark hallway.

"Don't you bloody change your mind," she heard Mike whisper. "Let's get out of here."

He pulled her into the hallway, then let go of her, and the two of them scurried up the church stairwell. They headed out the door towards the parking lot in silence and then slowed down once they were on the path. It felt good to be out in the fresh air.

"Well, that was a big waste of time," Pam said as she looked at her watch. "If I had known it was going to be a Bible study class I wouldn't have bothered to go."

"I'm just glad we escaped," he said as they walked down the pathway. "She droned on for so long, I could barely keep my eyes open."

Pam laughed.

"Can I offer you a ride?" Mike asked. "I'm pretty sure you are going to find any excuse to say no, but the next bus doesn't come for another twenty minutes, and as a fellow parent who is paying Mrs. Price $3.00 an hour, I can't, in good faith, let you waste another dime waiting for the bus."

Pam wanted to tell him that she only paid $2.00 an hour, but she nodded instead and took him up on his offer. They drove without talking. Mike turned on the radio. The station was playing oldies.

Pam sat in the passenger seat tapping her foot along with the music. This was the music she grew up on — 1960s girl groups, Motown, and hippie rock. She liked reggae and calypso, of course, but she loved American rock just as much.

Mike was surprised to hear her humming along to Cream's "I Feel Free".

"I didn't peg you as a Cream fan," he said as they turned into the complex's parking lot.

"I grew up listening to American pop," she said. "Like most Jamaicans."

"They play this stuff in Jamaica?" he said. "I thought you people only listened to reggae. I mean, not trying to offend or anything, but rock is white people's music."

"Correction," she said. "Rock 'n' roll was *black* people's music before you white people came along and copied us."

"I stand corrected." He chuckled as he parked the car.

They walked through the parking garage and stood awkwardly by the basement entrance to the elevator, waiting for it to slowly make its way down. Pam kept her gaze on the elevator floor indicator. She looked over at Mike. "Thanks for the ride. I appreciate it."

He smiled nervously before looking at his watch. "Well, nothing much came out of it," he said. "If this elevator takes any longer we might have to pay Mrs. Price for the next hour all the same."

Pam laughed.

"Do you want to come over for some coffee, since we have an hour to waste?"

"Sure."

"Really?" he said. "I didn't expect you to say yes."

"Why not?" she said.

The elevator finally arrived.

When they got to his apartment he opened his door but stopped. "Can I be honest with you?" he asked.

"Sure," she said wondering why his face was turning red. He was acting strangely.

"When I offered you coffee I honestly thought you wouldn't take me up on my offer," he said. "The truth is, I ran out of coffee this morning. I was trying to be nice."

Pam started to laugh at him. He looked so embarrassed. And then his face started to relax and he started to laugh as well.

"I have coffee at my place," Pam said, shaking her head. "Meet me on the balcony in ten minutes."

They sat on their respective sides, Pam on her orange folding lounge chair and Mike on his milk crate, with a carafe of coffee sitting between them. She had brewed some of the Blue Mountain coffee she got for Christmas. It was a special blend from Jamaica that was hard to find in Toronto. Only a few West Indian grocers carried it. It was the only luxury item she allowed herself to splurge on.

"This is good," Mike said as he let the coffee drift down his throat. "What brand is this again?"

"Blue Mountain. It's a Jamaican coffee."

"Wow, you drink this stuff all the time in Jamaica?"

"No," she replied. "The tourists do. I mainly drink tea."

"Is your tea any good?" he asked.

"It's alright," she replied. "Almost as good as the coffee."

Mike smiled as he enjoyed his cup. It was the first time both of them had put down their invisible shields and just talked to each other. He had missed having a normal conversation with another adult. Especially an adult who shared his lack of parenting skills.

"Is Nolan your only child?"

"No. I have a fourteen-year-old daughter. She's with my wife."

"Why doesn't your oldest live with you?" Pam sipped her coffee. "Not to be nosey or anything, but most single parents usually have all the kids or none."

"It's just easier for each of us to care for one instead of both," he said swiftly. "If I could afford a house without working two jobs, then I could be there for both of my kids. Hell, maybe my wife would appreciate it and take me back."

"Is that why she left you because you didn't have a house?"

"No, that wasn't it. And she didn't leave me. I left."

"I'm confused. You left your wife and you want her to take you back? Is this a Canadian thing?"

"I left after we had a huge argument," he said cautiously. "I hoped she would come to her senses so we could work things out, but as you can see that hasn't happened yet."

"What was the argument about?"

"She wanted to go back to school," he said with a sigh. "I didn't think it was the right time for her to go back, not with the kids being so young, but she wanted to get her degree and have a career. She claims I wasn't being supportive, which is bullshit since I work my ass off to give her everything."

"But wait!" She sat up. "Your wife went back to school to better herself, maybe even get a good job and bring in more money and you couldn't get behind that? Backside! To be a white person."

"Oh, here we go."

"No, seriously," she said trying not to laugh. "Funny enough, I would kill for a man who'd want me to stay home and raise the pickneys. I mean what black woman hasn't wanted to put her feet up and let her man do all the hard lifting."

"Well aren't you the anti-feminist," he laughed. "Don't you want to *have it all?*"

"Fuck feminism," she said curtly. "Feminism is a white thing. Whenever a white woman asks for a raise she's being a feminist. A black woman asks for a raise and all of a sudden we're lazy niggers asking for a handout."

"Wow," he replied as he stared at her. "I guess I thought all women…working women were feminists."

"Hate to burst your bubble, but black women were never invited to the party," she said. "And anyway, we've always been workers. I'm probably the only Jamaican you'll ever meet with one job. Most of us have at least two jobs and a few side hustles just to keep food on the table."

They sat for a moment in silence as he looked at the bottom of his coffee mug. He had never given any thought to what it was like for a black woman to survive. The conversation had gotten too deep too quickly. Mike didn't know how to respond or what to say next. Was he supposed to feel bad for being a man? Or for being white?

"Look, let's not colour this evening with all this real talk," she said. She leaned across to pour more coffee into his mug. "Life is too short."

"Agreed," he said. He sat back, savouring the new cup of coffee. "Funny, though...funny that you're the first black woman I've met with only one job and I'm probably the first white man you've met who has two jobs and at least three side hustles."

Pam spat out her coffee as she burst into a high-pitched laugh.

"Just be careful," she said. She dabbed some of the coffee that had dripped from her lips. "Someone may confuse you for a Jamaican."

Mike laughed harder than he had laughed in a long, long time. He handed her another napkin. He looked at her and smiled. He liked it when she laughed. She was prettier when her face lit up.

They sat comfortably watching the courtyard lights turn on. Mike glanced down at his watch. He didn't bother to mention that they were closing out their second hour on Mrs. Price's clock.

7

T he spring had marked a thaw between the two families, and the summer manifested an unlikely friendship between Pam and Mike. The two didn't see eye to eye on many things, but they began to recognize that they might have more in common than they'd been willing to admit. They tried to give the parenting classes a real go but, after another two sessions, they ended up skipping the meetings and instead used that time to sit on the balcony comparing notes about St. Augustine, their kids, and the fact that Mike needed more furniture for his apartment.

"I don't get it," Pam said. "You've been in your apartment for how long and you still live on card tables and milk crates? What are you waiting for?"

"I guess I'm waiting for Meghan," he said. "If I break down and buy furniture, then it's one step further away from reconciling. I'm not ready to give up on my marriage."

"No one says you have to, but the least you can do is stop living like squatters," she said. "The bums under the highway have more furniture than you."

"Well, what if I buy all this furniture and we work things out? Then what?"

"And what if that never happens?" she rebutted. "If she's not banging down your door by now, she's not going to bang down your door any time soon."

That night Mike lay awake on the mattress next to Nolan and thought about what Pam had said. It was true. He had been living on hold, hoping his life would go back to normal, hoping that by the summer he would be back in his own bed, next to his wife. He looked up at the crumbling ceiling above him. He was fuming. Nothing had changed. Meghan acted as if everything was okay, while he and Nolan and Dana had to take a backseat to her dreams. What bothered him most was that it looked as if she was going to break her promise to Nolan. From the beginning, she had promised him that they'd all be back home together by the end of the school year, but now that time was quickly approaching and she'd started saying she needed more time to think.

"Get dressed," Mike said groggily the next morning. "We're going to see your mother and sister."

▶

THEY DROVE in silence down the 401 towards the Don Valley Parkway. A month ago, Meghan and Dana had moved downtown to be closer to Meghan's college campus and Dana's new high school.

Nolan was excited to see his mother but, because his father seemed angry and because he didn't want them to get into another fight, he was nervous. Another argument would only push his mother farther away from them.

They exited the DVP, taking endless side streets through the downtown district. They passed the flashy bright lights of Honest

Ed's and the crowds of tourists filtering in and out of the Eaton Centre. Then they circled around the block a few times.

"Do you know where you're going, Dad?" Nolan asked.

Mike continued to drive in silence.

After what seemed like forever, they pulled into a quiet neighbourhood of small family homes and apartment buildings and parked by the side of the street. Kids were playing at the end of the street. Mike found the building and, when a kid came rushing through the entrance, he grabbed hold of the door and they went inside and up to the apartment. His father banged on the door.

"Mike!" Meghan said. "Nolan! Is everything okay?"

She was dressed in the satin robe his father had bought her for Christmas.

"Everything is fine." Mike peered into her apartment. "We were in the neighbourhood."

"Please come in," she said. "Nolan, it's so good to see you, my darling." She pulled him into her arms and squeezed him tightly.

Nolan grabbed on. He was so glad to be in her arms again. He missed the way she smelled and moments like this, when she would run her fingers through his hair.

"My goodness, you've gotten so big," she said as she pulled away to take a closer look. "What has your father been feeding you?"

"Mac and cheese," he said, smiling. "And oxtail."

"Oxtail?" She laughed. "Since when did you start eating oxtail?"

"Mrs. Price makes it every Friday," he said, looking around the apartment. "She says oxtail and beans will make me taller."

"Well, she may be right, because you're growing like a weed." Meghan smiled at Mike.

"Hey Nols, why don't you hang out while I talk to your mom," said his dad, patting him on the head.

"Mom, can I watch TV?"

"Sure, sweetie," she said. "It's in my bedroom. The first room on the right."

Nolan slowly walked through the apartment. His mother's bedroom had the same furniture from their old place but somehow the new way she had arranged the room made the furniture look brand-new. Even the old television set looked bigger and better. He turned it on and stretched across her bed as he watched a repeat of the WWF match he and Simone had seen the previous week.

Mike and Meghan hovered by the front door. Mike felt like a deliveryman waiting for a tip. He didn't know what to say.

"I'm a little surprised to see you here," Meghan said. "Do you want to come in?"

"Yeah sure," he said, walking into her quaint apartment. "Your place looks nice."

"It's not much," she replied.

"More than us," he said, under his breath. "Looks like you're doing well for yourself."

"Can I offer you some coffee?" she asked. "I have some brewing."

"Sure." He followed her into the kitchen. "How's Dana doing? I was hoping that she would be home so I could see her."

"She's sleeping over at a friend's house this weekend." She added, "I have finals so she's staying the weekend to give me time to study."

"You know she could have stayed with me." He poured himself a cup of coffee. "I don't get to see her much anymore."

"Mike, she's a teenager. She'd rather spend the weekend with her girlfriend than hang out with her dad."

"Well, Nolan misses her," he said. "He misses you too, Meghan. He needs to see you more than a few times a month."

"Are we going to do this now, Mike?"

"Whoa! I'm not saying anything but the truth. Just because your life has changed doesn't mean your role as his mother has."

"Jesus, you don't think I know that?" she snapped. "I'm under a lot of pressure right now. I don't need this."

"Look, I didn't come here to fight with you."

"Then why are you here?"

"I have no idea," Mike said. He poured the rest of his coffee down the sink. "I came over hoping we could talk. Maybe come to some kind of understanding. What the fuck was I thinking?" He headed towards the front door.

"Mike, where are you going? Nolan is still here."

"No shit!" he said. He opened the door and was in the hallway when he yelled back: "Spend time with your fucking son. I'll be back for him tomorrow."

Meghan caught up with him on the staircase.

"Mike, I'm studying for my finals!"

He watched her trying to keep her robe shut.

"Goddamn it, Mike, why are you being such a fucking prick?"

He could hear her still screaming at him even when he got outside the building. He sat in his car for a moment. He turned on the ignition. And then he started to laugh. Hearing Meghan call him every name in the book seemed so comical. He felt a little vindicated that he'd left her fumbling. The look on her face! Soon he was laughing so hard that tears were streaming down his cheek.

He put the car in drive and took off, but his fits of laughter made it almost impossible to continue. At the first red light, his laughter quickly turned into heaving sobs, and it was only when the driver behind him started to honk his horn did he snap out of it and realize the light was green. He was barely able to pull himself together. He hadn't cried that hard since his mother died when he was six years old.

He remembered his mother lying in the hospital bed dying of cancer, and his father pulling him aside, telling him to *man up and quit crying like a girl*. Since then he had been automatically on *man-up* mode, taking care of his father before he lost his battle with cancer. Taking care of his family, his home, and church. He was always the caretaker and now he was seeing his family slip away and he was helpless.

On his way back to North York, he made a U-turn at the IKEA store, Pam's words about getting furniture ringing in his mind. He walked through the aisles, planning just to look around, but ended up buying furniture for his living room, a bunk bed for Nolan, and a proper kitchen table.

He spent Saturday afternoon quietly assembling the furniture. With his head down, he barely heard the light knock on the balcony door. Simone stood with her face pressed against the glass. He gestured for her to come in.

"Hi, Mr. Mike!" She sat in the armchair that he had built earlier. "Where's Nolan?"

"He's at his mother's place this weekend."

"Oh," she said, disappointed.

"You guys are as thick as thieves," he joked. "Can't go a day without seeing each other."

"Yes I can," she said. "I just thought he ran away or something. Is this new furniture?"

"Yup," he replied.

"It looks nice. Nolan's going to like it."

"You think so?"

"Yup," she said as she got up to leave. "Bye, Mr. Mike."

By the end of the evening, he had assembled everything and marvelled at how different the apartment looked. It felt like a home. He wanted that for Nolan — he didn't want them living on hold.

The next morning, Pam came over.

"Not bad," she said commending him. "Simone told me what you were up to. You know what? I think I have something that will make it even better."

She went back to her apartment and brought back a beautiful pastel painting of an untamed beach. They hung the artwork in his living room. It looked good against his eggshell white wall.

"This painting always reminds me of the beaches in Jamaica that haven't been overrun by tourists," she said. "Much nicer on your wall than in the back of my closet."

That afternoon, when Mike went to pick up Nolan he brought Simone with him, hoping that Meghan wouldn't curse him out completely in front of one of Nolan's friends. He pressed the call button.

"Hi Dad," Nolan said. "Mom says I have to meet you in the lobby. I'll be right down."

Mike tried to smile at Simone.

As they drove home, Mike chuckled at Nolan showing her the caterpillar he had found. The two friends chattered all the way to the complex about everything they'd missed the twenty-four hours they'd been apart from each other. When they got to their apartment, Mike gently guided Nolan ahead of him and waited for his surprise.

"Whoa!" shouted Nolan. He and Simone started running from room to room. "What the heck!"

"You like it?" Mike asked.

"Yeah, I do," he said, grinning from ear to ear. "Whoa, I have a bunk bed?"

"You and your sister have bunk *beds*," he said, watching the two children climb onto the top bunk.

"This is so cool, Dad! Everything is so cool!"

"I'm glad you like it, buddy."

He hadn't seen Nolan smile this much in a long time and was starting to feel really good.

The kids jumped down from the bunk and Nolan carefully held out the caterpillar.

"Dad, can we go outside and get some leaves for the little guy?"

"Sure."

Mike went back into the living room and saw Pam sitting on her end of the balcony reading the paper. He went out to join her. The heat of the late sun hit him as he slid open the balcony door.

"Did he like the new furniture?" she asked.

"Yup," he said, sitting next to her.

"Good."

Silence.

"You got the sports pages there?" he asked her.

She looked around in her stack of papers and handed him the section. They sat quietly, reading the paper, as their kids laughed and yelled in the courtyard below.

8

T he end of the school year couldn't come soon enough for Simone. The muggy heat had arrived early, sending her a sweet reminder of Jamaica's balmy summers. She remembered whole days lazily perched on the steps of her Auntie's veranda, sticky from the mangos she ate right off the tree as the sun's fire soaked through her skin.

She grew restless in the final weeks of school, daydreaming of all the things she would do with her freedom with Nolan and Kester. But her dreams were quickly dashed when Pam received another letter from the school, this time directly from the principal.

"Why are you giving these white people any excuse to beat you down?" yelled Pam. She boxed Simone's ears. "Do you realize that they want to fail you?"

"I hate that school. It's so boring and everyone there is so stupid. I want to go back to Jamaica."

"Well, that's not going to happen," Pam yelled back. "You refused to do the work. Now they're saying you have to make it up during the summer."

"That's not fair!" she cried out. "Lots of kids in the class don't do their work. Mrs. Zennewich just hates me! She's always giving me a hard time."

"Mi don't make the rules," Pam said, exhausted by the whole argument.

▶

PAM HAD KNOWN this would happen. She'd sensed it the first time she'd met with Simone's teacher. Now she had to meet with Simone's teacher and the school's principal. They were wrong about Simone, but she realized that no matter what she said they were not likely to change their minds.

She sat in the principal's office and he showed her Simone's incomplete class work. Several pages of vocabulary colouring assignments and pages of simple addition and subtraction stood between Simone completing the second-grade and having to go to summer school. She argued that it was ridiculous to make Simone go to summer school over a few missed assignments, but Mrs. Zennewich was adamant that Simone wasn't ready to move on from the second-grade.

"But she's a smart girl!" Pam showed them Simone's old school transcripts. "She was an 'A' student with first-class honours. Just look at her grades from her school in Jamaica."

"While I'm sure the schools in Jamaica do a good job teaching at a rudimentary level, this is a Canadian school," the principal said, placing the transcript on his desk. "Many of our immigrant children find our level of education difficult."

"All I see are colouring sheets and learning to add one plus two," Pam criticized.

"I'm sorry, Miss Allen, but it's more than her work," the teacher said. "She doesn't pay attention in class and is often ill-mannered."

"Do you force all your ill-mannered white students to go to

summer school?" Pam interjected. "This is crap, and you both know it!"

"Miss Allen, the bottom line is simple," Miss Zennewich said. "Either Simone goes to summer school or she repeats second-grade."

Pam threw herself back in her seat and looked at their apathetic faces. She got up and left before the tears of frustration began to stream down her face.

▶

"THEY'RE NOT FAILING Simone because she's a dummy," Pam yelled loudly. She was sitting with Mike on the balcony as their children watched television in her apartment. "They're failing her because they don't like her and that's not right!"

Mike looked at the letter from the principal and sighed. He had received the same letter from Nolan's teacher, recommending that Nolan go to summer school, but he had done what he usually did. He'd charmed Nolan's teacher, who was on the church's board, and arranged for his son to volunteer at the church in lieu of summer school. He didn't dare tell Pam that Nolan wasn't in any danger of failing. He knew no good would come from it.

"Can they even do this?" Pam continued. "I never hear of a school just fail a student like that."

"The schools up here are tougher," he said, placing the letter on her chair. "They're not like the schools in Jamaica."

"Give me a break," she scoffed. "Simone was learning her multiplications when Nolan was still trying to figure out his colours. These Canadian teachers don't know what they're doing."

Mike couldn't disagree with Pam there. He was also frustrated with the teachers. They were still using the same lesson plans he'd been given when he was a student. It irritated him that for the first two months of every school year, Nolan would be reviewing work from the previous year.

"Well, what are you going to do about it?" he asked her.

"I don't know what to do," she said. "I tried talking to them. I even called the school board, but no one is calling me back."

"If the school board is as incompetent as the teachers then you're going to be waiting a long time for that call," Mike said. "You know, summer school is not the end of the world. At least that's free childcare for most of the summer. I'm going to have to pick up extra shifts at the bar just to be able to pay Mrs. Price to look after Nolan this summer."

Pam quickly looked at her watch and bolted from her seat.

"Oh shit, Mrs. Price will be here any minute and I'm not dressed yet," she said, grabbing the letter. "I asked her to watch Simone tonight."

"You got a big date or something?" he asked.

"Yes, if you must know," she said. "Caleb is coming by to pick me up. He's taking me out to dinner."

"He's back?"

"Yes," she said smiling. "He returned a few weeks ago."

◀◀

CALEB HAD MOVED to Montreal shortly after their argument over Simone. He had tried to smooth things over with Pam but she'd refused to speak with him. He had finally given up, and came to say goodbye. His uncle had opened a grocery store in Little Burgundy, he told her, and he was moving to Montreal to help out.

"I love you, Pamela. But I think we need this time apart so we can figure things out...so you can figure out what you want."

"Well, go then!" she said. He reached for her hand. She quickly pulled it away. "Just don't expect me to wait around for you."

"Don't be that way," he said.

She left him standing in the living room alone. He could hear her bedroom door slam shut.

Simone had been no better. She'd spurned his parting gift. She had finally gotten used to him and now he was leaving her to deal with her mother alone. She sat on her bed pouting. Caleb smiled awkwardly when she turned up the volume of her radio. He realized that it was no use. The two of them were alike and there was no getting through to them when they acted that way. He placed Simone's gift on the coffee table and left.

When he closed the door behind him, Simone went into the living room and found his gift. The brand-new diary had a bright purple cover with pearly white pages. She opened it to find a note slipped inside the cover.

In case I don't see you when you finish your other diary. Here's a new one for your collection.

Simone took the diary into her mother's room. Pam was lying on her side, quietly weeping. Simone went over to the bed and crawled in beside her and listened to her cry herself to sleep.

And then Caleb suddenly returned with a bouquet of roses and a bottle of wine as if no time had passed. "Sugar, I'm back for good! Come nuh and help me celebrate my new teller job with Scotia Bank!"

Pam promptly slammed the door in his face.

"You left me when I needed you the most," she yelled at him when he called her at work the next day. "How do I know you're not going to do that again?"

"I won't," he pleaded. "I love you, Pamela. You know that."

He kept phoning, and every time she hung up the phone, her whole body shook with anger. Her co-workers were looking at her. They were secretly rooting for Caleb after six dozen roses now sat in the break-room trashcan.

Then one day all the calls stopped. Pam came to work and there wasn't a bouquet of flowers waiting for her. There were no messages on her desk. At the end of the day, she sat in the restroom crying, realizing that he had finally given up. She cried the entire bus ride home and looked so pitiful that the driver stopped to make sure that she was okay.

She cursed herself for being so stubborn. Caleb was the only man in her life who accepted her for the way she was. He knew her heart. He knew what could make her scream out in laughter and what could shut her down. He knew what her silence meant and respected that sometimes she just needed her space. He was the one man that she trusted and she believed she loved him even more than herself. Yet she had thrown him away instead of greeting him with open arms.

Her heart was completely shattered by sadness.

She had to pick up Simone at Mrs. Price's. She looked a mess and didn't want to deal with the old woman prying into her business, wondering why she was so upset, but she had no choice. She wiped back her tears, hoping her eyes were not too red, and went into the apartment. Caleb was sitting on Mrs. Price's couch playing checkers with Simone and Nolan with a plate of cake balanced on his lap.

She did a double-take through her blurry eyes.

When Caleb got up and smiled at her, she ran into his arms without even thinking and kissed him the way she should have kissed him the moment he came back to her.

"Ewww," Simone said, covering her eyes. "You guys are gross."

Pam laughed. Caleb was looking into her eyes.

"I don't want to spend another night away from you," he whispered. "You hear?"

Pam nodded as he held her.

▶▶

THE WEEKS after their reunion saw a different side of Pam. She was happier. Her constant scowl was replaced with a radiant smile. Simone was also overjoyed that Caleb was back in their lives. Her mother seemed less controlling; she focused less on her and more on Caleb. But, most important, they started to feel like a family.

"Simone!" Caleb yelled one morning. "What's this I hear about you having to go to summer school?"

She came into the kitchen and shrugged.

Caleb was frying bammy on the stove and she snagged a hot piece from the serving dish.

"Ouch!" She dropped the cassava bread back on the plate. "My teacher hates me and just wants to punish me. She's always picking on me."

"My teacher hates me," he mimicked. "She's always picking on me."

"That's not funny," she said as she sucked her burnt finger.

"Wow, if looks could kill, I would be six feet under right now." He handed Simone a plate and dished out some of the bammy and fried fish for her. "Little darling, you are probably the smartest girl I know, so you need to stop blaming everyone and realize that you created this problem."

"No, I didn't!"

"Is who always getting in trouble for not paying attention in class?" he asked.

"But that's because she teaches the same thing all the time. Why do I need to hear the same stuff over and over again?"

"Is who always talking fresh to their teacher?" he said.

"But she asks some stupid questions."

"But! But! But!" Caleb said, teasing. "Is who di teacher? You or this Miss Zenith…"

"Mrs. Zennewich," she corrected.

"Yes. Mrs. Zennewich," he said. "Is she not the teacher? Is she not in charge of the class?"

"Yes," Simone said, scowling. She sat down to eat her breakfast.

"Okay, then...then you must respect your teacher and her rules."

"But I shouldn't have to go to summer school." Her eyes glistened. She wiped away a tear that escaped down her cheek.

"I'm not saying you deserve to go to summer school," he said. "I think your teacher is an eediat for even saying that you need it, but if it means not repeating the second grade then you just need to make the best of it."

Simone put her head down. She was the only student in her class going to summer school. While all of her classmates were enjoying their vacation, she would be stuck in a stuffy classroom, "learning" how to add and subtract.

"You still writing in that diary I gave you?" he asked.

Simone shook her head.

"Well, see," he said brightly. "That's your problem. You take your frustrations out on your poor teacher when you could be writing stories about the evil Mrs. Zennewich."

Simone laughed out loud.

"Instead of talking back to your teacher, use that fire to write about the mole on her cheek that has whiskers as long as a cat and her wrinkled hands with all those warts."

"She doesn't have a mole or any warts," Simone sang out. "But she does have bad breath."

"Well there you go," he said joyfully. "She got bad poisonous breath. Next time you're dealing with her or anyone that gets you mad, write about them. Write stories that trash them or stories that have a better outcome."

"I guess," she said. "But I still hate that I have to go to summer school."

"Listen, summer school is going to be fun," he said. "You get to hang out with your friends instead of messing around with old Mrs. Price all day long. From what your mother told me, your class goes on a field trip every Friday. Doesn't that sound fun?"

"Yeah, I guess. I just don't want people thinking that I'm dumb. Only dummies go to summer school."

"Then let this be the last time you have to go." He sat across from her, grinning. "Don't give these white people any more excuses to keep you down. You hear me, gyal!"

"Yeah, I hear you."

"Come nuh," he said. "Let me see you smile."

Simone made up her face.

"Jeeesus! What an ugly smile," Caleb said, laughing.

▶

THE FIRST DAY of summer school Simone peeked into her assigned classroom, still embarrassed that she had to go at all. All she could hear was Kester in her head, laughing and saying that only the dummies went to summer school. She could believe it. Cathy Moretti was sitting in the back of the class giggling with her cousin Vivian. Cathy and Vivian certainly acted dumb — they were notorious for disrupting class and fooling around.

Simone stood by the doorway, ashamed that she was being lumped into the same group as the Moretti cousins. She wished Nolan was with her. It would have been bearable. But Nolan was volunteering at the church. She envied his luck. She would do anything to be able to sweep up a dusty old church instead of spending the summer at school.

When the bell rang, a loud voice said: "Is this my class? Because students in my class know that all talking ends the moment the bell rings."

Simone was a little surprised. Miss Olivia Gardiner was her summer school teacher? She had only known Miss Gardiner as St. Augustine's school librarian. She was also the first black Canadian she had met.

Miss Gardiner was a seventh-generation black Canadian, born

and raised in Sherbrooke, Quebec. She had graduated from Teachers College five years before but, due to the recession, she had moved to Ontario, hoping to land a better-paying job with the Metropolitan Separate School Board.

"Are you planning to join us, Miss Allen?" she said. "You're not going to learn anything standing by the doorway."

Simone sat down at the front of the class, looking around at the different students as her teacher introduced herself and wrote her name on the blackboard. There wasn't another child like her. Other than her teacher, she was the only black person.

She felt the sting of tears running down her cheek. She quickly wiped them away. She didn't want her first day of summer school marred with tears. She felt worse when she realized that her desk was right in front of the teacher and she slouched, wishing she could disappear.

"Okay class, let's get started," her teacher said. "Open your mathematics book to page five."

It was the same work she had sat through in Mrs. Zennewich's class. The same work she'd mastered in Jamaica. She rolled her eyes as Miss Gardiner spent each morning reviewing simple addition and subtraction. She tried to stay awake but the stifling heat and her wandering attention made it real hard.

"Miss Allen, are we boring you?" asked Miss Gardiner.

Here we go again, Simone thought to herself.

"Yes, Ms. Gardiner," she responded before realizing that she had said it out loud. She felt her face flush when some of the students giggled.

"Yes, we're boring you?"

"I'm sorry, Miss, but I already learned this last year with Mrs. Zennewich," she said. "And before, in my last school in Jamaica."

"You're from Jamaica?" her teacher asked.

"Yes, Miss, from Manchester parish," she replied proudly.

No one had ever asked her where she was from or anything about Jamaica. Nolan thought it was cool that she was from the island and was always trying to copy her accent, but that was as far as it went. Most of her classmates teased her accent and funny sayings. She was always trying her best to sound more Canadian.

"How lovely," Miss Gardiner said. "I visited there once and stayed in Negril. A beautiful country with wonderful fruit. What was the last thing you learned before you came to St. Augustine?"

"We learned our multiplications and division," she replied, smiling brightly. "I can multiply up to twelve and divide double digits. When I left we were going through adding fractions."

"I see!"

Simone sat up, surprised that she hadn't been chastised for complaining.

Next morning she was no longer working on subtraction and addition. Miss Gardiner started her on simple fractions, which, over the week, morphed into more complicated fractions. By Friday, Simone was working on algebra equations, and Miss Gardiner gave her logic questions to work on over the weekend.

▶

IT INFURIATED Ms. Gardiner that they would place a student like Simone in the second grade when she should have been in the third or, at the very least, in a split second/third-grade class. It was typical of the schools in the district. The administrators treated immigrant students like they were stupid. In the wrong grades, they would be unchallenged and bored. And some of the school's smartest students would end up repeating a year simply because they didn't know English or because their accents were too thick.

She was thrilled to see the progress Simone exhibited in such a short time. She was definitely a special child and, if she were properly placed, she would excel in school. She went to Mrs. Wilson, who was the acting principal for the summer session.

"Sorry to interrupt, Mrs. Wilson. I was hoping to speak to you about Simone Allen, one of the students in my summer session."

"Yes, Miss Gardiner, Simone Allen...yes?" The vice principal rested her elbows on a large stack of papers that sat on her desk. "Wasn't she in Mrs. Zennewich's second-grade class last year?"

"Yes, the very one," she continued. "I've been working very closely with her over the last few weeks and, I have to tell you, she's a very bright girl. Here's the thing. I took a look at Mrs. Zennewich's notes and I think Simone was misplaced. In fact, I believe she should have been placed in the third grade when she came to St. Augustine."

Mrs. Wilson sat quietly for a moment, then she went to her cabinet and pulled out a file. After quietly perusing it, she looked up and smiled.

"It's honourable the way you speak out for your students, but her file says quite the opposite. Her teacher writes of how disruptive and belligerent she is. In fact, if it wasn't for the new policies banning us from failing students, she would have remained in the second grade for another year."

"Mrs. Wilson, with all due respect, I believe that she was wrong," she said. "Simone is the type of student who needs to be challenged. It's probably the reason why she was acting out. We know what happens to students who are not stimulated intellectually. If you see the work she does you'll see that she's a smart girl!"

"Do you have examples?"

"Yes...yes, I do," she said, placing Simone's work on her desk.

Mrs. Wilson flipped through the pages as if she was sifting through a magazine. She stopped when she came across the algebra homework.

"And you were there while she was working on these equations?" she asked.

"Well, not all of them. Most of them she worked on independently—"

"How do you know she didn't get help or even cheated?"

"Why would she cheat? She has no incentive to cheat or pretend to do the work." Miss Gardiner noted the look of scepticism on Mrs. Wilson's face. She took a deep breath and smiled to mask her frustration. "I've seen her work through a problem and she grasps math very well. She was way ahead when she came from Jamaica. Their school system is—"

"Oh, I know what kind of system they have in Jamaica, and I can tell you that it's as primitive as their locals. I hate to break it to you but you have to watch these Jamaicans. You're Canadian-born so you don't realize how sneaky they can be."

Miss Gardiner felt her anger rise and clenched her teeth. She had always worked with people like Mrs. Wilson. A generation of Canadians dying out from the herd. They truly hated the changing landscape, so many people from all over the world migrating to Canada. They felt threatened by these new Canadians with their own cultures, religions, and ways of life — believing they would never assimilate to the Canadian way. Mrs. Wilson was scared of the future, of what Canada would turn into. She fought against the emerging changes any way she could.

Miss Gardiner took a deep breath and smiled sweetly. She couldn't lash out at the aging administrator. She had to be the "good Negro librarian," a term Mrs. Wilson once used to describe her when she was trying to pay her a compliment.

"Mrs. Wilson, why don't you test her?" Miss Gardiner said carefully. "Allow her to show you what she's made of."

"I really don't have the time or resources to test Miss Allen," she said. "I'm swamped just getting the upcoming school year together."

"Haven't they assigned a principal to St. Augustine yet?" asked Miss Gardiner. She knew that Mrs. Wilson was vying for the position, which was why she had agreed to run the summer session. She wanted desperately to impress the school board.

Mrs. Wilson shook her head.

"The board is always thrilled when there is an exceptional student in their district," said Miss Gardiner. "Can you imagine the praise this school would get if you were able to identify a student like that?"

"Ha! I see what you are doing, Miss Gardiner," she said before pausing. "Look, I know that your heart is in the right place, and if I had the funds I would test her, but the school board is tightening up our spending. The best I can do is place her in the third/fourth split in September and, if she's as bright as you claim, her teacher will revisit what attention needs to be spent on her."

"Mrs. Barrett is the teacher of that class," Miss Gardiner said, alarmed. "I've worked with her and she is hard on her minority students. I'm pretty sure she will not lift a finger to help Simone."

Mrs. Wilson was frustrated by the whole conversation. She had known Sharon Barrett for years. She wasn't the most pleasant woman to be around, but she was a good teacher with good values. She too was angry about the influx of more and more students with very little help in terms of resources from the school board.

Miss. Gardiner could tell that her comment about Mrs. Barrett had crossed the line.

"Mrs. Wilson…Martha, I'm not asking you to treat Simone any different than any of the other students," she said. "I'm just asking you to be fair."

"Here's what I'll do," the older woman said. "I will put her in Mrs. Barrett's class and make a strong suggestion that she be given both third- and fourth-grade curriculum. That's the best I can do. Now, if you don't mind, I have a lot of work to complete."

Miss Gardiner left the meeting despondent. She hated how the system allowed bright children to fall through the cracks based on where they came from or the colour of their skin. The last thing she wanted to do was cry racism and be *that* black teacher, but these students needed an advocate. Someone to fight for them.

She went back to her classroom and looked at Simone's work.

She had to find a way to bring change to the school without alienating the Mrs. Wilsons and Mrs. Barretts. She just couldn't figure out how to do it without a fight.

▶

SIMONE ACTUALLY ENDED up enjoying summer school and loved having Miss Gardiner as her teacher. She felt at ease having a black female teacher again, especially one who didn't make her feel that every word that came out of her mouth was wrong.

Each night she came home eager to tell Caleb and her mother about all that she had learned and was starting to feel excited about her school. Even Nolan was envious as he listened to Simone go on about all the fun they were having: the trips to the zoo, afternoon picnics at Edwards Garden, playing dodgeball every recess. Nolan even wished he wasn't stuck in St. Augustine's nave, polishing the wooden pews.

After summer school had finished, Simone and Nolan had the month of August to enjoy their freedom before the new school year began. While they still had to stay close to Mrs. Price's during the day, they could spend most of their time outside with the other building kids. The courtyard was their clubhouse by day and a haven from their parents in the evening. All fights and disagreements were handled in the courtyard. They shared snacks stolen from their pantries and traded toys pulled out of their toy trunks. It was a marketplace of amusement until the sun dipped into the horizon and the streetlights came on.

The older kids would stay out later, hanging out in the courtyard until their parents hollered at them to get off the streets. They played music on their ghetto blasters, reclaimed lengths of cardboard from the dumpsters to break-dance on. Simone and Nolan would watch them from the balcony. They could barely hear the music but had a bird's-eye view of the action below.

The breakers bent their bodies without any effort, shattering all rules of dance convention. The building kids crowded around hollering in excitement when someone performed a head-spin or did a windmill, with their bodies melded together to the beat of Africa Bambaataa's "Planet Rock". For Simone and Nolan, every move they made was magic.

If they were lucky, the breakers would come out earlier in the day and Simone and Nolan would find any excuse to run downstairs to watch up close. Sometimes Kester would be on the scene, wearing his big sunglasses and a green velour tracksuit with a bright blue stripe along the side of his pants. He had become the B-Boys' mascot and he popped out doing the worm and moonwalked across the cardboard.

Simone and Nolan got Kester to teach them every move he knew. On the weekends, he would come to the building and the kids would hide away in Nolan's room practising. They spent hours perfecting their moves, planning to start their own breakdance crew when school started.

Simone begged her mother to buy her a tracksuit for her birthday. The school board had ended the mandatory uniform rule and students now had the option to wear regular street clothes. Simone badly wanted the red tracksuit she had been eyeing at Simpsons department store. Pam laughed and said that only hooligans wore those trashy outfits, but Simone would not give up. And then Nolan started on Mike and, after a week of wearing their parents down, both Simone and Nolan ended up with tracksuits as part of their back-to-school outfits.

Simone, Nolan, and Kester entered the third-grade looking so "fresh" and so "slick". They started every sentence with "Yo", called each other "Guy", and had the kids in their class clamouring around Kester's Walkman to listen to Grandmaster Flash's "The Message". Soon enough, other kids were begging their parents to buy them sneakers and tracksuits.

For Simone, it was the best beginning to the school year. She was no longer the new student that had shown up mid-year. She was not just another student either. She was now part of the Breaker Crew.

Mrs. Wilson wasn't pleased with all the commotion. She was having a hard time getting up to speed as acting principal and seeing this group of kids dancing on a cardboard mat made her nervous. Any time kids started gathering to make a show of their skills, she would quickly descend on them and make them disperse.

One day that first week, Simone decided she was ready to demonstrate the leg jump. The girls in her grade were eagerly gathered in the washroom waiting to see her perform this feat or die trying and, as they all cheered her on, Simone felt her heart soar.

"You ready!" she yelled.

"Yeah!" they yelled back.

She grabbed onto her right foot, pulled her left leg, jumping out from under the hole she'd created. She proudly displayed her signature move. The entire bathroom erupted in cheers as she balanced herself and became steady on her foot. It was perfect. It was the first time she had been the centre of anything and she happily basked in it. A smile spread across her face. She couldn't believe that she had actually performed the move perfectly.

She asked them if they wanted to see her do it again, this time to the beat of "The Message". She started rapping the song and moving to the beat. It was her moment. As the beat played in her head, she grabbed firmly onto her right foot. But, just as she was about to jump out again, her left foot tangled with her trousers and she fell flat on the wet tile floor.

The girls in the bathroom didn't know what to do. Simone was sprawled on the floor moaning. Many ran out screaming, while a few tried to help until Miss Gardiner came into the bathroom, rushed to Simone and turned her over to find a purple goose egg forming on her forehead.

"Oh, Simone," she sighed. "What in the world were you thinking?"

"I don't know, Miss."

She helped Simone to her feet and took her to the administrative office. "Sit here while I get you some ice. I'll have to call the school nurse."

Simone sat next to Ilene Cheng, a chubby girl with long jet-black hair and bangs that hung just above her eyelids, who sat stiffly on the bench with one hand on top of the other, resting on her lap.

Mrs. Wilson came barrelling in, the school's secretary following quickly behind her, and dropped a stack of files on her desk. The secretary informed Mrs. Wilson that Ilene had been misplaced in the second-grade class and had been waiting since mid-morning to be placed in one of the third-grade classes.

"Can this wait?" Mrs. Wilson bellowed. "Right now I don't have the time to deal with this. Send her back to her class and I'll deal with it later."

Ilene's face flushed and her lips pursed tightly. She started to mumble angrily to herself, then looked over at Simone and gasped.

"What happened to you?" she said in a thick Mandarin accent. "You have a big lump." She pointed.

"I hurt myself trying to do a leg jump." Simone winced as she traced the bump with her fingers. "I hit my head on the bathroom floor."

"Well, that was dumb," Ilene responded. "And the bathroom floor is dirty. Why would you do that?"

Simone gave her a sour look.

Miss Gardiner came back with a towel and ice. Then Mrs. Wilson called her into her office and reprimanded her for fooling around in the girls' restroom. "No more break dancing on school grounds! Am I making myself clear?"

It had been a short run for the Breaker Crew but it had solidified Simone as a legend — the student who'd performed the leg jump and nearly died doing it. When she came back to class, several classmates ran over to her to examine the swelling on her forehead. No one had ever seen a bruise so gruesome before and wanted to get a close look.

"Wow," said Brian Kepler. "I think I can see it moving."

"That's disgusting," Sarah Jane said before she quickly ran back to her seat.

"I can't believe you did it twice," Yvette squealed. She hugged Simone. "You are so brave."

Simone looked over at Nolan a few rows in front, but he didn't look back. She called out to him but he ignored her. The other kids by her desk wanted her to retell the entire incident.

"Settle now, lunchtime is over," yelled Mrs. Barrett.

She was a tall woman who wore her white hair in a short perm and always dressed in a polyester pantsuit with a floral blouse. It was a look she hadn't changed since leisure suits had come into fashion a decade ago.

"And, Miss Allen," she continued, looking squarely at Simone, "don't you think you've wasted enough time today?"

"Yes, Mrs. Barrett," she said sheepishly.

Despite the throbbing pain, Simone couldn't stop smiling. On the ride home, the entire bus was buzzing about her leg jump maneuver. A crowd of kids followed her and Nolan off the bus, chanting her name, trying to egg her on to do the stunt again, but Nolan said "No way" and told everyone to go away.

"What's up with you?" Simone asked him as they walked towards their building.

"That was a really dumb thing you did," he said. "Now Mrs. Wilson is banning us from even breaking."

"Yo, why are you mad at me?" she barked back. "Both you and Kester do head spins all the time in the schoolyard! What's the difference?"

"The difference is that you could have really hurt yourself," he said, touching the swelling on her forehead. "It was stupid."

Simone flinched as he traced the lump with his thumb. The two stood by the elevator door. Nolan was still touching her face. She didn't know what to say. She wasn't used to someone caring about what happened to her.

"Yo, you should have seen how I landed with the first leg jump," she snapped back as they walked into the elevator. "It was amazing. Swoosh. But the second one was booty. Never doing that again."

"You better not," he laughed as he pressed the button for their floor.

9

M ike sat on the balcony, in the dark, drinking his beer. Laughter was coming from Pam's apartment. He looked at his watch. He didn't know why he even bothered now that Caleb was back in the picture. Pam was almost twenty minutes late and he felt foolish, sitting around, waiting for her to come out for their evening ritual. It had been their thing — she would bring out her mug of ginger tea and they would sit for hours arguing while he sipped his cup of coffee.

Most of their discussions were political in nature, with topics ranging from the federal government to the state of the economy as the recession continued to sweep through the nation. He enjoyed debating the issues with Pam and was pleasantly surprised at how well read she was on Canadian politics. They talked about how many of their friends were scrambling to find work after being laid off, and they worried that the economy would sink further before it got better.

At the end of each night, they would ease into their favourite topic — their kids. It was the moment he waited for. It felt so good to have someone to connect with who understood the strains of being a single parent and who understood the seeds of doubt that constantly sprouted within him.

It wasn't just their children that gave him a sense of commonality. Their lives seemed almost poetically parallel. Both of their mothers had died when they were young children and, during their teenage years, both had been left orphaned when their fathers passed away. Both knew what it was like to grow up quickly, trying to navigate without a compass. They understood each other, which made their late-night chats ever more meaningful as the weeks went by, but all of that changed with the return of The Great Caleb.

The late-night conversations were shorter and less lively. Pam was no longer happy to sit around and debate an article he'd read in the paper or to discuss Meghan cancelling her weekend with Nolan again. The friendship they'd cultivated over the last few months took a backseat to her renewed relationship with Caleb.

Mike looked at his watch again and decided to call it a night. As he got up to leave, the light on Pam's side of the balcony came on. She walked out with her favourite purple mug and plopped down next to him.

"You're not going in, are you?" She smirked at him. "Caleb just left. I got caught up talking to him. I didn't realize how late it was."

"So lover boy has his own home?" He sat back down. "Here I thought he'd moved in with you and Simone."

"Not that it's any of your business, but yes he's planning to move in," she said calmly as she sipped her tea. "I thought you liked Caleb?"

"I have nothing against him," Mike said, forcing a smile. "I mean if you're okay being treated like a test drive, who am I to comment?"

"Excuse me?"

"Look, I'm an old-fashioned kind of guy," he said. "I mean I thought you wanted better for yourself. A single woman living with a man seems a little slack, don't you think?"

"I'd rather live with someone I love than marry just to make people like you feel better," she spat. "And, just to be clear, Caleb doesn't cheapen me because we're not married. He treats me well and loves Simone and we don't need some paper telling us that!"

"If you live together, sleep together, and carry on like you're married then you might as well get married," he said. "A woman who lives with a man ends up with a shitload of bastards to pawn off on the system. It's the same old story. The man leaves for some reason or other and the woman ends up having to manage all by herself with the good ole government paving her way."

"Your family is just as broken," Pam retaliated. "You got married. You had kids the old-fashioned way. How's that working for you? You know, instead of shitting on me for being happy, maybe you should figure out how to keep your own damn family together."

She quickly got up from her seat and went back into her apartment, slamming the balcony door behind her.

Mike sat quietly in the dark fuming. It was easier to criticize Pam and her relationship with Caleb than it was to admit that things between him and Meghan had derailed. He wished he hadn't run Pam off. He needed someone to talk to. Someone to help him make sense of how his marriage had suddenly dissolved.

Pam's balcony door slid open again. He didn't say a word as she sat back in her seat. He could barely look at her.

"I can't seem to get my marriage back on track," he finally admitted out loud. He looked out at the kids in the courtyard break-dancing and he started to tremble. "I don't know what I'm going to do if I lose her."

Pam carefully took the beer bottle from him and placed it on the ground. She held his hand, squeezing it until the trembling stopped.

"It will be okay," she said.

He nodded. The teenagers below were cheering as one took centre stage, breaking to the music.

"Don't these kids have a curfew?" he said.

Pam laughed. She sat back, keeping his hand in hers, as they strained to listen to the music.

▶

"MY MOM IS MOVING to Nova Scotia after the Christmas holidays," Nolan told Simone while they were watching television on Mrs. Price's bed, waiting for her weekly prayer meeting to finish.

"What do you mean?" Simone bolted up on the bed. "Are you moving too?"

"Nah, just my mom and sister," he replied, staring at the screen.

"Oh," she said. "Why aren't you going?"

"I don't know. I guess she doesn't want me there."

He hadn't seen his mother the entire summer, not since that impromptu weekend his dad had set up with her. They had only spoken a few times over the telephone. That morning he had been elated to hear her voice and excitedly told her all about break dancing and his friends and his favourite songs.

"That's great, honey," she said. "Sounds like you're having a good time!"

"Mom, when can I see you?" he asked. "I haven't seen you and Dana in so long!"

"I know, Nolie, that's why I'm calling," she said. "I'm hoping to have you spend Thanksgiving weekend with Dana and me."

"That would be awesome!"

She then went on to tell him about the new school she would be attending in Nova Scotia. How the program was one of the best in the country and they were giving her a scholarship so that she could go to university and get a bachelor's degree. When he asked if he was coming, she paused before telling him that it was best that he stayed with his father.

Nolan told Simone everything. She handed him her last Oreo cookie and the television remote.

"Well I'm glad you're not moving to Nova Scotia," she said.

"Ya, me too, I guess," he replied.

He slid to the floor in front of the bed and flipped through the stations until he landed on "Press Your Luck". He knew Simone wanted to make him feel better, but he couldn't stop thinking about his mother moving away. He couldn't understand why she didn't want him with her. It didn't help that he'd seen his father in tears after having a really big argument with her over the phone. He had never seen his father cry before and it scared him.

He continued to watch the game show but barely batted an eye when a contestant won $5,000. Simone lay on the edge of the bed, messing with his hair. He usually hated that and would swat her away like a pesky fly, but this time he sat unmoved as she braided his curly locks.

"I know how you feel," she said to him quietly. "I know what it feels like to be left behind."

She then started to talk about what it was like to be without her mother and never meeting her father. How her Aunt Marva had raised her and how much she missed her aunt and Jamaica. She talked about how scared she had been coming to Toronto by herself, and she said that, if she had her way, she would find her father and stay in Jamaica forever. She talked about her very first plane ride and how bumpy it was and that she almost cried thinking that the plane would crash, but that it wasn't so bad because the flight attendants were really nice and gave her lots of candy.

"Maybe the same thing will happen to you," she said. "Maybe your mom moving to Nova Scotia will be a good thing. You'll get to ride on a plane, just like me."

Nolan sat quietly and listened. He turned away from her. He

didn't want her to see him crying. She went on to talk about how scared she had been of snow, wasn't that funny? She laughed when she told him that she had thought the cold would hurt her skin but, after her first snowfall, she loved it. It was the thing about Canada that she liked the most. She talked about Caleb coming into their lives, how it felt like her mother had abandoned her again, but once she got to know him she ended up liking him as well.

Mrs. Price called out to let them know that dinner was ready.

"Come on, I'm hungry," Simone said getting up. "I think Mrs. Price made barbecue chicken for dinner."

"Thanks, Simone," he said as they walked out to the living room. She looked over at him and nodded.

"Lawd Jesus," Mrs. Price cried out, laughing when she saw Nolan's hair. "Simone, what did you do to this poor boy's head?"

▶

MIKE WATCHED Nolan tear into the slice of pizza he'd brought home for dinner. It was from a pizza parlour by the Eaton Centre. The slice was as big as Nolan and Mike had wanted to cut it up into smaller pieces, but Nolan insisted on eating the thing whole.

It had been a long day. He had worked, then met Meghan at a coffee shop by the shopping centre, and he was still processing the entire meeting. He had to force his anger back, keep it at bay.

"Mike, I'm not here to fight," she had said. "I want to make things right."

"How is moving to the Maritimes going to make things right, Megs?" he said. "You're tearing our family apart."

"Please keep your voice down. Everyone is looking at us."

"I don't give a rat's ass who's looking at us. In fact, let them look. Everyone should know that you're leaving your kid behind and breaking up our family."

"Mike, I'm doing what's best for our family. I wasn't happy, okay! Every day I felt like I was drowning. I'm going to university, Mike! I never thought in a million years that I would be good enough to get into a university, let alone get a scholarship."

"I don't understand," he'd said quietly. "I thought our family meant something to you?"

"It did...it does." She'd placed her hand over his. "But right now I need this more."

"So what about the kids?" he asked her point blank. "Do we just swap them during the holidays and call in when birthdays roll around? Dana is going to be so far away from me — and what about Nolan! He will never see you!"

"Mike, the kids will be fine," she said. "Dana is excited about going to high school in Halifax. She's treating this like an adventure and Nolan will come to understand."

"How the hell do you know that? You know you really are a selfish..." He had stopped himself, not wanting to turn the conversation into a shouting match. "If you were around long enough you would know that he is not okay with this. He doesn't understand why you're leaving him and, frankly, I don't get it, either."

"You never did," she said. "That's always been your problem. All you ever see is your end of things. How everything affects you. You never cared about how I felt."

"So your answer is to just pick up and leave and everyone is supposed to get used to it! And what about me? Do I get a say on what happens to us — to our marriage?"

"What marriage?" she said. "Our marriage has been over for a while now. It was over the moment we separated."

"Well, isn't that perfect," he said, feeling his voice tense up. "You seem to have everything planned out for everyone."

He'd got up to leave. There were tears in her eyes.

"Don't do it like this," she said, trying to pull him back.

"Unless you are going to take it all back and fight for us, then I don't want to hear it," he said.

Mike couldn't stop rerunning the shouting match. He barely touched his own slice of pizza. Instead, he lit a cigarette and smoked in silence and watched Nolan eat.

Nolan looked up at his father. "Did you see mom today?"

"Who told you that?"

"No one." He squirmed. "I overheard you on the phone with her. Did you tell her not to move away?"

"Nolan, I tried…"

"Yeah, but did you try hard enough?" Nolan's eyes were wet. "Mom likes flowers and toffee. Did you bring her some flowers?"

"Buddy, flowers are not going to fix this. I don't know what to tell you…"

"Why doesn't she want us anymore?" Nolan said, looking at him. "Why doesn't she want me anymore?"

Mike could see the hurt in his boy's eyes and he felt his entire body go weak when Nolan broke down in tears. He held onto Nolan tightly as the young boy wept in his arms. He tried to convince him that his mother still loved him but deep down he wasn't sure how she felt about them. He felt just as lost and hurt as Nolan.

"Are you and Mom getting a divorce, Dad?"

"I don't know, Nols," he responded. He felt his own tears blur his vision. "All I know is that it'll be okay. I promise that we'll be okay."

10

"He doesn't live far," Nolan said to his father. "And it's the best neighbourhood for candy."

Nolan and Simone were pleading with Mike, pestering him all the way back from the trash chute. Halloween was three days away and they had been invited to trick or treat in Kester's neighbourhood. Mike was too exhausted to think. He had just come home from a particularly difficult day cleaning the chemistry labs and he only had an hour before he had to start his evening shift at McKinney's.

"Nolan, I'm not in the mood to talk about Halloween," he said gruffly. "I just got home and don't have time to deal with this."

"But Dad, it's Simone's first Halloween," Nolan said. "She's never gone out before and in Jamaica they don't even celebrate Halloween. Can you believe it?"

Mike looked at Simone, who lowered her eyes on cue, and then back at Nolan, who quickly saddened his face.

They had planned their ambush right down to the very minute and the last detail. They had mentioned it to Pam first but were now wearing Mike down because Pam hadn't immediately agreed to let them go. Despite his appearance of being a tough disciplinarian, Mike was the weaker of the two. He always gave in when Pam wasn't around. He was the one who snuck them candy and took them out for pizza. If all else failed, they would enlist Mrs. Price, who always seemed to have a way of making their parents fall in line.

"Come on, Dad! Kester's older brother will be there," Nolan whined. "Please!"

"I don't know, buddy," said Mike.

The three walked into Mrs. Price's. Pam was at the dining table waiting for Simone.

"Pam, what do you think?" Mike said, sitting next to her.

She turned to him with an annoyed look on her face. "Mi spend di laas ten minutes ignoring dem pickney and now dem a work pon yuh? Unuh giving mi a blasted headache! Jeee-sus!" She rubbed her temples. "If it means they stop their nagging then my answer is yes!"

Mike chuckled slightly before he turned his attention back on the two children.

"Well, since I'm outnumbered I guess it should be fine." He sighed. "But I'm coming to supervise."

Simone squealed with excitement. She hugged her mother and then Mike. The two children then ran off to Mike's apartment to rummage through Nolan's old Halloween costumes to see what they could wear.

For Nolan, it was business as usual. He had gone trick-or-treating since he was old enough to walk. But, for Simone, it was her first time walking around in a costume to get free candy. She had decided to go out as Wonder Woman and spent the next day gathering items for her costume. Her pink jump rope would make a good lasso and she stuck gold stars on her red and blue swimsuit.

"Are you crazy?" Pam said, looking up at her daughter's home-made costume. "Did you forget how cold it is in this city? I will take you to the store and get you a proper costume. One where you won't freeze your behind off."

The night before Halloween, Pam took Simone to Bargain Harold's where the costume aisle was practically stripped clean.

Simone looked through the racks, despondent at the choices that were left. There were barely any costumes in her size and the only ones that were decent were too expensive.

"Look! Here's a good costume for you to wear," Pam said pulling out a bright yellow and green rayon number. "There...this is big enough for you to wear over your snowsuit."

"But, Ms. Pam, this an ugly monkey costume," she said, studying it.

"No, man, this from *Planet of the Apes*. That was a big-time movie." She placed it against Simone's body. "This will fit you nice."

"But it's ugly," said Simone as she looked through the rest of the costumes. "Isn't there something else I can go as? Couldn't we go to another store?"

"No, Simone! I'm not traipsing up and down the street for a costume," Pam said firmly. She had been feeling sick all day and wasn't in the mood to argue. "It's either this or nothing at all."

She saw Simone's disappointment. She sighed as she watched her daughter put the costume into the shopping cart. She felt bad. Simone's costume wasn't as fancy as the other kids or as fun as her Wonder Woman idea.

"Simone, isn't the whole purpose of Halloween to scare people? This is definitely scary and, look, it's a girl monkey. Come nuh, no one is even going to know that it's you under there."

Simone shrugged her shoulders and they continued up the aisle to the cashier.

The next night Simone sat on Nolan's bed playing video games before going out to trick or treat. Nolan couldn't stop giggling at Simone's costume. It was hard for him to keep a straight face watching her fidget with her mask.

"Shut up, Nolan." She banged on the controllers, trying to get Mario to jump over the barrel.

By the time they got to Kester's neighbourhood, Simone had forgotten about her costume. She was just happy to be going door-to-door with the other kids, getting her bag quickly filled up. She couldn't believe how much candy the homeowners gave her.

The three kids ran up and down the streets, giggling hysterically. Some of the homeowners opened their doors dressed in costume and Simone jumped every time someone yelled "boo!", and she screamed when a man dressed as Jason from *Friday the 13th* chased them, and she ran to Mike in tears, and he tried to assure her that the knife wasn't real. But she held onto his hand as the others went to a few houses without her.

"Come on, Simone," Kester said, laughing at her when they came back from another house. "Stop being a chicken. That house over there is giving out whole Aero bars."

That piqued Simone's interest. The house was decorated with jack-o-lanterns on the lawn. She quickly let go of Mike's hand and grabbed onto Nolan's arm, dragging him to the house. She wasn't about to miss out on a whole Aero bar.

Mike continued on with Kester's father, a giant of a man who didn't speak much, and Kester's older brother, Omar.

"Yo, your Dad is scary," whispered Nolan to Kester. "Does he talk?"

"Nah, he doesn't talk much to white people," Kester said. "He also hates Halloween. The only reason he's taking me is because my mother had to work tonight and my brother is an idiot. He didn't want him losing me."

"How can anyone hate Halloween?" Nolan asked. "It's the only day you get free candy."

"Yeah, I guess," Kester said

"Ms. Pam hates Halloween, too," Simone chimed in. "She thinks it's a waste of money giving out free candy. She bought some nasty candy to give out. I stole some but put it back when I ate one."

They all laughed as they continued to the next house and turned up a driveway with creepy music and mist coming from a fog machine.

"Hey, Simone, why do you call your mother Ms. Pam?" Kester asked. "Is she your sister or aunt or something?"

"No, stupid!" she said. "She's my mother! Not that it's any of your bee's wax."

"Then why call her Ms. Pam?" he asked again. "It sounds weird."

Nolan looked at Simone. He had always wondered the same thing but didn't dare ask.

"I don't know," she finally confessed. "It's what everyone calls her and she's never told me not to call her that. I mean...when I first met her I didn't know her. It was weird calling her Mummy."

"I get it," replied Kester.

"Yeah, it makes sense," echoed Nolan. "Sometimes when I'm really mad at my dad I call him Mike. He hates that."

They all burst into giggles.

"Yo! Your dad's name is Mike?" asked Kester. "For real?"

"Yeah, why?" asked Nolan.

"My dad's name is Mike too," Kester laughed. "That's funny."

"Come on you guys," yelled Omar, who was already at the end of the street. "We still have two more blocks to go."

An hour later, the children had covered nearly three streets on both sides and they headed back to the car. Simone and Nolan had stuffed their bags with candy. Mike was surprised at how much loot they'd got.

"Let's trade when we get home!" said Simone.

"Next year I'm bringing my pillowcase," Nolan said, getting into the car.

"Not me," Simone said. "I'm bringing a garbage bag."

Mike chuckled as he listened to them recount their entire

evening. By the time he pulled into the building's garage both kids had passed out in the back of the car with their hands and faces sticky with candy. When they got to Pam's apartment, Nolan was barely standing up and Mike had to carry Simone into the apartment.

"Come in," Pam whispered. She pulled in her robe. "How was it?"

"They had a good time," Mike said. "Simone's candy is in my car. I'll bring it by in the morning."

He placed Simone on her bed and Pam removed her boots, costume, and snow pants. She then covered her with a blanket. She was fast asleep with a smile on her face.

"She's dreaming of all that candy she's going to eat," Mike joked.

"I bet she is," Pam said. "Thank you, Mike! This really meant a lot to her."

"Anything for little Splimoney," he said.

They walked back to the living room. Nolan was asleep on Pam's sofa.

"Come on buddy, let's go! You're too big for me to lift you. Let's go." Mike tried in vain to rouse Nolan.

"Leave him," Pam said. "He can stay the night on the sofa. I'll make sure he's up for school."

"Are you sure?"

"Yes, man! He'll be fine." She went to the hall closet and pulled out a blanket and pillow for him. "It's the least I can do. I was feeling so lousy earlier and you taking Simone really helped me out tonight."

Mike smiled as he watched Pam take off Nolan's shoes before tucking him in with the blanket. She made sure he was snug and tight in his spot so he wouldn't fall off the couch. The way she fussed over him reminded him of the way Meghan used to tuck Nolan in at night. Pam glanced over at him and he looked down. They hadn't talked much since their argument.

"Mike," she called out. She followed him out of the apartment and into the hallway. "I just wanted to tell you...I'm just...I'm sorry for getting upset with you before. I didn't mean to say those things about you and your wife. It was wrong of me and—"

"Meghan and Dana are moving to Nova Scotia," he interrupted. "She's going to Dalhousie University to get her degree. She got a scholarship and everything."

"Oh, Mike," Pam said. "I had no idea. I don't know what to say."

"I don't know what to say either," he said, trying to laugh it off, avoiding eye contact with her. "It is what it is, I guess...it's just...I can't seem to wrap my mind around the idea that my marriage is over."

"I'm so sorry, Mike. I'm so very sorry for the both of you."

He smiled brightly as he wiped away a tear.

Pam held him as he tried to laugh off the pity party she was giving him but when she continued to hold him his whole body went limp. He attempted to *man up*, but as he pulled away from her embrace, her lips brushed up against his. He froze for a moment, then she moved in closer and purposefully kissed him. The moment was brief. Not long enough to turn into anything but a friendly reminder that he wasn't alone.

"You're a good man, Mike," she whispered to him. "One day she will realize it."

She then quickly went back into her apartment, shutting the door before he could respond. He stood in the hallway stunned, listening to her fasten the locks on her door. Part of him was in shock that she had kissed him, but another part was shocked at how much he had liked it.

Mike put on a pot of coffee. It was going to be another long day. He had just added another job to his full schedule. It wasn't enough that he worked part-time from Monday to Friday as a janitor for Ryerson University, or that he worked three evenings a week as a bartender at McKinney's, but now he was officially the weekend maintenance worker for a few of the area's Catholic churches.

He watched Nolan at the table, quietly playing with his cereal.

"Come on, Nols." He messed with his son's curly locks. "It's not like you're by yourself. Stop being so dramatic. Between Mrs. Price and your little girlfriend next door, you have plenty of company."

"Geez, she's not my girlfriend, Dad! I hate when you say that!"

"Okay…okay, buddy," Mike said, smiling. "I'm just teasing you."

"Dad, just tell the truth. Are we running out of money or something?"

"No…no, nothing like that." Mike wanted to keep busy, especially when he was upset. It had always been that way for him. Pick a goal, stay the course, and keep working. "I'm just working hard so that we can finally get the hell out of this dump and buy a house," he continued. "Maybe a Glenview townhouse by the mall."

"The Views," Nolan cried out. "God, I hate that place."

"Watch your mouth, Nolan." Mike smacked the back of his son's head.

"Ouch." Nolan rubbed his head. "I'm just saying that place sucks!"

The Views was a small townhouse complex across the street from Glenview Mall or, as Mike called it, "The Rich Mall". It was one of the few places close to the school that was affordable. It was also a haven for divorced single mothers who used their alimony and child support to purchase the two-bedroom town-homes.

"It's a nice place and closer to school," he said as he poured his coffee. "You wouldn't have to take a bus to school anymore. It would take you minutes to walk home. Plus, don't some of your classmates live there?"

"Yeah, well, all my friends are right here," Nolan said. "Plus, I don't think Mrs. Price is going to take a taxi over to The Views to watch me while you're working."

Mike stood there for a moment. He hadn't thought of that. His plan was clear and simple. He would buy a house. They would have more space and he would work like a dog to make the payments.

"Come on now, can't you let a guy dream?" he joked. "It's a long way off, anyways. By the time I get the down payment you'll be old enough to buy your own home."

"Yeah, whatever," Nolan said, clearing his plate from the table.

Nolan tried not to make a big deal of his dad's new job, but now, with his mother and sister leaving for Nova Scotia, he felt even more alone. As for The Views, it was only the prissy girls in his class who turned their noses up at everyone who didn't live there. They acted like they came from better neighbourhoods, even though many of them relied on government assistance just like he and his father did.

He walked to the balcony and noticed that Simone was out there doing her homework. She was always doing her homework on the balcony when the weather was nice, but today it was freezing cold and windy. She sat with her coat and gloves on as she worked on her math.

Nolan slid open the sliding door only to have a gust of freezing wind blow into the apartment. He quickly closed the door and ran over to the hall closet and grabbed his winter jacket, gloves, and book bag.

"Not your girlfriend, huh?" Mike said.

Nolan ignored his father but gave him a nasty look as he slid the door closed.

12

"Pregnant!" Pam said. She looked around the examination room of her doctor's office. "Are you sure?"

"Quite sure," her doctor said. "We'll have your blood work back in another day or so but, from what I can tell, you are about ten weeks along."

"Pregnant," she repeated in shock.

It wasn't any news that she'd expected. She had felt funny ever since Halloween, but thought she'd caught Mrs. Price's stomach flu. It all made sense, though. She had been an emotional wreck all week. First kissing Mike out of the blue, and then crying uncontrollably afterwards.

On the bus ride home from work, she tried to determine what to do next. She knew that Caleb would be happy that they were having a baby — he always talked about them starting a family — but a small part of her wished it wasn't happening so soon. They had just started living together and she'd wanted to wait a few years to see how the relationship was going before taking such a big step. They hadn't even talked about marriage, and now a baby was in the picture.

When she got home, she asked Mrs. Price if Simone could

sleep over. She wanted private time to tell Caleb that he was going to be a father. She started to relax when she imagined what kind of father he would be. She had already seen how he was with Simone and knew she didn't have to worry. She sat at the kitchen table, waiting.

When Caleb came in from work he had the biggest smile on his face.

"Hey baby," he said as he swooped down to kiss her. "How was work? Where's Simone?"

She looked up at him. She had planned to tell him over dinner but was anxious about the whole thing, so she decided to get it out of the way before her nerves took over.

"She's sleeping over at Mrs. Price's house," she said. "Caleb, I'm pregnant! Ten weeks pregnant."

Caleb's face drained of all colour. It wasn't the reaction she had expected from him. She'd assumed he would be excited, but instead he looked sheepishly at her.

"I'm sorry," he said meekly. "I'm just in shock. Things were going so nice for us. I just didn't factor in a baby just yet."

"I...I thought you would be more excited," she said, regretting that she had told him so frankly. "I thought you would be happy."

"No, baby, I'm happy," he said. "I just had plans of us doing it differently. Getting married, buying a house, and then having kids. That's all."

"Do you think that I wanted it to be like this?" she said, crying. "This is not how I wanted to do it again."

"Come here," he said, pulling her into his lap. "Please don't cry. Look....look, I want to show you something."

He pulled out a piece of paper from his wallet. He carefully opened it up and placed it on the table.

Pam looked at the paper, confused.

"Do you see that receipt?" he said, kissing her cheek. "That's a receipt for the down payment I put for an engagement ring. I don't have all the money for it yet, so they are holding it for me until I make the final payment."

"What are you saying, Caleb?" she asked him.

"I'm saying that you are the woman I want to spend the rest of my life with. I want to make you my wife."

"Caleb, I had no idea."

"Real talk, Pamela," he said. "I want us to have it all. To get married and have a truck-load of children. I don't want to be like my parents who never got married. I was just hoping that I would have the money saved for all of that to happen."

"I don't need fancy," she said. "All I need to know is that you'll be here for us."

"I will," he said, kissing her. "You never have to worry about that."

The next morning Caleb was back to his old excitable self. He stood in the kitchen dancing a slow wine with his wooden spoon as reggae music blared. He was cooking his specialty — poached eggs smothered with hollandaise sauce with a splash of pepper sauce sprinkled on top of a slice of bammy and a side of callaloo. Simone wandered into the apartment enticed by all the excitement, but before Pam had a moment to tell her daughter, Caleb blurted out the news.

"Sweet girl, your mother is having my baby!" he yelled over the music.

"What?" She turned the music down.

"God, Caleb," Pam said, rolling her eyes. "Are you going to chat our business to the whole building?"

"Yes, I am, because Simone is going to be a big sister and the whole building needs to know," he said as he grabbed Simone and started dancing with her. "And they need to know that I'm going to marry your mother and we soon be a family."

"Aren't you both too old to be having babies?" Simone said.

"Listen to her," Caleb laughed. He playfully danced Simone around Pam, who sat there beaming.

Caleb set Simone down and then rubbed and kissed Pam's belly. They started discussing baby names.

"That's great news." Simone sulked towards her bedroom.

"Aren't you hungry?" Pam asked. "Caleb made a nice breakfast for everyone."

"No. I had breakfast at Mrs. Price before I came home," she lied. "I have homework."

They both ignored her. She looked at them giggling to themselves and felt her eyes sting with tears. She couldn't understand why she felt so low or why she felt hurt by their joy but, in that instant, she felt like she was being left behind by her mother all over again.

▶

"AFTER AN INCISION IS MADE, *along the anterolateral, a trocar is then inserted. Once the arthroscope is properly inserted at the joint, the knee is distended with sterile saline solution...*"

"That's so gross," said Nolan.

He and Simone were sitting on the edge of Mrs. Price's living room sofa. Mrs. Price had finally had cable installed. She had more channels than anyone could imagine. Channel-surfing, they'd stumbled on the Surgery Channel and had been instantly hooked on the televised surgeries being performed. The program barely had any commercials, with only the lone narrator and the constant beeping from the medical equipment for sound. By the end of the week, they had seen cataract eye surgery, a hip replacement, and a brain tumour being removed. Today was knee surgery.

"Ew, the inside looks like chicken," Simone replied as the surgeon suctioned out the blood from the surrounding muscle tissue. "I can't believe that's what they did to Mrs. Price."

Mrs. Price had slipped on a patch of ice after the first ice storm of the season, which led to a knee replacement. Her youngest daughter, Esmeralda, or Esma, had moved in to help her mother while she recuperated.

"What are you two watching?" asked Esma. She walked in from the kitchen. "Jesus! That's disgusting!" She quickly turned the channel to *Let's Make a Deal*. "Don't you both have some homework to do?" She plopped on Mrs. Price's armchair.

"Nope," replied Simone coldly. She glared at Esma.

She hated that Esma always walked around like she was the queen of everything, moving things and snooping through Mrs. Price's drawers. She wished Mrs. Price wasn't stuck in her bedroom.

"Well, find something to do," said Esma. "Go outside or something."

They didn't need to be told twice. The two quickly got up and put on their coats and headed out the door.

"Make sure you're back before your parents come for you!" Esma yelled after them.

Nolan and Simone ran to the elevator and pressed the button. They were excited. They had been cooped up inside for the last week while the snow continued to fall heavily.

"Where do we go?" asked Simone.

"Come on," he said as the elevator opened. "Let's be explorers."

Nolan pressed the button for the top floor. They started to play tag in the stairwell that went even farther upstairs. When they got to the top of the stairs, there was a brick holding a door ajar. The door led to the building's rooftop. They opened the door and climbed over the brick, making sure that it stayed in place so they wouldn't get locked out. The wind blew strongly. They went to the edge and peered over the side.

From the top, they could see the entire complex. They could see the McCarthy boys holding their mother's hands as she walked through the snow. One of the twins ran off, but their mother grabbed him quick, slapping his behind swiftly before dragging them both into the building. They could see the other kids playing in the snow, trying to erect a snow fort. They watched these kids being chased inside by a stray German Shepherd.

"I never knew we had so many trees," said Simone as a gust of wind blew snow in her face. "Let's get out of here before we get blown over the edge."

"Let's go downstairs and find a tree for a tree house," said Nolan excitedly. "I want to climb the one behind the dumpster."

They raced back down the roof stairway, screaming like someone was chasing them. They ran into the open elevator and headed for the lobby. Nolan pressed every button before they dashed out of the elevator car. They headed towards the cluster of trees by the dumpster and Nolan began climbing the big maple tree.

Simone was a little hesitant. The tree trunk was wet and icy. She never was one to climb trees. Her heart was pounding. It was so much freedom at once that she just wanted to burst. She climbed up behind Nolan and reached as high as him. They both sat in the crutch of the branch.

"Whoa, you can see into those apartments from here," said Nolan. "This would make an awesome spot for a tree house."

"Yeah, it would be great," she said. She swung her feet and looked at the ground below. "We should make it a clubhouse."

"Yo, that's a great idea!" he said. "You, me, and Kester can be the first members."

"Ugh...Kester," she said. "I don't know why you are friends with him. He's such a dummy."

"That's what he says about you," Nolan said, grinning. "Come on, let's go home before it gets dark."

Simone remained sitting on the heavy branch and let the cold air blast against her face. It was bitterly cold but she didn't mind. It was nice up in the tree, with no one calling her name or knowing where she was. Just complete silence.

Nolan turned to her. "What's wrong, Si?"

"I can't get down," she said. "I mean...I don't want to get down."

"You want to stay up here?"

"Yes," she said. "My mother would never climb up here. She hates being high up. She would never reach me."

The two of them sat quietly looking at the sun slowly setting. It was going to get dark soon and she knew her mother was going to be home shortly, but she didn't care.

"She's having a baby, you know?"

"Really? Wow! That's kind of cool, right?"

"Not really. She gets angry a lot more because of the baby."

"Ya, I can tell...I mean I can hear her through my wall sometimes," he replied. "But my dad does that too! They all yell."

"Not like her," she said, tracing the scratch on her face she'd received that morning. "It's different...I can't do anything right."

She wanted to tell Nolan how bad things had gotten with her mother. The constant yelling. Her arm getting twisted when she didn't move fast enough or being boxed in the ears any time she talked back. Before, it didn't happen when Caleb was around, but now her mother didn't care.

"I just want to stay up here forever," she said.

"Umm...okay," he said. "I'll stay with you so you won't get scared, but if we stay up here you can't tease me if I pee my pants."

"That's so nasty," she said, squinting at him.

"I mean it. I'll stay if you want me to."

"I know," she said, smiling back at him, before they made their way back down the tree.

▶

"YOU ARE LIKE A SLUG," Pam screamed at Simone. "Do you know what that is? A slob on the ground that is useless. Pick up the garbage and take it out to the trash chute and don't have me tell you again!"

"Fine!" Simone yelled, slamming doors as she went into each room to collect the garbage. She stomped back out into the living room but ended up dropping the big garbage bag. She started to cry as she picked up the dirty tissues and banana peels from the carpet.

Just then, Caleb walked into the apartment. "What happened now?" he asked.

Simone brushed past him, slamming the front door.

"She's impossible, Caleb," Pam said. "Her whole purpose in life is to piss me off but mi gonna fix her business if she comes back with that stink attitude of hers."

Caleb sat down at the dining table. He sighed loudly as he watched Pam chopping onions, slamming the knife into the counter, yelling about Simone talking back to her and taking her sweet time to collect the trash.

"Today, for example," she continued. "Mi tell her to eat her lunch and stop wasting mi blasted food. She come home with her food still in her lunch pail."

"She's a kid, Pamela," he said. "Kids do the complete opposite from what we want. We were the same way."

"Noooo, not me!" she said adamantly. "When I her age I did exactly what mi fadda tell me. He say jump an mi ask how high an if me can cum back down. When mi her age, mi haffi wash all mi own dirty draws, iron mi clothes and fix mi own dinner."

"Chups! Yuh nuh let her mess with di stove or di iron. How she gwan wash har draws wen yuh have a fit if she go inna di basement?" he asked, trying to lighten the mood.

"That's not my point, Caleb," she said. "Everyone spoils that child! Aunt Marva, Mrs. Price...you! That girl came with too many bad habits."

"But yelling at her and slapping her up is not going to change those habits," he said. "It's making her act up even more because,

123

no matter what she does, you still yell at her. You push her too hard and one day she's going to push you right back."

"Well, then she can leave this household if it comes to that," she said as she chopped the onions even more furiously.

Caleb got up from his seat and calmly took the knife from Pam and continued to chop the onions himself.

"Go sit down," he said.

She kissed her teeth at him.

The apartment was becoming too cramped for the three of them. He could only imagine how stressful it was going to be once his mother arrived after the baby was born. He knew it was only a matter of time before things got worse.

He had resumed driving a taxicab at night, hoping the extra income would give him enough money for a down payment on one of the townhouses at Finch and Leslie. He hoped that with a little more space, a backyard for Simone to play in, and his mother staying with them, things would be less stressful for Pam.

"Pamela, you need to calm down," he said as he poured the onions into the pot of oxtail she was cooking. "You get what you put into your relationship with Simone. You come at her angry, she will only respond in anger."

"There you go trying to sound like that damn foolish Donahue," she scowled.

"Well, if that's the case, he sounds like a smart man." He covered the pot. "I know this is hard right now but you can't stress yourself so much. That baby and you need to keep calm."

"I know," she said, wearily rubbing her stomach. She was almost five months and her patience was starting to wear thin with juggling work, Simone, and her pregnancy. She wished Caleb would help out more, but his dream of moving them out of the complex seemed to be his sole purpose in life.

"And try to be softer with Simone," he added as he slipped his arms around her. "She's not even nine years old and you have her acting like an old lady. She's a kid. She's supposed to have fun.

She's supposed to run around with her friends and get into a little trouble."

"Yeah, well, do you think she could be a kid and not move like a slug?" she snapped back. "She's slower than molasses."

"And you're too quick with your temper," he said. "Just relax, man!"

Pam looked at him and he made a face. She started to laugh, but then Simone walked back into the apartment, and her mood quickly turned sour as she watched the girl stomp back to her room, slamming her bedroom door.

13

S imone sat quietly after completing Mrs. Barrett's math test, but then she started to play with her pencil, waiting for the rest of the class to finish.

"Simone, stop that racket!" Mrs. Barrett said. "Shouldn't you be concentrating on your test and not disrupting the class?"

"I'm all finished, Ma'am."

"Well, then spend the time checking your work," Mrs. Barrett told her.

"I did that, Ma'am," she replied.

"Well, then sit still. Better yet, go over to Miss Gardiner's class with this note."

"Yes, Ma'am," she said excitedly. She loved going to Miss Gardiner's classroom.

Miss Gardiner was now the ESL/Special Education teacher. Her classroom wasn't like the other classrooms. Instead of rows of desks and a plain blackboard, hers was carpeted with a few round tables students could sit at. It was like a playroom, with lots of storybooks, puzzles, and even a dress-up trunk. She taught ESL students for a few hours in the morning and in the afternoon focused on students with learning disabilities. The ESL students had just been dismissed and were heading back to their regular classes when Simone arrived, and Miss Gardiner was cleaning her blackboard before the next session.

"Good morning, Miss," Simone said cheerfully.

"Good morning, Simone."

"I have a note for you from Mrs. Barrett."

Miss Gardiner took the note and walked back to her desk and sat down. She looked up at Simone beaming at her. She placed the note on her desk without reading it.

Simone could tell that Miss Gardiner wasn't in a very good mood. Usually, they would have a bubbly conversation about Jamaica or how she was doing in school, but this time she seemed distracted and upset.

"Is everything okay, Miss?"

"Everything is fine. Don't mind me. I just have a lot on my mind."

◄◄

THE WEEKLY STAFF meeting had aggravated Miss Gardiner. She had brought up her plans to ask the school board for extra funds to test students who showed the potential to be gifted, but she had been shot down.

"Not this time," Mrs. Barrett said. "As our school's liaison, I have bigger fish to fry, like trying to make sure that our new principal is familiarized in the ways of our school. That's our first priority. Not some meaningless test for a bunch of foreigners who can't take the time to learn English properly."

Miss Gardiner stood up in response.

"Many of my students have a high aptitude for learning, but are being held back for not mastering the English language. At least four students are far ahead of the average in mathematics. But it's not just the ESL students," she went on.

"There are other students who are extremely bright. Take Simone Allen, for example. She's a student in your class and I worked with her over the summer. She shows exceptional promise and would be a prime candidate for a gifted program."

"Miss Gardiner, are we really doing this right now?" Mrs. Barrett smiled stiffly as the other faculty members looked on. "I have a lot of students who are just as bright as Simone, who also deserve to be recognized, but that's not how we do things at St. Augustine. We don't give any student special treatment."

"But I'm not asking for special treatment," she said. "I'm only saying that students like Simone go unnoticed because we're not given the right tools to properly identify them."

"Miss Gardiner, you seem to have an affinity for Simone Allen," said Mrs. Barrett coolly. "Is it because she's black that you find it necessary to bring her up?"

"No...not at all!" she started to stutter. "I'm just pointing out that—"

"You are new to teaching," Mrs. Barrett said, interrupting her. "Let me say this for your own good. The school board doesn't appreciate teachers favouring students because they are the same race. That's not why we hire black teachers. You might want to think about that the next time you wish to bring up Simone Allen."

Miss Gardiner felt completely flustered. She looked around at the other teachers, and they turned away from her. She knew that many of them were just as frustrated as she was at the way the school was being managed, but not one of them would speak up. She felt helpless.

▶▶

THE NOTE SENT by Mrs. Barrett was to inform her of another

student she planned to transfer to the ESL class. Miss Gardiner crumpled the letter, tossing it in the trash.

Simone was playing with the Chinese medicine balls she kept in a case on her desk. She laughed a little as she watched the girl trying to master them.

"It's like this," she said, picking up the metal balls and swirling them in the palm of her left hand.

"Let me try," Simone said, taking the balls from her and slowly swirling them until she got the hang of it. "I did it! Where you get this, Miss? I'm going to ask my mother to buy me some."

"Take them," she said.

"Really?"

"Absolutely!" she said as the lunch bell rang. "You better get back to class."

"Yes, Miss," she said, collecting her new prize. "Thank you, Miss Gardiner."

Miss Gardiner got up from her desk and hurried out of her classroom to get her lunch. She collided with the new principal, Abe Nikolaos, in the hallway.

"Mr. Nikolaos!"

At the age of thirty-five, Abraham Nikolaos was one of the district's youngest principals. Despite his youth, his reputation for swiftly reforming troubled schools had grabbed the school board's attention. His last high school had been one of the worst in the district and he'd turned it into one of the best, and he had built an advanced program for the many Asian students he had actively recruited.

"Miss Gardiner, I'm so glad I ran into you," he said, handing her a notebook. "Do you have a minute? I would like a word."

"Yes, I have some time," she said, holding her books in her hand. "What can I do for you?"

"Well, as you may know, many of the district's Special-Ed and ESL students will be transferred to St. Francis where they have a better facility and more faculty."

"Am I getting transferred?" she asked. They continued to walk down the hallway.

"No, no, no," he said. "I'm looking to make some changes for next year at St. Augustine. The school board wants to consolidate the area's Gifted Programs under one roof and I think our school would be the perfect campus."

"That would be incredible," she said, taken aback. "This school sorely needs a program like this. We have so many students who would be great candidates. I just wish more teachers were on board."

"What do you mean?" he asked.

"Frankly, Mr. Nikolaos, I'm having a hard time getting support from some of the teachers. Especially with regard to our foreign students."

"That has been my experience, too," he said. "I felt it the moment I walked into this school. Unfortunately, it's becoming increasingly difficult to get any faculty interested in my ideas. What would you suggest?"

"If you give me thirty minutes, I can tell you exactly what could help," she said. "In fact, I think my suggestion might help get that gifted program you want for this school."

Over the next month, Miss Gardiner and Principal Nikolaos arranged for the entire third and fourth grades to be given a beta test during school hours in the gymnasium, monitored by a school-board appointee. The results showed many students scoring well above the provincial average.

After an emergency meeting with the school board, Mr. Nikolaos got permission to change things around. Mrs. Barrett and Mrs. Peters were asked to switch classes. Instead of teaching the third/fourth-grade split class, Mrs. Barrett would now teach the third grade, while Mrs. Peters would be instructing the smarter third- and fourth-graders. Mr. Nikolaos hoped this would help them prepare for the new gifted program that was going to be implemented at St. Augustine the following year.

Miss Gardiner smiled at Mr. Nikolaos while he went over the new changes at the next staff meeting. She was especially happy to see Simone Allen finally properly placed, together with the other gifted students, in Mrs. Peters' class.

▶

SIMONE SAT on top of the dryer, waiting for the clothes to dry. Her mother had finally entrusted her to do the laundry on her own. She'd brought the clothes down and separated them, making sure not to mix the colours and whites. She'd carefully poured the bleach into the sitting water for the whites, and now the clothes were to stay in the dryer for precisely one hour. She sat like a pit bull on the dryer, making sure no one messed with their laundry. It was the perfect time to work on the short story her new teacher had assigned.

Simone and a handful of students had sat the three-hour test, and then had been transferred to Mrs. Peters' new third/fourth-grade class. Mrs. Peters was short, mousy, and serious about their class work, but she was nice and fair and didn't yell like Mrs. Zennewich, nor was she mean like Mrs. Barrett.

Simone was glad to be out of Mrs. Barrett's class. Her former teacher had a knack for finding ways to diminish her in front of the class. She always called her out for talking during quiet time or when she didn't complete her homework correctly. She constantly reminded everyone that Simone had gone to summer school, and, even though Simone worked hard as she could — completing four pages of math homework when the assignment was two pages, or drawing an African jungle filled with every mammal when the homework was to draw one — Mrs. Barrett never praised her. She was only singled out for bad things.

In Mrs. Peters' class, she didn't feel the pressure of being under the teacher's microscope. Her new teacher treated her like everyone else. She was expected to do her work, and, if she were caught talking with a classmate during class, both of them would be threatened with detention, not just her.

Her new class was the smallest in the school with only eight third-graders and ten fourth-graders. That was nice, but she quickly realized that she was no longer the smartest student in the class. Several students were either just as good as her or even better. Sarah Jane and quiet James Chow and Ilene Cheng were in the class, and they were pretty smart, too.

Simone and Ilene were assigned seats together, but Simone despised Ilene, who always corrected her English any time she mispronounced a word; and Ilene hated Simone for laughing out loud anytime she got a question wrong. Both girls were bright daughters of immigrants who lived under the iron thumb of their strict parents. Yet neither recognized how alike they were and, despite their similar backgrounds, they preferred to be bitter rivals.

Despite the mid-year upheaval, Simone and her classmates quickly adapted to their new teacher and routine. They were more engaged in their lessons and enjoyed the challenging work Mrs. Peters gave them. It was the teachers who seemed to have the hardest time adjusting to the changes.

At the end of the first week, an angry Mrs. Barrett showed up at Simone's class with five of her students close behind her. The two teachers ended up in a heated argument, with Mrs. Barrett threatening to contact her union rep about her over-populated class. She had decided to take matters into her own hands and transferred five of her students to Mrs. Peters' class — one being Nolan O'Shea.

Mrs. Peters' students sat at their desks, giggling, as Mrs. Peters and Mrs. Barrett battled loudly in the hallway; then Principal Nikolaos arrived to try to mediate the situation.

"I don't care what the union rep has to say," Mrs. Peters said.

"You can't just dump your students without proper notice. I don't even have desks for them to sit in."

"That's not my problem," said Mrs. Barrett as she huffed away down the hallway. "*He's* the principal. He's the one who decided to change things around here. Let him figure it out."

"I'm sorry for all of this, Beth," Principal Nikolaos said. "Bear with me and I'll get this all straightened out."

"It's okay, Abe," said Mrs. Peters. "Sharon has always gotten away with being a bully around here."

"And I'm sorry for that," he said. "I appreciate your patience."

Simone was thrilled that Nolan was in the same class as her. As the school's janitor swiftly brought in desks for the Barrett Five, she excitedly waved at him and he waved back while Mrs. Peters frantically tried to figure out how to get books and supplies for her newest students.

Notorious troublemakers and best friends Daniel Peebles and Brian Kepler sat with Nolan in the back. The chatty Moretti cousins, Vivian and Cathy, sat directly behind Simone and Ilene. Simone could hear Ilene mumbling to herself in Cantonese and then heard her whisper how much she hated the Moretti cousins before slumping in her seat.

The Moretti cousins were just two of twenty Moretti students who had attended St. Augustine. Over the last ten years, every grade and class had had a Moretti student. Being a St. Augustine teacher meant having to deal with their loud, overbearing, and obnoxious parents, who ran practically every facet of St. Augustine that required volunteers.

Some of the fourth-graders turned around and snickered at Vivian and Cathy. They were the only Moretti students in the third grade, and they claimed fame by boasting about their older brothers who were the resident schoolyard bullies. Neither girl was particularly pleased about being in Mrs. Peters' class. Despite who their brothers were, they were still teased for being held back in the first grade.

"Faccia di culo! What are you looking at?" Vivian snapped at the students sitting in the fourth-grade section, looking at her. She then turned and made a face at Ilene. "I can smell your egg rolls from all the way over here."

"Mangia merda," laughed Cathy, picking dirt from underneath her nails. "Turn the fuck around, chink!"

Ilene quickly turned away, her face burning bright red. The two cousins continued to speak Italian to each other in low voices. Occasionally Mrs. Peters looked up at them with a scowl on her face, but the girls continued to whisper and giggle.

"Simone," Vivian whispered.

Simone tried to ignore her. Mrs. Peters was in a foul mood and she didn't want to be lumped in with them as being a troublemaker.

"Simone!" Vivian whispered again. She threw an eraser at her.

"What!" Simone said. "I'm trying to do my work!"

"You're friends with Nolan, right?" she asked. "Cathy is in love with that brutta faccia."

"Shut up, Viv," Cathy said, hitting her leg.

"Ouch, stop it! That fucking hurts."

"Vivian and Cathy Moretti," said Mrs. Peters. "Since you have no interest in finishing your math problems, go to Miss Gardiner and finish your work there."

"Yes, Mrs. Peters," they said in unison.

"Simone, have lunch with us later," Vivian called out from the doorway.

At lunch period Simone sat with Cathy, Vivian, and a swarm of girls while they grilled her about her friendship with Nolan. The cousins even offered her their Nutella sandwiches.

Simone was confused. It was as if every girl had suddenly become her best friend. She didn't understand all the attention until Yvette and Angie told her that most of the third-grade girls had a huge crush on Nolan. By the end of the week, Simone was so annoyed by the constant questions that she started to wish that she didn't know Nolan at all.

"Here." She passed him Tammy's envelope with his name written on it.

It was too cold to sit on the balcony and finish their homework, so they were at Simone's kitchen table, while Pam was in her bedroom talking on the telephone.

Tammy had cornered Simone during recess, begging her to take the note to Nolan. Simone instantly refused. She had already been in trouble twice that week for talking in class.

"I'm not your personal mailman, Tammy."

"Puleeeeaaaase, Simone! It's an emergency. I'll give you anything you want!"

Tammy was a pudgy girl who lived in The Views next door to Sarah Jane. She was known for being boy-crazy and spent most of the time playing with her curly red hair and daydreaming about her crush of the week. When she heard that Simone and Nolan were neighbours, she quickly set her sights on Simone as her own Cyrano de Bergerac.

"He's standing right there, Tammy," Simone said. "Why don't you just give it to him yourself?"

"No way," she screamed. "I can't! I don't want him to know that I like him."

"You give him notes all the time. What's so different about this one?"

"In the other notes I was asking him about his favourite TV show or song but this one is different," she said. Her face turned cherry red. "Come on, Simone...please, I'm begging you. If I give it to you then I won't chicken out."

"Fine," she said snatching the note. "But I want two packs of Hubba Bubba...the strawberry flavour."

"Here...here, I only have one pack, but I'll bring the other on Monday." She pulled the gum from her bag.

Nolan recognized the writing right away. The heart instead of the "a" was a dead giveaway. Tammy Willows had been sending him notes the entire week, even after Mrs. Peters had threatened detention to anyone caught passing any more messages. He opened the pink envelope and a whiff of perfume escaped. He rolled his eyes at Simone as he crumpled the paper.

"I want to read it," Simone said. She grabbed the note before he could throw it in his bag. "She's giving me two packs of gum for this. I want to see what the big deal is."

She un-crumpled the note and smoothed out the page carefully before reading it in her most stuffy Canadian accent.

Hi Nolan,
Will you be my science partner?
Circle your answer below:
♡ Yes
:(No

"Lawd Jesus, she fool, she fool," Simone said mimicking her mother's favourite expression. "So what are you going to tell her?"

"Man," he said. "I don't want to be her partner."

"Well, you'll hurt her feelings if you say no." She handed back the note. "You know she likes you."

"Yeah, well, she's too late," he said smartly. "I already have my science fair partner."

"Yeah, who?" she asked.

"You, stupid," he said, teasing her. "Duh!"

Simone smiled as she punched him on the shoulder. She hadn't planned on being his partner but was a little smitten that he wanted to be hers.

She delivered the message to Tammy during recess, but Tammy refused to give her the second pack of gum. "That was a dirty trick, Simone!" she yelled. "You are supposed to be my friend and now you're his science partner?"

"It's not my fault he said no. I'm not the boss of him!" Simone yelled back. "You and everyone else need to stop bugging me about Nolan. If you want to talk to him then talk to him yourself and leave me out of it!"

Tammy stormed off and Simone could see her whispering to her friends and they all looked at her and shook their heads.

She was sick of the entire deal. She sulked off to the other side of the school, where the kindergarten kids played and sat by the fence and started to cry. She didn't know what made her feel so sad. Usually, she brushed off situations like this.

A tennis ball rolled up to her feet. She picked it up. Ilene Cheng was walking towards her. Ilene was the last person she wanted to talk to. She didn't have the strength for another fight.

"Why are you crying?" Ilene asked bluntly.

"Just leave me alone," Simone said.

"Well, can I have my ball back?"

Simone threw her the ball.

Ilene caught it. She walked away but turned and looked back at Simone who sat on the ground digging a hole in the grass with a stick.

"Do you want to play?" she asked. "I'm just throwing the ball against the wall. I made up my own game. I call it whip ball. I pretend it's the face of someone I hate and try to whip the ball as hard as I can against the wall. You want to play?"

Simone stopped digging her hole and looked up at Ilene and nodded.

At the wall, Ilene handed her the ball and Simone whipped it as hard as she could. It felt good. She was smashing Tammy's face against the wall. Simone caught the ball and then threw it again. This time it was Sarah Jane's face. Ilene caught the ball and threw it hard and caught it and smiled at Simone.

"That was Cathy's stupid face," she said laughing.

▶

"I DON'T GET IT," Simone said.

She and Pam and Caleb were at the kitchen table feasting on Swiss Chalet chicken that Caleb had brought home for dinner. It was the first time in a long time they had all sat down as a family for dinner. Caleb worked most nights and Simone spent most evenings with Mrs. Price while her mother rested after getting back from the hospital.

"What don't you get?" Caleb gave Simone a silly look.

"Well, you work at a bank, right?" she asked.

"Yes."

"And working at a bank pays a lot, right?"

"Yes, I guess you can say it pays well."

"Well, then why work as a cab driver at night?"

"Well, Ms. Nosey, the bank pays well, but it's not enough for what I need," he said, grinning. "We have big things coming our way. In a year, we'll be moving out of here and into a house. That's why I'm driving a cab. Caleb the cab driver. Maybe I'll own my own fleet of cars and start a side business."

"Okay, Caleb the cab driver," Simone laughed.

Pam smiled as the baby kicked. She looked on as Simone continued to laugh and joke with Caleb. She could feel her back stiffening and got up to stretch. "Alright, silly people," she said loudly. "I'm going to take a walk downstairs and pick up some ice cream."

"Mint chocolate chip," begged Simone.

"Nah mon, rum and raisin," countered Caleb. "That's real ice cream."

"I'll get both," she said, smiling at them.

"Yay," squealed Simone. "Thank you, Ms. Pam!"

Pam wandered around the complex for a while before heading to the convenience store. She didn't have many opportunities to explore the complex grounds and the weather was mild and almost spring-like, even though the crunchy ice beneath her feet said otherwise. She looked up into the night sky at the bright twinkling stars. The night sky looked like a *National Geographic* photo. It was beautiful and calming.

She wandered over to the playground, where she could see Mike sitting on the swing set, smoking a cigarette. Since her pregnancy, they hadn't had much time for each other. The occasional hello as they passed in the hallway was all the conversation they'd had in weeks. The cold winter weather didn't help matters either. With the freezing winds blowing against the balcony doors, neither of them wanted to venture out and so their evening coffee breaks had come to an end.

"What are you doing out here?" she asked as she sat down on the empty swing beside him.

"Nolan is having his weekly phone call with his mother." He took a long drag from his cigarette. "I didn't feel up to being in the room while she blew smoke up his ass."

"I guess she already moved to Nova Scotia," she deciphered.

"Yup, her and Dana are pretty much settled in. How about you and your new baby and your perfect new family?"

Pam shook her head. Mike was being nasty to her. She stood up to leave.

"No wait," he said, grabbing her hand. "I'm sorry...I'm just in a lousy mood right now."

Pam looked at him. His face looked haggard. She put her hand softly under his chin, lifting his face up. "You look bad, Michael O'Shea. You're not sleeping much these days?"

"I've turned Jamaican," he said, smiling. "I now have three jobs."

"Lawd Jesus, three jobs? No wonder you look so tired," she said. Her laugh turned into a hearty belch. "Oh, excuse me. I've been having the worst indigestion. Worse than when I was pregnant with Simone."

She sat down again on the swing and pulled some Tums from her pocket.

"My Gram used to tell me that heartburn during a pregnancy

meant a baby with a full head of hair," Mike said, tossing his cigarette butt into the snow bank.

"Well, then this one must have a massive afro." She laughed through another belch as she tried to adjust herself on the swing.

For a moment they sat in silence.

"What do you think about Mrs. Peters?" he said.

"She seems okay. Better than Mrs. Barrett. That woman is always screwing up her face like she smelt her upper lip."

"Believe it or not, she was a teacher when I went to St. Augie," he laughed. "We used to call her Mrs. Battle-Axe behind her back."

"Oh, so you're the reason she's so miserable," said Pam. "I don't know how she has lasted so long being a teacher. She seems to hate her students. Never a kind word from her mouth."

"Don't tell anyone, but I'm actually related to her," he said.

"Backside!" she howled.

"Yup, she's my father's brother's daughter."

"So she's your cousin!"

"Shhh...it sounds like we're related when you put it in those terms," he replied. "And please don't tell Nolan. If he knew he would want to switch schools."

"How does Nolan not know?" she asked. "Doesn't he notice her at family gatherings?"

"To be honest, since my father passed, I haven't really kept in touch with that side of the family," he said. "I don't really know my mother's side either. The only family I had was Meg and the kids."

"I catch what you mean. All my family died off a long time ago," she said.

They continued to sit silently looking up into the night sky.

"I guess that's when you know that you're an adult," he said. "When your family is no longer your anchor."

"Or when there's none left," added Pam.

14

"Where's Simone?" Kester asked.

Nolan and Kester were riding the school bus to the complex. Nolan had begged his father for weeks to let Kester sleep over and Mike had finally relented. It was the first time he'd had a friend over since his parents had started living apart.

"She's sick," Nolan said as he sifted through Kester's latest pack of baseball cards. "She's been out for the last two days."

"No wonder it's been so quiet at school," Kester joked.

The two boys laughed. When the bus pulled up to the stop, they ran up the path and into the stairwell, climbed up the eleven flights, and then raced down the hallway to Mrs. Price's door. They walked into the empty apartment.

Nolan went into the kitchen and opened the fridge door. He pulled out the jug of milk and some cookies from the cupboard. As they sat eating at the kitchen table, Mrs. Price came into the apartment.

"That poor baby," she sighed. She walked into the kitchen to wash her hands. "She's sick as a dog."

"Can we go over to visit her later?" asked Nolan.

"No, baby." Mrs. Price shook her head. "Simone is still way too sick. Do you have any homework?"

"I do, but it's Friday!" Nolan protested. "Kester's here...can't I just do it later?"

"Your father told you to finish your homework before he picks you up," she reminded him. "The sooner you get it done, the quicker you get to go out and play."

Nolan sulked as he pulled out his math homework. Simone usually helped him, which made the work go faster, but, with her out sick, he knew it was going to take him a while to get through it all.

"But what about Kester? He's going to be bored sitting here waiting for me."

"Nolan, stop troubling yourself about Kester. He can watch TV in my bedroom while you finish your work." She pulled out more cookies for Kester before sending him away to watch television.

Kester stuck his tongue out at Nolan.

Nolan glared back at him. Kester usually got away with everything when it came to Mrs. Price. He was her favourite.

▶

MRS. PRICE HAD KNOWN Kester's family for years. In Jamaica, she had lived next door to his grandmother, Beverly, before she got married and moved to Toronto. When Mrs. Price finally made her way up to Canada, she'd been heartbroken to find out that her childhood friend had died after a stroke.

As the years went by, she watched Beverly's daughter, Cicely, grow up to be a beautiful young woman, and she celebrated Cicely's marriage to a fellow Jamaican, a mechanic named Michael. The young couple moved into the building next to hers after the wedding and Mrs. Price became part of their family — a replacement for Beverly.

Mrs. Price was with Cicely for the birth of all her children and kept in touch with them when they moved to their four-bedroom house. When Cicely found herself pregnant again with their fourth child — the unwanted one — they all referred to him in jest as 'the accident', but when he was born they named him Kester.

It always bothered Mrs. Price that Kester was regarded as an afterthought. He was the runt of the family — short and maaga. His parents ignored him and he was a prime target for his older brothers' relentless teasing and tormenting. Mrs. Price often sat behind them at the Pentecostal church they all attended. The older boys would lick their nasty fingers and stick them in Kester's ears. If she sat close enough to them she would box the back of their heads, quietly cussing them out in patois.

Through it all, Little Kester remained her darling. He visited her whenever he came to the neighbourhood to play with Nolan. She often laughed to herself when she eavesdropped on the two boys playing. Little Kester always had a big mouth around Nolan, acting like he was a big man, but it was all an act. He barely talked at home with his family. When his father was around, with his booming voice and heavy hand, Kester was timid and fearful.

It pleased Mrs. Price that he felt comfortable enough to be his true self at her place. That's why she spoiled him with treats. Why she always slipped him a dollar when no one was looking. Why she turned a blind eye when she caught him dressing up in her clothes.

Her heart sank the first time she caught him wearing one of her dresses. She ran into her room and ripped the yellow dress off him. He started to cry. Of course, he didn't understand why she was so angry. He was too young. It crushed her seeing him reduced to tears. She didn't want to come down hard on him the way the others did, so she hugged him and tried to explain why it was bad for little boys to wear dresses.

"But I want to be like my mommy," he said. "I want to be beautiful like her!"

Mrs. Price thought the phase would pass as he got older, but instead it became a routine. She didn't know what to do. She didn't want to make an issue about it with his parents. It was only dressing up. It could be their secret.

But that night, while Mrs. Price was fixing a mug of tea and Nolan was doing his homework, she forgot Kester's routine. It slipped her mind until she noticed that the TV in her room had been quiet for a long time. If Simone had been there, she would have been in the bedroom watching television with Kester and nothing would have happened.

Nolan got up after finishing his homework and, before she could stop him, ran to her bedroom and threw open the door. She quickly followed him, but it was too late. Kester was twirling around in one of her old dresses.

Nolan stood in shock with his mouth gaping as Kester danced around in her baby-blue button-down dress. It was the one she had worn as a girl. The one she kept to remember her youth.

He spun faster and faster.

She called out and Kester looked up.

Silence.

"GET OUT!" he screamed when he saw Nolan. "GET OUT! STOP LOOKING AT ME!"

He quickly pushed Nolan out the room and slammed the door.

"Kester," she said calmly through her bedroom door. "Come nuh. It'll be all right. Open the door."

After a few minutes, Kester opened the door and, dressed in his own clothes, fled the room.

"KESTER!" She hobbled past Nolan but couldn't keep up. By the time she got to the front door of her apartment, Kester was already down the hallway. He ran past Mike and quickly disappeared down the stairwell.

"What in the world is going on?" Mike said. "Where is Kester going? I thought he was sleeping over at our place tonight."

"Lawd Jesus! I don't know what is going on with that boy," she said, looking to Nolan. "I need to call his madda."

"Of course, Mrs. Price. Absolutely!" said Mike. "Is everything okay?"

"Yes man!" she said. "Nothing to bother yourself over."

"Okay then," he replied. "Come on, Nolan."

"Much thanks," she yelled out.

She didn't wait to see them out. She rushed to her bedroom. She felt sick with worry over Kester. She needed to make sure he was okay. She went to her bedroom to call his mother. Her old light-blue dress was crumpled on the floor. She suddenly sat on the bed with tears in her eyes.

"Oh, Kester," she said to herself. "God Almighty!"

▶

EVERYTHING HAPPENS ON A FRIDAY, Simone had once told Nolan.

It was a theory that she had thought up the day she got into a fight with Mikey Moretti. Every schoolyard fight. Every car accident. Getting a lousy grade from your teacher. The day you break your leg or skin your knee. Everything seemed to happen on a Friday. Nolan had laughed and said she was crazy but this Friday, after he walked in on Kester, he started to wonder if she was right.

He was too scared to talk to his father about what had occurred and he couldn't go back to Mrs. Price's apartment to talk to her. He didn't know what to do. He thought about calling Kester but was afraid to talk to him. He didn't understand what was happening to his friend. "There's no way Kester would wear a dress," he thought. "It must be a prank, a joke. Why had he dressed like a girl? Did he like boys now? Was he a fairy? But this is Kester. He's the coolest person I know. He's all about Eddie Murphy and basketball, not acting like a girl. Why would he act like a sissy?"

That night he could barely sleep. He got out of bed and snuck out to the balcony. He needed to talk to Simone and hoped that she was awake. Her room was on the balcony side of her apartment so he quietly walked over to her window. It was unlocked. He opened it and slipped into her room. Her bedroom smelt like a fog of vapour rub and steam as her humidifier hummed. He went over to her bed and shook her slightly.

"Simone," he said as quietly as possible. "Simone."

After a few attempts, she woke up, groggy from her cold. "Nolan, is that you?" she asked. "What time is it?"

"I don't know," he replied. "It's late."

"I'm sick, Nolan and too dizzy to talk. Can this wait until tomorrow?"

"Simone, if you saw me do something really bad, like kill a cat or steal something from the convenience store, would you stop being my friend?"

"Nols, you're not making any sense," she said rubbing her eyes. "Did you kill a cat?"

"No, I didn't," he said flustered. "But if you did see me do something like that, would you? Would you stop being my friend?"

"No, stupid," she said. "I would make Father Paul sprinkle holy water to take the devil out, but I guess I would still be your friend. Why are you asking me such a dumb question?"

"I saw Kester wearing a dress today," he blurted out.

"What? Say that again?" Simone sat up. "Did you say that you saw Kester wearing a dress?"

"We were at Mrs. Price's apartment," he said quickly. "I was doing my homework in the kitchen while he was watching television in her room and when I went over to her room...that's when I caught him wearing it. He was spinning around in a blue dress!"

"Come on, stop fooling."

"Simone, I'm not joking."

"So wait, he had a dress on and everything?" she asked again. "Are you sure you saw what you saw?"

"With my own eyes."

"Wow!"

They sat for a moment, staring at each other.

"There are some people like that in Jamaica," she said. "There was a woman...I mean a man, who lived down the street from my Auntie's house. He walk pon di street in drag. Auntie always made me turn my head. She said people like him are sinners and need a good whipping."

"Really?" he said. "Did they beat up on him?"

"Not really. Sometimes kids would throw rocks at him. Not to kill him. Just to mess with him. He was a little sick in the head so most of the time everyone left him alone. But Kester don't seem sick in his head. I mean...I don't think he is — is he?"

Nolan didn't know how to answer her. He had known Kester longer than she had. He should know everything about him, but now he felt like he knew nothing.

"Did he see you?" she asked him.

"Yeah, and he ran out of Mrs. Price's apartment," he said. "I guess I should have called him but I don't even know what to say."

"I don't know what I would say either," she said. "I mean he's an anti-man...a batty boy. In Jamaica, they would kill him just for putting on the dress."

"Really?" he said. "I mean up here they would beat up a sissy but I don't want Kester to get killed. I mean it's just a dress, right?"

They sat there as the wind picked up outside. It wasn't the kind of conversation he thought he would ever be having with Simone.

"Are you still going to be friends with him?" she asked.

"I don't know."

"You know, Nolan, if it was me I wouldn't be friends with him because it's weird that he dresses like a girl," she said. "But you've been best friends with Kester since kindergarten. If you were the one wearing the dress would you want him to still be your friend?"

"Yeah...I guess," he said. "I guess I would."

"Well then, be his friend," she said yawning.

"What if people find out?" he said. "I don't want people to think I'm some gaylord or that I wear dresses like him."

"Who's going to find out?" she replied. "I'm not going to say anything to anyone, are you?"

"No, I guess not," he admitted.

"Well then, don't worry about it," she said.

She lay back on her pillow and yawned again as she closed her eyes. He sat next to her for a moment. He wanted to talk more but he also started to yawn. He realized that, if he stayed any longer, he would fall asleep.

"Hey, Simone. Are you asleep?"

"Mmm hmm," she said. "I'm asleep."

"Okay." He forced himself out of her bed and headed to the window. "Just checking...Night."

"Night," she replied before falling back to sleep.

By Monday morning, Nolan had come to realize that, despite everything, he didn't want to lose his friendship with Kester. He didn't understand what would make him want to dress like a girl, but it didn't matter to him anymore. Kester was his best friend. Things could still be the same, as long as he didn't think or talk about it — Kester could still be the same old Kester.

On the school bus that morning, his heart started to pound when he saw Kester sitting alone. He quietly sat next to him and forced a smile. Kester just looked at him. Nolan tried to say something but couldn't even muster up a simple hello.

"Kester," bellowed Simone as she plopped in the seat in front of them. Kester turned away and stared out the window. "You don't hear mi talkin' to you?"

"What!?" he snipped.

"Some of the older kids are playing British Bulldog during lunch," she said, without missing a beat. "You coming to play with me and Nolan?"

"I guess," he replied.

Simone looked at Nolan and gestured at him to say something.

"Yeah, it will be cool," Nolan said nervously. "We used to watch your older brothers play all the time, right, Kester?"

Nolan waited for him to reply but he continued to stare out the window. Simone turned around and opened up her reading book. The two boys remained silent the rest of the trip. When the bus finally pulled up to the school, Kester was the first to bolt out of his seat and out the door.

"What's up with him?" whispered Simone. "It's not like you're the one wearing the dress."

At lunch recess all of the third- and fourth-grade students geared up to play British Bulldog. It was a tradition for students to play after the first thaw of the year, when boots were no longer required but the fields were still muddy. Simone had always heard about the game but had never seen or played it. Nolan excitedly described the game to her.

"Someone stands at one end of the field," he said. "Then the person who is 'it' yells, 'British Bulldog' and everyone has to run past the end of the field without being caught. If you get tackled, then you join the other side and have to catch the others. Kind of like a zombie attack."

"Well, that's stupid," Simone replied. "Isn't that just tag?"

"I guess it's like tag," he said. "But with a field and mud."

All the kids stood bouncing on the soccer field as Mikey Moretti, the biggest and strongest fourth-grader, waited at the end of the field by the goal post. Nolan looked to see where Kester was. He was hoping to talk to him before the game started, but Kester slipped in right before everything began.

"British....Bulldog!" yelled Mikey, and all the screaming students ran across the field. Simone got by and so did Nolan and Kester. The majority of the kids were able to bypass Mikey, but some of the unlucky ones ended up being tackled to the ground by his gigantic body.

Simone's adrenaline was pumping as she watched kids getting pummeled by him. The slippery mud didn't help much, and some of the kids skidded as he toppled on top of them. By the time they reset for the next round, the group of kids that were now "it" looked filthy and scary as they all yelled out "British...Bulldog" in unison.

Simone ran fast, hoping that none of the kids would notice her. She and Nolan jumped over mud puddles in order to avoid slipping. Kester was one of the first to make it across the field, with Nolan and Simone right behind him. They stood there laughing as they watched Peter Kelsey try to give Donny Frisco the slip. He would have made it too, had he noticed Mikey Moretti coming at him on his left side. He went down like a ton of bricks. All the muddy boys piled on top of poor Peter.

When they got ready for the next round, there weren't many of them left. She was the only girl that hadn't been tackled. Cathy and Vivian were already out. Cathy was rubbing her sore rump. Mikey had taken her out hard.

Next round, Simone was not so lucky. She and Kester were both tackled, leaving only Nolan and a handful of other kids. James Chow had tackled her, but, instead of violently pulling her down, he gently pushed her with two hands. She smiled at him as they high-fived each other. She was glad that she wasn't being chased anymore.

Soon a new round was underway, and Cathy and Vivian chased Nolan. They giggled as they tried to catch him, but he was quick and dodged them like an expert. He nearly made it to the end, but was tackled by Kester.

As he attempted to get up from the wet muddy ground, Kester pushed him back down. Nolan laughed a little and tried to get back up, but Kester pushed him down even harder. Before he could do anything, Kester was punching him in the stomach. Nolan tried to push him off, but Kester continued to hit him.

Simone ran over and tried to pull Kester off, but she slipped in the mud and they both went down. Kester was so mad at Nolan. Nolan was angry, too. Simone could see blood pooling out of his nose, spilling down his lip. She stayed sitting in the mud next to Kester and then he started to cry uncontrollably. The game stopped as people came over to find out what was happening.

"What's going on?" asked someone.

"Is Kester hurt?"

Simone timidly put her hand on Kester's shoulder as he continued to sob. Nolan looked completely bewildered at what was happening, but he joined her and Kester and crouched down and patted Kester's shoulder.

"Hey, man," he said. "Don't cry, it's okay."

Everyone stood around watching Kester cry.

"What's wrong with him?" asked Mikey Moretti.

"Nothing!" said Nolan. "Come on, Kester." He grabbed Kester's arm to help him up.

Kester stumbled a bit before he pushed Nolan's hand away. "Leave me alone!" he said before limping towards the school.

Soon the recess bell rang and the game was officially over. Many of the kids ran back to class before the second bell rang. Simone and Nolan walked silently behind Kester.

The next day Kester didn't come to school. He was out sick the day after that.

▶

MRS. PRICE WASN'T SURPRISED there was trouble between Nolan and Kester. She wanted to talk to Nolan, but Simone was always there until Mike came by to pick him up. She didn't have an opportunity until the end of the week, when Pam picked up Simone early and Mike was working late.

"Nolan, I'm going to come out with it and I expect to get the truth," she said calmly as he was eating his dinner. "What has happened to you and Kester since last Friday?"

"Nothing happened," he said weakly.

"Really?" She sliced cucumbers onto his plate. "It looks to me that you two are not as friendly anymore. What happened with that?"

Nolan shrugged and started to play with his food.

"Well, here's what I think," she said. "You walked in and saw Kester in a dress and it was a shock. That's what I think."

"You...you saw him too."

"Yes, man!" She walked over to the stove. She was cooking a pot of hambone soup and watching for the pot to boil. "So what else 'appen?"

"I don't know," he said quietly. "I saw him dancing around in that dress, then he started yelling at me to get out. Then he just left."

"Is that all?" she said.

"We got in a fight at school," he replied. "It's like he hates me! He won't talk to me and I don't know what I did. It's not like I said anything to anyone. I didn't even bring it up."

"Nuh baby, you didn't do anything wrong. Kester has always been a special child. He's always been touched with that affliction."

"Affliction?" said Nolan.

"Yes, darling," she said, hesitating. "Since he was little, always prancing around like a little girl. Playing with his sister's dolls. Putting on his mother's lipstick. Putting on my church hat and heels, dancing around the apartment. When he got old enough to understand how wrong it looked, he was scolded by his mother. Boy, she beat him one time so bad that he missed school."

"I remember when he missed a week of kindergarten," said Nolan. "He said he had chicken pox. He was in so much pain when he came back."

She paused, remembering Kester's frail body covered in welts from the beating. "Lawd, I pray for dat family every day. After that, he started staying with me after school, until they moved away."

"Oh…I didn't know that," Nolan said quietly.

"It's why he's always trying to act like his brothers," she said. "He's trying to be more like them. I hoped he would grow out of this but now it looks like he might not."

"Does he know that you know?" Nolan asked.

"We don't talk about it, but he knows," she said. Tears welled up in her eyes. "I just pretend that I don't see it. I just turn the other way and pray he stops all this nonsense. But until then, Nolan, I need you to be his friend."

"I tried, Mrs. Price," he said. "But he won't talk to me."

"Give him some time, baby. Maybe you catching him will put a stop to this, once and for all."

The next week, Kester returned to school and was back to his old self — cracking jokes with everyone and breaking and playing basketball. When he saw Nolan he ran up to him, punching him on the shoulder, as if nothing had happened. "What's up, man?"

Nolan wasn't sure what to do or say. He wanted to pull him aside and yell at him and ask him what was going on, but Kester had a frightened look in his eyes. A look that said, *Please don't tell anyone. I'm sorry about what happened, just don't tell anyone.* So Nolan just smiled at his best friend and said, "Hey, dude," trying to sound as normal as possible.

Kester's tense face immediately softened and relaxed.

The two of them walked into school together, laughing about the crazy weekend Kester had had. His brothers had taken him to Dunlace Park, where they rode their bicycles all day, and then they'd gone to Becker's, where they stole popsicles and stuffed them down Kester's pants. Nolan laughed at Kester demonstrating his popsicle waddle.

A few minutes later the bell rang. The boys high-fived each other.

"Meet you at recess?" Nolan asked.

"Yeah, see you then," replied Kester.

Kester seemed to walk like he was some big gangster, Nolan thought. His swag was almost comical. He'd never really noticed it until now. The way Kester was always trying so hard to act like a man.

15

The freezing rain had been heavy in the night and ice still lingered on his windshield. He had tried all morning to scrape it off, but, with the weather still so cold, the most he could do was scratch off enough to see. Throughout the day, he had done a good job managing the slippery roads, taking his time despite irate passengers who demanded that he drive faster.

"No sir," he said with a big smile. "I rather get you there late and in one piece than on time and in a body bag."

His tips had been very light that day.

His final fare was off the books. A young boy hailed him from the middle of the street. He should have passed him and kept going but the kid's red frozen face softened his decision and he pulled over.

The young boy told him that he had skipped school to visit old friends in the city. His mother had just remarried and they had relocated to Barrie, where his stepfather worked building houses. He had lost track of time, missing the last train back. A ride like that should have cost almost a hundred dollars but the kid only had thirty dollars to his name. He felt sorry for this child, who worried that he wouldn't make his curfew.

There was no way he could leave him stranded. He wouldn't want his own child to be left helpless. "Okay. I'll take you home." He sighed.

By the time he reached the highway, the kid was fast asleep in the back of the cab. He turned the radio down. The young boy looked comfortable on the soft leather seat, with the warmth of the car blanketing him, soothing his frozen toes.

On the road, the blurry lights of merging cars danced in front of him. After half an hour he started to feel his eyes weaken and his lids grew heavy. When his car started skidding he woke up to see another cab filling the windshield, honking frantically before colliding into Caleb head on.

The two taxicabs crumpled on impact, and both drivers were pinned in their cars. The young boy was thrown from the vehicle into a snow bank. By the time the emergency units arrived, all involved had died. The boy died instantly with a broken neck and back. Caleb was the last to be pulled from his car; soaked in his own blood, with his eyes wide open. He was clutching the Polaroid of Pam and Simone that he kept in his visor.

▶

PAM SAT in her living room, agitated by how many people had come back after the funeral service. All of Caleb's relatives were sitting around her. Mike was off in a corner, looking uncomfortable between two of Caleb's co-workers. She hardly knew any of the people and wished that she had rented the church's community room instead of opening up her apartment to so many strangers.

She tried to show gratitude for the outward show of love for Caleb, but actually felt anger at them for smiling and laughing. Didn't they know that her fiancé, the father of her unborn child, lay dead at Mount Pleasant Cemetery? How was she going to manage raising two children alone?

At times, Caleb's older sister or one of his brothers would sit with her, but she barely spoke to them. It was daunting listening to everyone share stories of Caleb. Things she didn't know about him, like his love for gardening at his mother's home in Jamaica and his obsession with James Bond films. Things she would have known in time if they'd been given the chance.

Pam looked at her watch. It was almost six o'clock. Caleb's mother, Annalise, was sitting quietly at the kitchen table. She had arrived from Jamaica in tears and hadn't stopped crying since. Caleb was her youngest and favourite child. He was the one who had stayed home the longest, and, even when he had eventually moved to Canada, he'd sent her money every week with a letter telling her the latest news.

Annalise had been excited about moving to Canada to help with the baby. It was her fourth grandchild and probably the last she would see in her lifetime. She was slowing down and had been looking forward to spending the rest of her days with Caleb and his new family, although she hadn't been entirely thrilled about Pam. She felt that Pam came with too much baggage, with a grown child and hardly any family of her own to count on. Despite her reservations, Annalise had eventually given her blessing. As long as Caleb was happy, she would be happy too.

But now her son was gone, and she didn't know how she would fit into her unborn grandchild's life. Pam was so cold and unfeeling.

Reggae music played on the stereo as guests mingled. It wasn't loud or inappropriate, but it was suddenly overwhelming for Pam, who only wanted the gathering to end.

Caleb's eldest brother Phillip sat on the sofa nursing his rum and Coke, the third that evening, not including the two spiked coffees he'd drunk that morning. He noticed how quiet Pam was. He felt sad for her and wanted to do something, so he went into

Simone's bedroom and pulled the unopened crib box into the living room. He set it right at Mike's feet and sat clumsily on the floor to open the package.

Pam looked on in shock as he haphazardly started pulling out the pieces.

"I'm not going to let my brother's baby come into this world with no crib," he said. "Come on, white boy, help me put this son-of-a-bitch contraption together."

Mike looked at Pam. Her face was red. "It isn't the right time to put together the crib, man," he said, but Phillip insisted on doing it. He used his teeth to open the bag of nuts and bolts and the pieces flew out and scattered across the wooden floor.

"Enough!" Pam cried out. She stood up. "No more. I can't take any more. Please, everyone...just leave."

She pushed past all the guests and ran into her bedroom, slamming the door behind her. The tears streaming down her cheek soon turned into heaving sobs and she fell to the floor, the magnitude of what had happened to Caleb finally pushing her grief to the surface. She could barely breathe, with the weight of his death suffocating her.

She pulled herself onto the bed and crawled under the blanket. Between sobs, she heard the front door open and close several times as guests left her apartment. When it was quiet, she surrendered to exhaustion and fell asleep.

She dreamt of Caleb lying next to her in their bed. They lay facing each other under their white paisley sheet. It was as if they were in a tunnel, with the sheet floating slightly above them. At first, she was scared that their cave would swallow them whole. She felt trapped and started to panic and tried to take huge breaths.

He smiled at her, which put her at ease, and she slowed her breathing and calmed down. He lightly touched her face. She felt sadness enfold her and she wept as she looked at him. She wanted to tell him that she loved him. That she missed him and couldn't make it without him. But any time she opened her mouth to plead for his return, she was mute. She tried harder to speak, but nothing but cries managed to surface.

Caleb continued to smile at her. His smile was so bright that his beautiful radiant dark complexion beamed brightly as well. She winced at his brightness. It hurt her eyes. She turned away for some relief. She could still feel him behind her. She could smell his cologne and felt his waning breath against the back of her neck. She reached for his arm. She wanted him to wrap it around her and to feel him one last time, but, as she reached for him, he disappeared.

"Caleb," she whispered in her sleep as she felt a kick jarring her lower back. "Don't leave me. Please don't leave me."

She felt it again. It was harder and caused her to wake up suddenly. She was sweltering beneath the blanket. She slowly sat up in her bed and realized that it had all been a dream.

She looked around her dark room and felt another kick as the baby moved inside her, pressing against her bladder. She got up and stumbled to the bathroom. When she returned, Annalise was sitting on the edge of her bed.

"What time is it?" Pam rubbed her eyes.

"It's a little after 10:00 pm. Everyone has left. It's just the two of us. Come sit next to me, Pamela." Annalise patted the spot on the bed. Pam sat next to her like a dutiful daughter-in-law. The old woman took her hand. "I'm going back home soon," she said.

"I'm sorry that I got so angry earlier, but you don't have to leave," Pam said.

"I know that, but you need some time to grieve and you can't do that with all of us on top of you, day and night. But don't worry. I promised Caleb that I would be here to help when the baby arrived and, if you still need me, I will be here."

Pam nodded as the tears streamed down her cheek.

"Caleb was a good son. A good son," Annalise said. She attempted to wipe back a tear with her hand, which was stiff and bent from years of crippling arthritis. "He was loved by every-body. I don't think I've ever met a person loved as much as he was. I guess that's the only consolation I have — that and my grand-baby." She sighed as she patted Pam's hand. "I want you to think about having the baby come back with me to Jamaica," she said quickly. "Not right away, but a few months after he's born. I will stay with you and then take him back with me."

Pam listened to Caleb's mother's plans. She suggested that it could be temporary, a few years, until the child started grammar school. Then they would see from there what would be best.

"But he's my baby," Pam said. Her voice quivered. "He needs me."

"What can you do for this child that is better than what I can offer?" Annalise asked frankly. "I'm a lonely woman who has a big empty house in the country. I can spoil that child and give him everything he needs. A good education. Lots of family all around. You're a single mother dealing with plenty right now. Who is going to take care of the baby when you go back to work? Have you thought of that? Simone is old enough to take care of herself but this little one needs more than the sitter down the hall."

Tears started to stream from Pam's eyes. She couldn't speak. She saw her life repeating itself. The same conversation. The same decision. It had been easier back then. Before Simone was born, she'd been young, scared, and alone. It had made sense then to leave her child behind and get a fresh new start, but she wasn't sure if she could do it again.

"He's the only thing I have left of Caleb."

"Lawd child, mi nuh gonna keep him away from you! Yuh a 'im madda and he will know it," she said, patting Pam's hand. "I'm getting on in years and I want to use this time to see him grow and tell him everything about his father."

Pam sat there, unable to respond.

Annalise eased herself off the bed. She placed her hands on Pam's shoulder. "Please take some time to think about it," she said.

"I'm going to leave on Monday and head back home, but I'll be back. In the meantime, just think about it."

Annalise walked out of the bedroom.

Pam didn't know what to think. Her soul felt drained from the funeral, and now this question weighed heavily on her. A deep sadness filled her as she lay back on the bed. Annalise was right. It was too hard for her to take care of the baby by herself. Her stomach churned as she thought back to all those years ago, when she'd sat in Aunt Marva's kitchen discussing Simone's future.

Go to school and make something of yourself, she remembered Aunt Marva saying. *Once the baby is born you can start over.*

⏮

WHEN SIMONE ARRIVED PREMATURELY, on a hot August morning, Pam had been certain about her decision to give her up. She had needed a clean break and desperately wanted to put the past behind her. But the hospital urged Pam to nurse Simone for at least three months to help restore her weakened immune system.

During that time, Aunt Marva grew attached to the baby, and, when the baby was strong enough, she wanted to raise Simone herself.

"She blood," Aunt Marva said to Pam. "No matter the circumstance, she bound by blood. We don't turn our back on our own. We raise our own. You hear me?" She softened her tone. "Come nuh, none of this mess is a reflection of you. No matter what 'appens always remember that! What you need to do is go to Canada and finish your education. Get a fresh new start where no one knows you. I'll care for Simone and when you're ready, you can come claim her."

Pam had quietly agreed to it and, when Simone was nearly five months old, she had left Jamaica. Her aunt had made all the arrangements, enrolling her in a nursing school in Toronto. It was a profession many young Jamaican women entered, but Pam hated the idea of becoming a nurse. After the first week, she dropped out and applied to the University of Toronto's business administration program. It was a difficult program but gave her the necessary distraction she needed to move forward.

In the beginning, she lived like a shut-in. She didn't know the area and was nervous being around so many strangers. She would only leave her small boarding room to attend classes and then retreated home to focus on her studies. Throughout the year, Aunt Marva called to check on her. Pam would lie and say that everything was fine, but in her heart she was miserable. She missed her baby.

Pam had never thought she would miss Simone, but her body continued to ache for her child. She missed the way she smelt — the sweet jasmine fragrance that comforted her. She craved the past moments when she had held Simone. The way it had felt every time her daughter cooed and smiled before peacefully falling asleep in her arms. Yet, despite how much she longed for her, Simone also served as a reminder of the past year and of the truth that leaving her behind had been her only chance to start over.

She needed more to distract her. Her studies weren't enough to keep away the nightmares she still coped with and the baby she was trying to forget. When school resumed, Pam decided to venture out more. She joined the campus' Caribbean Association and forced herself to make friends.

By winter break, she had become close friends with Daphne and Linda. Linda was a native of Jamaica, but had lived in England for most of her life. Daphne had been born and raised in Barbados, but had come to Canada to become a doctor. Both of them were a year ahead of her and felt sorry for the shy timid country girl. She was so young and lost, even after a year in Toronto. They instantly took her under their wings, dragging her to campus parties and association functions.

She loved hanging out with the two girls. They knew nothing of her past and didn't really ask much about her. Their only concern was what they were going to wear to the next dance and who was going to be there.

In the beginning, they tried to set Pam up with dates, friends they thought would be perfect for her. They teased her for being shy, but found it strange that she refused to even dance with men at parties.

"What's your deal, love?" asked Linda as they walked back from one of the parties. "You only fancy women?"

Pam shook her head. She didn't want them to think she was queer, but she wasn't ready to tell them why she didn't dance with men. She laughed it off.

"Wait nuh, dear heart," Daphne said. "Yuh a virgin?"

"Rawtid, why didn't you say something?" Linda asked loudly, before Pam could respond. "Mi forget you still a freshy but mi never peg you a virgin."

Pam quickly nodded. She didn't want to lie, but she'd rather lie that she was a virgin than tell anyone the truth.

"Girl, we'll fix that for you," Daphne said. "We'll make sure you meet a nice boy at the next bashment. Not some ragga fool but a really good gent. Someone who will take you out and keep his hands to himself."

"But to meet someone you have to at least dance with them," Linda advised. "Don't be so standoffish. Smile a little. Flirt a little. Dress a little better. You're young and have all the time in the world to land a husband. Right now you need to have fun!"

The next evening they went to another dance and Pam tried to swallow her fears as the first man asked her to dance. She was terrified when he put his arm around her waist. She wanted to pull away from him. But he was gentle and didn't force himself on her the way she'd expected. Instead, he kept a respectable distance. After a few more dances, Pam started to feel more relaxed. No one was lurking in the shadows and she made Linda and Daphne promise that they would always come and leave together.

She started to smile more. It had been a long time since she'd genuinely smiled and it felt good feeling happy again. She also never drank. That was a big rule she had. She brought a flask filled with water and took sips from it when she wanted to feel like she was part of the crowd. While other women were getting sloppy and drunk, she kept her wits about her. She was surprised at her ability to handle the men who came on too strong. She started to shed her shy demeanour and she found her voice. When a dance partner got too fresh, she told him so, but if there was a man she was interested in, she let him hold her a little tighter. It felt good to have control again.

In time, she got a part-time job at the university library. It wasn't much but it gave her a little pocket money. She bought a few nice party dresses. Her favourite was a chiffon blue dress that she wore often. It brought out her light brown complexion and made her chestnut brown eyes sparkle when she laughed.

By her second summer in Toronto, she was completely transformed. She wasn't anxious to run home to her little room, and she soon forgot the troubles of her past. Instead, she focused on the few boyfriends she kept at bay. She only dated nice respectable boys who took her to the movies, bought her dinner, and didn't keep her out till dawn.

She attended the Jamaican Associate picnics, where she met many Jamaican-Canadians. A lot of them were students like her, while others were working Jamaicans trying to bring their families and children over to live in Canada. By the end of the summer, she had gone to so many picnics and parties that she couldn't keep her schedule straight.

The biggest party was the annual Caribbean festival, Caribana. She attended her first parade as a bystander, but, by the following year, she became bold enough to join Daphne and Linda as dancers for one of the mas bands from Barbados. The three women dressed in sparkly blue and yellow sequined costumes and headpieces and danced the day away, their glittery golden bodies sweltering in the muggy heat.

Pam started to love Canada. Despite its brutal winters, it was her salvation. The carefree days, the friendships she'd gained, the nights she was wrapped in some man's arms on the dance floor — those were real moments she could hold onto. It was only on a few occasions that her past would come crashing around her, leaving her despondent for days. A moment in a grocery store when a fellow Jamaican swore that he knew her from back home. Or she would open her mailbox to find a letter from her Aunt Marva with a picture of Simone stapled to a money order.

The last letter she received from her aunt was the day before she graduated from university. It was a card congratulating her and a Polaroid picture of her four-year-old daughter. The little girl was in pigtails with bright green ribbons as long as her hair. The young girl looked right into the camera, as if she was unsure of what to do. Her eyes were open wide, and her mouth showed a smirk rather than a smile. Pam looked at the picture and her heart stopped. Simone had her big round eyes, button nose, and full lips, but to her, this girl looked like a stranger.

She started to panic as she crumpled the picture in her hand. She went back to her room and lay on her bed, wishing she hadn't opened the letter, and her chest started to heave as the weight of the moment sat on her like an anvil. She tried to breathe, but tears streamed down the sides of her face.

She's a bright thing Pam, the note said. *You would be so proud, my dear. She is everything like you, when you were a child.*

She couldn't bear to read on.

The next morning she barely made it out of bed for the graduation ceremony. She would have missed it entirely if Daphne hadn't been planning to pick her up. She had to pull herself together. She took a long hot shower to settle her nerves and brushed away any tears. When the others asked her why she seemed upset, she told them she was sad that her late father wasn't there to see her graduate. That excuse seemed to work. Her friends simply took her at her word.

A week after her graduation, Pam went to the phone booth down the street from the new apartment she rented with Daphne and Linda. She dialled her aunt.

"Mekhace Simone, come quick!" Aunt Marva said. "Your mummy is on the phone!"

"No, Auntie," Pam said. "I don't have much time. Please, I need to tell you something."

"Yes, dear," her aunt said through the crackling connection. "Go on with it before they cut us off."

"I've moved from the boarding house." She twisted the phone cord around her finger. "I've moved into a new apartment with a few girls from school. The place is nice and clean, so you don't need to worry."

"That's very good," she said. "I worry about you all alone. It's good that you have some girls to live with. Wait a moment while I get my address book."

"Auntie…wait."

"Yes, dear? What is it?"

"I don't have an address to give you," she said, stumbling. Her index finger was now blue. She slowly unravelled the cord. "I'm sorry, Auntie, but…I'll call and check in from time to time. You'll still hear from me."

Silence.

"Is that what you want?" her aunt asked. Her voice sounded so weak.

"It is," she said, trying to stop herself from crying. The crackling line filled in the gap. "I have to go, Auntie. I promise to call back soon."

"Goodbye, my dear," Aunt Marva said. Pam heard the line click.

She stood in the telephone booth for a while, unable to move.

She wasn't certain that she had made the right decision. Part of her wanted to call her aunt and take it all back, but instead she stumbled out of the booth.

▶▶︎❘

Now, many years later, she lay in her bedroom faced with the same predicament and pondering the same question again. She felt herself crumble as she wondered if it was best to send her baby to his grandmother. She couldn't imagine giving up another baby, and, when she looked at the empty side of the bed, her entire body trembled. She had to stifle her cries with her pillow as she felt him gently jabbing her from inside her womb.

16

Nolan was going to spend Mother's Day in Nova Scotia. His mother had called the week before to tell him that she was flying him out for the weekend. Not only was it his first time in Nova Scotia, it was also his first time on a plane! He tried to contain his excitement in front of his father, but he couldn't stop grinning, and it was hard for him to keep calm.

Mike forced himself to stay positive as he walked Nolan through the airport to his gate. He tried to seem genial about the whole plan, but inside he was seething. He had been doing all the heavy lifting with Nolan while Meghan lived her life, without much concern for either of them. When she missed Nolan's birthday, he had called, yelling at her: How could she let Nolan go to bed that night without even giving him a phone call? Since then, she had tried to be more attentive, but most of the conversations between her and Nolan barely lasted ten minutes, with Nolan doing most of the talking.

This idea of Nolan spending the weekend with them was suspicious. Something felt wrong — but he had nothing to complain about. It was what he had been harping on for months — for her to spend more time with her son. He was briefly tempted to join Nolan in Nova Scotia, but he knew that would be a disaster. So he hugged him and reminded him to be on his best behaviour.

"Don't worry, Mr. O'Shea," said the airline rep. "He's in good hands."

Nolan sat right up front, next to the cockpit. He couldn't believe how big the plane was. He looked back at all the rows of seats filled with people, bubbling with anticipation.

The plane ride lasted around two hours, which wasn't nearly long enough. Yet, the moment the doors opened, he jumped out of his seat and headed to the gate. His smile was wide when he saw his mother and sister standing by the entrance holding a big homemade sign with "WELCOME NOLAN!" on it.

"Mom! Dana!" he yelled as he ran to them.

The three of them embraced. His mother's eyes were filled with tears.

"You look so much like your father," she said. She touched his hair. "You must be an inch taller. Where did my little pudgy guy go?"

"Mom!" Nolan looked up at her, smiling. She looked a lot softer than he remembered.

"You got big, bud," said Dana, messing with his hair. "Come on, let's get out of here before they send you back to Toronto."

The ride to their home in North Preston seemed to fly by as Nolan chattered from the back seat all about his flight and Dana sat in the front seat, fooling with the radio.

"Wait," said Meghan. "I love this song. Leave it there!"

It was an old John Lennon song about his mother that Meghan used to sing all the time. She was a huge Beatles fan and any time a radio station played one of their tunes she always turned it up and sang along.

Finished with describing the flight, Nolan talked endlessly about his friend Simone and about Simone's stepfather dying.

How much he had in common with her. Their break-dancing group. The time she nearly cracked her head open.

"Aren't you young to have a girlfriend?" teased Dana, turning around.

"She's not my girlfriend," he said. "She's just a friend."

"Calm your nerves," she said, swinging her arm back and punching his leg. "She goes to your school or something?"

"Yeah," he said. "She lives next door to us."

"Wait, the Jamaican woman's daughter?" she inquired.

"What Jamaican woman?" Meghan asked. "I didn't know your father had Jamaican neighbours."

"Simone and her mother are from Jamaica," he said nonchalantly. "No big guff."

"Does Dad know that you are hanging out with your little Jamaican girlfriend?" teased Dana.

"Yeah, duh," he said rolling his eyes. "But she's not my girlfriend. She's just my friend. Dad is friends with Pam too. That's Simone's mom."

"Really," said Meghan, her eyes darting to the rearview mirror.

"Dad and Pam hang out all the time," Nolan said. "Mostly on the balcony."

"Your father is friends with a Jamaican woman?" she said. "A black Jamaican woman?"

"Mom!" Dana said. "That is so rude!"

"No, that's not what I meant...I'm just a little shocked," she said. "I mean it's great that he's made new friends and all. It's just he's always been...well, he's never had a black friend before."

"Hey Nolan, did you say that Simone's stepfather died?" asked Dana. "What happened?"

"Oh yeah," replied Nolan. "Caleb got into a car accident up in Barrie. A guy fell asleep while he was driving and drove into him."

"Oh wow," said Dana. "That's horrible."

"Yeah...it was really sad," Nolan said. "Simone cried a lot. Pam did too! They were supposed to be married this summer."

"I'm sorry to hear that, honey," said Meghan.

"I feel really sad for Pam," said Nolan. "She's having a baby soon and now the baby isn't going to have a dad."

"That's tough," Meghan said. "Poor woman."

"Yeah, bud, that sucks," Dana agreed.

The rest of the drive they rode in silence, with Nolan looking out the window at the flickering lights of highway cars passing by. By the time they arrived home, he was fast asleep. He hardly felt Meghan lifting him in her arms and carrying him inside.

Their house was a white wooden craftsman home, and, the moment they got in, Dana quickly left for her friend's house. Meghan was disappointed, but Nolan was fast asleep, anyway. She laid him in the bottom bunk in Dana's room.

She stroked the hair out of his face. His hair was wavier and longer. She missed his curls. As he adjusted his body to get comfortable, she could see the beginnings of his adolescence and felt a sharp pang of regret. It was going to be like this now. Stolen moments. Playing catch up every time she saw him.

▶

THE NEXT MORNING, Nolan woke suddenly, jarred from a fitful sleep. For a moment, he thought he was back in his own bedroom, but then he remembered that he was with his mother. A smile spread across his face. He could hear her muffled voice talking to his sister in the kitchen. But soon he could tell that they were fighting.

"What the hell, Mom," he heard Dana say. "It was your deal to leave and drag me with you. You wanted things to be different."

"You're too young to understand, Dana," his mother responded. "It's not that easy. I can't just shut off my feelings like that."

"I understand a lot," Dana said. "You're jealous because he's moving on with his life and now you're pissed. It's like you want him to be as unhappy as you!"

The front door slammed. Nolan stood by the bedroom door, unsure if he should even go into the kitchen. He made his way there anyway.

"Hi there, handsome." Meghan wiped her hands with the dish-towel. "I'm almost finished the pancakes. Are you hungry?"

"I can eat," he said, flashing her a smile.

"I can eat," she said, imitating him. She laughed. "Listen to you, Mister Comedian."

"Yeah, well," he replied. "Where's Dana?"

"She's out," Meghan said. "She'll be back soon."

He could tell his mother didn't want to say much more. He stood by the stove watching her grill his pancakes. She added blueberries in the shape of a happy face. He hated blueberries, but didn't want to say so. He was just happy to have her cook him breakfast the way she used to.

They ate breakfast together, Nolan excitedly repeating his adventure of flying for the first time, but, when she asked him about school, his excitement waned. He told her that he didn't like school and hated having to always do homework, but didn't mind the projects they worked on. He said his partner for all of his projects was Simone. She was smarter than him so he knew he would always get a good grade working with her.

Meghan sat quietly listening to him prattle on about his other best friend, Kester, whose family was also from the island. She was mildly amused that Nolan's best friends were Jamaican and wondered how much it bothered Mike that Nolan played with black children. She wondered, too, if this Pam woman was the reason Mike was easier to get along with lately.

"So tell me about Pam," she said. "What does she look like?"

"She's really pretty...like Miss America," he said. "She's smart like Simone and sometimes helps me with my homework if Dad is busy."

"She sounds like a nice person," Meghan said.

"She's okay," he said. "Sometimes she's mean, but mostly to Simone. She's always yelling at Simone."

"Does she yell at you?"

"No," he said. "She's really nice to me. She yells at Dad a lot."

"Really?" she said. "She yells at your father?"

"Yeah, they're always sitting on the balcony arguing about God and the Prime Minister, our teachers..."

"I see."

She was curious about Mike's relationship with Pam. She had never heard of this woman and, from what Nolan was saying, there was something going on between her and Mike. A small part of her wanted to ask if Pam was his father's girlfriend.

How convenient, she thought to herself. *A girlfriend who lives next door. They've probably slept together.*

"Does she come over a lot?" she asked.

"Not really. Sometimes we go over to her place for dinner. She's a great cook."

"Really?" she said. "What does she cook for you?"

"Some Jamaican stuff, like ackee."

"Acne?" Meghan repeated.

"You're saying it wrong! It's Ack-EE," he said, laughing at her pronunciation. "It looks like scrambled eggs but it's actually a fruit. Crazy, huh? Dad's favourite is jerk chicken. His face gets so red when he eats it, but he eats it anyways."

Meghan didn't pay much attention to the story. All she could concentrate on was this woman she didn't know who was cooking for her husband and her son, helping her son with his homework, and who looked like Miss America.

It's not as if she wanted Mike back. She was finally living her own life and doing everything she wanted to do. She was enjoying her new program and loved the house they lived in. This was her first time on her own. Even though she had to manage Dana, her daughter felt more like a roommate than someone she had to care for. She felt free. She didn't have to ask Mike's permission to fart and she was happier than she had ever been. But maybe Dana was right. Maybe she didn't want to see her husband happy.

She wished Dana understood why she'd had to leave instead of believing that her mother had broken up their perfect family. Dana never saw that Mike was so overbearing and authoritative that it stifled her, never heard their nightly arguments over finances. Dana didn't see how content Mike was being mediocre, not ever venturing out to do more with his life.

It worried her that her children might never understand her feelings. She hoped that one day they would, but maybe it was already too late.

Nolan was smiling at her. She smiled back at him. Just then the front door opened.

"Hey bud," said Dana, rushing in and ruffling his hair as she grabbed a piece of bacon from his plate. "Did Mom tell you what we're doing today?"

"Nope," answered Meghan. "I was just about to fill him in on our plans."

"What plans?" he asked with his mouth filled with eggs.

She started to list things on her fingers. They were going to go to the harbour and visit the Maritime Museum. Then a surprise. Then they were going downtown for dinner at her favourite Chinese restaurant. And then....

▶

IT WAS one of the best days of his life. He loved Halifax, especially the harbour. He had never seen so many boats. He just ran up and down the docks. Meghan had even arranged for them all to take a cruise around the harbour. After dinner, the three of them were walking silently towards the car when he grabbed hold of his mother's hand. It still felt soft and squishy like he remembered. When he was little he used to call her Squishy Hands. It was getting dark when they finally made it back to the house.

Meghan pulled out the tub of Neapolitan ice cream from the freezer and started scooping. Dana's favourite was strawberry, Nolan's chocolate, and Meghan's all three.

They giggled as if they were all kids. They reminisced about the past. Meghan reminded Nolan how, when he was little, he called his sister Danny and how angry he became when they finally told him that her name was Dana, not Danny. They talked about their old place in Willowdale with its big yard in the back, just behind the highway. Dana shared a story of her father cutting the grass while she stood behind him holding the cord so he wouldn't roll over it and electrocute himself.

When it was finally time to go to sleep, Nolan and Dana headed up to her bedroom. He wanted to sleep on the top bunk this time.

"Good night, Nolan," she said.

"Hey, Dana."

"Ya?"

"Do you think you and Mom will come back home soon?" he asked. "I mean after she gets her degree and everything. Do you think you guys will come back to Toronto?"

"I don't think so, bud," she said.

"Maybe I could come and stay with you guys for the summer," he said. "I can bring Dad next time and he can see how great it is over here."

Dana lay in bed, listening to her brother plan ways to get his father to visit. Even though Nolan had grown up so much since she'd last seen him, he was still childlike and naive. He still believed in Santa Claus and the Easter Bunny and that his parents would get back together one day.

Dana knew that was never going to happen. Their mother was already seeing someone. She barely stayed home these days. Dana wouldn't dare say anything to Nolan because he would tell their father. The less they knew, the better.

She wished she lived with her father. She missed Toronto and her old friends. In Toronto, she'd believed that her parents' separation was a temporary lapse of judgment, a fight between them that went on longer than it was supposed to. But, once in Halifax, she realized that her whole world had changed. She had begged her mother to let her go back to Toronto and live with her father, but Meghan wouldn't have it.

"Mike wouldn't know what to do with you. Have you seen his apartment? It's barely furnished as it is."

"So why is it good enough for Nolan?" she'd yelled back.

"Because you'd be a pregnant dropout within the year. Nolan is a boy. He needs to be with his father. A daughter will never survive without her mother, but a son will do okay."

Dana had wanted to call bullshit, but Nolan seemed to be doing okay living with their father. His grades were fine and he seemed happy.

She could hear him breathing deeply. He had fallen asleep. She wanted to wake him and tell him the truth — that their family was fucked up and nothing would ever be the same again. That he was better off living with Mike and not with their mother, whose only concern was finishing school.

But she let him be. She didn't want to ruin the short time they had together. She wanted this weekend to be perfect for him.

▶

THE NEXT MORNING, Nolan and Dana surprised their mother with a lavish Mother's Day breakfast of toast with jam, bacon, fried eggs, sliced tomatoes, and a side of baked beans. Meghan sat up in bed eating her feast. She quietly listened to her children happily banter back and forth. She missed seeing them together like this.

Nolan looked up at his mother. "You okay, Mom? Is the food not good?"

She gently pushed his hair off his face and smiled at him. "No, everything is wonderful," she said. "I'm just full right now. Why don't we clean up so that we can do some more sightseeing before your flight?"

"Cool." Nolan beamed. He kissed his mother's cheek, then jumped off her bed and ran to get dressed.

They spent most of the day hiking the Salt Marsh trail. Dana brought the new camera that Mike had sent with Nolan for her birthday. She shot almost fifty pictures, mostly of Meghan and Nolan walking along the trail. After a long afternoon of hiking and a picnic lunch, they headed back to the car.

"Did you have fun, Nolie?" Meghan asked him. "I know I did."

Nolan looked at his mother with a bright smile. He hugged her and nestled his head into her chest. He could hear her heart beating and squeezed her closer to him. He didn't want to let her go. "Mom," he said. "You love me, right?"

"Of course I do, baby." She grabbed his hand and kissed it. "A million times over."

"Do you love Dana more than me?"

"I love both my children the same," she said softly.

"Then why is she here with you and I'm not?" he said rapidly. Tears streamed down his face. "Why can't I live with you and Dana? There's a lot of room and I clean my room on my own without Dad even telling me. Plus, we can always have days like this. We can hike all the time. We can go to the docks and watch the ships come in. I'm quiet, too, so when you're studying it would be like I'm not even around."

"I don't know what to tell you, Nolan," she said. "It's complica—"

"What about the summer?" he asked. "No one has school in the summer. I can stay with you then."

"Baby, listen to me," she said. "Your dad needs you. He would be so lonely without you. Do you understand what I'm saying?"

"Yah," he said, wiping his eyes with the back of his hand. "Even if you had a million dollars you wouldn't want me here with you and Dana."

"No, honey," she said. "That's not true. I would...I do."

"Forget it," he said, pushing her away. "Let's just go. I want to go home now."

He ran off to the car.

Meghan looked after him. She watched Dana hug her brother as he cried in her arms. He was too young to understand. How could she tell him that she had been too young when she started having children and that, if she had it to do over, she would have waited? She would have lived her life. Travelled the world. Fallen in love a few times before settling down.

All she could do was look at him crying, with tears of her own trickling down her cheeks, and hope that he knew she loved him. That she would always be there for him but couldn't right now.

The ride to the airport was solemn. Dana attempted to change the mood by engaging Nolan, but he sat in his seat, gazing listlessly out the window. Dana ended up turning on the radio. John Lennon's *Mother* was on rotation again.

The haunting lyrics drifted through the car. A song about a man grieving the loss of a mother who abandoned him years before. They were still fifteen minutes away from the airport. The tension felt thick and heavy. Meghan turned off the radio midway through the song but the lyrics still ran through her mind over and over as they silently drove to the airport.

▶

MIKE LOOKED BACK at his son and could tell that something was wrong. He wasn't in the best mood after waiting two hours for Nolan's plane to arrive, the flight delayed until late in the evening.

"Nolan, I'm talking to you," Mike said. "What's wrong with you?"

"Nothing," mumbled Nolan.

"I asked how are your mother and sister?" he said for the third time. He didn't really want to hear about Meghan's wonderful life in Nova Scotia, but anything was better than his son's attitude.

"They're fine, okay?"

"Fine? Just fine?"

"Yeah, fine," he said looking out the window.

"What the hell is your problem?"

"Nothing," Nolan yelled back. "Just leave me alone!"

"Leave you alone? Nolan, I don't see you for the whole weekend and you come back with such a damn attitude."

"Why does she hate us, Dad?"

They pulled up to the stop sign by their apartment building. He had hoped that the trip wouldn't bring out the resentment he knew Nolan had towards his mother. Despite how angry he was with Meghan, it broke his heart seeing Nolan so full of bitterness.

"She doesn't hate you, Nols," he said. "Your mother loves you very much. I promise you that. She just needs to do things her way."

"It feels like she doesn't want me," he said.

Back home, Mike kissed Nolan on his forehead and told him to go to bed. It was late and he had school the next morning.

When he was sure Nolan was fast asleep he went into the kitchen and poured himself a tumbler of whisky from his private stash above the refrigerator. He didn't usually drink. His own father had drunk too much and that had turned him off it. Many nights he had watched his father pass out on the couch.

He finished his drink and poured another. It was a warm spring night, and he decided to sit outside. He picked up the bottle and the phone and dragged it to the balcony.

"Hello?" he heard her say on the other end of the line in her crisp, cool, unassuming voice. It infuriated him. She sounded as if she didn't have a care in the world.

"Don't fucking call him again," he said. "You're not doing him any favours. Just fuck off and leave him alone. We don't need you anymore. Do you hear me?"

With that, he slammed the phone on the cradle. The phone rang back, but he didn't pick up. He didn't want to get into another argument with her. He couldn't stomach any more of her bullshit. She called a few more times until he picked up the phone and left it off the hook. He then poured himself another whisky and sat drinking on the balcony in the dark.

The next morning Pam came out wrapped in a wool blanket. Mike was passed out on her orange chair, a half-drunk bottle of whisky next to him. She shook him awake.

"Hey," he said. "What time is it?"

"Almost six in the morning," she said. "Did you spend the night out here?"

"Looks like it," he said.

A flock of birds flew over the complex, shifting their flight pattern.

He hadn't seen much of Pam since the funeral. Her face looked thin. She was almost eight months along but seemed small for someone who was about to have a baby.

"You're not eating much," he said. He got out of her chair and sat down in his own. "You're wasting away."

"How do you know what I'm eating?" she said. She sat down.

"Because I know what it's like," he said. "When my mother died I barely ate for weeks."

Silence.

"I was about six years old when she died," he continued. "And I refused to eat a thing. My father didn't notice. He barely ate anything either. I think I must have looked like a four-year-old famine victim when my relatives visited and forced me to eat a decent meal."

"Do you remember her?" she asked him.

"Who? My mother? Honestly, I don't remember much about her. I remember a few things but not what colour her eyes were or the way she sounded. I guess if I'd known she was going to die, I would have paid attention to those things."

"Well, it's probably better that you didn't know her," she said quietly. "Less painful."

The birds flew all around them, then disappeared behind the building.

"I don't know if that's true," he said. "I wish I could remember how she was. To be honest, she is a mystery to me. My father barely talked about her and I was too afraid to ask."

"Why?"

"Talking about her was a 'no-no' in my house," he said quietly. "Even though he was a tough son-of-a-bitch he couldn't handle even saying her name. That's why he didn't stay in touch with her side of the family. He wanted to forget her. Now history is repeating itself with Nolan and his mother. It must be my family's curse. *May your men never know their mothers and always be raised by their fathers.*"

"Then I guess my children have my family curse," Pam said, shivering. She pulled her blanket close. "*May your children be raised by anyone but their mum.*"

"What do you mean?" he asked her.

"Caleb's mother offered to take the baby back to Jamaica and raise him," she said. "And...and I'm thinking about taking her up on her offer."

"What!" Mike said sharply. "What the hell, Pam! You can't just hand off your baby to some stranger."

"She's his grandmother."

"And you're his mother! What makes her better at raising him than you?"

"You don't get it," she said. "What kind of mother can I be to him?"

181

"Any kind of mother," he said. "Look, if I had my way, I would have traded everything just to have my mother in my life. If you send your baby away, you are going to damage him the way your relationship with Simone has been damaged."

"My relationship with Simone is not damaged," she said.

"You really think so?" he asked. "Why does she still call you 'Ms. Pam'? What kid calls their mother by their first name, anyways? And don't feed me that crap about how it's done in Jamaica. Mother is universal. It's the first word a child learns."

"I'm scared to do this on my own."

He could see the fear in her eyes. "What are you talking about," he said. "You've been doing it alone with Simone for almost two years."

"It's not the same. I've never really taken care of a baby before," she said. "Dealing with Simone is easy, because all I need to do is make sure she's fed, clothed and gets an education."

"Well, it's the same for a baby," he said.

Pam gave him an impatient look.

"Okay...it's not the same thing. It's hard and it's tricky and it's messy but it's worth it. Trust me, Pam...and you won't be alone. You'll have Simone to help, and Mrs. Price isn't going anywhere... plus you'll have me. I'm here."

Pam looked at him, her head on one side as if she wasn't sure if he was still drunk.

"When my mother died, I could have gone to live with any relative," he said. "I asked my father why he didn't just send me to live with my grandmother or my mother's sister who had a brood of her own and he said, 'Because you're my kid. I raise you, not some stranger.' I never forgot that. It was the one thing that made me proud to call him my father."

The birds flew back to their end of the building. Mike and Pam watched them flock together, dazzled by how quickly they moved as a unit, despite the quick changes to their flight path. They looked on silently, mesmerized by their dance.

17

It was the last week of school and probably the most jovial part of the year. The final days of school meant no home- work, projects, or tests. Gym classes were extended, and every afternoon there was art class. During lunch, students got to watch a film in the library, and recess was a little longer to allow students to enjoy the sunshine. The culmination was the last day, which was designated as Play Day.

Play Day, a long-standing tradition at St. Augustine, was filled with non-stop activities to celebrate the end of the school year. An assortment of kids from every classroom were placed into several teams, from grade one all the way to grade seven. Grade eight kids were chosen as captains, and all morning the teams had to complete obstacle courses, play dodgeball, fight epic tugs of war, and run races around the track. Everyone wanted to win the tournament. After the events but before the judging, the children were treated to a hot dog lunch, which included a can of pop, a bag of chips and a snow cone with all sorts of flavours, then they spent their extended lunch hour creating team posters with the remaining art supplies.

Simone, Nolan, and Kester were on three different teams, but that didn't stop them from having the best times of their lives. In the previous year, none of their teams had won. They swore that this year one of them would be on a winning team.

As the students competed, Principal Nikolaos played popular music over the P.A. system. He walked around the schoolyard cheering and jeering teams through his bullhorn. He enjoyed seeing the chaos and the children's excitement. After lunch, the kids gathered in the gymnasium for the announcement of the winning team. Principal Nikolaos beamed at the sea of faces. Everyone clapped and chanted wildly for the results of the tournament. Kester's team had won the most points, and they all ran on stage and received their goody bags.

Simone sat with her team on the gym floor, disappointed that they hadn't won. Her team had played well but was a few points shy of the lead. Kester ran up to show her his loot. The bag was filled with candy, bubble gum, a pack of team cards, and a few old books retired from the school library. Nolan joined them. He wasn't too happy that his team had lost, but he shrugged it off and started claiming first dibs on the candy.

When school ended, the three decided to walk home instead of taking the school bus. They felt older now that they were moving on to the fourth grade. They would no longer be in the little yard with all the younger kids. In September, they'd be allowed to play in the big yard with the older students — and this, they all agreed, meant more than their final grades.

They got to the complex way before the bus, and the entire playground was deserted. It was as if the whole world had disappeared and they were the only ones left. They had free range on the monkey bars, swings, and the slide.

After running themselves ragged, they sat on the top of the monkey-bar dome, nearly ten feet off the ground, eating the rest of Kester's candy.

"This was the best day ever," said Kester. He gleefully pulled out his trading cards. "The best!"

"Easy for you," scowled Simone. "Your team won, or cheated."

"Ha!" laughed Nolan. "Simone, your team was the biggest cheater. I thought you guys were going to get in trouble when Mrs. Barrett caught Mikey pushing the other team down during the egg race."

"I hate Mikey Moretti," she said loudly. "He's a disgusting fat fuck!"

"Oh my God, you said the F-word," Nolan said in shock. "Don't let Mrs. Price hear you."

"I only save butt-whipping words for people who deserve it," said Simone. "And Mikey is a fat fuck who is probably going to repeat the fourth grade again."

"I hope not." Kester shuddered. "That fat fuck always pushes me in the morning line."

"Fat fuck," repeated Nolan.

"Fat fuck," Kester continued.

They all laughed at their new freedom to curse without repercussions. They watched the bus pull up, and then the rest of the students were running into the playground.

"I'm going to miss you guys," said Kester. "We're spending the summer in Jamaica with my cousins, but I'd rather stay here with you guys."

"Me too," said Simone. "My mother is going to be on maternity leave the whole summer, so you probably won't see much of me either. Are you still going to Nova Scotia for the summer, Nolan?"

"Don't think so," replied Nolan stiffly. "Dana is coming home for the summer so I'll probably stay here. She promised to take me to Canada's Wonderland."

"Lucky," Kester and Simone said in unison.

"Jinx!" they both yelled.

"Double Jinx," Simone countered.

Kester frowned at her; he kept quiet, waiting religiously for someone to say his name three times.

"Well, you could always come to Wonderland with us, Simone," said Nolan. "I'm sure Dana won't mind."

"Yeah, well, my mother will mind." Simone picked up a comic book from Kester's loot bag. "She expects me to help with the baby."

Kester, in the meantime, was frantically motioning one of them to say his name. He was nothing but dedicated to the game of jinx. Simone looked over and stuck her tongue out at him.

"Kester, Kester, Kester," said Nolan.

"You fat fuckers," he said to them.

As the playground thinned out, they climbed down from the top of the dome and made their way to the big-kid swings. The three of them pumped the swings, racing to see who could reach the highest. The warm wind caressed their faces as they practically flew off the swings to land on the soft green grass. They lay on the ground for a little while looking up in the sky. The heat from the sun tanned their faces.

"Kester," Simone called out. "Why do you wear dresses?"

Nolan sat up and glared at Simone, but she turned away from him and looked at Kester for an answer.

"I really don't know," Kester replied. He squinted and quickly covered his eyes from the sun's blinding light. "All I know is that it makes me feel better when I do."

Silence.

"What about your parents or your brothers or sister?" she continued. "Do they know?"

"I...I don't think they do," he said. "I mean, I think my sister does, but she doesn't say anything. I think she's scared of what my dad will do."

"I heard Esma talk about a man who was that way," Simone said. "He had to move to England and live with his aunt. She said that he had to stay in hiding for a week before they could smuggle him on a plane to England."

"Why did they have to go do all of that?" asked Nolan.

"Cause they were going to kill him," said Simone. "Chop him up with a machete."

Nolan looked at Kester, his eyes wide.

Kester had got quiet. He started pulling out blades of grass from the ground.

"I better go," he said shortly afterwards. "My mom is making burgers for dinner tonight. I don't want to be late for that. See you guys later!"

"Bye," they said in unison as he disappeared up the path with his book bag slung over his shoulder.

Nolan and Simone got up and started to walk back to their building. Nolan stormed ahead of her. She tried to catch up.

"What's your problem?" she said to him at the elevator. "Are you mad at me because I asked about the dress? I figured you told him that I knew."

"I'm not angry that you said anything," he said. "Okay, a little angry — but I'm more angry that he was fine talking to you about it. I'm his best friend! Why do you get to talk to him about it?"

Nolan started pressing the button harder, trying to get the elevator car to come quicker.

"I dunno," she said. "I mean...I'm not his best friend or anything, or his sister, or Mrs. Price, or anyone. I guess it's easier for him to talk to me than anyone important to him."

"But why did you have to go on about that guy who went to England," he said as the elevator finally opened up. "I mean no one kills you for stuff like that, right?"

"In Jamaica they do," she said. The elevator door slowly closed. "You're not allowed to be a faggot in Jamaica."

▶

IT WASN'T the most exciting summer for Simone. What started off as an exciting few days of non-stop gallivanting halted when

Pam's high blood pressure forced her to stop working. The doctor worried that the stress of Caleb's death was putting a strain on her health and requested that she take an early maternity leave.

Simone tried to help her mother. She learned to cook meatloaf and spaghetti for the days when her mother was too ill to feed them. But Pam was constantly aggravated by everything. Her short temper had an even shorter fuse. Simone tried to ignore her mother's constant nagging and yelling, but she really wished she had gone to summer school again.

When her mother slept, she sneaked over to Mrs. Price's house to play board games with Nolan. One day Mrs. Price knocked on Pam's door and suggested that Simone spend the days with her to give Pam a break.

"So I can give you what's left of my money? Simone is fine here with me this summer. She doesn't need to be hanging about when she has plenty to do at home."

"Is for dis baby that mi keep mi un-Christian thoughts to myself," said Mrs. Price. "Mi nuh say nothing that will cause me to rile myself up."

The only times Pam seemed calm were the evenings she spent on the balcony with Mike. They talked endlessly about everything and anything. When it got late, Pam would try to spark another topic of conversation so that they could linger longer. She was afraid to face another sleepless night. She still hadn't decided if she was going to let Caleb's mother raise her baby. Annalise had called a few times to see how she was doing and to make arrangements, but Pam told her that she needed more time to think it over.

Simone wasn't sure what was going on. She listened to the telephone conversations, trying to decipher what was being decided. Then she overheard her mother arguing with Mike and Mike trying to convince her that sending the baby to Jamaica to be raised was wrong. Simone was dumbfounded.

"Ms. Pam, are you going to send me away with the baby?" she

asked her mother one morning while they were in the laundry room washing clothes.

"Who told you that?" Pam continued to fold the clothes on the large counter.

"I overheard you talking to Nolan's Dad," she confessed. "I couldn't sleep last night and you were both arguing pretty loudly. I wasn't trying to be nosey but — I'm just wondering if you are going to send me to live with Grandma Annalise?"

"Don't call her that. She's not your grandmother," she said, sharply. "And no, I am not sending you away with the baby."

"But you are planning to send him away? You're going to send him to Jamaica?"

"I'm thinking of it," she said. "No decision has been made."

They continued to fold the clothes in silence. Simone hated that her mother would do this again. She began to wonder if there were other siblings tucked away with different grandmothers. Secret siblings that she didn't know about and who didn't know about her. She felt sorry for her unborn brother. It wasn't his fault that Caleb died. Why should he be punished and sent away?

"Well, if you send him away, send me with him," she said. "He shouldn't grow up thinking his family doesn't love him. I want to make sure he knows me."

Pam was stunned by Simone's request. She had never given a thought to her daughter's connection with the baby. A lump formed in her throat.

"It's not easy raising two pickneys with no help," she said. "You're too young to understand."

Pam started to shake and the tears streamed down her cheeks. She sat down on the chair by the washer. Simone looked at her and started to cry, too. She had never seen her mother lose control. Even after Caleb's death, she had remained stoic, cold, and more hostile than ever. Mrs. Price said it was her hormones and the impending due date that was causing her to be so angry, but this weeping frightened Simone more than her moody outbursts.

She moved timidly to her mother and placed her hand on her shoulder, but Pam swiftly brushed her off and stood up and started to yank the clothes from the dryer.

"The clothes are not dry," Simone said, trying to help her mother.

"Just leave them alone," Pam screamed. "Go back to the apartment and leave me alone."

"But I want to help." She tried to take her mother's hand.

Pam pulled away, pushing Simone into one of the dryers. "I don't need your help," she said, wiping her face with one of the towels they'd just washed. "Just leave me alone!"

Simone rushed out of the laundry room and ran to the elevator. She repeatedly pressed the elevator button. When it finally arrived, she pressed the top floor. As she rode up, she burst into tears. She couldn't stop crying. Her breathing began to stutter, then she started to punch the elevator wall.

When she got to the top floor, she ran to the stairwell and then up to the roof, opened the door and ran out to the edge, and looked over while tears burned her eyes. She could see the side of the building with the trash dumpsters below. She missed Jamaica, her Aunt Marva, and especially Caleb. She missed him the most. He always knew how to make everything better, but he was gone. She envied him so much. She wished she were with him.

She peered over to see how far it was to the bottom. The nasty smell wafting from the blue steel dumpster bins below was strong. If she jumped and landed on them, would she still smell the stench when she died? She didn't want to die smelling the rotting garbage, but she figured it wouldn't matter. Rotting garbage would be better than the ache she felt in her heart.

She stepped up to the ledge and instantly felt dizzy. She looked down. She imagined herself lying there alone with all of her bones broken. She started to cry, wondering how long it would take for her mother or anyone to notice that she was gone.

"No one would even care," she said to herself. "She won't care. She would probably throw more garbage down the chute on top of me."

She imagined the escovitch fish her mother made for dinner landing on her face as she lay dead in the bin. She started to cry even harder. She didn't want to smell like fish. As she contemplated jumping from a different side of the building, she felt a heavy hand pull her down from the ledge.

"What the hell are you doing up there," yelled a man. "Are you trying to get yourself killed?"

Carl Alden, the building manager, was holding her, dragging her back down from the rooftop to the stairwell.

"Damn kids. This area is off bounds. Don't you know how unsafe it is to be that close to the edge?"

Simone nodded.

"Aren't you Mrs. Price's granddaughter or something?" He was breathing heavily and his pudgy fingers gripped her arm. "She's not going to be pleased when I have words with her."

Simone didn't say a word all the way to Mrs. Price's. Mr. Alden banged loudly and they heard the shuffle of footsteps before Mrs. Price opened her door.

"Keep your granddaughter off my roof," he bellowed as Simone slipped behind Mrs. Price. "These kids need proper supervision. This building is not a goddamn playground."

"Well that's your damn problem," Mrs. Price shouted back in defiance. "You too damn cheap to put proper locks on di doors. When are you planning to fix di front doors and dem slow blood-claat elevators? Don't worry bout mi pickney and worry more about this nasty building!"

She then slammed the door on his bright red face before turning to Simone.

"What the raas are you doing on the roof?" she yelled.

Simone threw herself down and cried into the chesterfield pillow.

"Lawd Jesus, what 'appen now?"

Simone sat with Mrs. Price for almost an hour telling her about the argument she had had with her mother and how she wished Caleb hadn't died and that she wished her mother was the one who was dead.

"Don't say dem evil tings, baby," Mrs. Price said. "Never wish that on yuh madda. No matter how you feel, she's the only one you have. Yuh hear mi!"

"Well, I hate her. She never wanted me here in the first place. She doesn't want either of us. She wants to send the baby to Jamaica and probably wishes she could send me too."

"Shhh...shh...don't say such things."

Simone snuggled in Mrs. Price's arms and the old woman started to rock her gently. She could smell her cocoa butter cream as she laid her head on the old woman's chest, and she started to calm down.

"I know she's not the easiest person to love," said Mrs. Price. She grabbed a tissue from her pocket and wiped Simone's runny nose. "God knows she's a miserable woman, but things will change. I promise you."

Simone nodded.

"You know, you in your family is your mother in her family."

"What do you mean?" sniffled Simone. She looked up at Mrs. Price.

"I knew your Aunt Marva a long long time ago. We both grew up in the same parish," she said. "She raised your madda the same way she took care of you. Ms. Pam never really knew her own madda. She died when she small and her fadda passed not long after. The same Auntie you lived with was her only people. She had no one to really show her how to raise you right."

"You knew my family?" Simone asked Mrs. Price. "Did you know my father?"

Mrs. Price sat still. She sighed heavily before she kissed Simone's forehead. "No, baby, I don't know him," she said. "And you shouldn't mind yourself over him either."

"But if I could find him, I could live with him," she said. "He would love me. He would want me around."

"Stop your foolishness!" Mrs. Price said, abruptly. "You may not see it now but she does love you. In time she will warm up to you and it will be better. She's just hurting right now. It's been hard for her with Caleb gone."

"I miss him."

"I know, baby. And so does your mother...remember that."

That evening Simone returned to the apartment carrying two plates of food.

"Where have you been?" Pam asked calmly. She was sitting at the kitchen table, drinking her tea and reading the newspaper.

"The apartment door was locked so I went over to Mrs. Price," she said.

Her mother continued to read her paper.

"She sent some food for you." Simone placed the peace offering on the table. "It's rice and peas with some oxtail."

"Thank you," she said. "Put it in the refrigerator."

Simone did so, then came back to the table and stood there. She thought back to what Mrs. Price had said earlier that afternoon. She wanted to look into Pam's eyes and see a woman who barely knew her own parents. Someone who hurt as much as she did, but Pam never looked up from her paper.

"I hope you didn't go over there telling her our business," she said tersely.

"No, I did not," she lied.

"Good."

Simone quickly went into her room and closed the door behind her. She pulled out the diary Caleb had given her from underneath her mattress. The notebook still looked brand-new, even though almost every page was filled with everything that had happened to her. Every thought, problem, dream, and secret. Every memory lived in her diary. Now she only had half a page left to write on.

Dear Diary,

I don't care what Mrs. Price says. I still hate my mother.

PART II

18

Maureen Meunier was on the telephone, loudly organizing her daughter's upcoming wedding, glancing at her watch, ignoring the unfinished report. It was the inventory report Pam needed for her afternoon meeting with the hospital's director.

Pam had been leery about employing the middle-aged woman. Maureen was a former nurse from Sunnybrook Hospital, whose resume showed an unexplained two-year gap, but Mike had vouched for his favourite cousin, telling Pam that she was perfect for the position. Whether that was true or not remained to be seen.

Pam had a lot to prove as a new manager. She had been running the department for less than a year and, despite knowing she was the best person for the job, she worried that the hospital board would regret promoting her. She felt like she had to work twice as hard just to make sure everyone knew it all wasn't a fluke. As head of administration for one of the largest hospitals in Toronto, she didn't have the time or patience to deal with any slacking off.

"Maureen," she finally yelled out from her desk. "I need you, please."

Maureen quickly hung up the telephone. She strolled in and sat in front of Pam's desk. She looked exhausted.

"Yes, Pam," she said. "What do you need?"

"How is the report coming along?"

"I'm working on it," she said. "It'll be done by the end of the day."

"Maureen, I told you that I needed the report by lunchtime," Pam said. "We had this discussion just this morning."

"Well, I've hit a snag with the calculations and it's taking a lot longer than I thought."

She always had an excuse for why she couldn't get a project done. The previous week she'd stayed home, claiming she was ill. The month before she couldn't get a report done because she was learning a hospital program system she had sworn she was an expert on.

"The only snag I've seen is that you've been on the phone instead of working," Pam said sharply. "I expect the report completed before my one o'clock meeting."

"Fine," she said. "You'll have it by one."

At lunchtime, Maureen was still working on the report. Pam was furious. She was forced to cancel her meeting with the hospital's director.

She called Maureen into her office at the end of the day.

"I'm sorry," Maureen said, "but I just don't understand how to get the calculations. There were a lot of parts you didn't show me properly."

"Maureen, I spent several weeks training you, specifically on how to complete this report. What didn't I show you?"

"Well, you weren't making a whole lot of sense. I can barely understand what you say half the time with your accent, and you talk too fast. It's distracting."

"You've had three weeks to tell me that you didn't understand how to complete this report and you choose to tell me this now?" Pam said, raising her voice. "Get this report done, Maureen! I don't care if you have to stay here all night. I want it completed and on my desk first thing in the morning and if you have any questions, go back to the mountain of notes you made while I was training you."

When Pam left the office, Maureen was still sitting at her desk, working through the report. Why would Mike even recommend her? Pam usually respected his opinion. He had never steered her wrong, yet his cousin was a complete disaster.

The car ride home didn't help settle her nerves. By the time she reached her empty apartment, she was glad to have the solitude to unwind. She threw her shoes to the side of the hallway, went into the kitchen, and opened the refrigerator, hoping there would be some wine left from the night before. There was nothing but the jerk chicken marinating and a casserole dish of potato salad.

She turned on the oven and then filled her electric kettle with water. She was dealing with a growing headache and, as the water boiled, she looked for the ginger tea she'd bought from the Jamaican grocer earlier that week. She was glad that she'd thought to buy a few boxes. Ginger tea was her saving grace for stressful days like this.

As she stood by the kitchen counter, sipping her tea, she felt a little better, though her head still throbbed. She turned when she heard the key rattle in the front door. It was Simone and Caleb Jr. coming home from Mrs. Price's place.

CJ was in senior kindergarten and Simone would soon be heading into her final year at St. Augustine. The children had just come home from spending the summer with CJ's grandmother in Jamaica. It had been their annual trip since CJ was two years old.

Deciding to raise CJ herself had not been a difficult decision to make. The moment he was born, she had looked into his sweet face and instantly fallen in love with him. In every way, he favoured his father — the curly jet-black hair, light brown eyes, and infectious laughter sent flashes of Caleb back to her. Initially, Annalise had been upset that CJ wouldn't be living with her, but, after several heated arguments, she was persuaded that, if she ever wanted to see her grandson, she had to let her plan go.

And so Simone and CJ spent the summers in the sleepy coffee town of Swaby's Hope in Manchester. For Simone, it was a dream come true, going back home each summer. She had missed Jamaica so much, and was glad for any opportunity to visit.

That first summer in Jamaica was a beautiful dream for her, except for one thing. She could see that Annalise was only interested in spending time with CJ. She hadn't counted on entertaining another child. But, any time Annalise attempted to show him any affection, CJ cried for his mother and clung to Simone. Simone didn't mind. She felt protective of her brother and it made her feel like a grown-up, being in charge. But she could tell that CJ's rejection hurt Annalise's feelings. At night, Simone would take CJ out of the bed they shared and the two would crawl into his Granny's bed to sleep. In the mornings, Simone greeted Annalise with a kiss and a hug and held her brother up to do the same. By the end of the first visit, CJ was no longer shy around his grandmother and Simone's relationship with Annalise blossomed as well, so much so that Annalise made Pam promise that Simone would join CJ each summer.

Pam could hear her children arguing the moment they walked into the apartment. She wasn't in the mood to deal with either of her kids right now. Her headache throbbed steadily, and they were too loud.

"Keep it down," she said.

She watched Simone getting frustrated over her little brother not taking off his shoes fast enough and pinching him when he complained that he couldn't untie his laces. The two were polar opposites. Pam loved her son's sweet and silly disposition, while she cringed at Simone's lack of humour and miserable demeanour. If she wasn't dealing with a massive headache, she would have cussed out her eldest, but she didn't have the strength.

"Simone, when the oven beeps, place the chicken in the stove for an hour. I'm going to lie down."

"Yes, Miss Pam." she said, trying to take off her jacket. "Come on CJ, leggo mi hand, nuh!"

"Come lay down with Mummy, CJ," Pam said. She grabbed hold of him and hugged him tightly. "Did you have a good day?"

"Yes, Mommy," he said, smiling at her. "Did you have a good day?"

"No," she said in a funny voice before she kissed him all over his face.

Pam lay next to CJ and watched him. She loved to watch him sleep. It was the only way she could sense Caleb's spirit. He favoured Caleb so much — the way his eyelids fluttered and his gentle snores. This helped her during the hard moments when she ached for him.

The smell of baked chicken, wafting through the apartment, gently woke her from her nap. She stretched out to find that CJ had already left. She could hear him playing with his Hot Wheels in the bedroom he shared with Simone. She wandered into the living room and could see Simone talking with Nolan on the balcony.

It was no surprise to see them huddled together. They hadn't seen each other the entire summer and usually were inseparable for days each time Simone returned home from summer vacation. But, for a short moment, Pam noticed something different about them — something she had never considered before.

During the summer Nolan had had a noticeable growth spurt that made him much taller than most of his classmates. He was bulkier and thicker, which made him clumsier. She was used to his new physique and him accidentally knocking everything down, but she hadn't noticed Simone catching up.

Simone was no longer that little girl who wore the colourful beads at the bottom of her braids. Her short lanky body had gotten longer and had filled out. Her breasts were perfectly shaped; they had blossomed from cherry pits to perfect rounded mounds. She had new curves. Pam couldn't help noticing how much Simone looked like her when she was that age — a lifetime ago.

She continued to watch the two of them, fascinated by how much they had grown. Simone stood by Nolan with her arms awkwardly crossed over her chest, obviously self-conscious about her breasts. Pam smiled a little to herself as she remembered what it had been like when her own body started to change.

Simone's cream-coloured T-shirt seemed too tight on her and her long legs made her blue-mesh shorts too short and inappropriate. Pam made a mental note to take her to Zellers to buy her better-fitting clothes. As she tried to figure which day she could take Simone shopping, she was startled by *it*. The moment the two childhood friends suddenly turned into awkward gangly teenagers. She had to adjust her eyes, unsure if she had just imagined it or not.

Nolan was leaning against the balcony railing, listening to some story Simone was telling him. He seemed drawn to her, as if she was telling him secrets of the universe. His face glowed as he laughed at some joke she made. Simone had started to relax and placed her hand on the balcony railing. Nolan noticed and looked down at her hand. Not quite sure what to do, his fingers lightly caressed the top of her hand. Simone looked up at him with a slight smile on her face.

Pam could see the chemistry brewing between them. She was about to call Simone back into the house when she saw their hands interlock.

She froze for a minute.

She had had the "talk" with Simone about sex after her first period and had sternly warned her to keep her legs closed to boys, but nothing had prepared her for this moment. Simone had transformed from the little girl she'd picked up at Pearson Airport all those years ago into the young woman holding hands with the boy next door.

"Simone!" she called out. The two quickly pulled their hands away from each other. "I hope my chicken isn't burning."

Simone rushed into the kitchen.

"Hi, Pam," greeted Nolan. When he walked into the apartment he nearly hit his head on top of the balcony doorway.

A little smoke was coming from the stove. Pam inspected the chicken over Simone's shoulder.

"Hi, Nolan," she said. "Humph, Simone, you're lucky my chicken didn't burn too much or I would have given your behind some licks."

"Ewww Mommy, you said you were going to lick Simone's butt," squealed CJ. "That's gross!"

Simone and Nolan started giggling. The combination of "licks" and "behind" brought out the silliness hidden beneath their adult bodies.

"Chups," Pam said as she scraped the chicken from the baking pan. "Simone, get the table ready for dinner. Nolan, are you eating?"

"No — actually Dad is taking me out for pizza," he said. "I was hoping Simone could come with us. We're celebrating my new job."

"You have a job?" Pam asked. "Doesn't your father work enough jobs already, now he has you working too?"

"Ha, ha — yes, Ma'am," he laughed. "I'm in charge of delivering *The Star* every morning to all the apartments in the building."

"Really!" she said. "Isn't that a pretty big job to do before school?"

"Yes," he said proudly. "But I'm only in charge of our building so it shouldn't be too bad. My supervisor says that if I do a good job he'll see if he can expand my job to Building 3 during the summer. That'll be a whole extra $10 a week."

"Well, good for you," Pam replied. "Maybe I'll renew my subscription."

"Miss Pam, can I go with them?" interrupted Simone.

"Yes...yes, you can go," she said. "Now that you made a mess of my chicken."

"I want to go too," whined CJ.

"No, CJ!" Simone yelled gruffly. "You can't come with us."

Pam shot her a look as she picked up CJ. She hated how harsh she could be with her brother.

"If you go, baby, who is going to have dinner with me?" said Pam. She nuzzled CJ. "Plus, you have to take your bath. It's almost bedtime."

"Okay, Mommy," he replied, and he kissed her cheek hard, over and over. "I'll never leave you by yourself. Who's going to protect you from monsters?"

"You are, my sweet boy," she said. She watched Nolan and Simone get ready to leave. "Make sure Mike doesn't have you out too late."

Pam made a mental note to have a frank conversation with Simone. She didn't want her to turn into some "fast gyal" — even if it was lanky, clumsy Nolan from next door.

▶

SIMONE AND NOLAN headed to the elevator. They were to meet Mike at the building's roundabout. They didn't say much as they walked down the hallway.

Simone was still startled by Nolan holding her hand earlier. She kept replaying the moment in her head as sparks continued to run throughout her body. She didn't dare reach for his hand. She wasn't sure if he'd really meant it and she didn't know how to show that kind of affection to another person — especially a boy.

Nolan's heart had been pounding ever since he'd grabbed her

hand. He'd tried so many times to reach out to her, but had always lost his nerve. Simone wasn't into the mushy stuff. She turned cold anytime anyone showed a little affection. But that evening, alone on the balcony, he had finally found the nerve. The moment he touched her hand an electric pulse surged through his body. It was so intense that he almost pulled his hand away. He had never felt anything like it. Not even on the nights he lay in his bed dreaming of her.

His dreams were a source of embarrassment. He would dream of her skinny honey-kissed brown legs, or her peach-coloured lips smiling at him, and wake up to discover the sticky wetness. He was mortified the first time it happened. He wanted to ask his father about it, but instead he hid his pyjamas until he had a chance to do his laundry. But he couldn't help going back to thoughts of her. He liked thinking of her. Dreaming of her. It was all he was able to do all summer while he waited for her to come back from Jamaica.

When Simone had finally returned, he almost didn't recognize her. He'd wanted to run up and hug her like he usually did but he could tell she was a little embarrassed. She stood awkwardly, folding her arms over her chest. He'd tried not to stare. She had changed over the summer. She had gotten taller and her waist seemed smaller, her hips wider. She no longer wore her hair in several tiny braids; now one long ponytail hung down her back.

They stood by the elevator, waiting for it to arrive. They didn't dare interrupt the silence that engulfed them. When the elevator finally opened, they bumped into each other as they attempted to enter at the same time. Awkwardly, they quickly moved away from each other, carefully trying not to touch. She let him go in first.

He winced.

Wasn't she supposed to go in first?

He felt like a dork as he quickly pressed the lobby button. They stood at opposite ends of the elevator, terrified to even look at one another. As the door started to close, someone cried out to hold the elevator. Nolan pressed the button to keep the door open, and the Wang children from down the hall gleefully piled in, their pregnant mother waddling after them, pushing Nolan closer to Simone as she pressed the button for the basement.

The two of them looked at each other and giggled.

Nolan then lifted his head to the elevator's ceiling and took a deep breath as he grabbed Simone's hand again. Simone felt her heart leap into her throat. Nolan exhaled, hoping that Simone didn't hear the heavy thumping in his chest.

▶

MIKE WAS FINISHING off some paperwork at the little office he had at Ryerson when the phone rang. He immediately regretted picking up when he heard Maureen's voice. He looked over at the time and sighed deeply when she immediately went into her weekly rant. He loved his cousin, but at times wished they weren't related.

Growing up, the two cousins had been inseparable. Maureen had become an older sister to him, especially after his father's death. But, as the years piled on, his fun-loving older cousin had turned into a bitter pain in the ass. It started when she married Loïc Meunier, a francophone graduate of McGill University. A true jackass who hated everything Anglo-Canadian, yet he'd married the very Anglo-Irish Maureen.

As the years went by, Mike had grown tired of his cousin and her overbearing husband.

"Typical of you Irish to quit. I should know," he remembered Loïc ranting, after Mike announced that he was quitting school. "I go to school with too many of you. Fuck, I married one so I consider myself an expert, no? You Irish take no opportunities.

You just shit on them. And you are no exception, Michael! Why not finish school and go to university?"

The four of them were at McKinney's, a local dive down the street from Maureen and Loïc's house. Meghan was pregnant with Dana at that time, and they had just married and had moved into their duplex not far from the bar.

"Not my speed, man," responded Mike.

"Mickey, stop being so bloody stubborn!" Maureen chirped. "With a baby on the way, you need to at least graduate high school."

"I've had enough school and I'm ready to join the real world, raise me some kids, and fucking live my life."

"You sound like one of those dumb American country singers," Loïc said. "Don't be like those stupid fucking Americans. Finish school. Go and get a degree. McGill has a great engineering program. You're a smart guy. You can swing it."

"Look, I'm a very smart guy, but I'm also a broke one too," he spat back. "Anyways, you're killing my buzz, man..."

"This is supposed to be a celebration, not a debate," interrupted Meghan. "Let's all just give it a rest and toast to new beginnings. Whatever they may be."

Mike had been happy when Maureen and Loïc finally called it quits, but Maureen continued to be as opinionated and bitter as her ex-husband.

"Meghan needs to go back to school and get her degree," Maureen remarked one morning, when the three of them were sitting in his kitchen eating donuts. "She's a smart girl, and can you imagine the amount of money you can pull in if both of you were working?"

"Stay out of it, Maureen," Mike said. "Megs doesn't have time for all that. She's busy raising Dana plus, if she's off at school, who's going to watch your precious Amber during the day?"

"Fuck you, Mikey," she said, smiling at him. "Okay, but I'm just saying Dana is not going to stay a little kid forever. One day she's going to go to school and then what?"

"Then we'll have another one, then another," laughed Mike. "A whole brood of O'Sheas terrorizing the streets."

"Speak for yourself," said Meghan. She lit another cigarette. "One more and no more."

"We'll see," Mike had said. He remembered caressing her stomach and noticing how beautiful she was. She had a glow and confidence about her that shone through. It was the best time of their marriage. A time when they were young and passionate about everything. Now here he was, still separated from his wife, sitting at his desk and listening to his cousin rant about her horrible day with her nag of a boss.

"She's a haughty bitch who needs to know her place," Maureen yammered. "Are you even listening to me, Mikey?"

He hadn't been paying much attention. From the moment she got hired, she'd been calling him weekly to complain. It began with a few disparaging remarks, but, as the months rolled by, the snide remarks had turned into full-out rants that often lasted an entire lunch hour.

He regretted telling Maureen about the position. He'd made the mistake of mentioning to her that his friend was in charge of hiring for the position at the hospital. After that, Maureen hounded him for weeks to put in a good word for her. He reluctantly talked to Pam, practically begging her to meet with Maureen.

"What happened now?" he said, hoping that this rant wouldn't last long.

"She has me here working on some bloody report that she could have done herself," she said. "Telling me to get it done or else."

"Well? Isn't that your job?" He was looking up at the clock. He had promised Nolan he would take him out for pizza and it was getting late.

"I don't understand how it's helpful to her meeting," she said. "I mean, who the hell cares how many goddamn Tylenol pills were dispensed month to fucking month."

"Well, it's useful to her," he said in annoyance. "Look, Maureen, I have to pick up Nolan—"

"Useful, my ass," she continued. "If I was running that damn department people like her would never be hired. I'm seriously thinking of placing a complaint with HR."

"A complaint for what?" he asked. "For doing your job? Come on, Maureen, give her a break. Pam's a good person."

"What is that supposed to mean?" she said. "And how do you know her name is Pam?"

"Maureen, are you fucking kidding me? Pam, my neighbour! She's your boss. I recommended she hire you for the job!"

"She's the contact you had at the hospital?"

"Who did you think it was, Maureen?" he said looking at the time again. "Pam is my neighbour and she also did me a huge favour hiring you, so do me a favour and try not to fuck this one up, okay?"

"Wait…has she said anything about me?" she asked.

"Goodbye, Maureen," he said, before hanging up the phone.

Mike drove back to North York pissed off. His cousin wasn't the smartest tool in the shed, but he'd never pegged her as a complete idiot.

How could she not know that Pam was my friend? he thought to himself.

But then it dawned on him that he didn't really talk about Pam to anyone. It wasn't that it was a big secret — it just wasn't a big deal. Pam and he had been friends for so long that he just assumed it was common knowledge that they spent time together. But, as he thought it through, he slowly realized that it was plausible that Maureen had been in the dark.

Over the years his relationship with Pam had gone from casual acquaintance to a close confidant. He worked so much he didn't have time to socialize with anyone else. His main focus was Nolan and, after a while, it felt normal to spend time with Pam while their children played together.

Even his relationship with CJ had become that of a surrogate father. When CJ was old enough, Mike took him to his Little League soccer matches, cheering along with the other parents when he scored a goal. He often dropped CJ off at pre-school on his way to work in the mornings. Many of CJ's teachers just assumed that Mike was his father, and he never saw any reason to change their perception.

They were their own strange family. Running errands together, eating dinners together, celebrating birthdays together — sharing their most private moments. Mike never felt the need to explain their relationship because he wasn't dating Pam and they weren't involved sexually. They were just two single parents helping each other out as they raised their children the best way they knew how.

As he turned into the roundabout, he could see Nolan and Simone sitting out front waiting for him. He looked at the car radio and realized that he was almost thirty minutes late.

"Look who's back from sunny Jamaica! Welcome back, Splimoney," he called out to Simone.

"Good to see you too, Mr. Mike," she said, smiling back.

"Where's your brother?" he asked. "He's not joining us for dinner?"

Simone crawled into the back seat. "He's having dinner with Miss Pam."

As Nolan followed behind her, Mike looked back, about to call his son out. Nolan usually sat up front with him. He noticed the two of them were holding hands.

"Oh God," he mumbled to himself as he drove off.

▶

LATER THAT NIGHT, after the kids were settled, Mike headed over to Pam's apartment through the balcony door. He tapped lightly before entering. Pam was in the kitchen scouring her baking pan.

"Hey," he said as he sat down at the kitchen table.

"Hi," she replied. "Do you want some coffee? I just made some for myself."

"No I'm fine," he said. "I'm...hmmm...did you notice..."

He couldn't find the proper words. The last thing he wanted was Pam throwing a fit over something as innocent as holding hands.

"Sorry, what's that?" she asked.

"Nothing...I mean...how's it going with Maureen? Are things going well?"

"Honestly? No!" She sat down with her cup of coffee. "I know that she's your cousin and all but..."

"...She's a pain in the ass," he said.

"Yes!" she said. "Look, I'm trying to work with her but she doesn't want to even try to do her job and, frankly, I'm at the end of my rope. I can't have someone working for me who doesn't respect me or the work I do."

Mike sighed loudly and got up to pour himself a cup of coffee. Pam never spoke much about her job. She usually kept her work life separate, especially now that Maureen worked in her department. He hated to be put in the middle, but it *was* because of him that Pam and Maureen were working together.

"Maureen has always been a difficult person to deal with," he said. "But she's been dealing with a lot lately. Her ex-husband hasn't been helping with Amber's wedding, so she's on the hook for the entire party."

"Trust me, mi know. She's constantly on the phone planning this wedding instead of doing her work."

Silence.

"Look...I hate to ask you this but can you be a little patient with her?" he said. "The wedding is in another few months and I'm sure after it's over she'll be better."

"A few months! Are you joking, Mike? This coming from a man who goes on and on about how everyone in the world is a lazy bum — everyone except you Irish, of course."

"I have never said anything like that." Pam gave him a condescending look. "Okay, okay, but not in a long time."

"Just last week you complained about the Wangs down the hall," she reminded him. "And I quote, 'Fucking chinks need to stop breeding and get off their lazy asses and get a bloody job.' You know, the craziest thing is that your cousin is probably the laziest person I've ever met and yet you want me to give her a few more months to turn her shit around? That is some real white privilege right there!"

Mike put his head on the table. He hated arguing with Pam, especially when she was right. Maureen was the most unreliable person and he wished he had never mentioned the job to her.

"Okay...okay, you're right," he said. "Maureen takes the cake as the laziest fucking person in the city — in the world! Pam, I'm asking you as a friend to just give her a break. She needs this job."

"Well, I need my sanity," she mumbled. "Do you know what she told me today? She said that she didn't understand the instructions I gave her because I have a thick accent."

"Well, you do." He laughed weakly. "I can barely understand you most of the time."

"Ha, ha, ha," she said.

Silence.

"Look, I'll talk to her and tell her to do her job," he said. "Come on, Pam, give me a break."

She stood there thinking for a moment. "Alright, alright," she said.

Mike got up and hugged her, giving her a gruff kiss on her cheek. "Thank you, Pam!"

"But before I promise you anything, you need to do something for me," she added.

"Whatever you want! Anything!"

"If you haven't already, make sure you explain to your son what will happen if he sticks his dick in my daughter," she said.

Mike stood there stunned.

Pam looked steadily back at him. She slowly sipped her coffee.

He quietly nodded before heading back to his apartment.

19

It was the last Sunday morning before school started. Mike usually took Nolan, Simone, and CJ to St. Augustine for mass while he spent the morning performing his weekly maintenance upkeep at the church. It was his "penance" for not actually going to mass. He sat in his car, waiting for the kids to come out.

He watched as they emerged from church with their friends from school, girls flocking around Nolan. He frowned slightly.

After his conversation with Pam, he knew he had to say something to his son — but what? He felt hot under the collar as he tried to figure out how to tell a boy with raging hormones that holding hands with the girl he has a crush on was a recipe for trouble.

It was easier for Pam. She was more straightforward. She'd told her daughter, point blank, that if she started having sex she would beat the horniness out of her. That made Mike laugh, but he knew that she was serious. They had seen many of the young girls in the building get pregnant. At least three of them were about to give birth, one as young as fifteen — all of them Jamaicans.

He knew Jamaicans had sex early and often. Pam had Simone when she was barely seventeen. But the last thing he wanted was Nolan getting Simone in trouble. He had to figure out a way to quietly dismantle any budding romance without being the bad guy.

Mike searched the crowd for Simone and her brother and quickly spotted them on the church steps. Simone was engrossed in one of her Danielle Steele books, with her brother beside her busy scarfing down Timbits.

He honked his horn to let them know that he was there, and Simone and CJ ran to the car, while Nolan lingered behind. Sarah Jane Ryden seemed to be talking his ear off. Maybe Sarah Jane could be a good distraction. Someone to keep his mind off of Simone. A girl who would be a good influence.

He had known Sarah Jane and her family for years. Her mother Claudia and Meghan had both volunteered at the school and had become fast friends. They still kept in touch, even with Meghan in Nova Scotia.

Sarah Jane was almost as tall as Nolan now and her golden strawberry blonde hair fell down the middle of her back. Her mother still dressed her in the same preppy skirt with a white blouse and penny loafers that had been her uniform since kindergarten.

When Nolan finally joined them in the car, Mike insisted that he sit up front.

"I'm dropping Simone and CJ off before we head out to run some errands."

"Can Simone come with us?" asked Nolan.

"Not this time," said Mike. "Pam wants them both home so she can get them ready for school on Tuesday."

Simone sat quietly in the back seat, reading her book the whole way to the complex, where she and CJ left the car. Mike waited for them to get into the building lobby before he drove off. He wasn't sure what to say to Nolan. His own father had given hım a hasty five-minute talk about sex and had thrust a pamphlet about abstinence at him. It hadn't helped much since Meghan had ended up pregnant with Dana in his senior year.

As they merged onto the highway he turned on the radio to lighten his mood. The Bangles' "Hazy Shade of Winter" was playing, and he hummed along as he weaved through traffic.

"So Sarah Jane still goes to your school, eh?" he asked. "She's still a pretty thing."

"I guess." Nolan was staring out the window, not paying much attention.

"You guess?" Mike said. "She's gorgeous and smart, too, if I remember."

"So? Simone is smarter than most of the girls in our class."

"Yes, but we're talking about Sarah Jane, not Simone."

"Sarah Jane is a big pain in the ass," Nolan said. "She's always bugging me about everything."

"Maybe she likes you. You ever thought about asking her out to the movies or something?"

"Sarah Jane? No way, Dad! I hate those Glenview girls. They're not my type."

"Your type?" Mike chuckled as they pulled into the Scarborough Town Centre. "Well, well, well! Nolan has a type. What does Nolan O'Shea look for in a woman?"

"Jesus, Dad," Nolan said, blushing. "You're being weird."

"No, seriously!" he laughed. "I want to know."

Nolan started to say something but then hesitated. He tried again but stopped.

"I don't know, Dad."

"Come on, Nols, you can trust me. Anything you say will stay between us and Babs."

Nolan sat for a moment longer. He looked at Babs, the air freshener hula girl that hung from the rearview mirror. He poked at it and she started to dance; a faint citrus scent lingered in the air.

He took a deep breath and started to tell Mike how much he liked Simone. He went on about how he had liked her for almost two years and that he was scared she wouldn't like him back but that recently she let him hold her hand. He wondered if that meant she liked him too. He then told his father that now that he was going into grade eight he was thinking of asking her to be his girlfriend but was confused because Simone hadn't talked to him all morning. He worried that he might have said something or done something that might have gotten her mad.

"Do you think she was mad that I was talking to Sarah Jane?" he said suddenly. "She hates Sarah Jane...like since the second grade. Maybe I should ask her."

"Wow," was Mike's only response.

"Do you think I should ask?"

"Look, Nols, Simone is a great girl," Mike said. "You have been friends — best friends — for as long as I can remember, so it's only normal for you to like her, but she's not the one for you, bud."

"What do you mean?" Nolan asked.

"Look, I'm going to lay it to you straight," he said. "In a few years, Simone is going to be the type of girl that men will go to when they want to get an easy piece of tail. Not a girl you would seriously date or even marry. You're a big boy and you know all about sex — you do, right?"

"Yeah...yeah, I do," he said. "Pretty much."

"Well that's good," he said relieved. "Then you know that sex is a big deal and when you start holding hands and dating and kissing it leads to sex. You have sex with a girl like Simone and it will be great at first, but the thing about these Jamaican girls is that they're fertile as hell. Is that what you want? You want to have sex with a girl who is going to get pregnant the moment you pop your dick in? You see all these girls in our building? Half of them are pregnant or having more babies with different guys. That's why you need to be careful when it comes to her." Mike paused for a moment. He glanced at Nolan, unsure if he had heard a thing or if he was going to pop his old man in the mouth. "She's a smart girl," he continued. "So maybe she might not be one of those girls, but her mom had her when she was young, and if she's anything like her mom the same could happen to her."

"I thought you liked Pam and Simone?"

"I do!" Mike said. "This is coming off wrong. I'm not saying she's a bad person or anything. I'm just telling you the way things are and you need to be aware of that. Someone like Sarah Jane — well she's different. She comes from a good family. She knows better and wouldn't let things get too far."

"Sarah Jane had three boyfriends last year and half the boys at school swear that she's done it already," Nolan said bluntly. "Simone and I spend most of our time listening to the radio and doing our homework. She's not that kind of girl, Dad! She won't even let me sit on the bed with her these days. I have to sit on the floor every time I'm in her room."

"Okay...okay, that's good!" replied Mike. "That's exactly what you're supposed to do. She's your friend. Hell, she's practically your sister, and that's my point, Nolan. She's nothing more than a friend.... And so maybe not Sarah Jane, but there are plenty of other girls in your grade that would be a better choice for you. I'm not saying that you shouldn't be friends with Simone. We all love her... I'm just saying that you need to JUST be friends with her. Okay?"

"Sure, Dad," he said. "I understand."

Mike studied him for a moment. He had given in too easily. He knew that his son was pacifying him just to end the conversation. He was his mother's child, and they were still a lot alike. No matter what he said, Nolan was going to do what he wanted. He had to do more than just talk to him. He needed to take action.

Early the next day, when Nolan left on his paper route, Mike headed to St. Augustine's before work. No one was around except for good old Mrs. Wilson, who was retiring soon but still acted like the school's watchdog.

"Michael O'Shea," she greeted him. "You are looking well. How is the family?"

She had been his teacher back in the day and was very familiar with the O'Shea family.

"Well, that's why I'm here, Mrs. Wilson," he said. "I'm hoping that I can talk to you about Nolan."

▶

THE FIRST DAY of school was always a nerve-racking experience for Simone. She didn't know why it gave her butterflies but, like clockwork, every time it came around, she felt sick to her stomach. She worried that she wouldn't like her teacher, or feared that this year she would fail all her subjects. The one thing she could count on was Nolan. But this year he was nowhere to be found. His apartment was quiet.

Pam had already left for work, so Simone had to take CJ to the bus stop early and wait with him for the kindergarten bus to arrive. After CJ left, she waited with the other students for the regular school bus. Still no Nolan.

That Sunday morning, before mass, her mother had read her the riot act about boys. She had practically accused her of being "fast," which led to a huge argument. During the service, she'd felt mortified that Nolan might have heard the commotion through their paper-thin walls. She hardly listened to the homily. Her mother had treated her like she was planning to spread her legs to every boy in the building. She had barely even thought about dating, let alone sex.

Usually, when Pam yelled at her, Nolan would sneak into her bedroom to make sure she was okay. They would play cards and she would get out her anger, whispering how much she hated her mother. By the third hand, he would say something to make her laugh and, by the fourth hand, she would be calm enough to go to sleep. Sunday evening, he hadn't come to her room. Yesterday, Labour Day, she had wanted to see him, but had to go with her mother and brother to a Jamaican Canadian Association barbecue.

When the bus arrived, she boarded and, just as it was about to pull away, Nolan ran up to the stop, panting. He got on, pulling his book bag off, and walked right past her to the back of the bus, where Brian Kepler sat. She turned to call him, but quickly turned around, too embarrassed to say anything. She wished Kester was on the bus. They usually all sat together, but his family had recently moved to a new neighbourhood, and he was on a different bus route.

When they finally got to school, Nolan was busy talking with all the other boys.

Simone suddenly felt out of place. She looked around the schoolyard, amazed; everyone seemed to have changed over the summer. The girls had all styled their hair like Paula Abdul and were dressed like Debbie Gibson. The boys were sporting rocker T-shirts and acid-washed jeans and were calling each other "guy". She felt silly in her drab white blouse and navy blue plaid skirt.

Yvette and Angie were standing by the stairs. Both girls had moved from the complex a few years back and lived in the same neighbourhood as Kester. She smiled when they gleefully waved at her.

"Simone!!!!" Angie cried out. "Girl, you got boobs!"

Simone blushed, but lost a bit of anxiety when they pulled her aside to show her the new lace bras that their mothers had bought them.

"How was your summer?" asked Yvette. "Did you go to Jamaica again?"

"Yeah, and did you meet any cute boys?" Angie chimed in. She pulled out a pack of gum. "Do you want any?"

"Sure." Simone nodded. "Jamaica was fun."

"Yeah, so did you see any cute boys or what?" demanded Yvette, clearly more boy-crazy than the previous year.

Angie handed out pieces of gum.

"There weren't any cute boys there," she finally admitted. "Just me and my brother with my Granny Annalise. How was your summer?"

"Oh my God, I'm in love with Jordan Knight," squealed Angie. "Yvette loves Joe, but I lo-oo-o-ve Jordan."

"Who?" Simone asked in confusion. "Do they go to our school?"

"No silly, NKOTB!!!" she said excitedly. "New Kids on the Block."

Angie opened up her jean jacket to show a T-shirt with a picture of five boys, each in his own colourful square box.

Simone looked at the shirt and didn't really understand the big deal.

"You know, 'Please Don't Go Girl,'" sang Yvette as she danced around with Angie. "Girl, they must not know about New Kids in Jamaica. You came back just in time."

"Their album comes out today and Yvette's mom is taking us to Sam's to buy a cassette," screamed Angie. "I'm so EXCITED."

Simone forced a smile. She still didn't really understand what they were going on about and found them so bizarre at times. She often had to remind herself that, even though Yvette and Angie's parents were West Indians, they were a lot more Canadian than most island people and they got more excited about pop groups and boys than she did.

"Simone, we're going to buy a blank tape and make a copy for you," said Yvette. "My ghetto blaster has a double cassette so it's no biggie."

"No, it's okay," she said.

"No, it's fine," Angie said, jumping up and down.

Simone had never seen Angie so excited. She was dancing

around, flailing her arms, and she nearly struck Simone, who moved back to avoid her and ended up crashing into Nolan.

"Whoops, sorry, Nols," she said. "That was a close one."

He grabbed onto her so that she wouldn't fall. "Tell me about it," he said. "What's up with them?"

"They're all excited about some white boys," she laughed. "New Kids on the Corner — or something like that."

"Ooooh, New Kids on the Block," he corrected her. "Yeah…I hate those guys."

Simone laughed out loud, but then quickly covered her mouth. She hated her smile and had, just this summer, realized how big her teeth looked. She felt like an orangutan every time she smiled.

"Hey, so are you ready for Sister Roger's class?" he asked her. "I hope she's not too bad this year. Dana had her in grade eight and almost failed everything."

"I'm a little nervous," she said.

"You're always nervous the first day of school," he said before hearing his name being called. "Hey, Dennis is calling me. I'll see you later. Save me a seat, okay?"

Simone watched Nolan head over to his friend. He turned back and smiled at her before talking to Dennis. She smiled at him and took a deep breath. She started to feel herself calm down.

After the bell, the students rushed into the school, all heading to their previous year's classroom. The first day always started out as a mini-reunion before they were assigned to their new teachers. Classmates chatted loudly about their summer vacations and which teacher they hoped to get. Simone took her old seat, with Nolan in the desk behind her. She turned to talk to him, but was interrupted by Mr. Saddler.

"Alright, students," he shouted over them. "Let's settle down. I'm going to call your name. When you are called, come up and get a slip. This year we have two classes, Sister Rogers' class in Room 13 and Mrs. Brickett in Room 21. Once you're called, I want you to get your stuff and head over to your assigned classroom. I trust that, as young adults, I don't need to remind you to go straight there. Correct?"

"Yes, Mr. Saddler," they all said.

"Good," he said. "Let's begin."

Simone was the third student called. She quickly picked up her bag and headed over to Sister Rogers' classroom. When she entered, a small woman with wiry grey hair and a warm smile greeted her.

"Welcome Miss…"

"Simone Allen," she replied.

"Yes…Miss Allen, please have a seat anywhere on the left-hand side of the room."

Simone took a seat in the front. Several more students arrived. Ilene Cheng came in and sat behind her. Sarah Jane sat in the front row adjacent to Simone. James Chow took the seat next to Sarah Jane, who was not too pleased.

Simone was really hoping Nolan was just late, but, as the final students made their way to their desks, she started to worry that he wouldn't be in her class.

"Mrs. Rogers," said a deep voice. "I was sent over from Mrs. Brickett's class."

"That's Sister Rogers," she corrected him. "You must be Nolan O'Shea?"

"No, ma'am…I mean Sister…I'm Sean Malcolm," he said. "I'm new to the school. Mrs. Brickett said that Nolan is now assigned to her class and that I was to come over to yours."

The new student was probably the tallest boy in the entire eighth grade. He towered over Sister Rogers as he handed her his slip showing the class change.

"Well, that's fine, Mr. Malcolm. Have a seat next to Miss Allen up front. And welcome to St. Augustine, young man."

Simone had never met anyone as handsome as the new boy. Her heart fluttered a little when he sat beside her. He smelt of Ivory soap and peppermint.

"Hi," he said, extending his hand. His smile lit up his entire face. "I'm Sean."

"Hi, I'm Simone." She quickly covered her mouth, hoping that he hadn't noticed her toothy grin. "Simone Allen."

"Nice to meet you, Simone Allen."

Sister Rogers started handing out the textbooks they were using for the year.

All of the girls in the class had noticed Sean. Some of them were whispering how lucky she was to be sitting next to him. Her face got warm. At first, she was a little embarrassed, but soon was elated to be sitting next to the cutest boy in school.

By lunchtime, she had forgotten that Nolan had been sent to Mrs. Brickett's class. In fact, Simone had forgotten how love-struck she had been over Nolan, not more than a few hours ago. She sat with Angie and Yvette during morning recess with a dreamy look on her face.

Before lunch, the students were given their first assignment for the school year — to interview their seat partner and write a short essay about their likes and dislikes.

Just as Simone and Sean started to discuss their project, the lunch bell rang.

"Ah, man," he said looking at the classroom clock. "Do you think we can interview each other after school? I want to check out the track at recess."

"Sure," she said. "Why don't I come with you? That way we can at least start our project."

During recess, the two of them walked around the school's track. Sean told her he had been a big track and field athlete in his old school.

Simone told him that she was born in Jamaica and had moved to Canada when she was seven years old. She told him that she loved to read and that she kept a journal under her bed. She also told him that she hoped to be a writer one day.

Sean confided that he wasn't much of a reader. "What's your

favourite book?" he asked her as they walked their third lap. "I've only read a few Hardy Boys."

"I've read a lot of Nancy Drew books," she said. "But I really like the Danielle Steele novels. I read all of my mom's copies."

"That's cool," he said.

She then went on to list her favourite songs and food and the best trip she had ever taken. That was one of her annual summer trips back to Jamaica, but they were all the best, really. Sean said he was jealous and wished he could go to Jamaica every summer. He had always wanted to learn how to surf.

The afternoon went by in a daze. After school let out, Simone and Sean sat together on the school steps and she continued to interview him.

Sean Malcolm's family had recently moved from Nova Scotia, where the majority of his family still resided. He was from a long line of coal miners, but his father had broken away from the tradition to become a banker. They had moved to Toronto when his father became manager of a small branch in North York. Sean's hobbies included his favourite sport — hockey. He had played hockey for five years and dreamt of going professional after high school. Simone hung on his every word and asked him so many questions that the time flew by.

By the time she got home, it was almost five o'clock. She was late picking up her brother from Mrs. Price's apartment, but was too busy being on cloud nine to notice the time.

"Nolan was looking for you," Mrs. Price said. She greeted Simone with a warm kiss on her forehead. "He didn't see you on the bus this afternoon."

"Oh yeah, I was working on my assignment with my project partner," Simone said. "We had to finish it up. It's due tomorrow."

"Homework the first night?" asked Mrs. Price. "They are certainly getting you ready for high school."

"Sister Rogers is tough," said Simone. "She even gave us a pop quiz in math."

"And how you do?" asked Mrs. Price.

"I aced it," she said confidently.

Mrs. Price beamed as she patted Simone on her shoulder.

"CJ, come nuh!" Simone yelled out to her brother. "I have to get dinner started before Ms. Pam comes home."

CJ ran up to his big sister and gave her a big hug and they quickly said their goodbyes to Mrs. Price before heading across the hall. Simone went straight to the kitchen and poured out a can of spaghetti sauce in a pot and started boiling water for the noodles. At the kitchen table, she began writing her essay on Sean Malcolm.

A soft tap.

Nolan was standing on the balcony by the sliding glass door.

"Hey," she said, poking her head out of the door.

"Hey," he said, smiling sheepishly. "Long time no see. Can I come in?"

"I'm sorry, Nols, but my mother told me that I can't let anyone in the apartment unless she's here," she said.

"Yeah...my dad said the same thing to me." He frowned a little. "Can you come out on the balcony, at least?"

She looked back at the stove. "I can't," she said. "I have pots on the stove going and I have to keep an eye on them."

He looked disappointed. "Okay, I'll catch up with you later," he said, as he reluctantly headed back to his apartment.

▶

NOLAN JUST WANTED to hang out for a minute, but he knew the rules. Mike had told him the previous night that, because they were now teenagers, they couldn't hang out alone. It bothered him that his father didn't trust him, but he didn't want to get Simone in trouble.

He wished they had the same teacher; then they would at least have an excuse to do homework together. But now he was in Mrs. Brickett's class. He didn't mind being in the other class, Kester and most of his friends were there, but he would have rather been in the same class as Simone. Simone was his best friend. She knew everything about him and laughed at his corny jokes and knew how to make him smile even when she wasn't trying to be funny. The feelings he had for her ran deeper than a simple crush.

He sat at the kitchen table and opened up his math book, but couldn't concentrate on his homework. Just then the front door opened and his father came in with two sub sandwich bags in his hand.

"Hey, buddy, how was the first day of school?" Mike placed the sandwiches on the table.

"It was okay," he said. "I didn't get Sister Rogers this year. I got Mrs. Brickett instead."

"That's great!" his father said. "She's a great teacher."

"I guess." Nolan picked up his book bag from the table.

"Hey, we're about to have dinner," his dad said. "Go wash up while I grab some pop from the fridge. Do you want root beer or Coke?"

"I'm not really hungry, Dad. I'll eat later."

"Oh...okay, buddy," he replied.

Mike watched Nolan sit on the couch and felt a twinge of regret. He was relieved that Mrs. Wilson had come through, getting Nolan into a different class than Simone, but he didn't want to see his boy unhappy. It was all for the best. He had spoken to Pam the previous day about how they would handle their kids' friendship. They both agreed that Nolan and Simone were getting older and needed boundaries. No hanging out in their bedrooms alone; no going to the movies unless other kids were there or if CJ tagged along. Mike hated having to be so strict. Pam, on the other hand, could care less. She just didn't want her thirteen-year-old daughter bringing home any babies.

20

Nolan felt isolated from everyone. He woke up every morning, rushed to get his paper route finished, and often had to walk to school because he'd missed the school bus. By the time he got to school, Simone would be already hanging out with Angie and Yvette, who spent every waking moment talking about New Kids on the Block. He never had lunch with her now that they were in different classes and, during recess, he was too busy playing soccer and basketball with the rest of the boys.

During one recess break, while he was shooting hoops, he saw Simone sitting alone on the side of the hill reading Danielle Steele. It was one of the last warm days of the season, so he abruptly left his basketball game to go sit with her. But, by the time he'd made his way through the yard, Sean Malcolm was sitting next to her.

He didn't think much of the new kid. Sean seemed more muscle than brains. He was a good athlete, but not that great at school. Yet everyone else seemed enamored with him. All the boys in his class flocked to him to talk about hockey while all the girls hung around him and giggled at every lame joke he made.

The following weekend, he planned to hang out with Simone, no matter what. It would be their final bike ride before it got too cold. Kester had invited them over to play video games and both his father and Pam had agreed to let them go by themselves. It had been a few weeks since they had done anything together and he was excited about their plans, even if it was just a bike ride.

Saturday morning, as they pedaled, Nolan kept looking back to see if Simone was still behind him. She wasn't in a good mood. When they stopped at Becker's to get a freezie, he noticed a gash on her cheek.

"What happened to you?" he asked, pointing to the cut.

"Nothing," she said.

"That doesn't look like nothing," he pressed. "I didn't see that yesterday. Did you get it last night?"

"I don't know...I guess," she said as they rummaged through the freezer at the convenience store. "I'm getting purple, which one do you want?"

"Orange... Hey, did you get that from your mom?"

She fished out the orange freezie and passed it to him. "Can you stop asking me stupid questions?" she snapped. "Let's get to Kester's before this melts all over me." They paid for their popsicles and headed back to their bikes.

"Si, you can tell me," he said.

"Would you stop bugging me?!"

"Tell me! I won't tell anyone. I promise."

"You want to know what happened? My mother slapped me because she thinks that I'm boy-crazy and that I'm going to do dirty stuff with you and bring home babies. I don't even like you that way! There! Are you happy now!?"

Nolan felt like he'd received a firm kick in the gut. He could barely look up at her.

"I'm sorry, Nols, I didn't mean to say it like that," she said. "I like you, but the way she goes on, you would think...it's just too much! I can't deal with her always yelling at me for everything!"

He felt horrible that Simone was getting into this much trouble. He couldn't understand why their parents were making such a big deal about it, and now she no longer looked at him the way she did when they first held hands. She seemed angry and upset.

"Look," she continued. "I'm just tired of everyone accusing me of doing things that I never even thought of doing in the first place. Plus they don't even know that you like Sarah Jane and that I like another boy."

"Wait, I don't like Sarah Jane."

"Well, I just assumed you did," she replied. "You're always talking to her and she definitely likes you, so I just thought that you liked her back."

"No way!" he said. "I mean she's okay and everything, but I don't like her that way. Which boy do you like?"

"I don't want to say," she said. "You're just going to make fun of me like you always do and you'll probably tell Kester who will tell the whole world. Plus I don't even think he likes me."

"Come on! I promise I won't tell anyone," he assured her. "Did I tell anyone when you stole that bag of chips from Becker's last summer?"

"Dummy, that was you," she laughed.

"Yeah, well you ate half the bag, so you're just as guilty."

He missed moments like this. The easy way they were able to talk to each other that always erupted into giggles and horsing around.

"We better get going," she mumbled, with the freezie hanging from her mouth. She hopped on her bike and rode off.

"Hey, you didn't tell me who you liked," he shouted.

Shortly afterward, they found themselves in Kester's neighbourhood and rode along the sidewalk towards his house at the top of the street. Nolan hated this uphill part of the ride. His legs ached as he strained to keep his bike going. Simone eventually got off hers and walked it up the hill. They passed an assortment of houses — two-level detached homes, duplexes, bungalows, all mixed in with Ontario Housing townhouses. It was an older area that had recently seen an influx of middle-class families from the Caribbean.

By the time they got to Kester's house, they were both panting and sweating. Nolan laid his bike on the driveway and headed up to the door to ring the bell. They stood there for a moment before the door finally opened a crack and Kester looked out.

"What's up, Kester?" Nolan said.

Nolan and Simone could hear shouting coming from inside.

Kester looked behind him. "Hey guy, it's not a good time," he whispered.

Simone sat down on the front porch, trying to catch her breath.

"Listen, can I meet you guys at the park?" he said.

"But I thought we were playing video games," Nolan said. "What gives?"

Simone looked up at Kester after hearing more shouting coming from behind the door and quickly realized that it wasn't a good time for them to be there.

"Come on, Nolan," she said forcefully. She pulled him from the doorway.

Before they could get to their bikes, Kester's big brother, Omar, stormed past them. Kester's father barrelled out behind him with a belt in his hand. The two men continued their argument in front of the house. Simone wanted to get out of there but they were blocked by the commotion. Nolan looked from Simone to Kester. He didn't know what to do. Omar was just getting hit over and over with the belt.

"You want to stay in my fucking house?" Kester's father yelled. "Then get a goddamn job."

He continued to hit him, but then Omar suddenly overpowered his father and took the belt from him.

"Don't fucking touch me," Omar screamed. He threw the red

leather belt over the hedge. "I don't need this bullshit and I don't need to stay here."

"Well go, then," yelled his father. "Move from mi premise. Ah fe mi house you squat in, you piece of shat."

He swung at Omar, but Omar ducked. Kester's mother rushed out of the house. She was mortified that the fight had spilled into their front yard.

"Lawd Jesus, gwaan inside before the blasted neighbours call the police!"

But instead of that calming things down, the two men ended up on the ground wrestling, as Omar tried to punch his father.

Suddenly, Omar's father hauled him up by his neck and threw him against the garage door. Kester's mother screamed as Omar charged at his father. She ran to the side of the house and came back with the garden hose and sprayed them both, yelling at her husband to go inside.

Kester's father looked around, dripping with ice-cold water. He was astonished to see that he had an audience and went inside, slamming the front door.

"Omar, go down to your uncle's!" Kester's mother yelled.

"But Mom..."

"Mekhace, go now and stay there until your fadda cools off! Don't have me repeat myself," she said more forcefully, before going back inside.

Kester looked over at Omar. He felt bad for his brother, who stood trembling as he wiped the blood that dripped from his nose. He went over and put his arms around his shoulder.

"Hey Omar," he said quietly. "Do you want to come hang out with us or something?"

"Get off me, Kester," Omar said, shoving him aside.

The three of them watched Omar stalk off and kick over the recycling bin before disappearing down the street towards his uncle's house.

"Let's get out of here," Kester said.

They rode their bikes up and down the streets, with Kester leading the way. They never left his neighbourhood and often he would circle back, checking to see if his father's car was still in the driveway. After the fourth lap, they ended up at Dunlace Public School, the elementary school in his neighbourhood. The school was attached to a public park with a tennis court and two sets of play yards. Kester rode down the grassy hill to the edge of the park next to an enclosed wooded area and Nolan and Simone followed. He got off his bike and led them to a hole cut in the fence.

"Come on."

They followed him through the opening. Neither of them had ever been to this part of the park. The area had tall trees and it got dark as they walked down the steep path. It got quieter the deeper they went in. Simone swatted at the mosquitoes that buzzed around her.

They finally came to a big oak tree. The base was old and its roots curved up out of the ground. Nolan tripped on the root and landed on a pile of muddy leaves. When he looked up, he saw a plank fastened to a branch in the tree. It was almost a tree house, but without any walls or ceiling. It was just a wooden plank that was large enough for the three of them to sit on.

Kester started climbing the tree. Nolan and Simone followed him up. Nolan sat on one side of Kester and Simone sat on the other, not sure if they should talk or just be there quietly.

"Crazy shit, huh?" Kester finally said, as he pulled off a small branch. "Omar and my dad are always arguing and stuff."

"What were they arguing about?" asked Nolan.

"Just the usual. Omar not getting a job and staying out all night with his girl, Rita."

Simone stared down at her legs. She swatted away a few mosquitoes that buzzed around her.

"What happen to your face," Kester said, laughing. "That's a huge gash. Did you get into a fight with Mikey Moretti?"

Simone didn't say anything. Nolan could tell that she was upset about what had happened with Omar.

"Yeah, and you should see what he looks like," Nolan responded on her behalf. "The fat fuck."

They continued to sit in the tree, throwing pieces of branch, trying to see who could throw the farthest. None of them said much, and, after an hour, Kester reluctantly decided to go home. They all said goodbye, with Kester taking a back way home, while Simone and Nolan made their way across the park.

"Hey, Simone, wait a second." Nolan stopped his bike.

Simone circled around him before braking.

He hesitated for a minute, not sure what to say. He was so overwhelmed by everything that had happened, but knew he needed to tell Simone how he felt. He wanted to tell her that he liked her and that he wanted her to be his girlfriend — even if it had to be a secret. Even if it got them in trouble.

For a moment they looked at each other. Then he reached out and pushed some of her hair behind her ear before he moved in to kiss her. She quickly turned away before his lips touched hers. He didn't know what was wrong. Not long ago they had been holding hands and now she seemed to be repulsed by him.

"Nolan...I can't...I don't want my mom..." she said, stumbling on her words. She looked up at him. "I'm afraid."

"Why are you afraid?" he asked. "I really like you, Simone."

"You don't get it! My mother would kill me if she even thought that we were doing stuff like kissing. For you, it's no big deal. Your dad is cool and never gives you a hard time, but my mother is a different story."

"Whatever," he said getting back on his bike. "I'm sure if I was that other guy you like, you wouldn't have a problem with your mother."

"Nolan, that's not true!" she shouted out as he rode off. "Nolan...wait for me!"

They rode the entire time in silence. Simone tried to talk to him in the elevator, but he brushed her off.

He got even angrier as he walked into the apartment, slamming the door behind him. Pam and Mike were sitting at the kitchen table.

"Pam, I hate to ask you this, but do you mind giving us a minute?" his dad said.

"No man," she said, "go see what's wrong with him." She stepped onto the balcony. "I have to get dinner ready anyways."

"Okay," he said. "I'll talk with you tomorrow."

Nolan went into his room. He sat on his chair and began throwing his tennis ball against the wall. The angrier he got, the harder he threw the ball.

Mike opened his door. "How was your bike ride?" He sat on the bed. "Did you guys have fun at Kester's place?"

"I don't want to talk about it."

"You seem pretty mad, buddy," his dad said. "What happened?"

"I said I don't want to talk about it," he yelled. "Can you just get out of my room? I want to be alone."

Silence.

"Look, if you want to talk, I'm in the kitchen." he said.

"Sure." Nolan whipped the ball against the wall.

He was done talking to his father, to Simone, to anyone. All he wanted to do was whip his ball as fast and hard as he could. Hard enough to punch a hole in the wall.

21

"**C**OME ON, SIMONE," yelled Mr. Saddler in frustration. "This is not a step ladder, it's a layup. You can't do a layup under the basket! Do it again!"

Simone panted as she ran back to the free throw line. The confrontation with Pam earlier that morning was still on her mind. She still felt the sting of her mother's slap. Fortunately, Pam's ring had not left a gash this time, but she felt so hurt. She didn't understand what was going on with Pam. Anything Simone did seem to lead to an argument. The biggest resulted in being forced to join the basketball team. Simone hated playing basketball, but Mr. Saddler was determined to create the best girls' team in the city.

He was the school's energetic and hard-nosed athletic director, one of several teachers whom Principal Nikolaos had hired after many of St. Augustine's teachers were forced to retire or given a pink slip. Mr. Saddler was fanatical about re-building the school's sports program and making sure that St. Augustine became renowned for its athletics. He was strict with his students and wasn't afraid to stand up to their parents. Many parents complained about his no-nonsense approach and military methods. Moreover, they were not thrilled that a black man from Barbados was hollering at their children.

Yet, despite the parents' objections, his students loved him. They first obeyed him out of fear, but they eventually appreciated his tough demeanour, and then seemed to gravitate to him naturally. He was one of the few teachers unafraid to think outside the box. While many teachers were fine with recycling the same lesson plans each year, Mr. Saddler made his lessons interactive and engaging. He led them on impromptu adventures through the schoolyard, collecting samples for science classes, and had his students put together a school newspaper to help them with their writing.

He initiated the "Week of Sportsmanship", making it mandatory that each student try out for track and field or volleyball, basketball or soccer. The entire school — with no exceptions. Some parents called the principal to complain, but Mr. Nikolaos fully supported his teachers and asked the parents to trust Mr. Saddler's methods, which proved to be successful. Over the past three years, the school had gone from last place to first in their district and this year they had cracked the top ten in the city.

Simone, however, always dreaded the event, even though she had been tested for every sport and was a natural athlete. She hated sports. She hated watching them, playing on teams, and even just talking about them. Mr. Saddler didn't care how she felt. All he saw was how easily she could clear the high jump bar, the way she controlled the soccer ball, and the ease with which she dribbled across the basketball court. He took it upon himself to make sure that she always tried out for the teams and participated. He even went as far as to contact Pam to express the importance of athletics for Simone: she could use her gifts to get scholarships for universities in Canada and possibly colleges in the United States.

Now Simone stood in the gymnasium, hands on hips, completely out of breath, praying for a twisted ankle — anything to get her off these teams. She ran the layup again, hoping that if she just got the basket he would let her rest.

"Good," he said, clapping his hands as she swooped the ball into the net. He walked up to the three-point line. "Very good, Miss Allen. One more time for good measure."

She looked over at him with venom in her eyes. She wished she had the guts to throw the ball at his head, but she didn't dare.

"Mr. Saddler, it's 4:30 and my mother is waiting for me outside," said Yvette.

Mr. Saddler looked up at the clock. "Alright…that's enough for today. You all can go home!" he barked. "But not you, Miss Allen. I want to speak with you in private."

Simone rolled her eyes as she slowly walked to the three-point line. He looked down at her, shaking his head. She knew she was going to catch shit from him.

"Simone, you are probably the brightest student in this school, but the laziest athlete I have ever met," he chastised her. "Do you realize what you can do with your talent? Not only can you get into a good university, but you may just get scholarship money to boot! But to do that you need to be on top of your game."

"Yes, Mr. Saddler," she said.

"Yes, Mr. Saddler," he mimicked. "Get out of here before it gets dark. Do you have a ride home or do you need a lift?"

"No, I'm good," she replied. "I'll make it home on time."

"Alright, good then." He picked up his clipboard. "Go home and rest up for the game."

Simone grabbed her bag and headed out the gym. Her body was aching. She wished she had taken him up on his offer of a ride. She hobbled to the back door of the gym and, when she opened the door, she nearly stumbled over Sarah Jane Ryden and Sean Malcolm, who were huddled together on the steps kissing.

"Watch where you're going, Simone," Sarah Jane snipped.

"Watch where you're sitting," Simone fired back.

She was too embarrassed to even look at Sean. For weeks she

had thought that he liked her. He constantly flirted with her, passing her funny notes during class. He was also on the boys' basketball team and sometimes, during recess, they would practise together on the court.

She felt like an idiot. She had spent so much time daydreaming and hoping that he liked her, and all the while he liked Sarah Jane. She felt a sick feeling in the pit of her stomach as tears formed.

"Simone, wait!" Sean said. He scrambled to his feet and ran over to Simone.

"Yes?" she said.

He caught up to her. "Can you do me a favour?" he said. "I was going to walk over to your building to give Nolan back his basketball shoes. I borrowed them for gym class — do you mind?"

Simone angrily looked at Nolan's smelly sneakers — there she was playing messenger again.

"Sure," she said grabbing the shoes from him. "Bye."

She walked home fuming, thinking back on all the times Sean had spoken to her and slowly realizing that any time he talked to her it was because he needed something. Every conversation started off with a compliment, but ended with a question about homework or an assignment they were working on. The notes he passed weren't him being flirtatious but questions about what the teacher was talking about.

How could I be so stupid?

By the time she was in the elevator of her building, her anger had turned into an ache and, when she got to her floor, she walked up to Nolan's door, wiped back the tears, and knocked.

"Here," she said, shoving the sneakers at him. "Sean asked me to give them back to you."

She turned and got to her door and then the tears started to spill out.

"What's wrong with you?" he asked, as she fumbled with her keys.

Her tears turned into uncontrollable sobs.

Nolan came up and hugged her. "Come on," he said, leading her to the stairwell.

He held her hand as they walked up the four flights of stairs to the roof. They hadn't been up there very often since Simone had got in trouble for being too close to the edge, and now the roof had barriers so that no one could ever fall over.

They sat on a stack of milk crates left there by the teenagers in the building who went up to the roof for a smoke. There were butts everywhere.

They sat silently. She looked down at her shoes. Her throat felt raw and dry.

"What happened, Si?" he asked her. "Are you okay?"

"I'm okay." She used her sleeve to wipe away her runny nose. "I just feel so stupid."

"What do you mean?"

"Did you know that Sean and Sarah Jane...are..."

"Yeah," he said. "Everyone knows."

"Well, I didn't know," she said. "How long have they been going out?"

"Since the beginning of school, I think," he replied.

He looked at Simone curiously. "It's hard not to notice. Sarah Jane always has her arms draped all over Sean and he always has that stupid grin on his face...Wait! Sean is the guy you like? He's the guy you have a crush on? He's a complete doofus!"

"Never mind," she said, getting up from the milk crate. "You're making fun of me."

"No wait, I'm not...I swear," he said, grabbing her hand. He held it for a while trying to find the right thing to say. "If he's too stupid to see you the way that I see you then he is a doofus."

"Thanks, Nolan." She looked at him as she wiped her eyes. He had always been a great friend to her and she was glad that she was still able to tell him about her feelings. "I just feel so stupid about the whole thing. I really thought he liked me."

"I know how you feel," he said shyly. "It's hard when you like someone who doesn't like you back."

Simone felt bad. She looked up at him and he looked away.

"Nolan...I....I..."

"It's okay," he said. He was caressing her index finger with his thumb.

Silence.

"Do you want to come over and play video games? My dad just got me the new Zelda game and it's been kicking my ass all week."

"I can't," she said, slowly pulling her hand away.

She could tell that he was hurt by her rejection. She didn't want to hurt him again. She liked him, just not the way he wanted her to. All she wanted was for them to go back to just being best friends.

He turns away, not wanting her to see his face burning red because she has hurt him again and it feels horrible, and then she quickly runs up and kisses him on his cheek and he grabs her, holds her tightly, feels her heart beating against his. He dips down and kisses her soft lips. When she breaks away, he catches her and presses her against the closed door and starts to get hard. He kisses her again, this time slipping his tongue inside her mouth, her legs are weak.

They slide down the door as his hands find their way under her top and cup her breasts. All he knows is he wants to see them, wants to smell them and taste them, so he pulls her top off and she shivers.

At first, she doesn't know what to do. He has engulfed her with his lips and their tongues are playing and she is moist and her heart beats so hard that she can't breathe, and when he grabs her hand and pulls it towards him, placing it in his pants, she can feel his penis hard and strong, and when she squeezes it slightly he moans softly and she does it again and again. All he wants is to pull off her panties and stick his...

"What are you guys watching?" yelled out CJ.

Simone and Nolan had been sitting on the floor in Mrs. Price's bedroom in front of her television. Nolan quickly turned off the set and ran to the VCR to retrieve the cassette.

"Can I watch?"

"No, you can't," Simone said sharply. She turned her brother towards her. "Go back into the living room and stay with Mrs. Price."

"She's asleep and I'm bored. Come play with me?"

"Isn't GI Joe on right now?" Nolan reminded him. GI Joe was CJ's favourite show. "Why don't you go and watch with Mrs. Price."

"Oh yeah," he said. He grabbed his toy and ran back to the living room.

"That was close," Simone said.

Nolan had already put the tape back in his knapsack. It belonged to Kester's brother, Omar, who had left it behind when he went to live with his uncle. Kester had spent the entire week bragging about how dirty the movie was and telling Nolan that he had to watch it.

Both of their parents were out for the evening, so Mrs. Price was sitting for the three of them. Mrs. Price wasn't as spry as she used to be. She constantly complained about her aching joints and she was partially deaf in her left ear. At times, the kids would find her fast asleep in her armchair in front of the living room television set.

"It was kind of weird," Nolan said. His face turned beet red thinking about what the man in the movie was doing to the girl.

"I know what you mean," Simone agreed. "I didn't like it. I felt dirty just watching it. I mean is that what sex is supposed to be like? Isn't it supposed to be romantic?"

"I guess," he responded. "It wasn't what I thought it was supposed to be."

The way Kester had described it, Nolan had expected he would turn into some crazy sex machine that wanted to have sex all the time. At first, he was excited by the way the two characters were kissing and touching each other, but then, instead of arousing him, it started to scare him. He didn't know if he wanted to do those things with Simone or any girl right now.

He wondered if he might hurt a girl if he touched her breast or if his dick was too small. The guy in the video had a pretty big penis by comparison.

For Simone, the sex scene wasn't anything like the ones she'd seen in other movies. She loved the romantic foreplay in films like *Dirty Dancing*, but the video they'd watched seemed so private.

"I don't think I want sex to be like that," she said. She crawled onto the bed and sprawled out on her back with her head dangling off the edge. "At least not for a long time."

"I know what you mean," Nolan said. "I don't think I'm ready for that kind of stuff either. I mean…it just seems like a lot to figure out."

"But I think that's what makes it dirty," she said, turning to face him. "It shouldn't be something you need to figure out. I think sex should be something that just happens."

"Simone, can I tell you something?" he said to her. His face got bright red again. "Sometimes I want to do some of the things in the video. Sometimes I dream about those things. I can't help myself…it just pops up in my head all the time."

"Really?" she said. "Not me. I don't want to get pregnant. My mother thinks that's what's going to happen to me if I even think of those things."

"My dad says the same thing," he said.

"Well, I wish everyone would stop worrying that I'm going to get pregnant just by looking at a boy."

"Or by kissing," he said.

"Exactly! The way Miss Pam goes on, you would think that if I just kiss a boy I'm going to get all hot-to-trot and start having sex," she complained. "I can kiss you right now and that doesn't mean anything — watch!"

She leaned in and kissed him on the lips.

At first, Nolan didn't know what to do. He wasn't prepared for her to kiss him. But after a few seconds, he gave in and pulled her closer to him as he kissed her back. He had never kissed a girl before. He tasted the cherry lip-gloss she wore on her lips and felt a warm flush throughout his entire body. He started to feel a little bolder and opened his mouth slightly, slipping his tongue into her mouth.

She pulled away sharply, stunned. She looked at him, slightly frowning, but she didn't want to make a big deal of it, so she leaned forward and returned his kiss, sharing her tongue with him.

He began to pull her off the bed and their teeth gently clashed as the intensity started to pick up. Chills rushed down both spines.

"See," she said breathlessly, after pulling away from him. "It's just a kiss and that's it. You don't see me taking off my clothes trying to have sex with you, right?"

"Right, it was nothing."

"Exactly, nothing."

22

"I don't really give a shit," he could hear Pam yelling at Simone. "Your school comes first."

Mike heard Pam slamming down her coffee mug on the counter. He was sitting outside on the balcony, reading his paper. It was never hard for him to overhear an argument from their apartment. It happened often and loudly.

"But it's not school, it's just a lousy basketball game," Simone yelled back. "Yvette only has a birthday once a year. Why can't I just miss this one game?"

"Because you made a commitment to be on the team."

"No, I didn't! I don't even want to be on the team. Mr. Saddler is making me. I hate basketball. I hate sports!"

"Unuh, keep your voice down," Pam said. Her eyes narrowed as she glared at her daughter. "The whole building can hear your tongue."

"So! Do you think I care?"

Pam slapped Simone with the back of her hand. "You think you're grown and can talk to me like that?" She slapped her again. "Don't you ever fucking talk to me like that again or you'll feel more than the back of my hand."

Mike could hear Simone whimper.

"Go and take out the fucking garbage and then go to your room. I don't want to see you for the rest of the night."

The bedroom door slammed, which made him jump up a little. He hated when they slammed their doors. It always made the entire balcony rattle.

After a while, the balcony door slid open. Pam was going to be in one of her moods. He wished he'd gone back into his apartment when he first heard the argument. The last thing he wanted was to hear Pam drone on about Simone. But it wasn't Pam, it was Simone. She sat on the other side of the balcony.

"Hey, Splimoney," Mike said, startling her. "Hey, honey. I'm sorry, I didn't mean to scare you."

She turned away from Mike without a response and went over to the little storage case, where they kept the box of garbage bags and wrestled out a bag.

"Sounds like you two were having a doozy," Mike said, trying to make light of the situation.

"Mmm hmm," she replied.

He noticed the cold stare she gave him and he smiled, hoping that would ease the tension. He hated seeing her so upset and wanted to say something to make her feel better.

"Well don't let her get you down," he said. "Maybe Nolan can practise with you on the weekend. The weather is still warm enough. Or I can even drive you both to the basketball courts at the Y."

"No, thank you." She picked up the garbage bag and headed back inside.

Mike sighed. After some time, Pam came out with a cup of coffee and a major attitude. She threw herself down on the chair next to him. Once again, he cursed under his breath for not hiding when he had the chance.

"So what was that all about?" he asked. He focused on his paper.

"She's getting too grown," Pam began. "Always talking back to me like she's paying rent."

"She's a teenager," he said. "They're all like that."

Of course, his simple reasoning would not penetrate Pam's mood. He really didn't know what to tell her. She had been handling a short fuse ever since the end of summer.

"Saddler shouldn't be calling you about Simone," he continued. "Sister Rogers is her teacher now, not him, and if Simone doesn't want to play basketball, that's her right."

"You white people. What do you know about it anyhow? She's a good player and he thinks that if she keeps it up she could be good enough to get a scholarship at any university."

"Yeah, but if she doesn't like it, how does that help her?" he said. "If she wants to quit, then let her."

"Like hell! I don't have money to put her through university. Maybe a year, but that's it. She needs some kind of scholarship just to get by."

"You sound like my wife," he said. "Simone is still in elementary school. You have years to figure it out."

"And what are you going to do when Nolan all of sudden tells you that he wants to go to university?" she asked. "Maybe he'll want to attend a fancy school like his mama and become a doctor or a lawyer. You're already working three jobs just to pay the rent. Are you going to sell your blood next?"

He hadn't thought much about what Nolan wanted to do with his life. He always saw Nolan and himself as cut from the same cloth. Nolan would go to high school, graduate, and then work as a mechanic somewhere, or even get into construction. Like him, his son was great with tools and had a knack for fixing anything he could get his hands on. Mike never imagined him wanting to do something else.

"Nolan is not that kind of kid," he said. "He hates school and probably only needs a high school education, anyways."

"Oh, you think so, huh?" she said. "Each year more of these

kids are graduating and going off to university. There is nothing in the job market for them if they stick to their high school diploma. But keep telling yourself that and let me know how that works out for you when he's thirty years old and still living with you!"

He knew Pam was right. Dana had graduated high school a few years before and was still having problems getting a decent job. The most she could get was a job working as a waitress at a diner. No one was hiring anyone with just a secondary education. She now had to go to community college just to be considered for receptionist and bank teller jobs.

Mike sat quietly as he tried to digest what Pam was saying. Most of his cousins' children had already finished college or university and, even for them, the job market was very competitive. But he couldn't fathom sending Nolan to university. Despite the government subsidizing the tuitions, it was still too expensive. Also, he still held onto the idea of buying a house.

"God, Mike! Don't look so down," Pam said. "Nolan is into basketball, maybe one of the universities will give a skinny white boy a scholarship to play for their school."

▶

By October, the cold winter air had found Toronto. Simone and Nolan were not prepared for how cold it had suddenly gotten, especially the mornings when they missed the school bus. Today, they had bundled themselves up, but they were still shivering as they headed to school on foot. They walked in silence up the hill.

Earlier that morning, Nolan had walked in on Pam and Simone having a fight. Simone had left an egg boiling on the stove and it had exploded all over the kitchen and splattered her mother's new suit.

"I've told you over and over to mind the stove when you are

using it. One day you're going to burn the whole damn building down."

"Well, then buy cereal."

Pam grabbed Simone by the collar of her blouse and flung her across the kitchen floor. CJ came in crying before Pam stormed out, leaving Simone whimpering.

He was glad he didn't have that kind of relationship with his dad. Mike didn't spend every waking hour hounding him about his schoolwork or get upset when he came home with a bad grade. His mother, however, was a different story. He'd heard her yelling at his dad on the phone. She called constantly, now that she had graduated from university and was working full time as an accountant, screaming about his slipping grades and how Mike was always out instead of being home.

"Everyone but you is raising Nolan," she'd said the other day. "He needs you to be his parent, not his goddamn roommate."

"Isn't that rich," Mike had spat out. "You get your fancy degree and now you come back, guns blazing, telling me that I'm a bad parent? Where were you all this time?"

"That's not fair, Mike," she said. "I've always been there for Nolan and you know that. If he doesn't improve, the guidance counsellor will only recommend a school like Mary Ward or Senator O'Connor, which will only stick him in general classes."

"Well, what's wrong with that?" Mike said. "You act like Nolan is going to get into some private school."

"Well, if he applied himself he could go to a really good high school," she retorted.

Mike chortled.

"You know what your problem is, Mike?"

"No, Megs, what's my problem?"

"You don't want anyone to do better than you," she yelled. "You're too damn afraid that everyone will pass you by and you know what? We all damn well should."

Dial tone.

Nolan watched his father standing holding the receiver, looking lost. He felt bad. He didn't want his problems with school to be a bone of contention between his parents. He still held out hope that somehow his family would get back together again. He felt childish for thinking that, but deep down he hated that his mother was never around or that his father worked so much to keep things afloat.

When Pam teased Mike for having so many jobs, it used to confuse Nolan. He always thought that having more than one job meant you were a hard worker, but then Mrs. Price explained to him why a Jamaican having so many jobs was a joke and not a compliment.

"It's simple, baby," she said. "When you don't have the proper education, you don't have the luxury of working one job. You always have to get two or three jobs just to make enough to get by. The ones who get a good education don't have to worry about that."

Nolan didn't want to be like his dad. He didn't want to have to work day in and day out just to put food on the table. He didn't want to spend the rest of his life scraping the bottom of the barrel.

As he walked along with Simone, he could see his warm breath puff out like smoke. He tried to make rings, but his teeth chattered any time he opened his mouth. Simone was shivering, too, as she walked beside him.

"Hey Simone, how's it going in Sister Rogers' class?" he asked. "I mean…is it harder this year?"

"No, she's a lot like Mr. Saddler, just not as loud." She pulled out her extra pair of mittens. "Why do you ask?"

"Mrs. Brickett's class is just different," he said pulling his coat closer to his body. "I'm just not getting the stuff she's teaching us and it's getting harder to catch up."

"Maybe you should try studying at nights instead of playing video games," Simone smirked.

"Hardy har," he responded.

The cold brisk wind picked up and they continued to walk in silence. It was too cold to talk. As they turned the corner, they could see students starting to line up in the schoolyard. They ran up to the line just as Kester arrived.

"Yo guy!" he said, clasping hands with Nolan. "What are you guys doing after school? Do you wanna hang out?" he asked. "We can go to the mall or I can meet you at your place. I was thinking about visiting Mrs. Price and seeing how she was doing?"

"I wish I could," said Simone. "I have a stupid game tonight after school."

"Sorry, guy," said Nolan. "I have to study. We have our history test right after the Thanksgiving break."

"Yo star, since when did you study?" he teased.

"Since now," replied Nolan, as they walked into the school. "I want to get better than a C on this test. My mom is getting on my case about my grades."

"Well, then maybe I can come to your game, Simone," Kester suggested. "I can be the girls' sexy team mascot."

"Yeah...Not!" she replied. "The last time you came to one of our games, you were clowning me every time I missed a layup. Now Mr. Saddler has me practising layups all day long. I prefer to embarrass myself in private, thank you."

Simone smiled at Kester, waiting for his usual comeback, but something seemed off with him. She couldn't put her finger on it, but all of a sudden he looked so serious.

"Hey Kester, let's meet up at Mrs. Price's apartment after my game, okay?" she offered. "I have to pick up my little brother anyways and maybe we can get her to fry up some roti."

"I dunno. Maybe." His head was down as he followed Nolan into their class.

▶

KESTER SLUMPED into his seat as Mrs. Brickett started the day. It was his least favourite subject — math. On most days, he would feign interest, but today he was trying to figure out where he would sleep that night. For two nights he had hidden out in the backwoods and snuck into his house to steal food in the middle of the night. He hadn't slept at home since his father caught him dressing in his sister's cobalt blue church dress.

Since Omar's dramatic exit from the household, the only kids left were him and his older sister, Cindy. Cameron, his older brother, was married and had moved to Montreal, while Omar had joined the army a few weeks ago, the moment he turned nineteen.

No one was ever home. Cindy only got in by curfew and his parents often worked late, which left him alone most evenings.

Kester's life had been simple: For a few hours after school, he'd enjoyed the solitude of having the entire house to himself and doing what any unsupervised kid would do. He watched movies on First Choice, filled himself with chips and pop and played video games for hours. If he was bored, he would fool around in his father's liquor cabinet, taking nips from the Mount Gay Rum hidden behind the cans of pop.

After a while, he would get the urge. He would wander into his parents' room and look through his mother's closet. His hands would stroke the silky lilac blouse his mother had just picked up from the dry cleaner. The soft material tickled the back of his hand. He loved the way it felt against his skin. It made his body shiver.

He lifted the blouse off the hanger and slipped it over his naked chest. It was exhilarating, standing there in front of his mother's full-length mirror. Soon he dared to put on his mother's pencil skirt and, before he knew it, he was wearing her heels and her curly wig. He almost didn't recognize himself in the mirror. He looked and felt beautiful.

And then he discovered makeup.

After that discovery, he would rush home and open jars of face creams and fiddle with his mother's makeup, trying to mimic the faces he studied in his sister's fashion magazines. He became fascinated with eyeliner and mascara and he mastered the dramatic Cleopatra look. His favourite lipstick was the Smoked Rosette his mother never wore because it looked too pink on her. He thought the colour complemented his medium brown complexion.

Kester picked up the lipstick and pressed it against his lips. He smiled when he saw how perfect it looked. He pouted and posed in the mirror. He took his time and carefully applied a light-blue eye shadow. The last time, he put so much on that he ended up leaving streaks of blue powder all over his mother's white vanity table. He covered his tracks by blaming the mess on a runaway basketball. He knew that excuse wouldn't fly a second time, so he made sure that anything he touched was put back exactly where he'd found it.

He then slipped into his sister's dress. He'd had his eye on Cindy's dress since the moment she'd worn it to church in the summer. It was exactly like the Audrey Hepburn floral Givenchy dress in his mother's old pattern book.

Kester looked at himself in the mirror and couldn't believe how he looked. He wished he had a camera to take a picture so that he could secretly look at it whenever he had the urge.

On bad days, when he wasn't alone to play dress up, he felt like he was suffocating in his own body. He would daydream of his parents telling him that it was all a mistake. They would tell him that he was really a girl and not some impostor named Kester. Then they would embrace him and tell him that they loved him just as he was.

He twirled in front of the mirror and waited for the urge to go away and to feel strong enough to accept Kester again. He turned to the vanity mirror to look at himself one last time, but caught his shocked father standing behind him.

"What the ass?!" his father screamed.

His father grabbed Kester by the collar of the dress, slamming him on the vanity table, knocking all of the makeup, perfume bottles and creams on the carpet. Kester tried to run away but the heels caused him to slip. His father grabbed hold of him and punched the back of his neck.

He screamed out as he was pushed against the wall. He could feel his father's arm pressed tightly against his neck. It wasn't until his mother came in screaming and pulled at her husband that he finally released his grip.

Kester ran out, gasping for air, scurried into the bathroom and locked the door. He crawled into the bathtub, coughing, his throat burning, and curled up at one end of the tub. He could hear his father crashing his fists against the door and his mother threatening to call the police if his father didn't leave the house.

He heard his father strike his mother.

She cried after he hit her again.

Silence.

Kester flinched when he heard the front door slam. He started to panic, wondering if his mother was hurt. After a few minutes, he emerged from the bathroom and went into the kitchen. She had taken the ice tray out and was sitting at the counter making an ice pack for her bloody nose. She winced as she applied the pack to the swollen area. Then she started to weep.

"Mommy," he said softly. "Are you okay?"

He touched her shoulder only to have her shrug him away. As she looked up at him, he realized his face was still covered with her makeup, and he was still wearing his sister's dress that had been torn in the struggle. She shook her head. Her nose continued to bleed and he ran to the sink to get more paper towels.

"Take it off," she said, forcefully.

"Here, Mommy," he said passing her the paper towel.

"Mi say take it off!" She slapped his hand away. "Take off that dress and that makeup. TAKE IT OFF!"

"I'm sorry, Mommy," he said crying. "I'm so sorry!"

"You're a dutty disgrace to me and your father," she screamed even louder. "Get out this house!"

Kester cowered as her eyes darkened. He worshipped her beauty. She was the model of what he wanted to be. Yet her disdain for him made him feel like throwing up. He ran back into the bathroom and locked it behind him. He sobbed as he wiped the makeup from his face. When he looked back into the mirror, part of his face was clear and part still had makeup — half boy, half girl were sharing his soul, fighting for a piece of him.

When he'd wiped his face fully clean, he snuck out of the bathroom and put the torn dress back in Cindy's closet. He felt bad that it was ruined. The collar was torn and the back of the dress ripped along the seams.

He walked to his parent's room to knock on the locked door. He thought if he tried to explain to his mother about his urges she would understand, but he couldn't handle another rejection, so instead he took some food from the fridge and headed to the woods with his sleeping bag.

He had stayed in the bitter cold for two nights and gone to school just to have a warm place to be. He hoped his parents would come for him, but he hadn't heard from them, and no one seemed to realize that something was wrong. He felt even more alone when Nolan and Simone told him they had plans and couldn't hang with him.

After school, he walked home. It was Friday and he was scared to go back, but he didn't want to sleep in the woods over the weekend. When he got to the front door, he tried to turn his key in the lock but it didn't work. He tried the garage but that was also locked shut. He went around the corner to the basement window. A piece of wood was wedged in the window sill to keep the window closed.

He walked out to the backyard. He sat in one of the lawn chairs, staring out at his old swing set. He remembered his sister pushing him on the swings and how he would squeal for her to push him higher. Tears spilled down his cheek as he wondered if Cindy hated him, too. It would only be a matter of time before she and the whole world found out. Before everyone would turn against him and look at him in disgust.

He sat on the plastic chair until the tears started to burn his eyes. His eyes burned so much that everything looked blue and fussy. Suddenly the backyard became void of all sound. Not a voice, or a chirping bird, or a car could be heard. Everything was motionless, windless, the air stagnant. He lay back in the lawn chair. His stony eyes turned as black as an onyx pearl as he watched his body gently sway in unison with his old swing.

23

"She's got herself a boyfriend, you know?" said Mike, as he poured Maureen another beer.

McKinney's was small for a pub, but nicer than your typical hole in the wall. With only a simple television hanging from the ceiling, a few tables, and a long bar that stretched from the restroom to the front door, the bar was known to pack the house. But that Friday, McKinney's stood empty, with many of the regulars taking off early for the Thanksgiving weekend.

"Does that really surprise you?" she countered. "What did you expect? Just because you choose to live like a monk doesn't mean she needs to."

"Yeah, well, we're still married, for Christ's sake." Mike wiped down the counter. "Doesn't that count for anything? Nineteen fucking years and this is it?"

It was Dana who had let it slip that her mother was seeing someone. She didn't mean to mention it, he could tell. It just came out when he had fished a bit.

"Jesus, Mike, you sound pathetic — you really do," Maureen said. "You need to move on and keep it moving. Find yourself someone new. Someone who'll build you back up and make you feel like a man, because she's making you look like a fool. Look at you — letting her have one over on you. Don't get me wrong. I love Megs. We go way back and all, but you're family and you shouldn't be moping around pining after her while she's off fucking some guy."

Mike glared at Maureen. He resented her calling him pathetic. He had spent the night with a woman or two. But he still believed in his marriage and still believed that he and Meghan would find their way back to each other.

He looked up at the clock and silently cursed to himself. It was only 6:00 pm and he still had a few more hours until his shift was over.

"Maureen, you can go home now." He went to wipe down the end of the counter. "Don't you have some wedding shit to deal with?"

"All done, Mikey boy," she said, finishing up her beer. "The roses have been clipped, the dresses hemmed, and the groom is raring to go. Furthermore, I'm not here to see you. I'm here to see my boyfriend."

"Oh God, Maureen, you need to leave Tommy alone," he said, handing her another beer. "He's not interested in you."

Tommy Thornton was the owner of McKinney's. He had worked at the bar for as long as the place had been around. It used to belong to his great-uncle, Darbie McKinney, until Tommy bought the place after his uncle died. Tommy was the main reason Maureen came to McKinney's.

"Tommy loves me," she smirked, grabbing a handful of peanuts. "He just doesn't know it yet."

"For fuck's sake, Maureen." Mike leaned against the bar. "You've been at it for years and he has never even asked you out."

"Give him time, Mikey. He just hasn't noticed how much of a catch I am. Once he's through dating whats-her-name, then I'll give him the business."

"Give who the business?" said a voice.

Maureen quickly turned around. She smiled and her face burned red.

"Oh that would be you, Tommy," she replied. "I'm looking for a date for my daughter's wedding and I'm hoping you'll do me the honour."

At almost six feet, with broad shoulders and strawberry blond hair, dress him up right and Tommy was considered attractive. He smiled at her before taking a sip of her beer and grabbing a handful of bar nuts. "Aren't you a doll," he said, flashing her a flirtatious smile. "But I don't think my girl Lily would let me." Maureen tried to get off her stool, but fell over. "Whoa there," he said, helping her to her feet. "Maybe we should get you home."

"Give me a ride, Tommy and I'll convince you to dump that Lily."

Mike sighed. He'd seen it all before. He started to dry the wine glasses.

"How 'bout I do you one better and get you a cup of coffee while you tell me all about this wedding you're planning," Tommy said. He pulled out the coffee pot from behind the counter.

"Put a little brandy in it and you've got yourself a deal," she replied.

Mike half listened as Maureen talked endlessly to Tommy about the wedding and how beautiful it was going to be and the caterer they'd hired, who once planned one of Prime Minister Pierre Trudeau's fancy soirees, and the free-flowing booze and the cover band that would play classic rock during the reception.

By the time Mike's shift had finished, Maureen was in the middle of a diatribe about her job at the hospital and how much she hated working for Pam.

"That bitch is the only reason why I want to quit that lousy job. I don't know how she even got that title. She's severely unqualified and what kind of degree can you get from Jamaica, anyways?"

"I don't know, Maureen," Tommy drawled. "I guess someone

has to teach them how to cook and clean." He winked at Mike. "I hear those people are pretty good at that."

"Yeah, well, you would think I was her fucking maid," she said flatly. "But don't say a peep about Miss Pam Allen to Mikey or he'll piss a fit. He's in love with her or something."

"Oh, is that so?" said Tommy. He winked again at Mike. "You holding out on me about your little jungle bunny, Mikey? And here I thought Father Mike was about to take his vows."

"Oh, don't let his choir boy act fool you," she teased, turning to Mike. "He's probably fucking her every night. Did you know they're neighbours?"

"Well, well, well." Tommy laughed loud. "Tell me more."

"That's enough, Maureen," Mike said. He hated how crass she got when she drank. It was even worse when she was around Tommy. Her arrogance matched Tommy's cocky attitude, which always made him the bottom end of their jokes. "I'm leaving now, if you plan on getting a ride with me."

"Alright, lover boy," she said to Tommy, slurring her words. "I'm going home with Father...no...no... choirboy Mike, but I'm not taking no for an answer. If you must, bring your girl to the wedding, and I promise to be on my best behaviour. Scout's honour."

"I'll think about it," he said. There was a glint in his eye as he massaged her shoulders. "You just go home and sleep off this brandy."

Mike and Maureen began making their way out of the bar just as a group of women walked in, giggling. They looked like students from the local nursing school down the street. Mike looked back to see them swarming the bar. He knew Tommy's weakness was young girls. Women his age didn't usually make the cut.

He felt Maureen sigh deeply. She was a fool to chase after him.

"Come on Maureen," he said, linking arms with her. "He's not worth your time."

Maureen stayed silent as they walked to his car.

"You need to find a guy who looks at you and nobody else," he said, opening the passenger door.

"I know," she said. "But if Tommy would just give me a bloody chance then maybe I can make him look at me and just me."

"Maureen, you know I love you, so I will tell you the God's honest truth. Tommy is a charmer and the life of the party, but there's a reason why he's never been married."

"Yeah, I guess…but it kills me that I'm going to my own daughter's wedding alone. Who's going to want an old cow like me? All you guys ever want are younger prettier girls."

"I promise you, the right guy will come around. A guy like Tommy is only up for a chase, and the way you are with him isn't much of a challenge."

He waited for her to yell at him and tell him to shut up, but instead all he could hear was her snoring softly. He drove in silence. She wouldn't listen to him anyways — asleep or awake.

▶

SIMONE WOKE UP EXCITED. It was the Thanksgiving weekend. Then she remembered she hated Thanksgiving. It was just an excuse for everyone to eat her most hated food — turkey. It didn't matter who made it or how it was prepared, she hated the dish, and Thanksgiving was the patron saint of all things turkey.

Just as they'd done the last few years, Simone and Pam and CJ spent the morning across the hall with Mrs. Price. Despite her many ailments, Mrs. Price was still an extraordinary cook and Simone loved to help with the meal preparation, while her mother sat in the living room gossiping with Esma.

Esma was now married, with three boys of her own. She'd moved outside of North York, but still came every weekend to check up on her mother. After her mother's knee replacement, the hospital had made a mess of the paperwork. Pam spent a week with Esma trying to fix the mess. Since then, the two had become close friends.

This year Thanksgiving dinner was at Esma's house, so Pam, CJ, Simone, and Mrs. Price piled into Pam's Toyota that afternoon and headed across the city to Brampton. Simone had never been to Brampton before. No one from her school lived out that far. She couldn't believe how big and beautiful the homes were. Most were majestic cookie-cutter brown brick homes with two-car garages and twin peak roofs. The lawns were all perfectly shaped with hedges. It was nothing like the homes in Willowdale. The houses in her area were a mishmash of different styles. They weren't unified and structured. In Brampton, all the houses looked like little soldiers that stood tall and at attention.

"When I get older, I'm going to live here," she said.

Esma's home had a grand staircase with 18-foot ceilings and large windows that let the sun shine throughout the house. Simone's eyes travelled to the sitting room, which was decorated with old-fashioned furniture similar to the stuff that her Aunt Marva used to have in her parlour room in Jamaica. When they walked into the kitchen, Simone held her breath. This was the largest kitchen she had ever seen. It had a large marble-top island and two ovens fixed in the wall, one on top of the other.

"Esma, are you rich like white people?" she marvelled. She ran to look out at the huge backyard adjacent to the kitchen.

"Ha," Esma responded. "No, child, I'm just willing to live far enough out to seem rich. Go put those pies down on the dining room table."

Mrs. Price had wandered into the kitchen. She shooed everyone out.

"Mama, don't you need our help?" asked Esma.

"No dear," she said, kissing her teeth. "Unuh get out a mi kitchen. Simone a go keep mi company."

"Are you sure, Mrs. Price?" asked Pam.

"Yes! Yes!" she said, waving her hands. "I'll call for you if I need anything."

Mrs. Price looked on as Esma and Pam headed upstairs to look at her newly renovated bathroom. They could hear Esma gushing to Pam all about the changes and decorating improvements she had made. She rolled her eyes at Simone, who giggled.

"That girl is too quick with her money," she muttered. Simone glanced at Mrs. Price who continued to watch them until they disappeared up the stairs. "Everything okay with you and your madda?" Mrs. Price quickly asked.

"It's the same as always," Simone replied. "I do something wrong, she gets angry and…well…anyways, nothing changes."

Mrs. Price passed her a bowl of potatoes and she began peeling. She didn't want to let on about how bad it had gotten over the last few months. The arguments and licks across the head. The yelling and cursing.

"Don't worry yourself too much, Simone." She showed Simone how to peel the potatoes quickly. "In no time you will be going to high school and, before you know it, you'll graduate and head off to a good university."

"You think so?" asked Simone.

"Of course," she said, smiling at her. "You're a smart girl and any good university would be foolish not to have you. Just keep working hard, and in no time you'll be moving up and out."

"Yeah, well, Ms. Pam thinks that I'll probably end up pregnant, so I doubt it," she said. She went to the sink to rinse off more potatoes.

"Do you have a boyfriend?"

"No!" she said loudly. "It's…it's just…she thinks that I'm going to turn out like her. I can't even hang out with Nolan without her giving me the third degree."

"Ah," Mrs. Price said, humming to herself. "That's because the two of you can only spend so much time together before your little friendship turns into something more."

"Oh come on, Mrs. Price," she said, laughing. "You watch too many soap operas."

"Really now," she said. "So neither of you have ever kissed each other?"

"Well... no... I mean... we did once but that was to prove that we didn't like each other."

"Oh, I see," Mrs. Price teased. "So what was the outcome of your little experiment?"

"Nothing," she said blushing. "Nothing was the outcome. We're just friends! That's it!"

"Okay. Just as long as it stays that way. You're a beautiful girl and, in a few years, you will have the boys lining up around the block just to talk to you. Your mother is doing what every mother does. She's making sure that you stick to your studies and not mess with any of these boys — even Nolan."

"I guess."

She wanted to tell Mrs. Price that it wasn't Nolan she liked but Sean Malcolm, and he had broken her heart, but she still wished he would ask her out. But then her mother and Esma were coming down the stairs, and the doorbell was ringing, and soon the house was filled with relatives from all over the city. Mrs. Price had a huge family, with many visiting from Ottawa and Montreal. The kitchen became so crowded that Simone got bumped from kitchen duty and was sent to watch over Esma's three young boys and CJ. She wished Nolan was there instead of spending the holidays with his father's family. There weren't any kids her age and she quickly got bored being the babysitter.

When things started to settle down, and the kids were banished to the basement to play, Simone hid away in the sitting room with *Full Circle*, the latest Danielle Steele novel she'd borrowed from Glenview Library. It was about a woman's jaded views on love. It was the third time she had read it, but each time felt like the first. She'd fallen in love with the 1960s and wished that she'd grown up when Motown was everything and tie-dye was the thing to wear.

As she poured through the next chapter, she was startled by a wail from the kitchen. She put the book down and went to see what was going on. There was a crowd of people consoling Mrs. Price.

"Lawd God Almighty, why, God?" said Mrs. Price. She rocked back and forth. "No, it's not true. Lawd it can't be true. I just talked to Cicely a week ago."

"Come on, Mama," Esma said hugging her mother. "Let's go upstairs. You need to lay down."

"No!" She turned to her nephew David who delivered the news. "A lie you tell! Dis can't be true. David, is a lie you tell?"

"I'm sorry, Mama Price," he said, taking her hand. "I wish to God mi wrong but it's true. I swear to you, it is the truth."

"Oh my Lord in heaven, why he haf to do such a thing to himself?" Simone heard a woman say to another. "What could be so bad?"

"His sister found him," said an older woman. "He had a garden hose wrapped tight around his neck."

"I know the parents," said a man behind her. "The father is tough on all of them. I hear he just threw out the middle one not that long ago."

"Mrs. Price," Simone said. "What's wrong?"

Mrs. Price looked up at Simone, her eyes brimming with tears. She covered her mouth trying to stifle her cry. Simone suddenly felt uneasy. The entire room fell silent. What was going on?

"Oh, baby," said a woman who placed her hands on her shoulders. "Mrs. Price's nephew Kester died a few days ago. The poor boy hung himself in his backyard."

▶

265

THE DAYS FOLLOWING Kester's death left everyone deeply distraught. Pam had never seen Simone this emotional. She didn't know much about Kester, other than he was somehow related to Mrs. Price. But seeing Simone fall to her knees sobbing in the middle of Esma's kitchen had brought tears to her eyes. She'd wanted to reach out and pull her into her arms and make the pain go away, but all she could think to do was take her daughter home.

Nolan, however, laughed it off when Mike told him that Kester had died. He thought his father was telling one of his long tales. A silly joke to trick him or teach him a lesson, like the time he told him his bike had been stolen when he found it abandoned in the courtyard. But when he looked into his father's watery eyes and heard his voice crack, he realized it might not be a joke.

"I'm sorry, buddy," Mike said. He placed his arm around Nolan's shoulders.

"That's not funny, Dad," he said, pushing his father away. "Kester is home with his folks. It's probably some other guy named Kester."

"I don't know what to tell you," Mike said.

Nolan's face contorted as he tried to stop himself from crying. He was in a battle with himself to keep it together. Mike pulled Nolan to him.

"NO!" Nolan yelled, pushing him back again. "I just saw him on Friday. If he's dead, then how did he die?"

"Nols, he did it — he did it to himself. It's hard for anyone to understand. I wish there was something I could say to make this better."

"I don't want it to be better." He hated that his voice quivered. "I want my friend back."

He went into his room, slamming the door behind him. He punched his bedroom wall. He banged it again and again until he'd punched a hole through it. He screamed out from the stinging pain in his knuckles and from the throbbing pain inside, then fell to the floor. It felt unreal that Kester was gone. He rehashed their last conversation and how he'd brushed him off to study for some bullshit test. He should have noticed something was wrong.

He wondered if it was dressing in drag that had led Kester to take his own life. After that time at Mrs. Price's, they'd never spoken of it. It was swept under the rug in a neat tiny pile that would now never disappear. He should have reached out to Kester about it; maybe that would have helped. Nolan's entire body started to shake as he thought of it. His stomach twisted tightly and he rushed to his garbage pail and threw up. After a few minutes, he sat up, leaned against the garbage pail, and stared out the window. The sun had started to set. He crawled to the foot of his bed and lay on the floor, finally drifting off to sleep.

When he woke, he had a blanket strewn over him and a pillow under his head. The garbage pail had been removed and a glass of water and sandwich left on his desk. He drank some of the water but had no appetite for the sandwich. He looked up at the clock. 1:30 am.

The entire apartment was silent when he emerged from his room. The heat was on full blast. Feeling claustrophobic, he opened the balcony door and went out to get some fresh air. He stood looking out over the railing at the deserted courtyard for several minutes, then turned to Simone's side of the balcony. Her bedroom window was open. He walked across and looked in. She was awake, eyes glistening, her body at the end of the bed, her head hanging over the edge. He opened the window wide and crawled through.

They lay next to each other in complete silence. He listened to her laboured breathing.

"It's my fault," he said, finally breaking the silence. "I'm his best friend."

Simone didn't respond. She had spent the entire evening going over what she could have done to save him. If she had let him tag along to her basketball game, he wouldn't be dead. He would have teased her for her lousy layups and she would have called him an idiot, but at least he wouldn't be dead.

"I should have been nicer to him," she admitted to Nolan. "Let him come to the game. Or talked to him more about...about...you know."

Silence.

Nolan clenched his teeth trying to hold it in, but he couldn't. He burst into sobs as he turned his head away from Simone. She tried to squelch her own cries, but hot tears just streamed down the sides of her face.

After a while they both drifted off, their hands clenched tightly together.

▶

MIKE WOKE, startled by a loud sharp bang on the front door. It was the daily 5:00 am delivery of newspapers for Nolan's morning route. He opened the door and pulled the stack into the living room. He went into Nolan's room to wake him, but the bedroom was empty.

He went out on the balcony and over to Simone's window. He could see the two of them passed out on her bed. He stepped quietly through the window into her bedroom and gently shook Nolan.

"Nolan, wake up."

Nolan opened his eyes, looked around.

"Come on, buddy. Don't wake her."

He sat up. Simone was still fast asleep. Mike led him out the window and back into their apartment. He kept patting Nolan's back. He wanted his son to man up and be stronger than the grief he felt. The same advice his father had bestowed on him. But

Nolan just shrugged him off and stood for a moment, staring at the stack of papers sitting in the middle of the living room floor.

"Do you need help with your route?" Mike asked.

Nolan shook his head and started to trudge down the hallway towards his bedroom.

"Where are you going?" asked Mike.

"I'm going to bed," Nolan replied.

"What about your paper route? Aren't you going to deliver your papers?"

The door slammed.

Mike stood outside his room. He stayed by the door waiting for Nolan to answer. All he wanted to do was burst into the room and hold his son until the anger and pain went away, but he just stood by the closed door. Then Nolan turned on his stereo and heavy metal blasted through the door, and Mike gave up the idea of trying to talk to him.

He went back to the living room and sat on the chesterfield. He wished Meghan was there to help him. She always knew how to talk to Nolan. She always knew the right thing to say. He picked up a paper and folded it and wrapped it with a rubber band. By the third paper, his eyes had cleared and he saw the story at the bottom of the front page.

Kester's school picture, with the headline, *Grade School Student Found Dead After Missing for Two Days*. He dropped the paper on the coffee table. He leaned against the chesterfield as the thrashing sounds of Nolan's music filled the living room.

"Goddamn it! This is a bloody mess." Mike felt exhausted. He pulled everything out from underneath Mrs. Price's bathroom sink. Bottles of shampoo and cleaning supplies lay sprawled out on her bathroom floor alongside his tools. "Sorry for the coarse language, Mrs. Price, but Alden has no business running this building."

"Lawd God, I done say the same ting about that dutti ole nehgah," she scowled. "Chups! Fi mi money he tek every month but his lazy white behind do nothing around here. Do you think you can fix it?"

"The problem is that the pipe is clogged with probably years of hair stuck in the drain. I'll see what I can do." He wiped his hand with a dishtowel. "Can you get me a garbage bag or a bucket? Maybe I can at least get it cleared…and a hanger too, Mrs. Price… a wire hanger."

Mrs. Price went into the kitchen and came back with a plastic grocery bag and hanger. Mike placed the bag underneath before opening the trap. He bent the hanger and pulled out wads of greasy hair. After ten minutes the rusted pipe was clear and he tightened the trap in place.

"Do you have some baking soda and vinegar?" he asked her. "Also can you boil some water for me?"

Mrs. Price arrived with a box of baking soda, a bottle of vinegar, and a kettle of boiling water. Mike poured the water and baking soda down the drain and then more of the water and vinegar before sticking the plug in the sink.

"We'll give it ten to fifteen minutes," he said.

"Good, good," she said. "That will give me enough time to make you some coffee with that fancy machine Esma gave me for Christmas — and I made black cake this year."

"You're going to get me in trouble, Mrs. Price," Mike said.

He had a soft spot for Mrs. Price's rum cake. The first time she sent him a tin, he ate three hefty pieces and was tipsy before he even got to Maureen's annual Christmas dinner. Pam had laughed when he told her that the cake had given him food poisoning.

"White boy's eye longer than his belly," she teased. "You're supposed to cut a small piece like this."

She cut a piece the size of a small tea biscuit.

"Come sit," Mrs. Price said, motioning him to the living room. She served him the cake and he savoured it slowly, sipping coffee between bites.

"How is Nolan doing these days?"

"Nolan is Nolan," he replied.

"No!" she said swiftly. "Don't give me that 'Nolan is Nolan'. I haven't seen him in a long time. It's not like him to stay away for so long, and why he not delivering his papers?"

"He's been busy with school the last few months," he said. "Trying to get into a good high school."

"Mr. Mike, you think mi just fling off the turnip truck? I know that boy since he was too small to push the elevator buttons. There is something very wrong with him."

"I know," Mike finally admitted. "He's been out of sorts since Kester... well since Kester...."

"You can say suicide," she said with a sigh. "It's what happened

271

and we can't be afraid to call it what it was. It was a terrible thing what Kester did to himself but we can't tiptoe around it, neither. What you gonna do about Nolan?"

"He's fine," Mike replied. "He just needs some time to get over it."

"What he needs is someone he can talk to," she said. "Mi noticed that he doesn't keep company with Simone no more. Did they have a falling out?"

"No, it's nothing like that. It's complicated."

"Well, according to Simone, any time she hangs around him, her mother gives her shit." Mrs. Price rolled her eyes.

Mike sat there silently, finishing off his coffee.

"He's already lost his best friend," she continued. "Mi don't think things will get better for him if he loses another."

"He's fine, Mrs. Price," he told her. He popped the last of the cake into his mouth. "He's just being a typical moody teenage boy."

"Humph, you stay watch," she said unconvinced. "I've seen what 'appens to boys like Nolan. If you don't reach them early enough you risk losing them forever."

◄◄

THE OLD LADY WAS RIGHT. Since Kester's suicide, Nolan had been difficult to deal with. He rarely spoke and was ignoring his paper route. Mike had tried to pick up the slack for a few weeks, but he finally called Nolan's supervisor and informed him that Nolan would no longer be available to run the route.

Mike thought and thought about what to do, then he settled on a kind of plan. Amber's wedding was coming up; Meghan and Dana would also be in town for the ceremony. His master stroke was to arrange for Dana to stay with them.

But instead of the old Nolan re-emerging, an angrier Nolan

took hold. He spent most of the reception brooding in a corner, away from the other guests. Sarah Jane and her mother were guests at the wedding. Sarah Jane bounced over to see Nolan, but he ignored her, then blew up at her when she tried to get him to dance. Meghan scolded him for being rude, but that only made him shove in his ear-buds and turn up the volume of his Walkman. Dana was the only person who seemed able to reach him.

"Come on," she yelled over the band. She pulled his hand and dragged him out of his seat.

They wandered out to the veranda to get fresh air. The Bayview Golf and Country Club grounds were covered with frost. They stood in the freezing night air, huddled next to an outdoor heater. Dana lit a cigarette and took several drags before handing it over to Nolan. He shook his head and then sat down at a wrought-iron patio table still covered with snow from the previous day.

"What gives?" she asked, standing over him. "It's not like you to blow up at some innocent girl asking you to dance."

"Yeah, well she's one of the most fucking annoying girls I know," he said. "I see her every day at school. The last thing I need is to see her here."

"Whoa, tell me exactly how you feel," she joked. Nolan started to laugh a little. "Seriously, what gives?"

"Nothing. I just hate being here. I hate this city and everyone in it."

"Spoken like a true teenager," she said. "So you hate everyone, huh? What about your best friend? That Jamaican girl next door? Is she still around?"

"She's still there," he said.

"Well, that's good. What school is she going to after St. Augie?"

"Probably St. Joseph," he said.

"Oooh, the all-girls school, huh? You know what they say about girls that go to an all-girls school. They're an easy piece of tail."

"That's not fucking funny," Nolan said. "She's not like that."

"It's a joke, Nolan. You used to be able to take a joke! Now I'm not sure what mineshaft to avoid so I don't piss you off."

"Sorry."

"It's okay." She squeezed his shoulder. "Let's change the subject... you know Mom wants you to spend the summer with us?"

"Yeah, she mentioned it. I don't know if I want to spend the summer in Halifax."

"Come on." She smiled. "What else are you going to do, anyways? You just said that you hated Toronto. It would be a perfect time to come out and visit."

"Well, I hate Halifax more."

"Picky, picky," she said, taking a last drag before putting out her cigarette. "It's too bad. It'll probably be the last summer I'll be home."

"Why?" he asked.

"I'm turning twenty-one next year and I'm still living at home," she said. "Jesus, Amber is only a few years older and she's already married. I need to do something with my life. I'll be finished college soon and Mom wants me to get a job."

"Aren't you working at that restaurant?"

"Yeah, but don't bring that up with her. She's told me to either find a career or another place to stay. You have it good, Nols. You're still in school. Dad pays for everything. He doesn't bug you. Mom spends most of her time riding my ass about what I'm going to do after college."

"What does she want you to do?"

"She wants me to be like her and get a job slaving for some company," she said. "I want to be more like Dad."

"You want to work like a slave for nothing?" Nolan replied.

"No, dipshit." She hit the back of his head. "I want to do what makes me happy."

"No offence, Dana, but nothing makes Dad happy," he said.

"He works three shitty jobs and sits around dreaming about buying a Glenview townhouse so that Mom will come running back," he said. "Look, I'm going back inside. It's too cold out here. Who has a fucking wedding in the middle of winter, anyways?"

Dana remained outside to smoke another cigarette as Nolan walked back to the reception — back to his anti-social corner seat. She could see her father on the dance floor, trying to keep up with Maureen who was on her fifth beer and was louder than the band. She was stunned by her brother's revelation and hated that their dad was still hung up on their mother. Her mother had moved on ages ago, dating good ole Rich for almost three years now. Her parents were never going to get back together. Mike seemed to be the last holdout.

She headed back inside to the dance floor. The band was playing an old Billy Joel song, "Just the Way You Are". She remembered her father singing that song to her when she was little. It had always been her favourite.

"You don't mind if I dance with my dad?" she said to Maureen.

"Be my guest, doll." She kissed Dana on the cheek.

"God bless you," Mike said. "I love Maureen but she's killing my feet."

They watched Maureen drag some other poor individual onto the dance floor and laughed.

Mike held her close, softly singing along with the band. "Do you remember me singing this to you?"

Dana nodded. "You look handsome, you know that?" she said. "Some unlucky girl is missing out."

"Aw thank you, sweetheart," he said pulling her away to kiss her on the cheek. "Are you okay? What's wrong?"

"Nothing," she said. She buried her head back on his shoulder. "I just miss you."

They danced for a while longer until the song came to an end and the band started to play another Billy Joel ballad.

"Dad, what's up with Nolan?" she finally asked. "I've never seen him so angry."

"Nothing is up." He shrugged. "Your brother is just a teenage boy who thinks he's in love."

"In love?" she said. "With who?"

"His next-door neighbour."

"The little Jamaican girl — Cynthia…right?" she asked.

"Simone," he corrected her. They both looked over at Nolan, who was still sitting in his corner listening to his Walkman.

"Simone!" she cried out. "For the life of me, I couldn't remember her name."

"Yes, Simone."

"Well, why is he so moody about it?" she asked. "Did she reject him or something?"

"Well, no," he said. "It's just your brother has too much on his plate to be dating. He's got to get his grades up and it's just not appropriate for him to be in a relationship with her."

"Why? Are you dating her mother or something?" she joked. "Mom and I have always wondered what was going on with you and the Jamaican beauty queen. You know Mom is a little jealous of her when Nolan talks about you guys," she teased.

"Really?" he said. "I didn't think your mother gave a shit about what happens to me."

"Come on, Dad. You know that's not true. She just thought that you would have moved on since she…well…since she's moved on."

"Well, I didn't," he said. "And Pam and I are just friends."

"Well, then, what's the problem with Nolan dating her daughter?"

"The problem is that I'm a single father and Pam is a single mom," he said. "What with work and all, we don't have enough eyes between the two of us to make sure that two hormonal teenagers are keeping their legs crossed and their pants on."

"Jesus, Dad, a little less graphic, please," she said, squirming.

"What are you going to do anyways, chain him to a fence? At some point, he's going to do whatever he wants — with or without your permission."

"Well, I can try."

"Dad, you're better off giving him a box of condoms and a sex-ed pamphlet."

"Yeah, well, giving him condoms is just an open invitation," he retorted. "He's better off just not having sex, period."

"And how exactly did that work out for you and Mom?"

Mike let out a big sigh as he shook his head.

"It's not the same thing."

"Come on, Dad, it's all relevant," she said, forcefully. "You good Catholic boys live in a fantasy world in which all honourable young men keep their pants on until they get married. There are people getting AIDS and all kinds of sexual diseases just because some Vatican dope with an oversized cap is telling teenagers to keep their hormones in check."

"Okay...okay. Can we change the subject? This is not something I want to discuss with my daughter on the dance floor of a wedding reception."

"Fine by me! Let's change the subject," she smiled. "Why aren't you doing it with Pam the beauty queen?"

"Oh look, they're cutting the cake," he said.

"Okay, okay, I get the hint," she laughed.

Dana and Mike moved to the cake table to watch Amber and her new husband having a food fight with chunks of wedding cake.

"Classy," Dana mumbled to herself. "I'm going outside to have a smoke," she told her dad.

25

Even though Yvette and Angie were the only other black girls in her grade, Simone had nothing in common with them; but she needed a distraction from the loneliness she had felt since Kester's death, so she put up with them. They spent most of their time listening to Top 40 music and watching television shows about happy white families involved in dumb weekly shenanigans. Also, they were still obsessed with New Kids on the Block, which really annoyed her. When their antics became too much to handle, she gravitated towards Ilene Cheng.

Simone and Ilene remained competitive but, over the years, had become more cordial with each other. Once Simone got to know Ilene, she quickly realized that Pam was a cakewalk compared to Ilene's parents. Ilene's family had emigrated from Hong Kong barely knowing English, but expected her to be fluent in English, French, Mandarin, and Cantonese. They kept a laser focus on everything she did and were determined to put her on the fast track to medical school, with proficiency in ballet, chess, and piano; she also had to attend Saturday Chinese school.

The three of them were quickly becoming the only friends she had left.

Things between Simone and Nolan had unhinged since the suicide, and the glue that once bonded their friendship was slowly disintegrating. With winter weather's arrival, the balcony was covered in snow, so they no longer met there. Being in different classes kept them apart. The few times Nolan did ride the bus, he sat with the Moretti cousins or other boys from school. He always seemed quiet and distant. She was hurt by all this and confided in Mrs. Price.

"Baby, he lost his best friend in a horrible way," she told Simone. "Give him time. Soon enough you two will be batty an' bench again."

If the signal was strong enough, Simone often spent evenings alone listening to the *Quiet Storm* on the Buffalo radio station WBLK. Each night she would lie in her bed listening to callers dedicate their favourite slow jams to a lover that got away or to a crush they were too scared to approach. She loved the music and, like every teenager, she started making mix tapes of her favourite songs.

The music often left her thinking of Nolan and their kiss. She replayed the moment in her mind as the breathy vocals of "Between the Sheets" played, hoping he would sneak into her bedroom to kiss her again.

Each tape of love songs she labeled *RMofH*, "Reminds Me of Him". The tapes not only reminded her of Nolan, but began to act like a soundtrack to her life. The music's heavy bass and slow sensual melodic rhythm left her moist, while the tantalizing lyrics told her story better than she could ever tell it herself. But, by the last song of the evening, she was left in tears as she ended each day without him.

As the weeks went by, she slowly got used to just seeing him from a distance. It was her final year at St. Augustine and she didn't want to spend the rest of it pining for him. She was going to be attending St. Joseph in the fall, which meant a fresh start.

By March break, the winter thaw had begun. Pam wasn't able

to take the week off, so Simone and CJ were stuck with Mrs. Price during their holiday. Mrs. Price always had a full house during the week-long vacation. A few of CJ's classmates stayed with her. It was fun for CJ but left Simone bored. She spent most of the time riding her bike around the complex and hanging out in the playground, listening to her tapes on the Walkman she had received for Christmas.

Nolan spent most of March break locked in his bedroom, blasting heavy metal or playing video games. On that Friday, before school resumed, he played Mortal Combat till dawn and ended up sleeping most of the day. He woke up in the middle of the afternoon, hungry and bored. The sun was shining brightly, so he went out onto the balcony and looked down at the playground. The only person out was Simone. He caught himself smiling as he watched her walk towards the swing set.

He took the elevator down and wandered out of the building to the empty playground. Simone was sitting on the swing fully engrossed in one of her Harlequin Romance novels.

She looked up to see Nolan standing there in his Metallica T-shirt and black acid-washed jeans. He was no longer the boy whose favourite top was a Pac-Man T-shirt. He sat down on the swing next to her. They started to swing. Neither could muster the courage to talk about Kester or about the distance that had come between them.

After a while, Nolan reached over and held her swing until they'd both stopped. He gently pulled her off the swing and onto his lap. The wind swirled around them. He brushed away some hair that had blown in her face. He stroked her cheek and then kissed her.

Simone timidly put her arms around his neck, drawing him closer.

They embraced as they kissed, swaying gently on the swing. It wasn't as intense as their first kiss. This time it was slower and softer. They slowly pulled away from each other.

She smiled slightly. "Nolan... I... I...." She wanted to tell him how much she liked kissing him — how much she liked him, but Yvette and a group of kids were coming around the corner. She quickly got off his lap and sat back down on the swing next to him.

Nolan got up and started to walk towards the main road. Yvette's group came running towards the swing set, all chattering about a movie they'd just seen. Simone strained to see where Nolan was going, but was distracted by Yvette.

"Simone, are you listening?" she said. "I am so in love with Judge Reinhold. You have to watch *Vice Versa* with me. Will your mom let you go tomorrow?"

"Uhm...no...I mean...I don't know," she stammered. "Yvette, I have to go, but I'll let you know later, okay?"

She quickly ran down the back path but, when she got to the main road, Nolan was nowhere to be found. She couldn't tell which direction he'd gone in. Her heart was beating a mile a minute as she searched. She wanted her moment back. That cheesy romantic ending she'd read about in her books. She no longer cared what their parents thought. All she wanted was the old Nolan back. The one who would tickle her to make her lose when they played video games. The one who wasn't afraid to crawl into her room in the middle of the night to play gin rummy. The one who smiled at her for no reason. The one who wore a goofy PacMan T-shirt and held her hand on the balcony.

Nolan, however, was seconds from exploding as he rushed down the path and around the corner. All he could think about was Simone on the swing in her oversized white sweatshirt and short jean skirt that showed her thighs.

His mind flooded with thoughts of all the things he wanted to do. To reach under her skirt and pull down her panties, leaving her open to him. He thought of how it would feel to be inside her. He wanted her to straddle him while he fucked her.

He stopped to catch his breath and saw that he was nearly at

Sheppard Avenue. He felt sick to his stomach. Everything his father had told him was right. Things with Simone had suddenly changed into something he couldn't handle. She was no longer just the girl next door, but the girl he wanted.

It scared him, knowing how easy it could have been to convince her to come upstairs with him to his room. No one was home. They would be alone for hours. It would be so simple.

The long walk home helped clear his mind, but not his raging urges. As he took the elevator up, he knew that he had to do something drastic. When he got to the apartment, he went into the kitchen and dialled Sarah Jane's number.

He asked her out on a date. She told him yes immediately and by the time school started up again, Nolan O'Shea and Sarah Jane Ryden were "boyfriend and girlfriend".

▶

SIMONE STOOD IN THE SCHOOLYARD, broken-hearted, as she watched Nolan walk hand in hand with Sarah Jane. Angie was rattling on about her trip to Florida, but she barely paid any attention. How could Nolan have kissed her a few days ago, only to stand there now, laughing with Sarah Jane, pretending she didn't exist?

Her body trembled as she forced herself to walk into the school to the nurse's office, where she broke down. The nurse got up from her desk and embraced Simone, asking what was wrong.

Simone said she wasn't feeling well.

"Oh, my dear, it's probably your monthly visitor." The nurse smiled at her. "We all go through it. Would you like me to have your mother pick you up or would you prefer to lie down?"

"I think I'll just lie down."

"Okay. You rest and I'll let Sister Rogers know where you are."

Simone lay on the cot. Not even her misguided crush on Sean

Malcolm had hurt this much. This ache ran much deeper. It wasn't just an ache either. It left such a stale bitterness in her mouth.

All men are the same, Ms. Pam had once told Simone. *They want what's between your legs and if you don't give it to them fast enough they will quickly move on to the next slack one.*

"How's our patient?" the nurse asked cheerfully when she returned.

"I'm okay. Can I go back to class?"

"Sure, but you know that you can stay as long as you want. No rush."

"No, Ma'am," she replied. "I want to go back to class. I don't want to miss anything."

Back in the classroom, Simone sat down and opened her math textbook. She glanced over at Sarah Jane, who was smiling happily to herself.

"I heard you weren't feeling well," said Sean. "Are you better?"

"I'm fine," she said quietly.

"Well, that's good," he whispered back. "I wish I had some of that medicine you got, so I won't feel so shitty about Sarah Jane dumping me."

Simone looked over at Sean and could see the hurt in his eyes. He looked down at his textbook and continued to work on his math problem. Simone turned back to her worksheet and bit her lip hard enough to stop herself from crying. She started to see things much more clearly. She never wanted to feel that vulnerable and promised herself that she would never waste another tear on a boy ever again.

"Fuck 'em," she whispered to Sean.

When she saw he was stunned by her response, she laughed a little.

"You're right," he said, smiling at her. "Fuck 'em."

▶

"IT'S CALLED A DATE, Mike, it's not an engagement," scolded Maureen.

She was sitting on Mike's sofa, reading the newspaper, while he shaved his stubble in the bathroom.

"Yeah, but who goes out on a date at 11:00 at night?" he said.

"Someone who works the late shift," she responded, rolling her eyes. "She's a nice woman, Mike, and right now you need a nice woman to keep your mood up."

Mike had never felt lower. After years of being separated, Meghan had finally filed for divorce. It wasn't much of a surprise to Dana or Nolan. Meghan had wanted this the moment she got to Halifax, but it felt like a huge blow to Mike. He had always hoped that things would work out between them, especially since they had been so civil to each other over the last year. He'd even danced with her at Amber's wedding and reminisced about old times. He truly believed he had seen a glimmer of hope. Christ, she had allowed him to kiss her goodbye.

If Nolan hadn't changed his plans and had gone to Halifax for March break, Mike would have gone with him, hoping to reconcile with her. He'd even thought about moving to Nova Scotia — anything to rebuild his marriage. Meghan was the only woman he'd ever loved and she was moving on with her life, while he was left stagnant in the past.

"Look, Mike, she's pretty, engaging and has a wicked sense of humour — you're lucky to even have a date with Joanna," she said. "She is a gorgeous woman. Definitely your type."

"Oh God, Maureen, any time I hear that, it means she's a dog."

"Will you trust me, please?" she said, tossing the paper on the coffee table. "I wouldn't waste my Friday night watching your kid if I didn't think she would be perfect for you."

He walked out into the living room. "Yeah, well, I'm holding your feet to the fire if this ends up being a waste of my time."

"Well, don't you clean up nice," she complimented him.

He examined his new pair of blue jeans and the fresh button-down shirt. "I do, don't I?"

He had met Joanna at McKinney's. Maureen was right when she said that Joanna was a looker. If he had not known, he would have said she was much younger than thirty-eight. She had thick, long, wavy blond hair and crystal-blue eyes and wasn't much taller than him. He was thankful that Maureen hadn't matched him up with one of her Amazon girlfriends. She wasn't as brash as Maureen but could hold a conversation.

"I work in pediatrics," she told him when he asked about her job. "I used to work in labour and delivery at East General but, before my husband passed, I had to quit my job to take care of him."

"I'm sorry about your husband," Mike offered. He sipped his beer.

"Thank you, but he was a total son-of-a-bitch till the end," she said brazenly.

Mike looked at her in shock.

"I'm kidding. He was a great guy, but hated when anyone got all serious about his cancer. He always made light of his condition and I guess I'm keeping up that tradition. It helps. Especially after days like today."

Joanna explained that one of her patients had died that morning. It was brutal because it had been looking as if the little boy was finally going home.

"You care a lot about the kids you work with."

"Yeah, I guess I do," she said. "It's hard with kids — dealing with a five-year-old who won't live past next year is heartbreaking."

They sat there in silence as Mike drank the rest of his beer. He signalled Tommy for another round.

"Hey, do you want to get out of here?" she asked. "I live just around the corner and I have a great bottle of bourbon that I've been meaning to open."

The moment they got to her house she kissed him and his entire body surged when her tongue danced in his mouth. He barely had time to close the door behind him before she started unbuckling his belt. He anxiously pulled the zipper of her dress down before pulling it over her head and there she was, standing in her living room in a cream satin dress slip. He pulled down the strap, baring her soft milky shoulder. He kissed her neck as the rest of the slip cascaded down her body. She pulled off his jeans, then hauled him down onto her peach leather sofa. When she asked him if he had protection, he felt like a tool.

"It's okay. I have something." She reached for her purse and pulled out a condom.

She gently stroked him with her hands and then with her mouth before placing the condom on him. He moaned slightly as she straddled him, rocking back and forth as he entered her. He grasped her waist and felt himself go deeper and deeper. Gliding inside her, his whole body pulsated as he felt arousal reach a feverous peak. He cried out loudly when he came. He wiped his brow with her slip. She collapsed on his chest and laughed.

"You're funny," she said. She kissed him. "I like that."

They kissed some more before making love again. It was nearly daybreak when he left her place, promising to call that weekend so they could make plans. He gave his head a shake. He hadn't been with a woman for so long.

When he reached home, Maureen was fast asleep on the couch with the television station bars on the screen. He turned off the television and placed a blanket over her before heading to his room.

"I told you she would be your type," Maureen said sleepily.

26

The annual eighth-grade class trip was the highlight of the year for St. Augustine's graduating class. Each year, all of the area Catholic schools participated in the pilgrimage to Quebec City. Mike had arranged with Pam that he would see the kids off from the school parking lot and, at 4:30 in the morning, he and Nolan were knocking at her door.

"Wow," Mike said when Simone opened the door. "Looking sharp, Splimoney."

"Thank you, Mr. Mike," she said proudly.

She had visited the salon and had her hair straightened to show off her long bouncy locks, and the hairdresser had given her cute bangs. She wanted to look more grown up for the trip, especially now that she was going into high school. She wore a red plaid skirt with a white onesie tank top and a black jean vest. She even wore a small black top hat that she'd bought at *Le Chateau.*

When Nolan saw her, he almost didn't recognize her. He didn't know what to say. He wanted to say something nice to her, but lost his nerve.

"I'm so excited about this trip," she said to him. "Aren't you?"

"Yeah, I guess."

"Well, I'm all ready." Simone brushed past him to grab her duffle bag.

"Let me take that, little lady." Mike took the bag from her. "Nolan, get the door."

"Alright, Simone," said Pam. She was still dressed in her robe and slippers. "Have a safe trip and be sure to call me when you get there."

"I will," Simone responded as Pam gave her a hug.

When they arrived at the parking lot, the sun was just peeking out of the dawn sky. Students from three different schools milled about, saying goodbye to their parents as they boarded the buses.

"Wow, your hair is so long and soft," said Tammy as she touched Simone's silky hair.

"I love your skirt," said Sarah Jane. "I have one similar to that but my mother said it was too grown-up to wear on a school trip."

"Oh, that's too bad," said Simone. "My mom just loves it on me. She says that, since I'll be in high school soon, I should probably start dressing more like a teenager instead of like a little kid."

Sarah Jane's smile faded as she looked down at the poodle crocheted on the front of her own sweater.

Simone sat with Ilene, Yvette, and Angie on the bus. The four girls were going to be roommates for the next week and couldn't contain their high spirits. They spent the next few hours chatting endlessly about movie stars they were in love with and speaking in code about the boys on the bus they had crushes on.

After stopping for lunch, Simone noticed that the bus had a tape deck. She asked the driver if she could play the mix tape she'd brought with her. In no time, the busload of students was singing along to New Edition and Bobby Brown songs.

Simone, Angie, and Yvette danced in their seats. They showed Ilene the Cabbage Patch and the Wop. She started to get the hang of it when Salt-N-Pepa's "Push It" came on, but it was Rob Base's "It Takes Two" that got the whole bus chanting loudly how they came to get down.

Nolan sat in the back of the bus with Sarah Jane, Donnie Frisco, Brian Kepler, Vivian, and Cathy Moretti. They were the rowdiest group. They shouted over the music about baseball and whether the Blue Jays would ever take the World Series, and laughed hysterically, recapping skits from Saturday Night Live, and reliving Mortal Combat kills.

In the midst of all of that, Sean Malcolm traded seats with Ilene to teach Simone Rock-Paper-Scissors.

▶

A PANG of jealousy swept over Nolan, quickly ending his joyful mood.

He was glad when the bus finally pulled up to their accommodations. The last thing he wanted to see was Simone and Sean hanging out. As he was getting off the bus, the driver grabbed his sleeve.

"Hey. Your classmate...the cute black girl...she forgot her tape. Can you give it back to her?"

He took the tape and looked at the label, *RMofH Slow Jams.*

"Come on, Nolan!" Sarah Jane said. "Everyone is inside already."

He slipped the tape in his backpack and ran to catch up with the rest of the class.

Their trip to Quebec started with a show by Francophone Circus street performers in one of the local theatres, went on with a walking tour of Old Quebec City with a guide who gave a brief history of Lower Canada, and on the third day they visited the Citadelle and the Musee de la Civilisation, where they were told they should develop a deeper understanding of Quebec's history.

On the second to the last day, the students were bussed to the Quartier Petit Champlain to go shopping and practise their conversational French. Like most of her classmates, Simone's

French was not very strong and she stumbled over her sentences. Only Ilene was in her element, since she spoke French fluently, and she ended up being their personal translator.

By late afternoon, Simone had lost track of her friends. She wandered down the cobbled street and into a dress shop. There she saw many of her classmates looking around. A rack of evening dresses caught her attention. She pulled out a floral printed cocktail dress and pressed it against herself and looked in the mirror. The beautiful powder blue complemented her complexion. She checked the price tag and couldn't believe how expensive the dress was.

As she hung it back on the rack, she looked across the store to see Sarah Jane slip a black dress in her knapsack. She was surprised, then wondered if she could get away with it as well. None of the sales clerks were looking, so she started to roll up the dress.

"Really, child?" a voice whispered in her ear. "It's not even your size!"

Miss Gardiner stood behind her, shaking her head in disbelief.

"If you are dumb enough to steal a $300 dress, at least pick the right size. Honestly!" She hung the dress back on the rack.

She pulled Simone out of the store and quickly down the street, into an alleyway.

"Goddamn it, Simone. What the hell do you think you're doing? I have one right mind to call your mother and send you back to Toronto on the next train!"

Simone stood there, shaken. She had never heard Miss Gardiner yell. The fire in her eyes made her burst into tears. She looked down at her shoes, hoping that none of the other students noticed what was going on.

"Please don't tell my mother," she said. "I don't know what I was thinking."

"You weren't thinking," Miss Gardener said, gripping her arm. "Is it really worth ruining the rest of your year and your reputation for a lousy dress? I thought you were smarter than that. So disappointing!"

It was the first time she felt as if she had really let someone down. If her mother found out, she would beat her, scold her, and call her every name in the book, but she would eventually get over it because she was used to being treated that way by Pam. But disappointing Miss Gardiner made her feel ill. She was the only teacher in the school who always stuck up for her, even when other teachers wanted to hold her back.

"I'm sorry, Miss," she whimpered.

"Simone, I want you to listen to me and hear me." She ushered Simone out of the alley. "No matter what the Sarah Janes in this world get away with, always remember that you are black. You will never just get a scolding — especially here. Had you been caught, the police would have been called, and, instead of being sent home, you would have been arrested. Do you understand me?"

Simone nodded swiftly. They headed back towards the bus.

"You saw her?" Simone asked.

"Yes, I did. And so did Mrs. Brickett, who is pulling her aside as we speak. I don't understand you kids. You are here on a wonderful trip that so many students would die to go on and you do something like this!"

"I'm sorry," she said again. "I really am... what can I do to prove to you how sorry l am?"

"You know what you can do?" she said. "Do better. Once you go off to high school, there won't be many teachers like me to look out for you. High school teachers won't give a shit if you steal, do your homework, or even graduate."

"Yes, Ma'am." She could barely speak. She continued to look down at her shoes. She couldn't bear the weight of her teacher's anger. Miss Gardiner lifted Simone's chin and forced her to look at her.

"I expect great things from you, Simone," she said. "I always have, but all of it depends on you. Now get on the bus and sit there until we leave."

Simone started to board the bus, but turned and hugged Miss Gardiner.

"Alright... alright," Miss Gardiner said, hugging her back. "Go on."

Simone was grateful that Miss Gardiner had stopped her from making the mistake. All she heard on the bus ride back to the hotel was everyone whispering about Sarah Jane getting caught shoplifting.

Not only had Mrs. Brickett caught Sarah Jane stealing, but the shopkeeper had and called security. Sarah Jane had spent an hour in the security office while Mrs. Brickett wrestled with her French to explain that this was a young impressionable girl who usually never did things like steal. She was able to convince the security guard to let her off with a warning, but had been deeply humiliated and was furious with the girl. She made her stay in her room for the rest of the night, while the rest of the students went to the formal without her.

▶

AT FIRST, Simone hadn't been a fan of the purple velvet baby-doll dress her mother had bought her. Its long draping sleeves and rounded neckline seemed too dark and frumpy. But now, when she looked at herself in the lobby mirror, she thought the dress, with a pair of low-wedged heels and a choker, looked stunning on her.

"My goodness, don't you all look so grown up," gushed Miss Gardiner. She went around fixing ties and brushing lint off shoulders. The girls were pretty in their outfits, the boys handsome in their slacks, white shirts, and ties. Some of the boys even wore dinner jackets.

They all walked together into the dining room, overwhelmed by the beautiful room, with its gold and silver decorations. The tables were decorated with beautiful moss centrepieces, gold confetti sprinkled on top. Simone had never been to a fancy formal event and looked in awe at the crowded room.

St. Augustine had three long tables. Most of the girls sat at one, most of the boys occupied the adjoining table, and the rest of the kids sat with the teachers at the third. Right from the start, the boys acted silly and continued through the meal, while the waiters in tuxedos served rolls, buttered chicken, au gratin potatoes, and grilled peppers.

"Pardon me, would you have any Grey Poupon, kind sir?" Donnie asked a waiter. The entire table burst into laughter when the waiter returned with a small dish of the mustard.

"This place really is fancy," laughed Cathy Moretti.

The highlight of the meal was creamy chocolate mousse served with coffee. Many students ordered coffee, but screwed up their faces after tasting the bitter drink.

"You have to add sugar and cream," Simone told her table.

She drank Blue Mountain coffee every summer with Granny Annalise in Jamaica. She was an expert at making the perfect cup.

"Show me," asked Sean, who was sitting at the boys' table behind Simone.

Simone added sugar and cream to his drink.

Nolan fiddled with his dessert as he looked on. He wasn't having much fun. He'd spent most of the meal sulking as he watched Sean flirt with Simone.

"Hey, man," said Donnie. "So did Sarah Jane really try to steal a $1000 dress?"

"Yeah, I guess," he confirmed.

"Yo dude! That's crazy! I heard they were going to send her home," said Brian.

Nolan wasn't interested in what happened to Sarah Jane. He was watching Sean head over to the dance floor with Simone. A group of them began dancing, as the DJ played a string of recent pop music. He wasn't in the mood to join in, so he stood off to the side, watching Simone. He liked her dress, the way it twirled just above her knees, and her legs looked really long. His neck burned hot.

It was as if Simone was a completely different person now. Her looks had changed, she hung out with a new group of friends and the music she listened to was new. He reached into his pocket and pulled out her tape. He'd kept it and spent the past nights listening to the songs on his Walkman. It was cool and different from the music he listened to now. Each song she picked was like a story. A message that held a special meaning for her. A secret code he was no longer able to crack. He repeated the songs he liked over and over. Sometimes he let the tape play in its entirety but often he would rewind and play certain parts of a song. Parts that reminded him of her. It was a whole world of music that he hadn't heard before. About a dozen songs were listed, all in Simone's neat fine print. One of the songs had three stars next to it. It was the song he liked the most.

Simone danced with Yvette and Angie to Bon Jovi's "Living on a Prayer" blasting through the speakers. It was clear they all loved Jon Bon Jovi. Simone had danced so much that she had to stop and take a break. Her bun had come undone and her hair fell loosely around her shoulders. She went to the refreshment table and asked the waiter for a glass of water as she wiped her brow. She stood there sipping her water.

"Alright kiddies, this song is a request," said the DJ. "Find yourself a partner for the slow dance moment of the night."

When the song began, she immediately recognized Deele's "Two Occasions". Across the dance floor, Nolan was gazing at her, and she felt a smile spread across her face.

Nolan watched everyone partner up. Simone was alone, swaying a little as she listened to her favourite song. He started to walk towards her, sure of a dance, when he felt his arm being pulled.

"Sarah Jane," he said. "What are you doing here? I thought they made you stay in your room?"

"Mrs. Brickett isn't that much of a cow after all," she said, smoothing out her dress. "Come on, Nols. Ask me to dance."

Nolan tried to smile, but glared instead. Sean had just grabbed Simone's hand, leading her to the dance floor. He looked like a giant next to her small frame. They were careful not to dance too close, as the chaperones looked on, but Nolan could see Sean inching Simone closer to him.

"Nolan!" Sarah Jane yelled. "I'm fucking talking to you and all you can do is look at Sean and Simone."

The dance floor was flooded with kids dancing. He watched Sean kiss Simone on the cheek.

"Come on." Nolan grabbed Sarah Jane's arm.

He tried to walk out of the ballroom, but Mr. Saddler was blocking the door with the other chaperones. There was an exit door behind the DJ booth, so they weaved between the dancers and snuck behind the booth. He pushed open the door and led her into a dark hallway.

Nolan pulled Sarah Jane alongside him, while Babyface's vocals echoed throughout the shadowy corridor. He opened a door to find a crammed linen closet. He tried another door that was locked.

The next door opened into an empty supply closet. He pulled Sarah Jane in with him, kissing her forcefully. She pulled away, trying to get air. He had kissed her before, but never this roughly.

He took in the stunned look on her face, but all he could think of was Simone and the way her lips felt when they'd kissed in the park. He wished it was Simone with him, hidden away from the rest of the world. He wished it was her face looking back at him. He wanted to be with her.

He closed his eyes and imaged Simone as he gently kissed

Sarah Jane. The music could still be heard faintly as the blur of the keyboard bled through the walls. He slipped his tongue into her mouth, in and out, the way he did with Simone. He heard her moan softly as their tongues played. Her arms wrapped loosely around his neck. He pulled down the strap of her dress. She moaned again as his hands went up her dress and caressed her panties. He heard her gasp slightly when he began to pull them down.

His pants slid to the ground as he lifted her up and pressed her against the closed door. She yelped in pain as he entered her. Everything started to happen too fast and he felt her tightening up but he couldn't slow down.

"It hurts," she whimpered.

He started to lose control when he imagined that it was Simone he was fucking. He then pulled her to the ground and spread her legs wider and started to move in and out of her. He went faster, trying to go deeper. He could feel his heart explode as a deep grunt escaped him. Beads of sweat trickled down the sides of his face.

He heard Sarah Jane cry out as his entire body shuddered. He collapsed on top of her, unable to move. He wanted to pull out but he was still cumming. After a few seconds, he finally finished and rolled off her.

He slowly opened his eyes and realized what had just happened. He wanted to reach out to her and apologize, but his throat froze. All he felt was shame. Was he supposed to tell her that he loved her? Or kiss her? Or hold her hand? Nothing had prepared him for what needed to happen afterwards. No one had told him that, afterwards, he would feel awful. All he wanted to do was get out of there.

"I'm sorry," he stammered as he pulled up his pants. "We shouldn't have... I shouldn't have—"

"It was my first time," she quietly blurted out. "I... I thought you should know. I... I don't want you to think that I've done this before."

"It was mine, too," he admitted.

Nolan could barely look at her. He felt sick. He had wanted his first time to be with someone he loved or at least cared for. He had hoped his first time would be with Simone. He had not wanted it to be a frantic moment in a dark dank closet next to a bucket of dirty soap water.

After a while, they headed back to the banquet hall. No one had noticed that they had left. Simone was animatedly talking to Ilene. She looked over at him and smiled and waved. He continued past her to his seat, with Sarah Jane quietly in tow. He saw Simone's smile fade as they sat down, and she quickly turned away from him.

"Hey, they're going to play some RUN DMC soon," Sean was yelling to Simone. "Do you want to go back out and dance?"

Nolan tried to smile at Simone, but the tension in him had left him miserable. He just watched her and the rest of the students as they headed back to the dance floor.

27

The school year was coming swiftly to an end. Pam usually anticipated the summer's arrival with a sense of calm relief because it meant almost two months without any children underfoot, but this year was going to be different. She had a lot of vacation time banked away and planned to join them in Jamaica.

Pam had been stagnant during the five years since Caleb's death. She didn't date or really go out with friends. She worked long hours and the rest of her time was spent running errands or wrangling her children. She put on a strong front, but deep inside she was barely functioning. She was still plagued with sleepless nights and, having only her children to fill her time, she felt lonely. Her girlfriends were no longer in a rush to find the next party. Daphne and Linda were now married, with six children between them, so the best they'd been able to do was introduce her to the few single men they knew. The pickings were slim.

"You know you should really look into going home," said Linda, as they sat in her kitchen. "Don't be like my mother. She spent most of her life alone working and raising my sister and me. I don't think she's been with a man in decades and that is not an exaggeration! Why live like that when there are some real good men out there sitting pretty with good jobs."

"And with plenty woman," Pam added.

"Not all," Linda responded. "Take, for example, my cousin Dexter. He works as a solicitor, he makes good money, and isn't attached."

"Doesn't he have a son?"

"Yes, but the boy is practically seventeen," she replied. "Long past needing to be raised. Anyways, he's a good catch and looking for a good woman."

"I'm sure all Dexter is looking for is a visa," she said, laughing. "That's all they're after."

"And why not," said Linda, refilling Pam's mug. "The reality is you need a father for CJ. Mark my words, he will grow up wild without a proper father figure in his life, and Simone...well, Simone has never had a father to even give her an example of what a good man is."

"And you think I'm going to find that back home?" said Pam, unconvinced. "All the good and smart men left the island, Linda."

"Yes, well, if Dex isn't so smart, then why does he live in a big house in Kingston, with a second house in Montego Bay? Now that's a man worth looking into."

Her talk with Linda had germinated. Most of the single men she met in Toronto were either too young to take seriously or too old to still be playing the field. The few who were her age were saddled with so many different children from so many different women that it made her stomach churn. The last thing she wanted to do was crawl back to Jamaica to find a man, but the alternative of spending the rest of her life alone made her shudder. The least she could do was try.

▶

WHEN PAM TOLD Simone and CJ that she would be joining them in Jamaica, CJ danced around the room, but Simone's heart dropped. Their annual trip was one experience her mother couldn't ruin for her. Two months away from Pam was always a welcome relief from the ten months of nagging, arguments, and licks. Also, Simone could be herself when she went back home. She was with her own people, who didn't treat her like an outcast. She ate the food she loved and talked the way she wanted without feeling out of place.

The week before graduation Simone, sat quietly at the dinner table, playing with her spaghetti and trying to figure out how to say what she had to say. She had found a way to get out of going to Jamaica but was terrified of her mom's reaction.

"Miss Pam, I need to tell you something," she said. "I got a job working at Laura Secord at Glenview mall."

"Yaaay!" squealed CJ. "Will you bring home ice cream all the time, Simone?"

"Wait, hold on," Pam said to CJ. She turned to Simone. "What job? When did you get a job?"

"I filled out an application for a summer job a while ago," she said. "I didn't think that they would hire me. I just thought I would try. Then the manager called me in for an interview. I went in, and I guess she liked me because she hired me part-time for the summer."

Pam looked at Simone, who continued to look down at her food.

"During the summer?" Pam said. "Do they have a Laura Secord in Manchester?"

"No," she said. "I was hoping you wouldn't mind letting me stay here this summer."

"Stay behind by yourself?" Pam laughed out loud. "You must think mi mad to agree to that!"

"No, no," she said. "I was just thinking that I could stay across the hallway with Mrs. Price while you and CJ are away. I really

really want this job. I want to save my money to buy a computer and, if I work the entire summer, I'll be halfway there. Please, Miss Pam."

Pam sighed as she got up from the table to empty her leftovers in the trash. She smiled slightly.

"You're growing up way too quick for me," she said. "I'm going to have to think about it."

"Oh thank you, Miss Pam!" Simone jumped out of her seat to hug her mother. "I promise that I will do everything Mrs. Price tells me. I won't be a problem. I'll go to work and then home."

"I didn't say yes, yet," she said, still trying not to smile. "I need to speak with Mrs. Price and think on it before I make a decision."

▶

SHE WASN'T THRILLED about Simone staying in Toronto, but she was proud of Simone's ingenuity and ambition. She had wanted to get a computer for Simone herself, but a good computer would cost two months of her salary. As the days grew closer, she realized that having Simone stay behind wasn't a bad idea. Nolan was spending the summer in Nova Scotia and, with Mrs. Price always on the watch, she figured that no harm would come of it. Having a part-time job would be good for Simone. It would teach her responsibility and give her a little pocket money.

"Under no circumstances are you allowed to gallivant around the city," she said to Simone as they sat in Mrs. Price's living room before she and CJ headed to the airport. "Mrs. Price and Esma are going to keep an eagle eye on you and will let me know if you get out of line. Do you hear me? I'm serious!"

"Yes, yes I know you are," Simone said. "You can trust me."

Pam looked intently at her and gave her a side hug before leaving.

"Mrs. Price has all my numbers," she said. "You call me if you run into any problems."

"Lawd, just go nuh!" yelled out an annoyed Mrs. Price from the kitchen. "You're going to miss your taxi and your flight and then cuss that we kept you from leaving. Go nuh!"

"Okay, alright." Pam grabbed CJ's hand.

"Bye, Simone," said CJ. He ran back to hug his big sister. "I'm going to miss you so much."

"I'm going to miss you too, CJ," she said. She kissed and squeezed him. "I'll see you soon."

"Don't forget that you promised to make me a triple scoop when I get back," he said. "Don't forget!"

"I won't," she said as the buzzer in Mrs. Price's apartment went off.

"It's the damn taxi driver," said Pam. "Come nuh, before he leaves us."

Pam waved to Simone up on the balcony as they climbed into the taxi. Her heart pounded as the car drove off.

"Six whole weeks," Simone sighed to herself as she collapsed on Mrs. Price's sofa.

▶

"SIX WHOLE WEEKS," yelled Maureen. She looked furious as she nursed her beer at McKinney's. "Un-fucking-believable! She barely does anything and now she's practically taking a two-month vacation while I have to do all of her work!"

"But isn't that what you wanted?" responded Tommy. "If I remember correctly you kept telling us that you would die for an opportunity to show the bigwigs that you can do a better job. Looks to me that your opportunity is knocking."

"Don't bother with her, Tommy," said Mike. "Nothing will ever make Maureen happy."

He poured ice into the bar's ice chest, then pulled Maureen another draft. The bar was starting to pick up as the Friday night crowd filtered in.

"Yeah, well, what would make me happy is if she got lost at sea," she said. "At least I have the summer away from her constant nagging. 'Blah, blah, blah, Maureen. I needed this yesterday, Maureen.' Nag, nag, nag!"

"Well, that's something, isn't it?" Tommy patted Maureen's hand. "Six weeks of peace and quiet, you being your own boss — you can pretty much set your own rules."

"Maybe you and me can have a long lunch, Tommy," she said, winking at him. "I mean now that I'm kind of in charge I can take off whenever I want."

"Maybe," he said, winking back.

"Oh, God," grumbled Mike. "Would the two of you screw already? This back and forth is getting old."

"What's eating you, O'Shea?" Tommy said, leaning against the bar, blocking Mike's path.

"He's been in a mood since Nolan left," Maureen responded.

"Oh yeah, that's right," said Tommy. "I forgot the kid was gone for the summer. Man, you should be over the moon! The whole summer to rev up your dating life."

"That's what I keep telling him," said Maureen gleefully.

"So what's the deal?" asked Tommy.

"The deal is that he's pissed that Meghan is moving in with her long-time squeeze," she said.

"Jesus, Maureen," snapped Mike. "Do you think I can speak for myself?"

"Sorry." She downed her beer and tapped on the empty glass. "It's not like I'm lying."

"I feel for you, Mike," lamented Tommy. "It's hard to get over a relationship that has lasted as long as yours. But you know what they say — the best way to get over a woman is to get under a new one."

"Here, here!" yelled Maureen. A loud crowd of women walked in and quickly swarmed the bar, all vying to talk to Tommy.

Mike could see that Maureen's time with him was up and that his attention would be solely on his giggling customers. Many of them were ten to fifteen years younger than Maureen and definitely much prettier and more fashionable than her. Already she'd gone quiet as she nursed the beer that Tommy had pacified her with.

He felt bad for his cousin. The two of them were in the same predicament. Still holding onto impossible ideas — that maybe one day Tommy would ask her out and that Meghan would return to him.

Meghan had decided it was time to file for divorce. He had tried everything over the phone to convince her not to go through with it, but she said she had made up her mind.

"I'm not ready," he'd said to her.

"Come on, Mike," she laughed. "We haven't been together in years. I think you're ready."

"No," he said. "I've given you space over the last six years and I've waited for you to come to your senses. I've done everything you asked. I mean, my God, Meghan, you could at least try to make things work between us."

"Are you being serious?"

"I am," he said. "We've never tried counselling or that therapy stuff yet. Maureen and Loïc at least tried."

"And look what came out of that."

"But at least they tried."

"I'm sorry, Mike, but I've changed. Everyone has changed and moved on except for you."

The tension continued when she arrived for Nolan's graduation ceremony. Meghan and Dana were to stay a few days afterwards before taking Nolan back for the summer. Mike booked a table at The Keg Steakhouse so the four of them could celebrate Nolan and give Meghan a reminder of the good old days. But his grand scheme dissolved the moment Meghan showed up to the graduation with her boyfriend Rich. It all came to a head in the church parking lot while Nolan and his friends looked on.

"Despite what you think, Meghan, WE are his goddamn family!" Mike yelled.

"Well, I'm not leaving Rich out," she fired back. "That's not right!"

"What's not right is bringing your boyfriend to Nolan's graduation!"

Rich stood by himself by the church entrance, far from the drama.

"It's okay, Dad," said Dana. "It will be fine with just the three of us. You don't want Rich tagging along, anyways."

"Thank you, Dana," Meghan said in a huff.

"He's a major dick and would probably end up ruining the entire dinner," Dana added.

"Let's go, Rich," Meghan yelled. She shot a look at Dana. "Make sure the both of you are ready for brunch tomorrow. I'll be picking you up at 10:00."

A few days later, Nolan was off with his mother and Dana and Rich to Nova Scotia. Dana had offered to stay and hang out for a few more days, but Mike insisted that he was fine. He hated the idea of stewing in the empty apartment, but didn't want Dana to see him come unglued.

28

The beginning of the summer had not been kind to Sarah Jane. Since their trip to Quebec, things had gotten weird between her and Nolan. She had hoped that their moment together would draw them closer but instead it pushed him away. It got worse when he told her that he was spending the entire summer in Nova Scotia with his mother and sister.

"But why?" she asked. She sat up in her bed and pulled on the cord of her Unisonic see-through phone. "I thought we were going to spend the summer together?"

"I can't," he said. "I promised my mother that I would spend the summer with her when I cancelled my trip in March."

"But I bet, if you tell her that you have a girlfriend, she might let you stay or... or shorten your trip," she said. "My mother will be at work most of the time, you know. I would have the whole house to myself... we can be alone. We can... you know... be alone."

"Look I have to go," he said, abruptly. "My mom and sister just got here and... I have to go."

By graduation, she was an emotional wreck. She had missed a few days of school and stayed mostly in her room listening to

Debbie Gibson on her pink boom box, curled up under her polka-dot bedspread, crying and hoping he would call her.

Her room was typical of a budding teenage girl. It still held the pink colours she'd loved when she was a girl but, instead of My Little Pony and Care Bears strewn everywhere, her walls were plastered with Kirk Cameron and George Michael posters. Her mother, Claudia, sat on the side of her bed. It was not like Sarah Jane to miss this much school. She lifted the bedspread to see Sarah Jane's pale and clammy face peering from her hiding spot. She looked just as she had when she was home with tonsillitis a few years back.

"This is rotten luck, Sarah, but I think you have the flu." She felt her forehead. "The doctor's office isn't open for another hour, but I'll call him to make an appointment."

Sarah Jane was an only child and had been Claudia's main focus since the moment she was born. She'd had everything she wanted in life. If she needed a telephone line in her room or tickets to a concert or wanted to go on an expensive ski trip, Claudia did everything in her power to make it so. She worked overtime at the bank or called her ex-husband, armed with a guilt trip in her back pocket.

Claudia had spent years moulding her daughter to be the perfect child — beautiful, popular, and smart. She relished the envy of other PTA mothers who clamoured for advice with their own children. She thanked God for giving her a good Catholic girl to raise.

What Claudia treasured the most was her close relationship with her daughter. Their open communication made them seem more like girlfriends than mother and daughter. Claudia confided in her daughter about her life and she absolutely loved when her daughter did the same.

They would curl up in Claudia's bed, eating popcorn and gossiping, and Sarah Jane would tell her mother about all the goings-on with the friends she kept company with and the girls in school she hated, the teachers she loved and the ones who gave her the creeps. Most recently, she had confided to her mother her frustration with Nolan and his infatuation with his Jamaican next-door neighbour.

"Sweetie, that's just a meaningless crush," Claudia had said. "He'll recognize quality soon enough. Just be patient."

Claudia hadn't been bothered too much by what Sarah Jane had told her. She knew her daughter was too mature for many of the boys in her class. But it concerned her that her friend's son was paying so much attention to trash like Simone, so she'd called Meghan in Halifax.

"Nolan and Simone?" Meghan laughed. "Claudia, do you have rocks for brains?"

"I don't know, Megs," sighed Claudia. "When's the last time you've really sat down and talked to him? He's a teenager now. Do you really know what your son is up to?"

"I certainly do. Nolan is a good boy, but he is his father's son, and I highly doubt he's pining over some black girl."

"Well, all I'm saying is, keep a close eye on your boy when you're here for grad. From what I hear, he's always around that girl."

"Well, I know Mike," she said. "If he caught a whiff of that he would quash it immediately."

"I'm just saying," she said. "Would hate for you to end up with a bunch of half-breeds crying out for Granny."

Claudia continued to sit at her daughter's bedside. She knew that Sarah Jane had had some kind of falling out with Nolan. He didn't call much anymore, and her daughter had been a mess ever since the trip to Quebec. One minute she was happy, then cranky, and the next moment she was weepy. She didn't know whether to call a doctor or arrange for an exorcism.

"Sarah, I'm going to call work and tell them that you're home sick." She caressed Sarah Jane's head.

"No! I'm fine! I have to go to the graduation rehearsal. I'm salutatorian and if I miss the rehearsal I won't have time to see Nolan before he leaves for Nova Scotia and I need to..."

Before she could finish her sentence, she threw up all over her bedspread.

"Jesus Christ," cried Claudia. She grabbed the wastebasket. "Sarah, you are not going to school today and, at this rate, I don't even know if you will make graduation."

Sarah Jane continued to heave out most of her breakfast, gasping for air. She collapsed back in bed and began weeping.

Claudia went to the bathroom with the wastebasket. She emptied the contents into the toilet, flushing down the puke and tissues. She placed the trash bin in the bathtub, turned on the hot water and hunted under the sink for the bottle of Pinesol. She combed through the cans of hairspray and bottles of gels and came across two unopened boxes of *Always* pads.

It was then that she started to piece it all together. The mood changes. The throwing up. The paleness. The weakness. She walked back to Sarah Jane's room and found her curled up in the fetal position.

"Sarah Jane, when was the last time you had your period?"

29

Nolan sat in the passenger seat of his mother's station wagon with his window rolled down. The afternoon air smelt of salt and fish. The strong aroma of Peggy's Cove lingered as they drove along the peninsula to a small farmer's market where Meghan liked to shop. She was planning to make her famous summer stew to celebrate the new promotion she had been working towards for the last year.

She was in high spirits as they took the long route home. It was an unusually balmy afternoon, but the evening promised to bring a gentle sea breeze — perfect weather for a late-night dinner under the stars.

Nolan had been in Halifax for nearly four weeks and, despite his early misgivings, the trip so far had been a welcome relief. Getting away from everything and everyone had given him a chance to catch his breath and think. Since the night he'd had sex with Sarah Jane, things had started to get away from him. He was glad he wasn't trapped in North York, with Sarah Jane clinging to him all through the vacation. Those last days he'd seen Simone across the schoolyard during recess, and he had wished she would drag him away from Sarah Jane's side so that he could confide in her that he had made a horrible mistake.

Sarah Jane had been sick with the flu on graduation day and had missed the entire ceremony, including giving her salutatorian speech. He felt sorry for her, but a big part of him was relieved that they'd said their goodbyes over the phone. He hadn't been sure if he could look her in the eye and tell her that he would write every day or call her once a week. He definitely hadn't wanted to promise her that he wouldn't talk to another girl — not when he was planning to break up with her once he returned from Nova Scotia.

He was also glad that he wasn't around Simone either. He had messed up everything with Simone and couldn't wrap his mind around how things had changed between them. Just last summer, he'd been counting down the days until she got back from Jamaica and this year, after graduation, he couldn't leave Toronto fast enough.

He sank into the peace and quiet of living in Nova Scotia. His mother bought him a used ten-speed bike at a garage sale and he spent most of his time riding around the area. He trekked out in search of solitude and freedom. At first just North Preston, then he found a bike path that took him through the Salt Marsh Trail and out of his area, with only a few apples in his backpack. At a special point on the trail, he'd find himself on a gravel path bordered by river stones that levied the waters on each side. He would often stop here and skip rocks across the water.

The pause silenced his world. There was nothing around but the strong wind blowing through the conifer trees and the steady pecking of the shorebirds. He stopped worrying about that night with Sarah Jane or his feelings for Simone. Riding the trail silenced everything.

That same feeling flooded him as he and his mother headed back from the market. He leaned out the window, closed his eyes and basked in the warm summer breeze.

▶

TURNING off the highway to their street, they could see a few of their neighbours sitting out on their porches, cooling down. They smiled and nodded politely. The people on their street were older black Scotians whose families had been living in North Preston for several generations. Meghan had leased her home from a professor who was teaching in America and needed tenants to occupy his family home.

At first, Meghan had found the area too quiet, though she liked the decent families that surrounded her. It wasn't an extravagant home, by any means, but on a student loan and now an accountant's salary with a loan to pay back, it was the best she could do.

Mike had fiercely objected to her living in North Preston, of course, because it was a predominantly black area.

She hated how Mike always found it necessary to tell her what to do. Even separated, she still felt his controlling presence, which is probably why she had stayed in the neighbourhood for as long as she had — she couldn't let him know that he was right. Now poverty and prostitution overran the area and drug dealers traded on every corner.

"It's time to move," sighed Meghan, as they drove up their driveway. "This is not the place I loved when we first moved down here. It's ugly and desolate and, frankly, not safe anymore."

"It's only now that you realize how dingy it is?" Nolan scoffed. "Nothing about this place has changed, Mom, and it's really not all that bad, anyways."

"Yeah, well, now that I have this promotion I think I deserve to live somewhere a little nicer, like Dartmouth." She turned to him. "You would like living in Dartmouth. The neighbourhoods are better and we can find a place big enough for you to have your own room. Plus we would be around people similar to us."

"You mean white people?"

"Yes, okay!" she said, exasperated. "Is there anything wrong with that?"

"No, I guess."

She stopped the car. "Look, I have lived around these people for a long time," she quipped. "It's no picnic. If I hadn't had to live on a shoestring budget for years I would have lived somewhere better."

"Okay, Mom," he said, getting out of the car. "I get it! Can we go inside now?"

"I just don't want you thinking that I'm some kind of racist like your father. He's the one that has a problem with them. I just want a better house, okay?"

"Okay, I get it, I get it."

"Okay, sweetheart." She tousled his hair before glancing at her watch. "Oh Jesus, it's late. Rich is going to be here soon and I haven't started dinner yet."

Meghan rushed into the house with her groceries, with Nolan straggling behind her. She immediately turned on the radio to the Saturday evening broadcast of local jazz bands. Nolan sat at the kitchen table, flipping through the sports section of the paper as his mother prepared the meal. After an hour, the stew was finished and Meghan began setting the table for dinner.

▶

THAT NIGHT, Dana and Nolan ate their stew at the dinner table across from Meghan and Rich. Dana, quietly wishing it was over, remembered Saturday nights when her parents were still together, sitting around her mom's shepherd's pie with cousins Maureen and Amber. After polishing off the entire dish, the kids would take their desserts into the living room and watch television, while the adults remained at the table smoking cigarettes and drinking coffee. Mike would bring out his old deck of cards and, if it wasn't too late, Dana would sit on his lap while the adults played rounds of gin rummy and talked politics and the latest gossip late into the night.

Now, at the overly decorated dining table on the hottest day of the year in Nova Scotia, she sat in front of a bowl of stew, glaring at Rich as he combed through the real estate pages. He was dressed in his usual navy blue vest, white dress shirt, and blue striped tie. She hated that her mother had invited him to move in with them.

From the moment they met, Rich had rubbed Dana the wrong way. He was arrogant and condescending. He was vice principal at the local Catholic high school and always felt the need to correct her grammar mid-sentence. He always corrected her mother as well, acting as if Meghan was one of his students.

"I don't know, Rich," Meghan said about one of the listings. "This one only has two bedrooms. I really want a three-bedroom for when Nolan visits."

"How realistic is it to buy a three-bedroom house when Dana will probably move out soon?" he said. "A two-bedroom would be best."

"Thanks, Rich," Dana said. She tore into a piece of mountain bread. "Love that you're already moving me out before you even move in."

"That's not at all what I'm doing, Dana," he said. "I'm just saying that you're a young woman who I hope has aspirations to be on her own."

"No... no, it's fine." She got up from the table. "I'll just move back to Toronto and live with my father."

Dana walked into the living room and flipped on the television. She turned the volume up, drowning out the music that was playing in the kitchen.

Meghan got up from the table and turned off the radio.

Rich shook his head as she returned to her seat. He didn't understand why Meghan would allow Dana to disrespect her in her own home. This was the main reason he had been reluctant to move in with them. He loved Meghan, but didn't want to deal with the drama she brought — the soon-to-be-ex-husband, the wilful 21-year-old daughter, and the sullen teenage son.

Nolan got up, set his dish by the sink, and went to join Dana in the living room. He sat next to her, turned on his Walkman, and rewound Simone's mixtape to the beginning and hit play.

Rich and Meghan began cleaning up the kitchen. Dana could hear them laughing. She looked over to see Rich whispering something in Meghan's ear. Meghan giggled and slapped his shoulder playfully.

The phone rang.

Dana jumped up from her seat, happy for the distraction. She picked up the phone and smiled when she heard her father's voice on the line.

"Dad!" she said. "How are you doing?"

"Hi, sweetie," he said. "Is your mom around?"

"Yeah, I'll get her. Is everything okay?"

"Everything is fine, hon," he said. "Just get your mom."

Dana handed Meghan the phone.

"Yes, Mike," Meghan said.

Her face went from annoyance to shock. She looked over at Nolan, who was staring at the television, still listening to his Walkman.

An hour later Rich, Dana, and Nolan were sitting in the living room in front of the TV, half watching the Blue Jays game, trying to piece together what was happening and why Meghan was still screaming at Mike on the phone in her bedroom.

"What the fuck is that supposed to mean," they could hear her hollering. "You are the primary. You're responsible, not me... Yes... Yes... No, Mike... NO, you fucking wait! Would you be blaming yourself if it was Dana? Oh, I'm sure... Well, maybe I should... you're a fucking prick, Mike. Do you know that? I... would you let me talk... FUCK YOU, MIKE!"

She slammed the phone down on the cradle. Dana and Rich looked at each other, not sure what had happened. Dana then turned to Nolan, who sat terrified and pale in front of the muted television set as a fight erupted on the field.

"Nolan, what the fuck did you do?"

▶

EACH EVENING, after her shift at Laura Secord, Simone would sit in Mrs. Price's living room and go over her savings bank book, daydreaming about the computer she was planning to buy. She had gone over in her mind how many shifts it would take and the type of computer she would buy. But, as the summer marched on, she realized that she would need at least four more jobs to afford even the cheapest computer. The most she could buy was a typewriter.

Now she sat in the far corner of the food court, feeling deflated as she pored over the Grand and Toy flyer, advertising computers. She barely noticed when Sean Malcolm slipped into the seat in front of her. Sean had a part-time job at Glenview Library, adjacent to the mall.

"Hey Sean," she said. She tossed the flyer aside. "Are you off or on a break?"

"I'm off," he said, stealing a chicken nugget from her tray. "Do you want me to wait for you?"

"Nah, that's okay. I still have four more hours. I took an extra shift so I can make more money. Did you know a word processor is $1700? It might as well be a million. There is no way I can afford a computer."

"What do you need a computer for, anyways?" He picked up the discarded flyer. "Do you even know how to type?"

"Hardy har, very funny."

Simone liked their easygoing relationship. It wasn't a

confusing mess like the one with Nolan. It helped that she no longer had a crush on Sean. Once she'd taken off the rose-coloured glasses, she'd realized that Sean wasn't all that dreamy. He was just a nice boy who chewed his food like a cow, snorted a little when he laughed, and had a crooked smile.

Sean, on the other hand, had grown to like Simone – a lot. It wasn't just that she was smart and pretty, she was easy to talk to. He liked her funny accent and the way she mispronounced words. He enjoyed their banter when they had breaks together. Most of all, he just liked being with her. He wished he had more time with her so that he could ask her out on a proper date and maybe even ask her to be his girlfriend, but his father had accepted a new position in Edmonton. By the end of the summer, he'd be moving across the country with his family, starting all over again.

"Can I ask you a question?" he said. "And promise that you won't get upset with me if I ask you."

"Yeah, sure," she replied. "Ask away."

"So — what was the deal between you and Nolan," he said. He quickly shoved a fry in his mouth.

She squeezed ketchup on top of her fries. "We're just friends."

"Come on," he said. "I don't believe you."

Simone looked at him. He tried to stare her down. She giggled when he broke her stare. She had never told anyone about her and Nolan. It never occurred to her that anyone would be interested.

"We kissed a few times." She touched her face. She felt it burn red hot.

She told him about the time Nolan kissed her at the park and how hurt she had been when he started to date Sarah Jane right afterwards.

"It's weird between us now," she admitted. "Sometimes I think we won't ever be that way again."

"Really?" he said. "I see the way he looks at you, even while dating Sarah Jane. I could tell that he still liked you. Everyone saw it. Trust me, even Sarah Jane knew."

"Seriously?" she said. It made her smile a little, knowing that Sarah Jane had been jealous of her.

"Yeah, seriously. You know what the craziest thing I heard about you both… well… maybe I shouldn't say."

"No, tell me! I want to know."

"Well… you know… everyone thinks that you guys did it," he said.

"What!" she yelled, spitting out fries. "That is NOT true!"

"Okay, okay — don't choke on your food." He laughed as he handed her a napkin.

"It's not funny, Sean." She snatched the napkin from him.

"I'm sorry. I don't want you to think that I believed that stuff. I just… I don't know, I just thought—"

"Oh, you thought I'm the type of girl who does it," she spat out. "Because I'm not, okay! I'm not that kind of girl and I wish everyone would stop thinking that."

"Simone, I don't think that! I promise," he said. "I guess I just thought that because of Nolan and Sarah Jane—"

"What about Nolan and Sarah Jane?"

"I heard that she got pregnant," he said, lowering his voice. "I guess I just assumed that…that you and him…well since she and him—"

"Wait, what do you mean she got pregnant? Where did you hear that?"

"From my mother. Sarah Jane's mom and my mom became friends after we started dating and, well…anyways, she called, hysterical, worried that Sarah Jane might be pregnant."

"Are you serious?"

"Yeah, my mom told me last night," he said. "She and my dad came into my room, asking me a lot of questions about Sarah Jane and me. They wanted to make sure that I wasn't doing it — which I'm not, but they weren't sure if Sarah Jane and I did — which we didn't."

"My God," Simone said in disbelief. "Are you sure?"

"Yeah," he said. He ate another fry. "From what my parents told me, Sarah Jane may end up getting an abortion."

"An abortion?" she asked.

"You know… getting rid of the baby," he said. "That's why she called my mother. My aunt used to run a clinic back home and knew of some places in Toronto."

Simone was stunned by Sean's revelation. She couldn't believe Nolan would do something as stupid as have sex, let alone get someone pregnant. Her heart sank. Nolan had seemed different. Before he left for the Maritimes he was much angrier and moodier than usual. She thought it was because of Kester's death. Neither of them had been the same since the suicide.

"I'm just glad that I avoided that train wreck," he said. "That could have easily been me or maybe even you."

"I have to go, Sean." She got up to grab her stuff. "My break is over and I don't want Mabel thinking that I forgot about my shift."

"I can stick around until you finish," he said, "and then walk you home or something."

"No… no, I'm good." She forced a smile. "I'll see you tomorrow."

"See you tomorrow," he said, sounding a little disappointed.

Simone worked quietly the rest of the afternoon. Her talk with Sean filled her thoughts. She couldn't understand how someone her age was able to have sex without getting caught. Wasn't Mike always around? She was sure Sarah Jane's mother was always around. She had seen her at every school function. Maybe Sean was just hearing rumours or his parents were mixed up. Maybe they meant Brian Kepler and Vivian Moretti. They had been going out since the beginning of the year and everyone knew that they were doing it. Some even swore that they did it after school by the willow tree, but Simone never believed that. Kids in her school were always spreading outrageous rumours. But, as the evening wore on, Simone knew deep down that what Sean had said was the truth.

On her way home, she pondered whether her mother had been right all along. Maybe Nolan had pushed her away because she wouldn't do those kinds of things with him. It made her sick to her stomach to think what would have happened if she had got pregnant. Then she stopped in her tracks and realized that Sarah Jane was probably not going to St. Joseph in the fall. It wasn't that she felt bad for her, but she couldn't stop thinking of how hard Sarah Jane had worked the entire year. It had been a neck-and-neck race between her and Ilene to be the top student in their class. While Simone had also been near the top, she couldn't keep up with the severe competition between the two girls. They were always vying for the top test score, best science project, even running against each other for class President. Ironically, they ended up tying for top student, with Simone coming in second and James Chow third, only losing to Simone by one percent.

What is Sarah Jane going to do now? she wondered. *Would she have to drop out of school and start back up a year later?*

She kept going back to what Sean had said about an abortion. She didn't know exactly what that meant, but she had heard enough during health class to know that abortions were bad. She couldn't imagine killing a baby, but Sarah Jane was too young to have one.

When she arrived home, she felt even more confused than ever. She didn't know what to do. She wished she had Nolan's number in Halifax. She had to speak to him. To find out what was going on. To scream at him for being such an idiot. To just listen to why he did it. To ask him what she could do to make things easier on him.

As she walked down the hall, she saw Mike coming out of his apartment, juggling a duffle bag and a cup of coffee while trying to find his keys.

"Hi, Mr. Mike, how's Nolan?" she blurted out. Mike was

scrambling to find his keys. He barely looked at Simone. "I haven't heard from him in a while."

"He's fine," Mike replied. He located his keys and started locking up his apartment. His eyes looked weary, as if he hadn't slept in a few days.

"I didn't get a chance to see him before he went to Nova Scotia," she said, following him to the elevator. "I don't have his telephone number. Would you be able to give me his phone number so I can call him up?"

"I'm sorry, Simone, but I'm late for work," he replied. "Can this wait?"

"Sure," she said. "Whenever you have a chance, Mr. Mike."

Mike scurried into the elevator that had just opened up. She waved goodbye, but he didn't seem to notice. He was too distracted to even notice that she had tears streaming down her face.

▶

MIKE HATED BRUSHING OFF SIMONE. She had always been a good friend to Nolan, despite all his fears, but he couldn't stop to talk to her, let alone try and remember Meghan's telephone number. All he wanted to do was finish off his shift at McKinney's and catch the flight out to Halifax that evening. Meghan had called a lawyer and filed for sole custody of Nolan. Mike was beside himself with panic. The thought of Nolan being taken from him made him out of sorts. He had talked to a lawyer friend of Maureen's, who had suggested that he get in touch with a colleague in Halifax.

He had been fighting with Meghan daily ever since they found out that Nolan had gotten Sarah Jane pregnant. Mike couldn't figure out how Nolan could have had a moment alone with Sarah Jane, let alone long enough to have sex. All they did was go to the movies and talk on the phone.

"You are the reason he's in this mess," Meghan said over and over to him on the phone. "You should have known that the two of them were in that kind of relationship."

"They were not doing it in my house," he replied. "Nolan is home every night and doesn't bring girls home. I made sure of that."

"Really, Mike? Because you fucked up somewhere with your foolproof system."

He had called Claudia, hoping to figure out how this could have happened. He'd tried to find a way to piece the whole thing together. To figure out where things went wrong, but Claudia ripped into him as well.

"What do you mean, am I sure?" she cried out. "The doctor says she's pregnant. The four home tests say she's pregnant. The second blood test I ordered, just to *be* sure, says she's pregnant. So trust me, Mike, she's pregnant!"

"I get it, Claudia, but I don't understand how it could have happened," he said. "And she's sure that it's Nolan who's the father? Because the two of them only went to the movies and the arcade. I never allowed them to come to the apartment without me being there."

"Unbelievable!" she screamed, into the phone. "Un-fucking-believable! Are you calling my daughter a whore? You need to look at Nolan and not my Sarah! He's probably used to fucking that little black bitch next door to you. Maybe you should examine how your son got my daughter pregnant, because I truly believe she was coerced into having sex with him."

"Come off it, Claudia," he shot back. "Your daughter has been waiting to spread her legs for Nolan since she grew tits. We all know that..."

Click.

Dial tone.

"Fucking bitch." He slammed the phone back on the cradle, nearly pulling the base off the wall. He wanted to call Claudia back and call her every name in the book, but he knew that it would result either in her hanging up on him again or her calling the police.

When he contacted the Halifax lawyer, John Mason, he was met with sombre news. He was told that, with circumstances the way they were, a judge could award custody to Meghan.

"I'm sorry, Michael," he said, over the phone. "It looks like an uphill battle. Even though you've raised Nolan all these years, the fact that he is fourteen and got a fourteen-year-old girl pregnant works against you. I mean, if the kids were older, say sixteen or seventeen, the case wouldn't get off the ground, but the reality is that this happened under your care."

"Come on, man," he said. "There has to be something I can do."

"Be at the hearing," Mason suggested. "Plead your side of the story. Tell the judge that you will reduce your hours at work and be home with your son in the evenings. Tell him that you've done the best you can, with the limited resources you've had, since your wife left you, but you'll do better to improve Nolan's home life."

"Okay, okay," he said. "I'll come. I'll leave tonight."

Next morning, Mike woke up in the motel he'd booked for the week. The sun was peering through the blinds onto his face. He had barely slept, worried that he wouldn't wake up in time for the 9:00 am hearing. He looked over at the motel clock. It was barely 6:30 am. He could have another hour of sleep, but he got up.

He tried to determine what to do next. His mind had been so consumed with the emergency hearing that he wasn't even sure how to get started that morning. He showered and shaved. He put on the blue suit he'd worn to Nolan's graduation and looked in the mirror and noticed how tired his eyes seemed. He didn't want to go to court looking hung over. He needed coffee. Something to perk him up.

He headed to the diner across the street and had breakfast and coffee. It was a nice diner, but a little yuppie for his taste. It had so many different types of coffee, he wasn't even sure if he was ordering a cup or a science experiment.

"Do you have any regular plain coffee?" he asked the waitress.

"Of course we do," she said. "Our specialty coffee for today is Jamaican Blue Mountain. It's a limited special, so get it while it's hot."

"Sure, I'll have a cup," he said.

She came back with a mug and the aroma reminded him of Pam and he instantly wished she was here with him and not in Jamaica. She would definitely know what to do.

After breakfast, he headed over to the courthouse. It was an hour before the trial and he sat in the lobby, hoping that his lawyer would recognize him. At 8:30, a man with a cup of coffee in each hand greeted him.

"Mike O'Shea, I presume?"

Mike nodded.

"John Mason." He handed him a cup. "I hope you like it strong because both of us need to be on our game if we're going to convince Judge Altan that this was a one-time mistake."

"What's he like?" Mike sipped the coffee. It was horrible. It tasted more like ground-up dirt than coffee. It completely ruined the taste of the wonderful cup he'd had earlier.

"*She* is a liberal gas bag who always has an agenda," he said. "I've stood in front of her many times, so let me do all the talking. Keep your answers short, and only speak to her if she addresses you."

They walked into the courtroom. Meghan was sitting next to her lawyer, with Rich behind them.

Mike felt his whole body tense up when he saw them. *Who the fuck does he think he is, showing up here.* He gulped more of the coffee to calm himself down.

Meghan glanced up at him briefly and whispered something to her lawyer. The lawyer peered over at Mike and then whispered something back at her.

Mike took a seat at his table next to John Mason and waited grimly for the case to be heard.

It felt like hours until finally the judge entered the courtroom and they all rose. Meghan's lawyer began the proceedings by arguing that Mike was in no condition to raise a fourteen-year-old teenager. He described Nolan as a depressed young man whose grades had slipped over the last year. He then presented copies of Nolan's previous report cards.

"What the hell is this?" Mike said to John. "He's not depressed."

"Let me handle this," John said. "Don't come off as defensive, okay?"

Meghan's lawyer then continued to argue that the result of the past year's neglect was an unwanted pregnancy in a fourteen-year-old girl and that it was due to lack of supervision, specifically by the father, Mr. O'Shea.

Mike's neck started to scorch.

When it was John's turn, he smiled at the judge and went into a compelling argument about Mike's parenting skills and how he was a good father to Nolan. He described how Meghan had left Mike to pursue an education in a distant province and, while that was commendable, she had made the decision to leave Nolan with Mike. He argued that she must have known full well at that time that Mike was capable of raising a young boy by himself and that her sudden change of heart now was pure selfishness. He described the past five years, demonstrating that Mike had done an exceptional job with Nolan. He had fed him, clothed him, and made sure he had ample care, without any help from his wife, even after she had graduated from college and achieved gainful employment.

Meghan O'Shea's claim for full custody, he went on, was purely out of spite. He said that Meghan had never had a role in Nolan's upbringing from the moment they separated and her threat for full custody was in response to Mike holding up their current divorce proceedings.

Mike could tell that the judge was listening intently to John's argument. He didn't feel good about the way Meghan was being attacked, but relaxed a little when his lawyer went on to talk about the pregnancy as being a mistake in judgment by all parties involved.

"I see," said Judge Altan. "And what plans have been made regarding the baby?"

"As far as we know, nothing has been decided on," stumbled John. He looked at Mike for an answer.

"My Lord, we have a written affidavit from a clinic in Peterborough, Ontario, indicating that the young woman Nolan impregnated had an abortion last week," said Meghan's lawyer. "Which will free Nolan from being morally or financially obligated to the child or its mother."

"Abortion!" Mike said. He stood up in court. "For God's sake, doesn't Nolan have the right to decide what happens to his kid?"

"Mike, sit down," John whispered under his breath.

"No, no... I want to hear what he has to say," said Judge Altan. "Continue, Mr. O'Shea."

"I'm sorry, your honour, but I'm Catholic and so is Sarah Jane and Nolan's mother and our entire family, and we don't believe in abortions," he proclaimed. "Nolan made a mistake, maybe, but doesn't he have rights?"

"Was Nolan informed about the decision?" asked the judge.

"Yes, your honour," stated Meghan's lawyer. He stood up to address the court. "Nolan agreed it would be the best decision, and he signed off on it."

"This is bullshit... bullshit," Mike yelled. "Meghan, the least you could have done was talk to me. This was a fucking decision that I should have been included in."

"While I understand your frustration, Mr. O'Shea, I ask that you please watch your language," Judge Altan reprimanded him.

"I'm sorry, your honour," he said weakly. "It's just not right."

"So tell me, Mr. O'Shea," she asked, "if the baby had not been aborted, would you expect Nolan at the age of fourteen to help raise the child?"

"Yes, of course," he said. "We would have done what was right financially and morally."

"And what if what's right for Nolan is to get an education?" she asked. "Wouldn't that be best for Nolan or for the young girl that got pregnant?"

"Look, I'm not saying that Nolan would have to quit school right away or anything," he said. "I'm just saying that for a few years I would help him and then when he was old enough he would do right by this baby."

John sat back down in his chair and flipped his pen on the table.

"Will he work..." she looked down at her papers. "...at a bar or as a university janitor or maybe hold several odd jobs like you?"

"If that means taking care of his responsibilities, then the answer is yes," he said defensively. "There is nothing wrong with making an honest living and working hard."

"You're right, Mr. O'Shea, there is nothing wrong with it," she said, in agreement. "Thank you, Mr. O'Shea. We will adjourn for now and resume tomorrow morning with my decision."

When she adjourned the court, Mike glanced at John, who was slumped in his chair. John took his glasses off and rubbed his eyes as Meghan, Rich, and her lawyer left the courtroom.

"I asked you to do one thing," he said. "To keep your goddamn mouth shut."

▶

ON THE TRAIN RIDE HOME, Mike sat in silence. He was glad there were barely any other passengers. The last thing he wanted was some stranger yapping in his ear, telling their life story when his own seemed to be crumbling around him.

The last few days had been his worst nightmare.

The judge returned a decision in favour of Meghan, claiming that Meghan's financial standing was better than Mike's. Her recent promotion and plans to move to a better neighbourhood were among the deciding factors. Also, a letter Meghan had written to the judge further explained why she felt Nolan would fare better with her. She firmly believed that, now that the baby was no longer a factor, Nolan should have the chance to start over in the loving, nurturing environment that she and her fiancé could provide in Halifax.

Despite her ruling, the judge did commend Mike on being a single father. She told him that most fathers would never take up that responsibility. She was sorry that, despite all he had done for Nolan, his financial status had led to a lack of supervision for his son, and she believed it would be best for Nolan to stay with his mother, where there would be two adults in the household.

She indicated that Nolan would stay with his mother for six months, and at that time she would revisit the case to see what improvements Mike had made. If Mike could then prove that he could properly care for Nolan, the decision might be reversed.

Judge Altan then addressed Meghan.

"Mrs. O'Shea, I truly believe that no parent can stop a child from being sexually active. But in this day and age, both you and Mr. O'Shea should have made it a priority to talk to your son about contraceptives and warn him about STDs. Children are subjected to sex everywhere they turn and it is up to the parents to properly guide them by informing them of the risks of being sexually active and provide them some sort of protection.

"By no means is this ruling a punishment of Mr. O'Shea. He has done the best he could. Had the young woman decided to keep the baby, I would have sided with him, allowing Nolan to return home to face his responsibilities. That being said, I believe that children Nolan's age should not be hindered by a poor decision. Nolan deserves a second chance and I believe that giving custody to you is that second chance."

The court was adjourned and Mike walked out, unable to grasp what had happened.

"This is not the end," John said. "It's a temporary ruling with some time for you to get your life situated. Find a better job that will keep you home more, and maybe purchase a house in a nice neighbourhood. Once the judge sees that you're making an effort she will rule in your favour."

"I'm done," Mike said. "I can't deal with this now. Meghan has gotten her way throughout this entire marriage and I'm tired of fighting her on everything."

"Don't give up, man." John patted Mike on the shoulder. "Don't give up on Nolan."

"I'm not giving up on Nolan. I... I just can't think about this right now."

The next day he went to see Nolan and Dana. He drove up Meghan's driveway just as Dana came running out the door. When she saw her father, she ran into his arms, sobbing.

"I'm sorry, Dad," she said. "I'm so sorry."

"It's okay, honey." He could see Meghan standing at the front door watching them. "Just have your brother come out. I want to talk to him before I head back to Toronto."

"Sure, Dad." She wiped the tears from her face, went back into the house, and called Nolan.

Meghan stood by the doorway, looking at him. He wanted to say something to her but there wasn't much point. Nolan finally emerged from behind his mother. She touched his head as he walked past her.

"Hi, Dad," Nolan said.

"Hi, Nols," he replied. "I just wanted to say goodbye before I head back."

"Okay," Nolan said, looking at the ground. Then he started to cry. He raised his arm to cover his eyes. "I'm so sorry, Dad. I didn't want any of this to happen. I'm so sorry for everything. Please don't hate me."

Mike pulled him into an embrace and kissed him on his forehead. "Hey, hey, Nolan. I don't hate you. I can never ever hate you. You made a mistake is all."

"Mom says that I'm going to live with her now," he whispered. "Why can't I come home?"

"I don't know, buddy," he said, trying to keep it together. "I wish I could change things but... look, I just need you to do good in school, okay? Keep your marks up and make me proud."

"Okay."

"We'll talk on the phone all the time and I'll definitely see you Christmas," he promised as he wiped the tears from Nolan's eyes. "And if you can't come back for Christmas, I promise that I'll come up myself. Okay?"

Nolan nodded.

Mike kissed his cheek hard and then pulled him into another strong hug before walking back to his rental car. As he drove away, both of his kids were watching. A guttural cry emerged as he looked back. When he was out of sight of the house, he pulled over to the side of the road and broke down.

▶

BY THE TIME the train arrived in Toronto, he was emotionally drained and physically exhausted. He walked up to the platform, duffle bag in his hand, and turned the corner. Pam was standing there at the edge of the platform, smiling at him. When he got close he hugged her tightly. They stood for a while, holding each other before he broke away.

"Come on," she said, linking her arm with his. "I'm parked somewhere around here."

Mike stopped and pulled her back. "Thank you, Pam," he said

feebly.

She looked at him and gently pressed her forehead against his before lightly kissing him on the lips. It was the kind of kiss that conjured a warmth that he had desperately sought and missed in Nova Scotia. A feeling he couldn't elicit from sex with Joanna or recreate with Meghan. He felt something rejuvenate in him, something that silenced his marred pride.

"Come on, old man," she said. "I'm hungry and you're treating."

"Okay," he said, sighing deeply, glad to be back in Toronto.

30

A few days after she returned from Jamaica, Pam's suitcase arrived. She could tell the bags had been rifled through. Some of her clothes and the bottle of Appleton Rum were missing.

"Typical," she said to herself. The reggae tapes she'd bought for Simone had been opened. She was glad that at least the tapes weren't damaged.

◀◀

IT HADN'T BEEN the glamorous getaway her co-workers would have pictured. The hour-long bus drive from Kingston airport to Mandeville was all stops and starts, and the bus was filled with commuters coming home from jobs in the capital. Pam felt uncomfortable sandwiched between strangers with CJ asleep on her lap. She wished that Annalise had picked them up from the airport, but she'd fallen ill with vertigo a few days earlier and hadn't been well enough to make the long drive.

"If yuh gwaan stay pon mi transport di return trip is $500 Jamaican dollars," said a voice.

Pam awoke startled and embarrassed. She had fallen asleep and the driver was shaking her by the shoulders. She and CJ were the only passengers left on the bus.

"We're in Mandeville?" she asked. She got out of her seat with the sleeping child.

"Yes, mam." The driver lit a cigarette.

"Thank you," she said, handing him five American dollars. "Can I trouble you to get our bags for us? They were placed underneath the bus."

The driver left their bags on the side of the road by the stop's bench. It was dusk, but she still recognized the main street. It looked exactly the same as it had fourteen years ago. The same shops and broken-up sidewalks. The same palm trees lining the block. It felt as if time had stood still, waiting for her to come back, right where she'd left off. She started to feel nervous as people walked past her. Would they remember her? Would they call her out by name? *Maybe if I return to Kingston and phone Annalise and tell her that we missed our flight, I can go back home,* she thought.

She heard a horn honk behind her. Annalise was waving frantically from the passenger side of a shiny brown Buick.

"Pamela!"

Annalise got out of the car and hobbled carefully toward her, steadying herself with a cane. Pam rushed to her so she wouldn't have to cross the street. She was shocked at how much Annalise had changed. Two years back, when she came to Toronto, she'd looked vibrant and healthy. Now she seemed frail and worn down and much older.

"Hello, Annalise."

They hugged warmly.

"You look good," the old woman replied cheerfully. "You got fat but yuh look good." She squeezed her as hard as she could and then turned to CJ, who was hiding behind Pam. "Lawd Jesus, Caleb Jr., you look so much like your fadda. He get big, eeh? Mi hope the clothes mi buy him still fit," she said, pulling him into a hug. "Come nuh! Granny miss you."

"I missed you too," he said, kissing her on her cheek. "Your hair is all white now."

"Yes, well, your Granny is getting old," she replied.

"Yeah, but you were still old last summer."

"CJ!" Pam said loudly. "Behave yourself."

"Leave him, a true he tell me. I haven't been by the beauty shop since I fell and now all mi grey come back with a vengeance." Annalise smiled at the man in the Buick's driver seat. "Look see, Arley, this is my grandson and his mother. Pamela, this is my neighbour Silvia's nephew Arley."

"Nice to meet you," said Pam.

Arley looked up at her and nodded, then climbed out of the car to retrieve their bags.

"Come, nuh," Annalise said, guiding them into the car. "Let's get going before it gets too dark."

The trip to her house took another twenty minutes. Annalise had a beautiful home in Swaby's Hope. It had been an old run-down plantation house that Caleb's father had renovated when they first purchased it. The house was painted light blue with white shutters. It resembled one of those old Southern American homes with its wrap-around porch and screen-covered veranda. Caleb had talked fondly of his childhood home. He had hoped that, when he retired, he would go back to Jamaica and live there again.

Pam carried their bags to the guest rooms. Hers had a large closet and a picture window and an attached bathroom. It was almost like staying in a hotel.

That night, Annalise had her housekeeper feed them a dinner of curry goat, rice and peas. Pam salivated at the aroma. The curry goat and potatoes melted in her mouth. The goat she bought in

Canada was frozen meat from New Zealand and never tasted this fresh. The curry, pepper, and flavour of the goat swirled in her mouth and she started to remember what she loved most about Jamaica. The food was better than anything she ever had in Canada.

Shortly after dinner, Annalise went to bed. After putting CJ to sleep, Pam took a long shower to wash away the day's grime and sweat. She lingered for a while as the nice cool water ran down her body. Afterwards, she sat on her bed wrapped in a bath towel, looking through her purse for her hand cream. A piece of paper fell out. The telephone number of Linda's cousin was scrawled on it. She had promised Linda that she would call him. She looked down at her watch. 9:00 pm.

"Well, let me get this over with and then I can toss this paper." She picked up the phone and dialed.

The phone rang and rang.

"Hello," she finally heard over the line.

"Yes, hello," she said, trying to sound very proper. "This is Pamela Allen calling. Am I speaking with Dexter Stewart?"

"This is Dex," he said. "What is it?"

"Sorry, I am Linda's friend." She started to stumble. "She told me to give you a call when I get into town."

"Linda who?" he asked.

"Linda… your cousin from Toronto?"

"You mean Belinda?" he said. "Yes, I know her. She's my Aunt's daughter. What about her?"

"She told me to give you a call when I got into town," Pam said. "I'm sorry, did I call at a bad time? I thought Linda had contacted you to let you know that I would be calling."

"No," he said.

"This obviously was a mistake," she said. "Linda gave me your number but… please excuse me for interrupting you."

"Wait nuh," he said. He rustled with the phone, then came back on the line. "You caught me dead asleep and I'm still a little sleepy. I'm awake now. Please start again."

"My name is Pam and I'm friends with your cousin in Toronto," she said. She paused to calm down. "She gave me your number and said to give you a call when I'm in town."

"I see," he said. "Look, I think I know why she gave you my number. It's nothing against you or anything, but my entire family has been trying to fix me up with some woman or another. It's starting to get embarrassing and honestly I'm too busy to deal with their nonsense."

Pam felt foolish sitting on the phone listening to this man chastise her. She wanted to slam the phone down on his ear. She couldn't believe how rude he was.

"Look, sah," she said. "As I said, this was a mistake." She could feel her blood continue to boil. "Forgive me for calling you and good night."

"Easy nuh," he said. "Mi wasn't finished. I was going to say that you sound like an innocent bystander to my family's foolishness. Where are you staying?"

"In Swaby's Hope," she said. "I'm staying with my family."

"Well that's not entirely too far," he said. "Tomorrow I have a meeting in Mandeville. There's a new restaurant I promised to visit called Little Ochie. We can meet there for dinner at 7:00 pm."

"Fine," she said.

"Good," he replied.

Pam stayed there on the line, unsure of what just happened. He had just hung up. This was probably the rudest man she had ever encountered. She wanted to call Linda and tell her how ill-bred he was and that there was a reason he was a successful bachelor — he successfully turns off any woman he meets. But she was too tired to deal with it. She promised herself that she would call him back the next day to cancel.

The next morning, Pam was awakened by CJ crawling on top of her.

"Mommy, mommy, wake up!" he yelled at the top of his lungs. "You promised that we would go swimming today. You promised that we would go first ting."

"First THING," she corrected him.

"First thing, Mommy!" he said, jumping up and down on her bed.

"Calm down, CJ! Just let me get dressed and get some tea and then we'll go."

She looked over at the alarm clock. It was almost 11:00 am. She had slept the entire morning. She staggered into the kitchen.

"I tried to keep him from waking you," said Annalise. "Come eat something before you go. Delilah saved some bammy and ackee for you."

After breakfast, Pam and CJ climbed into Annalise's car and Arley drove them to Treasure Beach. Annalise had hired Arley for the summer to take Pam around since she was unable to drive herself. He had been out of work for some time, so Annalise gave him odd jobs around the house to keep him busy and to give him some sense of worth while he struggled with unemployment.

Pam could understand why someone like Arley couldn't find work. Although Annalise had told her little, she'd found out that he was in his mid-30s despite looking much older. His burly and rough exterior resembled that of a sugar-cane field hand. He was also way too quiet, so probably wouldn't make it as a tourist driver. In Jamaica, the tourism industry was king. All you needed was a keen sense of the island's history and the ability to turn on your personality, just to make the frightened white people comfortable with your black skin.

"What do you do for a living?" Pam asked him as they drove.

"Odd jobs, Miss Pam," he said.

"No, I mean what's your trade?" she said.

"Odd jobs, Miss," he responded again before turning on the radio.

When they got to the beach, Pam relished the cool breeze. The day was getting hotter, but being by the sea instantly cooled them down. Arley stayed in the car reading his paper. He was under strict instructions to stay with them like a personal bodyguard.

Pam played in the ocean with CJ. She spent most of the afternoon teaching her son how to float on his back. Towards the end of the day she sat on the beach and watched CJ attempt it by himself.

"Look at me, Mommy," CJ cried out. He floated with ease. "I wish Mike was here to see me! Take a picture, Mommy, so you can show him."

"Okay, baby," she said. She pulled out her camera and took a picture of CJ by the shore.

She hoped things were okay with Mike. Since Meghan had asked for a divorce, he had started to spiral down. He seemed depressed and had broken off his relationship with his new girl-friend, claiming she was just a distraction. She'd thought about inviting him to join her and CJ in Jamaica, but had quickly dismissed the idea. She was there to meet someone, not have Mike there as a chaperone. Still, she felt bad that he was in Toronto, by himself, for the entire summer.

"Miss Pam, it is getting late, we need to leave," advised Arley.

"Oh yes." Pam suddenly remembered she'd completely forgotten to cancel her plans with Dex. "Let's go, CJ." She turned to Arley. "Can you drive me to Alligator Pond this evening?"

He nodded.

Pam was not looking forward to dinner with Dex. If he wasn't Linda's cousin, she would have stood him up, but the last thing she wanted was to make Linda look bad.

She dressed in her long bright tangerine summer dress, but barely had time to put on makeup. She just grabbed her straw hat to cover her newly washed hair and took a quick glance at the hallway mirror. If this date had been of any significance she would have pressed and styled her hair, but she left it wet and curly.

"Clean and presentable," she said to herself

She felt refreshed after the wonderful day at the beach. She'd forgotten how much she loved the feeling of sand between her toes and salt water against her skin. It was pure heaven.

Arley pulled into Alligator Pond. Little Ochie was packed with patrons. It seemed secluded and far away from the world, a nice quaint place by the sea and not a stuffy hotel restaurant.

Pam dismissed Arley, telling him that she'd probably get a ride from her date. She wandered into the restaurant and looked through the crowd. She wasn't sure if she would be able to make Dex out. Linda had only described him as bookish.

"Can I help you miss?" asked a cute hostess.

"I'm meeting someone here for dinner," she said, looking around. "His name is Dex Stewart."

"Oh, yes," she said. "He's been expecting you. Follow me."

Pam followed the hostess to a quieter part of the restaurant, away from the bar, where most of the patrons were watching a soccer game. She was slightly surprised when she arrived at his table. For some reason, she'd expected a short wiry man who looked old enough to be her father, but instead she met a man a few inches taller than her with a smooth olive-brown complexion and soft curly black hair. He was dressed in a well-fitted grey Italian suit, with wingtip shoes, and his cuffs were closed with gold cufflinks.

"You're over an hour late," he said, looking up from the newspaper he was reading. "I was just about to leave."

Pam froze. She glanced at the clock on the restaurant's wall. She squirmed. It was 8:15 pm. She felt a sting when she saw the scowl on his face.

"Well, hello to you, Dex," she said. She sat down and placed her beaded clutch on the table. "I'm sorry for being late, but I'm here now."

"Yes, well, let's order quickly." He dropped the paper on the table and waved the waitress to their table.

Pam looked at him angrily. She had barely even sat down and he was ordering dinner?

"I'm sorry, but can you come back when I've had a moment to look at the menu?" she said to the waitress. "In the meantime, I would like a soursop."

Dex sighed impatiently as the waitress left.

Pam tried to concentrate on her menu, but she couldn't hide her growing contempt for him. She had thought his impertinence on the telephone was a case of a bad first impression, but she was starting to see that this crude attitude was normal. Again, no wonder he was a forever bachelor. Any smart woman would run for the hills after dealing with him.

After ordering their meals, they sat in silence. At least he had put the paper down and didn't sit there reading it in front of her. They hunched at the table in complete silence until she figured that she was expected to start a conversation.

"So, you're a lawyer?"

"Yes," he replied.

"What kind of law do you practise?"

"Corporate and commercial law."

"Interesting," she said. "I know some lawyers. I work as the head of hospital administration at Toronto East Medical Centre. We work closely with our legal team when dealing with lawsuits."

Pam then told him everything she did at the hospital. There was hardly any interest from Dex. She told him about her children. He kept silent. She kept talking. Finally, their food arrived.

"How is your jerk lobster?" she asked him.

"Fine," he replied.

"Well, my red snapper is fantastic," she said. "You know you could participate in this date."

"You seem to be handling all the talking for the both of us."

"Are you always this rude?" She threw her napkin on her plate. She got up to leave the table.

"Pam, wait," he said.

She turned around.

He stood up from his seat. "You forgot to pay for your part of the bill."

Pam looked at him, furious, and pulled out some cash from her purse and threw it down on the table. She then picked up her drink and threw it in his face.

"You're a jackass and mi sorry for the woman that ends up with you," she said. "Go fuck yourself."

Pam left the restaurant fuming. She had never dealt with someone that rude and arrogant. She stood outside for a moment and then went back inside to ask the waitress to call a taxi for her. She had waited for nearly ten minutes when Dex emerged from the restaurant.

"You know you forgot your meal," he said, holding up a doggie bag.

She continued to look up the road, ignoring him.

"Look, I'm sorry for being a jackass back there," he said. "When I get annoyed I get mean."

She continued to ignore him until she saw her taxi pull up.

"I can't let you leave like this," he said. "At least let me drive you back to your place."

He turned to the driver, giving him ten American dollars.

"Sorry for the trouble, but we don't need a lift," he said.

"Says who?" she said, opening the taxi door. "Who the hell are you, anyways?"

"A regretful man," he said. He pulled her aside to let a group of British tourists take the taxi. "Please let me take you home."

She had no choice. It was getting late and the only money she had had gone towards the dinner. She motioned for him to go ahead to his car.

"Where are you staying?" he asked. "Not too far, I hope."

"Swaby's Hope," she muttered. "The first house off the highway."

They got into his car and drove off.

"You know this date wouldn't have been so bad if you weren't such an inconsiderate woman," he said. "You were over an hour late."

She looked at him scornfully. "Did you offer to give me a ride home just to piss me off? If that's your plan, then let me off right here and I'll walk the rest of the way."

"No...no," he said. "I just wanted to explain my behaviour."

"Well, if you want to know what I think, it's no wonder your cousin and your entire damn family tries so hard to pawn you off on some poor unsuspecting woman." She laughed bitterly. "They probably are sick of your pompous, arrogant ways and hope that some eediat woman will take you off their hands. Maybe make Christmas and Easter gatherings more bearable. That's what I think."

Dex looked a little hurt. Pam realized that she had hit a nerve and smiled to herself as they continued to ride through the night. After a few minutes, he pulled up to the house. Before she was able to close the door properly, he sped off along the dirt road. He did a U-turn.

"You jackass," she yelled after him, jumping back to avoid being run over. She picked up a rock and hurled it at his car but missed. She stumbled up the driveway and to the front door, hunting for the house key in her purse.

"Miss Pam," she heard a voice call out from across the yard. "Is that you?"

Pam turned to see Arley working on the Buick in the garage.

"Is that you, Arley?" she called out. She walked towards him. "What are you doing up so late?"

"Just cleaning out the car," he said. "Lots of sand is no good for a car."

"I'm sorry," she said. "That's our fault. Let me help you."

"No, Miss," he said. "It's no bother. It gives me something to do."

"No, man, I insist." She grabbed a rag and started wiping little specks of sand off the back seat. She couldn't believe how messy she'd left the car. "I guess he was right."

"Who's right?" he asked.

"The man that dropped me off," she said. "He said I was an inconsiderate woman."

Arley continued to clean.

"What? Do you agree?"

"Well," he said, trying not to offend, "I just think that you've spent too much time in Canada. Picking up their ways. I worked for the airport for almost ten years and the one thing I noticed is that the white people think that, because they're on vacation, the entire island is there to pick up after them."

Pam was at a loss for words. She wanted to argue that wasn't true, but she knew he was right. That attitude was the first thing she'd noticed when she arrived in Toronto. Canadians felt they were owed something. Now she was so used to feeling entitled that it was a shock to her system when she realized that she had forgotten the basic manners she had grown up on.

"I guess I didn't realize how much I've changed," she said, sitting in the back seat.

"It happens," he said. "Now that you're home it will all come back to you."

Pam laughed out loud as she wiped down the leather seats. The two of them continued to clean the car as she rehashed her date with Dex. Arley smiled when she told him that she had thrown her drink at him.

"But, Miss Pam, you should have thrown *his* drink."

"Chups, I really should have," she said. "That soursop taste nice."

He started to laugh heartily.

It was the first time she'd seen him laugh. He had seemed so quiet and serious.

"You know, Arley, I like this version of you," she said after they'd finished polishing the dashboard. "You have a nice smile when you use it."

"Well, that was very nice and considerate of you," he said, smiling.

"Any time." She yawned. "Boy, it's getting late. I better get some sleep."

He walked her to the door and stood by the gate, making sure that she made it inside. She turned to him and smiled before entering the house.

The next weeks flew by. Pam and CJ spent many days at the beach. Often they would pack a lunch and head over with a blanket and spend hours, while Arley remained in his car reading a newspaper until they were done. Sometimes he would run errands for Annalise and return to pick them up.

One very hot day, Pam could feel beads of sweat running down her face. Arley was sitting in the burning hot car, reading the paper, with all the windows down and doors open. She got up, shook the sand off her cherry-red one-piece swimsuit and walked up and knocked on the side of his car.

"Yes, Miss Pam?" he said, looking up from his paper.

"It's pretty hot out today."

"Yes, it is," he agreed.

"You know it's much cooler by the ocean," she said.

"Yes, Miss."

"If you insist on keeping watch over us, then you probably should come out this car before you get a heat stroke."

"That's okay, Miss," he said. "I'm fine here."

"Arley, you make me feel bad seeing you up here baking while you wait for us," she said. "We have plenty food. Why don't you come join us for lunch?"

He wasn't particularly dressed for the beach in his usual button-down white shirt and black trouser shorts and leather sandals. He looked out of place sitting on the blanket. Pam dished out a plate of stew chicken with rice and peas. He ate silently, watching CJ try to build a sand castle with his hands and an old coke bottle.

"You need something deeper and bigger to shape your castle," he said to CJ. "Stay here. I'll be back."

He went back to his car and returned with three of the large margarine containers he used for his lunches. He went down to the sea and rinsed out the containers, filling the largest one with water.

"The first thing you need to do is pour some water on the sand to make it stick," he said, showing CJ. "Then you gather up the sand like this and then shape it. I used to make sea turtles with sand. Do you want me to show you?"

"Sea turtles?" CJ asked. "Yes, please!"

Arley unbuttoned his white shirt, carefully folded it, and set it on the blanket. Dressed in his shorts and a white undershirt, he knelt down to help CJ with his creation. Pam sat on her blanket reading a magazine, peering over from time to time to watch what was going on. Arley's dark leathery skin and grizzled beard implied a man much older than he was. But in the hot glowing sun, he actually resembled an island version of Teddy Pendergrass.

Over the next hour, the two of them sculpted a large sea turtle, complete with a pebble-and-seaweed shell. CJ jumped up and down after they'd finished.

"Mommy, look... look what Arley and I made."

Pam got up and headed towards the sand turtle.

"Kiss mi neck," she said as she surveyed the creation. "It looks good."

"Mommy, take a picture of me with my sand turtle, please," he said, running back to the blanket to bring the camera.

"Okay, okay," she said.

He handed her the camera.

"Come in the picture with me, Arley," CJ said, pulling the man by his hand.

345

The two of them knelt down by the sand turtle and smiled as she tried to situate herself to get the best picture.

Her wrap slipped off as she tried to adjust the focus of the camera. She stood there in her swimsuit, her tanned body glistening from the heat of the sun.

As she adjusted the focus of the camera she stopped for a moment to admire Arley. She felt her face flush as his smile lit up his face. She liked the way the sides of his eyes crinkled when he smiled at her.

"Did you take the picture yet?" said CJ. He struggled to keep still for the picture.

She clicked the camera. "All done," she said.

She looked up at Arley and smiled a little, aware that he was looking at her toned legs and her perky behind. He smiled back, but quickly turned away and looked into the ocean.

"Okay," he said. He took a few deep breaths. "I think we better get going."

Pam looked curiously at him. He still stared off into the ocean. She suddenly realized why he was facing away from her. She giggled when she noticed him discreetly adjust himself.

On her last week in Jamaica, Pam left CJ with Annalise while she made a shopping trip to buy gifts and souvenirs. She sat up front with Arley as they took the hour-long drive into Kingston. She went to several shops, purchasing gifts for Mrs. Price, Mike, and her co-workers. The final stop was a small record shop on Temple Lane she had often visited in her youth. She was searching for reggae tapes for Simone.

As they were pulling out to drive back to Mandeville, Pam spotted Patrice's Restaurant, a small hole-in-the-wall that she had frequented with her father. It had changed a lot since the last time she had been there, but the moment the smell of jerk chicken wafted by her nose, memories came flooding back. She remembered coming to Patrice's after stowing away on a truck with friends to attend dances and house parties. Nights, after they would see ska reggae musicians like The Mighty Diamonds and Bunny Wailer perform live.

"Arley, wait... can you stop for a minute?" she asked.

"Yes, Miss Pam." He stopped the car in front of Patrice's.

"I'm hungry," she said. "Let's get lunch before heading back to Mandeville — my treat."

Pam stood in line with Arley. They each ordered a plate of jerk chicken with rice and peas and a helping of plantain on the side. They sat on a bench trying to balance their plates of food.

"What does a nice *gyal* like you know about *Patrice?*" he asked her.

"I was born and raised in Kingston," she said. "I went to school in Mandeville, but I grew up on these streets."

"What!" he said, laughing. "Unu foot bottom run dees streets?"

"Yes, sah," she said, laughing. She bit into a piece of plantain. "It was just me and my father for a while. We didn't live too far from here."

"Well, how did you end up in Mandeville?" he asked.

"I went to Carter Academy."

"That's a fancy school." He whistled. "You must be rolling."

"Not quite," she said. "My father died of cancer and left me some money for school. I didn't have any family except for my mother's older sister and so Carter was the best place to go."

"I'm sorry to hear that," he said, tipping back his ginger beer.

"Enough about me," she said, sipping from her bottle. "What about you? What is Arley's story?"

"Ah," he said. "Nothing interesting. I worked as an aircraft cleaner at Kingston International for almost ten years. I set to go to school to train as an aircraft technician, but ended up being laid off a few months ago. Now I'm trying to figure out what to do next."

"I'm sorry," she said.

"Nah, man, it's all good," he said, smiling. "God willing, I'm hoping to get my job back quick when the economy picks up and then work a few more years before I go back to school."

"Wait... why are you waiting?" she asked. "Why don't you just go back to school now?"

"It's not that easy," he said. "The program is four years and right now not even airport technicians are being hired."

"Who says you have to work at an airport?" she asked. "I'm not sure what it's like here in Jamaica, but, in Toronto, the most sought-after skill set are people who work in computers. If you feel confident enough to fix a plane, I'm sure you can fix computers."

"Computers," he said. "I don't even know anyone with a computer."

"Well, in Toronto that's all people are into," she said. "One good computer costs almost $5,000 Canadian."

"But wait." He laughed. "Mi can buy a nice piece of land for that price."

"Well, it's even bigger money to know how to fix them." She tossed her empty plate in the bin. "My hospital spends a small fortune on computer repairs. I'm sure there are classes you can take on the island to figure out how to fix them."

"I'm sure there is," he said, smiling at her. "You're a smart woman."

"Well, you're a smart man," she said.

Silence.

He looked over at her and she could feel herself blushing as he pulled her into a kiss. She wasn't sure what to do. It was probably best to pull away, but his lips felt nice against hers. She was warm and wet and breathless when she did finally pull away.

By the time they got back to Mandeville, it was raining. Unable to escape the storm, they parked by the side of the road as sheets of heavy rain poured on top of the car. The thunder bellowed and the lightning struck swiftly. Pam crawled on top of Arley, unable to wait for them to get back to the garage.

He wrestled with her blouse, then reached for the back of her bra and unsnapped it, letting her breasts hang before he hungrily sucked on them. Pam could barely contain herself. She unbuckled his trousers. She pulled them down to set him free and caught her breath as he grew stiff. There was so much of him, she didn't know how to even begin. He reached under her skirt and pulled her panties to the side, before lifting her on top of him.

She felt him enter her and moaned as the rain splattered against the car windows. She cried out as he moved faster and faster. He had gone deeper than any man had gone before. She bit his shoulder, trying to stifle herself. It was the most exhilarating thing she had ever felt. The way he pumped her up and down, starting off slow and then speeding up. Her entire body shuddered as he lifted her off him.

"I'm not done," he said. He reached behind her seat, releasing the catch to make it lie flat. "You're not finished."

He knelt on the floor and spread her legs apart with his hands. He licked her pussy slowly from the bottom to the top of her clit. Her entire body trembled. He probed his tongue inside her until she clenched and cried out. He pinned her down so she couldn't move. She whimpered as his tongue travelled back to her clit, where it danced around, making her so hot that she could barely breathe.

"Oh God," she cried. "Oh, my Christ."

"You ready for me?"

Her only response was a deep moan. He turned her around to enter her from behind and she felt him go even deeper, ramming her harder with each thrust, her body rocking as she begged him for more.

"Harder," she cried out. "Harder!"

He was hurting her but she wanted to feel the pain. She needed to feel something other than the emptiness she had been carrying in her since Caleb's death. But, instead of going harder, he slowed down. She didn't want him to stop. She wanted him to keep going. She needed him to keep going.

"Turn around and look at me," he said.

She turned and looked at him. He looked like a wounded bear.

"You are a delicate and beautiful woman and no one should ever rough you up like that," he whispered to her. "No one."

She started to cry as he kissed her lips softly and caressed her face. Then he laid her back and went inside her again, more gently and slowly.

She closed her eyes as he rocked her and cried out when she felt another orgasm. When they finished, she passed out, exhausted, nestled in his arms, as he kissed her sweaty brow.

They shared a few more evenings together before she headed back to Toronto. It had been the most incredible three days of her life. She had never felt more sensual or alive. Each time together brought her to ecstasy, and, just when she thought nothing could top the last time, he would bring her body to new heights.

Their last moment together was at the airport. As Annalise said goodbye to her grandson, Arley quickly and discreetly kissed Pam. He held onto her hand as long as he could.

Once they got settled in their seats, Pam looked out the window while CJ curled up next to her. She thought back to her first night with Arley and smiled as she recalled the way he thrust inside her, sending shivers through her body. She wasn't sure if she would ever see him again. They hadn't made plans to keep in touch, but she felt it was for the best. He was a man she had needed for the moment. Someone to stoke her fires and remind her that she wasn't dead yet.

They got back to Toronto at nearly midnight. She walked into the empty apartment, happy to be home. She put CJ to bed, then looked around to see that everything was still in its place. Nothing had burned down or been stolen or damaged. Life had continued, despite her being away for weeks. Her answering machine notification was flashing. She sat on the couch to listen to the calls.

The first message was from Mike, telling her that he needed a lift from the train station. His voice wavered, telling her that he had taken a last-minute trip to Nova Scotia.

I wouldn't bug you... it's just... I don't want to ask Maureen. A judge is forcing me to give up custody of Nolan and... I... I just can't deal with Maureen right now.

Pam, of course, knew that there were new problems between Meghan and Mike, but she was shocked that it had turned into a legal matter. She wrote down the time his train was coming in. She clicked on to the next message.

Pamela, it's me, Dexter... Linda's cousin, he said in his deep Jamaican accent. *I didn't know how to contact you and didn't think it would be a good idea to show up at the house you were staying... so I hope that you don't mind that I got your number from Linda. Okay... I just want to apologize for the way I acted.*

"Humph, yeah right," she said to the phone, about to delete the message.

...I was a complete ass and you didn't deserve to be treated like that, the message continued. *I'm going to be in Toronto the end of September and hope that I can take you out on a proper date... something to make up for the way I behaved.*

Pam was thrown off guard by his apology, which hinted at some sort of sincerity. She then laughed to herself. She lay back on the couch, lightly caressing herself. She thought about her predicament. Coming off a wondrous week with Arley, a man who had drawn her out of herself only to submerge her in the beauty of her own womanhood, made Dex's anxious message seem nectarous.

"Now the lawyer wants to make amends," she said, smiling to herself as she started to doze off. "Maybe there is something redeemable there."

31

Nolan sat at his desk and stared listlessly at the chalkboard as Mrs. Lanier, his math teacher, reviewed what would be included in the upcoming mid-term exam. While his peers ardently jotted down notes, he fiddled with a loose thread hanging off the sleeve of his blazer. Everyone, except him, was buried in their notebooks.

Nolan should never have been assigned to her class. Based on transcripts from his previous school, he should have been placed in the general class, but Mrs. Lanier had been instructed to do this favour for Vice Principal Rich Bevens.

When the bell rang, the students bent their heads and rushed to copy the rest of the notes before gathering their books for the next period.

"I expect to see your work, people," Mrs. Lanier said as the students headed out the door. "If I don't see your work, you won't see a grade."

Many of the students groaned. Mrs. Lanier's class was not the easiest at Holy Cross High School and none of the students were looking forward to the mid-term. It was notorious for being harder than the final exam.

"Mr. O'Shea, might I have a word?" she said.

"Yes, Ma'am." He rested his book bag on the desk.

"You realize that the mid-terms are coming up?" she said. "Are you ready?"

"Yes, Ma'am."

"Well, I really hope you understand the importance of this exam," she said. "You've failed the last four quizzes and if you fail this you will fail the class. Do you understand, Mr. O'Shea?"

"Yes, Ma'am," he repeated.

The next round of students was lingering in the hallway.

"Nolan, you seem like a nice boy and I know that somewhere there is a brain in there," she said. "But if you don't make a concerted effort, my next conversation will be with your mother. So please study for this exam. Can I get that commitment from you, Mr. O'Shea?"

"Yes, Ma'am."

Nolan sauntered down the hallway as the last warning bell rang out. Students were quickly running to their classes. He headed to his locker next to the gym and pulled out his science book. He looked at it and then shoved it back into his locker.

The sun was shining through the gymnasium's double doors. His fifth-period science class was supposed to have a quiz on the periodic table but he hadn't studied. He'd spent the entire evening playing video games. The last thing he wanted was to hear another lecture from Mr. Vyhovsky, who had been on his case since the first day of classes. He closed his locker and headed through the gym, across the slick shiny floor, leaving black streaks from his heavy boots. He opened the back doors and the sun shone brightly on his face.

He wandered to the bleachers, where he usually hid out until the end of the day. It was the one place that was safe from everyone. He sat on the cold frigid ground under the bleachers as the winter air tore through his blazer. The cold weather didn't bother him. Nothing seemed to bother him. He was in a constant state of mellowness, with a steady supply of weed in his back pocket.

Nolan and his mother had moved into a two-bedroom house with Rich. It was an older home with a nice-sized backyard and a decrepit greenhouse that needed to be torn down but was temporarily being used for storage. When they moved in, neither Meghan nor Rich noticed the few marijuana bushes that had been left behind — parting gifts from the previous owners.

Nolan recognized the plants from a pamphlet that Rich had brought home for him to read. The pamphlet talked about how to spot the plant, the dangers of weed, and the many ways teenagers disguised the drug. It turned out to be the perfect gift. Nolan then went to the public library and borrowed books on how to replant, cultivate, and prep his product.

He didn't intend it as a huge venture, just as a hobby to give him a personal supply. When he felt generous, he would pass a few joints to the students who joined him for a smoke at the ravine. But, by mid-semester, he had become the hook-up for every party and post-football game, though lately he preferred to smoke alone, especially now that he was down to his last few joints.

He rolled up his navy blazer, tucking it under his head like a pillow, before lighting up his joint. He took a quick hit as his mind continued to race: the pressures of being in a school he hated; having to drive in with Rich each morning and drive home with him each evening, enduring endless lectures about not skipping school and achieving higher grades. The next drag wasn't strong enough; his mind wandered to the baby that never saw the light of day. The part of him that was ripped away without anyone asking how he felt. His gut started to twist tightly. He took another drag, inhaling deeply. His mind finally started to fade away into the abyss.

"You're Vice Principal Bevens' kid, right?" a voice said, interrupting the mellowness he'd finally achieved.

A gaunt girl was sitting in the shadows behind him. She looked like a child wearing adult army gear. Her oversized green military jacket hung over her tiny wispy frame. She wore the usual kilt and white blouse with a pair of old muddy Dr. Martens. She was sitting there with a pocketknife, pieces of her hair sprinkled in front of her.

"He's not my father," Nolan said. He watched her cutting her bangs. "He's dating my mother."

"Like I care."

"Then why did you ask?"

"I'm not going to skip class with the vice principal's narc," she said, fiddling with the knife at her forehead. "Does this look even to you?" She sat up straight. Her bangs were uneven on the left side and seemed longer in the middle.

Nolan got up and walked over to her. "No offence, but don't you think you should do this in the girl's washroom in front of a mirror, or something?" He handed her his joint and took the blade from her. "Stay still."

He carefully cut away at her bangs to even out the mess she had made. Her face was very pale and she had sapphire blue eyes. He had never met anyone with eyes that colour. He wasn't sure if they were even real.

"There." He handed back the blade. "Now you look less retarded."

"Thanks, fucker," she said, taking a drag before handing back his joint. "So what's your name anyways? Something WASPy like Brad or Hunter?"

"Nolan." He took another drag before handing it back to her.

"That's your name?" she said, mocking him. "What is that? Irish?"

"Gaelic," he said.

"Humph." She picked up her bag.

"Yeah, well, what's your name?" he said. "Brittany, Tiffany or Debbie?"

"Not fucking likely," she said, trying to hide her smile. "It's definitely not fucking Brittany, it's Tessa... Tess."

She gathered up her books, placed the knife in her backpack, and got up to leave. He was a little disappointed. He was enjoying their banter.

"How come I haven't seen you before?" he asked. "Are you in my grade?"

"Not unless you're in grade ten," she said, lifting her heavy bag over her shoulders.

"I'm in the ninth grade," he said to her.

"Well, isn't that swell, Brad," she said smirking as she ducked out from beneath the bleachers. "Gotta go. See you around."

"See you around," he repeated. He watched her walk across the field. She was pretty in a Goth kind of way.

He was about to head back to his spot when he realized that she had left behind a booklet. He picked it up and opened it. It was a photocopy of another book. He flipped through the worn pages. Lines were highlighted, with notes in the margin. He looked back at the cover of the booklet. *Romeo and Juliet.* When he flipped to the second page there was another title — *Frisco's Last Stand.*

He perused the forward briefly before he got to the first page of the book and began reading.

It was the end of the civil war but only the beginning of the race war that would last a hundred years. We had trained for it, planned for it and now raised an army strong enough to combat it. On the night of September 16, 1965 we came out of our underground chambers ready to fight for our way of life. For us to take our rightful place in a land that was slipping away from our grasp.

He leaned back against one of the stanchions and smoked what was left of his joint as he kept reading. By the time he'd finished the fourth chapter, the entire campus was deserted.

"Fuck." He looked at his watch. It was nearly 5:00 pm. He scrambled to his feet, hitting his head on the seats above him. Rich was probably looking for him. He ran to the building, but all of the doors were locked and the faculty parking lot was completely empty.

"Shit," he said. He climbed the fence and headed up the walkway towards home. It got colder as the sun dipped down. He rolled the booklet and crammed it into his coat pocket.

▶

"HE STINKS OF IT, MEGHAN," Rich said. He stood in the kitchen, where she was washing up the dinner dishes. "He's not fooling anyone."

"For Christ sakes, Rich, he's fourteen," Meghan said. She felt exhausted. The argument had entered its second hour. "He doesn't even know the first thing about smoking pot. He's a kid!"

It was now almost eight in the evening and Nolan was nowhere to be found. Rich had waited at school as long as he could, then he had searched the entire campus.

"How can you say that," he said. "You just spent months and hundreds of dollars getting full custody of Nolan because you thought your husband couldn't hack it as a parent, and now all you can say is that Nolan's a kid? That's the best you can come up with?"

"Don't you dare criticize me!" She slammed a dish in the sink. "Who do you think you are, comparing me to Mike? I'm a fucking good mother, okay?"

"I know that you are," he said. "I'm not saying that…"

"Do you have kids?" she interrupted him. "Do you even know what it's like to be a parent? No? So don't lecture me about Nolan!"

"No, frankly, I don't know what it's like to be a fucking parent, Meghan." He headed for the door. "But I do know what it's like to be a vice principal to five hundred students and I know the signs and, if he doesn't pull his shit together, I'm throwing him out of school."

Meghan froze. She heard him slam the front door behind him. It wasn't the first fight they'd had over Nolan, but it was definitely the nastiest one. All week, Rich had been coming home with stories of meetings with Nolan's teachers to discuss his failing grades. The only class her son seemed to be managing was shop; in all of the others, he was either in danger of failing or he was already failing.

Meghan had slowly come to realize that moving him to Halifax had created a lot more difficulties than she had anticipated. With her promotion, it was becoming harder to juggle home and work life. Long evenings in the office were the new normal and, with Nolan's school work slipping, she didn't know what to do. She had expected that Rich would be helpful, since Nolan was a student in his school. She should've known better. When she'd suggested that Nolan attend Holy Cross, Rich had been firmly against it.

"It's not practical and will be a conflict," he had told her.

"How?" she countered. "You're not his teacher or even his father. He'll just be another student at your school."

"Who lives under the same roof as me," he reminded her. "It won't work."

"It will," she insisted. "Any issues with Nolan will come to me. You will be left out."

He finally gave in and agreed, on the condition that Nolan kept up his grades and gave none of the teachers any reason to complain. But, shortly after the first semester began, so did the problems. Complaints of him skipping classes, being unprepared, and not handing in school assignments plagued Rich's desk weekly and he tried to smooth things with his teachers by telling them of Nolan's upheaval from Toronto; but, now that the mid-terms were approaching, the teachers were slowly losing patience. Rich liked his reputation as a hard-nosed administrator and letting Nolan slide made him seem incompetent.

Rich was outside smoking a cigarette when Nolan came walking slowly up the hill. He quickly put out his cigarette as the boy got closer.

Nolan's face looked pale. "Hi," he said, shivering.

"Where have you been? I looked everywhere for you."

"I was at school," he said. "I was on the field reading and lost track of time."

"Reading... is that what they call it now?" Rich lit another cigarette.

"That's enough, Rich," Meghan said through the screen door. "Nolan, come out of the cold and have some dinner. Are you hungry?"

Nolan walked into the house.

Rich laughed sourly. "I'm going out," he said, pulling out his keys. He didn't want to stay in the house while Meghan tended to her baby boy. He hated the way she easily gave in to him. He couldn't stand there and watch her tussle his hair, desperately trying to alleviate her guilt by feeding him pot roast, mashed potatoes, and vanilla bean ice cream.

Meghan watched through the kitchen window as his car careened out of the driveway, narrowly missing the trash bins. She looked over at Nolan and began to see what Rich was talking about. Nolan's eyes were bloodshot and glassy and he had a vacant expression. She lifted his chin. He squirmed out of her grasp and sat down to eat his dinner.

"Are you unhappy, Nolie?" She sat next to him.

"I'm fine."

"I know this has been a huge transition, but you know it will get easier," she said. "It's getting better, right?"

"Sure, Mom."

"Would it help if you spent a weekend with your dad?" she offered. "Maybe you can see some of your old friends."

"I don't have any old friends."

The last thing he wanted to do was go back to Toronto and visit. Not when everything was as shitty as it was. If his father found out that he was failing school, it would send him over the roof. He didn't want another legal battle. All he wanted was for his world to stop spinning and for some normalcy.

"Okay, honey," she said. "Are you at least making new friends? I mean... I'm assuming you have some, right?"

"Yeah... yeah," he lied. "I've got tons."

"Really?" she said. "Maybe you should have a few over sometime."

"Sure," he said, finishing his dinner. "Do you mind if I head to my room? I have a math midterm to study for."

"Sure thing, honey." She reached to smooth out his hair.

She flinched when he jerked away from her. She watched him head upstairs and noticed that he'd left his book bag at the foot of the kitchen chair. Pangs of regret silenced her. She just picked up his dish and placed it in the sink as Metallica blasted from his bedroom.

▶

SIMONE SAT in Mrs. Price's living room, working on her algebra homework. It was the third weekend in a row that she and CJ were sleeping across the hall. Mr. Dex's visits were becoming more frequent.

When Pam had returned from Jamaica, she was like a giddy schoolgirl. She hummed and wore fun summer dresses that she'd bought in Jamaica. She cut her hair short in a Halle Berry pixie cut and started wearing a little more makeup. At first, Simone had been hesitant about her mother's new attitude. She couldn't help wonder when the other shoe would drop but, when she met Dex, she got why her mother was in high spirits.

This time he was staying in Toronto for nearly three weeks. Simone didn't mind being out of the apartment. Even though her mother was in a better mood, she preferred staying with Mrs. Price. It was her brother who had an issue.

"I hate being here." CJ tossed his basketball against the living room wall. "Why are we always here?"

"Stop banging the ball against the wall," Simone said. "You're going to put a hole in it."

"Whatever," he said. He let the ball roll under the kitchen table. "Why can't we go home? I want to play my video games."

"Why didn't you bring them with you?"

"Cause I didn't know we were going to stay here... again," he said.

"Well you have homework," she reminded him. "Go finish it."

She glowered at him until he finally gave in and pulled out his phonics book from his book bag and started his homework. Simone went back to her homework, but was distracted by voices from the hallway. She thought it was Mrs. Price coming back from the grocery store with Esma, but then heard her mother's voice. Pam was in the hallway with Dex.

She went to the door and opened it slightly. She could see them arguing. He held her wrist as she tried to open the door with her key. He grabbed the key and opened the door himself. Simone saw him grab her mother's hair and pull her head back and kiss her hard on the lips. She didn't like the way Dex was acting and she grew scared, until her mother started laughing and pushed Dex into the apartment.

She couldn't understand their relationship. She had overheard her mother tell Linda how she couldn't stand Dex and she even called him a pompous ass. Yet, every time he was in town, she would jump at his beck and call. She had never been so needy with Caleb. She had always seemed in control of herself. Yet, around Dex, she didn't act at all like herself. Dex had some kind of pull on her.

Despite her reservations, Simone didn't dislike Dex as much as her little brother did. CJ couldn't stand his mother's boyfriend. When they'd returned from Jamaica, CJ had talked of nothing but the beach and his mother and Arley. Simone had heard so much about him that when Pam announced that a gentleman friend would be visiting, she assumed it would be the illustrious and infamous Arley. Instead, it was Mr. Dexter Stewart, a handsome Kingston lawyer with the brightest teeth and slick black hair, who spoke like a white man. He was nothing like Arley, according to CJ.

Dex had very little patience for CJ. He said CJ was too noisy, had no manners, and was always interrupting. Pam answered his complaints by promising that, the next time he visited, he could have her all to himself.

Once they'd gone into the apartment, Simone crept into the hallway and placed her ear on the door to see if she could hear anything. Only laughter.

"What in the world are you doing, Simone?"

Mike was pulling out his keys.

"Hi, Mr. Mike." She turned to him nervously. "I… I thought I heard my mother in the apartment."

They could hear raucous laughter coming through the doorway. Then reggae music started to play.

"Well, it sounds like she's home to me," he said. "Are you staying at Mrs. Price's tonight?"

"Yeah," she said, moving away from the door. "We're staying the weekend."

"Ah, I see."

"How's Nolan doing? Will he be coming home over the Christmas holidays?"

"I hope so."

"Me, too."

She hadn't been told much by anyone about Nolan. Sean had been the only person able to fill her in on the whole pregnancy scare that seemed to be a whole lot about nothing. When school started up again, Sarah Jane was in attendance and seemed unscathed by the whole incident. She seemed no different from her usual self. She still sat with her nose in the air, above it all, although, after the first week of school, she vanished. Ilene told Simone that she'd transferred to Loretta Abbey Collegiate. Ilene wasn't sure why she'd left, only that some of the girls had heard things about her, which led to a fight in religion class. Simone felt bad for her. She'd never liked Sarah Jane, but conceded that, if such a thing could happen to Sarah Jane, then it could easily have happened to her.

Simone had got hold of Nolan's home address and telephone number from Mrs. Price. She'd left him a few messages over the summer, but he never returned any of her calls. She wrote him a long letter, telling him all about her summer job at Laura Secord and how excited she was about going to St. Joseph, but she never got a reply. By the time school started, she had accepted that, no matter how close they had been as children, Nolan had become a footnote to her past.

She focused on the future. She was excited about going to St. Joseph and was determined that high school would be a fresh new start. But going to the all-girl school didn't do much to ease her gently into the befuddling world of adolescence. Despite the change in scenery, all her old insecurities and hang-ups seemed to follow her around. She had tried to be more confident and make new friends, but she felt out of place. Everyone was in a clique and, while the more outgoing students were able to fit in, Simone felt like she was in a harried game of musical chairs, never able to snag that empty seat.

At eight hundred students, St. Joseph was one of the largest all-girls Catholic schools in the country. It boasted a six-acre sprawling campus in the middle of North York. The school was packed with so many students from the surrounding Catholic elementary schools that Simone rarely saw any of her old St.

Augustine classmates. Most of her friends seemed to have gotten swallowed up in the general population. In fact, the only class that had a familiar face was English class with Ilene.

If they had the same lunch periods, Simone would join Yvette, Angie, or Ilene. It was the only time she felt she could be herself, but, after a few months, they slowly started to change. Ilene was no longer interested in being the smartest student in the class. She still maintained good grades, but got a boyfriend after the first week of school and spent most of her time hanging out with his friends.

Over the summer, Angie and Yvette had morphed from being obsessed teenyboppers into self-proclaimed "rude gyals" who acted more Jamaican than she did. They spoke patois, slicked their hair back in tight ponytails, and applied heavy lip-liner. The most communication she had with them was the occasional head nod in the hallways. They travelled in packs with the rest of the slicked-back girls, sucking their teeth and reciting "Trailer Load of Girls" as their own personal anthem.

It was strange for Simone. She felt her whole existence standing still while everyone around her went full speed ahead. She was lonelier than ever and quietly kept to herself.

Moving under the radar was what she did best. She'd rather be a people-watcher than the one being observed. It was almost her superpower — the power of invisibility. The ability to quietly see the interactions of the faculty, the snide remarks made behind a girl's back, the way the cafeteria lady would dump the new food on top of the old food. She had the distinct opinion that her math teacher, Miss Campbell, had been either born male or was a very masculine lesbian.

She turned her power on her family and noticed how much angrier her little brother was than usual. It was a little bit of a shock, since she had always been known as the miserable one, but they did share half of the same genes. The anger that seethed in him seemed to grow more restless with Dex around.

It was more than just a young boy's jealousy of his mother's new boyfriend. He seemed angry with everyone. No one was safe from his outbursts; not even frail sweet Mrs. Price was immune. The only person who seemed to be able to handle his anger was Mike. He was the only adult CJ listened to. When his mother was too busy with Dex, CJ would often slip away to Mike's apartment and sit with him as they watched baseball together.

Mike had always loved CJ and treated him like his own son, but, now that Nolan was living with his mother, CJ filled a void in his life. Mike continued to take him to every soccer practice and attended every tournament he played in. If CJ started to act up, Simone would threaten to expose her little brother's bad ways to Mike. That would usually set him straight, giving her enough peace and quiet to finish her homework.

CJ's tantrums got worse when Dex decided to spend the Christmas holidays with them. Mrs. Price went to Jamaica for the holidays. She called it her "final trip home before her real homecoming," a proclamation she made every other year. Mike had hoped that Nolan would spend Christmas in Toronto, but ended up making plans to go to Halifax for the holidays. That left Simone and CJ with the happy couple.

Dex was nothing short of elaborate in his approach to their Christmas celebration. He showered Simone and CJ with every gadget and gift under the sun, saving the most expensive gift for Pam — an engagement ring. He proposed to her in front of them, on Christmas Eve, which left Simone shell-shocked. They had only been dating a few months.

"Oh my God, Dex," Pam said. "It's so soon."

"Not soon enough," he said, smoothly. "We're good for each other, and whether we do it now or wait a few more years, that will never change."

When Pam looked at Dex, she had tears in her eyes. Simone felt only shock. There was nothing but contempt in CJ's eyes.

"Maybe we should talk this over more in private," Pam said softly to Dex.

Dex looked over at them where they stood under the lights from the Christmas tree. The branches and lights cast shadows over the room.

"What's with the sour-puss expressions?" he said. "Pam, your children are some bright ones, eh! This is supposed to be a celebration, not a funeral. I just asked your mother to marry me and neither of you has anything to say?"

They sat in the colossal mess of glossy wrapping paper, unable to muster up anything to say to him.

"Anything from you, big man?" he said to CJ.

"No!" CJ said.

"Leave them, Dex," Pam said. "They are a little overwhelmed at how quick this is. This is the first real amount of time they've spent with you. Give them some time."

"Well, you two need to fix your faces because I'm going to marry your mother quick." He grabbed Pam by the waist and kissed her on the lips. "She's the only Christmas gift I want this year."

CJ just stood there, bubbling with anger. Simone could sense that he wanted to push Dex away from Pam, out of the house and back to Jamaica.

"Come on, CJ," she said. "Let's toss out all the trash before the garbage room gets full."

"That's a good idea," Pam said. She got up and went into the kitchen. "Let's get this place cleaned up before we head over to Linda's for dinner. I can't believe how late it is already."

As Pam occupied herself in the kitchen, Dex got up and grabbed CJ's arm. He stared directly into the young boy's eyes.

CJ stopped cold.

Simone could tell that Dex was squeezing his arm too tightly.

"Come on, CJ," she said, trying to pry them apart. "I said come on!"

"Talk and taste your tongue," Dex said to CJ as he finally relaxed his grip. "Listen to your sister, Caleb Junior. She's the smarter one."

Simone grabbed the trash bag and they swiftly picked up the wrapping paper and stuffed it in, then they headed out the door to the garbage room.

"I hate him," said CJ. His voice sounded throttled. "I hate his greasy muthafucking ass."

"CJ! Weh yuh get dem deh bad words from!?" she said. "Don't let Ms. Pam hear you talk like that."

She could tell that her brother didn't care. They continued to walk to the trash room as slowly as they could, in order to avoid going back to the apartment. It was Christmas. She didn't want CJ to be angry. She pulled him into her arms and squeezed him tightly.

"He'll be back in Jamaica by the end of the week," she said. "When he's gone, we'll talk some sense into her. She's not going to marry that greasy muthafucker! I promise."

CJ nodded. He looked up and tried to smile.

Simone squeezed his hand as they walked through a mountain of wrapping paper. The trash bin was full. They had to leave the bags on the floor. The whole room was already overflowing with garbage.

M ike waited by the counter of the car rental at Stanfield International Airport. It was a few days after Christmas and, after three delayed flights, he had finally made it to Halifax. He didn't want to be there, but he had no choice.

"What kind of bullshit is this?" Mike had said to Meghan, a few weeks before. He was on the phone from his desk at work. "The judge said that I'm supposed to have Nolan for two weeks during Christmas break. This is fucking nuts!"

"Well, I think it's too soon," she said. "He's settled here and shipping him to Toronto would disrupt the progress Rich and I have made as a family. Plus, he's working on a school project over the break. If he goes to Toronto, he won't get it done."

"What kind of school gives them homework during Christmas holidays?" Mike fired back.

"High school, Mike. He's not in grade school anymore."

"Yeah, well, this is my time, Meghan, and if I have to I'll fly up for the week…"

"It's not necessary."

"What do you mean, it's not necessary? Why are you trying to keep us apart? What's going on?"

"Jesus Christ, Mike! Everything is fine," she said. "I just don't want things to get confusing with you and Rich and Nolan."

"There is nothing confusing about any of this, Megs," he said. "You either get over yourself and let me spend time with my kid or Nolan comes home. I'm done with this fucking conversation."

"Fine! If you want to come all the way over, then fucking do it!"

Mike flinched when Meghan hung up on him. The entire conversation seemed off. It wasn't like her to be so evasive. He couldn't understand why she was being so difficult, especially since he had given up any further legal claims on Nolan.

His lawyer had told him that he had a pretty solid case for getting Nolan back, since he had reduced his hours at the bar and was now working full-time at Ryerson University. But Mike wasn't sure that fighting for custody was the best thing for Nolan. He seemed to be happy in Halifax. He talked on the phone about how much he enjoyed his classes and all the friends he had made. Maybe it would be bad to uproot him just when things had started to settle.

Regardless, his conversation with Meghan raised concerns. He wished Maureen and Meghan were on speaking terms. After the legal scuffle, Maureen had called Meghan and laced into her for the way she had handled the situation, calling her an absentee mother who was laying all the guilt on Mike when the real reason that Nolan was so fucked up was because of her. Mike appreciated his cousin sticking up for him, but then Meghan refused to let him speak to Nolan for two weeks after. It had been the most volatile four months he had ever experienced. Not even when they were miserably cohabitating had it ever got this bad.

After receiving the keys to the rental, Mike headed directly over to Meghan's new place – the house he had wanted to buy her. It stung seeing the old two-level Gothic revival house with its steeply pitched gable roof. The house had been recently painted pewter grey and the big yard was surrounded by a white picket fence.

He shut off the engine and sat in his car as static overwhelmed the music on the radio. He lit a cigarette and smoked, letting each drag linger deep inside. He thought about just leaving and coming back the next day.

A light tap.

Dana opened the passenger seat. "You lost, old man?"

Mike laughed. He reached over to give her a hug.

"Hey, sweetheart," he said.

She took the cigarette from him. "You know these things will kill you," she said. She took a drag before putting the cigarette out. "You're not getting any younger. You need to take better care of yourself."

"Ah well, we eventually all die, don't we?"

"Oh God, Dad," she said, rolling her eyes. "You doing okay?"

"Yeah, honey. "I'm doing good… better than expected."

Dana looked at him with pity. "Come on, they're all waiting for you," she said.

They walked in together. Meghan was setting the table and Mike felt uneasy the moment he stepped into her living room. He didn't know what to say. Then he saw Nolan coming down the staircase.

"Jesus, Nolan! What happened to you? You're a giant!"

"Hey, Dad," he said. "Did you just get here?"

"I did." He looked Nolan up and down. "My flight got in a few hours ago."

"Hi, Mike," said Meghan from the kitchen.

He turned and attempted a smile and silently nodded at her before walking into the kitchen to give her a brief hug.

"You don't look worse for wear. We're about to have dinner. Will you be joining us?"

"Of course he's going to join us, Mom," Dana said.

"Yes, of course," she said. "Dana, set another place at the table. Dinner is going to be ready soon."

"Where's Rich?" Mike asked. He washed his hands at the kitchen sink.

"Grand Manan Island," she said, making herself busy in the kitchen. "His mother hasn't been doing too well, so he's spending Christmas with her."

"Thank the Lord for small miracles," Dana mumbled to herself.

"I see," he said. "Do you need some help, Megs?"

"No… no. Just wash up for dinner," she said.

"Already done," he said, waving his wet hands in the air. "Let me make the salad. If I remember correctly, I was the designated salad maker in the past."

"Okay," she said taking a deep breath before handing him a head of lettuce to shred.

The O'Shea family dinner started out quietly. The four of them sat around the table, barely looking up at one another. Mike began eating his meal. The pot roast and mashed potatoes were as good as he remembered but with a sweeter flavour.

"This is interesting," he said, almost to himself. "It has a sugary taste."

"I stewed it in Coca-Cola," Meghan said. "Something I started doing a few years back."

"Hmm," he replied. "My neighbour makes a stew similar to this but she uses oxtails and kidney beans."

"Oxtails, Dad?" Dana said, turning her nose up. "Like the actual tail of an ox?"

"Well, actually the tail of a cow," he clarified. "It's just like any other part of the cow."

"God. Cow or bull or whatever, eating a tail sounds disgusting," Dana said.

"It's the best part of the cow, isn't it, Nolan?" Mike said.

"Yeah, I guess," Nolan mumbled.

"You guess?" Mike said. "Anytime Mrs. Price makes the stuff you are always first in line with your gigantic cereal bowl."

Dana and Mike laughed as Nolan sat there, his face turning crimson.

"Mrs. Price makes the best oxtail," Mike continued. "She cooks it all day and the entire floor smells of it, but in a good way. My favourites are the little dumplings she puts in. They're like little pillows of flavour when you get some in your mouth."

"Little pillows," Meghan said, laughing. "I'm sorry, Mike, but I've never heard anyone call dumplings little pillows of flavour."

Mike laughed along with her. He started to feel a little more comfortable.

"You should taste her curry goat and potatoes," he said. "Goat meat is usually pretty tough but when Mrs. Price is done it melts in your mouth like butter."

"Or pillows," Dana chimed in.

They all laughed as Mike told stories about the characters on his floor, especially the Wangs or, as he referred to them, the Wang Family Dynasty. He joked that the family seemed to have some Irish in them, given the number of children they produced each year. He swore that Mrs. Wang had been pregnant with her last child for over a year, which brought on a fit of giggles from Meghan and Dana.

"Mike, you need to stop," said Meghan, hitting Dana's back as she choked on her food. "You're going to put Dana in the hospital."

Mike turned to Nolan, who sat with his head down, playing with his food. He seemed a little uncomfortable with the entire conversation. It occurred to Mike that it might be because neither he nor Meghan had really discussed Sarah Jane with Nolan since the whole pregnancy came to pass.

"Okay, okay… I'll stop," he said.

"I bet that's what Mr. Wang said after the last one," mumbled Nolan. He instantly turned red.

Meghan and Dana looked at him, trying hard to suppress themselves, then erupted into laughter. A smile crept across Nolan's face, which soon spilled into an ardent laugh.

"Well, what do you know," Mike said. "He does have a funny bone."

After dinner, Dana left for her evening shift at the diner while Mike sat with Meghan in the backyard. The night air was crisp and he enjoyed his steaming mug of hot cider. Nolan sat on the steps of the back porch listening as they reminisced about high school and updated each other on family members neither of them had seen in years.

▶

NOLAN WAS BEWILDERED by his parents. It had been a while since they had lived in the same space without any turmoil. For so long, family had meant separate units, just to keep the peace. He wondered if this was what it was always like to have a family.

His mother seemed like herself around his father, laughing at his jokes and actually holding her own. When Rich was home, she trod lightly. Rich was the educated one who never let you forget it. It was exhausting, talking to Rich, because everything was always a debate, but seeing his parents sitting together, reminiscing about the past without all the usual tension, gave him pause to relax. His parents seemed almost happy together.

Nolan wandered back into the house, grabbed his keys and wallet, and slipped out the front door. He pulled his bike out of the garage, hopped on it and rode to Point Pleasant Park Beach to meet Tess and her friends. They were having the last bonfire of the year.

◀◀

THE DAY after their first encounter, Nolan had seen her sitting alone in the cafeteria.

He swooped in beside her. "You left this behind." He pulled out *Frisco's Last Stand.*

"Fuck, I was looking everywhere for that," she said, snatching at the book.

He held it above her head, out of reach. "That's some crazy shit you're reading," he said. "I mean you must have read this at least a few dozen times with all these sections highlighted. Is this for English class or something?"

"No," she said, finally grabbing the book from him. "But it should be required reading for everyone. It would fucking rock the establishment to its core."

"It's a book about a bunch of racists," he said. "I doubt the English department would go for it."

"Obviously you didn't read it."

"I read a few chapters. It's just a little far-fetched, don't you think? I mean a race war?"

"You, like most white people, have been asleep to the truth," she said. "We're already in a race war. Civil rights movement... affirmative action... just the idea that we can live in the same fucking neighbourhoods with them, is the war."

"Uhm... okay," he said.

"Think about it," she continued. "We're made to feel guilty, for what? For being race realists? For creating modern civilization? For fucking walking upright? The coons, the kikes, the chinks... they're all fucking bottom-feeders that stole our culture and our ways. Now they infest our society and want to brainwash us down to their level. That's the war we're fighting."

"That's a little extreme," he said. A few of the students, sitting nearby, turned their heads to look at them.

"You know what's extreme? Every time a white man loses a job to a fucking monkey."

"Shhh," he said. "Everyone can hear you."

"Do you think I fucking care? Look at this school. There is a club for the Chinese and Blacks but when you want to have a club for us it's an issue." Nolan noticed a few of the students moving away from their area. "Why should I be ashamed of being white? If we don't protect our ways we're going to be wiped out."

"Come on, wiped out?" He rolled his eyes. "You sound a little crazy, right now."

"Look, just read the entire thing," she said, handing him back the book. "It changed my whole perspective. Read it with an open mind, and if you can't find anything to agree with, then so be it."

He went home and started reading the book again, this time without being stoned. It was hard getting through. Part of him felt guilty reading it because the story was about killing all non-white races and even anyone who mixed with non-white races. The rhetoric made him uneasy, but he liked Tess — a lot. Despite her apparent hatred towards every other culture under the sun, he was attracted to her sarcasm and to the darkness in her. He liked her moodiness, as well as the way her eyes lit up whenever she smiled. He hadn't felt this way about a girl in a long time and was willing to play the part long enough to see where it went.

He found her in the library the next day, trying to sort through a stack of crumpled notes. She looked unhappy, scowling as she pulled at her hair. Her bangs were now even shorter than before.

"Interesting," he said, handing her back the book. "Very interesting."

She didn't say anything, just took it from him and shoved it in her bag.

"What's wrong?" he said. "Everything okay?"

"Yes... I mean no," she said. "I'm just stuck. I have this report due on *The Tempest* and I fucking hate this play."

"When's it due?"

"Tomorrow."

"Then worry about it tonight." He showed her the joint in his hand. "Let's walk around the track and open your mind."

She smiled, quickly getting her stuff together.

"You know you're a bad influence," she said as they walked towards the bleachers. "And you're a year younger than me. Shouldn't it be the other way around?"

"Yeah, well you can spend the day worrying about everything or an hour worrying about absolutely nothing," he said.

They smoked the joint in silence beneath the bleachers. They could hear the occasional whistle of the school's phys-ed teacher as a class played field hockey. When they were finished, Nolan closed his eyes and lay on the cold ground, letting his high wash over him. This was the best part, being able to let it all go. It was better than sleep. Better than being home around his family. It was even better than the feeling he got after jerking off in his bedroom, late at night.

Tess lay on top of him. He opened his eyes. Her face was soft and creamy, framed by her raven hair. Her eyes were so vivid. He smiled at her and closed his eyes again. She rolled off him and lay back, propping her head up as the sun filtered through the rows of metal seats above them.

Tess told him she had been born and raised in Nova Scotia to a single mother who worked at the Swiss Chalet by the pier. She and her siblings barely saw their father and the only time her mother spoke of him was to call him a piece of shit for running off.

She'd had a stepfather for a while, whom she grew up calling Dad. She described him as the most badass man she had ever known. He was a biker with tats all over his body that represented every major experience in his life. He would spend hours telling her about his tattoos and adventures. She said she grew up adoring him but he died during a botched robbery a few years back.

"So what about you?" she asked. "What's your story?"

"Nothing much to tell," he said. "I used to live with my dad and now I live with my mom."

"That's it?" she said. "I mean, did you have a girlfriend or some slut you slept with or are you a fag or something?"

"No," he laughed. "I had a girlfriend before moving here but we kind of broke up."

"Why?" she asked. "Did she cheat on you or did you cheat on her?"

"God, where do you come up with this stuff?"

"Seriously, why did you break up?" she asked again.

"She got pregnant," he said. "I found out when I was out here for the summer. I never went back to Toronto, so I guess we're kind of broken up."

"Wait, you knocked up some chick?" she said, getting up from the ground. "Holy shit, you're like thirteen, right?"

"I'm fourteen, okay," he said. "And she's not pregnant anymore. She had an abortion."

"Wow! She had an abortion?" she said. "Wow."

"Yeah... well," he said.

"Is that why you don't live in Toronto?" she asked.

"Yeah, kind of." He looked away. "My mom thinks she can keep a better eye on me."

She laughed. "Uhm, yeah, no offence but does she realize that you supply the entire school with pot?"

"Not quite," he said, smiling shyly. "She didn't even notice the weed left behind by the people who sold her our house. I doubt she even realized what it was."

"No way!"

"Yeah. Well, I ran out, so now I have to figure out what else I can do to keep sane." He sighed. "I mean it's boring as fuck out here."

"Yeah, well maybe we can find you another hobby." She smiled at him and grabbed his hand.

Nolan hesitated for a moment. It wasn't that he wasn't attracted to her, but it felt strange holding her hand. It was the same way he felt every time Sarah Jane had held his hand. It felt forced and controlled. He looked at her and smiled awkwardly before letting go.

"I better get going." He got up and started packing his bag. "I have to get to my last class. Rich... I mean... Mr. Bevens is meeting me right after."

"Yeah," she said. "Well, I'll see you around."

He walked out from under the bleachers.

"Hey, do you want to have lunch tomorrow," she called. "I mean... unless you have friends that you rather eat with or something."

"Sure, I mean... yeah, I'm available for lunch," he said. "See you tomorrow."

Nolan felt a little strange. It wasn't just the weed. He liked Tess a lot. She wasn't afraid to say what was on her mind and was funny, but he didn't really know her. Except that she hated anyone that wasn't white and for some reason reminded him of the Glenview girls he'd gone to school with, but with a little edge.

The next day, she was waiting for him outside his third-period class. She was wearing docks with purple socks, her kilt was rolled up at the waist, showing off her legs, and her black riding shorts had shimmery black skulls imprinted. She wore heavy cherry-red lipstick and dark eye makeup.

"Let's eat outside," she said after they got their lunch. "I want you to meet my friends."

He hadn't known that she had friends. Every time he saw her in the hallway or in the cafeteria, she was alone, so he was surprised when they headed out the cafeteria to see a group of kids sitting on the cold benches by the staff parking lot. There were four of them sitting around one of the picnic tables, eating their lunch.

Three of them were boys who seemed almost in uniform with their pant legs tucked into their boots, T-shirts of a punk-rock band visible underneath unbuttoned white shirts, and spiked leather bracelets and chains hanging down from their pockets.

The boys were bald or wore their hair closely shaven. They weren't allowed to wear rings in their ears and noses at school, though Nolan could see some piercings.

The girl with them was dressed similarly to Tess. Her hair was bright red and she had freckles sprinkled across her face. One side of her head was shaved off with the long hair on top pulled into a ponytail. You could see the tattoo of a Celtic cross at the base of her neck. Like Tess, her skin was pale and white, almost ghostly against the redness of her hair.

Nolan had seen these kids around school. One of the boys was in his math class. They usually kept to themselves and often took up the back table of the cafeteria — a place none of the other students used. The black students either sneered at them or avoided them, referring to them as "the skinheads" or "the Klan."

"Who's this?" asked one of the boys. He stared at Nolan intensely as he continued to eat his sandwich.

"This is Nolan," Tess said. "He's a new friend."

Nolan tried to smile, but felt uncomfortable. Not just from hanging out with them, but it was clear that the boy Tess sat beside was her boyfriend. He watched the boy wrap his arm around her neck in a chokehold and kiss the top of her head, and then release her and go back to eating his sandwich. Tess laid her head on his thigh like a little puppy sitting at the feet of its master.

"Nolan, this is Bryce, Kevin, Jules," she said pointing to the three other kids sitting around the table. "And this is my boyfriend Rowan."

"Hi," Nolan said.

"Hi." Rowan held out his hand.

Nolan could feel the intent to intimidate in Rowan's grip and his heart beat faster when Rowan looked him directly in the eye.

Nolan looked away and over to Bryce. "Aren't you in my math class," he said, trying to sound friendly.

"Yep," replied Bryce. "Are you ready for the exam?"

"No," Nolan said. "I fucking hate that class."

"Don't be a pawn in their game," Rowan said sharply. "Are you going to let the Chinks and Japs push you out of your rightful place because you hate math? Don't stay stupid in the one place you should be superior."

"That's right, brother," Kevin said. "Math comes easy to them but the theories and methods all came from us. We have to master it or they will master us."

"Amen," said Jules.

Nolan looked nervously at Tess, who was looking up at Rowan, entranced by every word.

"If you're having problems in your class, Bryce can help you," Rowan said as a matter of fact. "He's top in the class and knows this shit inside out."

"Yeah," Nolan said, nodding. "I would appreciate that. This class is kicking my ass."

"We always help each other out." Bryce smiled, reaching out to slap Nolan's hand.

Nolan smiled back. He sat down at an open spot and started eating his lunch. Moments later, they all began talking about the Leafs game that had been on the previous night. The conversation shifted and then the four boys were arguing whether it was better to shoot left-handed, or right-handed like most American hockey players.

Nolan told them his father swore that it all depended on when you start playing the game. They debated whether that was even possible. Tess and Jules whispered together and, when Tess glanced up at Nolan he winked back, as he continued to make his case that Maurice Richard was by far the best hockey player of all time, even better than Bobby Hull. By the time the lunch period was over, Nolan had made plans to meet Bryce after school to study for the midterms.

Nolan, Tess, and Jules left the others to walk back to their classes. Nolan smiled to himself when he heard Rowan adamantly stating that Richard was totally the better player.

"See what you did?" said Jules, back in the quad. "Now I'm going to have to hear this shit for the rest of the day. It was nice to finally meet you, Nolan."

She ran off as the warning bell rang.

"Well, I better get to class," Tess said. Her face had turned red.

"Yeah, me too," he said, smiling.

She turned and ran off. Nolan looked at her and felt a rush. He shook it off and closed his blazer against the gust of wind that wasn't there.

"She's so stush," Tina Sung said loudly to Yvette. Loudly enough for everyone in the cafeteria to hear. "She thinks her shit don't stink."

"She's always been that way," Yvette agreed. They both looked at Simone, who sat at the end of their table reading *Merchant of Venice* for her English Literature class. "Angie and I don't get her. At St. Augie, she was always putting on airs like she's better than everyone."

"That's not true, Yvette," said Angie. "She's always been my friend. You just don't like her because Sean Malcolm liked her instead of you."

"Whatever, Angie," Yvette said. "You're just as whitewashed as Simone. I get why you are. Your mother is half white so you can't help it. But she was born in Jamaica."

"*Raaatid!*" Tina got up laughing. "She born in Jamaica? Don't make me laugh. Miss Prim and Proper?"

She got on top of the bench and walked across it until she was at the end of the table where Simone was sitting. She then jumped down and sat right next to Simone with a smug look on her face.

"So, I hear you're a true bredren?" laughed Tina. "Mi doubt it."

Simone looked up, her heart beating wildly. Tina Sung was speaking to her, in her face again. She looked across the table at Yvette and Angie, who were watching the whole scene unfold.

Born to Chinese Jamaican immigrants, Tina was a notorious bully who made it her mission to make everyone's life miserable. She was known for picking a fight with anyone on any given day. Even the teachers would complain to the principal if they saw her name on their roster.

"Mi mean, yuh seem Jamaican," she continued in her fake patois. "Yuh seem like yuh people come from deh siem yard."

Simone looked down at her book as her heart continued to pound in her chest. Tina was a tenth-grade student who still had to redo several of her ninth-grade classes. They were in the same geography class, but Tina had spent most of the semester either skipping class, in detention, or sitting in the back of the room with her friends, being disruptive. Since the beginning of the winter semester, Simone had been Tina's main target.

"Does your black come off if I rub it?" She swiped at Simone's arm. "I mean you are whitewashed. That what your friends over there say."

"What are you talking about?"

"I heard that you're a slut, too," Tina continued, loudly. "That you like to give head to white boys. What does white dick taste like, whitewash? Is that why your skin keeps turning white?"

Simone's eyes burned. She started to pack her book bag. She turned away from Yvette and Angie so they wouldn't see her upset and reached for her uneaten lunch.

Tina flipped her tray on the floor. "Where de bumboclaat you tink you're going?" She pushed Simone. "Your stush bitch-ass needs to know what's up."

"Why are you doing this?" Simone said. "Why are you always messing with me?"

"I don't like your fake-ass," she said, kicking Simone's food.

"I've never done anything to you."

"So!"

Many of the students were watching now. She didn't want to fight Tina — it was the last thing she wanted to do. She was happy hiding in the background, but she knew that, if she didn't say something, Tina would continue to torment her for the rest of the year.

"Just leave me alone, Tina. Aren't you sick of being in the ninth grade two years in a row? Maybe you should stop bothering me and concentrate on getting to the tenth grade."

"Oooh," chorused girls throughout the cafeteria. Some of them were laughing. Tina looked around, embarrassed, then turned her bulging eyes her way.

Simone instantly regretted the dig. She eyed the cafeteria exit, hoping to make a quick getaway before things got worse, but, as she moved to leave, Tina struck the back of her head with her fist and then began pulling at her blouse.

Simone fought back. In no time, the two girls were on the ground with Tina on top of her punching the side of her head. Simone wasn't much of a fighter but was able to scratch Tina and rip out her dangling earrings during the struggle. There was so much yelling and screaming that her ears rang. All she could hear was muffled noise as Tina boxed her and tore at her hair.

Simone lay on the floor trying to cover herself. Tina got up and kicked the side of her head. Then the teachers broke up the fight and she felt two of them pick her up before she eventually passed out.

The next thing she was lying on a couch in the principal's office. The lights were dimmed, the blinds closed. Only a trickle of sunlight filtered through. Simone tried to sit up, but her head felt as if it was going to explode. She felt dizzy and fell back. She took a deep breath and tried to get up again. She could see her book bag lying next to her feet. Just as she was attempting to get off the couch, Sister Mary Helen, the principal, walked into the office with an ice pack.

"Lie back down, Simone." Sister Mary Helen handed her the ice pack.

Sister Mary Helen wasn't very popular with the students. She was known for giving swift and harsh punishments for the simplest infractions. If your kilt was too high, you were sent to the glass-enclosed detention room. If you skipped class, you spent an hour after school cleaning the school cafeteria. If you were caught fighting, you risked being thrown out of school. But Simone liked her. Simone worked as a student volunteer once a week after school, helping her organize the students who were forced to volunteer as part of their detention. Tina Sung was there almost every day.

"Simone, you are a good student. I don't understand why you would engage with someone like Tina Sung."

"I tried to walk away," Simone said. "She kept pushing me down. I didn't know what else to do."

"I know, my dear." She gently pulled the ice pack away. "That is a nasty bump on your head. Well, you don't need to worry about that girl anymore. Tina Sung has been expelled."

"Really?" Simone asked.

"Yes, indeed. This is the third fight she's been in this year and probably the worst one yet."

"What's going to happen to her?"

"To be honest, I really don't care. She's no longer my concern and, frankly, whatever happens to her will depend on what you and your mother decide to do."

"What do you mean, Sister?"

"Well, my dear, the police have been called and statements made," she said. "So it all depends on whether or not your mother plans to press battery charges. I hope she does. Tina doesn't need another school to terrorize. What she needs is the Toronto West Detention Centre."

Simone was silent for a moment. She was glad that she didn't have to worry about Tina anymore, but feared Tina's expulsion would be blamed on her. Despite her being a bully, most of the black students in the ninth and tenth grades were Tina's friends.

"Sister Mary Helen, I need to go home," she said, trying to get up from the couch.

"Not until your mother comes for you. She should be here shortly."

Just as she said that there was a heavy knock on the door and Dex stormed into the office.

"Let's go, Simone." He grabbed her book bag.

"Mr. Allen!" Sister Mary Helen said. "I would like to talk to you about the incident before you leave."

"What is there to talk about," he said. "I have eyes. I can see that Simone had the shit kicked out of her while your teachers looked on. Tell me, Sister, why wasn't she taken immediately to the hospital to check for a concussion? I don't know what kind of school you are running, but right now Simone needs medical attention and not a meeting about the incident."

Sister Mary Helen looked dumbfounded.

"Let's go, Simone," he repeated.

Simone sat quietly in the passenger seat of the car. She leaned against the ice-cold window and felt some relief as the window cooled her swelling.

She fell asleep.

When Dex woke her up, they were at the complex.

"I thought you were going to take me to the hospital?" she said.

"You're fine," he said. "You just need some rest. Plus, I don't have time to sit around in the emergency room just for some doctor to say that there's nothing wrong with you. It's bad enough your mother had me running to your school to get you."

"Thanks," Simone mumbled, sarcastically under her breath. At least he carried her bag to the elevator.

Her entire body felt tense and sore. When she got home her mother was sitting at the kitchen table helping CJ with his homework.

"Simone," CJ cried out. He ran up and hugged her tightly.

"CJ, go to your bedroom and finish your homework." Pam turned to Simone. "Are you okay?"

"Yeah, I guess," Simone said. "I'm just a little tired."

"Jeeesus, this cut looks bad," Pam said, examining Simone's swelling. "Maybe I should take her to the doctor."

"Simone's principal said that she was fine," Dex said. "She's just a little bruised. Nothing to worry about."

"Why do you get yourself in these messes, Simone?" She took a bag of frozen peas from the freezer. "This is the third time you've gotten into an issue with this girl."

"I try to stay away from her, but she's always coming for me." Simone winced as her mother placed the bag on her swelling.

"Well, no girl just comes for you for no reason," Pam said. "Somewhere there's a reason."

"Pam, we don't have time for this!" Dex glanced at his watch. "You're still not dressed!"

"Nearly done," she said. "I just have to finish my makeup. Listen out for Mike, he should be over shortly."

Simone had forgotten that her mother and Dex were going to a dinner at the Jamaican consulate to celebrate an award Dex was receiving in Jamaica that weekend. They were going to attend the dinner and then Pam would drive him to the airport afterwards to catch the red-eye home.

"I don't get how you can ask some strange white man to watch your kids," he said from the bedroom as he changed into his tuxedo. "He can't even care for his own child let alone your children."

"Well, Mrs. Price wasn't available tonight and he's all I got, so be nice."

The noise from CJ's video game filled the living room.

"Whatever." He went into the bathroom to brush his teeth.

"Well, if it bothers you that much, I can always stay home with the kids," she said, kissing his cheek. "CJ, turn off that video game and go finish your homework."

"Mommy, just let me finish this level," he yelled back.

Simone sat down next to her brother. She heard Dex spit out his toothpaste in the bathroom sink. Then he stalked into the living room, grabbed the cord of CJ's console, and ripped the plug from the wall.

"I thought your mother told you to turn it off," he said. "Go to your fucking room like you were told."

CJ looked up at Dex, startled as the man stooped over him. His eyes opened wide before he got up and ran into his room.

Dex signalled Simone. "You, too," he said.

Before she could obey, there was a light tap on the balcony door and Mike walked into the living room.

"Pam, your neighbour is here," Dex said.

"Thanks, baby." Pam came out wearing a long shimmering emerald evening gown. The dress was snug and fit her body like a glove. Both men were looking. She looked elegant with her short hair curled into a fashionable bob.

"Hi, Mike," she said, giving him a quick hug.

"Hey, Pam," he said, grinning. "Don't you look glamorous!"

"She sure does." Dex pulled her into his arms.

"Mike, you're a lifesaver," she said, putting on her coat. "I have to drop Dex at the airport after the dinner. I should be home around midnight. I wrote down his pager number if you run into any problems."

"Got it," he said, sitting next to Simone on the chesterfield. "What in the world happened to you, Splimoney?"

Dex opened the apartment's front door. He was met by two Ontario Provincial Police officers who stood outside the door.

"Is this the Allen residence?" asked the shorter officer. He showed her his badge. "We're here to speak with Simone Allen."

"This is the residence," Pam said.

"Are you Miss Allen?" asked the taller officer, checking his notebook.

"I'm her mother," she said. "What's going on?"

"Can we come in?"

"I'm sorry," she said, "but we're just heading out."

"Ma'am, we need to speak with Simone and this may take a while."

Pam looked over at Dex, who glanced at his watch and then glared at her. She didn't want to be the reason he missed his important dinner or his flight.

"Dex, why don't you head over and I'll take a taxi when I'm done here." She handed him the keys to her car. "I'll try to get there as soon as I can."

"You sure?" Dex asked.

"Yes."

"Okay, contact me if you need me," he said, kissing her cheek. "Don't be too long."

Mike backed away as the two police officers came into the apartment. "Pam, I'm going to stay," he whispered to her as she ushered the officers into the living room.

She nodded, pulling up one of the kitchen chairs.

"What is this all about?" she asked.

"We're here to serve a complaint against your daughter, Simone Allen," said the short officer, handing her the order.

Pam's eyes widened as she read it over. "Simone, this is an assault charge!"

"Miss Pam?" Simone said.

"Why is there a complaint against Simone?" she said addressing the officers. "She was the one who was attacked and harassed by that girl."

"Not according to Tina Sung and the witnesses who gave statements," the taller officer said. "Miss Sung and her mother are pressing charges against Miss Allen for battery. Witnesses claim that she started the fight."

"That's not true," Simone said. "She came up to me and knocked my tray down. The entire school was there. They saw her. She pulled my hair and kicked the side of my head."

"Well, according to the witnesses we interviewed you acted first," said the tall officer. "They said that you pushed her."

"I pushed her out of the way because she kept coming up in my face," she cried out.

"Officers, is she being arrested?" asked Mike.

"We're here to deliver the summons and take Simone's statement," the taller officer said. "We can take her statement here or at our offices."

"We can do it here," said Pam.

The officers spent the next hour talking to Simone. She described what had happened at the lunch table in the cafeteria. When the officer asked her what was said, Simone was quiet. She tried to remember, but couldn't quite.

"Miss Sung stated that you are known to have a lot of white boyfriends," said the shorter officer, reading from his notebook. "And that you had sexual contact with one of her friend's boyfriends. When Tina mentioned it in the cafeteria you got mad and hit her. Is that true?"

"NO!" she cried out. "I mean, I did get mad when she said those things to me but I have never done anything like that. I don't even have a boyfriend."

"Then why would you hit her?" He asked. "You admit you were angry?"

"I didn't hit her!" Simone blubbered. "I don't know why she's saying this! She's never liked me."

"Well, according to other witnesses we interviewed you're engaging in sexual intercourse on school property and..." he consulted his notes, "'Simone was angry because we were planning to tell the principal.'"

"I know it's hard for you to talk in front of your mother," said the shorter officer, "but it would be best if you told the truth."

"I'm telling you the truth." She looked over at her mother and then at Mike. "They're lying."

"Who are these witnesses you keep talking about?" Pam bellowed. "You keep referring to witnesses but we have no idea who."

The tall officer flipped back a few pages in his notebook. "Angie Michaels and Yvette Johnson," he said. "Do you know them?"

"Yes," Simone replied. The tears started to stream down her cheek.

"But these are your friends, Simone," Pam said. "Why are they saying this?"

"I don't know," cried Simone. "I don't mess with boys. I don't know why they are saying lies."

"Officers, have you spoken to the school? Have you talked to the other students that were there?" Mike asked. "It seems like you've only spoken with students that have a problem with Simone. I'm sure other students witnessed the whole thing."

"We plan to see the principal tomorrow," he said. "But, in the meantime, Miss Allen is expected to make an appearance in front of a family court judge tomorrow morning. The summons has the time and courtroom number."

"That should do it," said the shorter officer. "We'll contact you if we have any further questions."

When the officers left, Simone sat down on the sofa crying. She couldn't understand why this was happening. She had thought that Yvette and Angie were her friends.

"What the raas is going on with you?" Pam yelled. "You think you're big enough to have your ass out all over town?"

Simone looked up at her mother, who came over and gave her a swift slap across the face.

"No!!!" Simone screamed out. She tried to block the slaps that came down on her head. "They're telling lies."

"Pam, calm down!" Mike tried to pull her off Simone.

"Everything I said was the truth," she cried. "Why don't you believe me? Why do you always believe everyone else but me?"

"Pam!" Mike pushed her away from Simone. "This isn't helping!"

Pam sat down on the chair. "You're nothing more than a yard dog," she said evenly. "I didn't bring you here so you can act slack."

"I never wanted to be here," yelled Simone. "All you do is yell at me and hit me. I'd rather grow up on the streets in Jamaica than have you as a mother."

Pam stared at her darkly, a look of venom in her eyes. "You ungrateful little bitch," she said. "Well then let's see you manage on your own since you're grown enough to suck little white boy's dicks. Let's see how far your big mouth will get you when you're dealing with a judge tomorrow."

"Pam, you don't even know what really happened!" Mike said. "Simone is not that kind of girl."

"Just like Nolan isn't that kind of boy? Well, you keep telling yourself that!" She grabbed her purse.

"Pam, are you seriously leaving right now?" he yelled out.

"You bet I am," she said as she headed for the door. "She's a grown woman now. Let her figure it out."

Simone was curled on the carpet crying, her little brother trying to comfort her. Mike sat beside her. He told her that her mother needed to cool off and that everything would be fine in the morning.

▶

AT MIDNIGHT, Pam hadn't returned home. Mike tried to contact Dex through the pager number but didn't get a response. It was morning when he woke up on Pam's couch to find that she still hadn't come home. He picked up the summons that was still on the coffee table. The hearing was scheduled for 10:00 am in Courtroom B.

"Where's Miss Pam?" Simone asked. She walked into the living room with CJ. "Is she still gone?"

Mike nodded.

"Look, I'm going to be honest with you," he said. "I don't know where your mother is, but we're not going to worry about that right now. Right now I want you to help me get your brother ready for school. Okay?"

"Okay, Mr. Mike," she said. "Is she going to come back in time for me to go to the courthouse?"

"I hope so, honey," he said. "But don't worry. If she doesn't get back in time, I'll take you, okay?"

Simone nodded her head and she led CJ back into their bedroom to get ready for school.

Mike tried to call Pam's office. He hoped that Maureen would be at work but no one answered. He realized that it was still too early. He went back to his apartment and took a quick shower. He searched his closet to find something proper to wear. The only thing suitable was the navy suit he'd worn at Amber's wedding and at the court in Halifax. He tried to call Maureen again. He tried to call Pam's extension but it only went to her answering service.

Mike didn't know what to do. He didn't have a lawyer. He hoped that Pam would cool off and come to her senses in time. But, when he and Simone got to the courtroom, her case was the first on the docket and everything happened too quickly.

The judge looked at Simone. "Stand up, young lady," he said. "Where is your lawyer?"

Simone didn't know how to respond. She looked at Mike, who stood up to address the judge.

"Sir, she received the summons last night. We didn't have much time to get her a lawyer."

The judge glanced at Simone and then addressed the crown attorney.

"Donaldson, why is this defendant in my court a day after getting the summons? Is this a murder charge?"

"No, sir," said the lawyer, looking at his notes. "This is a battery charge. It must have been a mix-up, your honour."

"No matter," he said. "Arlene, call legal aid and have them send someone over. We'll take an hour recess."

Within thirty minutes, a young blond woman entered the courtroom and sat at the table next to Simone.

"Hello, Miss Allen," she said. "I'm Christine Baxter."

"Hi."

"Hello," she said to Mike. "Who are you?"

"I'm Mike... Mike O'Shea," he said. "I'm Simone's neighbour."

"Where are her parents?"

"Her mother is on her way," he lied. "She's running late."

"Okay, well, hopefully she'll be here soon," she said. "Give me a minute to look over everything."

Simone and Mike nervously looked on as the lawyer perused the notes in her file. After about ten minutes, she looked up at Simone and smiled.

"Your friends don't seem to like you very much," she said. "Battery is a serious charge, but I will do everything I can to challenge the police report. In the meantime, the only thing the judge wants to hear from you is guilty or not guilty. Then we'll get you home, okay?"

"Yes, Ma'am."

Just as Christine had said, the judge asked her to indicate her plea.

"Not guilty, sir," she said, quietly.

"Who is Miss Allen's parent or guardian?" he asked.

Simone's lawyer whispered in Simone's ear. Simone whispered back. The lawyer turned to Mike. "Why isn't she here?"

Mike whispered that Pam would be there any minute.

"Your honour, I have been told that Simone's mother is running late," Christine stated. "We're expecting her shortly."

"That's the problem with these girls," he said, shaking his head. "No one seems to be responsible for them."

"I'm here, sir," Mike interjected.

"And who are you?" the judge asked.

"I'm Simone's neighbour, Mike O'Shea," he replied. "I... I'm usually her guardian when her mother is away."

"Your Honour, he's also listed as an emergency contact at her school," Christine continued.

"That's not good enough, counsel," said the judge. "Is there a legal guardian present?"

"No," she replied.

"Typical," he muttered. "Well, until her mother appears before me I'm going to remand Miss Simone Allen to Toronto West Detention Centre. Madam Registrar, have a social worker meet with Simone before she is taken into custody."

"Wait, what does this mean?" cried Simone.

"I don't know, sweetheart," Mike said. "We'll fix this, okay?"

"I don't understand," she said, looking from Mike to her lawyer. "Where is my mother, Mr. Mike? Please call my mother. I didn't do anything. I didn't do anything. She came up to me and beat me up and I have to go to a detention centre? Please don't let them send me away. I didn't do anything."

Mike felt helpless as he watched Simone being led away.

"Wait here," he said to the lawyer. "Her mother's office will be open. Let me try her again."

"Okay... I have twenty minutes before I have to run to my next meeting. I can't wait for long."

"One second," he said, rushing to the payphone.

He dialled Pam's office, but again it went straight to voicemail. He hung up and dialled Maureen's number.

"Maureen Meunier's desk."

"Maureen, it's Mike," he said frantically. "Is Pam there? It's an emergency."

"Hi Mike," she said. "I just got back from a meeting with her boss. Apparently, there was a family emergency in Jamaica and she skipped town. She won't be back for at least a week."

"Wait! What?" he said. "Did she give you a number for anyone to reach her?"

"Nope, but she did say to him that, when she landed she would phone, and leave a number. What's going on?"

"I can't talk about it right now," he said. Simone's lawyer was motioning to her watch. "When she calls back with a number, please call me as soon as possible. Leave the number at my house, okay?"

Mike's mind was spinning. What was she thinking, going to Jamaica while her daughter was sitting in a detention centre? Pam and Simone had a rocky relationship and for years he'd kept silent over her harsh disciplinary methods. He chalked it up to a cultural difference in parenting, but, since she'd come back from Jamaica, there seemed to be a ceasefire between the two. Pam was preoccupied with her new relationship with Dex and Simone was busy at school. Mike had thought things were getting better. He'd never imagined that she could sink this low. This was throwing Simone to the wolves.

"Mr. O'Shea, I really have to go now," said Christine. "Here's my card. Please contact me when you hear from her mother."

"Wait... wait a minute," he said. "She's only fourteen years old. We can't just leave her in there. I know Simone. I've known her since she was a little girl. She's not the kind of kid who gets into fights. She gets straight As and volunteers at school and even has a part-time job. This is a huge mistake."

"I get that, Mr. O'Shea, but, unless I can get other witnesses to corroborate her side of the story, then it's her word against theirs," she said. "Look, I have to be in another court proceeding. It should only take a few hours. Why don't you give me until the end of the day and we can regroup this evening at my office. The address is on the card."

Mike nodded. He watched her rush down the hallway with her briefcase. Here he was in another courtroom, feeling defeated. It was the exact same feeling he'd had when he lost Nolan. The only thing he could think of doing was head back home to wait by the phone and hope that Pam would call. When he got home, he called Maureen, but she didn't have any new information. He wanted to tell his cousin everything, but knew that would only add fuel to the fire. He went over to Mrs. Price's to see if she'd heard from Pam, but she was shocked that Pam had left for Jamaica, and she got into a real state when Mike reluctantly told her what had happened to Simone.

"Jee-sus! Why the raas didn't you tell me sooner?" She picked up the phone and dialled out. "Esma," she yelled into the mouthpiece, "mi not staying quiet no longer! That low-down bitch done broke the last straw."

The next thing Mike knew, Mrs. Price's daughter, her son-in-law and his brother were in her kitchen. Esma's brother-in-law was a lawyer who had just moved back to Toronto from New York. Mike tried to explain that the court had assigned Simone a lawyer and showed them the business card.

"What she look like?" asked Mrs. Price. "She old, young, white, black?"

"What does it matter?" he asked. "She seems to know what she's doing."

"Oh, she's white," said Esma. "Probably blonde. Look, Mike, I'm not trying to sound harsh, but we've seen too many of our friends and family get railroaded in this so-called justice system. If we leave Simone up to this lawyer, she's going to be in there for a year before everything gets figured out and, in the end, she'll end up getting deported."

"Deported?" he said in shock.

"Yes, deported," she reaffirmed. "She's not a Canadian citizen.

Pam applied for her to get her citizenship, but it's not official yet. This needs to be handled before it gets out of hand. Kevin is an experienced immigration lawyer. He's been involved in cases like this for years."

"What I need is to meet with her principal," Kevin said to Mrs. Price.

"She goes to St. Joseph," Mrs. Price answered.

"Good," he said. "Pass me the phone."

By the end of the afternoon, Kevin had arranged a meeting with Simone's court-appointed lawyer, the crown attorney, and Sister Mary Helen.

The principal was furious. "I don't understand how your office could have screwed this up," Sister Mary Helen said to the crown attorney. "Simone was the one harassed and beaten by that girl. She's one of my best students and if you had taken the time to talk to me I would have told you that. The police officer I called after the attack interviewed at least ten students and five faculty members who witnessed the entire fight."

"I understand that you are angry, but..." he said, trying to interject.

"Furthermore," she continued, "why wasn't Tina Sung arrested?"

The crown lawyer looked over his paperwork for a moment before answering. "So we are not discussing a plea deal?"

"Most certainly not," said Kevin.

"It seems there was a mistake on our part," said the lawyer. "We had two separate units dealing with the incident and neither was aware of the other. It's an unfortunate mistake..."

"Yes, it is unfortunate," said Kevin. "Quite a serious mistake. I'm assuming that you are going to get to the bottom of this immediately?"

▶

ANGIE, Yvette, and their parents were summoned to the crown attorney's office, where they were informed that if they did not tell the truth they would be charged for making false claims and hindering due process. It was Angie who folded first. She broke down in tears when she admitted that Simone was actually the victim. Yvette then started to cry. She said that she had been telling Tina for weeks that Simone had done things with white boys in their old school. Both of them finally admitted that none of the stories were true and that Tina had had it in for Simone from the moment she met her.

The next morning, the crown attorney called an emergency session with the judge and explained everything.

"It is a shame that these lies have caused this young lady hardship," the judge said in his ruling. "I will grant a dismissal and extend my apologies to Miss Allen. However, I still have not seen the mother. Is she in court today?"

Kevin and Christine looked at each other.

"No, your honour," Christine said. "It seems that she had to go to Jamaica for a family emergency."

"Shouldn't this be an emergency?" he said, reviewing his notes. "It states here that police officers spoke directly with her and that she understood that her daughter was to appear in court yesterday. What kind of emergency would make her leave for Jamaica?"

"We are not certain, your honour," Kevin said. "We're still trying to locate her."

"Well, it seems we have a problem," he said to both attorneys. "Unless you provide her mother or a legal guardian, Simone will stay in the detention centre until Children's Aid can come up with a solution."

"Your honour, we have several people who are willing to step in until her mother returns," said Kevin. "People who have known her for several years."

"That is commendable, but we have a process," he said. "I can't in good conscience hand her over to just anyone without going through the proper channels. Does she have grandparents or a father who could step in?"

"No, your honour," Christine replied.

"Then you know the deal," he said. "File the proper paperwork and we'll meet in a week."

"I don't understand," Simone cried out. "Why can't I leave?"

"That is all," the judge said, banging his gavel.

Simone was visibly trembling and tears streamed down her cheeks. "I don't want to go back to the detention centre."

"It's okay, honey," Mrs. Price said to her. "You'll be out soon. Just be patient and we'll clear things up, okay?"

"But I didn't do anything wrong," she said crying as she was escorted out of the courtroom. "I didn't do anything."

Mrs. Price broke down as Simone was led away. Mike sat down next to her. He turned away from Mrs. Price, unable to watch the old woman cry. He could feel his own teeth clench as Simone disappeared behind the courtroom's side door.

PART III

34

He sat under the dock, holding onto the piling, as the waves splashed against him. It was dark and cold and his boots were full of mud and sludge. The sirens grew louder and louder. He didn't know if he could hold on for much longer. A splinter from the piling had gone into the palm of his hand and he clenched his teeth against the excruciating pain.

"Be a soldier," he kept telling himself. "Be a fucking soldier."

This was his test. The proof that through it all he could survive. If he could evade the police for a while longer and not die of hyperthermia, he could make it through anything. This was no longer some story in a book, it was the real deal. It was the war. The war that raged in his head, that filled his day and fuelled his nightmares.

He could hear the cops walking overhead. He could hear their radios with directions from their precinct dispatcher.

"Four white male suspects and a female suspect at large. Suspects in their late teens, early twenties. Description of the male suspects, bald with tattoos on the backs of their skulls. Female suspect has brunette hair and several ear piercings…"

He stopped breathing. One of the police officers was right

above where he was hiding. He held onto the cross-brace beneath the dock, hoping that it would soon be over, but the cops just stood around up there. Then suddenly a big light shot from a passing boat and blinded him. His first instinct was to shield his eyes but he knew he would fall into the sea. Instead, he shut his eyes. As the light shifted, he looked around and could see the others holding on in their spots as well. But Tess was barely holding on. She'd been mid-climb when the cops had arrived. He wished he was over there with her, helping her cling to her post. She should have never come. He should have forced her to stay behind, but only Rowan had ever been able to tell her what to do.

The others were steady and calm. None of them looked scared. They looked pensive and focused as they waited for the cops to move on.

A moment later, the noise of the radios disappeared, cars started to drive away, and nothing but silence and the probing beam of the boat were left.

Rowan signalled all of them to keep quiet and stay where they were. Nolan wasn't convinced that it was over yet, but he was sure that Tess couldn't hold on. She was slipping. He watched her try to grasp onto a cross-brace, then she screamed and fell into the waves below.

"Tess!" He jumped in after her.

Soon the light from the boat found her and cops were shouting out commands. They all let go into the ice-cold water. Trying to swim to shore, Nolan kept looking around for Tess, but the spotlight had lost her and it was too dark to see anything. He swam toward the lights along the bay and then he made out the others climbing onto the beach. He saw Tess pull herself up from the freezing undertow. She was on her hands and knees, coughing up water, unable to scatter with the rest of them. The police caught up with her first. They dragged her out of the sea and cuffed her. She was like an animal trying to break free, screaming at the top of her lungs.

He started to swim away from shore, against the frigid cold waves that threatened to suck him under. His arms burned as he struggled against the massive pull of the sea. He knew that, if he didn't get out soon, he would drown from pure exhaustion. He gave up. He let the waves carry him to shore. He was farther down the beach than where the cops were. He saw them apprehend Rowan and Kevin, but it seemed that Bryce had gotten away. Once on shore, he ran as fast as he could, stumbling on the rocky beach until he got to a wet marsh.

The sirens and radio and voices grew faint as he ran. He knew they would keep looking for him and that it would only be a matter of time before they picked up his trail. His teeth chattered as he ran. He stopped for a moment and took off his boots, emptying out the water, sludge, and seaweed. He put his boots back on, tightening his laces before covering them with his cargo pants. He decided to ditch his trench coat. It felt like a dozen heavy wet blankets on his back. He tossed it into a blue metal trash barrel before he pulled the wet hoodie over his slick bald head.

He continued running until he got to the road. At first, he wasn't sure where he was, but he kept going and came to a bus stop. Miraculously, a tour bus had pulled up. He snuck aboard with the crowd, leaving the area. An hour later he turned onto his street. The lights were still on in the living room. He went around back, in through the side door, and straight to the laundry room where he took off his wet clothes. He searched the dryer and found a pair of Rich's clean boxers and an undershirt.

He walked upstairs and into the kitchen where his mother sat at the kitchen table. The room was filled with police and the moment they saw him they tackled him.

"Don't hurt him," his mother screamed. She tried to pull one of the police officers off him.

"Back off, Ma'am."

They pinned Nolan to the ground and cuffed him.

Nolan could see his mother being dragged back by one of the female officers and escorted into the living room. Her eyes were drained and her face was pale. The police officer read him his rights. They pulled him up and took him out of the house just as Rich's car pulled into the driveway. Rich got out of the car and stood, arms folded, and watched the police put him into the patrol car.

▶

MEGHAN AND RICH waited in the police station while Nolan was processed and booked for battery. His arrest had come at the worst possible time. Meghan was in the middle of an audit at work and battling the flu. She sat in the precinct, her eyes red and puffy from crying and her throat burning from an infection. She was miserable. Rich had tried to get her to stay home while he bailed Nolan out, but she'd insisted on going with him. Rich reached for her hand, but she quickly moved it away, blowing her nose as an excuse for the rejection.

"It's going to be okay," he said to her. "Bob is one of the best attorneys and he'll get these bogus charges dropped."

"Bogus?" she said hoarsely. "He's being charged for nearly beating a homeless man to death. Do you understand, Rich? This isn't some scuffle in the school's cafeteria or a barroom fight that got out of hand. This is serious."

"Did you call Mike?" he asked.

"No."

The last thing she wanted to do was tell Mike that Nolan was in trouble again. After the first few scrapes with the law, Mike had stopped lashing out at her for letting it get this far. She no longer needed the reminder. She'd realized how bad it was the moment her son came home with his head fully shaved with *14/88* inked on the back of his head.

Meghan had no idea exactly what it all meant and had tried to chalk up Nolan's subculture activities to teenage angst. But after months of him hiding out in his bedroom with the lights turned off and daunting punk music piercing the walls, she had evicted him from his second-floor bedroom to the newly soundproofed basement. It was the move to the basement that she believed was the moment she lost him.

He had painted the entire basement black, adding a few horrifying posters to add colour to the bleakness. There was a poster of Hitler addressing a crowd of supporters, and one of a punk band that he listened to daily, and a poster of dead Jewish bodies being stockpiled in a ditch. When Meghan saw these, she immediately regretted her decision, but Rich told her to be reasonable.

"Let him be! He's a boy trying to find his way to being a man."

"Are you kidding?" she said, pointing to the poster of Hitler. "Is this what you call being a man?"

"Yes and no," Rich argued. "He's discovering himself and his culture."

"What fucking culture?" she yelled. "This racist bullshit is not his culture. This is not what he grew up seeing."

"No, but maybe that's why he's acting out." He went on: "White kids are made to feel guilty for their culture, their history, their presence. It might not be the right choice of imagery. It's nothing I would recommend, but I understand it."

"So you're saying that you're fine with this?" she said. "Posters of Hitler, looking like a skinhead — this is what you think he should be focusing on?"

"Of course not," he said. "But when my black students study Malcolm X and spout 'black power' I don't condemn them."

"Hitler killed millions of Jews," she yelled.

"So they say," he responded. "Look, I'm not saying that he needs to go around terrorizing the neighbourhood. I'm just saying that knowing history, the good and bad, will help shape him."

Tears stung her eyes as she sat in the police station remembering the past eighteen months during which she could have stopped Nolan. Times she wished she had called Mike for help. She should have told Rich to shut up every time he and Nolan sat around the dining room table discussing the plight of the white working class in Canada. And then there was Tess, the scary girl who dropped out of high school a year before Nolan dropped out.

Tess had been the greatest influence on Nolan. It was clear to Meghan that he was infatuated with her and would probably follow her to hell if asked. He never introduced her as his official girlfriend, but Meghan knew there was a lot going on between them. There were many mornings when she saw Tess sneaking out of the basement, wearing one of Nolan's T-shirts. She knew for certain that they were sleeping together when the basement toilet overflowed and at least ten condoms floated up. She knew there had been another pregnancy scare when she rummaged through Nolan's knapsack looking for drugs only to find a pamphlet from a clinic that performed abortions. She'd never said a word. Confronting him would only mean admitting that she was as bad as Mike or worse than him. Worse because Mike hadn't allowed Nolan to become a skinhead — she had.

"I need to call Mike," she finally admitted to Rich. "He needs to know."

"Do you think that's necessary?" Rich responded.

"My son is looking at possible jail time, Rich. It was necessary two years ago."

35

"Get your feet off the table," Dex said to CJ. They were sitting in the living room watching the Celtics play the Bulls.

"I have my socks on."

"I don't care if they were blessed and sprayed with holy water, it's a disgusting habit. Move them!"

CJ reluctantly moved his feet. He scowled at Dex. His stepfather ignored his glare and continued to watch the game while he sipped his rum cream. Basketball was the one thing they had in common. The one thing they might have bonded over.

Dex always had something critical to say during the games. If CJ liked a particular player, Dex would find ways to bash that player. He always made a big story of how he had played basketball all through his university days, which made him the resident expert. It annoyed CJ, who often found himself silently wishing he was next door at Mike's place watching the game.

CJ's pants started to buzz. He pulled out the beeper his mother had got him for Christmas and smiled when he recognized the number.

It was a bone of contention between Dex and Pam.

"He looks like a drug dealer with that pager," Dex once said to Pam.

"You have a pager, Dex," she said. "No one sees you as a drug dealer."

Dex stared at him. It was the middle of winter and CJ was walking around wearing a black tank top with his jeans hanging off his ass showing his underwear. It infuriated him. It also infuriated him that Pam always had an excuse for her precious CJ. The way she doted on him, buying him expensive shoes, clothing, and even a CD player for no reason at all. Dex couldn't understand how she could be so strict with Simone, while CJ got away with murder.

"Where you going?" he asked CJ, who was putting on his Air Jordan sneakers. "Your mother will be home soon."

"Yo, I'm just going downstairs," he said. "Jojo forgot his math homework. I'm lending him my textbook."

"Don't you think you should take your textbook with you, eediat?" Dex threw the math book at his feet.

CJ kissed his teeth as he picked up the textbook.

Dex was ready to get up and strike him, but Pam walked into the apartment.

"Hey baby," she said, smiling at CJ. "Where you going?"

"Just down at Jojo's," he said, kissing his mother on the cheek.

"Well don't be too long. Dinner will be ready soon."

Pam dropped her briefcase by the door. She sat next to Dex and hugged him.

"Hello, my love," she said, softly nuzzling his ear.

"Hi," he said.

He continued watching the game. He didn't feel like engaging her. His drink was finished. He got up to fix another.

"That boy better get home quick," Pam said as she followed him into the kitchen. "He spends too much time gallivanting with Jojo and not enough time in the books."

"Humph," Dex grunted. He turned off the television set. "I'm going to watch the rest of the game in the bedroom. Call me when dinner is ready."

Pam watched his back as he walked into their bedroom, closing the door behind him. She pulled out the bag of rice. It was going to be another evening eating alone.

▶

CJ FLEW down the eleven flights of stairs and was panting by the time he got to the basement. He headed to the laundry room where he could hear the machines buzzing and found her sorting her clothes. A big broad smile spread across his face as he stood behind her and wrapped his long arms around her shoulders.

"Jesus, CJ, you scared the shit out of me." She turned around and gave him a hug and kiss on his cheek.

"Sorry Si," he said, laughing. He sat on the counter next to her clothes. "You just started?"

"Yeah, just putting a load in the wash. Tell me something, CJ, and be serious, okay? Is it really necessary to dress like you're auditioning for Jodeci?"

"Please," he said bigging up his chest. "They dress like me!"

"Oh God," she said, kissing her teeth. "I don't get it. It's freezing outside and you act like you're going to Caribana."

CJ laughed as he picked up one of her school shirts and started buttoning it. It was their Wednesday ritual. CJ would make some sort of excuse to his mother and keep his big sister company while she did her weekly laundry. They would spend the hour catching up. Sometimes she would help him with his homework, other times they would just talk.

◀◀

AFTER THE BATTERY charges had been dropped, Simone spent 17 days, 16 hours and 23 minutes in the detention centre before she was finally allowed to go home. It had been an uphill battle. No one had been able to get hold of Pam for several days, and it wasn't until she finally contacted Mrs. Price to check up on CJ that she finally heard that Simone was in trouble and needed her help. Pam's only response was, "Let her rot" before she abruptly hung up on the old woman.

With no other options, Mrs. Price hired her in-law Kevin to get her temporary guardianship over Simone. A new family court magistrate was assigned to the request and, despite the urgency, the judge insisted that Pam be given a few more days to respond to the petition before they made the guardianship final.

The day after Pam came back from Jamaica, she was served with a subpoena. She attended the hearing, but didn't say a word to anyone and only answered "Yes" when the judge asked her if she understood that Mrs. Price had made a petition for guardianship. She barely looked at her daughter when the judge asked why she was not fighting the petition.

"She's trouble and an ungrateful child," she responded directly. "She's a big woman now and if Mrs. Price wants to raise her, then so be it."

Tears streamed down Simone's cheek as her mother walked out of the courtroom with Dex. Kevin drove them back to the apartment where Mrs. Price comforted her.

"It's for the best," she said. "Your mother has some demons that she continues to battle. Demons she thinks will go away, but, no matter where she go, they will always follow her. You better off, baby."

Things quickly changed. CJ was no longer allowed to go over to Mrs. Price's house. Pam enrolled him in an after-school program and, for a long time, Simone didn't have any communication with her brother until one afternoon he wandered into the basement and found her doing laundry. He was excited to see his sister. He tried to speak to her but she pushed him away.

"Please don't ignore me, Simone," he said. "I hate that I can't see you. I hate that Mommy won't let you come home. I wish she would let you come home."

She continued to fold her clothes. "Well, I'm glad that I don't live there anymore," she said. "I'm much happier where I'm at."

"I'm not," he said. "You know Mom and Dex got married a few weeks ago."

Silence.

"Is he still bothering you?" she asked him.

CJ didn't say anything. He didn't want to tell his sister that Dex had punched him in the gut a few days ago when his mother was at work, or that he'd kicked him the month before. Or the really bad time when Dex was "playing around" and sat on top of him until he was gasping for air.

"Nah," he lied. "He's a dummy. I just stay out of his way."

"I know you're lying," she said. She cupped his face and looked him directly in his eye. "Listen to me, okay? If he hurts you, come to Mrs. Price. I don't care what Pam says. You just come and I'll protect you, okay?"

"I miss you," CJ said. "Why can't you talk to Mommy and just tell her you're sorry so you can come home? You don't have to mean it. Just tell her what she wants to hear."

Simone took a deep breath and pulled him into a hug. She then grabbed his hands and kissed it.

"I'll tell you what," she said. "Why don't we meet in the laundry room once a week. Does she still work late on Wednesdays?"

CJ nodded.

"Good, then you come down here after school while I do laundry and we can catch up." She smiled down at him. "We can talk about anything you want or play cards or I can help you with your homework."

"I'd like that," he said. "You know, it's better when you are with us."

"I know," she said. "But it's better for me when I'm not."

⏪

THE WHOLE ORDEAL with Simone hardened Mike's feelings towards Pam. He hadn't recognized the woman he'd seen in the courtroom. The one who ran off with her boyfriend and left her daughter alone and scared, then came home and disowned her.

The woman he knew was the one who had picked him up at the station when he'd come home from Halifax, distraught over losing custody of Nolan. That woman had taken him to a nearby bar, where they'd had a few drinks. That was the woman he knew.

She'd lain next to him and held his hand when he'd cried through the early hours of the next morning. She'd turned to him when the sun rose and kissed him and told him that everything was going to be okay. Her body gave him warmth and she didn't push him away when he hungrily kissed her back.

He remembered that morning vividly. The way she gave herself to him. The way his body felt when she wrapped her legs around him as he entered her. A moment he hadn't expected but desperately needed. He spent the entire morning making love to her, purging himself of the sadness that bored a hole in his soul. They had connected in a way that neither of them had expected.

But all of that changed when Dexter came into the picture. The feelings they had for each other quickly vanished. Pam got swept up. He'd tried to move past it, but that morning with her had changed him — Pam had changed him.

"Did you see the notice from the building?" It was a few days after Simone's release from the detention centre. Pam had joined Mike on the balcony to have a smoke and to show him the pamphlet that she had found in her mailbox. "Looks like the building is finally fixing these ramshackle balconies."

The new owner planned to redo the outside of the buildings, to transform the dreary greyish walls to a sleek black, and upgrade to brand-new metal balconies. The balconies would no longer extend the length of two apartments; instead, each apartment would have its own private area.

"It's going to make the place look much better." She passed him the pamphlet. "Give it a little class."

"I don't get you," he said. "You act like nothing has happened. Like everything is business as usual. What the hell happened with you and Simone?"

"I don't want to talk about it," she said.

"No, Pam. You owe me that much," he said. "Do you know what it was like for her? To be locked up for something she didn't do? You just bailed on her. We didn't know where to find you and, even when you knew those girls were lying, you still kicked her out." Pam sat unmoved. She lit her cigarette. "Pam, are you listening to me! Why can't you admit that you got it wrong? She's a good kid. A good student. She doesn't run the streets or give any trouble. I don't even think she has any friends. Why are you treating her like shit?"

"You don't know what you're talking about," she barked at him. "She has been a problem from the day she born. I *never* wanted her. I was *never* given a choice."

"What are *you* talking about? We all have choices."

"Not me!" She got up from her seat. "I'm done with this conversation."

"No!" he said, grabbing her arm. "What the fuck does that even mean — what choice weren't you given?"

"Just drop it, okay," she yelled. "Let go of my fucking arm."

"Pam, tell me," he said. "It's not her, is it? This hatred you have is not about her."

"It's always about her!" She pulled away from him. "Every time

I see her face, I don't see my child. I see the men who raped me! I hear them laughing as they held me down and pried my legs open. You tell me how I'm supposed to love her when all I can remember is that. You tell me!"

Mike sat in disbelief. "Pam, I didn't know... I'm so sorry," he stammered. "Why didn't you ever tell me?"

"Why should I tell you? You think all Jamaican women are whores who spend their nights fucking every last man on earth. Isn't that what you tell your son? Why don't you tell him about the girls that get forced on, huh? Do you ever tell him about that?"

Pam looked away from him. The cigarette she held burned slowly down to its core.

Mike took it from her. He lit her another cigarette as it started to rain lightly. She took a few drags to calm herself down, then began telling him about the night that changed her life forever.

◄◄

IT WAS a few years after her father died of leukemia. With the money he had left her and some help from her Aunt Marva, she was sent to Manchester to attend the private school in Mandeville. It hadn't been an easy adjustment. Pam was still grieving her father's passing as well as trying to navigate being on her own.

As time went on, she started to find her smile again. She made a few friends that she hung out with — girls who also lived at the boarding school. She soon became one of the more popular students and, by the time she turned sixteen, she was like any other girl. She wore makeup, styled her hair like Tammi Terrell, and, on the weekends, she would sneak off to Kingston to listen to the latest local Jamaican musicians. But what should have been the most whimsical and exciting moment of her youth turned into the most horrific night of her life.

Pam was one of the few students who remained at the school

during the Christmas holidays. She would have preferred to travel with her Aunt Marva to London, but she had exams and wanted to stay behind and study. She wasn't too dispirited by the idea of remaining on campus. She had the company of her best friend, Julie, who had convinced her parents to let her miss their annual Christmas trip to Miami.

The girls were invited to Headmaster Lewis' home for Boxing Day lunch. It was an annual tradition for the students who stayed behind. The students were joined by the headmaster's son, Jason Lewis, who had come home from the University of Cambridge with three of his friends, who were visiting Jamaica for the first time.

Everyone knew of Jason, who was a former student. He was virtually a legend. Besides his status as the headmaster's son, his natural athleticism had granted him the title of captain of most of the school's sporting teams. He had always been voted president of the school's Welcoming Club. The academy's pamphlets still featured his handsome, smiling face.

The moment Pam and Jason crossed paths they were drawn to each other. Pam had assumed that, because his father was a white man from Manchester, England, Jason would be just another Brit, but when she heard his deep Jamaican accent she knew he was an island boy.

Jason was obviously very attracted to her and made it a point to let her know. He sat as close as he could to her during the lunch.

Pam was nervous, but tried to stay calm whenever he looked in her direction. His tall muscular body, his wavy brown hair cascading over his forehead, his dancing light brown eyes — all made her heart pound, and she hung onto his every word as he addressed the others and answered his father's questions. It didn't matter that they barely spoke to each other during lunch, the attraction between them was strong enough without words getting in the way.

"What is your name?" he asked as he walked her and Julie back to the dormitory.

"Pamela," she said sweetly. "Actually, my friends call me Pam."

"Pam," he repeated. "That's a pretty name. Well, Pam, I didn't get a chance to speak to you at lunch, but I hope we can rectify that. My friends and I are going to a dance. I'm showing them around. Would you like to come?"

"I don't know. I...I would love to, but curfew is early tonight because of the holiday," she said.

"Come nuh," he said, kissing his teeth. "Find a way to meet us and bring your friend, too. My friend Dennis fancies her."

Julie blushed and he smiled at her. Pam looked over at her friend, unsure of what to say. Julie's eyes were wide with excitement. They arranged to meet him and his friends around 10:00 pm, after everyone else had gone to sleep.

The night started out okay. They walked along the side of the road, Jason and his friends with Pam and Julie. The girls giggled at the boys, who were dressed in matching black slacks, white dress shirts, and beige dinner jackets.

"But wait," Pam said. "Dem dress like de Wailers. Backside!"

The two girls kept giggling as they walked, but, after a while, Julie whispered to Pam, "Which house party be this far? I don't know about this, Pam. This don't feel right. If they know it's going to be far, why they don't arrange for a ride?"

"Hush, nuh," Pam said, hoping that Jason hadn't overheard them.

Jason and Dennis walked over. While Dennis talked to Julie, Jason and Pam went on ahead.

"You look really nice tonight," Jason said to her.

"Thank you."

"Pam," she heard Julie cry out. "Pamela!"

"Yes," she yelled back. "What is it?"

Julie ran up to her and pulled her aside and whispered in her ear, "Jason's friend is a toad. He place his dirty hand on my bum."

"Julie, relax," she said. "He's only having fun with you. Plus we're almost there. Let's just get to the party and stay for a bit and then we'll ditch them and head back to the dorm."

"Okay." She linked arms with Pam. "But twenty minutes, tops."

When they finally got to the house, the party was in full swing. Music pulsated through the walls and every room was jam-packed. Pam and Julie looked around, thrilled, watching couples holding each other tightly in the biggest room.

Jason led Pam into the crowd of bodies and swooped her up in his arms. At first, she was nervous. She wasn't used to being so close to a boy. She relaxed when he began caressing the small of her back and they danced for a long time before she realized that she hadn't seen her friend in a while.

"Where's Julie?" she said, looking around the room.

"She's in the main room dancing with my friend Gil," he said. "It's getting a little hot in here. Do you think we can step outside for a minute?"

"Yeah, sure," she said. She fanned herself as they walked out the back of the house. "I thought I was going to faint in there."

"Well, we can't have that happen," he said.

They strolled down the path for a few minutes in silence. Pam was a little nervous when he grabbed her hand.

"Tell me about yourself," he said. "Who is Pam?"

She blushed as she looked at him. "Well," she said. "I'm sixteen and I love music. My favourite right now is Jimmy Cliff. He's the best. Do you listen to his music?"

"Not really," he said. "I don't really get a chance to listen to any good stuff in England."

"That's too bad," she said. "Have you seen any good flicks lately?"

"I watched *Godfather II* recently," he said. "Have you seen it?"

"I don't think I've ever heard of it," she said.

"That's okay," he said. "Jamaica always gets films a year later. You'll see it in a few months."

Pam laughed.

They passed a small field with high grass.

He squeezed her hand.

He stopped and kissed her. She had never been kissed before. His lips felt soft against hers.

"Come with me." He pulled her into the field. "I want to show you something."

Pam didn't want to stray too far off the road. It was too dark and she was getting worried; she hadn't seen Julie for hours.

"No, it's getting late, and Julie is going to be mad if she doesn't find me."

"She won't, I promise," he said holding onto her wrist. "It's okay."

She tried to squirm out of his grasp, but as she struggled his grip grew stronger and soon he was pulling her off the road and into the bush on the edge of what looked like a private farm. He was practically dragging her.

"What are you doing," she yelled. "Leggo mi arm."

"Come nuh," he said, lifting her up. "It won't take long."

She screamed. He continued to drag her farther away from the road. Then she could hear laughter coming from up ahead. Her heart stopped when she made out his three friends drinking beer, all wearing ski masks over their faces.

Jason tossed her on the ground. She was winded. Then she couldn't tell which one was Jason. They all wore masks. All four looked the same.

She tried to run away but was surrounded. She screamed out until one of them punched her, knocking her out cold. When she came to she could hear the murmur of their voices.

"What's the point of this if she's bloody unconscious?" said one of them.

"Wait… wait, I think she's waking up."

Pam tried to focus on the dark figures above her. She tried to get up but was slapped down. She began to cry when someone dragged her over the grass. One of the men barked at the others to hold her down.

"Who goes first?"

"He picked her out," said another. "He gets the first time."

"Do you think she's a virgin?"

"I doubt it," she heard Jason say. "But no matter."

She felt her arms being pinned down by the weight of someone's legs. She started to violently fight and scream out when she heard a truck passing on the road, but the boy on top of her muffled her cries with his hand.

"I can either fuck you awake or out cold." She could feel his stale breath on her. "So I suggest you shut the fuck up."

"Fuck, man, hurry up," said one of them.

"Well, if you hadn't let the other one escape, we could have taken care of this quickly," said another.

"We got time," she heard Jason say. "There's no one for miles."

Someone's hands pulled off her underwear. She tried to squirm and keep her legs closed but was dealt another slap across her face, and then she felt her legs being pried open. She cried out as one of them swiftly entered her. A sharp tug. She screamed in pain. As he went faster the pain intensified.

"Oh God, she's definitely a virgin, mate," said the one raping her. "Oh fuck! Oh fuck!"

For nearly two hours the men raped her over and over. At one point, one of them decided it would be funny to relieve himself on her, so he pissed on her hair. She lay there crying as his urine ran down her face. Another suggested that they jam her up with one of the broken beer bottles.

"Are you crazy!" she heard Jason say. "We're not trying to fucking kill her."

"Well, I want another turn," said another. "I can still go for another hour."

As Pam lay on the cold ground, praying for the nightmare to end, she heard a light rustling behind them. The sun was rising and several people were approaching down the road, maybe heading to the farm to work, and soon they were crossing the field. None of the men noticed the oncoming workers until it was too late.

"What the raas!" yelled one of the workers. "Get off her!"

Pam's eyes were swollen, but she felt the workers pull the rapist off her.

"Don't let di other ones get away," she heard a female worker yell.

A loud yelp. One of the workers sliced at her assailant's arm with his machete. Screaming. Another machete took out a chunk of his posterior. Pam felt dizzy and sick and couldn't get up from the ground. All she heard before she blacked out was the faint sound of screaming ringing in her ears.

▶▶|

"I WAS in the hospital for nearly two weeks," she told Mike. "They broke my ribs, my arm, and tore me up so badly that I had to have surgery. All three of Jason's friends were arrested and charged. But only one was found guilty. The other two were acquitted."

"How is that possible?" Mike asked her. "They caught them in the act."

"They caught one in the act and the other two claimed they were just standing around watching." She cleared her throat, trying not to cry. "I guess the judge couldn't justify charges because there were no witnesses and, because they wore masks, I couldn't tell who was actually... I... I just couldn't tell, so I had to accept that at least one of them went to prison."

"But what about Jason?" he asked. "Wasn't he charged too?"

"Well, Jason was a smart one." She cleared her throat again. "When the field workers arrived, he ran off. When I gave my statement to the police they went to question him. Jason's parents insisted that he was with them the entire night."

"But there had to be witnesses at the party," said Mike. "Didn't anyone come forward and say they saw him with you?"

"Some people remembered seeing a few white boys, but no one knew who they were," she said quietly. "In the end, I couldn't prove anything."

"But he walked you to the field," he said. "You were able to hear his voice. Wasn't that enough?"

"They took his parents' word over mine. Julie told the police that she only saw the other boys. She told them Jason never came with them. She testified that it was only the other boys that were with us."

"I'm so sorry, Pam," he said, holding her hand. "Did you ever find out what happened to him? To any of them?"

"No," she said. "I never went back to the school. The only thing I did hear was that Headmaster Lewis resigned afterwards and moved back to England, but other than that I haven't heard anything about any of them since."

"My God, Pam," he said. "I don't know what to say."

"Do you want to know the worst part?" Pam whispered. Tears were streaming down her face. "It wasn't having to leave school or everyone in Jamaica knowing what happened to me. It wasn't even finding out that I was pregnant or having no clue which one of those bastards was Simone's father. The worst is that every time I look at Simone all I can see is them."

Mike held her and she broke down in his arms.

"It was bearable when she was younger," she murmured. "She looked like me when I was young. But as she got older it became harder to see myself in her. All I could see was their smug faces, and the only thing I wanted to do was to punish them — to punish her."

"But Pam... don't you see? She's only a child, not your rapists." She sat, folded in his arms. "I know that it's hard for you to deal with the past, but you can't keep blaming her for something she's not even aware of. She's as much of a victim as you are." He gently kissed the top of her head. "I can never pretend to know how you feel, Pam. But know that she is more like you than them."

"Don't ever say that!" Pam sat up and pulled away from him.

"Say what, the truth?" he asked. "She never knew her father and probably never will — thank God! Everything she is, it is because of you. Her sensibility, her no-nonsense behaviour... that's all you, Pam! No matter how much she reminds you of that night, she will always be your daughter."

"She is nothing like me and will never be like me. Never!" She quickly moved away from Mike and headed back inside her apartment.

Mike watched her join Dex in the living room and pulled away from view. The last thing he wanted was to get into a confrontation with Dex. He stood out of sight and watched Pam hug Dex, who seemed more preoccupied with the television than with her.

Mike stepped to the railing, hoping she would notice him waiting for her. She got up from the couch and walked to the balcony door and swiftly closed the blinds, leaving him alone in the dark.

36

Simone stood in front of the girls' bathroom mirror and carefully applied her eyeliner. The light in the bathroom wasn't the best, but the other bathrooms were much worse. She was attempting to make her eyes more exotic, going for the Cleopatra look Ilene had shown her the day before.

She looked at herself, somewhat satisfied, and then started to draw the eyeliner on the bottom lid. She hated that part. It always made her tear up and she blinked excessively.

Simone wasn't used to putting on so much makeup but she wanted her first date with Patrick to be perfect. Perfect hair to go with her perfect makeup to match her perfect look.

Yesterday during lunch period, Ilene had given her a month's worth of makeup lessons in an hour-long tutorial. Ilene had become the school's go-to expert after spending the previous summer taking cosmetology classes, an eighteenth birthday gift her parents had reluctantly given her, and now she was charging students for doing their makeup. There wasn't an image she couldn't recreate and, for a small fee, she could give you the "Gina" look, the "Fly Girl" look, the "Beverly Hills 90210 Princess" look, but her specialty, dubbed the "Anemic," made a student look haggard and sickly, which was pretty much a get-out-of-school-free card.

Ilene had always been about her hustle. She knew that anything she wanted in life required a little bit of smarts and a whole lot of ingenuity. It was the thing Simone had always envied about her. Only one thing ever fazed her or stopped her: a project partner who didn't pull her own weight.

◄◄

BY THE END of the ninth grade, Simone had been failing her classes. She was having difficulty focusing. Her whole world was falling apart. It was only when Ilene cornered her in the cafeteria that she realized how critical things had become.

"What the hell is wrong with you? You were supposed to meet me in the library to go over our presentation. Where were you? You didn't even show up to class. We're lucky we got an extension, but if you are just going to flake, then I'll do the presentation without you."

"Isn't that the whole point of blowing off a presentation?" Simone said, smirking.

"It's not funny, Si," Ilene said. "You may not care about your grades anymore but I care about mine."

"I'm sorry," Simone said.

"What's going on with you? First, you leave school for almost a month and then, when you come back, you act like nothing matters."

"Whatever," she mumbled. "Look, everything is fine, okay!"

"I know that you are failing," she said. "And I know for a fact that if you don't get your shit together they're going to make you repeat the ninth grade."

"So! Why does it matter to you?"

"It matters plenty to me, Si," she said. "Remember our plan last year? We were going to be the best of the best, go to Queens, become doctors, open our own practice and rule it all. Did you forget?"

How could she forget? The two of them, sitting in St. Augustine's schoolyard on the hill, watching the eighth-grade boys play touch football. They'd spent many recesses mapping out their dreams and futures.

Simone looked at her friend. "I don't live at home anymore. After the fight with Tina, my mom kicked me out. I was placed in juvy until they figured things out."

"Holy shit, Simone. Why didn't you tell me?"

"I don't know. After the fight, I didn't really want to deal with it."

"Well, no one knew what happened to you," she said. "One day you and Tina were rolling on the cafeteria floor and the next you both disappear into thin air and even Yvette and Angie switched schools. Where are you living now?"

"With Mrs. Price, my neighbour. She used to take care of Nolan and me when we were kids."

"So where is your mother?" she asked. "Do you see her?"

Simone shook her head. "She still lives across the hall, but she acts like I don't exist."

"Are you kidding me?" she said. "What the hell!"

"Yeah, so now you see why I really don't give a fuck about our presentation," she said, kicking the piece of trash that had fallen out of her coat pocket. "What's the point?"

"The point is that you're smart, Simone, and what you're doing is fucking stupid," yelled Ilene. "Seriously, did she really kick you out because of that fight you had with Tina?"

Simone nodded.

"Well, then you're better off without her." Ilene linked arms and steered her to the benches outside the cafeteria. "You can't let her win! You can't let any of them win."

"Everyone believes that stuff Tina said about me," she said. "I'm not some fucking ho. I don't do that shit. I don't fucking suck white boys' dicks!"

Ilene looked around uncomfortably. "I know, Si," she said quickly. "I know you're not like that. I've known you since the third grade. And if I thought for a moment that you ran off with some white boy from Buffalo and got arrested for prostitution…"

"What the fuck!" Simone yelled out. "Is that what everyone is saying?"

Ilene laughed a little. Simone started to laugh as well. Soon both of them were laughing so hard that they had to hold onto each other for balance.

"Fucking idiots," Simone said.

"Fucking ass-wipes," Ilene added.

"Look, I'll be in class," Simone promised. "I won't let you down."

"Simone, forget about letting me down," she said. "Don't let yourself down. You're always telling me how your mother treats you like a loser but, by giving up, you're proving her right."

"Thanks," Simone said sarcastically.

"Well, am I wrong? You're basically telling her that all the times she treated you like shit were fucking justifiable. Don't let her do that to you. Throw it back in her face."

▶▶

BETWEEN GRADES NINE AND TEN, Simone had to go to summer school to redo math. The following year, tenth grade, was the most gruelling yet; she had to attend night school to replace the classes she'd done poorly in. But, by the time she made it to eleventh grade, her GPA was at a 4.0 and, for the first time, she made the high school honour roll.

Now she was in her final year, preparing to go to the university of her choice and was seeing a guy that thought she was worth talking to. It didn't matter that her mother continued to ignore her when she saw her in the hallway. Or that the only family she could rely on was Mrs. Price's. Or even that there were still a few idiots who believed that she gave blowjobs for quarters.

She looked down at her watch. It was almost 4:30 pm and the next bus was in twenty minutes; Patrick's shift finished at 5:00 pm and she wanted to be there the moment he got off.

They were going to the movies. He seemed nice. Not like the last one. The last one would call her and they would talk for hours, then she wouldn't hear from him for a week or more. This went on for nearly two months. Patrick was different. He called her all the time. He was tall and dark with a goatee. He worked as a stock boy at IKEA and was saving his money to buy a car. She'd met him over the spring break while she was working at the ice cream parlour. He hung around for nearly three hours talking to her between customers. Every so often she would sneak him a cup of vanilla ice cream. His family was also from Jamaica, but he'd never been to the island. By the end of the afternoon, he was affectionately calling her "baby girl," and that had become his pet name for her.

They had talked a lot over the last few weeks. He admitted to her that he'd dropped out of school the previous year but was taking night classes so he could get his GED. He told her that he'd be glad to be done with school. She laughed and told him that she felt the same. She told him that she was finishing her last year, but didn't mention that she was going off to Queen's in September. She didn't want to scare him off.

Last week, he'd walked her home after work and held her hand all the way. His hand felt slim and rough. She couldn't help wonder what it would feel like on her bare skin, but then she was nervous when he kissed her in the lobby of her building, worried that someone would see him slip his tongue in her mouth.

"The walls have eyes and ears," she'd said. "I don't want people telling my grandmother that I'm out here making out with you."

"Then meet me on Friday night," he said, smiling back. "We can go to the movies, where it's dark and more private."

Simone looked into the spotty mirror as she dabbed on her dark mauve lipstick. She blotted her lips with the bathroom's cloth roll towel before taking a final look at herself. She examined the large gold hoop earrings. They had started to fade. They were the last good pair she had.

"Ten minutes," she said to herself, and ran out the bathroom and down the empty hallway, out the door, and across the parking lot, carefully avoiding puddles from the afternoon shower. She didn't want any mud splashing her school uniform. She was out of breath when she got to the bus stop. She looked up the street and sighed in relief when she saw that the bus hadn't arrived yet.

Her socks had slipped into her Dr. Martens, so she sat on the bench outside the bus shelter, untied the laces, pulled her socks up, and scrunched them back down on her boots. She barely noticed him, but when she glanced over at the other side of the bench, she felt a shiver of fear.

He wore military-style Dr. Martens laced up his shins, grey camouflage cargo pants tucked into his boots, and his head was shaved. Her heart started pounding and she quickly averted her eyes, praying the bus would come soon and that he wasn't taking the same one. She wanted to get up from her seat, but didn't dare move. Instead, she searched her bag for her keys. A key was the sharpest thing she had with her.

He sneezed, which startled her. Her bag fell on the ground. Her Walkman, cassette tapes, and makeup tumbled out of her bag by his feet. As she dropped to her knees to retrieve her belongings, he reached down to help.

"Simone?" he asked, as he handed her a tape.

She looked up to see Nolan next to her. She wasn't sure it was him until he smiled and the sides of his eyes crinkled.

"Oh my God, Nolan!" she said. "I... I didn't recognize you."

She couldn't believe this was the same boy she had run up and down the streets with. He looked older, thinner, and a little intimidating, but he still had that smile. The smile that had always put her at ease.

"Ha ha," he said, pulling his black hoodie over his head as a few raindrops fell. "Yeah, I changed my look a little."

"A little!" she said, catching her breath. She looked him up and down. "More like a lot! You scared the shit out of me."

Nolan looked at her sheepishly. For the first time, he felt embarrassed by his looks. He could feel his face burn red hot as he handed her another cassette tape. He hadn't expected to bump into Simone, but, when their eyes locked, her warm smile allayed his tension.

Simone frowned as raindrops began to splash down on her. She looked up at the dark clouds.

Nolan wanted to give her his jean jacket, but remembered that the back of his hoodie said, *Die nigger, die* and showed a skeleton hanging from a tree. He didn't want her seeing that.

"Let's go in there," he said, pointing to the empty bus shelter. "It looks like it's going to pour in a second."

They bolted into the shelter just as sheets of rain poured down. Simone shook the water from her hair. She felt mascara running down her cheek and cursed as she pulled out a tissue and dabbed her face. Nolan laughed a little.

"What's so funny?" she said.

"Nothing. You look different, too," he said. "I guess I'm not used to Si with makeup."

"Yeah, I guess we both look a little different." She chuckled.

"How have you been?" he asked her.

"Same ole, same ole," she said. "What happened to your hair? You use to have so much."

"Yeah, decided one day to shave it off," he said, a little self-consciously.

Silence.

"So do you still live in the building?"

"Yeah, but I'm living with Mrs. Price now," she said. "Got a little too crowded over there."

"Oh," he said.

"So are you here visiting your dad?" she asked. "How long are you sticking around?"

"Just here for the night," he said, looking down at his feet. "You still go to St. Joseph?"

"Yup," she said. "I'm finishing off my OAC year."

"So you're thinking about university?" he asked. "What school are you going to?"

"Got accepted by all three of my choices," she said. "But I'm planning to go to Queen's."

Nolan stood around as she rambled on about attending Queen's University in the fall. He held his breath and watched her. The way her head tilted to the side when she spoke and the way her lips moved, he barely heard a word. After all this time, she still rendered him speechless and his heart still galloped a mile a minute. As she continued to talk, his mind went back to that moment in the park, on the swings, when he'd held her in his arms. The moment their lips touched that night in Mrs. Price's room. The day he first held her hand.

"What about you?" she asked, breaking his reverie.

"What?" he asked, confused. "Sorry?"

"What about you?" she repeated. "Which school are you going to?"

"Oh… I'm taking a break," he lied. "Not sure what I want to do yet."

"Oh," she said.

The rain stopped. Her bus was hurtling down the street. She looked down at her watch. It was almost ten minutes late. She picked up her bag. Their reunion was far too brief. She wished she could stay and catch the next bus but she didn't want to keep Patrick waiting.

"Well, this is me." She smiled at him. "It was really good seeing you, Nolan."

"Wait, you're not heading home?" he asked, walking with her to the bus door.

"No... I'm meeting a friend."

She got on the bus and made her way to the back corner. She looked out the window at him and, when he waved goodbye, her heart sank. She couldn't believe that she had wasted the entire time going on about school when the one thing she wanted to say was left unsaid.

She could see him about to put his headphones back on and banged on the window to get his attention.

She opened the window. "Nols," she shouted. "I wrote you after you left. Why didn't you write back?"

He stood there, speechless, as the bus started to pull away. She quickly faced forward, hurt that he'd said nothing, and put on her headphones, blasting her music.

He didn't know why he was too scared to answer her, why he couldn't admit that he didn't write her because he was in love with her and was too afraid to do anything about it. If he had answered her, he would have confessed everything. About being a skinhead. About facing a lengthy jail sentence for holding a homeless man down while Rowan beat him unconscious.

He would have told her that for years he had been angry at her for rejecting him, at his dad for letting him slip away, at Kester for taking the easy way out. He would have told her that his life would have been much better if she had still been in it. And that, the moment she'd sat next to him, his entire body, heart, and soul, had ached for her. But, as the deafening sounds of thunder rolled above and the speeding bus faded out of view, he knew it was too late and his chance was gone. As his own bus pulled up, he wondered if he would ever get to answer her question or if he would ever see her again.

▶

"NOLAN, WHAT ARE YOU DOING HERE?" Mike embraced his son. "Your mom didn't tell me that you were coming."

"It was a last-minute trip," he said. "Can I come in?"

"Come in." Mike gestured him into the apartment. "I'm just about to sit down for some dinner. There's plenty, if you're hungry."

"Yeah, I'm a little hungry," he said, dropping his duffle bag on the floor. "Thanks, Dad."

They sat at the dinner table eating in silence.

"So how long are you in town for?" Mike asked. "You're more than welcome to stay as long as you want."

"Thanks," Nolan said. "I'll just stay the night. I'm headed to Buffalo."

"Buffalo, huh?" Mike replied. "Too bad! Simone still lives in the building. She would have loved to see you. She moved in with Mrs. Price, you know."

"Yeah, I know. I saw her earlier."

"You did, did you? And did she run for the hills after seeing your new look?"

Nolan laughed a little but his father wasn't smiling.

"What's going on, Nolan? I haven't seen you in two years, and you show up out of the blue on your way to Buffalo?"

"Well, your visits to Halifax have become few and far between."

"And I hear you'll probably be going to jail for awhile?" he continued. "Did I get that right?"

Nolan looked away as his father stared him down.

"What the fuck happened to you?" Mike said. "I thought this get-up was just some phase you were in. The crazy music, the tattoos... but to go and attack some guy. That's insane, Nolan."

"It's a war out there." Nolan continued to eat. "The most we did was rough him up."

"Nolan, you nearly killed him," Mike yelled. "The man you so-called 'roughed up' is still in intensive care. I don't know what war you think you're fighting, but it's a delusional one. The crap you're following is a fucking lost cause. Pure and simple."

"Oh, come off it, Dad," Nolan said. "You yourself said that Canada is turning into a fucking toilet with every garbage immigrant getting in. That's all I'm fighting for. I'm fighting for us."

"Let's get one thing straight," Mike said. "You are not fighting for me. I may have my views about the way this country is going, but only lunatics take it this far. The son I raised would never raise a fist to anyone. Hell, your best friends for most of your life were blacks. How can you go around saying this shit?"

"Things change," he said. "I was just too brainwashed to see the truth."

"And what truth is that, Nols? Because the only truth I see is that you are heading down a road that's either going to lead you to prison or put a bullet in you."

"It's not going to come to that," Nolan said. "You don't know what the fuck you're talking about."

"No?" he said. "So why did the RCMP show up at your mother's this morning looking for you. Oh yeah, she calls me when you fuck up. Did you know that they can revoke your bail? You shouldn't be here. Your mother could lose her house! Did you think of that?"

"Look, I didn't think it would get to this," he yelled. "This is fucking bullshit. All I did was hold the guy down."

"Yeah, well, it doesn't matter what you did, Nolan," Mike said. "All they see is a gang of Neo-Nazi fuckers beating the shit out of some homeless guy — and you want to know the kicker? You didn't beat up some immigrant. You dumb fucks beat up some old white guy. Do you hear me, Nolan? Your so-called race war ended up with you beating up one of your own."

▶

435

SIMONE RUSHED up the hill to IKEA as the rain poured down again. She was almost twenty minutes late. Patrick was standing by the loading dock smoking a cigarette. He smiled when he saw her approaching.

"Hi," she said. "Sorry for being so late."

"It's okay," he said. He grabbed her hand. "I'm just glad that you made it."

She looked at him and tried to get back the excitement she'd felt an hour ago, but all she could think about was Nolan and how she wished they'd had more time together.

"Hey, baby girl, what's going on with you?" he said. "You seem upset."

"I'm sorry. I'm just soaking wet. I think I'm coming down with something."

"Are you saying that you don't want to go to the movies with me?" Patrick said. "I was really looking forward to this."

"No... no. I just need to get somewhere warm, so I can dry off."

"If you want, we can skip the movie and head over to my place. My mom is home, but she won't mind."

From the moment she met Patrick, she'd wanted him. He was the total package — tall, dark, and handsome. Any other day, she would have jumped at the chance to go home with him, but at that moment she wasn't in the mood.

"Next time," she said. They walked back to the bus stop. "Let's just go to the movies. I've been looking forward to seeing *Speed* all week."

"All right," he said, disappointed. "But sometime soon I want to introduce you to my mother."

He was always talking about his mother. She figured that he was using his mother as an excuse to get her over to his house. His mother worked nights as a nurse and was rarely home. He'd let that slip the first time they talked. If she went over to his house to "meet his mother" the only thing she would meet would be in his bedroom beneath the sheets.

They sat in the dark crowded theatre. Patrick nuzzled against her neck. Simone squirmed away from him, trying to watch the film. When he reached over and started to kiss her neck she tried to ignore him. He whispered in her ear that he wanted her tongue to slide up and down his dick. He wasn't bothering at all with the movie.

"I can get you in the mood," he said. "I can get you so wet that all you'll wanna do is fuck me."

He placed his jacket over his lap and quietly unzipped his trousers, reached for her hand and pulled it under his jacket.

"Stop it!" she said. "What are you doing?"

A few people shushed them.

"Get a fucking room!" said one.

Simone got up from her seat and grabbed her bag. She made her way out of the row and towards the theatre door.

"Simone!" Patrick called out to her. "Simone, wait!"

She turned and saw him coming after her, but he'd forgotten that his pants were still unzipped. His trousers dropped to the floor exposing his dick hanging out his boxers. Some of the people in the back row giggled as he struggled to yank his slacks back up.

She quickly ran out of the theatre and caught the first bus that came down the street. Her throat felt raw and scratchy. When she got to the apartment, her whole body was hot and sweaty.

Mrs. Price insisted that she take off all her wet clothes and get into a hot bath. Afterwards, she rubbed Simone down with Vicks, made her dress in her winter pyjamas, and then bundled her up with blankets and brought her a bowl of Red Beans Soup. It was their usual Friday night meal and Simone was so glad to have a bowl. After the soup, she passed out.

She woke up the next morning to Mrs. Price talking loudly on the phone.

"Yes, sah," she said over and over. "Yes, nuh, I will keep an eye on your place. You just take care of Nolan and God bless you."

Simone walked in as Mrs. Price hung up the wall phone.

"Lawd Jesus," she said. "Mi never tink mi see the day."

"What's going on, Mrs. Price?" Simone said. "What's going on with Nolan?"

"Nothing to concern yourself with."

"I saw him yesterday, Mrs. Price," she said. "I know there's something wrong. Just tell me!"

Mrs. Price looked deep into Simone's eyes and shook her head, mumbling to herself.

"You children disappoint me," she said. "Promise me that you will never let things get so bad that you end up down a road you can't come back from. Promise me that?"

"I promise," she replied.

"Mi serious now," she said. "I know you are keeping your time with some no good nehgah. You don't think I know? The only ting that needs to be pon your mind is going to damn university! Not wasting time with some lazy dropout."

"Okay," Simone said. "He's just a friend, anyways."

"Yes, well, they all start off as friends. That's the problem."

"What happened to Nolan, Mrs. Price? He never said anything to me when I saw him."

"That's because he's not going to tell you that the police after him for beating up some poor soul." She started washing the dishes, attempting to scrub last night's soup pot. "Or that he's lucky that he didn't kill the man."

"I don't understand," Simone said, sitting down. "I don't believe it! Nolan would never do that!"

"That's not what his fadda tell me. Nolan is not the same boy, Simone. He fall into the wrong crowd over the last few years."

"I didn't know," she said.

"Why would you know?" Mrs. Price sighed. "That boy should have never left to live with that trash he calls a mother. When he was with his father he never got into trouble like this. His father kept a watchful eye on him and when he couldn't, I did. I practically raised that boy, and the boy I raised would never strike a man."

Simone sat at the table listening to Mrs. Price tell how Nolan had fallen in with a brutal gang of thugs that had been terrorizing the streets and that Nolan was planning to cross the border and skip bail, that his mother was in a state, and that Mike was really mad.

"Mr. Mike is taking Nolan back to Halifax," she said. "He's going to be in Halifax for a while so I promised to look out for his place while he's gone."

"Does that mean Nolan is going to jail?" Simone asked.

"Don't know, baby," she said. "He's due in court next week."

Simone kept quiet and let Mrs. Price ramble on. She should have realized that something was wrong the moment she saw Nolan's scary, rough look. Something didn't seem right, but his eyes had fooled her. His steel blue eyes with the smile lines that lit up his face when he looked at her. Right then, he was the same old Nolan — with less hair and more chains. The same person. No matter what Mrs. Price was saying, she had to believe that the boy at the bus stop was the one she knew — the one she grew up with.

▶

MIKE SAT in court once again with Meghan and Rich, this time to hear Nolan plead guilty to being a party to the offence of assault. Mike's stomach churned as he stared at the back of Nolan's bald head. His hair had started to grow back, but the tattoo was still visible.

The defense lawyer had said nothing could be done for Nolan. The homeless man was on life support and it was looking like he was going to die.

The only thing on the table was to agree to a guilty plea; accessory to assault would guarantee him thirty-six months, but he would avoid future charges of battery or, worse, manslaughter if the victim died. The only condition was that he testify against Rowan. It was Rowan they really wanted. They had tried to get him on other charges in the past, but he always managed to get off.

Several witnesses, ranging from some homeless people, to a couple walking by, to the security guard who called the police, had seen Nolan try to pull Rowan off the victim. Many of them recounted how Rowan had turned on Nolan and kicked him in the gut several times. A few had heard Rowan scream at Nolan that he wasn't his brother and accusing him of sleeping with "his woman."

"The both of you are fucking trash," were the words they recalled Rowan saying right before the police sirens closed in.

According to the witnesses, Rowan had pulled Tess away, she had been terrified, and all the assailants had run to the pier.

Nolan had sat down with his attorney and the crown prosecutor to listen to the plea deal: thirty-six months with early parole after two years if he testified against Rowan.

His lawyer agreed but added another condition: "Nolan's nineteen and has his whole life ahead of him," he said. "By the time he gets out, he'll barely be twenty-one. Expunge his record after his release and you have yourself a deal."

"You can't charge Tess either," Nolan said in a low voice. "I won't agree to anything unless you let her off. She didn't do anything. She wasn't even supposed to be there."

The crown attorney looked at Nolan. He looked down at his notes.

"Fine," he said. "Do we have a deal?"

The next day the judge agreed to the deal. An hour after Nolan was given his sentence the homeless man died and Rowan was brought up on charges of second-degree murder.

▶

MIKE WALKED QUICKLY OUT of the courtroom, found the closest bench and sat down to try to pull himself together. He looked up at the ceiling and prayed. He prayed to God to knock some sense into his son, to wake Nolan from this nightmare he seemed to want to live in. But mostly he prayed that Nolan would be safe in prison.

Meghan stood in front of him. She looked pale, her eyes glazed. He wanted to say something to make her feel better, but he didn't have it in him to comfort her. They had been divorced for almost four years and it wasn't his place to comfort her anymore.

"Mike," she said. "Nolan gave this to me to give to you. Can you please take care of it?"

Mike took the tightly folded piece of paper and shoved it in his pant pocket. He tried to smile when Meghan asked him to join her and Rich for dinner.

"I can't. I need to catch the next train to Toronto."

He remained sitting on the bench as he watched Meghan join Rich and walk off down the hallway.

His mind filled with regret. What had gone wrong with Nolan? He felt the weight of his own loneliness and for the first time in a long while he wished Pam was by his side.

On the train, he looked for Nolan's note. It was gone. He searched his bag, his wallet and all his pockets in vain.

▶

THE NOTE LAY on the floor beneath the bench outside the court-room until late in the evening when the night janitor noticed it. He unfolded the paper and adjusted his glasses.

You asked me why I never wrote back. I was afraid. I ruined every-thing between us and I didn't know how to fix it. It should have been you. It always should have been you. I think of you every day. Please don't give up on me Simone. Don't forget me.

The janitor turned the paper over. Only "Simone" was written on the other side. He crumpled the paper and tossed it in his trash cart before continuing down the empty hallway.

PART IV

37

P am read through the letter for the eighth time. This wasn't another complaint notice, an unhappy patient disputing a bill, or some lawsuit mistakenly sent to her instead of legal. She couldn't just forward the letter straight to another department. The letter was certified and personal and it had come from the Jamaican Embassy.

Dear Mrs. Pamela Stewart (née Allen),

This letter is an official notice to inform you that there is a joint trust account that has been set up through the Royal Bank of Canada in Kingston, Jamaica for you and your daughter, Miss Simone Allen. It is imperative that we contact you or your legal representative regarding this account and its terms. We are unable to reach Miss Simone Allen and hope you can assist us with locating her. Please contact me at the telephone number provided below.

Sincerely,
Thomas Clark
Embassy of Jamaica, Toronto

Pam jotted down the telephone number and placed the letter in her purse. She told Maureen to hold all her calls, she didn't want to be disturbed, then went into an empty conference room where she closed the door and called the number.

"Embassy of Jamaica, this is Margaret speaking. How may I direct your call?"

"Mrs. Pam Stewart for Thomas Clark, please," she said and waited while the operator transferred her call.

"Hello," said a gruff voice. "This is Mr. Clark."

"Hello, Mr. Clark, my name is Pam Stewart. You sent me a letter..."

"I know exactly who you are," he said abruptly. "I was the judge on your case twenty-three years ago."

Pam held her breath as she sat on the phone. She slowly exhaled. "I don't understand what is going on. Your letter states that I have a trust account that I need to claim. What is this about?"

"To be quite frank, Mrs. Stewart, I really can't say, but our embassy was charged with finding you and your daughter regarding this matter."

"I see."

"I'm going to give you a number for the law firm that contacted us," he said. "You'll need to speak with a Ms. Linda Carson at Phillips Watson Wilson. They will tell you exactly what this is all about."

"Thank you." She jotted down the information.

"Mrs. Stewart," he said.

"Yes, Mr. Clark?"

"Do not hesitate to call the embassy if you need any further assistance," he said. "We are always available for a daughter of Jamaica."

"Yes sir," she said.

Pam sat in the conference room for several minutes, then picked up the phone and dialled Maureen's extension to tell her that she was not feeling well. She wanted to go home and call the law firm in private. She needed to figure out what was going on without anyone breathing down her neck. CJ was still at school and Dex had left first thing that morning and wouldn't be home until late that night. She thought about calling him, but quickly changed her mind. She was glad he wasn't home. The last thing she wanted was to see him.

The previous night Dex and CJ had fought. During their stupid argument, she intervened, trying to calm them down. Dex forcefully pushed her up against the wall, then stormed out of the apartment. She'd tried to tell CJ that Dex had had a little too much to drink, but her son only shook his head in disbelief and retreated to his room.

Pam arrived at the empty apartment and called the number and was promptly transferred to the lead barrister, Linda Carson.

"The trust was set up a few months ago by Lord Jonathan Lewis," she said. "He charged us with the task of setting up a trust and locating you, but it was only when you applied for your husband's citizenship that we realized that you had changed your name."

"But Lord Jonathan Lewis… Lewis," Pam said, confused. "Wait nuh, are you speaking of Headmaster Lewis from my old school?"

"Yes, I believe that is how you would know him," she said as a matter of fact.

Pam sat on her bedside dumbfounded. She had not heard this name in years and the idea that her rapist's father was searching for her sent a sickening feeling to the pit of her stomach.

"What does he want?" she said.

"Yes… well, it seems that he has set up a trust," the lawyer said. "The trust is a total of fifty thousand pounds, and names you and your daughter as equal beneficiaries. As I stated, we've had a hard time locating you. We hope you can assist us with contacting your daughter…"

"Why the hell is he giving me all this money?" she interrupted.

"I have not seen this man and his family in years and out of the blue you contact me with this?"

"I'm sorry, Mrs. Stewart," she said. "If you let me explain, I can give you all of the details. As I understand it, this money is to make up for any hardship you and your daughter have endured over the last twenty-two years."

"Are you serious?" Pam was trying hard to keep her anger at bay.

"Yes, Ma'am," she continued. "However, there is one major stipulation. Lord Lewis wants to ensure that there is never ever any mention of you and his son; that period of your history will remain sealed. This trust is not an admittance of paternity of Simone Allen by his son. The stipulated seal is merely an assurance that you will not discuss in any way at any time Mr. Jason Lewis and/or his family."

"This is hush money," she spat out in disgust. "He's asking me to keep quiet about the time his son and his friends raped me. He's trying to shut me up."

There was a long silence.

"I'm sorry... I had no idea," came the far-away voice.

"I'm sorry, I've forgotten your name. Miss... Miss..."

"Ms. Carson."

"Well, Ms. Carson, I don't know why they feel they need to contact me now, but you tell Headmaster Lewis that the price is not high enough for the hell his son put me through."

Pam hung up the phone. Tears were streaming down her cheeks. Now she wished Dex was home. If she had told him he would know what to do. If she had told him.

She went over to Dex's side of the bedroom and pulled out the bottle of rum hidden in his nightstand. She stumbled into the kitchen and poured herself half a tumbler, then went out onto the balcony and sat drinking until the bottle was nearly finished. She looked over at Mike's apartment and silently cursed. Since the renovation, she no longer had access to him. All she could see was the siding of the balcony wall.

It was getting late and she knew she had to pull herself together. She replaced Dex's rum and made a mental note to go to the liquor store and buy another bottle. She stopped in her tracks. Why now? All these years, she hadn't heard a word from the Lewis family. Jason had never been charged, so why did her silence mean so much to them now? Pam took out the letter and dialled the Jamaican Embassy. She was on hold for a while before Mr. Clark came on the line.

"What can I do for you, Mrs. Stewart?"

"Mr. Clark, you said you were the judge on my trial," she said. "Can you explain to me why the father of one of the men who raped me is giving me nearly fifty thousand pounds?"

"What are you talking about, my dear?"

"Mr. Clark! You know exactly what I'm referring to."

A long silence. "As I remember, the Lewis name was not mentioned at the trial. But let me say this, Mrs. Stewart, just between you and I, England is gearing up for their next Parliament elections and it might be that your benefactor is cleaning house before the campaign."

"I don't understand," she said, more confused than ever. "What does this have to do with me or my daughter?"

"My dear, this is off the record," he said. "But this has everything to do with you and your daughter. I suspect that whatever you might have to say about the past will spoil Jason Lewis' political aspirations."

"Political aspirations?" she said hoarsely. "Is that why they want me to agree not to discuss the rape?"

"Yes, daughter," he said. "That is exactly it."

Nolan jolted from his sleep, gasping for air. He sat up, expecting to be in his cell, but groggily realized that he was back in his bedroom in Halifax. It happened from time to time. He would wake up disoriented after a sleepless night of tossing and turning from the same recurring nightmare.

He lay back down, trying to process the dream before it faded into his subconscious. It always began the same way, in Toronto on Pam's side of the balcony during a winter storm. He was lying on the white-and-orange plastic chaise lounge with Simone nestled in his arms. Her favourite faded brown blanket covered them, shielding them from the brisk swirling snow and wind. They clung to each other until the blizzard settled, with only a few flakes drifting down.

The last snowflake would land on her lips and he would kiss it, melting their lips together while he unbuckled his belt and pulled down his pants. She would moan his name as she ran her fingers through his hair. Each lock of hair would come out in her hands. She would seem unfazed by it as he continued to kiss her.

Next moment, he would be bald again, dressed in his sleeveless skull T-shirt, black torn jeans, and tightly laced Dr. Martens,

Simone tracing her fingers over the *14/88* tattoo on the back of his head. But, instead of Simone, it was Sarah Jane.

He would anxiously look for Simone and then see her teetering on the balcony railing, wrapped in her blanket, but he couldn't reach her because there would always be someone pulling him back. His father or his mother, sometimes Tess, would wrap their arms around his neck, keeping him from her and, just as he finally broke free, Simone would look at him and smile before slipping off the balcony. He would rush towards the siding of the balcony, falling over the edge after her.

He always awoke from his dream in a panic with his heart racing and his pillow soaked in sweat. He'd gone to the prison doctor, who had prescribed him anti-depressants and the dreams had gone away, but, after his release from Springhill, they returned to plague his nights.

He'd been warned that being home would be a shock to his system. He was no longer an unhinged teenager but a felon, who would be tethered to his crime and his conviction long after his release.

After he was paroled, he was sent back home to his mother's house, since halfway houses in Halifax were filled to capacity. His stepfather and his mother could barely look him in the eye. Relationships that had been strained by distance were now strained by fear.

When he returned home, nothing of his past remained. Meghan had cleared the basement of his books, music, and even his toiletries, and left them at the dump. All he found were a couple of pairs of blue jeans and a handful of T-shirts and sweaters his mother had bought him long ago at K-Mart. The basement had been converted to a storage unit, and he was back in his old room on the second floor with only a twin bed, a night-stand, and a chair by the window. It was as bare as the cell he'd spent the last two years in.

He hadn't expected a homecoming party or even tears of joy,

but the coldness of his reception had left him feeling forsaken. During his incarceration, Meghan had accepted a few of his calls, but had not had enough courage to visit. Rich and Dana visited him at first, but, after a few months, only Dana continued to come regularly.

After his release, Dana tried her best to bring normalcy into his life. She invited him to stay with her on weekends and talked her boyfriend into getting him work at his construction site. All in an attempt to get him back on track, she told him. Back to the way his life should be.

▶

"HE'S DIFFERENT," Meghan whispered to Dana one Sunday, while they were in the kitchen washing the dinner dishes. "He barely utters a word to Rich or me. He just stays in his room, staring at the ceiling, or parks himself on the sofa watching TV. Sometimes he seems even more hostile and angry than he was before."

"It's going to take some time. He's still adjusting, Mom," Dana replied. "It's not easy for anyone to bounce back after being in prison."

"I guess," she said. "But the few times he says anything he is so charged with rage. He went to *Needs* last night and came back bitching about some black kid stealing a handful of gumballs. It's always about how much 'they' get away with."

"It's just talk, Mom. He's just frustrated about everything. Now that he's working, he'll make some money and won't feel so helpless."

"I don't know if it's just talk, Dana." Meghan handed her the last dish. "It was just talk before and look how things turned out. I love Nolan, but I can't go through this again. If he keeps going like this, he's going to end up back in jail."

Tears drifted down Meghan's cheek. She sat on her kitchen stool.

"Mom, Nolan is responsible for Nolan," Dana said. She took her mother's hand in hers. "I think that's what's eating him. He knows that all of his mistakes stem from the decisions he's made. He's just not coming to terms with it."

"I should have done something years ago, when it all started," Meghan said. "But I didn't want your father to say 'I told you so.' I let my goddamn pride get in the way and now look. He used to be my sweet boy. Now it scares me how much he's changed. I... I have no idea how to fix him."

"Talk to him, Mom. The only thing you never did was talk to him. Try talking to him."

"I tried," she said. More tears spilled down. "But it's hard. Sometimes I wonder how things might have turned out if I had just left him with his father."

"I know, Mom. Sometimes I wonder the same thing."

"When Nolan got that girl pregnant, I hated your father so much," she admitted. "He was screwing everything up and I wanted to prove to him that I was the better parent. Boy, did I show him."

"Do you really think that if Nolan was with Dad he wouldn't have found some way to screw up his life?"

"I don't know what to think. All I know is that something in him is broken and I can't stomach watching him spiral out of control again."

▶

NOLAN STOOD in the parking lot of the labour centre, waiting for the various construction companies to cherry-pick workers for their jobs. He hated this process, standing with a mixed bag of guys, especially when he was usually at the bottom of the pile —

the only meaningful skill he had learned in prison was how to lay tile.

Dana had helped him get the job with her boyfriend's company, but the job paid peanuts and all he got to do was hold up a "slow" sign for twelve hours a day. He was laid off after a few months, which left him still on parole and jobless and ineligible to expunge his record until he'd completed his sentence. In the meantime, nobody was looking to hire a felon, despite all the work programs set up to help ex-cons. His only options were to either pick up odd jobs or break parole and find work in Toronto. The latter would be a stupid move that he wasn't willing to make.

Some black men were huddled off to the side, drinking steaming coffee from their thermoses. He sipped the cold cup of coffee Dana had given him at the diner and tried to move away from them. He didn't want to hear them carrying on, laughing, acting like they didn't have a care in the world. Their loud quips back and forth made him seethe as he tried to focus on standing out in the crowd for the foremen looking for workers.

When he first joined the morning ranks, he'd thought he would get a job easy despite his lack of skills. He was white, educated enough, and determined. Yet he always ended up left behind.

"I need someone who can handle a jackhammer," said a foreman.

Several men shouted out.

"Johnson." The foreman pointed to an older sturdy black man. "I also need plumbing and electrical."

Several more hands shot up.

Before Nolan could say anything, another truck behind him was calling for dry-wall installers for a residential job. He quickly turned around, but was too late.

"Do you need anyone to lay tile," he yelled out. "I can do tile."

"So can everyone here, white boy," laughed one of the younger construction workers from the bed of one of the trucks.

Nolan could hear the group of them laugh as the truck pulled out. He could barely control his contempt as he watched the last truck disappear.

▶

"DID you ever think about going back to school?" Dana asked. They sat out on the back porch of the house she and her friends rented. "You have to come to the table with more than your lily-white ass."

Nolan shrugged and continued to drink his beer.

"Nolan, you can't honestly think that being a felon and having zero skills is going to put you on top of any hiring list," she continued. "And before you go into one of your fucking white power speeches about blacks stealing your jobs, try getting your GED first."

"Well, fuck it," he said. "I'll just wait until my probation is over and go back to Toronto."

"That's not going to solve your problem. You need a job to stay on parole."

"Yeah, well, whatever," he mumbled. "It's all bullshit."

"You know what, Nolan, I'm so fucking sick of everyone coddling your stupid ass!" she said. "Poor Nolan came from a broken home. Poor Nolan had to move to Nova Scotia. Poor Nolan got caught up with the wrong people. Well, fuck that!"

Dana got up and walked back to the kitchen. Nolan felt the entire back porch shake as she slammed the door. He got up and stormed into the house after her.

"What the fuck is your problem," he yelled at her. "You think I wanted all of this?"

"Come on, Nolan! Are you really asking me that?" Dana replied. "Who are you trying to fool? You should be grateful that your dumb ass didn't end up with a longer sentence like those fuckers you hung out with."

He glared at her.

He had been luckier than the others. While he was paroled after two years at Springhill, Bryce and Kevin received five-year sentences, and Rowan ended up with ten to twenty with a chance of parole.

"All I hear from you is 'poor me, all the blacks get everything while the white man is a dying species.' It's pathetic! You're the one who dropped out of school. You were the one who went to prison for beating up a homeless man…"

"I didn't fucking beat him up," he screamed. "Okay?"

"Oh, my mistake, you held him down, didn't you? Do you even hear yourself? At what point do you start holding yourself accountable! Take Sarah Jane, for example…"

"Whatever. You don't know anything about what happened between me and Sarah Jane!"

"Did you even call her to see how she was doing?" Dana said. "Do you even fucking care that, because of you, Claudia and Mom haven't spoken in years! Does any of it matter? And speaking of Mom, she is terrified to be alone in the same room with you!"

"That's not true. What the hell does she have to be afraid of?"

"Well, I don't know, Nolan," Dana said. She was crying now. "Maybe because you came back more hostile than before? Maybe she was always scared of you? I mean, you're tatted up with white power on the back of your fucking head! Attacking people just to show everyone how big your balls are and for what!? Where has it gotten you? Was it fucking worth it?"

He said nothing, just looked at his sister, who was trembling as she gripped the kitchen sink.

"I love you, Nolan," she continued. "You are my baby brother and I would do anything to protect you. Maybe that's the problem. Maybe we've all been protecting you for so long you can't figure shit out on your own. But you know what scares me the most? Despite everything you've done, you still haven't learned a damn thing. You refuse to fucking change."

Nolan looked at his sister. She had always been there for him. He was frustrated and angry over the whole conversation, but he felt alone and didn't want to lose Dana, too. He reached over for her hand, but she quickly pulled away.

"Nolan, I think you should go back to Mom's place this weekend," she said.

"Come on, Dana," he said. "Don't do this."

"Right now, I can't do *this*," she said. "I'll ask Jeremy or Stu if they can give you a lift home."

She went up to her room. Nolan didn't want to sit alone in the kitchen, waiting for her roommates to drive him home, so he got up and left through the back door.

As he walked down her street, he realized he had forgotten his gloves and toque but didn't bother to go back. By the time he got to Dartmouth, the wind was slicing through him. His fingers ached and felt numb, but pain was a welcome relief to Dana's harsh words, which were still ringing in his ears.

39

Reconnecting with Joanna was probably the last thing Mike counted on happening. After their brief time together, he had abruptly ended things when he lost custody of Nolan. Joanna had moved on and found another rugged Irish-Canadian man to charm. The last he heard, she'd got married, but the relationship had ended in a messy divorce.

And here she was at McKinney's, as beautiful as ever in a floral wrap-around dress, her soft shiny hair cascading down her back.

"So what's good here?" she said, winking.

"The bourbon is always good." Mike smiled at her, lifting the bottle from the shelf and pouring her a drink. "Are you here on a date?"

"Nope," she said, carefully sipping. "No date."

"You meeting up with Maureen?"

"Wrong again," she said playfully. "I'm here to take you home, Mike O'Shea."

Mike laughed.

"You're not seeing anyone, are you?" she asked.

"Nope," he said. "But I'm working."

"Okay," she said, finishing her drink. "I'll be at my place when you're done here. You still know where I live, right?"

Mike closed up for the night and sat alone in the bar, enjoying an old-fashioned. The bar-back finished mopping the floor and turned off the main lights.

"Good night, Mike," said the young guy.

"Good night, Frankie. Get home safe."

It was nearly 2:30 am. He sat in the dark trying to figure out why he was stalling. Joanna was a beautiful woman who wanted him. It wasn't as if their relationship had ended in some huge fight, coupled with tears and ultimatums. It had stopped as casually as it had begun, but something felt off. Something was missing, he thought, as he slowly sipped his drink.

After finishing, he carefully washed the eight-ball, leaving it on the bar to dry under a paper towel. He looked down at his watch and saw that it was 3:00 am. She would still be awake and would forgive his tardiness. But he convinced himself that it was too late to go over to her place and locked up before walking back to his apartment.

It was chilly this early in the morning, but he liked the brisk wind against his face. It made him more determined to get out of the cold and into his own bed. The trash left on the grounds swirled through the courtyard of the complex. The strength of the wind and the long shift at the bar had left him exhausted; he had to use every ounce of strength to open and close the building's side door.

He managed the eleven flights of stairs. He didn't mind the hike. He preferred the stairs to the elevator. He took the stairs mainly for the exercise, but also to avoid Pam.

Things between them were strained and Mike didn't really know how to fix it. He wanted to be there for Pam, especially after she'd told him about the rape, but since that night she'd been cold towards him. She treated him like a stranger — especially when

Dex was around. The only thing he could do was accept it. She was living her life and he needed to live his.

At the top of the final flight of stairs, he could see a little figure curled up in the corner by the door. It startled him. Was it some homeless guy who had snuck into the building, or a drunken tenant? As Mike got closer, he recognized the bright white sneakers and realized it was CJ curled up asleep.

"CJ... CJ," he said, jostling the sleeping boy. "What are you doing out here? Does your mom know you're out here?"

"She's not here," CJ said, wiping the sleep from his eyes. "She's in Jamaica for the week."

"In Jamaica? What about your stepfather? Isn't he looking for you?"

"Probably," he replied. "Or maybe not. He told me that if I came home late he would lock me out, and I came home late."

"I see," said Mike, helping him up. "Well, you can't stay out here. Come on."

As they moved to the door, the light above the exit sign shone brightly on CJ's face. His eye was swollen and purplish, with a little bit of blood coming out of the corner. Mike stopped him dead in his tracks. CJ squinted as Mike turned him.

"CJ, what the hell happened to your face? Who did this to you?"

"Nobody. It's nothing."

Silence.

"Was it Dex? Did he do this?"

"No... no, man," CJ said. "It's not like that."

"CJ, if Dex is doing this, you can tell me." He looked at the swelling. "If he's fucking doing this to you, I will stop it now."

"No... it's nothing." The boy was panicking. "It was some punk who jumped me for my shoes. It's nothing. I swear!"

Mike looked down at CJ's new pair of Jordans and knew he was lying.

"Do you think I can use your bathroom?" CJ said. "I really have to go."

They walked the long hallway to his apartment. The moment Mike opened his door, CJ bolted to the washroom. Mike went into the kitchen and pulled out the first-aid kit.

"Sit down," he said when CJ came out of the bathroom. "Come on, now."

CJ reluctantly sat down at the kitchen table. The sun was slowly breaking through the buildings to the east. Mike pulled out a bottle of alcohol rub and swabs.

"Are you going to tell me the truth?"

"I'm telling the truth. It was just some punk I ran into on the way home. I swear!" he pleaded. "Can we just drop it?"

Mike nodded. He'd known CJ long enough to realize that they weren't going to get anywhere. He tilted CJ's head up to the light and started to wipe the area clean with rubbing alcohol. CJ screwed up his face as Mike cleaned the area and applied ointment to the cut. He went into the freezer and pulled out a bag of frozen peas.

"Here," he said, handing him the bag. "This will help with the swelling."

CJ placed the makeshift ice pack timidly on his swollen eye. Mike felt overwhelmed, watching him in pain. He grabbed hold of him and pulled him into a long bear hug. At first, CJ laughed nervously, but, as Mike held him tighter, he felt the boy loosen up and hug him back.

"My boy," Mike whispered. "Look, it's almost morning. Go and sleep in Nolan's old room. If Dex isn't worried that you haven't been home yet, he's not going to care much if you're gone another couple of hours."

CJ nodded. He walked into the room and shut the door. Mike looked up at his clock. It was too early to do anything. He was glad, in that moment, that the building had installed private balconies. It was the only thing keeping him from going into Pam's apartment and beating her husband to a bloody pulp.

▶

PAM SAT IN THE TAXICAB, heading home from her trip to Jamaica and going through a mental list of what she wanted to do for CJ's upcoming graduation party. It was still several months away, but she was anxious to get a head start. She planned to book the complex's newly renovated party room for the occasion.

She was one of a handful of tenants in units still under rent control. The only problem with her situation was that, while all the other units were being upgraded into luxury apartments with new floors and appliances and renovated bathrooms and kitchens, Pam had to be content with outdated fittings and appliances. It didn't matter. Her apartment was a bargain and, right now, the best place to host a graduation party.

Pam had a lot more to celebrate. Her trip to Jamaica had been worth it. Prior to her trip, she had hired a Jamaican private investigator, recommended by Mr. Clarke. Within a few months, the investigator revealed that Headmaster Lewis had been working behind the scenes to fix every disaster his son had left in his path. He'd paid off all of the witnesses at the party who had identified Jason, the worker who thought he'd seen the headmaster's son, and all of Jason's university friends, including Roger McAllister, who ended up going to prison a few months for the rape. He'd even paid off Pam's friend Julie.

The thing he hadn't planned on was Pam getting pregnant. When he heard about it, Headmaster Lewis had contacted Pam's aunt, who refused to speak to him, but changed her mind when a huge cheque was sent to cover Pam's education abroad. Pam had always thought her aunt had funded her entire education with the money her father had left.

Aunt Marva's neighbour and closest friend confirmed that Headmaster Lewis had even secured Pam's visa for her to go to school and to work in Canada. After the baby was born, her aunt told Headmaster Lewis that the baby would be given up for adoption and she never heard from him again.

The Lewis family went back to England and Jason Lewis went on to have a lucrative career as a barrister, got married, and had a few kids. But, when he entered the world of politics and decided to run for Parliament, he obviously began to worry that his political career would be dead in the water if the Pam Allen rape case started to bubble up.

The private investigator reported everything he could dig up on Jason Lewis and his family. According to his sources, Jason Lewis was a favourite to win in his riding. He was a popular and charismatic politician with important backers willing to fund his entire campaign. During the vetting process, Pam Allen's name began to surface, setting off red flags. Whispers of a possible "love child" in Jamaica started to dampen his chances. And, if there was a child, there was DNA. Jason had sworn to his backers that this was all a huge misunderstanding, but they were reluctant to go forward until they had definite proof that he wasn't involved. Now his lawyers were ready to have Pam declare that Jason wasn't involved in the rape, all for the sum of £50,000.

After hearing the entire story, she'd gone to Thomas Clark in tears. "It kills me that once again he's getting off so easy, but it's £50,000. I don't know what to do. What should I do?"

"Pam, be smart." Tom Clark pushed the box of tissues across his desk. "You survived and went on to have a great life, so don't shed any more tears."

"Mr. Clark, you have no idea what my life has been like since Jason Lewis," she said. "He destroyed everything."

"What really did he destroy Pam? List everything."

"My schooling, my... my reputation, my relationship with my own daughter," she said.

"Can you get any of that back?" Clark asked her. "And before you answer, I want you to seriously think about what I'm asking. Can you recoup anything that you've listed?"

Pam sat in his office, silently wishing her life had been different. Seething anger had lived inside her for years and heavy bouts of depression and panic attacks continued to plague her. She hated her daughter, who didn't even know the reason why.

"No, Mr. Clark," she said calmly. "I can't get any of it back."

"Then you have to ask yourself, what is it all worth to you? What is the pain he gave you, the hatred, the anger... how much is that all worth?"

"Definitely not fifty thousand pounds," she said. "A hell of a lot more than that."

Mr. Clark looked steadily at her.

"You're saying that I should ask for more? No amount of money is going to fix anything."

"But it will fix him," he replied. "Why should you be the only person that is burdened with hardships because of Mr. Lewis' actions?"

Pam had gone home that night to ponder Mr. Clark's advice. She wanted Jason Lewis to pay for what he did to her, but where was the true satisfaction when any amount she could imagine would be a drop in the bucket for him? She wanted him to feel her pain. She wanted to humiliate him the way he had humiliated her all those years ago. She wanted to gut him the way he had gutted her innocence, leaving her bitter and filled with hatred and distrust.

She did the only thing that made sense to her. She hired the best lawyer she could find and, through him, demanded that Jason Lewis fork over £1 million. She knew it was a lot and that he might never pay it, but she wanted to send a clear message that she wasn't some piece of trash that could be played with.

Jason's lawyers immediately rejected her offer but sweetened their initial offer by raising the amount to £500,000. Pam's very resourceful lawyer started to dig into Jason Lewis' finances and found that he was worth nearly £6,000,000 and, that if it came out that he had fathered an illegitimate child, he would lose lucrative endorsements he needed to secure his run in the election.

Pam's lawyer then countered with £1.5 million and included a picture of Simone when she was ten years old and a promise that neither Pam nor Simone would demand a paternity order. It was a defining moment for Pam when Jason Lewis quickly agreed to all her demands, though she found little solace when she went to Jamaica to sign the agreement. Part of her wished that she had demanded more, just to dig at him a little deeper, but, after months of negotiating the settlement, she was happy that it was finally over.

▶

PAM HOPED Dex would be home. She'd taken an earlier flight than planned so that she could tell him the great news about the money. She had never told him about the rape. She still wasn't sure how he would react to it and had decided to tell him that the money was an inheritance from a distant relative.

She was surprised to see Mike outside his door. It was not like him to be hanging around in the hallway. As she got closer she could see that he was hot and ready for a fight.

"Mike, you look mad as shad," she said. "What's going on?"

"I need to speak with you." He opened his door. "Right now!"

"Okay... okay," she said. "Let me just drop my suitcase—"

"No. This can't wait." He took her suitcase from her and headed into his apartment. "I need to talk to you before I see his fucking face because I'm ready to rip him apart."

"What are you talking about?"

"I'm talking about that fucking man you call a husband!" He

slammed the door. "Do you know where your son has been sleeping for the last three nights?"

"No—"

"Well, the first night he was sleeping in the stairwell, scared shitless that his stepfather was going to beat the crap out of him. Then he spent the last two nights in my apartment."

"What are you talking about?" Pam repeated. "Dex has never laid a hand on CJ — I would know."

"You're either a fucking liar or blind. Don't forget that I live next door to you. I can hear when a pin drops in that apartment. I hear the way he talks to CJ. I know that he roughs him up — and don't fucking try to deny it because I hear you screaming at him to stop. Where do you think CJ goes after he gets into an argument with Dex? The only reason I don't come over to fucking smash his head in is because CJ is terrified of him."

Of course, the walls were thin. She felt her face turn red. "Mike, what happens between CJ and his father is none of your business. Neither is how Dex disciplines CJ."

"Pam, are you kidding me? CJ is every bit my business. He has been since the day he was born. I may not be his biological father but I've always been there for him."

"Well, Dex is his father now," she shouted back. "Dex is trying to raise my son to be a respectful black man, something you would never be able to do for him."

"That's a load of bull," he said. "I know men like him. He's a bully!"

"Mike, you don't know anything about him. At times they argue, but all kids fight with their parents."

"Not like this," he said. "Kids don't get black eyes after arguments."

She looked at him in disbelief. It had been always tense between CJ and Dex. She had made sure that Dex would be working most of the days she was away. He had just started a new job with a real estate agency and was busy showing two big listings.

His career as a lawyer hadn't manifested the way they had hoped. He'd tried working from Canada with his Jamaican clients but, after a year, his clientele list had dried up. He took the Canadian bar exam, hoping to start up his own practice in Toronto, but corporations in Canada were not keen on working with an unknown Jamaican lawyer. Pam persuaded him to get into real estate, where he could use his experience in contract work and hopefully make big commissions. He wasn't much of a salesman and hated the idea of selling houses, but he got his license to appease her, and the market was finally showing an upswing.

"Where is CJ?" she asked. "Is he here?"

"No. I drove him to school this morning. I didn't want him here when I talked to Dex."

"Mike, I don't want you involved in any of this."

"I can't stay out of it anymore," he said. "You've known me long enough to know that I'm not going to sit around and let him pounce on CJ."

"He's my husband and CJ's father."

"Stepfather," he interrupted. "Please stop calling him his father."

"Stepfather, okay? Look, Mike, I know how much you care for CJ, but going for Dex is going to make things worse for him and me. Just let me handle this. Please, Mike! Promise me that you'll stay out of it."

"Only if CJ spends the afternoons with me," he said. "I don't want him home alone with him. He can hang out with me at work or help me at the church on my days off. Make up some excuse. Tell him that I got him a part-time job or something. I don't really care. I just don't want him alone with that son-of-a-bitch."

"Fine! Are you happy now?" She stormed out of his apartment. Safe inside her apartment, she leaned on the closed door, breathing hard, then realized that she had left her suitcase behind.

A few knocks on the door.

She opened it swiftly. Mike stood there with the bag in his hand.

"Thank you! Thank you! Thank you for my bag. Thank you for pointing out what a horrible mother I am. Thank you, Michael O'Shea! Thank you!" She dissolved into tears.

He walked her into her apartment and sat her down on the sofa. "Pam, you know more than anyone that I'm not a perfect parent," he said. "I've made my fair share of mistakes with my own kids. But the one thing I appreciated while I was bullshitting through it all was having you there to set me straight. I only want to do the same for you. I'm always going to tell you when there is something wrong with CJ. I can't help it... but I'm sorry that I yelled at you—"

"I'm just mad at myself." She wiped her eyes with the side of her hand. "I know Dex can talk rough with CJ, but I swear to you if I had known that he was beating him... I would have never left CJ home alone with him."

"Talk to CJ," he said. "He's scared of Dex and won't say anything to me but maybe if you approach—"

The locks on the front door rattled. Dex walked into the apartment.

"What do we have here?" he said sarcastically. "Another neighbourly pow-wow?"

"Just leaving," Mike said. "Pam, tell CJ that I expect to see him right after school tomorrow."

"Okay," she said.

As she closed the door, Mike grabbed her hand and squeezed it.

Dex was fixing himself a drink in the kitchen. She turned to see him drain the glass then pour himself another.

"So what did fix-it Mike want?"

"Nothing," she said. "CJ asked him for a job and he came by to tell me that he had some work for him."

"It's about time that boy gets off his lazy ass." He turned on the television set. "Prince Caleb spends too much time playing those damn video games. Hey, when did you get in? I thought you were coming home this evening?"

"I took an earlier flight," she said, unsure if now was the time to share her news. "Annalise is doing much better, so I left a little earlier. How was it with CJ?"

"The usual," he said, his eyes glued to the television. "I didn't see much of him the entire time."

Pam looked at him, giving him a chance to tell her what had happened with CJ, but he just continued to watch the local news program. She took her suitcase and headed to the bedroom. She felt sick to her stomach. If she was just dating Dex, it would be an easy decision. She would dump him. She should have done it the moment he uttered a negative word against her son.

She thought back to the days she was dating Dex. He always "teased" CJ. Had it been all in good fun? An older father figure riling up the young one? Toughening him up for the real world?

Dex had been a successful Jamaican lawyer and prominent in the community. She'd been dazzled by him. She'd decided that he was a good man.

She struggled to keep herself from crying as she opened up her suitcase and pulled out the trust documents. Nothing fit in her life anymore — not her daughter, not her relationship with Mike, not her husband, and now she risked losing her son. She picked up the phone and dialled. Now it was even more important that she continue with her plans. She no longer had a choice.

"Hello?" she said. "I need the telephone number for Simone Allen in Kingston, Ontario."

40

Simone snuggled into her oversized armchair, settling in for the night. She was studying for her last exam. She had spotted the dark brown leather chair a few years back at a yard sale, several patches masking the tears and cracks. The broken-down chair was bigger than any armchair she had ever seen but smaller than the typical love seat. She was proud that she had talked the seller down from $200 to $50.

The chair had long been a sore point for Simone's roommates and friends. They swore that they would torch, sell or shank it to bits if she didn't get rid of it. But it was her first big purchase and it suited her small frame, and despite its worn-out exterior, it was as comforting as a warm blanket. Simone had spent many nights in her chair, falling asleep while staring out the picture-pane window at John A Boulevard.

The moment she arrived at Queen's University, she'd hated living on campus. She always felt out of place alongside rich kids who took for granted that they had parents who paid their way. While she worked three jobs to afford school, they drained their accounts on booze and partying and were satisfied earning passing grades. She dealt with their noise and sloppy messes. She tolerated the lack of privacy and intrusive questions about her personal life.

During frosh week, she made the mistake of admitting to her floor-mates that she didn't know who her father was. Several students thought it was hilarious and played "Find Simone's Daddy," naming every celebrity who could possibly be her father. She'd tried to laugh it off, but hated being the butt of everyone's jokes, so she started to spend more time in the campus library, away from the chatter.

One afternoon, a few drunken students crashed into her room and she had to call campus security to remove them. From that moment on, she was labeled "anti-social" and a "stuck-up bitch." Her roommate complained to the residence board and requested that she be evicted, claiming that Simone's attitude was ruining her first-year experience.

The last straw was when her second-year roommate touched her hair and Simone struck her. It had been a huge ordeal, with the residence board threatening to remove her from residence for her violent outburst. Rather than wait for the board to rule her fate, Simone took matters into her own hands and found a sublet in "The Student Ghetto". A homesick Chinese student had moved back to Hong Kong after frosh week and the girl's father was desperate to find another student to take over the four-year lease. Although the place came with a roommate, it was the perfect opportunity. She was eager to get off residence and he was eager to have the whole rent paid.

Simone's roommate was a Taiwanese girl who barely spoke English. Her name was Lucy and she was never home. During their first year together, Simone could count on one hand the number of times she actually bumped into Lucy.

Simone enjoyed her solitude, which she celebrated by purchasing her first piece of furniture, her leather chair. People came and went, but her armchair was a constant presence. The chair gave her a sense of peace and calm. It represented freedom and the fortitude she'd felt in making decisions for herself.

At the end of her third year, Lucy decided to move in with her boyfriend. Simone knew that she would need a new roommate, but hated that her perfect solitude would be interrupted by some unknown factor.

Her prayers were answered in the form of Jessica Bennett.

They met in the library one Friday evening toward the end of the school year. Simone was studying for her anthropology exam and sat across from a young woman with long blonde hair piled in a messy bun on top of her head. She glanced at Simone over her black-rimmed glasses, then slumped in her chair, carefully perusing her binder full of notes as she proceeded to chew the cap of her pen.

As they were quietly studying, one of Simone's old floor-mates came in with some friends, all very tipsy and loud.

"Hey, Simone," her floor-mate cackled, stumbling over with her books. "Guys, this is the girl I was tellin' you 'bout." She was slurring her words. "Isn't she so goddamn fuckable? I'm so fucking jealous of her fat-fat booty. I wish I had ass and tits like her."

Simone turned red. She gathered her books to leave.

"Fucking look at her hair," the girl said, touching Simone's hair. "She's like a white girl in a black girl's body."

"Do you mind shutting the fuck up?" Jessica said, from across the table.

"Who the fuck are you?" Her former floor-mate turned to the blonde girl with deep dimples and cold green eyes. "I'm talking to my friend and you're interrupting us."

"This is a library, not a fucking pub!" she said. "Do us all a favour and file your ass out of here." She pointed across the room.

The drunken girl looked around. A security guard was headed in their direction.

"Fuck this," she said to her friends. She slammed her books on the table before stumbling off.

The security guard walked up to their table and looked squarely at Simone, about to say something, when another disturbance from the drunk group attracted his attention. He quickly moved on.

"Thanks," Simone said.

"It's nothing," she said, sitting up. "That cunt is in my world lit class. I fucking hate that bitch."

"We're in the same class," she said. "I'm Simone."

"I thought you looked familiar." She reached out her hand. "I'm Jessica. I think we're also in the same anthropology class, right?"

"Tuesday night class with Professor Gillis?"

"Yup, the very one. Are you ready for his exam?"

"Not really."

"Me neither." She sighed, flipping through her notes. "I thought this class was going to be easy, but it's one of my hardest courses. Hey... if you don't mind... do you want to study together? You know... help each other out?"

"Yeah, sure." Simone moved her stuff closer to Jessica. "A lot of this stuff seems to be going in one ear and out the other."

The two of them spent the first hour discussing the chapters that the exam covered and then the next two hours talking about themselves.

Jessica had grown up in Bridle Path and had attended private schools most of her life. She opted to go to Queen's University instead of the University of Toronto for the sole purpose of escaping her over-protective parents.

After that night, they quickly became good friends. Simone liked talking to her. Jessica had an edge about her that Simone gravitated towards. Her sarcastic yet humorous personality was a great foil to Simone's dry sense of humour.

Simone was overjoyed when she found out that Jessica was looking to move off campus. It was perfect. Simone needed a roommate, someone she didn't mind hanging out with, and Jessica's parents would only allow their daughter to live off campus if she had a roommate.

Living together was a good fit for the two women. Jessica was always dragging Simone out with her and, in turn, Simone brought Jessica to hip-hop concerts and poetry slam performances, which introduced Jessica to a world of black culture she'd never known existed.

When Jessica's birthday was marred by her parent's pending divorce, it was Simone who took her on an impromptu trip to Montreal to cheer her up. It was Jessica whom Simone confided in when bouts of depression left her crippled with nightly panic attacks. It was Jessica who helped Simone come to grips with her pain when letters she'd sent to her brother were returned unopened.

Their friendship was further solidified during what they dubbed "zombie hell week," when Ontario experienced the worst ice storm in decades. They spent that week bundled up in layers of sweaters and blankets in front of their television set watching old movies between newscasts reporting on the storm.

Now, with their final year at Queens coming to a close, everything was about to change. Simone looked around at all the moving boxes cluttering their tiny living room. She was excited about her yearlong internship at Prisdel Productions, while Jessica had finally agreed to go to law school at the University of Toronto. Jessica's only condition had been that her father buy her a two-bedroom condo for her and Simone to share, and he surprisingly complied without a complaint.

The condo was in the heart of downtown Toronto, close to the subway line, Harbour Front, and the SkyDome. It was much bigger than any apartment Simone had ever lived in and she would pay very little in rent. She couldn't pass up the chance.

"You're not taking that with you?" Jessica gestured to Simone's chair. "I'm pretty sure there is a rat colony living in it."

"Either it comes with or I keep my ass in Kingston," Simone quipped as they packed the kitchen dishes. "Plus I caught your fat ass asleep in it last week."

"I'm not going to lie." Jessica laughed. "That chair is comfy as hell but seriously, Si, who the fuck hated you so much that they sold you this piece of shit?"

"Well, if it makes you feel better I'll keep it in my room," she said, wrapping newspaper around the only two wine glasses they had left.

"I get it," Jessica said, giving her a look. "So you and your friend can fuck on it in private?"

"What friend?"

"Bitch, the same friend you've been talking to since I moved here," she rattled off. "The same friend you had staying here while I was home during spring break. The same friend that ate my peanut butter cups."

Simone started to laugh. She had forgotten to replace Jessica's stash before she got home. Jessica knew how much she hated them and was smart enough to figure out that Simone had company while she was gone.

◀◀

IT HAD BEEN a while since she'd been in a significant relationship. At the end of high school, she had messed around with Patrick, but that had quickly fizzled. She'd tried to get into the social game and meet someone, but school occupied most of her time and there was no one that she was attracted to.

Early days at the sublet, she'd started to hang out with a neighbour — an Italian woman named Lia. They'd met at the famous garage sale down the street and found they lived in the same building. She had instantly liked Lia because she'd convinced her that the chair was a beautiful piece that she should snag before anyone else did.

Lia had helped her bring the chair home. It took them nearly thirty minutes to lug the beast back to the building and, after they had managed to get it up the two flights of stairs, they laughed and hugged each other at their accomplishment.

After that afternoon, they often chatted in the hallway when they bumped into each other. Brief conversations turned into lengthy discussions over coffee in Simone's kitchen. Simone learned that Lia was a graduate student attending Queens. She was studying to be a teacher and was almost finished with her master's degree.

The friendship had turned into something more serious after they attended a small film festival together. That night, they ended up curled together on Lia's sofa, polishing off two bottles of Pinot.

Simone had never thought she would find a woman attractive, but Lia wasn't an ordinary woman. She was bright and witty and voluptuous, with a curvy hourglass figure and long thick wavy brown hair. Any time they walked down the street together, Lia got most of the attention from men openly lusting after her. Lia loved flirting with them and basked in their attention. Simone found it hard to believe that a woman as beautiful as Lia, who could get any man she wanted, was interested in her.

Their first intimate kiss came from Lia. Simone was timid. She didn't know what to do with herself, but, when the kiss got heated, she started to respond.

"All this time I thought you were so stiff," Lia said when she pulled away. "Is this the first time you've been kissed?"

"Yes," Simone said. "I mean... the first time by a woman."

Lia laughed. "Your kiss was very sensual and passionate."

Simone didn't know what to say. Lia thought she was a good kisser. Part of her was a little embarrassed, while part was a little elated.

"Canadian girls are an interesting bunch," Lia continued. "On the surface, you are as rigid as the Americans when it comes to sex. In Europe, we're much freer. You just love and enjoy life, whether it is with men or women. Life is too short to stifle your heart."

"Where I come from, they kill people that are gay," Simone said. "Being gay in Jamaica is like a death sentence."

"Then don't go back to Jamaica," she said, sitting next to Simone. "Be where you can freely find and experience love. Who wants to be around so much hate and destruction? It's easy and wonderful to fall in love. It's when you force it away from you that there is so much mayhem."

"Says the woman who fled Italy for the cold winters of Canada."

"I know," Lia agreed. She laughed. "I don't know what I was thinking."

Simone covered her mouth and they both let out a hearty laugh.

"Why do you do that?" Lia asked. She pulled Simone's hands from her face. "You have such a lovely smile. It makes you very pretty. Much more beautiful than me."

"Are you kidding?" Simone said. "You're probably the most stunning woman I have ever met. I don't think I could ever come close to being as beautiful as you."

"That's not true," she said pulling down Simone's hand again. "Sei una donna molto bella. You have a... what do they call it in English... café latte... milky coffee complexion and gorgeous curly hair. I bet you half the women you know are secretly jealous of you and the other half want to fuck you."

She looked into Simone's eyes. It always made Simone self-conscious when anyone looked at her. She could feel her face growing hot. She turned away. Lia reached out and took her chin, turned it towards her and softly kissed her lips. Lia leaned her back on the couch. Simone wanted to stop, but, before she knew it, they were kissing intensely.

Her entire body was aroused by Lia's touch, but she felt timid and closed her eyes as Lia pulled off her camisole and lifted her skirt, slipping her fingers inside to reach her g-spot. Simone panted. She felt a deep sensation travel up and down her spine. Lia released her and continued to kiss her inner thigh, moving up between her legs.

Lia's tongue slowly licked her pussy, sparking every nerve in her body. She had never felt anything like it and felt paralyzed as Lia's tongue lightly caressed her clitoris.

"Oh my god," she said, gasping slightly. Her back quickly arched. She felt Lia's tongue circle around before travelling to her centre. "Wait...wait...stop...not there."

Lia obeyed and moved to kiss Simone's outer thigh before making her way to Simone's breast, up to her neck, to kiss behind her ear.

"Kiss *me* down there," Lia whispered. She lay back on the couch.

Simone nervously moved her lips down Lia's body, kissing her soft skin. She was uncertain if she was doing it right and tried to mimic what Lia had done. She let her tongue guide her.

Lia moaned when she touched the tip of her clit. "Don't stop." She gripped the couch.

Simone felt a mixture of excitement and power, and, when Lia cried out, she felt a small but acute satisfaction.

Lia let her orgasm sweep her away and, at the end of it, they both collapsed on the floor with Simone wrapped in Lia's arms.

Simone's body still felt electric. She was turned on, but terrified by it all.

"How did it feel?" Lia asked when they'd finally caught their breath.

"Strange... but nice. And a little scary."

"It's always scary the first time you make love," she said.

Simone hadn't thought of that. It bewildered her that this was the first time she had had a significant sexual encounter with someone. She felt flustered when she thought about it, but then her lips curled into a smile.

"What's so funny," Lia asked.

"Nothing. I was just thinking of all the things my mother told me about sex. She warned me that my first time would probably get me pregnant."

"Well, the good news is that you can't get pregnant licking my pussy," Lia replied.

Simone burst into a fit of giggles. Lia was right. She didn't need to worry about that at all. She reached for Lia's hand and pulled her back down, kissing her deeply. Lia stroked the small of Simone's back. She lay back and Simone made love to her again.

Their relationship was something Simone soon treasured. She relished her ability to live a normal life, interrupted only by ventures across the hall to the private fantasy that now started to consume her. Hidden away from the prying eyes of friends and family, she was content with concealing their relationship and Lia was patient with Simone, recognizing her private nature. Lia never pushed her into anything that would scare her away but, being the free spirit that she was, she hoped Simone would one day feel comfortable enough in their relationship to go public.

Lia had come out to her family years before and, after a long time, had gained their acceptance, but for Simone coming out was going to be a slow and impossible process. After two years with Lia, Jessica was the first person she told – on the night before they were to move to Toronto.

"Wow, I had no idea you were a lesbian," Jessica said in disbelief. "I mean, I figured you were dating someone, but I just never realized…"

"I don't want to categorize myself that way," Simone said. "It's not like that."

"So you're not a lesbian?" Jessica taped up another box of

kitchen dishes. "I mean... what do you call it then? Are you bi?"

"I don't know," she said. "I guess I just don't want people to call me anything. You get called that and then that's all you end up being."

"You prefer women, but don't want to be labelled a lesbian?" said Jessica. "Sounds like you're either really confused or don't know what you want."

"Well, you always wanted to be a writer, but then you decided to study law. Have you given up on being a writer?"

"No... but that's not the same thing."

"Hear me out," Simone said. "You still want to be a writer, but, for now, you're putting things on hold until you get this law degree and then you will see where things go, right? Well, that's exactly what I'm doing. I'm just enjoying whatever this is and for once I'm not trying to define it or ask anyone's permission."

"So then why be so secretive about it all?" Jessica asked.

"Because the less people know about me, the less they have to say about me."

"Okay... so this mystery person... woman," she said, correcting herself. "What happens to her now that we're moving to Toronto?"

"Nothing," Simone replied. "She knows that the internship is going to take up most of my time and that I'll have to visit her on the weekends. It'll work."

"So I don't get to meet her?" Jessica asked. "I mean, I know you want to keep her a secret and all, but don't you think she'll want to visit you in Toronto?"

"I'm not ready for that," she said. "Too many prying eyes in Toronto."

"You mean your mom," Jessica said. "It's a big city, Simone."

Simone sat silently as she wrapped the last coffee mug. She hadn't seen her mother in years and was still grappling with the strange phone call she'd received earlier that week. Pam had been surprisingly pleasant. She'd invited Simone to her brother's eighth-grade graduation. But Simone was wary. The last thing she wanted was her mother rejecting her again. She didn't know if she could deal with another blow-up between them.

"Anyways, how long do you think she'll want to stay in the shadows?" Jessica said as she taped a box shut. "I'm pretty sure relationships work the same gay, straight and in between. You can't hide her forever. Eventually, she's going to want more."

"All I want is peace," Simone said. "Do you know what I mean? I just want to live my life without everyone weighing in on what I should and shouldn't do. I've spent my entire life dealing with everyone's opinion of me."

"I get it," Jessica said. "It's not an easy thing to come out to friends and family, which is why I'm honoured that you told me."

"Yeah, well…" mumbled Simone.

"No, seriously, Si," she said. "We've been friends for a little while and, if this woman makes you happy, then I'm happy for you."

"I am happy," she said.

"So you're not going to tell me who she is?"

"Hell, no," Simone said, laughing. "You're too damn nosey."

"Bitch!" Jessica said, throwing a kitchen towel at her.

◀◀

NOLAN SAT at the counter of the diner where Dana had worked all through school. He was waiting for his lunch order of a ham sandwich with an apple and a bag of chips. He nodded to the diner owner, who still remembered him and who, in the past, had given him odd jobs when he was struggling for work.

After months of standing in cold parking lots, hoping to get a construction job, his luck finally had panned out in the most unpredictable way. The only black foreman in the area had taken pity on him and hired him into his crew.

Jake Lassman was an older man with leathery skin and a gruff way about him. He wasn't the most pleasant person that Nolan had met, but he seemed to take a liking to Nolan.

At first, he found the pace a little daunting. Jake's crew were fast and prompt, and Jake held high expectations for anyone on his team and did not forgive those who wasted time. Nolan was expected to do anything asked of him, even if it meant getting coffee for the all-black crew slugging away at the site. Though he hated being the errand boy, he kept his head down, hoping to hold onto this job long enough to get off parole and move back to Toronto. He needed money so he could get out of Halifax and he was a few months away from his parole being up.

Not much for socializing, he was quickly nicknamed Frosty for his bald white head and for always eating his lunch away from the rest of the crew. In the beginning, the guys ribbed him, trying to find ways to get under his skin, and there were moments when he wanted to clobber them.

"Hey Frosty," said Freddy, one of Jake's younger crew members. "I saw your mama last night."

"Yeah? What of it?" Nolan replied. He continued sorting his tools.

"I don't know, man," Freddy said, laughing. "Yo Mama so white, she gets a tan just opening the fridge door."

The others on the crew started laughing as Freddy continued.

"Yo, Frosty, your mama is so white that, when she went to the north pole, she got lost," he said to a roar of laughter. "Frosty's mama is so white she makes the Holy Ghost say 'Gawd Damn'."

Nolan started to laugh a little. He remembered playing the dozens with Kester, who remained the reigning champion. The real sparring had always been between Kester and Simone. In the end, Kester always had the best line to shut the whole game down.

"Hey, Freddy," he said. "Yo mama is so stupid that she called me up last night and asked for my number."

Nolan could hear some of the crew chuckle as Freddy tried to act like Nolan's slam was nothing.

"Yo, Freddy," he continued. "Yo mama so stupid, when she went to take the 66 bus to Penhorn, she took the 33 twice instead."

"Ah shit, Freddy," said one of the other crew member, "That's your Mama for sho."

"Yo, Freddy," Nolan said as he placed the tools on the bed of the truck. "Yo mama is so dumb, I told her to do the robot and she came crying, thinking that C3PO knocked her up. Yo mama is so stupid she put Purina in her drawers to feed her pussy..."

The entire crew stopped dead in their tracks as Nolan continued to bash Freddy's mother. Freddy stood there stone-faced as Nolan rattled off line after line.

"Hey Freddy," he said, saving his best dozen for last. "Yo mama is so stupid that the first time she used a vibrator she cracked her two front teeth."

The entire crew burst out laughing. Nolan smiled. Freddy stood there stiffly, looking around in wonder to see all of his co-workers patting Nolan on the back.

"Fuck this," Freddy said. "That's not funny."

"Come on, young blood," one of the older men said. "You know he got you good. You can't be no bitch when playin' the dozens."

Nolan walked over to Freddy with his hand extended. Freddy stood there for a moment, his eyes glaring, but then a slight smile spread across his face and he reached out to shake.

"That last one was foul, Frosty," he said. "Funny, but foul as hell."

After a few weeks on the crew, Jake told Nolan that he had a knack for plumbing. It was the first time Nolan had ever been glad that his father had dragged him around to the various parishes every weekend. He had an encyclopaedic memory for all the small fix-it tricks his dad had used for difficult issues, including plumbing, on church job sites. Jake took Nolan under his wing, teaching him other things that he eagerly picked up from job to job. He was a fast learner and was soon putting up drywall, laying cement, and working on simple electrical work. By spring, Jake had started to take his apprentice to smaller jobs. He told Nolan that he could be the jack-of-all-trades and work the off-hours jobs he didn't have time for.

"I trust that the time you were in jail was not for stealing," he said to Nolan as he sized up a paint job at a private home. "I don't want you making me look bad by going into these white people's houses and stealing their shit."

"No, Jake," he said, laughing. "You know I'm white, right?"

"That don't mean shit," he said. "These days it's hard to find good trustworthy white boys."

Nolan laughed awkwardly as they pulled their equipment off the truck. They were painting the exterior of an old two-story country house off highway 215. The house stood by the Minas Basin and the sea winds had torn off much of the paint over the years. The owners were away on vacation and wanted the house painted while they were gone.

The house was much taller than most they dealt with and it took most of the morning to finish the front. By noon, the two of them were sweating. They stopped to take their lunch break. It was nice sitting out in the sun.

Jake opened up his huge lunch pail. Nolan laughed to himself at Jake's feast. His wife always prepared his meals as if she was building him a personal picnic. The tuna sandwiches were Saran-wrapped separately, the lettuce and tomato slices carefully placed in paper towels to take away excess moisture. The man hated a soggy sandwich and his wife went to great lengths to make sure his sandwiches were perfect.

Nolan opened up his own lunch pail and pulled out his copy of *Mein Kampf*. He had been reading the autobiography of Adolf Hitler over the last few weeks and was preoccupied with the book.

"What do you have there?" asked Jake as he picked up the book. "I never took you for someone interested in this kind of stuff."

"Just something to pass the time," he said. "Have you read it?"

"A very very long time ago," he said, handing him back the book. "A long-winded book from a long-winded man."

"He was a very complex man," Nolan said. "I mean, set aside some of his policies…"

"How in the world do you set aside his policies?" Jake said, raising his eyebrow. "Young man, you won't learn much about life from that book. He was a madman responsible for the destruction of six million Jews and God knows how many other people."

"Do you really believe that?" Nolan asked. "I mean I think that number is wildly exaggerated. Plus, they were the usual casualties of war."

"I was a young man stationed in Germany during the reconstruction," Jake said. "One of the ugliest times of my life. I saw bodies lying in ditches and on the sides of the road. You couldn't tell if the bodies were grown men and women or children. Many of them were just skin and bones. No sir. I wouldn't call any of what happened an exaggeration. I would call it the ugly truth."

They finished their lunch in silence.

The next day Jake dropped a copy of Viktor Frankl's *Man's Search for Meaning* on top of Nolan's lunch pail and walked over to the supplies to take a quick inventory. Nolan reluctantly picked up the book. He looked at the cover. The book seemed familiar. He tried to rack his brain for where he had seen it before, and then remembered that it had been assigned for religion class in the eleventh grade. He remembered that class because it was the only one he'd had with Rowan at Holy Cross.

⏮

ROWAN WAS SLUMPED in his chair at the back of the room when Nolan walked in. Nolan had planned to skip the class to hang out with Tess, but Rich had already warned him that, if he missed another class, he would be kicked out of school. He didn't really care if he was expelled, but he didn't want to catch shit from his mother. They hadn't been getting along lately and it was either toe the line or deal with her nagging him. He chose the former.

Nolan nodded to Rowan as he went to the empty seat in front of him. He could tell by Rowan's expression that he wasn't thrilled to be there either. They had been friends since the ninth grade. These days Rowan spent half his time in the gym working out and the other half ignoring teachers, not really trying to finish school.

It wasn't that Rowan was a poor student. In fact, he was probably the brightest in his grade. He had an aptitude for learning that should have placed him in a better school or at least in some sort of gifted program, but his attendance was shoddy and his attitude poor. He had spent so much time dealing with his strung-out mother and being bounced from house to house that school was an unnecessary burden. Nolan had heard about Rowan and his mother from Tess, who had been to their house and met the woman a few times. She said his mother belittled him every chance she could. It was hard to imagine anyone belittling Rowan. He came off as if nothing moved him.

Religion class was supposed to be a bird course for the students, which was why everyone showed up. As long as you showed up, the teacher would assign readings that were never reviewed and you would spend the course either catching up on your other classes or sneaking out after attendance was taken.

It was the only reason Nolan attended the class and Rowan tolerated it. But, this semester, they were being taught by Brother Morley, a young priest from New Brunswick who had come with the idea that he was going to actually teach. They all looked at him like he was crazy when he said he was going to review and grade every book report and essay. A few planned to complain to the principal when he informed the class that each week there would be a quiz on the material they would be reading.

The first assignment was Viktor Frankl's *Man's Search for Meaning*. Nolan looked at the cover of the book and couldn't make out what it was about. The image was of an old man who looked as if he was pondering something deeply.

When Father Morley gave the class time to begin reading, Nolan pulled out the sports pages to check the baseball scores. At the end of class, he walked out with Rowan.

"Great class, eh?" Nolan joked.

"Yeah, whatever," Rowan said. He seemed upset. "The whole thing is a fucking joke."

"Yeah," Nolan said, trying to find something witty and crude to say about Brother Morley. "I mean didn't he get the fucking memo?"

Rowan snickered.

"What they need is a class that tells the truth about the Holocaust," Rowan said.

"Holocaust?" Nolan asked.

"You don't fucking read, do you? The book Morley assigned is about the Holocaust," Rowan snapped at him. "I didn't know this school assigned fiction outside of English lit."

"Yeah, man," Nolan said, still confused. "I know what you mean."

"No you don't," Rowan said. "You have no idea what I mean. Did you even read that crap he's ramming down our throats? Fucking people like him are the problem. They're trying to brainwash us with this liberal kike bullshit, they want us blinded to the truth."

"And what truth is that?" Nolan asked.

"That the Holocaust wasn't real," he said "It's bullshit that six million Jews were gassed by the Nazis. The narrative is always shaped by the victors."

Nolan wasn't sure what to say. He hadn't paid much attention to the Holocaust and didn't feel like he could say anything one way or the other. He had never met a Jewish person or anyone who was actually in the Holocaust. He just smiled and nodded as Rowan went into his usual diatribe about the Jewish conspiracy.

"This is why we're where we are today," he said. "The sooner we understand that, the better."

"Yeah, man," Nolan said. "You can't trust anyone these days to tell you the truth."

"Absolutely, brother," Rowan said. "Not even your own bitch."

"Who, Tess?"

"Especially Tess," he said. They stopped at Rowan's locker. "She thinks I'm stupid, but I know she's fucking other guys."

Nolan went quiet.

"She thinks that I don't know, but I do," he said, pulling out a textbook. "I can smell their cocks on her breath."

Nolan felt his face get warm as Rowan searched his locker. He hated when Rowan talked about Tess like that. It was common knowledge within the group that he always had other girls on the side. No one ever said anything. Not even Tess, who would cry on Nolan's shoulder when she caught him with one of them. Nolan had tried to convince Tess to break up with him, but, no matter how Rowan treated her, she stuck with him; he had this strange hold over her.

Instead, she would show up at Nolan's house in the middle of the night, tap on the basement window, and then spend the night. She would just lie next to him, not saying a word, but, after a while, she would go down on him.

Nolan felt bad that he was fooling around with her. Rowan treated him like a younger brother and had become one of his closest friends. He figured it was because he was easy to get along with and didn't talk much that Rowan gravitated to him. Being with Tess left him feeling like a traitor, but he found it hard to say no to her.

"Don't worry, Nolan," Rowan said, pulling him into a playful headlock. "I still love her. I just can't trust her. But I'm not worried. She can keep whoring herself to the entire school if she wants. As long as I know the truth, that's power, man."

The bell rang for the next period. Rowan and Nolan said goodbye and made plans to meet up after school. Nolan went to his locker and shoved the Viktor Frankl book to the back of his locker before heading to his next class.

▶▶│

NOLAN SAT on the front lawn of the house he and Jake were painting. He looked at the book Jake had given him. He couldn't remember if he'd ever got around to reading it for class. He stuffed it in his bag, not wanting to seem rude.

During the long bus ride home, he started the first chapter, inwardly jeering, but, after a while, he became engrossed in the easy storytelling style. The descriptions of life in the concentration camp were similar to stories he had heard before, but Frankl's personal account captured his attention. It went beyond the gruesome details to give examples of how Viktor had used mind over matter to give him hope during the bleakest moments.

He read a little bit each evening, on his way home from work. At the end of the week, just as the bus pulled up to his stop, he finished the book. He got off the bus, flipping through, looking for a quote that had stuck in his mind. When he found it, he read it over several times.

We who lived in concentration camps can remember the men who walked through the huts comforting others, giving away their last piece of bread. They may have been few in number, but they offer sufficient proof that everything can be taken from a man but one thing: the last of the human freedoms—to choose one's attitude in any given set of circumstances, to choose one's own way.

He read it over and over by the side of the road until his throat felt raw and his vision started to blur with tears. He could hear his sister's words mingle with Frankl's.

Despite everything you've gone through and done, you really haven't bothered to learn a damn thing.

Their words started to resonate with him. For a moment his world stopped spiralling out of control. He stood by the streaming traffic and started to see things clearer.

As long as I know the truth, that's power, man.

He wanted something different for himself. He didn't like the person he had become or the anger he harboured. He couldn't understand what he was angry about anymore, only that it left him constantly exhausted. He wanted something in his life to mean something.

He started up the street to his mother's house, but stopped and turned back to the bus stop and waited for the bus to swing back around. He hopped on it again and headed downtown. He went to the public library and sat for a while figuring out what he wanted to do.

He went to the information desk and asked for the Toronto white pages. He looked through the book, found the number, and jotted it down, then looked around for the closest phone booth.

"Good day," said a voice. "You've reached the automated service for Sheridan College. Please press 1 if you know the extension you wish to reach. Dial 2 for Sheridan's financial aid, Dial 3 for the admission office…"

Nolan pressed the number three and waited, listening to the hold music. It was a while before someone came on the line.

"Hi," he said anxiously. "Can I get some brochures on your construction and maintenance program…or just anything about your plumbing and electrical programs?"

He listened as the woman listed the programs available and he jotted them down on a scrap of paper he found by the phone. She asked if he would like brochures for any of the programs.

"Yes, please," he said. "All of them."

After his probation ended, Nolan decided to stick around and work full-time for Jake. He learned as much as he could on the job and even took his GED and graduated from high school.

That spring, Nolan and Freddy started up a renovation business. Freddy had an eye for potential and a talent for renovations and Nolan had the quick mind and necessary skills to see a job through. They pooled their resources and purchased a 700-square-foot foreclosure that should have been demolished years before. It was a small nothing of a place that happened to be situated close to Dalhousie University.

"We have to think big, Nolan," said Freddy as they walked through the tiny house. "You wait, this little shit-hole is going to take no time to fix and flip."

"I guess," Nolan said, unsure if it was worth sinking the little money he'd saved into this shack. "It's just I can't even see anyone but a serial killer wanting to fuck with this place."

"Come on, man." Freddy pulled down the plywood covering up the kitchen window. "This place isn't that bad and, when we're done, not only are we going to get multiple offers, but you'll want to live here."

The two of them carpooled into work for Jake and then worked on the house every evening and from sun-up to sundown on weekends. By the time they had hauled most of the garbage out and cleaned the house up, they started to realize just how much it would cost to get everything up to code.

"Fuck me," Freddy said, as they went through a laundry list of repairs while grabbing drinks at Mackenzie in the North End. "We have to spend every last paycheque to get this done."

"It's not that bad." Nolan reviewed the list. "If we just stick to basic features and keep the look neutral we can get this done in two months."

"Yeah, well, I was hoping to get it done in two weeks."

"What's the rush? It's two months, not two years."

"My girl is pregnant," Freddy said, finishing his beer. "She's due in six months."

"Wait, which girl?" Nolan asked. "Kelly?"

"Nah, man," he said, wishfully. "I stopped fucking with Kelly a while back. It's this Jamaican girl from Dalhousie… Amaya."

"Ah, man, congratulations… I guess," Nolan said, trying to suppress his laughter.

Freddy glared at him.

"I'm sorry, man, but weren't you the one telling everyone that you would fuck any woman but a Jamaican woman?"

"Hellz yeah," he said. "Fucking fertile motherfuckers. She swore up and down that she was on something. They have some voodoo thing they do to sperm. I swear! Their pussies are like witchcraft. Fucking pulls you in and messes with you."

"I think that's all women." Nolan gestured to the bartender for another round. "I grew up around Jamaicans and it doesn't work like that."

"You wanna make a bet? One minute I'm checking Kelly and

then Amaya shows up with her round tight ass and breasts for days."

"How did you meet Amaya, anyways?"

"She's Kelly's roommate," Freddy said.

"Ah, so you got greedy." Nolan laughed. "That's not some fucking voodoo. That's you, fuck for brains."

"Yeah, well," he said. "Shit happens."

"Look, I know how it is," Nolan said. "I had the same troubles myself."

"No shit? You knocked up a chick?"

"Yeah, two actually." He nodded. "Well actually technically one. Right before high school, I got my girlfriend pregnant but she had an abortion. Then I thought I got another girl pregnant but it ended up not being mine. It was her boyfriend's."

"So she got greedy," Freddy said, laughing.

"Yeah, something like that. Look, I started strapping my shit up after that!"

"Yeah, I guess that would have been helpful to hear three fucking months ago! But seriously," Freddy said, "you fucked up a girl? Shit! I guess Irish motherfuckers are just as bad as Jamaicans."

Nolan laughed. He finished his drink.

Freddy sat quietly looking at his glass. "I think I'm going to marry her," he finally said. "It's the right thing to do. I mean she's a good woman. She's smart and funny and feisty... like real feisty. I just need this flip to work, man. I've put everything in."

"Freddy, it's going to work out." Nolan patted his friend on the shoulder. "You are one of the best in the city. Between you and me, we'll get this place back to its former glory and sell it."

"Okay, damn it!" he said. "We fuckin' got this!"

Nolan walked back home after he left the bar, cursing himself for not telling Freddy that he was moving back to Toronto at the end of the summer. It had been his plan the entire night, but hearing about the baby made him table the conversation for another time.

As the weeks flew by the scrap house on Courtyard Avenue was transformed into something special. Within six weeks they had added the final touches. Nolan was extremely proud of the project and invited his mother to come see their handy work.

"Oh my God, Nolie," Meghan said. "This is incredible... I mean really incredible."

"Thanks," he said, beaming, as he showed her the kitchen. "We were lucky to get most of the stuff wholesale and a lot of help from Jake and the crew the last week."

"Honey, I can't believe that you guys did all of this." She wandered through the house. "When you first told me about this I thought it was a bit risky... but this... this is amazing."

"I wish Dad could see it before we sell," he said. "I think he would get a kick out of it."

"I'm sure he would," she said. "Why don't you stick around a few more years? You and Freddy could make a great business out of flipping houses."

"It's tempting," he said. "But I need to go back to school. I have so many ideas of what I want to do and if I get more training I can start bigger renos. Toronto is a big city with a lot of older houses. I can definitely do more down there."

"Well, we'll miss you, but I think you're right." She hugged him. "I'm proud of you, Nolan. I know that I haven't told you that lately."

Nolan smiled as he hugged his mother tightly. She gave him an extra squeeze as she looked up at him. It had been a long time since they'd talked like this. It had been a while since he didn't see fear in her eyes.

▶

Pam put the finishing touches on the cake for CJ's graduation party. All the decorations were in place and the balloons were still floating up toward the ceiling of the new party room adjacent to the building's new pool.

CJ had wanted the works for his party. Pam spared no expense and booked the room and the pool, and she even hired a hip-hop DJ, despite Dex's objections. He'd told her it was silly to spend so much money on an eighth-grade graduation, but she was proud of her son. He was not only graduating from elementary school, but had been accepted to St. Michael's College. She wanted to show him how proud she was and demonstrate to the world that she could afford to send her son to one of the most prestigious private schools in the province.

The only thing she needed was Simone to sign off on the terms of the trust. Pam had tried to get her lawyer to separate her deal from Simone's but that term was non-negotiable. Either they both agreed to the non-disclosure clause or the entire deal was off.

Pam headed back up to the apartment. She had asked Simone to come by before the party so they could have a moment to talk. She wasn't sure how she would broach the subject. Except for the phone-call invitation, it had been years since they'd spoken. The last thing she wanted was to tell her about the circumstances that led to the trust. Talking about the rape was something she swore she would never do again. The only thing she needed from Simone was her signature.

When she got to her floor, she found Simone sitting on the ground outside her apartment. She was stunned to see how much she had changed over the last four years. Her loose curly hair, her clothing, and even the makeup she wore had a bohemian feel that softened her look.

"Simone," she called out as she walked towards her.

"Hi," Simone said. "Am I early?"

"No... no." Pam smiled at her. "I told you the right time. The party starts in a half hour. I was hoping to catch up before it started."

"Catch up?" Simone mocked. "Why would we do that, Miss Pam?"

"Why don't you come in," she said, ignoring Simone's tone. "Do you want anything to drink?"

"No," she said, walking into the apartment. "I'm fine."

"Okay, well, why don't you have a seat. I'm going to make myself some tea."

She glanced back from the kitchen as she put the kettle on. Simone was wandering around the apartment, touching the sofa that she'd once sat on; and then she walked out onto the balcony and over to the wall on Mike's side.

"They've made a lot of changes here," she said, joining Simone on the balcony. "Some good, some bad."

"So where's CJ? I was hoping to see him before the party."

"Mike took him to get his hair cut," she replied. They walked back into the living room. "He should be back shortly. You are growing your hair out."

"Uh huh," Simone replied. "Been growing it for awhile now."

"Well, it looks nice. You always had nice hair."

"Must have gotten that from my father."

Pam cringed.

Simone picked up Pam's wedding picture that stood on the side table. "Where's Dex?" she asked.

"He's in Jamaica this week," Pam lied. "He had last-minute business that couldn't wait."

She had no idea where Dex was. After their latest fight, he'd left and hadn't been home for two days. Actually, she was relieved. She didn't want his miserable mood ruining the celebration.

"Simone, I wanted to talk to you before the party because I have some documents I need you to sign," she said carefully. "I had a joint trust put together for you and your brother that I need to access. CJ was accepted to St. Michael's College and will be going there in the fall. I need to access the funds for his tuition."

"He's going to St. Michael's?" Simone said. "That's great!"

"Yes." Pam breathed a sigh of relief. "He's been working hard for the last couple of years. Dex and I are really proud that he got into the school."

"Okay," Simone said. "Sure. Just send me the paperwork and I'll sign it."

"I have it here." She picked up the folder from the dining room table. "I was hoping you could sign it today. Esma is going to be here and she can notarize the whole thing. That way I can send it in and have everything processed by next week."

Simone took the paperwork and glanced at it. "Why do you have a trust set up for me? I mean, with everything that happened, you made it clear that you didn't want anything to do with me."

"That was then," she said. "I know that we've had a lot of issues in the past—"

"No, you've had issues in the past," Simone interrupted. "I've just been the victim of your issues."

Pam sat quietly.

"And I'm sorry for that," she said. "I tried to do the best I could by you."

"The best you could?" Simone laughed. "You threw me out of your house and left me in juvy for weeks. If it wasn't for Mike and Mrs. Price, I probably would have been there for months."

"I was given wrong information," she said. "I thought that you were—"

"You thought I was some slut passing myself to any and every guy. And, even when it came out that those girls were lying, you still hung me out to dry. Why?"

"I don't have answers for you, Simone," she said. "All I can say is that I made a mistake and I am trying to make it right."

"How, Miss Pam?" Simone could feel her jaw tightening. "How can you make up for eight years of keeping me away from my brother? Or ignoring me when we met in the hallway? And what about the last four years? I've been in school without any help from you. Tell me again how you can possibly make it right?"

"I'm trying to make amends now," she said. "I wasn't a perfect mother. When you have your own children you'll understand the pressures."

"I don't think I can ever understand," Simone said. "When I was little you treated me like crap and you have ever since. Before I do anything for you, I deserve to know why."

Before Pam could respond, CJ and Mike came through the front door.

"Simone!" CJ yelled as he ran to his sister. "Yo! What are you doing here?"

"Splimoney, when did you get back in town?" Mike said.

"I officially moved back last month," she said, hugging her brother. "I got a year-long internship at this production company. I start in the fall."

"Oh shit!" CJ said. Mike gave him a look. "I mean snap. Oh snap, Si... that's the best news ever! Are you going to live with Mrs. Price?"

"No," she said. "I'm living downtown with my college room-mate. We have a place on Spadina."

"Moms, Simone has to come to my party," he said. "You have to come. It's this afternoon."

"Of course Simone is invited," she said. "That's why she's here."

"Hey, CJ, I actually can't stay," Simone said. She smiled as she handed him a small box with a card. "I was only here to drop off your graduation gift and to say a quick hello."

"Come on, Si," he said. "Just stay for a little while."

The doorbell buzzed. Mike went to find out who it was and the laughter of kids could be heard over the intercom.

"Looks like your friends are here," Simone said. She hugged him. "Don't worry, we have plenty of time to catch up. I'm heading out right now. I'll walk you down."

Simone gave Mike a hug, promising to stop by. She barely looked at Pam. It was clear that a simple olive branch wasn't going to solve things.

"Pam, what just happened?" Mike asked when they'd left. "Are you and Simone talking?"

"Trying to," she said, putting the documents away.

"It's a start," he said kissing her on the cheek. "Give it some time. It's not going to happen overnight."

"Yeah," she said, trying to shake off her disappointment. "Come on, let's go downstairs before these kids tear the place apart."

▶

DEX WALKED into the apartment and was glad that it was empty. He'd spent the last few days drunk in a hotel room with a strange woman. Right now, he couldn't remember leaving the hotel, let alone meeting the woman.

He went into the fridge, looking for something cool to drink. He was thirsty all the time. All he could find were a few cases of sodas stacked on a shelf. He cracked one and downed it, then reached under the sink, pulled out the hidden bottle of vodka, and poured himself a tumbler.

The living room was a mess, with decorations scattered on the dining table and the floor. He had to stop for a moment and squeeze his eyes shut before he realized that CJ's graduation party was happening today. He poured himself another drink and walked out to the balcony.

Looking over, he could see the entire party in full swing. There were almost fifty kids down there, many of them splashing around in the pool. He peered over, looking at some of the pretty young girls dressed in two-piece bikinis. He started to think about how different it was when he was a kid. Girls didn't walk around in such skimpy clothing, but this was Canada. In Canada, anything goes.

He squinted and spotted Pam coming out of the party room with a platter of burgers to grill. He watched her carry them to the table next to the barbecue and wondered if he should go down to help, but he stopped when he saw Mike join her, holding a bag of ice.

Mike poured ice into the cooler as Pam stood around, talking to the other mothers. Mike placed his hand on her waist and whispered something in her ear.

He drained the vodka bottle. He hated how close they were and was suddenly sure they were lovers. Once, in a drunken rage, he had accused Pam of sleeping with her "Irish boy" and Pam had vehemently denied it, laughing off the accusation. She'd ended up pleasuring him. Now he wondered if it was her way of throwing him off.

He hated CJ working part-time with Mike, helping him do odd jobs. He hated Mike taking CJ to his soccer games on the weekends. He hated Mike.

Dex staggered across the living room and made a detour to the bathroom. He stumbled as he tried to pee in the toilet. He fumbled, pulling up his zipper. Feeling lightheaded, he sat down to steady himself and dozed off.

He was roused awake when he heard the front door open and shut. At first, he thought that he was imagining it, but then he heard a girl's voice in the hallway.

"Are you sure no one is here?"

"Baby, it's okay." A boy's voice. "Everyone is downstairs and no one knows that we left."

CJ's bedroom door closed.

Silence.

The faint sound of giggling. Dex got up and tried to regain his balance, angry that CJ had brought some girl up to his room while his mother was downstairs playing house with the next-door neighbour.

"What the fuck is going on in there?" he said, banging on the door. "Open the fucking door."

The door quickly opened and a short blonde girl ran out adjusting her bikini top. She ran past him and out the front door.

"Why the fuck did you do that?" CJ yelled. "What is your fucking problem?"

"My problem is you." Dex grabbed CJ's arm. "Who do you think you are bringing some girl up here? You think you're a man now? You think you can stick your little pecker in some little bitch under my roof, huh?"

"Get out of here with that! What do you know about my fucking junk, old man?" CJ was laughing at him. "I got a piece on me all the honeys want. You're a fucking slob that smells like piss. Why don't you take your drunk ass back to whatever hole you crawled out of?" CJ pushed him aside.

Dex grabbed him by his shoulders. "You think you're some big man?" He punched him. "You think I can't fuck you up?"

CJ pushed him off and swung at him. He landed a punch on the side of his face.

Dex just threw CJ onto the coffee table, which crumbled beneath him, then picked up the leg of the broken table and swung it, hitting CJ in the chest. He heard the sickening crunch. CJ attempted to crawl away. Dex hit him on the back and then the side of his head. CJ tried to shield himself from the blows, then fell back as Dex continued to bash him with the leg of the table.

"What are you doing?" Pam screamed. The young girl darted behind her. "Get off him, Dex!"

CJ was quiet on the ground so Dex turned and grabbed Pam by the neck and slammed her against the wall. He could hear the young girl screaming. Then Mike was all over him, landing punches hard in his face. His hatred for Mike just boiled over, but he was too tired to fight any more. Mike quickly pinned him down on the couch.

Dex turned his head to see Pam slumped on the floor, moaning, next to CJ's body. Mike was calling out to the boy but there was no response.

"Call 911," he heard Mike yell out to the frightened girl. "Get help, now!"

And then he blacked out.

42

"Would you stop fidgeting, Freddy?" Nolan said. They were at a Second Cup near Dalhousie University. "You're making me nervous as fuck."

"It's too high," he said. "She's asking for too much. Ain't nobody gonna fuck with us when they see the price. We're going to be stuck with this shit-hole."

"Freddy, stop," Nolan said in frustration. "My sister knows what she's doing, okay? Just give it a rest."

"Yeah, so how many houses has she sold, man?" he asked. "She just got her license. I don't even know why I let you talk me into letting her sell it."

Nolan was also anxious about the sale of the house. This was his last weekend in Nova Scotia. He was moving to Toronto on Monday and he wanted everything about the house settled before he left. He needed that cheque to pay his tuition. Sheridan had already given him another extension.

"Yo...Yo, here she comes," Freddy said as Dana walked into the Second Cup. "Fuck man, she looks pissed. I knew this wasn't going to happen."

Nolan looked at his sister. Dressed in a navy blue suit and

carrying her computer bag, she looked professional. Dana had begged him to let her sell the house. She had just gotten her license and was working for a small real estate company in Dalhousie. He'd thought it would be a good idea to have her sell it, but now, looking at her face, he wondered if she was way over her head.

"Hey," she said, kissing him on the cheek. "Hi, Freddy."

"What's up, Dana?" Freddy grimaced. "I can tell by your face that nobody bit."

"What?" she asked. "No...no...I sold your house."

"What!" Freddy said. "Then what's wrong?"

"I'm just pissed," she said. "I should have held out for more. I think I could have gotten them to go higher."

"How bad was it?" Nolan asked, worried that they hadn't got their listing price of $100,000. "How much did you get for it?"

"Nolan, the whole thing was insane! We had seven bids this morning," she said, frowning at both of them. "My ass is numb from sitting at my desk on the phone all day. I had to get my boss to help me with the negotiations. She had never seen anything like it."

"Dana, how much did you get for the house?" Nolan asked.

"The accepted bid was $170,000," she said. A huge grin spread across her face. "I sold your house for fucking $170,000... $70,000 over asking price."

"Yo... Yo, Dana," Freddy said. "Are you fucking with us?"

"Nope," she said, pulling out a manila file folder. "I should have asked for more."

"Oh my god," Freddy whooped. He stood up and hugged Dana, lifting her off her feet. "Jesus Christ, that's way more than I thought we would get for that shit-hole."

"Well, that house you call a shit-hole just gave you guys a handsome profit." She beamed at Nolan. "You guys did good."

"I can't believe it," Nolan said in shock. "They paid that much?"

"Yup, and in cash." She showed them the banker's draft. "I just wish I could have asked for more. The new homeowners were stoked about the finishes. The work you did was amazing. I almost wished I put in a bid."

"See, man?" Freddy said. "This is why you can't go to Toronto yet. There are so many houses we can flip. In no time we could be making *boku* cash."

"He's right, Nolan," Dana said. "The market is flooded with houses that could use major renovations. If you guys flipped a few more like this, you could pull in a ton of money."

"Listen to your sister, Nolan," Freddy said. "This woman knows what she's talking about."

"Freddy, you are the brains in all of this," Nolan said. "I don't have the experience to know half the stuff you know. This place wouldn't have gone anywhere if you weren't working on it. You got the vision. I'm just your glorified helper."

"Come on, man," Freddy said. "You know a lot more than you think. I can fix shit but you have a way of making stuff flow. You designed the entire layout. It was your idea to knock down the living room wall and put in a breakfast counter and it was your idea to refinish the fireplace."

"Well, after I finish school I'll be even better," Nolan said. "That's what I gotta do, man. Then, you can join me in Toronto where all the money is at."

"That's what I'm talking about," Freddy said, sharing a palm slap with Nolan. "My girl is already harping about moving to Toronto. Speaking of which, I need to bounce. We have our Lamaze class in an hour."

"All right, gentlemen," Dana said. She pulled out the contracts for them to sign. "Let's get down to business."

After Freddy left, Nolan walked Dana to her car. The wind had just picked up, and it looked as if it was going to rain. They made it to her car just as it started to pour.

"Are you sure I can't give you a lift home?" she said. "You are going to be soaked by the time you catch your bus."

"I'm good," he said.

"Okay, then." She smiled at him. "Hey, Nolan?"

"Yeah?"

"I'm really proud of you," she said. "Like, seriously, the house is amazing, and you're making the right decision to go back to school."

"Thanks, Dana." The rain started to come down harder. "I'll see you on Sunday at Mom's, okay?"

"See you then," she said.

Nolan watched her turn the corner before he started to jog down University Avenue. When he looked at the time he saw that the bus had already left and he decided to walk. The rainstorm stopped as he headed up Barrington Street towards a string of public houses in Mulgrave Park. When he got to the last townhouse, he went up the walk and banged on the screen door. He waited a minute before the door opened.

"What are you doing here?" asked Tess from behind the screen. "I told you to stay away."

"Tess, let me in," he said. "Just for a moment."

She sighed and opened the door. She gestured him into the living room, which was littered with toys and laundry.

"Where's Kyle?" he asked, as he sat on the couch. "I want to see him."

"Nolan, he's asleep," she said. "Look, you can't keep showing up here like this."

"I just wanted to say goodbye to him," he said. "And I wanted to give you some money."

He handed her an envelope.

Tess looked in the envelope and quickly handed it back to him. "I can't take this, Nolan."

"You need the money, Tess." He placed it back in her hands. "Please, take it."

"You have to stop doing this. You have to stop giving us money and coming over to see him. He's not your kid."

"I promised to be there," he said. "I get it that you're with Rowan. I'm not trying to get you to change your mind, but he's in prison, and I want to help."

"It would have helped if you'd kept your mouth shut," she snapped. "Then maybe Rowan wouldn't be in prison for the next ten years."

"Don't do this, Tess," he said. "With or without my help, Rowan would have gone to jail. If I didn't testify, you would have ended up giving birth to Kyle in prison. Is that what you wanted? Look, just take the money and use it to pay bills or buy something for Kyle. I want to make sure that you're okay before I go." He reached for her hand and held it for a moment before letting go. He put the money on the coffee table and turned to leave.

"Nolan, I know that you mean well and I wish to God things had turned out differently." She handed back the envelope again. "If I had my way, you would be Kyle's father, but you're not, okay? I can't have Rowan finding out that you're coming around doing things for us. Do you understand? I can't deal with that, okay?"

"Okay, I get it."

"Goodbye, Nolan," she said, walking him to the door.

He walked down the front porch stairs, then stopped and pulled the envelope out of his jacket. He sealed it, wrote her name on the front, placed it in her mailbox, and continued down the street.

▶

PAM SAT IN HER BEDROOM, unable to focus. She had been working from home for nearly a month while Maureen helmed the ship. The hospital's director had insisted that she take some time off, but she didn't like being away from work completely and asked if they would allow her to work from home. She looked at the report that Maureen had sent her, and nothing made any sense. She picked up the phone.

"Why isn't there a cancelled cheque for the Bethany account?" she said. "I see the first three, but the last cheque is not on file."

"Good morning to you, too," said Maureen. "I'm doing good. Thank you for asking."

"Not now, Maureen. I'm not in the mood."

"It should be in imaging," Maureen said. "I put it in myself last week."

"Well it's not listed here, and I can't close out this account without it," Pam said. "I'm looking at the file right now."

"Well, like I said, I personally dropped the copy of the cancelled cheque in the imaging bin," Maureen snapped back. "It probably got delayed by the vendor."

"Find it," Pam said. "I don't care if you have to go to Iron Mountain yourself. Just find it!"

Pam hung up the phone and slammed her laptop shut. She hadn't been in her right mind since her morning call with the last specialist. She should've logged off then for the rest of the day.

It had been nearly two months, and CJ's condition hadn't changed. After three weeks in the hospital, the doctors had said he was stable enough to be transferred to a nursing facility. Pam knew that meant that CJ would be in a vegetative state for the rest of his life. She had spent weeks contacting every specialist in Canada and the United States, hoping to find one that would give her hope that CJ had a fighting chance. They prognosticated varying degrees of rehabilitation, but none of them could see him being independent again. She wasn't willing to accept that CJ would never be able to walk again, never regain mobility or speech, but none of them promised anything; all of them had come to the same conclusion — it was a miracle that he had survived at all.

After hanging up with Maureen, she went into CJ's room and broke down. She tore down his posters, smashed his stereo system, and hurled CDs against the wall. She slipped on one of the broken CD cases and fell to the floor.

She crawled to the bed in pain, lay across the bare mattress, and looked up at the cracked ceiling for almost an hour until the front door opened, and she heard Mike calling out as he walked down the hallway.

He looked at her and went away, returning with a garbage bag. He sorted through CJ's room, tossing anything that was destroyed, then lay next to her.

They both stared at the ceiling, listening to the sounds coming from behind the wall. The new next-door neighbours were having an argument about whose turn it was to cook dinner.

"They have no idea how easy they have it," Mike said. "No kids to worry about."

Pam couldn't trust herself to speak.

"I remember having those arguments with Meghan before Dana was born," Mike said. "Petty arguments that I could barely remember the next day. Man, what I wouldn't do to have those hardships back. The luxury of fussing over nothing."

After a while, the argument died down. Mike reached for her hand and squeezed.

"It's done," she said, clearing her throat. "The specialist from Houston reviewed all of his tests and agrees with the others. I'm out of options. He's going to spend the rest of his life laying in a bed, unable to talk or move."

"I'm sorry, Pam," he said. "I'm so sorry that all of this is happening."

"Yesterday, while I was visiting him, he looked up at me," she said. "I told him that I was going to make sure that he gets the best care so he can get better sooner. He just looked at me blankly as if he knew that none of it was true."

"There is still rehab," Mike said. "He may not be the boy you knew before all of this, but rehab will give him some of it back."

"But I want all of him back," she cried out. "I don't know if he's even there anymore."

"It will take time," he said. "Don't give up because God knows he's probably giving up on himself. He needs you to keep fighting for him. Keep praying for him."

She nodded.

"Did you talk to Simone yet?"

"I can't," she said. "I can't deal with that right now."

"Pam, you need the money," he said. "You don't have any other options."

"What do I say to her?" She wiped back her tears. "I can't get her to sign the trust agreement unless I tell her the truth. And she won't sign it knowing that it means she'll never find out who her father is."

"But Pam, it's the only way you can get a hold of the money," he said. "If you want CJ to get the best care possible he needs to be in St. John. Simone will see that, and she'll understand."

"She'll hate me, Mike," she said. "She'll never forgive me for forcing her to sign away her father's identity — even if it is for CJ."

43

"You're talking blasted foolishness," Mrs. Price said. "How is quitting your job going to make things better for CJ?"

"How am I supposed to go on with my life while he's lying there, fighting for his?" she said. "He needs me right now."

"No, Simone, what he needs is for you to be strong," Mike said. "Missing this opportunity is not going to improve his chances."

"What if something happens to him and I'm not there?"

"Nothing is going to happen to him, Si," Mike said. "CJ is not giving up on himself, so you can't either. When he gets better, he's going to want to hear about all the great things you're doing."

It had been three months since Dex's attack on CJ but it felt as if it had happened yesterday. She felt so helpless, but she knew that Mike was right. She had spent the last four years working towards an opportunity like the Prisdel internship. Quitting it to keep a bedside vigil was not going to change CJ's circumstances.

She was one of four students out of nine hundred applicants accepted into the coveted yearlong program and, when she stepped into the Prisdel boardroom, she started to feel truly excited. She sat down and introduced herself to the intern next to her.

Hubert Bublik, a Ukrainian-Canadian, had just graduated from McGill University in Montreal with an architecture degree and aspirations to work in film. He had spent the previous two summers interning with American production companies, working as a production assistant.

She took an instant liking to the six-foot giant. Even sitting, he towered over her five-foot-seven frame. He had a stylish, bookish look that complimented his ruddy complexion and wavy brown hair. He reminded her of a male version of Jessica with his snarky, witty comebacks and dark sense of humour. He was also the first openly gay man she had met and she felt an easy rapport with him.

Another intern took Simone completely by surprise.

"Oh my God, Simone!" Ilene Cheng could barely contain her excitement. "What the hell! I didn't know that you were interning here. Is the entire St. Augustine population working for Prisdel?"

"What do you mean?" Simone asked. "Who else is here?"

"Your best friend, Sarah Jane Ryden." Ilene snickered. "She arrived in full form with her nose stuck in the air. She tried to pretend that she didn't remember me. Can you believe it? She's still a prissy bitch."

Simone laughed, just as Sarah Jane entered the boardroom and took her seat. Sarah Jane was obviously stunned to see Simone speaking with Ilene. Simone politely smiled and waved. Sarah Jane quickly looked away.

"Well, forget about her," Simone said. "I'm just happy to see you. Did your parents threaten bodily harm for not becoming a doctor?"

"Ha," Ilene said. "I told them that, if they didn't let me do this internship, I wasn't going to medical school. To be honest, I can't stand the sight of blood. I would make a horrible doctor. After this internship, I'm either going to marry rich or get a job at Prisdel."

"You and everyone here," Simone said.

They spent the next four hours filling out forms for human resources and watching the company's employee onboarding video. The orientation ended with lunch. As Simone freshened up in the bathroom, before lunch, Sarah Jane came out of a stall.

"Look, about Nolan and me. Nothing came out of it. It's not like I had the baby or anything — I just don't want everyone knowing what happened." Simone said nothing. "Do you still keep in touch with him?" Sarah Jane continued. "That prick never even bothered to call me... even after everything."

"I haven't really seen much of him since St. Augustine," she said. "We kind of lost touch after he moved away."

"The way he always went on about you, I thought you guys were closer than that," Sarah Jane said, laughing. "And all this time I hated you because Nolan had the biggest crush on you."

"We were just friends."

"Could have fooled me," said Sarah Jane. "I guess in the grand scheme, things are never exactly the way they seem."

"Yeah, I guess." Simone watched Sarah Jane touch up her flawless makeup.

After lunch, the four of them were assigned to their departments. They would rotate positions every eight weeks to train in several areas. Ilene's first assignment was in post-production; Sarah Jane was assigned to the location department, where she would work on their newest show, *Gifted Gardens*; Hubert was assigned to the art department to work on scripted programs, while Simone was assigned to work with the production secretary.

She had the glamorous job of making photocopies, processing receipts for expense reports, connecting with the legal department, and filing away documents. She also became the resident expert on the temperamental switchboard whenever the receptionist was on break or out sick.

By the end of her rotation, she was so glad to be moving on. She didn't mind working behind the scenes, but was longing to get her feet wet with real production work. She'd been envious of the others, who all seemed to be doing much more exciting work. The four of them sat in the conference room, waiting for their monthly update with the head of the HR department.

"Well I don't know about you, but I'm about done," said Hubert. "I hated working under Miss Cynthia. Do you believe that she has me calling her Miss Cynthia? Not Miss Delroy or Cynthia but fucking Miss Cynthia."

"What's wrong with that?" laughed Simone. "In Jamaica, we addressed everyone that way."

"Does it look like I'm driving Miss Daisy?" he said. "I'm white, damn it!"

"And so is Cynthia. What's your point?" Ilene laughed too. "You're such a drama queen, Hubert!"

"That's Miss Drama," Simone quipped. "Look, I would trade calling her Miss Cynthia for answering the phones, any day."

"Cheryl out again? I thought she was back from her vacay," said Hubert.

"She's out sick," Simone lamented. "She threw her back out."

"Bad luck," Sarah Jane piped in. "Jonathan promised me that he'd talk to Cynthia about keeping me for the next rotation. He said I'm the best intern he's had and that the show is way too important to change the formula now."

"Well, aren't you special." Hubert turned his back on Sarah Jane. "Anyways, Ilene, how is post-production?"

Simone tried to stifle her laugh. The main reason she loved Hubert was how much attitude he gave Sarah Jane. It was clear he couldn't stand her. The moment she'd started trash-talking Simone, he promptly called her a two-faced bitch to her face and ever since then, Simone has cast him as her best friend.

"It's fun, but a lot of work," Ilene responded. "I'm working with this chick named Felicia, who was an intern a few years ago. She works full time now."

"You mean that black girl in editing?" asked Sarah Jane. "I can't stand her. Every time I give her dailies to edit, she's always placing them at the bottom of the pile. When I go back to ask if she's done she just puts it back at the bottom."

"My kind of girl," Hubert mumbled under his breath. "Felicia is good people. I had drinks with her a few weeks ago. She's a little loud, but aren't we all?"

"Well, I wouldn't know," Simone said. "The only people I've been in contact with are the folks in accounting and the FedEx guy."

"Poor Si," Hubert said. "We'll have to rectify that! A bunch of us are grabbing drinks tonight. You need to come out with us."

"Ugh… I want to, but I promised to meet up with my room-mate for dinner. She just broke up with her boyfriend and I'm trying to keep her mind off of getting back together with him."

"Well, bring her," he said. "I'm bringing my roommate, Timothy."

"Your roommate, huh?" Simone said, winking. "Is that what you're calling him?"

"For now," Hubert said. "So far he fares better as a roommate."

"I hear ya," she said.

Rhonda, the head of human resources arrived. "Okay people, let's keep this short and sweet," she said. "Rotations are up, but I have some bad news for a few of you. There have been a lot of changes recently, and so not everyone is going to switch their roles. Sarah Jane, Jonathan has asked to keep you around. To keep him happy I'm letting you stay on his team for another round."

"Thank you, Rhonda," Sarah Jane said, smiling.

I'm pretty sure he's fucking her, Hubert passed the note to Simone.

Simone giggled a little, quickly covering her mouth.

"Hubert, I'm going to put you in post-production, primarily in our editing suites. You'll be reporting to Felicia Richards. Ilene, you will be placed in the art department."

Ilene beamed.

"Simone, unfortunately, you'll need to stay put for the time being," said Rhonda. "Cheryl has put in for a leave of absence and, since you seem to be the only person who can handle the phone system, we need you to cover her. Just for a month or so."

"But can't I just show the others how to use the system? It's really not that hard."

"Maybe next time. For now, we need you at the receptionist desk." Rhonda looked at her watch. "Okay, people. That's it for now. I'll send a calendar reminder for our next meeting."

"Just think of the important service you're contributing to everyone, Simone," Sarah Jane jeered. "Someone has to man the phones." She walked out of the conference room.

"Fuck her, Simone," said Hubert. "The good news is today is Friday and tonight we're going to get wasted, have a great time, and maybe find someone to fuck if we're lucky. You in?"

"Yeah," she said. "It just pisses me off. I'm like the only black person in this place—"

"What about Cheryl?" Hubert said.

"Or Felicia in editing," Ilene chimed in as they walked out of the conference room. "And Mr. Stevens in the mailroom."

"I love Mr. Stevens," Hubert said happily. "He's always trying to fix me up with his niece. I don't think he's figured out that I'm more hot for his nephew."

"Okay, one of four people," she corrected herself. "The point I'm trying to make is that I'm the only black student intern and I'm the one answering the phones."

"So what are you going to do about it?" Ilene countered. "You're an intern. The whole point of this program is to do shitty jobs until you land a full-time position."

"Yeah, well, this is not what I signed up for," she replied. "I didn't move back here to learn how to transfer calls."

"I get it," Hubert said, hugging her. "Look, if you want, you can show me how to work the board. That way I can help out."

"Really, Hubes?" She smiled. "You would do that for me?"

"Bitch, please," he said. "I'm playing... I'm playing. You name the time and place and I'm there for you. Okay, enough talking. Some of us have real work to do around here."

Simone gave him a dirty look. "Very funny."

"We're still on tonight?" he asked. He gave her a sloppy kiss on the cheek.

"Yeah," she said. "I'll be there."

▶

MIKE SAT at a table in the back of the Swiss Chalet, nursing a beer. What was taking Nolan so long?

Mike hadn't seen much of him since Nolan had returned to Toronto. He was glad to have his son back. He had even hoped he would move back into his old room, but Nolan had insisted on staying close to the school. Mike was just happy that they were in the same city, but today he was annoyed that his kid was late again for dinner. Just as he was about to flag down his waiter and order, Nolan came rushing to the table.

"I was about to give up on you. You're twenty minutes late."

"Sorry, Dad," he said, taking off his jacket. "I came straight from class. I didn't realize how bad traffic was going to be."

"Maybe you should invest in a cell phone." Mike handed him a menu. "It's 2001, for god's sake. Even I have a cell phone."

"Don't have cash to waste," he said, looking over the menu. "What looks good?"

"Everything," Mike said. "Did you get in touch with Tommy about the job at his brother's construction site?"

"Yeah, I start Monday." The waiter came by to take their order. "Just the double leg dinner and a Labatt, please."

"The same for me," Mike said. "Well, I'm glad that worked out. Does that mean that you're officially in the apprenticeship training program or do you have to wait until next semester?"

"Talked to my advisor today and they were willing to keep me in the program," he said. "No harm, no foul."

"Humph, you're lucky Tommy's brother came through for you," Mike said, unconvinced. "Not everyone is willing to hire someone with a prison record."

"Yeah, well, I guess I'm lucky it all worked out," Nolan said. "You need to relax, Dad. In a year, I'll be finished with the program and, if my luck continues, I'll be my own boss soon."

"Easier said than done," Mike said. "You did good renovating that house and was damn fortunate to get it sold, but I know a lot of skilled and hard-working men like you who get rejected for loans because a small prison stint pops up on their record."

"I get it, Dad," he said. "I fucked up and it's going to bite me in the ass everywhere I turn, but does that mean I shouldn't try?"

"No, of course not." The waiter brought their drinks. "I just want you to know what you're up against."

"I'm trying to turn things around," Nolan said, pulling a flyer from his pocket. "This was posted on our community board at school. It's an open casting call for contractors."

Mike looked at the flier and frowned as he read the description.

"Is this for a television show?" he asked. "Why would you be interested in this?"

"It's a home improvement show," he explained. "The work is pretty good. They go to different homes and complete renovations. They're looking for students who want to volunteer."

"Looks like they're looking for free labour," Mike said. "Do you even get a stipend?"

"Yeah, we get $50 a day," said Nolan. "But that's not important. I get to work on a lot of different projects and get a ton of experience."

"Well, it looks like you've looked into this," he said, handing back the flier. "You need as many hours as you can get."

"Speaking of which, do you need help this weekend at St. Augustine?"

"Not going this weekend," Mike said. The waiter brought their food. "I'm taking Pam to see CJ."

"Oh yeah?" Nolan said. "How's he doing?"

"The same," Mike said, pouring sauce all over his food. "Pam is hoping to arrange for him to start rehab in the next couple of weeks. The place is really good, but so damn expensive."

"How's Simone holding up with it all?" Nolan asked. "Do you guys see much of her?"

"Not really," Mike said. "She visits her brother once a week but she's still a little distant with her mother."

"That's too bad," Nolan said quietly.

"Nolan, if you want to contact her, I have her cell number," Mike said. "She would probably love to hear from you."

"Nah, it's okay," he said, turning slightly red. "I'll catch her at the next St. Augustine reunion."

"Sure. Well, if you're curious, she's actually doing pretty good. She got a place with a roommate, not too far from Harbourfront. She's working as an intern for some company. I can't remember what, but anyways, she seems to be pulling her own."

"That's good," he said. "I'm happy for her."

"Mmm hmm," Mike said, looking at his son.

▶

SIMONE STRETCHED her legs while she watched Lia get dressed. It had been a month since they'd seen each other. The last few hours had been spent making love, both trying to mask the tension brewing between them. It had been difficult maintaining their long-distance relationship. Promises of calling each other nightly and seeing each other every weekend were not kept. Long phone calls had been reduced to short phone calls a few times a week, and Simone had made only a few visits to Kingston. It frustrated Lia that Simone was so unavailable. She told her she missed being with her so much that she was contemplating moving to Toronto.

"Wouldn't you like that? It makes no sense being away from each other like this." Simone kissed her. She pulled off the bra Lia had just put on. "You keep distracting me," she said, pushing Simone away. "I'm talking to you about moving to Toronto and you don't say anything!"

Simone sighed as she lay back in bed.

"There is nothing to say," she said. "I work almost fourteen hours a day. I'm barely home as it is. You moving here isn't going to solve things."

"Well, are you going to at least introduce me to your friends?" Lia said. "You keep me like a canary under lock and key. We go nowhere. See no one."

"That's not true! I've introduced you to Jessica."

"No… no, you didn't! We bumped into her in the elevator. And she introduced herself to me."

"What about Hubert and his roommate, Timothy?" Simone said. "You met them. And you also met Felicia."

"Simone, do you take me for a fool? Felicia and the whole gay brigade don't count." She slid off the bed and started getting dressed. "Does your mother even know about me?"

Simone got up and fished for her robe. She didn't want to have this conversation with Lia. Her relationship with her mother was volatile enough. She didn't need to add any more fuel to that fire.

"You can't answer," said Lia as she pulled up her jeans. "For someone who claims to love me, you have a horrible way of showing it."

"I haven't told my mother about you because she doesn't know about me," she said.

"Well, then tell her today," Lia said. "You're meeting her for coffee, no? Bring me with you and introduce your girlfriend to her. Rip that band-aid off, already."

"Easy for you," she said. "Your entire family knows about you."

"What are you talking about, easy?" she said. "When I came out to my family, my mother spit on me and my grandfather refused to speak to me. I was ostracized from most of my family. Only my brother stood by me. God bless him because, if it wasn't for him, my mother would still hate me."

"Yeah, well, that's not my family," Simone said. "And with everything going on with my brother she's the only family I have left."

"So, you're going to hide in the closet for the rest of your life?" Lia said. She reached for her purse. "Pretend that you're not gay to your family?"

"Why is it so damn important that she knows?" Simone snapped. "Why can't you just accept that I will never tell my mother?"

"Because that's how you start, with family. You hide me up here, too afraid to walk down the street with me," she yelled. "If we could just live like a normal couple, then I would be fine with it, but you're too damn scared to be seen with me. What are you afraid of?"

Simone sat on the edge of her bed in silence. She was more than afraid to be in public with Lia — she was terrified. In Kingston, it wasn't an issue. The few friends they shared knew they were a couple. But, back in Toronto, she felt like she was living in a fishbowl. She didn't want to take any chances.

"You don't know my mother," she said. "I can't go and tell her about us. She wouldn't understand."

"Well, I don't understand, either." Lia picked up her overnight bag. "This is Diana all over again. I came out to my family because I thought Diana was the love of my life. Instead, she was a bloody coward and couldn't do the same for me. I'm not going to go through the same thing with you, Simone."

"Where are you going?" Simone said, following her into the

living room. "Give me time, Lia! I'm not as brave as you. I can't be forced out like that. I'm not ready."

"Simone, I love you. I'm willing to shout it out from the rooftop but you... you treat us like a disease."

"Don't leave. Please."

Lia stopped. She barely lifted her head to meet Simone's eyes. "I can't do this again. I can't be stuck in the closet with you while you try to figure out if being with me is worth the risk."

"Please, Lia. You know I love you."

"I know you do," she said. "But it's not enough."

Simone followed her out the door to the elevator, but quickly ducked back into her apartment as one of her neighbours came walking down the hallway. She closed the door behind her, reached for her cell, and called Lia, but her call went straight to voicemail.

She looked at the time and realized that she was late meeting her mother. After getting dressed, she splashed cold water on her face, grabbed her purse and jacket, and rushed out of the condo and up the street to the coffee shop. She was shocked to see Mike sitting beside her mother.

"Hi," she said. "I'm sorry I'm late."

"Hi, Simone." Mike got up to hug her. "You look well."

"I'm doing my best," she said. "I'm surprised to see you. Is everything okay?"

"Yes," Pam said. "I asked Mike to join us because—"

"I'm just here as a friend," he said. "For the both of you."

"Okay." Her eyes darted from Mike to Pam. "But I can't stay long."

Pam looked nervous. Her hand was shaking, "It's about your brother," she said, her voice wavering. "I need to talk to you about his care."

"Did something happen?"

"No, nothing has changed," she said, pulling out documents. "Simone, I need you to look over these documents and then we need to make arrangements to meet with my lawyer to sign. I don't have the money to care for CJ. Once you sign, I can unlock funds... to get him better care."

Simone picked up the documents and read through them. She could see her name and her mother's name, but she didn't see CJ's name anywhere. She re-read the first page and got to the paragraph that said the Lewis Estate was the benefactor.

"What is this Lewis Estate?"

Pam shared a look with Mike. He smiled slightly and nodded at her.

"Jason Lewis is one of my rapists," Pam said. "He and three other boys raped me when I was sixteen years old. He contacted me because he is running for a seat in the English parliament and doesn't want... this involvement coming out."

"Rape?" Simone said. Her face went pale. "What do you mean, rape?"

"I can't go into details about it." Tears were starting to slip down Pam's cheek. She picked up a napkin from the table and dabbed at her eyes. "Saying this much... this is hard enough."

"Is he my father?" Simone asked. She looked squarely at her mother, who turned away.

"I don't know. There were four of them."

"Then why would he set up a trust fund..." she looked at the paperwork, "...for the both of us?"

"To make sure that we never talk publicly about the rape or anyone involved in the rape," Pam said. "And that includes neither of us ever asking for a paternity test of any kind."

"Wait... wait a minute!" Simone's voice started to carry. "So what about the three others? Any one of them could be my father. I can still rule them out, right?"

"No," Pam said, gripping the napkin. "Any inquiry into the other potential fathers may uncover that he's your father. You can't inquire even if there is a chance that it's not him."

"But that can't even be legal," she said. "I'm not going to sign this. I have a right to know who my father is. I've been asking about him my entire life and now I have a name. Why would I give up a chance to know who he is?"

"Why would you want to?" Pam said, pushing away the napkin. "None of them have ever shown any interest in you or taken care of you or even admitted what they did to me. They don't deserve to know you. They're monsters and you're better off not knowing who your father is!"

"So is this what these documents are all about?" Simone cried. "I'm supposed to just sign on the dotted line and leave a whole part of me in the dark?"

"Simone, it's a lot of money," Pam said. "After taxes and lawyer fees it will be at least a million dollars each. Think of how that can change all of us. You and your brother."

"I don't care about the money," she said. "Don't you get it? That doesn't mean anything to me."

"Really? So you're not drowning in college loans?" Pam said. "You don't have rent to pay? Food to put on your table? You can't afford to pass this up."

"Is the money all that matters to you?" she said. "You don't care about me or how I feel. You just want to get your hands on the money."

"Yes, right now that's all I care about," she said. "Because every penny I can get means a better life for CJ. I can't afford to send him to these specialists and have him stay in his current nursing home without this money. So, yes, all I care about is the money because that's all I have to help your brother."

Simone turned away from her mother and stared out the front door. She held onto the legs of her chair and tried to take a deep breath. She felt her hands shake and her body tremble. She looked at her mother, then quickly turned away again. She couldn't bear the weight of her mother's glare.

"Don't I matter?" she asked. "You have shut me down every time I asked about my father. You gave me nothing."

"Because I had nothing to give! What could I have told you? How would you have me explain? Do you think you would have been better off knowing what happened?"

"By making me sign this, you are asking me to give up ever knowing who he is," she said. "You are asking me to stay in the dark, when all I want is to know about me... my past. Who I look like. Who my grandparents are. Do I even have siblings?"

"Simone, you do have a sibling and he is the only family that matters right now," Pam said. "That should be enough."

"I can't do this right now," she said getting up.

Pam got up, too, but Mike motioned for her to sit down.

Simone rushed outside, but Mike followed and grabbed her elbow before she could cross the street.

"Don't, Mike," she said, pulling away from him. "Don't try to make excuses for her. I'm done."

"Simone, I know you're angry—"

"No, you don't know!" she yelled. "You don't know what it's like to spend years being treated like a mistake. Always knowing, that no matter how well you did in school, how hard you tried to follow the rules — nothing counted! Now... now she comes back into my life, not because she's sorry that she was a bully or that she treated me like shit, but because she wants something from me. Did she tell you that, before that asshole nearly killed CJ, she tried to push those same papers on me? This is all about her trying to cash out."

"Okay... I get it," he said. "But, no matter what you think or feel, we have to think about your brother. That's what's important, and the reality is that your mother can't afford St. John. His treatments are expensive and your stepfather drained her accounts to cover his legal bills. If she's forced to put CJ in a second-rate nursing home, he won't last a year."

"Don't do this, Mike," she said, nearly crying. "You're asking me to choose between my brother and knowing who my father is."

"No, Simone, I'm not," he said. "I'm asking you to choose your brother and give him a fighting chance over finding out which one of those bastards shares the same DNA as you."

She covered her mouth with the back of her hand, as she started to cry. People walking past were looking at her. Mike tried to reach out for her, but she pulled away and stormed back into the coffee shop.

"You want me to sign," she said. "Give me the number of your lawyer and I'll go and sign, okay? You'll get what you want and we can go back to having nothing to do with each other."

▶

SIMONE LAY ON THE FLOOR, watching the ceiling fan spin slowly, eyes burning with tears. She could barely see the wobble. Her cell rang; Lia's number was on the screen. She picked up. Lia said she was back in Kingston. Simone told her what had happened earlier that afternoon at the coffee shop, angrily cursing her mother.

"But, in the end, it's for your brother," Lia reminded her. "That's all that matters."

Silence.

"Am I going to see you next weekend?" Simone said. She sat on the floor of her bedroom cradling the phone. "I promise it will be different."

"Simone, I think we need to take some time apart. I don't mean permanently, just some time. The drive back gave me perspective on things and I think I need to go home and see my family."

"I'm sorry about our fight," Simone said. She sat up anxiously. "Let me come up tomorrow. I'll even take Monday off."

"No, honey," Lia said. "This is something I've been thinking of doing for a long time. I think it would be good for us to have some time apart to get our heads on straight."

"Please don't leave while things are in limbo with us. I want to work things out."

"And we will," she said. "After I get back."

When Simone hung up, it felt like her whole world was coming apart at the seams. Every thread she pulled, more of her life unravelled.

▶

"It's for the best," Jessica told her later that evening, as they sat in the living room drinking vodka shots. "Don't get me wrong, Lia seems like a nice woman and I get why you're attracted to her, but long distance isn't working for you guys. Plus, she's your first lesbian experience. And maybe the reason why you were a little hesitant about introducing her is because you weren't really ready to be in a serious relationship."

"I guess." Simone downed her fourth shot. "I really never thought of that."

"No matter whether it's with a girl or a guy, it's always the same thing." Jessica got up and went into the kitchen. "At our age, getting deep with anyone is a recipe for disaster. Maybe in ten or fifteen more years, but not now. Shit, I have two more years before I finish law school. I need to be concentrating on my career and fucking, not who I'm going to spend the rest of my life with."

Simone laughed. She pulled her hair into a ponytail and looked up at Jessica, who was back in the living room with a box of short-bread cookies and an open bottle of wine.

"You need to play the field a little so that, when she gets back from Italy, you'll also have a better perspective on things," she said. She had a mischievous look on her face. "Maybe you won't want a relationship with her. Or maybe sex with anyone else will be so bad that you're willing to tell the whole world just to get a piece of that ass."

"Jess, did anyone ever tell you that you sound like a guy when you're drunk," Simone said, laughing. She opened the box of cookies. "You're so fucking vulgar."

"That's my point, Simone," she said handing her a glass of wine. "Be vulgar sometimes. Bring home a girl that you don't know and fuck her in the kitchen. Hell, fuck a guy just for kicks — just do something crazy. Star in a porno and then mail it to your mother as a proper 'fuck you'. Just do anything to put some life back in you."

"You're a mess," Simone said, laughing. "I think being a lesbian is pretty out there already."

"Wow… wow!" Jessica said getting up. "Did you hear that?"

"Hear what?" Simone asked as she looked around. "I didn't hear anything."

"You just called yourself a lesbian." Jessica covered her mouth, a shocked expression on her face.

"You're an idiot," Simone said, throwing a cookie at her.

"No, seriously, Simone," she said, catching the cookie. "You have never, ever referred to yourself as gay, lesbian or even curious. You've always danced around it. Maybe there is hope for you, yet."

Simone thought a lot about what Jessica had said. She had always steered away from doing anything that might appear unseemly. No matter where she was, she feared her mother would leap from behind her and lash out. That hadn't changed since elementary school or high school or when she lived with Mrs. Price; her mother still made her anxious.

The next morning, she woke up with a nasty headache and the realization that she couldn't sit around anymore, living half a life. She got out of bed and changed into sweats and a T-shirt and pulled her hair into a ponytail. She went through her closet and dug out her sneakers. She hadn't run since high school, but she felt that she needed the fresh air. She grabbed her wallet and her CD Walkman and started out. She ran all the way to the subway and then took the train up to North York. She got off at York Mills station and ran down York Mills Road to Bayview Avenue.

When she got to the complex, she pulled out her earbuds and walked around the grounds. She jogged past the tree that she used to climb with Nolan and lightly touched the trunk. She wandered into the courtyard and looked up at Mike's balcony. The sun was shining brightly. She shielded her eyes, hoping to see Nolan. She turned away, her face warm. She wasn't sure if it was warmth from the sun or embarrassment.

She stuck her earbuds back in her ears before continuing down the path towards the main driveway. She ran up the sidewalk.

▶

NOLAN QUICKLY LOOKED at the jogger as he and his father drove up the driveway. He strained his neck to get a better view, but, by the time he'd turned all the way around, the jogger was too far away. He watched her get smaller and smaller until she disappeared from view.

44

The camera light shone brightly in his face. He wanted to shield his eyes, but didn't want to drop the dry-wall adhesive. Just as he was finished with the top row, he heard "cut" and stood still, unsure if he should continue with the next row or stop everything until they'd reset the scene. The director wasn't happy with the lighting. He needed the set brighter and yelled out for more light. Nolan touched the portion that he'd glued; he didn't want it to dry out, so he just kept going, hoping that he wouldn't catch shit.

Nolan had been working on the home improvement show for nearly a month and he still wasn't used to being in front of a camera. It was daunting, a slow steep curve, and nothing like the construction work he'd been doing. The show was in its fifth season. The production coordinator described it as a renovation show for people who had tried it on their own and now needed the experts to come in and fix their butchered homes.

The host, Mackenzie "Mac" Stevens, was a well-known contractor who had renovated some of Toronto's most prestigious homes over the last three decades. For years, he'd hosted a small program on TVOntario, giving viewers tips on how to complete simple home repairs. When reality television started to take off, Mac found himself on cable, hosting the new home improvement show — *House Helpers*.

Canada's lovable but cranky host was always battling the "young folks" on how a house should be rebuilt. He hated "yuppies" who wanted to tear down historical structures and homeowners who were determined to have the most expensive features, yet would go crazy when the project went over budget.

Viewers couldn't wait for Mac to blow a fuse in front of some unsuspecting homeowner who didn't know a nut from a bolt. This was reality television at its best. The drama of chaotic and emotional renovations followed by the stunning results: picture-perfect homes for clueless homeowners.

Nolan recalled sitting with his father, watching Mac Stevens rewire a ceiling fan or retile a bathroom floor. He was anxious to tell the guy how much his old TVO show had meant to him and his dad, but, on his first day, he was warned that Mac never conversed with anyone unless it was on camera or when the production coordinator brought his lunch.

Nolan was contracted to intern on the show for six months. It was long hours and, coupled with his class work, it left him with no time for himself, but he loved every minute of it. It wasn't being on television that excited him but working on the homes and being a part of the finished product. At times, he would volunteer to come in on weekends to help, just to be a part of the magic that was Mac Stevens.

"You know the cameras don't roll on the weekends," Mac barked at Nolan. "And we don't pay you, either."

"Yes sir," Nolan said. "I'm here to learn."

"Well, I don't need students," he said. "I need workers."

"Yes sir," Nolan said. "What I mean is that I want to be here to learn and contribute, even if it means picking up coffee or getting lunch or digging a trench…"

"Okay, okay," Mac interrupted. "Pay attention to what I need and you can stay. No bullshitting. We're here to get the job done."

The weekend work was different from the day-to-day work. Everything was more relaxed and Nolan was given tasks that fit his expertise. Mac was also different. He wasn't completely unapproachable. The same motley crew that barely spoke to him while filming was relaxed and everyone sat around during lunch, laughing and conversing.

He was also humorous and easygoing with the homeowners who flocked to the site, bringing him treats and gifts. It was a different world. All week long he would snap at the homeowners to get their budget together, but on the weekends he played with their children as he calmly went over tile samples. It left Nolan bewildered. He hesitated before approaching Mac at the end of the day.

"I just wanted to thank you, Mr. Stevens... for letting me work with you. I've been a fan for years and it's been an honour just being a part of this."

"Where you from, O'Shea?"

Nolan quickly removed his ball cap.

"I'm from Toronto, originally," he said. "My father is a building engineer, but has a lot of experience working as a contractor. He taught me a lot of what I know."

"Really?" he said. "Why go to Sheridan then?"

"Well... I... I worked on a house that my buddy and I successfully flipped and... and I wanted to learn more," he stuttered. "I'm hoping to go into the reno business."

"Interesting," Mac said, putting away his tools. "So you renovated a house and now you want to take over the world?"

"Something like that." Nolan chuckled. "Any advice?"

"I'm assuming you've worked with other crews before," he asked. "Something outside of lights, camera, action."

"Yes sir," he said. "I got most of my experience working in Halifax."

"Halifax, huh?" Mac grinned. "I got my start in Halifax. Was born and raised there. Got the hell out as soon as I could. Listen... if I had to give any advice it would be to get out of this work if you're doing it for the money. If that's the case, you'll end up being a slave to it. Working in this industry is like finding a good woman. It's not easy to find the best fit but, when you do, you have to love every part of it. The complicated and the mundane."

He fastened his tools to the bed of his truck and climbed into the cab. Nolan wanted to know more, but Mac was preparing to drive away. He didn't completely understand what Mac meant by loving everything.

Mac stuck his head out the window. "Your application said that you worked for Jake Lassman," he said. "How long did you work for him?"

"A little over a year," Nolan said. "Do you know him?"

"He taught me everything I know," he said, turning on the ignition. "You should thank him. I wouldn't have picked you otherwise."

Nolan watched Mac drive off. He'd had no idea that the old man had worked with Jake, but it made sense. They were both meticulous about everything. Mac was old school about the process, just like Jake, carefully planning out everything to the last detail.

The next day, Nolan was eager to speak to Mac again. He wanted to know how Mac knew Jake. He wanted to hear stories about his mentor and to bond with his hero, but, when he got to the set, a gruff cantankerous Mac emerged, barking orders at everyone. His moment with Mac was maybe a one-time thing or a weekend thing. He kept his head down and got to work, hoping the old man would see him and want to speak with him. But, by the end of the day, it became apparent that it wouldn't happen. When the weekend rolled around, Mac wasn't on site. He wouldn't be on site for another few weekends while he went around the country to work on different projects.

Nolan was a little disappointed, but relished the fact that Mac had chosen him from all the candidates that had applied. He called Jake to let him know he was working for Mac, but Jake was notorious for never picking up his phone. Nolan chuckled to himself. The two men were a lot alike — hard to talk to and hard to get a hold of.

He spent the next several weeks working diligently on every project he was assigned, mostly in Toronto, but he jumped at the opportunity to help out during spring break on the Vancouver set.

He instantly took to Vancouver. It was a different vibe from Toronto. Spacious, and with a natural beauty that took his breath away. He spent his free hours exploring Stanley Park and looking at the horizon. The North Shore Mountains held a stark echo of Nova Scotia and the city had much of the feel of Toronto, but slowed down.

When spring break was over, he was assigned to the Vanguard home on Queens Street, one of Toronto's oldest houses, whose renovation was going to be launched as the flagship episode of the season. It was a huge production endeavour; the main crew had worked on the home for the entire year, with the assistance of plenty of reconstruction specialists. Mac and the producers told everyone to be on their 'A' game.

"I chose you all for this particular project because I trust that you'll get the work done," he said earnestly to the group. "So, if you are not sure, ask someone! I don't want any mistakes on this."

The last leg of the restoration would finish by the end of Nolan's internship. Because this was a historic home, the work was more gruelling than all previous projects; there was so much red tape involved. Mac had to fight the city to get special permits for every crucial update to the home. There were times when work had to stop for days. Once taping was on hold for a week until a permit went through to remove a pillar from the basement. This was to be the most difficult project in the show's history, but, when it was complete, the Vanguard House became the talk of the town.

The work Mac and House Helpers did on the home was featured in several magazines and the finished house was even visited by the premier of Ontario. Nolan was proud that he'd had a small hand in the restoration, and he started to understand what Mac had meant when he said that you had to love every part of your job. Tedious work became just as thrilling as intricate work. He'd never thought that pouring cement, making sure it was level, or painting walls perfectly would excite him, but these mundane jobs were his contribution to the whole experience, and he was sad when it all came to an end.

Before the last day of his internship, he was able to get Jake on the phone, and his old boss laughed when he heard that Nolan was working with Mac. Nolan asked what he should get Mac as a thank-you gift.

"Well, my nephew has a thing for scotch," Jake said. "He's partial to Balvenie single malt."

"Wait — nephew? You guys are related?"

"Mac is my older sister's son. He was born over here, but moved to Toronto years ago. When he was a young blood, I took him in my crew and taught him everything he knows."

"Wow," Nolan said. "I would have never guessed that in a million years."

"My family is a rainbow," Jake chuckled. "How's it going out there anyways?"

"I can't find the words to tell you how great it has been," he said. "I've learned so much in class and on set. I just wish that it wasn't coming to an end."

"Well, when can we see the show?" Jake asked.

"The season begins the end of the summer," he said. "I think the first episode is the job we did on the old townhouse we tore down to the studs. That was some good work."

"Sounds like you found your place."

"Just as long as I can find more work," Nolan said. "Hey, how's Freddy doing?"

"Freddy is well. The baby is getting big. Almost six months already."

"Wow, that went fast," he said. "I wish I could have gone to the wedding. I feel bad that I couldn't get away."

"I'm sure he understands," Jake reassured him. "It was a pretty small affair."

Just as Nolan was going to ask Jake how he was doing, the operator interrupted — his calling card only had a minute left.

"I'm sorry, Jake, but this thing is going to cut me off soon," he said.

"That's okay, young blood. Send my best to Mac when you see him."

"Will do. Tell the guys that I said 'hello'..."

Dial tone.

He wished he had money to add to the call but he was flat broke. The truth was the work he'd been doing wasn't paying the bills. He had to start finding real work, now that the internship and his classes were coming to an end. He barely had money to purchase the Scotch that Jake had recommended. He knew he would have to ask his father for a loan.

At the end of his last day on site, the crew threw a quick "thank you" celebration for the interns. Nolan gave Mac the bottle of scotch.

Mac looked at the label and laughed, patting Nolan on the back. "I see that you spoke to my uncle," he said. "This is a pretty good bottle."

"I did," Nolan said. "He told me to tell you hello... this is your favourite, right?"

Mac was still chuckling. "This is *Jake's* favourite scotch," he said. "It's an inside joke I've had with him ever since I went dry. I've been sober for over twenty-five years."

"I'm sorry," Nolan said, feeling foolish. He adjusted his baseball cap. "I had no idea."

"Young man, no need to apologize," Mac said. He called over one of the production assistants. "This bottle is meant to be shared, Nettie, get some cups for everyone. I want to make a toast."

Everyone on the crew was given a paper coffee cup. Mac himself poured the shots, leaving a double in Nolan's cup.

"You drink my share," he said, winking.

He raised his water bottle and the crowd quieted down.

"Nolan here was nice enough to pick up a bottle of the finest Scotch made anywhere," he said. "I thought it would be only fitting for us to share a drink after another successful season. You all worked your asses off over the last six months and I appreciate that. So here's to all of you and for a job well done."

"Here, here," they all cheered, downing their shots.

"Thanks for the drink, Nolan," everyone said.

"Good luck with everything, Nolan."

"It was fun working with you, babes." A giddy production assistant kissed him on the lips as she passed by.

Nolan laughed, touched his lips, then went to retrieve his tools. As he was gathering his stuff, Jonathan Andrews and Cynthia Delroy came up to him. He was a little surprised to see them. He only knew them as 'the suits' — Mac's name for them.

"Nolan, I don't think we were ever properly introduced. I'm Jonathan Andrews and this is Cynthia Delroy." They shook Nolan's hand. "We're with Prisdel Productions. We produce *House Helpers*."

"Yes, I know," he said. "It's nice to be able to thank you for letting me have this opportunity. It's been great working here."

"Well," Cynthia said, "we were hoping that you would be interested in staying on with us full-time. We'd like to have you on board here and also available to work on other programs when we need you."

"We're one of the few production companies who hire their own construction staff," Jonathan added. "And when we see individuals who are as committed as you are, we go the extra mile to secure them."

"Wow, I don't know what to say," he said.

"How much longer do you have left with your school program?" Jonathan asked.

"I've completed one year of the program," he said. "I'm not able to afford another year."

"Well, we offer some of our people help with that," said Jonathan. "And the ability to hone your craft, if you are willing to keep learning."

"Absolutely! That would be amazing," he said. "I can't believe this."

"Mac speaks very highly of you," Cynthia said. "He was the one who recommended that you stay on with the crew. All of us are impressed with the work you've put in this season, but Mac was especially impressed."

"I'm floored," he said. "Just tell me where to sign up and you can count me in."

"Perfect," said Jonathan. "My assistant will contact you to set up a conference call and we'll go over the details."

"Welcome to Prisdel Productions," Cynthia said as she shook his hand again.

◄◄

"PRISEL PRODUCTION, HOLD." Simone pressed the hold button. "Prisel Production, hold. Prisel Production, sorry for keeping you on hold, how can I direct your call?"

She had been at the front desk fielding calls all morning, annoyed at being the full-time receptionist once again. After weeks of sick leave, Cheryl had returned to work only to quit the next day and Simone was asked to remain on the switchboard until they could find a replacement. Then they hired a full-time receptionist and Simone was assigned as a production assistant on *House Helpers*. But, before she knew it, she was back on phone duty after the new receptionist unceremoniously quit.

"Prisel Production, hold," she said. She pounded the transfer button when placing another caller on hold. "Sorry to keep you holding, how may I direct your call?"

"To whom am I speaking with?" said the voice on the line.

"My name is Simone," she said.

"Simone who?"

"Simone Allen, Ma'am," she said, annoyed. The other lines were lighting up. "I'm sorry, but can you hold?"

She placed the caller on hold, continued to transfer more calls, and lost the call. She just kept going. In a quiet moment, after a string of calls, Cynthia Delroy walked into the lobby.

Simone hadn't conversed much with the boss. She split her time between the Vancouver and Toronto locations and wasn't often in the office. You would never guess that Cynthia was an award-winning filmmaker. She looked so ordinary, like someone's aloof grandaunt. She'd started off working in the art departments of several production companies and then, after ten years, had begun making documentaries.

After years of filming around the world, she started Prisdel Productions with Jonathan Andrews. It started off as a traditional production company, but fell into the world of reality television when partnered with an American production company to create a show about a cross-country marathon called *The Chase*. The show became so successful so quickly that she and Jonathan decided to create more reality-based television programming on the Canadian side of the border.

Simone attempted a smile at Cynthia but the woman looked upset as she brushed past the receptionist desk and into her office, slamming the door. The phones started to ring again. A few minutes later, Rhonda from HR rushed into Cynthia's office and, after twenty minutes, came out and walked over to Simone.

"Simone, Cynthia has asked me to cover the phones," she said. "She would like to speak with you."

"With me?" Simone asked. "Is everything okay?"

Rhonda tried to smile, but the look on her face suggested otherwise.

Simone rushed to Cynthia's office and knocked lightly on the door.

"Come in and have a seat, Simone," Cynthia said, without looking up.

She was dressed in skinny black dress slacks with a lilac floral silk blouse that complemented her silver-white hair. Simone quietly sat down. She watched Cynthia complete an email, then glanced through the glass door at the receptionist desk and regretted not bringing a notepad and pen. She felt ill prepared. Beads of sweat dripped from her hairline.

Cynthia finally looked up from her computer. "Simone, how long have you been interning with us? Nine months now?"

"Yes, Ma'am. Nine months."

"Don't you think that's enough time to learn our culture here at Prisdel?" she asked. "And wouldn't you also say that's enough time to learn how we answer calls at the switchboard?"

"I'm sorry, but I don't understand."

"I called earlier this morning and your telephone manners are atrocious," she said. "You are impolite and you barely say the name of the company correctly. It's not Prisel Production. It's Pris-del Productions! Pris-del Productions with a 'd'!"

"That's what I've been saying!"

"This company prides itself on its professionalism," Cynthia continued. "When you answer calls I expect you to clearly say, *'Good morning, welcome to Pris-del Productions, my name is Simone Allen, how may I direct your call.'* And you do not drop calls. When I called this morning you dropped my call."

"I'm sorry... I didn't realize," she stuttered.

"Well, you've been working the phone systems for nine months," Cynthia interrupted. "Wouldn't you agree that is plenty of time to learn how to answer calls?"

"Yes... yes, Miss."

"Okay, then do better!"

Simone felt her neck burn as she watched Cynthia scroll through her blackberry. She could feel tears forming. Then she realized that the conversation was over and got up to leave. At the door she stopped and turned, waiting for Cynthia to look up at her.

"What is it, Simone? I thought we were done here?"

"I'm not," Simone said. "I have been busting my tail for months without once complaining. I'm an intern, so I get it! I don't get a say when I'm made to answer the phones 99% of the time. I don't get to be mad that you've never even acknowledged my existence until now, when you decide to rake me over the coals. I don't even get to be upset when all the other non-black interns are rotated around other departments while I continue to be the receptionist.

"So forgive me for saying this, but how dare you yell at me!" She kept going, even though she was trembling. "I came to Prisdel to work in production and the only thing I've learned is how to answer and transfer calls. I don't get paid enough for this crap, because you barely pay me at all. I have wasted the last nine months when I could have been working for another company that would have taken the time to mentor me. So you don't have the right to call me out for dropping your call. I get to call you out on this bullshit excuse of an internship. It's no wonder your receptionist was constantly calling in sick. She probably felt exactly how I do, having to be the local Kizzy instead of being treated like a human being."

Simone then quickly opened the door to escape.

"Ah who yuh tink yaah talk to?" she heard Cynthia say. "Yuh tink mi owe yuh nothin?"

Simone stopped as she heard Cynthia's thick patois ring in her ears. She turned around to see Cynthia leaning against her desk.

"Yuh dont tink mi know who you are?" she continued. "Mi know exactly who you are. Sit down, Simone."

Simone slowly came back to the desk. She was just a little confused by this white woman who spoke like a yardie fresh off the boat. She looked at Cynthia, who stared at her.

Then Cynthia let out a loud laugh. "Jeeesus! Mi haven't talked dat bad inna years. Gyal, yuh bring it out of me," she said, covering her mouth. "Miss Simone, you don't think that I haven't been watching you? Do you know why you have been relegated to the receptionist desk the entire time? Not because you're black or because you can't handle anything else, it's your damn attitude!"

"My attitude?" Simone said.

"Yes, your attitude," she said. "You are the most unpleasant person I have ever met. No please, no thank you. You don't smile. You sit at your desk with your head down and never look up when anyone walks past you."

Simone stood shocked. Her mother had always told her she was mean, she always complained about the scowl on her face, but to hear it from the CEO was humiliating.

"That's not fair," she said. "Anyone would be unpleasant if they had to work the phones day after day."

"Oh, my dear, that's a lousy excuse." Cynthia sighed. "In life, you have to learn to make the best out of a bad situation. I'm going to share the best advice anyone ever gave me! You will never love your job unless you love every part of it —from the mundane to the exciting. If you can't even try to fake liking working the switchboard, how are you going to enjoy running around getting coffee for producers? Or getting minute details right when setting up a location shoot; it can take days to arrange permission just to film in a location for a single hour. This industry, frankly, is not very sexy."

Simone stood silently in front of Cynthia's desk. She didn't want to seem ungrateful for her internship, but it was unfair that she was the only person being called out like this.

"Simone, when I was your age, I was working as a receptionist for a small film production company," she said. "I hated that job with a passion. I had just arrived from Jamaica and had high hopes of starting off at the top. I felt I was smart enough and worked harder than most people in the office, but I learned very quickly that attitude was everything. Getting angry held me back. So I embraced the job and became the best damn receptionist that company had ever had, and when they did eventually offer me a better position, I looked back at what I'd done with a lot of pride."

"But do you know how humiliating it is with the other interns?" Simone said. "They have been given work in every department and a chance to learn everything. I'm sorry, Miss Cynthia, I get what you are saying, but when this internship is over, the others will move on to better opportunities. When I leave, the most I can put on my resume is that I learned how to answer the phones."

Cynthia leaned back in her seat, looked up at Simone, and smiled. "What if you didn't have to go to another company? What if you stayed on with us as a full-time member of the Prisdel family?"

"I'm sorry, but if you're looking for a full-time receptionist then I'll have to pass."

"No, no," Cynthia said. "You are one of the brightest interns we've come across in a long time and, despite what you think about your experience here, and despite your attitude, you have a lot more to offer than any of your fellow interns. Only you and Hubert have been getting your hands dirty, and what I'm looking for are people willing to pull up their sleeves and do the work."

"So what are you offering me?" Simone asked.

"I'm offering you the whole experience," she said. "I'm offering my mentorship along with access to some of the best people in the field. You have what it takes to be a fine producer one day, but that won't happen until you lose some of the attitude and learn everything from the bottom up. That means answering the phones, knowing everyone that comes in and out of this office. Being a part of this company will take you further than knowing the best places to get coffee on Queen Street."

Simone nodded at Cynthia. She even smiled a little.

"See, there it is," she said. "There is a pleasant girl buried deep down in there. You stick with me and you'll get there."

"Can I ask you a question?" Simone asked. "I had no idea that you were Jamaican. Not one clue. Is that a secret or something?"

"No, man! It's no secret," she said. "I'm very proud of mi roots but I'm just like everyone else. I save my patois-speaking lovable self for my family and my professional Canadian diction for the professional world. But I'll tell you a secret: If you get enough Appleton in me during our Christmas party, my accent comes out nice and clear."

Simone laughed out loud. Her mother was the same way. Simone thought of it as the Bell Canada syndrome; her mother would cuss her in patios but the moment she picked up a call she quickly adjusted to her Canadian accent.

"Now that we have this all cleared up, I have a meeting in fifteen minutes that I need to prepare for," she said. "We will talk more later. Okay?"

"Yes, Miss Cynthia," she said smiling. "And thank you."

"You bet," she replied in her most Canadian accent.

Simone went back to her desk smiling, which took Rhonda by surprise. She sat back down and breezed through the calls for the rest of the day.

By Friday, things had already changed. The other interns were taking shifts on the switchboard. Ilene and Hubert actually enjoyed not having to run around and were happy for the break. Sarah Jane, on the other hand, wasn't thrilled about having to work the phones. By the end of her first day on the switchboard, she was in Jonathan's office complaining. Simone overheard her because his office door was open as she passed by.

"This is bullshit," Sarah Jane said. "I shouldn't be wasting my time on the phones. I didn't sign up for this. Isn't that what Simone does? I mean, it's more up her alley to do this kind of stuff."

"Keep your voice down, Sarah," Jonathan said. "I really don't want to hear any more about those fucking phones. Just give it a rest."

Obviously, the honeymoon had fizzled.

During the last week of the internship program, Cynthia invited the group to an all-staff lunch, where she announced that all of the interns had been invited to join Prisdel Productions full time, but that only Simone and Hubert had accepted positions.

"Ilene Cheng has accepted a position as assistant to the associate art director for MAC Cosmetics in Montreal," she said. There was applause from everyone. "I am so happy for her. She is a very talented young woman who will go far with MAC. Miss Sarah Jane has also elected to move on. Sarah has decided to travel for a year before joining the workforce."

"Yeah, I heard she was offered the receptionist position," Hubert whispered to Simone. "She wasn't too happy about that. I about died when I heard."

Simone looked over at Sarah Jane, who was maintaining her poise as Cynthia went on to wish her well in all her future endeavours.

"Hubert Bublik will be working under Jonathan as a production assistant," Cynthia said. "I'm sure he will continue to bring his vision and dedication to every project he works on."

Hubert beamed. Simone squeezed his hand. She was really happy that her friend was staying on, too.

Cynthia looked over at Simone. "I am personally very pleased to announce that Simone Allen has accepted the position of project coordinator with our production team. Most of you sitting here know exactly who Simone is and how helpful she has been handling the receptionist duties while we went through some personnel changes. Through it all, she persevered and showed that she is a team player. So please join me in officially welcoming Simone to the Prisdel family."

Simone blushed as the staff congratulated her with boisterous applause. She looked around at all of the people she had gotten to know that year. Cynthia was right — she did need to know the company from the bottom up if she planned to be a producer one day. Even though she hadn't worked with most of them yet, she knew who they were. Everyone, from the folks in accounts receivable to the production assistants, all the way up to the most senior executive producers, had conversed with her. Despite the rough year, her dreams were finally coming true. She felt Hubert place his hands on her shoulders.

After lunch, Hubert and Simone headed back to their desks to finish off the rest of their day.

"Don't forget we're toasting Ilene and our new jobs tonight at Marlowe's," Hubert said.

"What, you're not going to invite Sarah Jane?" Simone asked.

"Oh, I did, but she respectfully declined," Hubert said. "Thank God, because I wasn't going to try and be nice to that heffa this evening."

Simone tried to stifle her laughter as they watched Sarah Jane walk back to her desk. "I almost feel sorry for her."

"Pfft, please," said Hubert.

"I'm in, but I'm going to bum a ride with Felicia. We're finishing up a promo and she promised to give me an editing crash course if I help her log time codes."

"Nice," he said. "Which show?"

"*House Helpers*," she answered. "Have you ever heard of it?"

"I worked on it for a minute," he said. "Some geriatric dude doing renos. They seriously need to do something with it quick because, from what I heard, the ratings are taking a beating."

"Well, then, I better help Felicia make this the best promo ever," she said, laughing.

"Alright, catch up with you later, doll. I have to relieve Ilene from the front desk."

"Have fun," she said.

"Girl, we're going to own this bitch!" he said, running down the hall.

Simone watched Hubert high-five his new co-workers before disappearing into the lobby.

She went to her desk to finish up a few projects and pack up her belongings. Afterwards, she walked over to the editing suites to meet Felicia.

▶

NOLAN CHECKED AROUND and found the production secretary's office.

"Hi, I'm here to meet with Jonathan," he said. "My name is Nolan O'Shea."

"Oh, that's right," the assistant said. "I'm sorry, but he left early due to a family emergency. He asked me to give you this package. When you're ready to send it back, there's a shipping label and envelope in the package."

"Okay," he said, taking it from her. "Please tell him that I'll send it back on Monday."

"Will do," she said, smiling up at him. "He also said that, if you have *any* questions, you can call him on his cell. The number is inside."

"Thanks!" Nolan said, headed out. "Nice to meet you."

"No, the pleasure is all mine," she said.

When he left, one of the production assistants came up to her desk. "Carly, where did he come from?"

They watched him walk away, then looked at each other and

giggled.

"He's one of the new construction crew members hired to be on *House Helpers*," Carly said.

"Damn, his hot bald ass needs to work here and not out in the trenches," she said. "What a waste."

"For real," Carly said laughing. "If they add any more hot construction workers on this show I'm going to have to request a transfer."

45

Pam sat on the balcony wrapped in a blanket, staring off. It had been over a year since Dex had attacked CJ, yet each night was filled with nightmares more severe than those that had followed her rape. This was worse than the period after Caleb died. During those other times, she'd found ways to keep her depression at bay. She'd had a new country to get used to and school, then children to raise and bills to pay. She hadn't had time to focus on anything else.

But this time the pain and guilt were overwhelming. Most days, it was too hard to even get out of bed. The only thing that kept her pulse beating was knowing that her son was still alive. She had to be there for him, even if everything around her was falling apart.

Right after the attack, Dex called her from jail daily. Mike usually played interference, refusing the collect calls. But then Dex began sending her letters. The letters were often pleas for forgiveness, ending with a diatribe accusing Pam of causing it all. In one letter, Dex told her that if she had sent CJ to live with Annalise, their marriage wouldn't have been so shitty. In the next, he apologized for what he'd said, but then cursed CJ for making him hurt him.

After that letter, Mike made her promise that she would never open another from him again. When the next collect call came in from the prison, Mike accepted it and threatened to go down there and beat the shit out of him if he ever contacted her again.

"And you know what, motherfucker?" he yelled into the phone. "None of the guards would blink an eye, so keep contacting her and call my fucking bluff."

Soon afterwards, Mike changed Pam's house number and cell phone number and told Maureen to screen all of her calls at work.

The only time she felt a spark of happiness was when they made love. For a brief moment, she could let herself get lost in Mike's caresses and kisses. She would cry afterwards, as the bliss quickly faded.

"Pam, you need to talk to someone," he whispered to her one night. "You can't keep living like this. You can't keep shutting down."

"I'm afraid to," she said.

"What are you afraid of? What's holding you back?"

"I'm afraid that one day I'm going to realize that Dex was right. That I'm the reason why all of this happened. Even Annalise won't talk to me. She blames me for marrying him and letting him put his hands on CJ. I know that CJ blames me, too. I see it in his eyes every time I visit him. He can barely move his head but he finds the strength to turn away when I visit."

"Pam, I know it's painful, but you can't let it destroy you," Mike said. "CJ is angry at the world right now. He's not able to communicate with anyone and he feels stuck. The only way he knows how to get his anger out is the few things he can do to make you feel his pain."

"I can't do this anymore," she said, turning away from him. "It's too hard and I can't hang on anymore."

"Pam, you have to try," he said, kissing her bare shoulder. "For me… try for me because I hate when you talk like this. Please talk to someone."

"I'm scared to do it alone," she said, wiping back her tears.

"You don't have to." He pulled her back into his arms. "I'll come with you."

She nodded as she lay there.

When Mike fell asleep, she carefully got up from bed to get some air on the balcony. It was easier to sit outside and look out into the empty courtyard than to lie awake at night.

Each morning, as the sun rose, she had a choice, either to step off the balcony or go back inside. So far she had chosen the latter, but she didn't know how long she would keep making the same choice.

The next day, after a visit with CJ, Mike asked the doctors at the nursing home if they could recommend a psychiatrist that Pam could talk to. They advised him of a few doctors in the area, but also suggested a support group for family members dealing with patients with brain injuries.

"Do you really think that I'm going to talk my business to a bunch of strangers," Pam said, as Mike spread the pamphlets on her kitchen table. "How the hell is that going to help?"

"Pam, I don't know if it's going to help, but it's a start. You need to talk to someone and wouldn't it make sense to talk to people going through the same experiences as you?"

"I'm talking to you, aren't I?" she said. "That's enough."

"It's not enough talking to me," he said. "If it was, then you wouldn't be up all night and spending the entire day in bed staring at the wall."

"Well, going to this group session is not going to happen, okay!" she said, throwing the pamphlet back at him. "It's crap!"

"Pam, you promised!" He followed her into the living room. "You said you would try."

"Then you go and tell everyone your business," she spat back at him. "I don't know why it matters so much to you. It's my goddamn life!"

"You're my life, Pam!" he yelled, slamming his fist against the wall. "Don't you get it by now? With all the back and forth between us, have I not made it clear enough? I love you, Pam, and will do anything to make things right for you. If it was as simple as me dragging you to these sessions, I would have done it a long time ago, but that's not how it works. You have to want it for yourself."

Mike sat down on her couch and put his head in his hands. He had been her strength the entire year and it was starting to take its toll. She walked to the couch and sat down next to him. She hesitated, then she reached out and took his hands into hers.

His eyes looked heavy and weary when he turned to her.

"One of my biggest regrets," he said, "was not telling you from the very beginning how much I love you. I knew, deep down, that you knew how I felt, but I took for granted that you needed to hear it. Sometimes I wonder if I had just told you maybe it would have changed things. Maybe you would have never married Dex. Maybe CJ would be here as my son and not lying in a goddamn hospital bed. Every day I wonder if I did things differently, how much our lives would have changed."

"I... I had no idea," she said. "I didn't realize that you felt this way."

"I've been living with it for the last year," he said. "You're not the only one dealing with guilt." He looked up at the ceiling. "I need you to get better, Pam," he said. She could hear his voice weaken. "I need you to come back to me. Not just because I worry about you, but because I need you and so does CJ, and Simone tries to pretend that she doesn't, but she needs you, too."

Pam nodded as tears ran down her cheek. She placed her head on his shoulder. Mike leaned back on the couch, putting his arm around her.

The next day Mike was able to arrange for her to meet with

Dr. Sheen, who had been recommended by Maureen. Pam paced her living room the entire morning and smoked a whole pack of cigarettes before they left for the session. She felt the strain of her anxiety as they drove to the hospital. She wanted to tell Mike that it wasn't a good idea to see a doctor at the hospital you worked at, but she kept quiet. She didn't want to make any more excuses. She wanted to do this for Mike. It was important that she did it for him.

The following week she was placed on anti-anxiety drugs that helped her sleep through the nights. Mike and Pam started to attend a brain trauma support group once a month, where they met others like them who were trying to cope with it all. It helped to hear their stories and the group quickly became a wonderful resource for both of them as they navigated CJ's care. They learned about different treatment options, got tips on how to care for CJ and, most important, how to live life without the constant guilt.

46

"**G**irl, you missed a hella good party," Felicia said to Simone. They were having lunch with Hubert. "Everyone was at Marlowe's after the Screen Awards. It was epic."

"I think we closed the place down," Hubert said, as he picked through his salad. "*House Helpers* cleaned up, which pissed me off. We had to cover drinks for their entire crew. There's like a hundred of them compared to the thirty crew and talent we have on *Globe-Trot*."

"Well, what did you expect?" Felicia said. "Their crew is spread out all over the country. Whose bright idea was it to place that bet anyways?"

"Jonathan's," Hubert snickered. "That idiot honestly thought we were going to get best reality against a powerhouse like *House Helpers*."

"A guy can dream, right, Simone?" Felicia turned to her. "Girl, what's wrong? You've been mute the entire time."

"Sorry," she said, forcing a smile. "Did you guys have fun last night?"

"Girl, we just said that," laughed Felicia. "What's the deal with you? You haven't been yourself all week."

"Lia isn't coming back," she admitted. "She sent me an email telling me that she's staying in Italy for good. She's back with her ex."

"Wow," Hubert said. "She broke up with you through email? Who does that?"

"That's some fuckery right there," said Felicia. "Girl, you don't need that mess following you around anyways. She was drama from the start."

"No... no, she wasn't. She knew that it wasn't going anywhere," Simone said. "That's the problem."

"Yeah, but you guys were together for a few years," Hubert contended. "The least she could do was pick up the phone and speak to you."

"Yeah, well, I guess it doesn't matter now."

"What you need to do is to start dating again," Felicia said. "My cousin Delisha just broke up with her girlfriend..."

"Wait... Delisha?" Hubert said, laughing. "Who the fuck names their kid Delisha?"

"My Aunt BeTreena, bitch," Felicia said, giving Hubert a look. "Anyways, my cousin De-LISH-A just broke up with her girl and she's looking to meet someone new. You know how hard it is to date in this city."

"I don't know, Felicia," Simone said. "I don't even know if I want to date another woman."

"You're turning in your freak flag already?" Hubert asked.

"Lia done turned her straight." Felicia laughed out loud. "Lawd Gawd... I get it, girl. Personally, I think you should keep all your options open. I'm not always strictly dickly. Sometimes you need to just find that one person to connect with."

"Yeah, well, I thought that I was ready for that with Lia," she said.

"Simone, how old are you... twenty-three... twenty-four?"

Felicia asked. "Why the hell are you trying to settle down? You should be up in the clubs with anyone and everyone. You got that look that makes any woman or man want to hit that. You shouldn't be looking to get tied down. You should be having fun."

"You sound like Jessica," Simone said, laughing. "That's what she said when Lia first left."

"I knew there was a reason why I liked that white girl," Felicia said. "You don't need to be looking for the one. Just the one right now. The one right now will get you hot and bothered and put a smile on your face."

"Famous words from Aunt BeTreena?" Hubert said.

"Shut up, bitch." She hit Hubert with a cherry tomato. "Seriously, Simone. Let me call my cousin and you guys can meet. Nothing serious, just coffee or drinks and see where it goes."

"Alright," she said. "But I'm not promising anything."

She agreed to meet Felicia's cousin at *Spankings*, a small lesbian bar in Cabbagetown. The place was crowded for a Thursday night and Simone felt flustered, waiting at the bar, the music and patrons all getting louder. She wondered if the whole thing was a big mistake. She didn't know anything about Felicia's cousin. She wanted to bail but didn't want to hurt Felicia's feelings. She sat, wondering if she would even be attracted to another woman after Lia. Maybe her feelings for her were a fluke. Did she fall in love with Lia or with the idea of being with a woman? Lia made her feel special and safe during a time in her life when she had no one. Now that Lia was gone, she didn't know how she felt about anything.

She recognized Delisha from the picture Felicia had shown her. She instantly felt intimidated in her jeans and black tank top as her date walked up in a red mini dress with six-inch stiletto pumps.

"Are you 'Licia's friend?" she asked. "Simone, right?"

"Yeah," Simone said. The music started to pulsate through the bar. "I know we were supposed to grab dinner, but I feel so under-dressed. Are we going somewhere fancier?"

"Oh girl, no," Delisha said. "I'm coming straight from work."

"From work?" Simone said a little surprised.

"Not that kind of work," she said over the music. "I'm a dancer on videos."

"A what?" Simone yelled, competing with the heavy bass from the speakers behind them.

"A dancer in hip-hop videos... a video vixen extraordinaire..."

"A what?" Simone yelled. "Did you say video vixen?"

"Yeah, you know," she said, getting closer to Simone. "Those girls who dance in hip-hop videos. I just came off of a Bad Boy shoot. I didn't have time to change, so you get video vixen tonight."

"Oh, okay." Simone laughed awkwardly as Delisha set her Prada handbag on the bar top.

"It's not the steadiest work, but it helps pay off my student loans and it beats stripping." She pulled out a wipe and began taking off the heavy makeup. She pulled her hair back into a loose bun before putting on a pair of cat-eye glasses. Now she looked more like a sexy librarian than a dancer in a hip-hop video. "There, much better, huh?"

"Did you go to school here?"

"Uh huh."

"What school did you go to?" Simone asked. "I went to Queens."

"I went to York," she said. "I was hoping to be a grade school teacher, but fell into this gig and, well... the rest is history. What about you?"

"I'm a coordinator for a production company," she answered. "We produce mostly reality television."

"No shit," she said. "Like *The Real World?*"

"More like home improvement and travel shows."

"It's not like that boring shit 'Licia does?" she said, rolling her eyes.

"One and the same," Simone said. "We work for the same company."

"Oops, my bad." She sipped her cocktail. "I'm sure it's exciting if you have a passion for stuff like that."

"It can be," she replied.

Delisha pulled out her cell phone. As she watched Delisha scroll through her messages, Simone started to feel like the date was a huge mistake. She didn't have a thing in common with Felicia's cousin and couldn't believe she had actually agreed to go on a blind date with a woman whose name was Delisha. She finished her drink.

"Sorry about that," Delisha said, putting down the phone. "Look, do you want to go back to my place? This joint is too loud and distracting. What do you think?"

"S-Sure," Simone said.

"Perfect."

▶

WHEN THEY GOT to her apartment, Delisha pounced on Simone like a lioness in heat. She kissed Simone vigorously and then pulled off her dress, exposing perfectly manufactured breasts. She started to unbutton Simone's jeans. Simone was startled by how aggressive she was. It wasn't a style she was used to, but she didn't want to seem like a prude. She kept thinking of Jessica's advice to let go and let loose, so she grabbed Delisha's breasts. They felt big and firm. She slowly kissed them.

"Let's go to my bedroom," Delisha said. "It's more comfortable there."

Simone did as she was told.

She had to stop herself from laughing out loud at the red

velvet curtains draping all the way to the floor and the large circular bed with pink satin sheets in the middle of the room. The bedroom resembled a strip club.

"Come here," Delisha said to Simone from the pink bed. "Don't be shy."

Simone sat beside her, unsure what she was getting herself into, but when they began kissing, her body relaxed. She wasn't as forceful as before. The kisses now were much softer and more sensual.

"I don't like to give," she said to Simone. "Are you okay with that? My ex hated that about us but I'm not down for that."

"Okay," Simone said. "Why don't we just get to know each other? Take it slow."

"I don't go slow," she said, kissing her again.

Simone got nervous as Delisha reached into her pants and began to finger her. It wasn't the nicest feeling in the world and she wasn't getting turned on. Simone pulled her fingers out and continued to kiss her. Delisha leaned Simone back against the bed. She could feel Delisha's hand trail back down to her pussy. This time she felt a little vibration. Simone looked down at the small vibrator attached to Delisha's index finger. She knew about vibrators but this one looked almost like a claw.

"Lay back down," Delisha ordered. She pulled down Simone's jeans further. "This will feel nice."

Simone could feel her fingering her again and this time the vibrator took hold. Her body convulsed as Delisha expertly manoeuvred the device. Simone tried to regain herself but couldn't stop moaning once Delisha reached deeper. The vibrator swirled around her clit, causing her to cream. She cried out, a little embarrassed that she had cum so easily. It felt good, but she quickly pushed Delisha off once she felt another powerful orgasm. The intensity was starting to scare her.

"My turn," Simone said.

After they finished, Simone sprawled on the circular bed

staring into the large ceiling mirror fastened above them. She could see Delisha fast asleep next to her. The woman snored loudly. She felt around the bed for her cell phone to check how late it was and then quietly got dressed and left the apartment. She sent Delisha a text, telling her to give her a call.

Simone didn't feel bad stalking out in the middle of the night. She knew that it was nothing more than a hookup and was fine with that, but she wanted something more — something unexplainable. She wanted her world rocked to its core, to feel something more than the rush of a thirty-second orgasm. She wanted the desperation you feel when you're deeply in love; sleeping with some random woman wasn't going to get her there.

She wondered if she would ever know what it felt like to be in love — if there was someone out there meant for her.

▶

THE SNOW WAS DRIFTING down as Mike sat in his Honda Civic waiting for the 401 afternoon traffic to clear. He was losing patience. Toronto was becoming so congested that he had to start his commute earlier and earlier to get home to make his evening shift at McKinney's. It seemed that the only time traffic wasn't horrible was four in the morning.

He missed the way Toronto had been. When he was young, he knew where everything was, but so much of the city had changed. It had got big so fast that the vast spaces that once surrounded the city were filling up with developments. North York had also changed drastically. Everything was denser, with bigger shopping malls encroaching on smaller homes as taller and taller condos cluttered the skyline. Everywhere he turned, there was construction, with new train stations along new subway lines to link new neighbourhoods. Even his beloved St. Augustine church had been torn down and replaced by a new modern facility.

In time, he'd be able to manage the city's evolution, but the one change he couldn't put up with was the traffic. The miles of cars with strings of red brake lights in front of him, as he sat on the DVP, infuriated him; the traffic wasn't heavy because of an accident, this was just your typical volume of cars that clogged the parkway every afternoon.

When he finally got off the highway, the traffic on the main road wasn't any better. It took nearly twenty minutes just to drive the short distance to the complex. Almost home, the traffic stalled completely as the light snowfall turned into blistering flurries. He noticed a familiar figure pushing through the wind and rolled down the passenger side window.

"Simone," he yelled.

He watched her stop and then turn around. He waved and she walked up to his car.

"Is that you, Mike?" she said, trying to keep her balance. "Hi."

"Come in," he said, unlocking his door. "It's getting so bad out here. You shouldn't be walking in this mess."

Simone quickly got into the car, fitting in her heavy boots. She closed the door just as the light turned green.

"What in the world are you doing out here?" Mike said. "You're far from home."

"I was on my way to see Mrs. Price," she said. "I can't believe how bad it got. When I walked out, it was cold but the sky was clear. Now it looks like a snowstorm is about to hit."

"Well, I'm on my way home," he said. "If the traffic continues this way I'll get you there in about three hours."

Simone laughed. She pulled off her mittens to warm her frozen hands on his car's heating vent.

"You look well," he said, turning down the radio. "How are you doing?"

"I'm okay. Things are okay."

"Good. I'm glad to hear it."

They sat in silence for a moment as Mike navigated through

the slow moving traffic. When they stopped again, he looked at her familiar face. Her round almond eyes, distinct frown lines, and button nose were more and more like Pam's as she got older.

"Your mother misses you," he said. "I know that you don't want to hear that, but she does."

Silence.

The wipers continued to squeak against the windshield.

"She wasn't doing well for a while," he continued.

"Why? What's wrong with her?"

"She's been dealing with depression and anxiety," he said. "It's been rough for her trying to handle everything with your brother. She's on medication to help with all of it. She's even in therapy."

Simone continued to stare out the window.

He went on to describe the improvements her mother had been making. He told her that she was now back at work and was taking everything one day at a time. He looked over and could see her hand on the door handle.

"I know that you don't want to hear any of this," he said. "And I also know how hard it was when you were younger. When I first met your mother she was a pistol. Not an easy woman to get along with and probably the most opinionated woman I've ever met. But, when she finally let down her guard, I saw a woman who was fragile and scared and tired of always being the strong one."

"My mother fragile," Simone said. "She was nothing but scary to live with and she treated me like I was some disease she couldn't get rid of. She was hardly fragile or scared."

"Don't be too quick to dismiss how vulnerable she was, Simone," he said. "It's not fair, especially now that you know what she went through."

Simone turned away.

"The rape stripped her of everything," he said. "Try to imagine what it was like for her. She was young, practically on her own... to be assaulted that way. You don't bounce back from something like that. Especially when you go on to care for two small children without really dealing with it."

"So am I just supposed to forgive her because of all of that?" she said. "Just pretend that I didn't cry myself to sleep for the last ten years wondering why she hated me? Never mind all the times she walked past me and ignored me? No, not just ignored me… she pretended I didn't even exist. I'm supposed to just let that go?"

"No, Simone," he said. "I'm asking you to see it from her side. I'm trying to get you to see how difficult it was for her and how hard she's working to get better. But she can't do it alone. She needs you and, whether you like it or not, you need her too. You are both the same in so many ways. You don't see it, but you are."

Mike drove into the parking garage, glad to be out of the snow. He turned off the engine and looked over at Simone. He smiled at her and grabbed her hand.

"Si, the thing I love the most about you is that, no matter how stubborn you get, you always have the ability to stop and think things through," he said. "You've always been that way. All I'm asking is for you to think about what I'm saying, and when you're ready, go and see your mother. Talk to her."

Simone nodded. She got out of the car, then quickly stomped to the elevator and pressed the button. Mike stayed where he was to give her some space. He hoped that the little he had said would sink in.

PART V

47

Each morning, Pam would wake before the alarm went off and watch Mike sleep. When he opened his eyes, before he was fully awake, he always took a deep breath. If she smiled at him, he would let out a slow sigh of relief. If she didn't smile, he would wrap his arms around her and hold on, as if the strength of his love could heal everything. Some days were good. Some days were fair. But, after six years of being together, she couldn't afford to let the bad days take over.

Pam's medication for depression had worked at first, but, as the years went by, she continued to have relapses. In most circumstances, her relapses were managed by a change in antidepressants, but finding the right combination of meds became increasingly difficult. She often felt despondent and worn down, so she skipped taking the pills, hoping to find relief. She got into heated arguments with Mike over it. She knew he felt helpless, watching her go through her highs and deep lows. The treatment was working, she knew that, but the meds dulled her mind and, each time she came off them, their relationship suffered.

Her latest and worst relapse came after learning that Dex was being paroled. She had divorced him years ago, but felt unhinged knowing that he would be walking the streets again. He had contacted her and told her that he had changed, but Mike insisted that she get a restraining order to protect her and CJ. Yet despite all the precautions, she still felt helpless and her depression slowly crept back until it was almost crippling.

She was forced to take a six-month leave from work to get a handle on her life through day treatments. When her doctor finally gave her the clearance to go back to work, Mike was furious. He'd stand by her, but told her that he felt it was too soon. He didn't want the progress she'd made give way to the stress of her job.

When Pam came home, exhausted from work, Mike was there. He was there most evenings now, instead of pulling extra shifts at McKinney's. She walked up to him and sat on his lap. It had been a rough couple of weeks getting the new administration system up and running.

She had spent the last ten days training her staff on the new software for processing new patients. It had been a frustrating process for her to learn the program, but was an even more daunting task to get her department trained.

"Why do we have to change anything?" Maureen complained. "It's not like the work doesn't get done."

"Maureen, the new system will take us half the time to complete admittance. The old paperwork system was costing this department money in overtime. Simple as that."

"Well, can we expect a raise then?" said Christina. "I haven't had a raise in nearly three years and not for the lack of trying."

"I hear what you're saying, Christina. I understand what all of you are feeling," Pam said, turning to the group of them. "But I can't justify raises to the board if we're using overtime just to complete our daily work. Look, once everyone gets the hang of it, the new system will allow us to process a patient's file within an hour. So let's just get through this training first before we start talking about raises, okay?"

"I just wish you would have prepared us first before dumping it on us," Maureen quipped. "Especially me. I've been doing your job for six months."

"I'm sorry if my return to this department has inconvenienced you," Pam said. "The reality is, the decision has been made by myself and the hospital board. If you have any issues, we can discuss them further outside of this session. Right now, I want to get back to the training module."

During her leave, Maureen had been the temporary supervisor. She had approved vacations and allowed staff to leave early for appointments and staff had complimented her on how well she was running the department, even giving her suggestions on how to make it better.

Pam had returned to find that Maureen had changed several of the hospital's vendors, postponed annual projects, doubled expenses, and approved excessive overtime. Dr. Greene, the Chief-of-Staff, had called her into his office on her first day back and told Pam to put affairs in order. A departmental review was underway and she would be held accountable if the assessment came back negative. Basically, she was blindsided.

"You were gone and I made some executive decisions," Maureen said. They were sitting in Pam's office going through a laundry list of changes that Maureen had made. "Look, I was asked to be in charge because I've been here the longest and I'm capable of running this department."

"Maureen, you were just supposed to keep everything going! The chief of staff is demanding that someone be held accountable."

"What is that supposed to mean?" Maureen asked. "He wants me fired?"

"Maureen, at this point I don't know," Pam said, looking over the list of changes. "But Dr. Greene is furious and... what are these expenses for The Keg?"

"It was for our weekly staff meeting," Maureen said. "I thought it would boost morale in the department. Pam, I don't want to lose my job over this. I was doing my best. Everyone seemed to be so happy with the changes—"

"That's the thing, Maureen. Part of being a supervisor is making decisions that not everyone is going to like or agree with. Look, just let me figure some things out. I can't guarantee your ass isn't on the line, but I'll see what I can do."

Pam had tried to fix the mess that Maureen had made. She had asked Dr. Greene to go to the board to fast-track the implementation of the new administration program that was budgeted for the fourth quarter, suggesting that if they implemented the program immediately she could recoup funds by reducing her staff's overtime hours, which would get things back on track by the end of the year. Dr. Greene loved the idea and it was decided by the board to push it forward.

▶

"You need to stop this bullshit with Pam," Mike said to Maureen. He pulled his cousin into McKinney's backroom. "I'm fucking sick of it."

"What's your problem?" Maureen said.

"You need to lay off on Pam!"

"You drag me back here after a shitty week to fucking tear me a new one about your girlfriend... oh, I forgot... your neighbour. Because I don't see how she gets to leave for half the year and then waltzes back and dumps on all of my improvements."

"Maureen, she wasn't off on some vacation," he said.

"Yeah, I'm sure." Maureen mocked. "What happened, did Miss Priss break a nail?"

"Why are you so fucking mean?" Mike asked. "She took a chance on you and put up with you for years and all you can do is bitch and complain. You should be fucking helping her!"

"Oh, is that what she told you?" she said. "Is that what you both talk about after you screw her? Do me a favour and keep my name out of your mouth, when you talk to her."

"You know what, Maureen? I'm fucking done with all of this. The only reason she hasn't fired you is because you're my cousin. I'm always begging her to turn a blind eye despite your screw-ups. I'm tired of always trying to protect you. If you end up getting sacked, then that's on you."

Mike tore out of the backroom, brushing past his bewildered cousin. He stood by the bar counter and attempted to take an order from one of his regulars. A moment later, Maureen quickly walked back to her table and grabbed her purse before she rushed out of McKinney's. Mike barely flinched when he heard the bar door slam.

▶

"I DON'T GET IT, MIKE," Pam said to him the next evening while they were cooking dinner. "It's like she's a different person. She was actually nice during today's training session. She even helped some of the staff, who were having issues with the module. Did you say something to her?"

"Nope," he said as he set the table. "Not a thing."

"Hmm," she said.

Mike walked over and lifted her hair to kiss the back of her neck. "I love you," he whispered in her ear.

"I love you too," she said, tilting her head back to kiss him. "I'm almost finished with the stir-fry."

"Okay, I'll go wash up."

He wandered into the bathroom just as her cell phone rang. She looked at the number, but didn't recognize it.

"Hello," she answered.

Silence.

"Hello," she said again.

She was about to hang up.

"Why won't you take my calls? Are you with him?"

She froze, barely holding onto the phone.

"What do you want?" she said, trying to keep calm.

"You know what I want," he said. "I want my old life back. I want you back."

"That's never going to happen," she said. "Don't call here again."

She hung up just as Mike came back into the kitchen. She started to tremble. She held her breath, hoping that her hand would stop shaking. The vegetables were starting to burn.

"Are you okay?" Mike asked. "What's wrong?"

"Nothing," she replied. "Just my nerves. It's been a long day."

She forced a smile and started dishing out the food. Her heart was racing. She took several deep breaths to calm herself down, and then she walked to the table with their plates.

48

Dana and Freddy were standing off camera, watching Nolan shoot his segment with Mac. It was the usual routine—Mac grumbling about the homeowners wanting to change his plans and then Nolan sweeping in to show Mac how they could handle the changes without disturbing the budget.

Nolan smiled at them as the crew fixed the light for the next shot. He knew it was tedious for anyone watching. It was tedious for him, too, having to say the same speech over and over; the same problems they discovered and fixed weeks before. But that was the world of reality television. Bottom line, you had to make it interesting to keep the viewer's attention.

When Nolan had been approached to be a bigger presence on the show, he'd thought it meant giving him more screen time to paint a wall or install a sink, but Cynthia and Jonathan had other ideas. Viewers had started to notice the tall bald construction worker in the background. *House Helpers* had been inundated with inquiries about him, usually from female fans who wanted to know the name of the hot construction worker and whether he was single or not.

The producers joked about putting out a calendar that featured Nolan as Mr. February—something that showed off his rippling muscles and gave housewives something to drool over. But, as the ratings continue to spike, Cynthia and Jonathan realized that Nolan was more than just eye candy. He was an untapped commodity. They gave him more screen time. Soon *We Love Nolan* fan sites started popping up on MySpace.

Jonathan came up with the idea of having Nolan co-host the show with Mac to bring in a younger audience—the new generation of homeowners. The first few months were spent prepping Nolan through acting workshops and training in on-camera work. He had a low smoky voice that often became inaudible when he got nervous. He wasn't comfortable with a close-up focus on him and he didn't appreciate the stylist "reviewing his look."

"We have to do something about that tattoo on the back of your head," she said to him. "It's faded but still distracting, and the bloody thing looks like a swastika is hidden in there."

Nolan stared at his face in the mirror. His whole face was red. He had been using fade creams on his tattoo for years. He had thought that it wasn't noticeable.

"Lost a bet, huh?" she said to him as she examined it. "Look, the quickest way to hide it is to grow your hair out. That will cover it up."

Nolan spent the next few months transforming from the bald, reserved background worker with a clean-shaven face to a smart-looking co-host in jeans and a tight T-shirt. His hair was lightened to bring out his crystal blue eyes. The stylist insisted he keep his five o'clock shadow to complete the look.

"I don't like this new you," Dana teased. She and Freddy were sitting with Nolan at a nearby pub. "All this hair on your face and head. What happened to your dimples? You used to have adorable dimples."

Nolan and Freddy laughed as Dana pinched her brother's cheeks.

"Our boy is getting the Hollywood treatment," Freddy said. "Just wait till you see him walking around shirtless."

Nolan started to turn red.

"Oh God, Nolan," Dana laughed. "Please don't tell me they got you doing that."

"Just for the promos," he said. "They promised that it's only going to be for the promos."

"I swear, if I see you in *Playgirl*, I'm going to hurl." Dana shook her head.

"Can't hate on you, brother," Freddy said, drinking his beer. "If someone asked me to flash my incredible bod for a television show I would do it in a heartbeat. No questions asked!"

"Please don't." Dana gave Freddy a look. "But seriously, Nolan, you're a natural in front of the camera. I can't wait to see it all come together."

"Thanks! It's strange doing this, but I have to admit it's a lot of fun. Did you guys get a chance to check out the city?"

Shortly after Freddy and Nolan sold their flip, Freddy had gone into business with Dana. They flipped a few old houses, and then the venture quickly snowballed into a construction/real estate enterprise that would purchase a cheap property, renovate it, and sell it for a profit. Now they were in Toronto, looking to expand into a bigger market.

"Yeah, we checked out a lot of houses yesterday and a few more this morning," Freddy said. "You weren't joking. These areas are prime for flips. I'm seriously tempted by it."

"I'm still not sold," Dana said. "I mean, Toronto is a huge market, but there's also more risk."

"Yeah, but these properties will sell for ten times more than the ones we're dealing with in Halifax," Freddy pointed out. "This is where we have to be if we're going to grow the business."

"Have you talked Amaya into moving yet?" Nolan asked Freddy.

"In due time," he said. "I have to scope things out before we take that leap. I'm not coming to her until we have a solid plan."

"Isn't she due in a few months?" Nolan asked. "Do you think she's going to want to move after having another baby?"

"Fucking hell," Freddy said. "That should be reason enough to relocate. All her people are here and I'm going to need more cash flow if she keeps popping out these fucking babies."

"Don't blame Amaya," Dana said. "You should have snipped your junk after Julian was born."

"Why is it always the man who has to cut his shit?" Freddy said.

"Because a man can go on having babies until he's ninety," Dana said, giving him a sideward glance. "Seriously, Freddy, I love all your bad-ass children, but, after this baby is born, you seriously need to get a vasectomy, before baby number five shows up."

"Shit," he said, shaking his head. "If that ever happens, shoot me in the head."

Nolan laughed. "Which one?"

"Both," Freddy groaned.

▶

PAM WIPED CJ's mouth after feeding him applesauce. She smiled at him as she tossed the empty container on his food tray. It was a good sign that he was starting to eat again. He had been on feeding tubes for so long that she never thought she would see the day when he would eat normally.

He was in better spirits lately, too. The first few years had been rough. His depression was terrible. He refused to eat, communicate, or even move when Pam visited him. She knew that he blamed her for Dex coming into their lives.

They had been happy, the three of them, with Mike and Nolan. They were a family—unconventional, but still a family. Things had changed when Pam started to date Dex. She fooled herself into thinking that Dex was going to be a real father figure for CJ. A successful, educated man in her son's life. Not the stand-in neighbour. Not the Irish-Canadian guy who worked three jobs just to keep the lights on. She'd loved Mike deeply—she could admit it now—but she'd wanted more for her son.

As she sat by CJ's bed, she wished she could go back and change the past. Her constant state of regret was the source of her depression after Dex had attacked CJ. She spent most nights going over to the decisions she'd made and she finally realized that *she* was the only reason why she'd had no relationship with her daughter and why her son was left disabled. It had taken everything in her to pull herself out of her depression. The main motivator had been a moment with CJ.

Pam had dreaded visits with her son. They began and ended the same way, with him facing the wall, ignoring her. The only times he would interact with her was when Mike came along. When Mike was in the room, CJ's entire disposition changed—his face lit up and he smiled. It was the only time she saw him happy.

Mike would sit for hours recalling to CJ some mundane memory sprinkled with his wild imagination and using his gift for spinning long elaborate tales. CJ would always look him directly in the eye, captivated by Mike as he recycled those same funny stories. It didn't matter how many times he heard them, CJ always laughed.

On that particular day, she had felt particularly low. She was on new medication. She didn't feel up to visiting her son, but Mike had insisted that she come along. She stood awkwardly by the door, watching Mike tell CJ that Mrs. Price sent her love, followed by an update on how the Blue Jays were doing, and then go into one of his stories. The story he told was about the day CJ had learned to dance.

Pam remembered well. Simone and Nolan were planning to attend their seventh-grade dance and she was adamant that the two reluctant youths learn how to waltz.

"And quit complaining," she'd said, pushing the living room furniture out of the way. "Because neither of you are going to that party unless you can dance properly."

They'd just grumbled.

"I'm serious," she told them. "And don't look at Mike, because he has no say in the matter."

She spent the afternoon showing them how to hold each other properly. How to lock their arms in position and how much space should be between them. Nolan was the clumsiest kid she knew and was constantly tripping over Simone. Pam had tried to show them how to move their feet, but was soon frustrated.

She remembered CJ jumping up and down on the couch. He wanted to waltz with her and show the others that he was a good dancer. They all took a break to appease him and he had happily danced with her. Pam was quite amazed at how natural he was. He knew all the steps much better than Simone and Nolan did.

But, according to Mike's story, CJ's dancing was so good that he and his mother entered several ballroom competitions and travelled the world, winning first place in everything. CJ's dancing career was at its height when his mother twisted her ankle on a lizard that was crawling on the ballroom floor. She squished the lizard so badly that she still had the green slime stuck to the bottom of her shoe. CJ's career was done.

CJ laughed so hard that Mike couldn't keep a straight face and started to laugh, as well. The laughter became contagious, with Pam joining in with them. Soon the three of them were out of control.

"That's not how it happened, Mike," Pam said. "You're slipping, old man."

CJ stopped laughing and turned to his mother. Those had been his words to Mike from long ago. He stared at her for a moment and then smiled. It was the smile five-year-old CJ gave her when she would wake up to find him lying in the bed next to her. The same smile he'd given her every Christmas morning when Santa brought the gift he'd asked for. The one he'd had when he was with his friends at his graduation party before everything changed.

Pam started to cry. She walked over to him, sat next to his bed, and grabbed hold of his hand as she soaked it all in.

"Hi," she said to him. "I'm sorry it took so long for me to get here."

She wiped back her tears, then hugged him and laid her head on his chest. She looked over at Mike and smiled.

This was the turning point, the moment she felt his forgiveness for bringing that monster into their lives. Forgiveness for not seeing the abuse sooner.

Visits afterwards were a source of solace instead of dread. When she walked into the room, CJ would laugh and clap his hands instead of turning his head to the wall. The physical therapist noticed the change in him. He was trying harder during his sessions and was making so many improvements.

Pam sat with him for a little while longer, brushing his hair.

"I love you, CJ," she said. "You keep working hard and hopefully we can bring you home soon. Mike and I are looking into buying a house together. We're trying to find the perfect place that's not too far from your rehab but that's easy for you to get around. We're going to be a family. The way it should have been."

CJ looked up at her and smiled.

Pam caressed his cheek until he fell asleep. She kissed the top of his head, then lingered in the doorway, watching him sleep peacefully. She turned on his night light so his room wouldn't be too dark when the staff turned off the lights.

▶

LATER IN THE EVENING, before visiting hours ended, CJ was startled awake. He felt the presence of someone in his room. At first, he thought his mother had returned, but, when the shadowy figure loomed over him, he could smell the stale stench of cigarettes and liquor.

"What the fuck are you looking at?"

His eyes widened as he threw up a little in his mouth. Tears started to stream down as his eyes checked the door, hoping a nurse would arrive.

"Now you're crying like a little bitch," Dex said, slurring his words. "Keep crying because I'm going to kill your mother and that maggot she's fucking and, when I'm done, I'm coming back here to slit your throat."

As Dex got closer, CJ started to cry and grunt. From the corner of his eye, he could see one of the evening nurses by his door. She immediately turned on the lights in his room.

"Get away from him! Who are you? What are you doing in here?"

Dex pushed past the nurse and quickly left the room.

CJ heard the alarm go off and he started to whimper. Through the noise and commotion, he could hear the security guard talking into his walkie-talkie as he ran up and down the hallway, checking each exit and empty room. After ten minutes, the alarm was turned off.

CJ's heart continued to pound as the nurse, night manager, and security guard hovered over his bed.

"Should we call his parents?" the security guard asked the night manager. "Let them know what happened?"

"No... it's not necessary," the manager said.

"He smelt of piss and booze," said the nurse. "He's probably some homeless guy who wandered in."

"Yeah, but the poor kid looks terrified," said the security guard.

"Well, I doubt he'll show up again," said the manager. "And it makes no sense opening up a can of worms when nothing happened. The kid is just a little shook up. He'll get over it."

CJ lay in bed, tears streaming down his face.

The nurse leaned over at him and tucked him in for the night. "Don't worry, sweetheart," she said. She used a tissue to dry his tears. "All the excitement is over. Nothing to cry over. Just a homeless guy who got lost. Go ahead and get some rest, okay?"

She turned down his lights, accidentally turning off his night-light.

He trembled in the pitch dark.

49

"Wow, two months in Europe, huh?" Jessica and Simone were roaming up and down the aisle of Loblaws. "They don't give you much notice, do they?"

"Actually almost three months," Simone corrected Jessica as she pulled up to the tea section and grabbed four boxes of mint tea. "They really didn't have much of a choice. My American counterpart ended up quitting during pre-production. I'm up for it. I just hope that I can do a good job. I can't believe Cynthia is trusting me to run it."

"Well, you've been an associate producer for three years now, I'm surprised that it took this long," said Jessica. "I mean, how many gardening shows do you have to coordinate for her to trust you with the big stuff?"

"I've done more than gardening shows," Simone said, putting two more boxes of tea in the cart. "Don't forget *Sam's Sandwich Bar* and *Do It Yourself.*"

"Yay you," Jessica said. "All I'm saying is that now she's giving you some meatier stuff and it's about damn time."

"Well, this is definitely a big one," Simone said. "I'm still not feeling the title, *Trails - Destination Europe*, but I'm hoping we'll come up with a better one before we start shooting."

"It a show about biking across Europe," Jessica said. "I don't think you're going to find a better title. Si, why are we buying six boxes of mint tea?"

"Because you drink more tea than I do," Simone said. "By the time I go for a bag, there's only an empty box."

"I don't drink your tea," Jessica said. She put back three of the boxes. "I'm not wasting our grocery money on six boxes of tea."

"What the hell is your problem, Jess? You've been a complete bitch all morning."

Jessica pushed the cart up the aisle.

"It's Peter, isn't it?" she guessed. "You guys broke up for good this time?"

Jessica nodded. They continued to walk in silence.

"You know you once told me that getting deep with anyone is a recipe for disaster. Do you remember that?"

"It's not Peter that's making me feel like this... I mean... it is him but it's also everything else," Jessica said. "I'm just tired of feeling like my life is going nowhere."

"What are you talking about, Jess?" Simone said. "You are a successful lawyer at a prominent law firm. You're on track to becoming a partner and you just broke up with the biggest douche on the planet. Just that act alone is taking you everywhere."

"You don't get it, Si," she said. "I'm alone again! You know why Peter broke up with me? He said that I'm one-dimensional. That prick said that I can only handle one thought at a time and told me to lay off the peroxide and maybe I can handle a few more thoughts."

"He's an asshole and a bully who's mad that you landed his dream job," Simone said, hugging her tightly. "Don't listen to his bullshit, and, while I'm gone, please do not get back together with him. I swear, Jess, he's not good for you."

"But he fucks me so good," she said, smirking.

"I hope you're joking. I'm pretty sure we can find a vibrator that's a better fuck than Peter. I'm serious, Jess, while I'm gone, do not go back to him. You have to promise me."

"Okay... okay, I promise." She picked up a carton of eggs. "It's hard coming off a relationship."

"Trust me, I get it!"

She knew exactly how Jessica felt. She was twenty-nine years old, staring thirty in the face, yet she felt like she was still back in high school. She wasn't on great terms with her mother. Her career had been in a slump for the last few years, and she had a dozen disastrous relationships under her belt since Lia moved back to Italy.

Simone had developed a knack for bouncing from one woman to another, strictly for the sexual gratification, and, if any of the women wanted more, she would quickly end things. Jessica and Hubert often teased her, saying that they always knew she'd broken up with a girl any time she changed her cell phone number.

"I don't ask for much," Jessica said, as they got to the register. "I just want a guy with a big enough cock to get me off. Someone who's nice to me... like really nice, and bonus points if it's someone I can hang with. I'm done with dating just to get into a relationship. It's a fucking waste of time."

"Eventually, you'll want the relationship," Simone said. "You'll want your Prince Charming and everything that comes with it. You just have to find him. He's out there."

"I know he is, but for now I'm not even going to think that way. I'm fine with being with someone with no strings attached. Just a guy looking to fuck a girl who is looking to fuck a guy."

"Is that going to be your ad?" Simone said, laughing.

"Oh my God, I should totally put that on my eHarmony profile," Jessica said. "Maybe I can land a decent date."

As they pulled up to their building, Simone looked at her phone and realized that it was getting late. She had promised

Mike that she would go over for dinner. It had been more like blackmail than a dinner invitation.

Not long ago, Simone had met Nina online. A few emails, then text messages back and forth, then long telephone conversations, sometimes lasting all night. They had finally agreed to meet for drinks at a bar near Ryerson University.

By the time their drinks arrived they were making out in a booth by the restrooms like a couple of horny teenagers. The chemistry continued hot and heavy until Mike walked past with his tool-box.

"Simone," he said. "Is that you?"

Mike's entire face turned red as he looked down at her and her date. She sat still, mortified and unsure of what to say.

"Hi! My name is Nina." Her date extended her hand to Mike.

"Yeah... uhh... this is my neighbour," Simone said. "Nina, this is Mike. Mike, this is my friend Nina."

"Hello," he said, stiffly shaking her hand. "Well. I have to go and fix an issue in the washroom. It was good seeing you, Simone."

Simone rubbed her temples as Mike went into the restroom.

"What's wrong?" Nina asked. "He's just your neighbour, right?"

"You don't understand. He's not just my neighbour. He raised me. He's practically my father, and he has no idea that I'm a lesbian."

"Oh," Nina said.

"I need to talk to him," she said, getting up. "Do you mind giving me a minute? I promise that I won't be long, but I have to fix this."

"Take your time," she said. "I'm not going anywhere."

Simone went into the men's bathroom. She walked up to the stall he was working on and gingerly knocked on the side of the door. Her face still felt warm.

He looked up at her. "I guess I know why you chose to stay away from everyone the last few years," he said as he worked on the clogged toilet. "Don't worry, I won't say anything to your mother—or anyone else, for that matter."

"You're mad at me," she said. "This is why I didn't say anything. I didn't want you or Pam or Mrs. Price judging me."

"Who's judging you, Simone?" Mike said. "I'm certainly not. If you want to be a lesbian, that's your business. You're an adult and capable of making your own decisions. It's just disappointing that you're using it as an excuse to shut everyone out.

"Your mother—I get. There's a lot there that needs to be fixed between the two of you, but I've been like a father to you since you were a little girl. When Pam turned her back on you, I was the one who was there, but lately...well, the only way I know you're even still in the city is that I see your name on the logbook when I visit your brother."

"I'm sorry, Mike. I'm sorry that I haven't been around."

Mike got up off his knees. "Look, Simone, I just want to hear from you from time to time. It would be nice to know that you're alive and well, to know a few details, like you being a lesbian, and so on. Just so I'm not so shocked when I run into you with your... your special friends."

"Oh, God," Simone said, laughing. "You can call them my girl-friends, Mike."

"Okay, girlfriends then," he said snaking the toilet. "I'm just saying that there are people who love you and worry about you and it wouldn't hurt to pick up a phone and call us."

"Yes, Dad," she said. "I get it."

"Good," he said, smiling at her. "Now, since when are you a lesbian, because this is news to me. I always thought you were into boys."

"Are we really having this conversation?" Simone laughed, leaning against the stall's door frame. "Because this coming-out party is super awkward already."

"Alright, I'll lay off. You probably should get back to your date, anyways."

"Okay."

"And Simone… you know that you can always come to me," he said. "I'm serious. I'm here any time. I'm not going anywhere."

"I know," she said. "And I promise I'll be better at keeping in touch."

"I'm gonna hold you to it."

Which he did a few weeks later, upon hearing that she was going to be in Europe for almost three months. He insisted that she come over to Mrs. Price's apartment for Sunday dinner.

The small dinner ended up being a family reunion of sorts, with music playing and the dining table set up like a buffet, and Mike, her mother, Esma with her entire family, and some of Mrs. Price's church friends all showing up to wish her well. She felt like the prodigal child returning home, but, after a while, it felt like old times again as she caught up with everyone. She even spent time with her mother, who hugged her fiercely. She realized with a jolt that she hadn't seen Pam in years.

It wasn't like her mother to be so affectionate and happy. Seeing her with a constant smile on her face was a bit of a shock.

"I told you," Mike whispered to Simone when he passed by them.

She sat with her mother for nearly an hour, telling her about her work at Prisdel and how nervous and excited she was about going to Europe to organize production for *Trails*. She could tell her mother didn't really understand what she did, but that she was pleased she had a good job.

"I'm worried about CJ while I'm gone," Simone said. "He hasn't been himself lately, have you noticed? I'm concerned that he won't understand why I'm gone for so long. I don't want him to think that I left him. I've told him about my trip to Europe, but the way he's acting makes me think that he doesn't understand."

"I don't know what is happening to your brother," Pam said, holding Simone's hand. "He stopped eating and it looks like his doctor is planning to reinstate his feeding tube. Even Mike's stories don't make him happy like they used to. He barely responds to anyone."

"Has anything happened?" Simone asked.

Pam said she had talked to the nurses and to the facility's administrator, trying to figure out why CJ had suddenly given up. Mike suspected some kind of abuse and had requested a full investigation, but nothing came of it. The only thing they could do was make sure someone was with CJ daily so he understood that he wasn't alone.

"He'll be okay," Pam said. "Mike and I will visit him on your days. If you keep in touch, we'll make sure to tell him every day where you are."

Simone thanked her. Her ears perked up when she overheard Mike mention Nolan to Esma. She hadn't heard about him in ages and she excused herself from her mother so she could find out what he was up to. Loud knocking was coming from the front door. She went over to open it.

"Simone, is that you, baby?"

Dex filled the doorway, his massive build towering over her. He reached out for her. Simone quickly moved away, leaving him swinging in the wind, reeking of alcohol. She tried to shut the door in his face, but he pushed back, sending her flying against the wall.

"How nice! The whole mother-fucking gang is here. Where's my wife?"

Dex stumbled through the living room. Mike quickly pulled out his cell phone and dialled 911.

"I'm in apartment 1108, in 100 Bayview Crescent, and there's a..." he said before Dex boxed the phone from his hand.

"You were such a big man on the phone while I was locked up. What was it that you said? You were going to fuck me up if I called my wife again? What are you going to do now?"

He started to move towards Pam.

"Stay the fuck away from her," Mike said. "She has a

restraining order against you. You come near her and I will fucking kill you and the cops will nail your ass."

"You can't do shit to me," Dex said, laughing. "I'm a free man."

"You're on parole," Mike corrected him. "And part of your parole is staying the fuck away from us."

"Shut the fuck up! Pam, kindly tell this piece of shit that I'm not here to talk to him. I'm here to see my wife. Come on, baby, all I need is a few minutes to talk privately."

"Dex, please don't do this," she said. Her voice was quivering. "Just leave us alone."

"You heard her," Mike said. "Get out!"

"It's okay," he said, walking towards the door. "I'll talk to you another time, Pam. Maybe the next time you're visiting that faggot son of yours? Where's he at? St. John's, room six? You go there every Monday, right?"

Pam's face turned white. She looked as if she was going to pass out.

"You leave him alone!" She ran at him, flailing her fists. "Don't touch my boy! Do you hear me, Dex?"

Dex just pushed Pam off, tossing her on the floor.

Simone had never seen Dex this drunk and angry. She froze for a moment but snapped out of it when she heard a faint voice coming from beneath Mrs. Price's couch. She realized it was Mike's cell and quickly ducked down and reached for the phone. She ran into the kitchen and told the 911 operator what was happening, pleading for help right away, but, before she could confirm the address, she was interrupted by new screaming as Mike and Esma's husband Derek started fighting with Dex.

"Get the fuck off her," she heard Mike say.

When she looked back into the living room, Dex had a knife and was swinging wildly at Mike; then he lurched towards Pam and pulled her to him. He eased the knife blade against her throat.

Everyone moved back.

"You're fucking him, aren't you?" he growled. "I know you're fucking him. I know you were fucking him the entire time we were married."

"No, Dex! It wasn't like that," she said. "Please. Don't do this, Dex... you're hurting me."

"She's telling you the truth," Mike said. His face was white. "We have always just been friends."

"You think I'm fucking stupid? I see the way you look at her. You look at her the way all the men look at her."

"Please don't do this, Dex, it's not like that." Pam was choking. "Please put the knife down. You're not well."

"Do you think I fucking care anymore?" He was weeping now. "I have nothing else to lose, except you. Don't you get that, Pam?"

Mrs. Price came from behind with a heavy cast iron pot and hit Dex on the back of his head as hard as she could and he instantly fell forward, dropping the knife. Mike and Derek tackled him just as the police arrived. Several police officers took over and handcuffed him before he came to.

▶

As Dex was sitting on the floor being read his rights, Mike and Simone took Pam to the kitchen, away from the confusion.

"Simone, stay with your mother," Mike said. "I need to get something." He left Mrs. Price's apartment, but was back right away. "He violated his parole and maybe two restraining orders," Mike said, handing over the orders. "Today with his ex-wife and I think he's been to the nursing home where her son is. He's threatened both of them."

"Thanks," the officer said, as he pulled Dex up.

"Still acting like a little bitch," Dex said, laughing.

Mike went right up to Dex, close enough to whisper in his ear.

"Listen to me carefully," he snarled. "Do you think I'm worried about you? You're done! But don't worry because while you're rotting in prison playing with your dick I'll make sure she's warm in my bed."

Dex tried to rush him. Mike quickly moved back as the officers tackled him again. One of the officers Tasered him before he was removed from the apartment.

A few officers stayed behind to get everyone's statement. After a few hours, everyone had left, except for Simone, Mike, and Pam, who sat quietly in the kitchen.

"Mike, I want to go home," Pam said. "I need to lie down."

"Okay," he said, helping her up.

The three of them returned to Pam's apartment. Mike and Simone helped Pam to her bed. He went to the hall closet and pulled out an extra blanket and placed it over her. Pam was still shaking, even beneath the two blankets.

He went into the living room and could see Simone, busy in the kitchen making tea for her mother.

"Simone, I need to go out. Can you stay with your mother while I'm gone?"

"Of course," she said. "Are you okay?"

"Yes," he said, forcing a smile. "Just sit tight. I'll be back soon."

Mike got into his car and drove down Bayview turning on Cummer Avenue. It was late for visiting hours, but he had told the night staff that it was an emergency and that he needed to see his son.

He walked into the room where CJ slept and he turned on the bedside lamp. CJ slowly woke from his sleep and looked over.

"He's back in jail, CJ," Mike said carefully. "Do you understand me? You will never have to worry about him again. I swear on my life."

Mike continued to sit with him, holding onto his hand. CJ's eyes darted from side to side as he squeezed Mike's hand.

"Shhh," Mike said. "I'm right here. I won't go anywhere until you fall asleep. Okay, buddy? Just relax and try to go back to sleep. You're safe now."

A nurse walked in. "I'm sorry to interrupt, Mike, but it's after visiting hours and—"

"I know, Connie... I know," he said. "Just give me a few more minutes. Just until he falls back asleep. I promised him that I would stay until he falls asleep."

"Okay," she said. She left the room.

After a while, CJ finally closed his eyes and Mike felt his grip loosen as he started to drift back to sleep.

50

Nolan looked over at the alarm clock. It was almost five in the morning. He turned over towards the blonde sleeping next to him and sighed. He'd had one-night stands before, but this one was definitely the quickest turnaround. It wasn't common for him to go home with a woman he picked up at a Prisdel event and he usually waited until after the first date before sleeping with a woman, but he liked her. She was cute and funny and smart.

He sat on the edge of her bed, wondering if he should wake her before leaving or just pick up and go. He couldn't remember her name or what she did for a living, but he remembered that she had liked it when he went down on her and that she'd nearly cried when he fucked her.

He wondered if sleeping with random women was going to be his new thing. It wasn't like him to act this way, but it wasn't like him to go to industry parties and hang out with other celebrities, either. It was a new world he was learning to navigate.

He had only recently started attending events to promote *House Helpers*. The guy who puts up the drywall doesn't get an invitation. Only executives, on-air talent, and the production staff were expected to attend, but his circumstances had changed.

"You're on-air talent now, Nolan," Mac said, as they sat on his front porch. "That means you get to go to these shindigs while I get an evening home to myself."

"I'm not good at stuff like this. I don't know what to say to these people."

"Well, you better figure it out," Mac responded. "I'm not planning to stay on forever. To tell you the truth, Nolan, I'm not sure I'll be able to finish off the rest of this season. It's getting to be too much."

"What are you saying? Your contract is for another few years."

"No, the show is on air for another three years," Mac said. "My contract is up the end of next year and I'm ready to retire. I just finished renovating my cottage. The wife and I want to spend our golden years enjoying it, not travelling the country, trying to fix everyone else's dump. That's why you're the face of *House Helpers*. That's why you're attending all these events, schmoozing with the suits, and why they're having you do all those silly promos. In a few months, this baby is going to be all yours."

Nolan sat next to his mentor with a sick feeling in his stomach. He hadn't believed the rumours that Mac was about to retire. His stint on camera had started off rocky. He'd been sure he would be fired after the first day of filming, but now he was used to it. He could forget that the cameras were focused on him and just be his funny, charming self.

Nolan was good for business. The first aired show brought in the biggest ratings in *House Helpers'* history. Nolan O'Shea was on his way to becoming a household name and, by mid-season, he couldn't go anywhere without being stopped, whether it was a grocery store or gas station, or even lining up to get a cup of coffee.

One of the major perks was the attention he got from women, many eager to fuck him. In Halifax, he'd had to work hard just to get a number; now he merely had to look in a pretty woman's direction and he had a date. After a while, he grew tired of attending the events, seeing the same people, and he started showing up late and leaving early. But last night's party at The Radcliffe was Prisdel's biggest bash of the year and everyone was expected to be on time to smile for the cameras and mix with the media.

Nolan felt pretty comfortable as he wandered through the home. It felt like someone's house party instead of some cold, strobe-lit warehouse with music pulsating through the walls. The party was intimate, with small groups of people mingling amongst the silver-and-blue holiday decorations.

As usual, he met so many people that he couldn't keep their names straight and had the feeling he was introducing himself to the same people over and over. When he had a moment to himself, he went outside for fresh air, slipping into the staging area where the caterers were prepping. He wandered past the makeshift tent to the back end of the property. There he found a pond and a gazebo, and a pretty young blonde was sitting on one of the stone benches, smoking a cigarette and furiously typing on her cell phone.

"I'd hate to be the person on the other end of that text," he said, smiling at her.

She barely looked up at him. "You and the rest of the world," she said, as she continued to type. "My ex is the biggest jackass and he seems hell-bent on ruining my night."

"Sorry to hear that," he said. "Is he the kind of guy who has to have the final word?"

"Ding! Ding! Ding!" she said. "No conversation is ever done unless you agree that he's right."

"Sounds like a charmer." Nolan chuckled. He took a swig from his beer. "You know what might help? Turning your phone off. There's nothing that eats at a guy like that than ending a conversation before he does. I guarantee it."

"So true," she said. When she finally looked up at him, she gasped slightly. She looked at Nolan closely, almost staring at him. The spell broke when her cell started to buzz. She looked down again and quickly turned it off and tossed it in her purse. "It's cold as hell," she said. "Do you want to get out of here?"

"Yeah," he said. "Actually, I would love to get out of here."

They snuck out through the service area and hopped into his car. In the light, she was even cuter than he'd first thought, with deep dimples in each cheek and bright green eyes.

"I'm Nolan," he said to her as he took off. "I never caught your name?"

"I never gave it to you." She slipped her hand into his pants. "Make a left at the light. My place is just a few blocks away."

▶▶

SIMONE SAT at the missing baggage claim office, waiting for her suitcase. She was tired and hungry and it had been a hellish trip. She asked the airline representative for an update.

"Ma'am, the best I can do is take your information and have your bag shipped to you when we find it," said the woman. "But make no mistake, we will find it."

"Right! The only thing is that I have my house keys in my suitcase and I can't get into my home without them." Simone went back to her seat and plopped down. She took out her cell phone and realized that it was on its last bar. She sent a quick text to Jessica. A minute later she got her response.

Hey babes, I got you. The car is in the shop but I'm just finishing dinner with Bachelor #4 (aka. Mr. 16 Ounces). We can swing by to get you in an hour, if you don't mind waiting.

Simone chuckled. They'd been in constant touch while she was in Europe and Jessica had been on a dating rampage. She had slept with more guys in three months than in her four years at Queen's.

Last week, she'd claimed it was the most liberating feeling to get off without the hassle of caring. She had also assigned nicknames to keep the men straight. She described *Mister 16 Ounces* as a god with a 9-inch dick the width of a 16-ounce water bottle. The first time she'd slept with him, he could go in only part way because it hurt too much. The most they could do was six inches.

He's a workaholic and is never in town much but when he is it's like Fuckapalooza.

Simone rolled her eyes. So now she was going to meet the infamous Mister 16 Ounces. She had asked Jessica if he was "The One," but Jessica quickly shot that down.

He's the one for now, she typed back. *I'm not interested in a relationship even if his penis is magnificent. He's just my fuck buddy. Plain and simple.*

It had been difficult for Jessica over the last few months. She was working towards partnership at her law firm, but no one seemed to take her seriously. To everyone, she was the blonde who didn't have a clue but had enough of Daddy's money. It didn't matter how hard she worked or how many hours she pulled, she was always dismissed by her colleagues as a lightweight.

Simone could totally relate. Prior to the trip, she had tried to hammer *Trails* into shape. She'd been recruited after the New York coordinator had quit his job. She'd thought she would just pick up where he left off and make sure things ran smoothly. But, the moment she was brought onboard, she quickly realized that nothing had been booked and the entire production was in jeopardy.

She'd worked tirelessly for weeks before the trip and for nearly twenty hours each day, flying country to country, city to city, making sure the shoot wouldn't run into any issues. When a location was not ready, it was Simone who took the brunt of the director's wrath. Twice she had fights with the camera crew and the assistant director that left her in tears and on the verge of quitting. She was tempted to contact Cynthia to vent, but she knew her boss would only tell her to suck it up and just focus on what needed to be done.

After each day's shooting was complete, Simone kept to herself. She had to wrangle everyone and didn't have time to forge friendships. She rarely slept and, when she did have a moment to relax, she was plagued with panic attacks, worried that she had missed a minor detail. It was the loneliest three months of her life. Even lonelier than the weeks she'd spent in juvy.

Jessica's emails about her sex life were her only solace while she worked on *Trails from Hell*. She would quietly laugh to herself when Jessica talked about Bachelor #6, a cute student from Calgary who cried every time they had sex, or Bachelor #2, whom she'd met online but who catfished her by leading her to believe that he was some Internet titan instead of an overworked IT tech. Jessica ultimately felt sorry for the shy awkward guy and ended up having pity sex with him on their first date.

After the wrap, back in Germany, Simone opted to stay an extra week and explore Italy. It had been a dream of hers since university, but, most important, she had located Lia and wanted to surprise her. After all the years, she had never stopped thinking about her and was full of trepidation on the three-hour bus ride to Punta Ala, where Lia ran a small apartment building, renting rooms out to tourists. It cost Simone a small fortune to book a room for a few days, but it would be worth it if it meant seeing Lia again.

She almost didn't recognize her. Lia had cut her hair short and no longer wore her signature vintage summer dresses. Instead, she was in jeans and a button-down blouse. She still had her curvy figure.

Simone could barely muster a hello, she was so nervous and unsure of herself. It was only when she accidentally bumped into a display of brochures that Lia saw her.

"Simone? What in the world are you doing here?"

"I came to see you," Simone said. "Well, actually, I'm here for work. I still work for Prisdel... that internship... well, now it's a full-time career. Anyways, I had some time off and thought I would look you up."

She felt her throat tighten. She took a deep breath and smiled, but Lia just looked at her with concern.

"Simone, you shouldn't have come here," she said. "I have a new life. I'm back with Diana and we're living una vita calma. I do not want any trouble."

Simone's smile quickly faded. "Honestly Lia, I'm not looking to cause any problems between the two of you," she said. "I just thought it would be nice to see you again—as friends."

"Okay," Lia sighed. She handed Simone her room key. "As friends. But know that Diana doesn't know about you and I prefer it that way."

"Of course," Simone said. "Would it be possible to have dinner together? I'm only here for a few nights and would love to catch up. You can tell Diana that we are old college friends. Can't you?"

Lia sighed again.

"Va bene," she said. "Come for dinner tonight. Verso le 18:00."

"Perfect," Simone said, looking at her watch. "That'll give me some time to freshen up."

▶

LIA, Diana, and Simone sat around a small wooden kitchen table without saying much. Diana spoke very little English and Lia spent the first part of the dinner staring intently at her food.

"This silly," Diana finally said. "Entrambi avete dormito insieme in Canada, giusto? You two fuck, sì?"

Lia nearly choked on her food.

"It's no big deal," Diana said. She held up her hand. "Questo era nel passato. I not mad."

"We're friends," Simone said. "Lia's a very old and dear friend."

Lia translated.

Diana smiled and grabbed Simone's hand. "She's beautiful, no?" she said to Lia. "I can see why."

Simone frowned, which prompted Diana to burst out laughing. Soon Simone and Lia were laughing along with her; after that, the women talked freely to one another with Lia translating.

Diana explained to Simone that she and Lia had been best friends in primary school, growing up in the village of Castelsardo. They fell in love as teenagers. Keeping their love a secret was easy enough until they finished school, when Diana was given a choice: Either join the convent and be a Bride of Christ, go to university, or get married.

"I wasn't a good student like Lia," Diana said in Italian. "And I was too wild to be a nun. So I married a boy from our village. It was the worst mistake, but I was young and afraid. I didn't want to take any chances. I didn't want our families knowing about us."

"I thought they did eventually find out," said Simone.

"They did," Lia said quietly. "I wrote her a letter begging her not to marry and her mother found it. Next thing the entire neighbourhood knew our secret."

"Is that when you moved to Canada?" Simone asked.

She nodded. "The only relative who would talk to me was my brother, who had moved his family to Toronto years before," Lia said. "He enrolled me at Queen's. It was close enough for him to check up on me, but far enough so his neighbours wouldn't find out about his dyke little sister."

"I don't like that word," Diana said, scolding Lia in Italian. "That word makes us look dirty. What we had... what we *have* is beautiful. It's not dirty."

Lia smiled at Diana, then Simone.

"When I went home from Canada, I found out that my mother had stage four lung cancer with little less than a year to live," she said. "I spent most of that time caring for her, which is why you didn't hear from me. When Mama died, Diana and her daughter came down for the funeral."

"This is my Rose," Diana said. She pulled out her phone to show Simone a picture of her ten-year-old. "She's spending the holidays with her father right now."

"She's beautiful," Simone said.

"With Lia, it was as if no time had passed," Diana continued. "After the funeral, we talked all night and, by morning, we realized that our love was still strong. I ended my marriage and the three of us moved here to Punta Ala."

"Mama left me with a little inheritance," Lia said. "Enough for us to buy this place."

Lia and Diana looked so happy that Simone realized coming here was a mistake. She had secretly hoped that maybe there would be room in Lia's heart for her, but it was clear that there was no returning to the past for either of them.

"I'm glad that you found each other again," she said. "You deserve to be happy... both of you."

Lia translated and then said something to Diana.

Diana responded by getting up from her seat. "It was nice to meet you," she said slowly in English. She hugged Simone. "Buona notte, e buon riposo."

"It was wonderful to meet you, Diana," Simone said. "Buona notte."

"I'll be up shortly," Lia said in Italian as she kissed Diana goodnight.

After Diana went up the back stairs, Lia got up to clear the table. Simone stood and went to pick up her dish, but Lia swiftly took the plate from her.

"Leave it! You are a guest," she said. Lia continued to clear the table in silence.

"I don't mind helping, Lia," Simone said, unsure of what had just happened.

"Why did you come here? I was fine until you showed up."

"I'm sorry," Simone said. "I didn't think…"

"That's your problem," she said, placing the leftovers in the refrigerator. "You don't think. You never thought of how I might feel. And now you just show up and it's not fair to me or Diana or the life we have here."

"I… I'm sorry, Lia. I just wanted to see you. I missed you."

"And you don't think that I didn't miss you?" Lia said, slamming the fridge door. "I've missed you and loved you, but I moved on. I can't move on with you here. You're making me feel things that are supposed to be gone."

Simone felt her stomach tighten. She didn't know what to say. She had hoped that Lia would still have feelings for her, but, when she searched her eyes, all she saw was hurt and resentment.

"I know that you are here for another day, but you need to leave by the morning, and please, no more contact."

Lia placed the dishes in the kitchen sink and then headed up the side stairs. Simone flinched when she heard their bedroom door slam shut. She felt alone and abandoned in their kitchen. She went to the sink and washed the dishes as a gesture before finally retiring for the evening.

The next day she woke early, planning to see Lia and apologize for ambushing her. Instead, she was met by Diana, who greeted her warmly and said that Lia couldn't see her off. She was in bed with *something*. Simone couldn't understand. "Migraine," Diana repeated, and she realized that Lia would not be there to say goodbye. She tried to smile as she thanked Diana for being a gracious hostess.

She took the first bus back to Rome and cried all the way. She had loved Lia for so long, but her anger felt so foreign and painful. She tried to enjoy a few days in Italy's capital before heading back to Toronto, but couldn't. The country's beauty wasn't there for her. Her heart felt so heavy that she changed her flight and returned home a few days early.

Now she sat at the baggage carousel, waiting for Jessica. As she watched the battery of her cell reach 1%, the airline rep jogged towards her.

"Miss Allen, we found your luggage," she said, panting. "I'm so glad you're still here. If you would just come back with me I'll have you sign for it."

Simone nodded wearily. She went with the rep to collect her bag. When she finally exited the baggage area, Jessica was by the exit door cozying up to a tall guy in dark blue jeans, wearing a black winter parka. She suspected that it was Mister 16 Ounces and she chuckled to herself as she walked towards them.

"Jessica!" she called.

Jessica turned and waved.

Simone stopped dead in her tracks when the man in the black parka looked her way. At first, she wasn't sure, but, as she got closer and saw the crinkle in his eyes, she knew it was him.

"Nols?" She felt her heart leap. "Nolan!"

A huge smile spread across his face as he started walking towards her. Simone quickened her pace, almost running to him.

"Simone, oh my God," he said, hugging her, lifting her off the ground.

Nolan felt a collision of feelings ranging from confusion to excitement to a sudden nervous restraint—all wrapped in a familiar warmth. He looked at her and almost couldn't believe how much she had changed. Yet, when he looked into her eyes, he saw the girl he'd grown up with smiling back at him.

"You two know each other?" Jessica asked. "This is crazy!"

Nolan awkwardly put Simone down.

"Simone and I were neighbours as kids," he said. "I haven't seen her in almost…"

"Ten years." Simone completed his sentence. She looked at him, wide-eyed. "It's been such a long time."

"Has it really been that long?" he said, calculating.

"I think we saw each other briefly during my last year in high school," she said.

"You're right," he said. They all started to walk out. "Wow! This is crazy!"

Simone couldn't believe it was Nolan that Jessica had been talking about all this time. She started to feel a little awkward. Jessica had revealed all the intimate details of Nolan—her childhood friend. Her face felt beet red. She quickly pushed any thoughts of water bottles out of her mind as they headed out of the terminal.

"How did you both meet?" she asked them.

"This is the guy I was telling you about," Jessica said under her breath as she linked arms with Simone. "We met a month ago, right babe? I was Hubert's plus one at Prisdel's annual holiday party and that's where I met him… wait… holy shit! I'm so stupid! Nolan, Simone also works for Prisdel."

"Are you serious?" he said. "Why am I just hearing this? How long have you been working there?"

"A little over six years," she said. "I work in the Toronto office as a production supervisor." Simone let out a huge yawn and felt her eyes flutter. Jet lag was starting to take over. She loved seeing Nolan, but her exhaustion was catching up. "Excuse me, it's been a long day," she said, yawning again. "How about you? What are you doing at Prisdel?"

"I started off working for *House Helpers* in the construction unit," he said as they continued through the parking lot. "A few years back they got me on camera with Mac and now I'm co-hosting with him."

"Oh, man!" Simone said. "I know of *House Helpers* but haven't worked with a lot of the Canadian programs the last few years. I primarily coordinate our programs in America. I had no idea that you were on the show."

"Well, he's everywhere now," Jessica said as she grabbed his arm. "Don't be offended, Nolan, Simone's completely clueless about everything around her except her own projects."

They got into Nolan's car. Simone was laughing along with

Jessica, but was mortified by the whole scenario. Cynthia was constantly scolding her for being out of the loop. Her mentor was always telling her that, if she wanted to move up in the company, she had to be more aware of what was going on. It was the main reason she had taken the European shoot, to prove to Cynthia that she could widen her perspective and be trusted with any project they gave her.

"I really don't know many of the Prisdel folks myself," Nolan admitted. He started his car. "It all kind of happened overnight. One minute I'm painting a wall and the next I'm on camera, showing the world how to install a barn door. I'm just surprised that Dad never mentioned anything."

"Mike still calls it 'that production company'," Simone teased as she mimicked Mike. "'Splimoney, how's that production company you're working at? What do you do again at that production company?' I just smile and nod."

Nolan laughed out loud as they drove out of the airport. "He still calls you Splimoney, huh?" he said. "Well, at least he knows that you work somewhere. Mrs. Price still has no idea how to find my show on her cable box."

"You know Mrs. Price?" Jessica asked, trying to piece together their history.

"We all lived in the same building," Simone answered. "Before I lived with her, she was our neighbour across the hall."

"Kind of our sitter quasi-grandmother for years," Nolan added. "You know, Simone, she did mention that you were working in Europe."

"Yeah, we were filming *Trails - Destination Europe*," she said. "That's what I've been working on for the last few months."

"I just heard about that show," he said. "I met the director a few days ago. He's a pretty intense guy. A little neurotic for my taste."

"That's a huge understatement," she said, chuckling. "I'm just happy that it's all over with and I'm back home."

"So am I," Jessica said. She turned to Simone and winked. "We have LOTS to catch up on."

On the drive to Jessica and Simone's condo, Nolan gave Simone the Coles notes version of what had been going on since he returned to Toronto. He asked what she was up to, and she gave him a brief history of her days at Queen's University and her work with Prisdel.

"Is that how you ladies met?" he asked.

"We met during our second year at Queen's," Jessica chimed in.

Jessica then filled him in on her friendship with Simone. How they'd met at the university library and their move to Toronto.

As she talked, Nolan couldn't help but glance at Simone in his rearview mirror. A few times, Simone caught him. Each time, he would quickly look away, pretending that he was checking traffic. It was hard for him not to stare. The last real memory he had of her was their eighth-grade graduation. He remembered how she'd looked over at him when they called her name to get her diploma. He remembered that smile. He had touched her hand lightly as she walked past him to collect her certificate.

She had changed so much since then. He wasn't sure he would even have recognized her had she not called out his name.

They turned into the building's garage. Jessica was still talking animatedly about Queen's when Nolan glanced over again to see Simone leaning against the window, fast asleep.

"Looks like she's wiped," Jessica said. "Travelling twenty-four hours in economy will do that to you."

He parked the car and turned off the ignition. He hated having to wake her. She looked beautiful, asleep in the back, clutching her knapsack. He remembered the first time he'd watched her sleeping, the night after Kester died. The night he knew he was in love with her. Now he wondered if anything had really changed since then.

51

S imone wandered into the kitchen with her hair wrapped in a powdered blue headscarf. Still dressed in her checkered flannel pyjama pants and her favourite kimono robe, she looked around the apartment, a little relieved that Jessica was at work.

She'd barely slept that night. Mostly because of the time difference, but partly because of her impromptu reunion with Nolan. It had been years since she'd spoken to him and his reappearance stirred feelings she'd thought had gone away.

She felt a nagging queasiness in her stomach and started to look around for tea to settle her nerves. All she found in the pantry was an empty box. She searched for her hidden stash of ginger tea in the back, but it was clear that Jessica had finished that box as well.

"Damn it," she mumbled to herself.

She opened the refrigerator and found a bottle of Canada Dry, nearly finished, and drank the rest, but it still didn't do much to settle her stomach. She debated whether she felt up to running to the market to get more tea. The sun was peeking through the silvery clouds. It looked as if the rain was easing up.

Simone slid open the balcony door, took a deep breath of the cold brisk morning air, and soaked in her homecoming. She had been homesick the moment she left for Europe, and seeing the Toronto skyline made her grateful that this was the first day of her weeklong staycation.

She stared out at the traffic, going over the previous night in her mind. How could Nolan have been working with Prisdel Productions all this time without her knowing? Even Hubert knew of him, she'd discovered when she texted him that morning.

Jessica and Cynthia were right about her being out of touch with everything. She'd become so preoccupied with her own world that she barely noticed anything else. She never watched any of the other productions. She had no use for co-workers not directly involved in one of her shows; she didn't even learn their names. Felicia teased her relentlessly about it. She called her Ms. Stush, "*too good to grab drinks unless there was a production schedule attached to a martini glass.*"

She walked back into the condo, wondering how many opportunities she'd missed by being so detached from everything. She knew it was more than just being aloof. Deep down, it was the problem of not opening herself to anyone or anything. The difficulty of going outside her comfort zone, even for a moment, became the main source of her anxieties. Fearful that, if she strayed too far, her whole world would change. She preferred life to remain familiar and predictable.

As she slid the balcony door shut, she heard the key in the front door and looked at the time on the microwave. Almost 11:00 am.

"I thought you were in court all day," she called out. "Did you forget your laptop again?"

"She did," Nolan said as he walked into the kitchen with a white pastry bag and two hot beverages. "She asked me to bring it to her office. I'm meeting her after lunch."

Simone looked at Nolan, a little embarrassed being caught wearing a headscarf. She quickly pulled it off, stuffing it in the kitchen's cutlery drawer.

"I brought breakfast, if you're hungry," he said, placing the bag on the counter. "Bagels, cream cheese, and tea."

"She gave you a key," Simone mumbled, pulling her robe together. "What kind of tea?"

Nolan smiled as he watched Simone reach into the cupboard for plates. She was still grumpy first thing in the morning. Yet, despite her mood, her mismatched pyjamas, and dishevelled hair, he couldn't help admire how beautiful she had become. Her hair was longer and her body was supple, softer and curvier. She was not the stiff scrawny girl he remembered from all those years ago.

"I wasn't sure what tea you were into these days so I got peppermint and ginger to be safe," he said, trying to focus. "Jessica finished the last box a while back and I figured you would be hankering for a cup."

"Ginger, please," she said. "And thank you."

"It's nice outside." He handed her the ginger tea. "Grab a jacket and we can eat on the balcony."

She watched him out there, clearing a pile of newspapers from the small table, making space to put their food. The last person she had thought she would be having breakfast with was Nolan. Yet there he was, looking more handsome than she could have ever imagined. His hair had grown back lighter and wavier. His smile was even more infectious, which made her stomach queasy again. She quickly sipped her tea to ease the tension.

"I still can't believe how long it's been since I last saw you," she said, joining him on the balcony. "You got more hair now."

"Yeah, I decided to upgrade my look," he said, looking up at her shyly. He ran his fingers through his hair. "Being bald wasn't really working for me."

"Yeah, I bet. Probably a little too scary for small children and animals."

Nolan let out a small laugh that made Simone smile briefly.

"Here," he said, handing her the pastry bag. "They're still hot."

She opened the bag. "Where did you get these?" she said, pulling one out. "I haven't had a twister bagel in years. I don't even know where to find them anymore."

"The construction site I used to work at has a Chinese guy who makes them from scratch," he said. "I passed by it on my way over."

"You worked in construction?" she asked. "Was that before or after jail?"

"Wow!" he said. "You really don't beat around the bush, do you?"

His demeanour changed. He wasn't comfortable with the topic, but she wanted to know how he'd gone from goofy lanky Nolan to a bald scary assault felon. This had been on her mind since the car ride home and it hadn't seemed right to bring it up last night in front of Jessica.

"Well, inquiring minds want to know," she said to lighten the mood. "The last I heard, you got into some serious trouble."

"It could have been worse," he said. "The short of it is that I fell in with the wrong crowd and did a lot of stupid shit. Not my finest moment." He averted his eyes.

She could tell that the conversation was going south very quickly. The last thing she wanted was to turn his kind gesture into a hostile inquisition. She pulled apart her bagel and smeared cream cheese on it.

"God, this is great," she said after devouring a piece. The hard lines around her brow softened. "This takes me back."

"It does, doesn't it?" he said, glad that she had changed the subject. "You know what would make this even more perfect?"

"No," she replied, handing him the tub of cream cheese. "What?"

"Listening to the radio like we did when we were kids." He

pulled off the lid of his tea. "Do you remember blasting your ghetto blaster while we ate breakfast?"

"We thought we were so cool," she said, laughing. "Meanwhile we woke up half the building with 'Push It.'"

"That was my jam," he said.

She laughed at him.

"No, seriously, I had the biggest crush on Salt!"

"Stop lying. You did not!"

"What are you talking about!" he said. "Somewhere in my dad's place, there's a hidden shoe box of letters I planned on sending her. We're talking full-on marriage proposals."

"You're an idiot," she smirked.

They sat silently for a while, watching the cars scurry through traffic. A few snowflakes started to fall, but the sun shone through.

Nolan was glad. He didn't want their breakfast to end prematurely. "You know what else this reminds me of?" he said. "Our parents sitting out on the balcony at our old place."

"On those old ugly plastic lounge chairs," she reminisced. "Man, it didn't matter if it was raining or a blizzard, they were always out there, smoking and drinking coffee."

"Remember the both of us sitting on the couch playing video games and cranking up the volume just to drown them out?" he said.

She burst out laughing. "Oh my God, yes! They were always arguing about *every* article they read in *The Star*."

"Once I hid their papers for a solid week just so they didn't have anything to argue about," he said proudly. "I almost got my butt tanned when Dad found out."

"I should have thought of that," she said. "They both were a trip."

"Hey Simone, let me ask you something. Do you think our parents… ever… you know…did it?"

"My mom and your dad? The two of them getting down? God, I hope not!"

"I don't know, Si. There were plenty of late nights we were watching television and I didn't see them on the balcony."

"Stop it!" she said, screwing up her face. "I don't want to even picture it."

"Well, does it really seem that farfetched?" he said. "I mean all those hot, passionate, steamy political arguments."

"You need to stop or I'm going to hurt you," she said, throwing the crumpled bagel bag at him.

"Okay...okay," he said laughing. "But, seriously, if you think about it, they were kind of like an old married couple, anyways. Always running errands together. Doing stuff for one another. Dad was always taking CJ to his soccer practices so Pam didn't have to leave work early. And all those times Pam took me to get my hair cut?"

"I remember that! She took you to that black barber shop on Eglinton," Simone said. "I think you were the only white boy that had a fade-with-line design. Didn't one of them attempt to give you a Gumby?"

"Yes," he said feigning anger. "And right before picture day."

"Mike was so pissed." She giggled. "I think I still have that picture somewhere."

"Hardy har," he said, sipping his tea. "Don't forget I still have your seventh-grade picture, too. The one with all your braids sticking out like Buckwheat."

"Touché! Your secret is safe." She raised her cup.

"Wait...wait...do you remember the Sunday dinners?" he asked. "Better yet all the Christmas Eve dinners?"

"I do," she said. "My favourite was our first one together."

"Me too," he replied. "Your Mom cooked so much food we had to bring in our card table so we had somewhere to sit."

"That was a really good Christmas," she said. "Remember how hyper we were? We couldn't wait for Christmas morning."

"I blame the Jamaican black cake your mom fed us, right before bed." He laughed. "That would make any kid bounce off the walls."

Simone sat back, smiling to herself. She remembered those nights. They were the best memories she had of them all. Everyone sitting around, eating, playing cards, and listening to Christmas music. Even her mother seemed to loosen up on Christmas Eve.

"I never told you this, but one Christmas Eve I was bunking in CJ's bed," he said. "I got up in the middle of the night to use the washroom and I saw them together in the living room wrapping our gifts, talking and laughing. Neither of them noticed me, but when I went back to the bedroom I saw them in the middle of the living room slow dancing."

"Stop lying, Nolan. Those two were the definition of oil and vinegar. I would have believed you more if you said you saw Santa Claus."

"No, seriously, I remember it really well," he said. "It was weird seeing them that close, but actually it was kind of nice. It was rough for my Dad that year. He was going through a hard time with my mother and I hadn't seen him that happy in a long time. Sometimes I wished he would just divorce my mom and marry Pam."

"Really? You never told me that!"

"Well, you know," he mumbled, "it was pretty much the only time I saw him happy. Some of my best times were with you guys... I liked our family."

They sat in silence. Simone wondered if things would have been better with her mother if she had married Mike instead of Dex. How different all of their lives would have been.

"Si, can I ask you a question?"

"Sure," she said. "Shoot."

"Are you really a lesbian? I mean, did I miss the memo or something?"

Simone felt her face burning. The last thing she wanted to do was talk with Nolan about her sex life. She had hoped that Jessica hadn't mentioned it, but she knew her friend had a tendency to blab.

"I'm sorry, am I getting too personal?" he asked. "I shouldn't have asked... it's just that Jessica mentioned that she had a lesbian roommate, so, when I saw it was you, it kind of threw me for a loop."

"No...no, it's okay," she said. "It's not a big deal, I just prefer the company of women. I'm more attracted to them."

"Really?" he asked. "I guess I just don't get it."

"It's simple," she said. "The women I'm with don't judge, they don't hide their feelings, and they get me more than most men."

"What about Pam or Mrs. Price?" he asked. "Do they know?"

"God, no!" she said. "And I would appreciate it if you kept this between us. The last thing I need is them going off about who I'm sleeping with on the regular."

"Okay...okay, I get it," he said. "Look, if you keep my white Gumby picture under wraps, I'll keep my mouth shut."

"Thank you," she said, finishing off her last piece of bagel.

"I guess... I'm just a little stunned," he continued. "It's just... I've known you since we were kids and would never have guessed—"

"You only knew me for that part of my life," she said. "Things have changed a lot since I was thirteen."

"Apparently not everything." He handed her a napkin. "You have some spread on your face."

"A little more specific, please," she said, wiping her mouth. "Did I get it?"

"No," he said, picking up a napkin. "You're still the messiest eater I know."

They both laughed at his clumsiness as he tried to wipe the cream cheese off her cheek. She instinctually messed with his hair. His heart raced and Simone's smile started to fade as he gently caressed her cheek with his thumb.

"It's getting late," she said. "You probably should get Jessica's laptop to her."

"Yeah," he said. "The traffic gets crazy around this time."

"Yup." She got up from her seat and adjusted her robe. He continued to gaze at her. "It's on the kitchen table."

"What?"

"Jessica's laptop," she said. "It's on the kitchen table."

"Oh, right…okay," he said swiftly. "Thanks."

They cleared the breakfast dishes from the balcony, the ease and chattiness between them morphing into an awkward silence.

"Nolan, does all of this feel incredibly strange?" She walked him to the door. "We lose touch all these years and then, overnight, it suddenly feels like nothing has changed."

"I know what you mean," he said. "It's crazy that we reconnected this way."

"Tell me about it," she said.

Silence.

"I'm glad that you and Jessica found each other. She's a really good person."

"Yeah, she's great. We have a good time together…I mean…I like hanging out with her—"

"I know what you mean," she said, smiling at him.

He opened the door. "I guess I'll see you around?"

"Yeah. For sure," she answered.

She watched him turn towards the elevator but then he stopped and turned back to her.

"Si, it's really great seeing you again." He wrapped his arms around her and felt her slip her arms around him. He sighed and closed his eyes. "I've missed you."

As he held her, she nestled her head against his chest. She could hear his heart beating and suddenly felt a warmth she hadn't felt in years. She closed her eyes, wanting nothing more than to stay in his embrace. But she pulled away instead, using every ounce of her strength not to get lost in his arms. She then watched him walk down the hallway and disappear into the waiting elevator.

She took a deep breath. She couldn't go down that road with him. He was a warm memory, a familiar stranger, but she couldn't lose herself to him—not even if her heart demanded it.

52

"Okay, let me try and figure this out," Freddy said, trying to stifle his laughter as Nolan drove them down Dufferin Street. "You, a reformed hardcore skinhead, is now sweating a fine piece of ass from Jamaica, who happens to be a lesbian? Did I get that right? Because it really doesn't get any more fucked up than that."

"Can you cool it with the whole skinhead thing," Nolan said. "And I'm not sweating her. I'm just a little shell-shocked seeing her again."

"Frosty, I've seen you with all sorts of women back home and you've never been shell-shocked," Freddy said. "How fine is she?"

Nolan drove in silence.

"Ah shit, she's that fine, huh?" Freddy said. "Come on, dude! You used to be that guy who barely batted an eye trying to pick up every blonde Becky that walked by."

"I'm not like that anymore."

"Yeah, all the pussy comes running to you now." Freddy laughed. "Look, man, if you like this chick, then call her up and ask her out."

"I'm sort of sleeping with her roommate right now."

"Oh shit," Freddy said, laughing harder, covering his mouth. "Yo! You need to run from that, dawg. Run far away. I don't think you can handle that much pussy at once."

"Would you be serious, Freddy?" They pulled into the tile warehouse. "I'm not trying to get with Simone. She's just a friend I haven't seen in years."

"And whose fault is that?" Freddy reminded him. "Ain't that the same chick from your hood? The one you've been avoiding like a little punk-ass bitch? You knew where she was all these years, didn't you?"

Nolan turned off his truck's ignition. Freddy was right. He had been purposely avoiding Simone for years.

When he was in prison, he was angry because it looked as if Simone had ignored the letter he'd sent through his father. During a visit, he had asked his father about it, but Mike didn't know what letter he was talking about. Nolan figured that she never received his message and was probably in Kingston, living her life, not giving him a second thought. It was then that he realized how obsessive he had become.

After his release, living in Halifax made it easy for him to put her out of his mind, but, when he returned to Toronto, some old feelings started to creep back. He took extra precautions to avoid her. He never went to the complex if he could help it. He only met up with his father at a restaurant for dinner or at Mike's work.

He also started to date a lot of women, most of them perky, blue-eyed blondes—the polar opposites of Simone. After a while, he was able to silence the part of him that was infatuated with her and went on with his life, jumping from one bed to the next, which worked until one of the blondes happened to be Simone's roommate.

Now, after their short breakfast reunion, thoughts of Simone quickly filled his mind, leaving him completely sprung. He started to find reasons to see Jessica as an excuse to spend time with

Simone. He would show up at Prisdel for any reason on the off chance that Simone would be available for lunch.

Simone didn't mind it. She liked spending time with Nolan. It felt like old times, the two of them sitting on the couch, watching television or playing cards, waiting for Jessica to come home. It only got weird when Jessica came home with a date. It led to awkward moments of Jessica having to introduce Nolan to the latest bachelor she was about to bang.

"Si, Nolan is a great guy and everything, but it's weird having him here when I'm bringing someone home," Jessica complained. "And it's fucking hard to get off with you two idiots in the living room laughing."

"I'm sorry Jess," she said. "But that dude looked like some boy-band reject. Where did you find that winner?"

"Real funny," Jessica said. "Look, it's not cool anymore and it's pissing me off."

"So what do you want me to do?" she said. "Nolan is just here waiting to see you, hoping to get another spin on the Jessica train."

"Really? That's kind of sweet."

"Look, why don't you text me an hour before you come home with your dates," she suggested. "Then I'll make sure he's gone."

"Yeah...that may work. On the other hand, maybe he should stick around. You know...in case I have a bad evening."

"You're seriously a major slut," Simone said. "Don't you think you're taking this whole casual dating thing a little too far?"

"Are you kidding?!" Jessica said. "This is the most fun I've had in my life."

Simone rolled her eyes. She knew all too well how quickly the euphoric feeling faded after a one-night stand. The emptiness afterwards left you lonely and longing for a deeper connection. But having Nolan back in her life was slowly eroding that loneliness. He was her best friend again, her partner in crime and, unwittingly, he was helping her get over Lia.

She usually didn't talk about her love life to anyone other than

Jessica or Hubert. It was private and she liked it that way, but it was a relief being able to confide in Nolan again. She didn't tell him much but did confess that she was still in love with her ex.

"Is she the love of your life?" he asked.

She nodded. They were stowed away in Simone's room, playing gin rummy while Jessica said goodnight to her date. She shuffled and dealt out the cards on her bed.

He looked at her. "Why don't you like talking about her? Wait... is it Jessica? Is that why you won't say her name?"

"Oh God, no." Simone dropped a card. "Jessica is like a sister to me and, just to be absolutely clear, I've never had those kind of feelings for her."

"My bad," he said, laughing, as he picked up one of her discarded cards. "Then why so secretive? Who's this mystery woman?"

Simone sat for a moment trying to find the words. She picked up a card from the deck and then studied her hand for a moment before looking up at him.

"Because my relationship with her was sacred," she said. "It's hard to explain. I met her when I was starting to get my life together. I was making it on my own and it felt good being by myself. I didn't have to answer to anyone and, for the first time in my life, I was happy—pure, unabashed happiness. She was part of that."

"Was she the first woman... you know... that you were with?"

She nodded. "It's probably why I'm finding it hard to get over her," she said. "Being with her was the first time I felt loved."

"So then what happened? What changed?"

"She wanted more than I could give her," she said putting down her card. "I wasn't ready for the kind of relationship she wanted—your turn."

"And what kind of relationship did she want?"

"She wanted me to come out to everyone and be open about us."

Silence.

"Well, then, she really wasn't the one because, if she was, you wouldn't care who knew. You'd want the whole world to know that you loved her."

"What do you know about love, Nolan O'Shea?"

"I've been in love before. I know enough."

Nolan looked at his hand and put down a card, then picked up another. He looked at her and there was a smile spread across her face.

She picked up the card he'd discarded.

"Well if you know as much about love as you do about gin rummy, then you're going to be single for life, son—Gin!" she said triumphantly. "That's three games in a row. Take another shot!"

"This deck is fixed," he said sourly. "I'm shuffling the cards from now on."

"Go for it," she said, handing him the deck and the vodka bottle. "I'm still going to kick your ass."

He grabbed the vodka bottle and took a long swig.

After five more intense rounds, Simone fell back on her bed, completely plastered. "I gotta take a break... I'm–"

"Shhhh...shhhh, listen," Nolan said drunkenly. "Is she moaning?"

"I think she is," she whispered loudly. "No, no... I think that's him."

"He's not doing it right," Nolan said. "By now she would be screaming my name."

"Yeah, that's because you're strapped like a horse." Simone covered her mouth. "Oh my God, I can't believe I just said that."

"Is that what she told you?" he said smiling. "That I'm strapped like a horse?"

"No... more like a 16-ounce water bottle," she said as she tried to stop laughing. "She calls you Mister 16 Ounces. Fuck, I'm so wasted. You can't tell her that I told you or she'll kill me."

"Okay, I won't say a word," he said, lying back beside her.

"Don't let that shit go to your head, Romeo," she said. "Shhhh... I think they're done."

"That was pretty quick," he said. "I don't think I need to worry much about this guy. What's her nickname for him, anyways?"

"Not sure. I think this one is the Italian Stallion."

They both burst out laughing. Simone tried to shush him with her hands over his mouth. She howled when he tickled her. She slipped back and fell off the bed.

"Oh my God, Si! I'm so sorry," he said, laughing still. "Are you okay?"

Simone, sprawled on the floor, continued to giggle as Nolan tried to pull her back on the bed but ended up falling on top of her. She laughed loudly, then groaned in pain. He pulled her to him, both of them laughing hysterically.

They stifled themselves when they heard Jessica's bedroom door open and footsteps stomp past Simone's room. The front door slammed. They listened for a few minutes more.

"Did they leave?" Nolan asked, wiping the tears from his eyes.

"I think so," she said.

His cell phone dinged. He reached into his pocket and pulled it out. Jessica had sent him a text. He chuckled a little, then showed Simone the message.

You guys are fucking ass wipes.

We love you too, Simone texted back.

Whatever. I'll be back in the morning, fuckers.

The two of them burst into giggles again.

"My body hurts from laughing so hard," Simone said. "Lawd Jesus!"

Nolan repeated Mrs. Price's favourite catchphrase, and they started to laugh again. Finally, they gained control of themselves. Simone wearily laid her head on his chest. She closed her eyes and listened to his heart beating rapidly, then slowing its pace. They continued to lie on the floor. Nolan lightly stroked her arm.

"Simone," he whispered. "You asleep?"

"Mmm hmm," she answered. She started to yawn. "I'm asleep."

"Okay." He reached over and pulled down her bedspread to cover them. "Just checking."

"Night," she said.

"Night."

53

"I hope it's comfy," Mike said. He pulled out an extra blanket. "I know it's not as luxurious as you women tend to like, but, if you need some extra pillows, I do have a few more in my bedroom."

"No, Dad, this is great." Dana looked around Nolan's old room. "It's perfect for now."

"Well, I'm just glad that we're under the same roof," he said. "Even if it's only for a few months."

Mike smiled at his daughter as she unpacked her suitcase. She was moving in with him while her townhouse was being completed. She and Freddy had finally bitten the bullet and relocated their business to Toronto. It had been a hard sell to Freddy's wife, Amaya, who wasn't thrilled about uprooting their family. Freddy had to promise to hire help for her and take a yearly family trip to Jamaica to persuade her to move.

Dana was glad to get things moving. Halifax had served them well, but Toronto was a bigger opportunity. Freddy and his family had bought a big new house in Woodbridge right away, but it took her a lot of searching to find a house that would also serve as their office, and then she had to bid on ten locations before she finally lucked out and won one.

Those first months, Dana wondered if they had miscalculated the risks. The Toronto market was much more unpredictable than she'd thought. Houses were being snapped up at higher and higher prices and in record time. She worried that the market bubble was going to burst the moment they put up stakes.

"Just think big and stay focused," Nolan said to his sister. They were walking through her almost finished townhouse. "You got this."

"I hope so," she said. They went downstairs to the basement. "What do you think?"

"Freddy did an amazing job," he said, whistling. "It's too bad you're not flipping this one. You would get a lot for this."

"You're funny," Dana said. "If I thought that way, I would be flipping every house I moved into. I'm not trying to live with Dad forever."

"He would love it," Nolan said. "He's having a ball having you as a roommate."

"Well, it's not like I see much of him," Dana said. "He's never around. I'm pretty sure he doesn't even sleep in his bed sometimes."

Nolan chuckled as he continued to walk through the basement.

"What's so funny? Am I missing something?"

"The bathroom is a lot bigger than I expected," Nolan said, ignoring her. "Did you design it that way?"

"Stop changing the subject." She stood in front of him. "You know something. Does he have a girlfriend?"

"All I know is that this is a huge bathroom for a home office," he said. "You should have used this space as a kitchen and put the powder room over there."

"Nolan, I'm being serious. Spill it."

He smiled at his sister, then let out a huge sigh.

"This stays between us, got it? I think he's seeing his next-door neighbour. He's probably been staying at her place."

"Wait, the same neighbour he's had for years? From Jamaica?" Dana said. "The beauty queen?"

"Yup! He hasn't said a word to me and, if you ask him, he'll probably deny it, but I think it's been going on for a while."

They walked back up to her living room.

"I don't get it. What's the big deal! They're both adults. Why so hush-hush about it?"

"It's Dad being Dad. He still wants people to see him as the good Catholic boy who would never ever sleep with a divorcee."

"Are you serious? That is so stupid."

"To you it is, but, for him, what others think is important."

"He and Mom have been divorced for years. Why doesn't he just marry her? It's not like we're kids anymore."

"Pam had a very bad marriage and I figure she doesn't want to go down that road again," he said. "Her ex-husband was a nasty piece of work." He walked around, examining the crown moulding. "I'm sure Dad is fine with the status quo."

"I don't know, Nols. If he's hard up telling anyone that he and Mrs. Jones are shacking up, then how's he going to be fine with the status quo? Every man has his limit."

"And all this time I thought you were the sentimental one," Nolan said.

"I am, but I also remember Mom and Dad together," she said, earnestly. "He went along with anything Mom wanted, hoping that she would come back to him, and look how that turned out! I'm just saying I wouldn't be surprised if the status quo doesn't last."

Nolan had seen his father's relationship with Pam transform over the years. It started off tumultuous, but had eased into a solid friendship. Each had ventured into other relationships, but theirs seemed to stand the test of time. Dana hadn't seen Mike's devotion to Pam or how protective he was of her and CJ. But Nolan saw it. He knew how much Pam meant to his father.

"Jesus, I guess I'm the last surviving romantic in this family," he mumbled.

"You and Dad," she said. "Last of a dying breed."

▶

MIKE HAD a love-hate relationship with Saturdays. It was the only day in the week he and Pam could sleep in, wake up slowly, make love, and lounge in bed, eventually getting up to enjoy a cup of coffee together and read the paper quietly in the kitchen over a late lunch. It was his favourite thing—the peace and quiet of being together.

But, as the day stretched into the night, he had to get his head ready for work. He still worked at McKinney's every Saturday night and would get moody when five o'clock rolled around. It meant having to take his shower and put on work clothes to leave the warm nest and head to his evening shift.

"Why don't you come out?" he said, wrapping a towel around his waist. "We can spend the rest of the night together and I can finally introduce you to Tommy."

"No offence, but being in a bar with a bunch of drunk old bitter white men is not my idea of a good time," she said.

He dropped the towel and pulled on his underwear and jeans. "You converted me from my old ways," he said, lying on top of her. He reached under her robe. "Maybe the place could use your charms."

"Will Maureen be there?" she countered.

He kissed her neck, making his way down to her chest. "Uh huh. When is she not there?"

"Then I'll pass." She playfully pushed him off her. "There's only so much of Maureen I can take in a week."

Mike grinned as he crawled back on top of her to kiss her again. As they were kissing, the phone rang.

"It's Silvia," he said. He handed her the phone before heading out the door. "If I don't leave now, I'm going to be late. Wait up for me?"

"I always do," she said to him before turning her attention to her call. "Hi, Silvia! How are things?"

"Not good, Pam," the woman said. "Annalise passed this morning."

Pam sat up.

Annalise had been ill for a while and Silvia had been keeping an eye on her, keeping Pam up to date. Annalise had always blamed her for the attack on CJ.

"If he was with me he would have been safe," Annalise had said, the last time Pam called her. "A yuh brought that wicked man into his life."

Pam clutched the phone, unable to speak. She listened to the details of Annalise's final day and wiped back her tears. She steadied herself and told Silvia that she would come to Jamaica and help with the funeral arrangements.

"God bless you, Pam. Mi know you and Anna weren't on the best terms with what happened to that poor child, but it was her grief talking. She knew deep down you did the best by that boy."

Pam nodded.

It didn't matter what Silvia said, she still felt like she'd left things unresolved with Annalise. The same way her relationship with CJ felt unresolved; his feelings had seemed to sour since the last time Dex had shown up in their lives.

Dex had been arrested and sent back to prison with no expectations of parole. He was never going to hurt them again, but CJ still seemed angry with her. She prayed that in time it would get better—it had happened before. She was sure it would happen again.

When Mike returned home from his shift, Pam was on the

phone, making flight arrangements for the funeral. He held her hand as she told him about Annalise's death, wondering if it was a good idea for her to go to Jamaica alone. He worried about her relapsing.

After her last bout of depression, the doctor had changed her antidepressant medication one more time. She'd hated the new meds. They left her drained, with a low sex drive. She'd begged her doctor to put her back on the previous prescription, but he wanted her to give the drug a chance.

After some time, she'd started to come around again. She was happier than she had been in a while. Her sexual appetite had returned ferociously, with them both skipping work and locking themselves away in her apartment. Yet, despite this return to her old self, Mike still worried the trip would be too much.

"Are you sure that I can't go with you?" he asked her. "I can move my schedule around and get my shifts covered."

"No... no, I'll be fine," she said. "I promise. And I need you to be with CJ. I'm still trying to figure out how to tell him about his grandmother."

"I don't think it would do him any good to find out that she'd died," Mike said. "It would only upset him."

"You're right." She sighed. "The nurses say he's still a little jittery at nights. I'll be so happy to have him home with us, once the doctor gives him his six-month assessment."

"Pam, I know that you think they are going to approve him living at home, but I don't think that's going to happen anytime soon. He's still on his feeding tube."

"I know, Mike... I know," she said. "But I need to keep my hopes up. It helps when I keep positive."

A few days later, Mike drove her to the airport. She was scheduled to be gone for ten days, returning right after the funeral.

He was surprised how much he ached for her while she was gone. It had been a while since the two of them had been apart. He longed to feel her body pressed against his each night and missed waking up with her in his arms. The ache made him feel good about their relationship, though, and even giddy when he got up the nerve to tell Dana about her.

When Dana had stayed with him, he'd gone to great lengths to keep his relationship with Pam private. He felt he had to hold onto his moral virtue. He didn't want his family thinking that he was always next door, screwing the neighbour.

"You don't seem too surprised," he said to his daughter. She was over for dinner and he just came out with it. "I thought you would have some smart-ass remark for me."

"Come on, Dad," she said. "I'm happy for you. I really am. I'm looking forward to getting to know her."

"You might be able to on Saturday," he said. "She's in Jamaica for a funeral, but she's coming home tomorrow. I'm hoping to bring her to the opening."

"Do you think that's a good idea? Mom is coming down for the party and it might be a little awkward for her, meeting your girl-friend for the first time."

"Why would it be? I had to suck it up with Rich."

"Be nice, Dad," Dana said. "It's been rough for Mom since Rich left."

Meghan's divorce had been a surprise to almost everyone. She had fought hard for her marriage and had endured two years of couples therapy, only to have Rich announce that their marriage was not worth saving. Dana was frankly glad to see Rich finally leave their lives, but she hated how it had destroyed her mother.

"Look, I will never pour salt on an open wound," he said. "I still care for your mother, even after all these years, but I can't help feeling slightly vindicated that they broke up. What happened, anyways? Did she dump him?"

"Come on, Dad. Let's just drop it."

"Why?" he said. "I'm just curious; did she complain that he wasn't home enough? Or was he getting a little action on the side?"

"Dad! Just stop," she said. "I know that you're still mad at Mom for leaving you, but her life was no picnic after you guys divorced. Rich was a jerk, okay! He was a fucking asshole who talked down to Mom for years, and she just took it; and then, after all the years of grief and verbal abuse, he ended up leaving her. So don't make fun!"

"I'm sorry, honey. I had no idea. I just assumed... I'm sorry, Dana."

"She's gone through a lot the last few years," she said. "Just try and be nice—for me."

"Of course I will," he said, patting her hand. "She's staying with Maureen, right? I'm sure Maureen will be dragging her to McKinney's tonight. I'll be sure to ply them with drinks and make sure they have a great time."

"See, was that so hard?" Dana smiled at him. "I appreciate it, Dad."

That night he went out of his way to be pleasant to everyone in the pub. Tommy was usually McKinney's ambassador of pleasantries, while Mike would hustle to complete everyone's order, but that night Mike was in the best of moods. He was excited that Pam would be home soon.

She had told him on the phone how beautiful the funeral was, and that, despite Annalise's old criticisms of her, the rest of the family had embraced her with open arms. She felt at peace with the whole situation and was happy and looking forward to coming home. Anxious to have her back, Mike filled everyone's beer glasses to the rim and made every cocktail stronger than usual.

When Maureen and Meghan arrived, he showed them to the best seats at the bar and, as he'd promised Dana, was a perfect host and comped all of their drinks. Maureen was soon high and tickled by all the attention.

"Megs, if I knew that he would be this generous, I would have made you fly out here every weekend," she said, finishing her third beer. "Nice to see you in good spirits, Mikey!"

"Maureen, not even that nasty-nice attitude of yours is going to dampen my mood," he said. "Can I top you ladies off?"

"Thanks, Mike," Meghan said. "It's good to see you."

"And it's nice to see you as well," he said, helping another customer. "You're looking well."

Maureen playfully bumped shoulders with Meghan. They both watched Mike talking with one of his regulars. By the end of the night, when the last patron had left, Tommy, Mike, Meghan, and Maureen sat in the back booth talking. Maureen told story after story about the good old days. The one thing the O'Sheas were good at was spinning long-winded humorous tales.

"Come on, Tommy." Maureen dragged him to his feet. "You never dance with me. Show a girl a good time, won't you?"

"All right, all right," Tommy said, putting his arms around her waist as they walked to the jukebox. "But I get to choose the song."

Mike and Meghan sat at the booth, watching them dance to Bonnie Raitt's "I Can't Make You Love Me" as they nursed their drinks.

"Well, she finally got a dance out of him," Mike said. "He's in for it now."

Meghan laughed as she sipped her beer. "So tell me, what's going on with you these days? I've never seen you so happy. I'm assuming you have someone special that's making you smile this much."

"It's pretty obvious, eh? Her name is Pam. We've been seeing each other for some time now. Oh, and don't mention it to Maureen. The two of them don't really get along."

"Really?" Meghan said. "How come?"

"She's actually Maureen's boss," he said.

"She's Maureen's boss?" Meghan said. "The neighbour woman with the two kids?"

"One and the same," Mike said, laughing as Maureen corralled Tommy into another dance.

"I had no idea!" Meghan said. "You never talked much about her. Anything I've ever heard was from Nolan or Maureen. I didn't realize how close you were."

"It didn't start off that way," he said. "In the beginning, we couldn't stand each other. She had a mouth on her—actually, she still does, but the kids were friends and were in the same class. We also had a lot in common being single parents."

"It sounds like you have a lot of history together."

"We do." he said. "We lost our way for a bit. Nolan moving to Halifax... and she got married... anyways... things ended up working out for us."

"That sounds nice," Meghan said, clearing her throat. "I'm really happy for you both and... and maybe I can meet her while I'm in town."

"You just might," he said smiling brightly. "I'm hoping to bring her to Dana's shindig."

"You should!" Meghan said. "You should bring her."

"Really?"

"Absolutely. Why not?"

"Dana seems to think that it might not be a good idea," he said. "She thinks that it might upset you."

He remembered the awkward phone calls in the years before Nolan moved to Halifax. The snide remarks Meghan would make about Pam after her weekly talk with Nolan. Nolan had obviously told her a lot about Pam, because after each conversation she'd snap at Mike, reminding him that Nolan was their son and Mike should be taking Nolan to the barbershop to get his hair cut and Mike should be the one to help him with his overdue book reports, not some random beauty queen neighbour. He got the distinct feeling that Meghan didn't like hearing about her.

"God, no," Meghan said. "That's silly! I would love to meet her."

"Meet whom?" Maureen said. She and Tommy were back at the booth, holding hands.

"No one," Mike said, downing his beer. "You two finished two-stepping? Are we gonna call it a night?"

"Yes and no." There was a glint in Maureen's eye. "Do you think Megs can stay at your place tonight?"

"At my place?" Mike asked. "What for?"

Maureen gave him the look of death. "I invited Tommy over for a nightcap," she said. "I thought you and Megs would like to catch up while Tommy and I hang out for a few more hours, Michael."

Mike sighed. He looked over at Tommy, who had a grin on his face.

"Don't worry, Mikey," Tommy said. "I promise to make sure your cousin gets home safe."

"Jesus." Mike got up and started to clear off the table.

"Maureen, I don't think that's a good idea," Meghan said. "All of my stuff is at your place—"

"No, no, no," Maureen said adamantly. "It's fine. Mike knows that it's fine. He has a spare room... more than enough room for you to bunk."

"It's okay, Megs," he said, glaring at Maureen. "I don't mind."

"Are you sure?" she asked. "I don't want to be a bother."

"It's fine," he said.

"Perfect." Maureen clasped her hands together. "Okay, Tommy, let's go."

"Mike, you got the lights?" Tommy asked. He wrapped an arm around Maureen's waist.

"Yeah, sure," Mike said.

After a few minutes, the place was pitch dark. He locked the front door and pulled down the gate. The night air was chilly.

Mike zipped his jacket shut. "I hope you don't mind, but I usually walk home," he said. "It's not far."

"I don't mind," she said. "It'll sober me up."

They walked in silence up Bayview Avenue. There were not many cars out at 3:00 am in the morning, which made the silence deafening.

"Maureen must be on cloud nine right now," Meghan noted. "As long as I've known Tommy, she's been after him."

Mike grimaced as they headed to the lobby of his building. They stood for a while, waiting for the elevator to arrive. Mike looked over at Meghan and she tried to smile at him, but he swiftly turned away and pressed the elevator call button harder.

"Mike, if this makes you uncomfortable, I can call a cab and go to Dana's place. I really don't mind."

"No... you can stay at my place," he said. "Stay as long as you like. I usually sleep at Pam's anyways."

"Great." Meghan's voice was strained. "That works out perfectly."

Once inside his apartment, he showed her where the bathroom was and where to find all the extra blankets and pillows.

"If you need anything, I'll be next door," he said. "Sleep well."

"Thanks, Mike. I really appreciate this."

Mike went to Pam's place and turned on the lights. It was almost 4:00 am. He crawled into bed, but his head started to throb. Wide awake, he looked up at the popcorn ceiling, worried that having Meghan in his apartment was a mistake. He wasn't attracted to her anymore, but the idea of her sleeping in the bed he shared with Pam made him feel guilty.

He looked back at the clock and saw that it was 4:30 am. He needed to sleep, but his headache wasn't getting any better. He opened the drawer to Pam's nightstand and felt around for the bottle of Tylenol, but instead felt several bottles. He swore as he turned on the lamp. He began pulling out bottles of antidepressant medication. By the sixth bottle, he was looking at the labels, slowly realizing that it was six months worth of unopened pills.

He lined them up in chronological order as he tried to make sense of it. How had he missed it? When was the last time he saw her take her meds? He'd assumed that she was taking them at work.

He found the Tylenol and popped a few pills. He felt betrayed. Tired of all the years he had held her hand through her anxiety and got her help for her depression. He was tired of killing himself so that she would never find that dark place again.

As the sun rose from the horizon and morning came, his feeling of betrayal shifted to anger; he was consumed with a rage he hadn't felt since he'd confronted Dex. He looked at the time and it was almost nine in the morning. He got dressed. Her flight would be arriving in a few hours and he needed to get gas for her car before he headed over to Pearson. He was in the kitchen, making a strong cup of coffee, when the front door opened and Pam stood in the doorway wearing his favourite yellow sundress.

Her eyes gleamed as she dropped her bags and ran to him.

"I took an earlier flight," she said hugging him. "I couldn't wait to see you."

She kissed him lightly on his lips, but he turned his head away.

"What's wrong, baby?" she said.

"You want to know what is wrong with me?" He grabbed her wrist and dragged her into the bedroom. "What the fuck is this, Pam?"

Pam looked at the bottles scattered on her bedspread. She turned to him. "Please, Mike," she said. "Don't yell at me."

"What do you expect me to do? Why are you off your medication?"

"I couldn't do it anymore," she said. "I... I... didn't feel like myself and it was hurting us."

"This is hurting us, Pam!" He threw the pills at her. "You not taking your pills is killing us... it's killing me."

"I'm better. I haven't had an episode since I've been off them."

"Till when, Pam? Until the next time you have a bad day and crawl back in that dark place?"

"Stop screaming at me! You don't know what it's like being

drugged up. Feeling like your body isn't your own anymore. Constantly feeling like shit and not even having the energy to get up in the mornings. Not being able to be with you the way I should."

"Do you think I care about the sex?" he said. "That doesn't matter to me!"

"But it matters to me!" She looked up at him, tears streaming down her cheek.

He looked at her and sat on her bed. He loved her so much, but he didn't have the strength anymore, always wondering which days were going to be good and which were going to push her over the edge.

"I can't keep doing this with you, Pam," he said. "I'm always there to pick you up when you fall. I'm always there to catch you, but it gets to be too much, worrying all the time, Pam. It's too much!"

"Please, Mike. I need you."

"I need you, too," he said, kneeling in front of her. "I've never loved another woman the way I love you. You are my life and I want us to get married one day and bring CJ home and be a family. I want all of it, but not unless you go back on your medication."

"I... I can't," she whispered. She grasped his hands. "Please don't ask me to."

Tears were streaming down his cheeks, too. He gently pulled away from her and left.

"What do you mean they took my chair?" Simone said angrily. She stomped into Jessica's bedroom. "What the fuck, Jessica? Why did you let them take my chair? They had no fucking right."

"I'm sorry, Si," Jessica said. "The bug guy found the source in your chair. He said there was a colony living in there. They must have gotten in through one of the holes in the cushions."

Simone glanced into the living room. Hubert, Timothy, and Felicia were huddled on the couch. Simone's chair had been the butt of their jokes for years and they knew how sensitive she was about it. Jessica was trying to explain that the whole thing was out of her hands.

"That's bullshit," Simone said. "You're a lawyer... they had no right to take my property without... without at least telling me or giving me a chance to move the chair myself."

"Si, there was nothing I could do," she said. "It was a violation of the condo association—"

"Forget it!" Simone glowered at Jessica. "Where is it now? Is it in the trash?"

"Si, they tossed it in the dump. I'm so sorry. If you want we can go out and find another chair. I'll pay for it myself."

"Don't bother," she said, storming out of Jessica's room and into hers.

Her three friends looked on from the couch. Hubert got up and wandered towards Jessica's room.

"I didn't think she would be this mad," Jessica said. "Jesus! I thought she would understand."

"Just leave her for a minute," Hubert said. "Let me talk to her."

Hubert knocked lightly before going in. Simone ignored him. She was at her computer, furiously typing an email to the condo association.

"Really, Si," he said as he closed her laptop. "Are you really going to fire off a letter threatening to sue them? That chair was a hot mess. You should have dumped it a long time ago."

"It meant everything to me," she said. "I've had it forever. It was the first thing I bought with my own money. I met Lia when I bought that chair."

"Is that why you're freaking out?" Hubert said. "Simone, you're obsessing over this chair the same way you're still obsessing over Lia. When are you going to move on with your life?"

"That's easy for you to say," she said. "You're in a two-year relationship with Timothy."

"Relationship?" Hubert said laughing. "Timothy is just a long-ass one-night stand. He knows exactly where this thing between us is going and it's cool. When it's time, we'll move on and that will be the end of it. You need to do the same thing with Lia. Your love life has been at a standstill since forever. You don't even go out with us anymore. You just stay home watching television and playing old maid with Jess's fuck buddy. Seriously, Si, you're letting yourself go."

Simone tilted her head slightly and smirked as Hubert gave her the look. This was the look he gave people when their ten minutes on the pity express was almost up.

Hubert sat on her bed. "Look, Si, I get it. You're getting close to thirty and shit that didn't used to be a big deal is starting to become a huge deal. I totally get it. I'm sick of sitting on the sidelines waiting for one of these fuckers at work to retire. I want to run my own department, but I have to wait for my time to come."

"She has a family, Hubert," she said. "A family and a beautiful inn by the sea and even a kid. That should have been me."

"I don't think so," he said. "You know that's not the life you want."

"Then what kind of life do I get? The one-night stands with random strangers? That's not working for me anymore."

"Well, then regroup," he said. "Figure out what you really want because Lia is not it and neither is that fucked-up chair you've kept on life support. And you need to apologize to Jessica."

Silence.

"I know...I know," she groaned. She got up and headed into the living room. Timothy and Felicia stopped talking as she wandered over to them. Jessica looked pissed off. "I shouldn't have blown up at you."

"Yeah...well," Jessica said. Simone sat next to her and hugged her, laying her head on her shoulder.

"I was being a shit," Simone said. "I'm sorry."

Jessica nodded and hugged Simone back. "Well, I better make sure that I return that sweater I borrowed. I sure as hell don't want you blowing up at me like that again!"

▶

MIKE SAT in Dana's kitchen, hiding away from all the guests. It was impressive how many had turned up for Freddy and Dana's grand opening. They had renamed their business Courtyard Renovations and the new company was set to do more than just flip homes—the business plan was to be a full-service company that did everything, from acquisitions to renovations to real estate sales.

"Dad, what are you doing in here?" Dana asked as she rushed into the kitchen to show the caterers where they could store their extra bags of ice. "Everyone is out in the backyard. Is everything okay?"

"Yes, everything is fine," he said, nursing his Scotch.

"Then why are you hiding out in the kitchen with the caterers instead of helping me celebrate?" She looked at him with concern. "Come on. I need you out there with me."

"Okay, sweetheart," he said.

Almost a hundred people were gathered in the backyard. Mike realized that the party was just starting and he didn't feel like standing around all night with a fake smile on his face while his relationship with Pam was imploding. He'd walked out on her, gone back to his apartment, collapsed on Nolan's bed, and fallen asleep. He'd woken a few hours later to the smell of fresh coffee and bacon and instantly wanted to run back, lay his head on her lap, and tell her that he'd be there for her, no matter what she did. But he was too exhausted to go down that road again. He was sick of fighting her about her health and needed a little time away from her to clear his head.

He had forgotten that Meghan was still over and wandered out of the bedroom to find her in his kitchen making breakfast. She'd set the table the way she did when they were married: The middle filled with condiments, their two plates neatly centred on place-mats, a carafe of coffee between them. Mike sat down and she laid strips of bacon on his plate, brought out the frying pan and dished out hot scrambled eggs. She sat down next to him and whispered a quick prayer before they began eating.

He hardly had an appetite for anything. Given the paper-thin walls, Meghan probably had picked up what was going on between him and Pam.

After breakfast, he got dressed and drove Meghan back to Maureen's house.

"Okay," Meghan said as she unbuckled her seatbelt. "Thanks for putting up with me, Mike. I hope I wasn't too much of a bother."

"No... no," he said, realizing that he was being rude. "Not at all. It was nice having you over. Thanks for breakfast, Megs."

"That's the least I could do," she said, patting his hand. "Do you want to come in for a minute? Maureen sent me a text letting me know that she's gone for the afternoon. Probably out with Tommy."

"I probably should get going," he said.

"Mike," she said, placing her hand on his, "do you want to come in for a moment? Maureen is going to be gone for a while." She leaned over and kissed him softly on his lips.

He sat for a moment, slowly coming around to what Meghan wanted. She kissed him again. He started to kiss her back, feeling her lips part. His pulse raced, and before he could take a breath, they were heading up the stairs, ripping off their clothes. They barely made it to the landing before Mike was inside her.

Meghan cried out.

He grasped her shoulders and held her down as he pumped in and out of her before he collapsed. His face went white. He pulled out, dripping on her leg. "I have to go," he said. He left quickly without saying a word.

He drove back to his building and sat in his car for several minutes before he angrily started to punch the dashboard, cracking the plastic shield over the speedometer. He looked at his hand. It was covered with blood. He started to cry as he watched the blood drip over his car mat.

What had come over him? One minute he was anxiously waiting for Pam to come home, prepared to sweep her off her feet and maybe even propose to her for the seventeenth time in hope that her answer would change. And now he was alone in his car with a bleeding hand, feeling directionless as everything slipped away from him.

He looked at the wound and could see that the blood was congealing. His knuckles still ached and he knew he had to dress them, but he liked the throbbing. He needed to feel the hurt. It felt better than the blinding white betrayal that blazed deep in his heart.

He had arrived at Dana's feeling barely human.

"This handsome fellow here is my father," she said, introducing him to some broker.

"It's almost a family affair," Dana said to another guest as she linked arms with him. "Our dad taught Nolan and I everything about fixing houses, so you know it's in our blood, going all the way back to our great-grandfather."

Midway through the party, Mike saw Meghan and Maureen arrive.

Dana smiled when she saw her mother and walked up to them. "Hi Mom, Maureen," she said kissing each on the cheek. "Dad, why don't you hang out with the ladies for a bit? You seem like you could use a better distraction. You guys be nice to him, he's been unusually quiet the entire evening."

"What's wrong, Mikey?" Maureen said, chiding him. "Cheer up! Your little girl is about to make a bundle with this business of hers."

Meghan quietly looked on as he tried to force a smile. He lifted his empty glass to indicate that he was going to get another drink and walked away.

"What's eating him?" he heard Maureen say.

"Nothing," Meghan replied. "He's just in one of his moods."

Mike was occasionally joined by Dana during the party, but, for the most part, Nolan and Freddy kept him company, talking and laughing. Even so, he was still having a miserable time.

When most of the guests had left, Meghan came up to him

with a bottle of Forty Creek from the bar. She poured out two stiff drinks.

"Cheers," she said, clinking her glass against his before downing hers and pouring another. "You seem more wound up than before."

He remained silent and continued to nurse his drink.

"Mike, it wasn't that long ago that the both of us were happy together," she said. "For a while, we were everything to each other. Do you remember how it was when we were first married? How much we wanted each other? We couldn't wait for Dana to take her nap so we could sneak away to make love. We never could make it to the bedroom. Like today. Things always got out of hand."

Meghan stopped and he felt his face harden.

"Mike, it didn't matter whether we were in a good place or not, being together was always our saving grace," she continued. "And the one thing we could always count on was feeling that special connection afterwards. It was strong, getting us in trouble, at least twice. But for the first time since I've known you, I felt dirty afterwards. I felt like a woman who has knowingly slept with another woman's husband."

He looked up at her and watched her swallow a big gulp of her drink. He could see her eyes were filled with tears. She was trying to fight back her emotions.

"You love her, Mike," she said. "I never understood or cared that you were in love with her. It didn't matter to me because, no matter what happened... who we were with... you were always my husband. We would always have that connection. Now... now it's clear that whatever happened between the two of you this morning... well... you need to find a way to fix it because, as much as she needs you, you need her more."

"I don't know how to get past it," he said. "I don't know how to get back to where it was before everything went to hell."

"You just do, Mike," she said placing her hand on his. "The

biggest mistake I made with you was that I gave up on us too quickly. We should have gone through hell and back a thousand times before even thinking of giving up. If you love her, then tell her. Whatever it takes. Fight for her as hard as you can."

Mike nodded. He put his drink down, got up from his seat and placed his hand on Meghan's shoulder. He kissed her cheek and then left without saying goodbye to anyone. When he got home, he rushed up to Pam's apartment and walked in to find her at the kitchen table, sitting in front of a bottle of pills and staring out the window.

He knelt in front of her and held her hand and kissed it. Tears were streaming down his cheeks as he looked up at her. He could see that her eyes were red from crying. She gave him such a doleful look.

"Pam, I'm sorry about this morning. I should never have come down on you like that. It was wrong and I want you to know that—"

"Mike, you were right," she said. "It kills me to say this, but we can't continue to be together like this. Not when things aren't right with me."

"No, Pam," he said. "I overreacted—"

"Please… just listen to me. I spent the entire afternoon staring at this red pill… this tiny thing… it seems to hold my entire future in it." She drifted off and looked away for a moment. "I… I sat here trying to figure out if I could do it. If I could just take the pill that would save us. But I can't and that scares me so much, because not even your love is enough to make me want to get better. That's when I realized that I haven't been doing this for myself, I've been doing it for you. If I'm going to get better I need to want it for myself."

"Pam," he said, gripping the sides of her dress. "I don't want you to do this alone."

"I have to," she said. "I need to stop depending on you to be happy. It's not helping me and it's not fair to you."

"What does that mean for us?" he asked as his throat started to collapse on itself. "I can't lose you."

"You won't lose me," she whispered. "You're the best thing that has ever happened to me, but if there is any 'us' then it has to be when I'm in a better place – once I get a handle on me. I'm going to see my doctor tomorrow to talk to him about switching meds. Hopefully, he'll find a prescription that is better and... and I'm going back to therapy. Actually, I had an emergency session over the phone this afternoon. I'm not giving up on us. I promise."

He nodded. He looked at her and broke down with his head on her lap. She bent down and held him as his tears fell.

"I love you," she whispered. "I want you to know that, okay?" She lifted his head from her lap and kissed him on his cheek, got up and walked into her bedroom, locking the door behind her.

Mike sat alone at her kitchen table and looked down at the cup of cold tea that hadn't been touched. He reached for it to dump it in the sink and noticed that the red pill was gone. He wasn't sure what it meant, just that he had to trust her to be able to do it on her own, and pray that she would come back to him.

55

For the past six years, Simone had quietly continued her private Wednesday evening meetings with her brother at St. John's Nursing Home. The time was sacred to her. The nursing home staff expected her. Her co-workers covered for her. Her friends always worked around it.

The first few years had been hard. She'd watched her kid brother go through vigorous rehabilitation, only to gain limited mobility and speech. He was frustrated over his inability to talk or feed himself. He was not able to complete the simple task of lifting his arm to scratch his nose. The only way he could relay his thoughts was by a grunt, a guttural laugh or, if he had the strength, a hand clap.

On bad days, he would lie in bed, staring out the window with tears streaming down his face. Simone didn't know what to do on those days. The therapist recommended just talking to him, even though he wouldn't respond. She suggested that repeating stories often would help him learn and remember what was going on around him. Anything to keep him engaged and feeling like he wasn't forgotten.

It was tough. Simone had never been much of a talker. She

found herself rambling on about her day and then would wonder if he'd heard or even cared. But she kept trying and eventually he'd start to respond with a smile or laugh. It was those days that she cherished the most.

She would sit and have dinner with him and chatter on, then she would read to him. He liked anything science fiction so she read him everything from Ray Bradbury to H.G. Wells. His favourite seemed to be the *Hitchhiker's Guide to the Galaxy* series. When she read these he would laugh loud and long and clap his hands.

She loved to see him smile. She could see remnants of the old CJ trying to break through. The slight smile echoed that of the young boy she had grown up with.

That evening, she was delayed by an unexpected meeting with Cynthia after work. Her boss had called her into her office to let her know that there may be room in the budget to incorporate another producer position and that they were looking at her. It was a long shot, but Cynthia was confident that she could get the promotion. She didn't want to tell Jessica or Hubert, afraid to jinx it, but she was anxious to tell her brother. She knew it would make him happy.

When she arrived, he gave her a huge smile. It was the biggest smile she'd seen from him in years. She sat next to him and kissed his hand. He was in a very good mood and that made her even more excited to share her news.

"CJ," she said, "I have some amazing news! Can you hear me?"

His eyes wandered off to the brightly coloured painting on the wall. He grunted and then turned his head to her.

"Good," she said, smiling. "You remember my boss, Cynthia? Well, she told me today that they're looking to promote me and make me a producer."

He looked at her and gave her another broad smile and tried to clap.

"I know, right?" she continued. "It's everything I've been

working towards. They're also looking at other candidates, but Cynthia thinks I have a good chance. They won't decide anything for a while, but this is huge."

She talked on about her job and how she had dreamt of being a producer and that one day she hoped to start her own production company.

He smiled at her as he listened.

"God, I'm just going on and on," she said. "Your nurse said you had a good day. She said you completed your rehab like a champ."

CJ shrieked happily as he rocked back and forth. She had never seen him move his upper body so easily. She laughed and gave him a big hug.

"Oh wow," she said. "Is that what you've been working on? Good job, little brother!" He leaned his head to one side. "And I'm sure it helps that they just hired a cute therapist. Don't think I didn't notice." She smiled when he rolled his eyes at her. "Well, Pam is going to be really happy to see your improvements."

His smile quickly faded away and he turned towards the picture on the wall. She sensed that he was still angry with their mother. Mike had told her that he was refusing to acknowledge her again and that it was crushing Pam to see that his anger towards her still hadn't subsided.

"It's okay, we'll change the subject, okay?" she said. "I saw Nolan this morning! He's co-hosting a television show called *House Helpers*. I'm sure Mike has told you. CJ, you should see him. He's all Hollywood now and getting recognized everywhere."

CJ turned to her and laughed.

"All the ladies go crazy when they see him. He grew his hair out and has a whole lot of muscles now. He's not that skinny kid we used to know. Jess gets a kick out of it. They're kind of seeing each other and I'm not going to lie, but it's kind of weird living with Jess and seeing them together. I mean, I'm happy for them and everything, but it's still strange seeing them all lovey-dovey. I guess I'm just used to the old Nolan I would mash-up playing video games and... seeing him all grown and... well... it's been an adjustment. Anyways, his show has been doing great. You know what? The next time I come over I'll bring my laptop so you can watch an episode! They're talking about having him take over once Mac retires. It would be an amazing opportunity for him."

Simone trailed off and then sat silently for a while. CJ looked at her and she could tell that he wanted to share his thoughts and give her his perspective. It killed her that CJ had no way to speak his feelings. She grabbed his hand and squeezed it, then pulled out a book.

"I know you're not into kiddie books because you're a grown-ass man and everything, but you might like these Harry Potter books," she said. "The films are really good, but I bet the books are better. Do you want to give it a go?"

He grunted.

She began reading the first chapter of *The Sorcerer's Stone* about the young wizard who was forced to live under the stairs. By the end of the chapter, she was hooked. She read several more chapters, almost forgetting that she was there to entertain her brother.

"Wow, this is actually a pretty good book," she said, looking up at the end of the sixth chapter.

CJ's eyes were fixed on the ceiling fan, his mouth slightly open. The ceiling fan wasn't moving. She stopped for a moment and looked back at his face and then grabbed his hand and squeezed it. He remained still, staring at the fan.

"CJ? No, no, no. CJ! Please... no... not now... CJ!"

She ran out to get the evening nurse. The nurse called the doctor and when they arrived, they ushered her out of the room while they checked his vitals. When they came out, the doctor said that CJ was gone.

"But he was sitting with me laughing," she said.

Simone stumbled to the bench outside his room. The nurse sat next to her and gently patted her on the back.

"I don't understand. There has to be a mistake. He was doing so well. He did his rehab today and everything. We were reading a book and he was so happy and..."

"I know, honey," said the nurse. "Sometimes it happens that way. Sometimes they have a really good day before they say goodbye. The fact that you were with him when he died was a blessing. I'm sure it made all the difference to him."

"But I didn't get a chance to say goodbye." Tears spilled down her cheek and she started to sob. "He left without me saying goodbye."

56

Nolan went over to the condo after a chaotic day of shooting. The film crew's generator had broken down and production was halted for three hours before another generator had been located. His construction crew couldn't finish that phase of the project and the production team complained that they needed the footage before the weeklong hiatus.

At nightfall, they had to suspend filming and construction. Nolan was glad the day was over and he looked forward to having the next few days off. He hadn't seen Jessica or Simone in a few weeks and, when Jessica called him to spend the night, he jumped at the chance of simple sex with no strings.

When he walked in, he was annoyed to see Hubert sitting at the dining room table with Jessica, sharing a bottle of wine.

"Hey, Nolan," Jessica said. "I forgot that you were coming over."

His stomach twisted when he saw their solemn faces. "What's wrong?" he said. "Is everything okay?"

"It's Simone," Hubert said. "Her brother died."

"Oh, my God. What happened?"

"Not sure," said Hubert. "Doctor thinks he might have had a stroke. She's pretty devastated. She was with him when he died."

"Where is she now?" he asked. "Is she here?"

"She's in her room," Jessica said. "But, babe, she's not talking to anyone right now."

He walked down the hallway anyway and knocked on her door. "Simone, it's me. Can I come in?"

All he could hear was silence on the other side. He felt Jessica's hand on his shoulder.

"She might be sleeping," she whispered. "Talk to her in the morning, okay?"

"I can't believe he's gone," Nolan said as they walked back to the living room. "My dad was just telling me that he was in good spirits when he saw him on Sunday. Shit, he was laughing and trying to talk to me when I last saw him. I thought it was a sign that he was getting better."

"That's what Simone said," sighed Hubert. "That he was laughing and smiling with her right till the end."

"Oh, man." Nolan pulled his hands through his hair. "She needs to be out here. Not locked in her room."

"I know, hon, just give her a little time alone to process it," Jessica said. "She'll come out when she's ready."

"I need to call my dad," he said. "Excuse me."

He walked out onto the balcony and tried to call. The first few times it went straight to voicemail, but the third try got through. His father sounded distraught.

"Dad, I just heard about CJ," he said.

"Yeah," Mike said hoarsely. "Mrs. Price and I are here with Pam. She's not handling it well right now. Frankly, I'm not handling it very well, either. How's Simone doing?"

"I haven't seen her yet," Nolan said. "She's in her room."

"The poor girl was a mess when she called her mother earlier," Mike said. "I tried to convince her to come over or stay with Mrs.

Price tonight, but she insisted on going home. I'm glad you're there. Look out for her, okay?"

"I will," he told his father.

"Nolan, I can't talk for long. Can we talk more tomorrow?"

"Yeah, sure thing, Dad. Please tell Pam that I'm so sorry."

"Okay, I will."

Nolan walked back into the apartment. He thought about going to check on Simone again, but he knew that the only thing he could do was give her space. He joined Jessica and Hubert at the table and they talked quietly.

Hubert stayed for a little while longer and then left, after telling an unresponsive Simone that he would be back the next day. After a while, Jessica and Nolan went to bed. Jessica had a morning meeting that she wasn't able to cancel and she needed to wake up early to catch the train. After she fell asleep, Nolan lay awake. He tossed and turned until nearly 1:00 am, when he got up and went to the kitchen to get a drink of water. Still feeling restless, he went into the living room to watch some television, but he couldn't concentrate on anything.

He couldn't stop thinking about CJ. When he'd moved back to Toronto, it had hit him hard, seeing CJ. The kid he remembered so vividly was not there anymore. His eyes teared up as he thought about the few times he'd gone with his father to visit him. CJ got so excited when he saw him. He could tell, by the light in his eyes, that visitors made his hell a little less lonely. He wished he had gone to see him more often.

Walking back to Jessica's room, he heard movement in Simone's bedroom and opened the door slightly. She was on her cell phone.

"Hey Lia, it's me," he heard her say. "Please call me. My brother died and I... I... please... just call me if you can. I'll be up."

He watched her crawl under the covers, clutching her phone in her hand as she wept. It tore him apart to hear her cry. He went into her room and lay down next to her. He took the phone from her and placed it on the nightstand and wrapped his arms around her. She started to sob. She turned and buried her head in his chest.

"Shhhh, shhh, I got you, Si. I got you."

She cried in his arms until her voice grew hoarse and then they lay silently staring up at her wobbly ceiling fan, turning at a turtle's pace.

She could feel Nolan lightly caressing her arm. It calmed her to feel his touch.

"I should have been there," she said. "I shouldn't have left him alone."

"You were there for him," he said. "CJ didn't die alone."

"But I should have been there from the beginning to protect him," she said. "He asked me to stay at his graduation party and I told him I couldn't. I told him that I would catch up with him later, but it was just some lousy excuse so I could leave. I was angry with my mother. I was so angry and selfish. If I had just stayed…"

"Si, you had no idea any of this was going to happen," he said. "You can't put it all on your shoulders."

"I can't help it. It hurts so much, Nolan. My heart hurts so much."

"I know it does. It'll hurt like hell for a long time, but you have to hold on to the fact that he's in a better place now. None of us could imagine what it was like for him lying in that bed, day in and day out, not being able to move or communicate with anyone. I could see it in his eyes, what it did to him. How depressed he was."

"But he was making so much progress," she said. "He was trying to get better."

"I know he was, Si, but now he doesn't have to keep trying. He's free now."

Simone started to cry again, thinking about CJ not having to struggle anymore.

Nolan could feel the whole weight of the world on her and wished he could take some of it. He kissed the top of her head. She was finally drifting off to sleep. Moments later, he fell asleep, his arms tightly wrapped around her.

▶

SIMONE WOKE to sunlight streaming through her curtains. She opened her eyes to find Nolan fast asleep next to her. It was almost 6:00 am.

"Nolan," she whispered. "Nols."

"Hey," he said, clearing his voice. "Did you get any sleep?"

She nodded.

He took her hand. "I'm going to stay with you today, okay?" He pushed aside some of the curls that fell on her face. "I don't want you to be alone."

"It's okay… I'm okay. You being with me last night helped."

"Just like old times, huh?" he said. "Except without a window to sneak through and the all-night card games."

Tears started to spill down her cheek.

"Oh no." He used his thumb to wipe them away. "I'm sorry… I didn't mean to upset you."

"No… no, it's okay," she said, sitting up. "I just remember all those times, all those arguments with my mother—you were always there for me."

"That hasn't changed, Si. I'll always be there for you."

"You know, my whole world changed when you moved to Halifax," she admitted. "You were gone. My mother dropped out of my life. Everything that happened with my brother… it was so hard and lonely and I missed you so much. I missed you being there."

Nolan rubbed her lower back. He didn't know what to say. It crushed him, hearing her say that. He sat up and leaned in, gently pressing his forehead against hers. He kissed her tears as they slipped down her cheek. She closed her eyes, trying to hold them back as his lips brushed hers. He then laid her back on the bed and looked down at her. She opened her eyes and could see that he was there for her—only her.

Just then, Simone's stereo came to life with Ludacris' "Move Bitch" blasting from her speakers. Startled by his booming voice, their heads collided as Simone jumped up. She started to laugh, holding her sore forehead. He winced in pain and started to laugh as well.

"Jesus, that gave me a heart attack," he said, rubbing his forehead. "Si, you're the only person I know who needs a high-powered stereo as an alarm clock."

"Well, there's no better way to wake up," she sighed as Lauryn Hill and D'Angelo's "Nothing Even Matters" started to play. "Especially when this song comes on. This song always makes me feel better."

"Do you feel better?"

She nodded.

The vocals filled the room as they listened to the song play.

See nothin' even matters
See nothin' even matters to me
Nothin' even matters
Nothin' even matters to me
You're part of my identity
I sometimes have the tendency
To look at you religiously, baby
'Cause nothin' even matters to me.

He turned to her and held the small of her back. She reached for his hand, slipping her fingers between his as they continued to listen to the song. Nestled next to him, she started to fall back to sleep.

Her cell phone started to ring. She looked up at him. The phone continued to ring. She reached over him to see who it was and quickly sat up.

"Nolan, can you give me a minute? I need to take this."

"Yeah... no problem," he said, awkwardly getting out of bed. "I guess I'll be in the kitchen."

She jumped up to turn off her stereo. "Lia, give me a second," she said into the phone. "Nolan, wait!"

She crawled over her bed and knelt up next to him and embraced him. He held onto her and buried his face in her mass of curls.

"Thank you for staying with me," she whispered. "Thank you for not letting me go off the deep end."

"Anytime." He kissed the top of her head. "Okay, go and take your call. I'm dying for some coffee right now."

▶

JESSICA WAS IN THE KITCHEN, pouring coffee into her travel mug.

Nolan snuck up behind her and hugged her. "Good morning," he whispered.

"Good morning," she responded sullenly. "I missed you this morning."

"I was checking on Simone," he said. "She had a rough night."

"Is she okay?"

"I think she is. Well, at least better than she was last night."

"So I guess you were with her all night?"

Nolan turned her to him and looked at her, surprised. It wasn't like Jessica to be jealous. She had always maintained that she didn't want anything exclusive.

"What's wrong? Are you okay?"

"Oh, I'm fine." She pulled away from him to grab her laptop. "I'm just a little annoyed. One minute you're lying next to me and the next thing I wake up and you're sleeping in Simone's room."

"Are you serious, Jess? I had to make sure she was okay."

"I'm sorry... I'm being.... I guess it's always a shock just how close you guys are."

"Jess, for a long time Simone was my best friend. Any time she needs me, I'm going to be there for her. Can you be okay with that?"

"Yes, of course." She poured sugar into her mug. "You're right! Look, I'm sorry. I'm not the crazy jealous type. Where you sleep is none of my business."

"Do you want it to be your business?" he asked her. "Because we can make that happen, if that's what you want."

"God, no. I like the way things are... super casual."

"Okay," he said. "Just as long as we're on the same page."

"Absolutely. Look, it's getting late and I have to go or I'll miss my train. Is Simone still asleep?"

"She's on the phone talking to someone named Lia."

"Oh wow," she said, pausing for a moment. "That's big."

"Why?" he asked. "Who's Lia?"

"That's her ex," Jessica said as she packed her briefcase. "The one who broke up with her and moved to Italy to be with an old flame. Simone was a wreck for a while. To be honest, I'm a little surprised that she's talking to her at all."

"I didn't know that was her ex," he said. A pang of jealousy swept over him. It all made sense why she had called Lia in the middle of the night and why Simone was so anxious to speak to her when she called back.

"Well, I guess there are some things about Simone that you don't know." She walked to the door. "I know that you would like to think that Simone is the same girl you grew up with, but she's not. She's lived an entire lifetime since you were kids."

"Yeah, I guess."

"Listen, I don't have to work late tonight. Let's still hang out," she said. "I taped some *Lost* episodes. We can catch up on them and other things."

"Sure," he said, before she walked out the door. "Sounds like a plan."

He could hear Simone still talking to Lia on the phone. He felt foolish being jealous, but at that moment he couldn't handle her turning to anyone—other than him.

Twenty minutes later, he was sitting on the couch reading the paper when Simone came into the living room. He looked up at her. Her eyes were red and puffy. She seemed distracted as she walked into the kitchen and poured herself a cup of coffee, still dressed in her satin boxer pyjamas.

"Everything okay?" he asked.

She sat down next to him. "Not really." She turned on the television.

Nolan sat quietly as she mindlessly flipped through the channels. She finally settled on the World Fishing Network. There was a fishing contest in progress.

The distraction failed. Thoughts of her brother consumed her. She kept her eyes glued to the television, but, when Nolan moved closer to her, she let her head rest on his shoulder. The tears wouldn't stop falling.

Throughout the day, they sat together on the couch with barely a word shared between them. Each seemed able to sense what the other needed. When they were hungry, one would get up and make a sandwich for them to share. When they were thirsty, the other would go get a water bottle. They spent the afternoon flipping through the five hundred and eighty channels.

When Jessica returned home from work, the two of them were on the couch, watching Judge Judy, a bowl of dill pickle chips between them.

"Come on, you guys!" Jessica said. "You need to get out of your PJs. Get up and get some fresh air."

She opened the balcony door, letting a cool breeze rush into the stuffy living room.

"Why don't you both get up and get dressed?" Jessica pulled Nolan to his feet. "We'll all go out and get a bite to eat. My treat!"

"You guys go without me," Simone said. "I'm not feeling up to doing anything."

"Nope! You're coming with us!" Jessica insisted. "We won't be long. Just down the street at Firkin."

"Come on Si," Nolan said. "She's right. I'm starving and I know you must be, too."

Simone reluctantly got up and went to her room and looked around. She didn't know what to do first. She made up her bed. She went into the bathroom and took a long shower. The scalding hot water didn't lessen the ache in her heart, it just made her numb.

When she returned to the living room, Jessica and Nolan were on the couch waiting for her.

"Are you ready to go?" Jessica asked.

Simone shrugged. She picked up her wallet and cell phone. As they were heading out the door, her phone rang.

"Just a second. It's my mom." She picked up the call. "Hi, Mummy... oh hi."

Nolan watched her in the kitchen talking on the phone. Her responses were short. He could tell that she was trying to keep herself from falling apart. Tears streamed down her cheeks. She walked over to the dining room table, sat down and lowered her head, trying to hide herself.

"Yes, I'm still here. I will... but does it have to be so soon... okay... okay... alright. Yes... uh huh," she said. "He's right here." She sat up straight and turned to Nolan. "Mike wants to talk to you." She handed him her phone.

Nolan sat down next to her. He placed his hand on her shoulder. "Hi, Dad," he said.

"Nolan, the funeral has been scheduled for the day after

tomorrow." Mike's voice wavered. "Pam doesn't want to prolong the process and we were able to get CJ's uncles and aunt to come in today. Pam needs Simone to be with her to make some decisions."

"Of course," Nolan said.

"And that includes you," Mike said, his voice cracking. "We need the both of you with us."

Mike's voice stopped. He broke down. Nolan's eyes welled with tears as he heard his father sob. CJ was the boy he'd helped raise from infancy. The boy he proudly cheered for at every soccer tournament. The boy he sat with in the hospital and in the care home.

Nolan lowered his head and suddenly fell apart right along with his father.

Simone watched him cry. She reached out and pulled him to her.

Nolan listened quietly as Mike told him what he needed him to do. When he finally hung up, Simone wiped away his tears.

"What is it?" Jessica asked meekly. "What's wrong?"

"We both have to go home," Nolan said. "They're having the funeral in a few days and we need to be there to help with the arrangements."

"So soon?" Jessica said. "Oh wow!"

"Si, can you be ready in ten minutes?" he said.

She got up and headed to her bedroom.

"Is there anything I can do?" Jessica asked.

"Could you help Simone pack?" he asked her. "CJ's family is flying in tonight and tomorrow morning. My dad and I are going to be driving back and forth, picking everyone up from the airport. We need to leave as soon as possible."

"Absolutely," she said. "I'll go and help her."

"Thank you," he said, getting up. "Tell Simone that I'm bringing my truck around and will meet her outside."

"Okay, I'll let her know. Nolan, do you want me to come with you guys?"

"No… thank you, though. It's going to be crazy over there." He smiled at her. "You'll be at the viewing tomorrow, right?"

"Yes. I'll make sure everyone knows. Just text me the info."

Simone was standing in front of her closet, having a hard time concentrating. Jessica came right in and went into her closet and pulled out a pretty black sundress printed with silhouettes of blackbirds. She then handed her a pair of black slacks and a grey blouse.

"Si, do you want to wear your black flats or the suede pumps?" she asked. "Si?"

Simone just sat down on her bed and stared out her window.

"Come on, hon," Jessica said. "We're almost done. Nolan's waiting out front for you."

Simone got up and finished packing. She went down in a daze and climbed into Nolan's truck and they drove up the DVP to North York. Nolan stopped at his house to grab a few things and then they headed to the complex.

When they arrived, Mrs. Price greeted them at the door. She hugged Simone, who melted into the old woman's embrace. Pam was already sitting at the table with the funeral director. With her were Esma and Mike and CJ's uncles, Phillip and Steven. All of them were trying to sort through the information. Her mother seemed overwhelmed with the decisions in front of her and with everyone in the apartment.

"Mummy, go lay down," Simone said. "You're exhausted. Let me handle this, okay?"

Her mother nodded. She got up to hug her daughter before heading to her bedroom. The crowd thinned out when Mike suggested that Nolan take everyone next door to his apartment, leaving Simone, Mike, and CJ's uncles to go over the options.

▶

Simone finalized everything with the funeral director. She picked a black onyx casket with a cream velvet interior. She imagined her brother telling her to pimp it out, but they only had time for something simple. She picked his favourite song, "End of the Road," which he'd made her listen to over and over in the laundry room. She handled everything from choosing the photos of CJ to what food would be served at the repast. She was exhausted afterwards as she went over the details with her mother, who had just woken from her nap. It was the hardest production she had ever planned.

"This is fine," Pam said.

After the funeral director left, more people arrived. Nolan taxied cousins in from the airport. Esma's husband, with their children, went over to Pam and gave her a big hug. Simone looked over at the boys. They'd grown up together. They were all so tall now. She couldn't help imagining CJ dressing, looking or maybe talking like them, if things had been different.

By midnight, everyone was settled in for the evening. Simone stayed in her old bedroom at Mrs. Price's apartment. The room hadn't changed much. The bed still had the same blue comforter and all of her posters still hung on the walls. Even her old boxes of cassette tapes were still sitting in her closet, exactly where she'd left them. Nolan was sleeping on the couch back at his dad's apartment, where CJ's uncles and cousins were also staying. Mike and Pam sat on the balcony, just like old times, talking about CJ until the sun broke through the horizon.

57

The next day started off hectic, with Mrs. Price rising early to prepare a huge breakfast of ackee and saltfish, fried dumpling and bammy for Pam and all her visitors. Everyone crowded into her apartment, smiling and laughing to keep the mood joyful, and it rejuvenated Simone to feel such positive energy permeating the old familiar place as she sat down to eat.

Her mother sat quietly at the head of the table. She looked dazed as everyone buzzed around her. All the women fussed over her, insisting that she eat, while the men shared stories of Caleb, trying to make her smile.

Nolan walked in with the final out-of-town relative, CJ's Aunt Julie. She was the eldest of the siblings, whom everyone referred to as Sister. She'd lived in Birmingham, England, for over thirty years and hadn't been back to Toronto since Caleb's funeral twenty years before.

"Simone, my darling," she said with a crisp British accent. "I can't believe it's been so long. The last time I saw you was years ago in Jamaica. How are you holding up?"

"As well as can be expected," Simone replied, as she hugged Sister. "How was your flight?"

"Long, but I'm glad to be here with everyone." She grabbed Nolan's arm. "It was nice being picked up by this handsome bloke."

Nolan chuckled.

"Nolan and I had a wonderful conversation on the ride over." She linked her other arm with Simone's. "He tells me that he works in television."

"Yes, he does," Simone said. "He's a local celebrity around here."

"Very good," she said. "And from what I gather he's also very single!"

"No matchmaking today, Auntie." Simone steered Sister towards Pam and her brothers.

"Be careful with this one," Sister said, winking at Nolan. "She will steal your heart when you're not looking."

Nolan laughed out loud. Simone turned and punched him in the shoulder.

After breakfast, they all made their way over to the funeral home, where CJ's body was laid out for the viewing. The morning's jovial mood quickly dampened in the chapel. Simone sat in the back of the room as everyone went over to his open casket to pay their respects. She didn't know if she was strong enough to sit beside him.

Simone quivered, hearing her mother cry out. She couldn't bear it. Her throat closed off and her eyes stung as more tears began to slide down her cheeks.

"Si," Nolan called out to her quietly as he sat down in front of her. "Do you want me to come up with you?"

She shook her head swiftly. It had been easy to plan his funeral and choose his favourite song and greet everyone, but the idea of seeing his lifeless body scared her. She kept seeing the look on his face just after he died.

"It's okay," Nolan said. "Baby steps."

When the family had finished their private viewing, the casket was closed and the doors opened for everyone else to pay their respects. Simone got up and stood with her mother as she greeted guests. Friends of CJ, old teachers, his soccer teammates, and several St. Augustine parishioners were the first to arrive. As the hours went by, more people filtered in. The small room got so packed that the funeral home director opened up a false wall into another room to accommodate the overflow.

Simone and Pam talked to so many people, everyone seemed like a blur. Simone felt like a broken tape recorder as she robotically thanked guests for coming and for their condolences. Pam's co-workers arrived. Several of the doctors, nurses, and staff from her department brought flowers and condolence cards. Maureen was among them and gave Pam a warm hug.

"I'm so sorry about your loss, Pam. I'm praying for you and Simone. I can't imagine how you are feeling. At least you have Simone to lean on. I only have my Amber. I wouldn't know what to do if something ever happened to her. I would be an absolute mess…"

Pam stood emotionless, listening to Mike's cousin. Maureen meant well, but she always said too much when she got nervous and would eventually stick her foot in her mouth. Mike came quickly over to sidetrack her.

"Thank you for your condolences, Maureen," he said. "Come and get a coffee." Pam looked up at Mike dolefully and tried to force a smile.

Then all of Mike's Ryerson University co-workers came into the chapel. Mike was clearly surprised to see them. As he spoke with them, Dana arrived with Freddy and Amaya.

Simone stood next to her mother and watched Dana give her father a big hug. It broke her heart to see Mike in tears. It was amazing how much CJ had meant to everyone. She continued to smile and nod as they all told stories about him. She could feel the love they had for her brother in every warm recollection, though it still felt like a dagger twisting in her heart. She needed a break. When she turned to greet the next set of guests, she faced Cynthia, Hubert, Felicia, and Jessica, and burst into tears. She walked up and hugged each of them as they surrounded her.

The hours dragged on with no end in sight. It was so hot; the crowd grew larger and louder; overpowering music was being piped in over the PA system. Father Paul stood next to Simone, practically giving her his homily as he spoke to her about love and being called home. Her face felt strained and sore as she kept up a weary smile. She barely paid attention to what he was saying, but didn't have the energy to excuse herself.

"Excuse me, Father," Nolan said. "Do you mind if I steal Simone away for a minute?"

"Yes, of course," the priest said. He patted Simone's hand. "Please don't be a stranger, Simone. We're here for you and your mother."

"Thank you," she said.

Nolan led her into the empty service hallway and they walked for a while before they found an exit to the parking lot. Her head was throbbing and she was so grateful for the fresh air. They sat on the curb by the exit door.

"Have you eaten anything since breakfast?" he asked.

She shook her head.

"Well, you're lucky that you have an awesome friend who snagged the last Aero bar from the vending machine."

"Thanks."

Silence.

"It's overwhelming, huh?" he asked.

"It feels like this day is never going to end," she said. "It's been the longest day of my life."

"I know." He held out the last piece of chocolate. She reached out and took it. "I think it helps that we're all here together. It's nice seeing everyone come out. So many people loved him."

They sat and watched random people walk up and down the sidewalk.

She wished she could spend the rest of the time hiding out in the parking lot, but felt guilty leaving her mother alone. She patted Nolan's knee before getting up, then reached for his hand, helping him to his feet.

Nolan slipped his arm around her waist.

When they got halfway to the viewing room she stopped and hugged him. They stood in the middle of the hallway while she rested in his arms. The fluorescent lights began flickering sporadically.

"How did we last all this time without each other?" she whispered. "I don't think I would have gotten through any of this without you."

"You're stronger than you think."

"Nolan, no matter where we end up in life you'll always be my best friend. You'll always be the love—"

"There you guys are," Jessica yelled out to them from the doorway. "Everyone is looking for you. I think the viewing is almost over."

"I had no idea how late it was," Simone said.

"Wait," he said in a low voice. "Finish what you were going to say."

She gently touched his face. "It's not important. Let's head back."

"Come on guys!" Jessica said. "The hallway lights are fucking creepy."

Most of the visitors had left. Simone was glad, but she knew that this would be her last chance to say goodbye. She walked over to the casket as one of the staff members was collecting all of the flowers that surrounded him.

"Would you like to see him before you go?" the woman asked her.

Simone touched his casket lid lightly and nodded.

The woman pulled up a chair and then opened the casket.

He looked different. He had a waxy unreal look. His face didn't seem the same. Nothing about him felt the same. She placed her hand on his, hoping that would invoke a feeling or memory, but all she felt was emptiness.

Nolan was watching Simone with her brother. She sat perfectly still, holding CJ's hand. Nolan restrained himself from going to her. He just kept watch as she wept. Pam brushed past him and stood by her daughter.

"He shouldn't be here alone," Simone said. She felt her mother's arms around her. "Are they going to keep a light on for him? He doesn't like the dark. That's why I always left a light on for him."

"I know, baby. We all did."

Nolan stepped out of the room and closed the door, giving them privacy. His father was in the hallway, speaking to Hubert and Jessica.

"We're having a few close friends and family over," he said to them. "A small wake. I think Simone would appreciate you guys being there."

"Of course," Jessica said. "What time should we come over?"

"In about an hour," Mike said.

"I'll text you the address," Nolan said.

"Okay," Jessica said.

"Come on, let's get out of here," Hubert said to Jessica.

She nodded. She watched Nolan walk over and embrace Simone.

"I think we deserve about three stiff martinis first," she replied.

▶

WHEN JESSICA AND HUBERT ARRIVED, they heard reggae pouring down the hallway and walked towards the music. Neighbours stood in small groups, all chatting together outside the apartment doors. Jessica couldn't tell if it was a wake or a floor party. She looked at Hubert, who shrugged his shoulders and smiled as they headed to Mike's apartment.

When they walked in, they found the place filled with people talking and laughing over the loud music and children running in and out of the bedrooms chasing one another. It felt more like a family reunion with everyone gathered under one roof, but it was just people who wanted to take a moment to put aside their sadness and celebrate CJ's life. Amid laughter, food and drink, each of them told stories of the boy they had all loved.

Jessica and Hubert walked into the kitchen, hoping to find Simone or Nolan. They spotted Mike at the kitchen table, talking with CJ's uncles and cousins, drunkenly passing bottles of rum and whisky around. They were toasting CJ, toasting one another, toasting their favourite sports teams. They had drunk so much that their toasts sounded like incoherent ramblings.

"I want to say something to you, Mike," Phillip said. "I want to say it before I forget. I have been drinking all day and if I don't get this out now I will pass out and forget, so everyone hush! Someone turn off the damned music," he yelled. "Everyone quiet down!" He lifted his drink to Mike. "Yessah! I want to drink a toast to you, Mike." He staggered to his feet. "When my brother Caleb died you were this white guy who sat in the corner while we mourned him. Over the years you went from being that white guy to Michael the neighbour to our bredren Mike. You were a father to CJ when we couldn't and, while you are not blood, you will always be family to us! We recognize you, my brother. We recognize you!" Phillip lifted his drink high in the air.

The men in the apartment held their drinks up as they all saluted him.

Mike was in tears as everyone crowded around him, drunkenly patting him on the back.

Hubert and Jessica continued through the apartment and

scanned the crowd, looking for Simone. Esma remarked their lost expressions and came over.

"Hello there," she said. "You're Simone's friends, right?"

They both nodded.

"Welcome," she said, smiling at them. "Please let me take your coats."

"Thanks." Hubert handed her his blazer. "We were looking for her. Have you seen her?"

"I'm sure she's around here somewhere," she said. "I saw her with Nolan a while ago, but this place is a madhouse. Try next door at Pam's apartment."

Pam's apartment was just as packed, with guests sitting in every available spot. They were greeted by Mrs. Price, who insisted that they each grab a plate of food. Hubert asked if she had seen Simone and Nolan.

"Lawd, dem two probably sitting outside," she said, pointing at the balcony door. "Right through there. Mekhace, unuh fill your plates first before everyone nyaam all dis food. Eat something."

Jessica and Hubert smiled at each other. So this was the famous Mrs. Price. They had heard more about her from Simone than about Simone's own mother.

As they stood in line at the food table, Dana and Freddy arrived. Jessica waved them over. She and Hubert were relieved to see people they knew. They were starting to feel like outsiders crashing a party.

The four of them went out on the balcony. Simone and Nolan were sitting quietly next to each other on an old sofa. As they got closer, they could see that they were fast asleep, Simone's head resting on Nolan's shoulder.

Simone woke up when she felt someone sit next to her. She smiled when she saw that it was Hubert.

"Hi!" She yawned, then smiled. "You guys came! I'm so glad you made it. It means so much to have you here."

"Anything for our girl," Hubert said, trying to balance his plate on his lap.

"Nolan's out cold," Jessica said, laughing.

"He's been running on fumes the last two days," Simone said. "Sit! Sit! I'm going in to get something to eat."

Hubert and Jessica and Freddy started tucking in.

Dana sat across from her brother. He continued to snore. She shook her head and then kicked his foot. "Wake up, slacker."

He opened his eyes. "Hey," he said drowsily. Everyone laughed at him. "How long was I out?"

"Long enough," Dana said.

Nolan sat up. He smiled at Jessica, who was sitting where Simone had been. He then looked past her, searching the crowd. He spotted Simone in the kitchen, talking to some of the guests.

Jessica squeezed his hand to gain his attention.

"When you said that you and Simone were like family, I really had no idea just how much. Did you grow up with all of these people?"

"Pretty much," he said. "I haven't seen a lot of them in years, but, yeah, this was my life."

"I think I get it," she said. "Surrogate family of sorts."

He nodded.

Simone came back out with a beer and a plate of food for Nolan. He smiled and thanked her and started to eat.

Jessica squirmed. It hadn't even crossed her mind to bring him something to eat. In fact, she also hadn't really noticed how in tune Nolan and Simone were until now. She sat quietly observing the way they interacted with each other. The way Simone inattentively noshed off Nolan's plate while he intuitively handed her his beer to sip, each of them carrying on conversations with other people.

She also noticed the way Nolan looked at Simone. He always seemed lost in thought. Jessica wanted to believe that the feelings Nolan had for Simone were platonic, but it was starting to become clear there was more than shared history drawing them together.

As the night started to wind down, Jessica and Hubert said their goodbyes. Jessica offered Nolan a ride home, but he declined, saying that he was going to stick around until all the guests had left. Nolan could see that she was disappointed. He leaned down to kiss her and said that he was glad she'd come over. She smiled, now yearning for a little more time with him.

▶

AFTER SAYING goodbye to the final guest, Nolan wandered back into Mike's apartment. His father was passed out on the couch. He didn't have the heart to wake him. He thought about crashing in his dad's bedroom, but remembered that Pam was staying there. CJ's relatives had taken over every extra bed and couch in both apartments. He thought about going home, but he was too tired to drive.

He went across the hallway and sat in front of Mrs. Price's doorway, pulled out his phone. It was almost 1:00 am. He wasn't sure if she would still be awake. He sent a text, hoping that she would come for him. He leaned back against the wall and started to fall asleep. A few minutes later, Mrs. Price's door opened. Simone reached down for his hand and helped him to his feet.

He followed her into the apartment to her old bedroom. She tried to reach for the extra pillow and blanket on the top shelf of the closet but wasn't tall enough, so he pulled them down. He stood close behind her, offering her zero room. They chuckled briefly as he moved out of her way.

"Good night," he said, heading to the couch in the living room. "Get some rest, okay?"

"You too. Good night," she said as she closed her bedroom door.

Nolan collapsed on the sofa. He was beat from the long day but was distracted, knowing that Simone was asleep in the next room. He missed the warmth of her body and found it hard to fall asleep without her next to him. He drifted off, gazing at the dark hallway, wishing he had the nerve to go to her.

▶

SIMONE WOKE to the sound of Mrs. Price singing in the kitchen. She half expected Nolan to be next to her and then remembered that he had slept on the couch. She sat up. The pillow and blanket she'd given him were folded neatly on the edge of her bed.

She wandered into the kitchen. Mrs. Price was already dressed, brewing a pot of coffee. She looked lovely in the simple black dress she usually wore to funerals, with her hair pinned in an up-do and a black veiled hat. Simone kissed her on the cheek before she poured herself a cup of coffee.

"Good morning."

"Morning," Mrs. Price responded. She sat at the dining room table humming. "Did you sleep well?"

"A little. Where's Nolan?"

"He left an hour ago to go home and get dressed. He'll be back to take us to the church." Mrs. Price was looking at her with a mischievous smile.

"What?"

"I know that you and Nolan are not kids anymore," she said playfully. "But I hope you two were respectful in my household."

"Oh God, Mrs. Price!" Simone choked on her coffee. "It's not like that! There's nothing going on between us."

"Mmmm hmmm. It's getting late, so you better hurry and get ready. He soon come."

Simone watched Mrs. Price pick up her morning paper and open it to the city section, grinning to herself. She started singing the old reggae tune, "Everybody Needs Love." Simone shook her head and went back to her bedroom.

By the time Nolan returned, the place was almost empty. He and Simone and Mrs. Price were the last to leave for St. Augustine Church. Everyone else had gone ahead to make sure that everything was ready for the service. When they arrived, the church was packed for CJ's funeral. Simone was happy to see that so many people had come out to see him off.

Esma had arranged for members of her Pentecostal Church choir to perform at the service. Simone could hear them joyfully singing "Abide with Me" from their seats. She felt so uplifted by the beautiful and jubilant singing that she hoped the feeling would continue throughout.

As the service was about to begin, she and Mrs. Price sat on either side of her mother, with Nolan on the other side of Mrs. Price with his father. She looked over at Nolan. He gave her a reassuring smile as Father Paul and the altar boys started their procession down the aisle to the front of the church.

The congregation stood to sing the opening hymn, "How Great Thou Art." Simone picked up the program and started to sing along.

> *O LORD my God! When I in awesome wonder*
> *Consider all the works Thy hand hath made;*
> *I see the stars, I hear the mighty thunder,*
> *Thy pow'r throughout the universe displayed*

As she continued to sing the words of the hymn, the reality that she was saying goodbye to her brother started to sink in and, by the refrain, she could feel her throat weakening and her voice starting to tremble. She could barely whisper the lyrics as a pool of tears clouded her vision. She looked over at her brother's coffin as the congregation sang, "Then sings my soul, my Saviour God, to Thee, How great Thou art! How great Thou art!" her heart swelling as grief rushed through her.

Others around her were crying. As the singing grew louder, Pam collapsed in Mrs. Price's arms, weeping. Simone watched her mother in tears and bit her lip, trying to squelch her own cries. She didn't want the whole world seeing her break down. She wanted to run out of the chapel, but was paralyzed. She fought to stay on her feet, but she eventually stumbled and had to sit down on the pew. As the congregation continued to sing, she doubled over, sobbing.

She felt Nolan kneel beside her. He took her hands in his and helped her up. He walked her out of the nave into the sacristy behind the altar, where they sat down. She continued to cry in his arms as he gently rocked her. As the hymn came to an end, she started to calm down. He handed her a handkerchief.

"I can't go back in there," she whispered. "I don't know if I can do it."

"Yes, you can," he said. "And I'll be right beside you. I won't let you fall off the deep end, remember?"

She nodded. They sat a moment longer, listening to Father Paul begin the service. Nolan kissed her forehead before helping her to her feet and they returned to their seats. Her mother reached over and held her hand as Simone leaned into Nolan's arms.

▶

AS THE MASS CONTINUED, Pam started to zone out. It was the only thing she could do to keep herself from falling apart. She needed to stay numb. Her son had been her whole world and burying him was more than she could bear. She didn't know if she could handle much more.

The eulogy was the only part of the service that she paid any attention to. She had asked Mike to give it. He was the one person who knew CJ as well as she did.

She listened as Mike spoke about CJ and how he was a good kid who loved God, his Nintendo games, and his family—all in that order. The congregation laughed.

Mike went on to talk about CJ's achievements and the several city soccer tournaments he'd played in over the years. He told of CJ's hopes to play soccer professionally after high school and his dream of being the next Pelé. He told stories of the mischief CJ got into when he was young and how hard it had been to discipline him.

"If he was due for a wallop, he would give his mother a wink and a smile, hoping that she would go easy on him," he said. "It worked almost ninety-nine percent of the time. That kid always had his mother wrapped around his finger."

Pam started to laugh with the crowd. She wiped away her tears and smiled at Mike.

"That was how CJ was," he continued. "He was a sweet charming kid. You couldn't help but love him. He was a lot like his father that way."

Mike paused for a moment and then took a deep breath.

"I remember CJ was around four years old when Pam started telling him about his father. CJ never knew him and no matter how many times Pam showed him pictures or tried to tell him about Caleb, he was still confused. He couldn't understand how the world kept going with his father gone."

Mike stopped again. Tears streamed down his cheeks.

"He said, 'Mike, all kids should have their parents. The world can't keep turning if everyone loses their mothers and fathers'. I asked him why he thought that and he said, 'because it would be too sad to keep going.'

"I told him not to worry, he had lots of family and friends who would keep his world going. He liked that explanation. It was enough for his four-year-old mind to comprehend. But, as I stand here, I can't help wondering if maybe he got it right, because saying goodbye to CJ feels like the whole world has come to a complete halt."

Mike took a moment to look over at Pam and then at Simone.

"Pam… Simone, the only comfort I can give you, at this time, is that you have a church filled with family and friends who will keep your world going." His voice was weak. "We'll make sure that each day without him won't be harder than the last.

"There's an old Irish poem my father used to recite on the anniversary of my mother's death—*Don't grieve for me, for now I'm free! I follow the plan God laid for me. I saw His face, I heard His call, I took his hand and left it all…*"

Mike's voice trailed off.

Simone looked back at him with tears in her eyes.

Pam's smile encouraged him to keep going.

"*…Perhaps my time seemed all too brief—Don't shorten yours with undue grief. Be not burdened with tears of sorrow. Enjoy the sunshine of the morrow.*"

He stepped down from the lector's stand and walked to Pam, who got up and hugged him. He held onto her, afraid that, if he let go, he would fall to his knees. They sat down together, holding each other.

The funeral finished with the choir singing "End of the Road" as Mike, Nolan, and CJ's uncles and cousins carried his coffin out. Simone, with her mother and Mrs. Price, followed behind CJ's body.

At the repast, Simone sat with Pam in the church's reception room as people filed past, offering words of sympathy and consolation. Pam could barely look up. It was Sister who stepped in and responded on their behalf.

When everyone had left, Jessica sat with Simone holding her hand. They watched the janitorial staff clean up.

Nolan came up to them and bent down in front of Simone. "Si, it's time to go. Just one last baby step, okay?" He stretched out his hand to her.

That was the hardest step she had ever had to make.

Only the immediate family was invited to the cemetery. Pam didn't want strangers there as they buried her son. Father Paul said a prayer and blessing before the casket was lowered into the ground. Nolan held Simone's hand as she sat and watched her brother's casket disappear from sight.

Back at Mike's apartment, the mood was much more sombre than it had been the previous night. In the living room, the ball-game played on mute in the background. Early in the evening, everyone called it a night and Pam started to clean up. It gave her something to do other than lie in bed crying. Mike helped her go around the apartments with a garbage bag, picking up paper plates and cups. They made sure Mrs. Price's apartment was in order, washing any dishes left in the sink, making sure everything was neat and tidy.

As Mike collected garbage from Mrs. Price's balcony, Pam walked into Simone's bedroom and found Nolan and Simone fast asleep. They were still in their funeral garments, on top of the bed, holding hands, sleeping peacefully. She gently laid a blanket over them.

"I think I got everything," Mike said.

"Shhhh," Pam said. "Don't wake them."

They quietly walked out of the room and left Mrs. Price's apartment, locking the door behind them. Pam was chuckling as they headed back to Mike's place.

"What's so funny?" Mike asked, smiling at her.

"Did I ever tell you about the time when I caught Nolan asleep in Simone's room?" she said. "They must have been eleven or twelve, and there was Nolan asleep on the floor at the foot of Simone's bed. Simone was asleep at the edge of her bed holding his hand. You know, they always thought I didn't know when

Nolan would sneak into her room to play cards at all hours of the night, but I knew. I knew every single time he would come over."

Mike laughed with Pam.

"Nothing really changes, does it?" she said.

"Not really," he said. "The world somehow keeps going."

58

"Wake up, Simone! Wake up!!"

Simone emerged drowsily from her sleep.

"Happy birthday, sleepyhead!"

She groaned and turned over. 7:30 am. She pulled the sheets over her head and tried to ignore Jessica's shrill greeting. "It's too early," she grumbled. "Let me sleep."

Jessica pulled the sheets back. "Simone, you only turn thirty once and I'm not going to let you waste it by sleeping all day," she complained as Simone held onto the sheets. "Come on, wake up! I just got some shitty news."

"Okay… okay… what!" she said, annoyed. "What's going on?"

"I have to fly out to Winnipeg in a few hours. The fucking Emery Energy contract is falling apart," Jessica said. She sat next to her on the bed. "I'm so sorry, Si. I had our whole weekend planned and I feel like I'm letting you down."

"It's okay, Jess, you're not letting me down. I'm not much for birthdays anyways."

"Yeah, but this one is a milestone. You don't turn thirty every day."

"Honestly, it's okay," Simone said, yawning.

"I'll do my best to get back tomorrow morning... tomorrow afternoon at the latest, and we'll go to Caché," she promised. "They're having an R&B throwback night."

"Sounds like a plan," Simone said sleepily. "That'll be fun."

"Perfect. I'll call Hubert and make sure the queens can go. By the way, are you going to wear that snatch dress you have in your closet?"

Jessica was referring to Simone's tight black leather dress that had been hanging in her closet for months. She had bought it on a whim, but hadn't found the right occasion to wear it yet. Jessica often joked that her snatch would definitely find some action if she ever decided to pull the dress out of hiding.

"Yeah, I was planning to," she replied suspiciously. "Why?"

"Well, if you weren't going to wear it, I was planning to steal it," Jessica answered slyly. "Nolan fucking loves me in slutty sexy."

"Too much information, Jess," she said, pulling the pillow over her face. "Do I really need to hear this?"

"I'm just saying, if you're not going to put it to good use, I definitely can," she giggled. "Come on, I got Nolan to make us breakfast."

"Ugh, part of having a birthday is sleeping in," Simone complained as Jessica pulled her out of bed.

"Not when you turn thirty," Jessica teased. "And just to be clear, when my thirtieth rolls around I want fucking fireworks."

The two women walked into the kitchen just as Nolan was finishing up. He had prepared his father's famous breakfast for champions—scrambled eggs, corned beef hash, baked beans, sliced tomatoes, and a stack of toast.

"Happy birthday, Si! I hope you ladies are hungry because I made a shitload of food."

"Thanks, Nols," she said, giving him a side hug. "Wow, this is way too much. You really didn't have to do all of this."

He handed her a mug of tea. "That's what I told Jess, but you already know that your friend is a little bit nuts. She's a little obsessed about this weekend."

Jessica elbowed him. "Hey, this isn't just some random weekend. I would kill to have my birthday fall on Caribana. It's the ultimate party weekend. There's always some kick-ass party happening and it pisses me off that I'll be in Winnipeg for most of it."

"Don't worry," said Simone. "We'll do it up tomorrow night."

"Okay," she said. "Just promise that you're not going to flake out on me or anything!"

"You would think that we're celebrating your birthday," Simone said, rolling her eyes.

She sipped her tea. Her stomach churned as she looked at all of the food in front of her. She hated eating this early in the morning. And this was way too much. All she ever ate were her buttered cream crackers and tea. She looked up at Nolan, who winked at her before sliding across a plate of crackers. She mouthed "Thank you" to him as Jessica bemoaned her overnight trip to Winnipeg.

All in all, Simone was glad for the distraction of her birthday. It was driving her crazy, not knowing what was happening with her promotion. Yesterday, Cynthia and the rest of the executive producers had been locked in a meeting for hours to discuss promotions and no decision had been made by the time she had gone home. She desperately wanted this promotion. It was the boost she needed to pull focus from her grief. If she got it, her whole world would change. She would be forced to do something new and challenging instead of dwelling on her sorrow and loneliness.

Since CJ's passing, each day had been a struggle. Her friends had tried to fill that void by getting her out whenever they could. When Nolan was in town, he kept her company in the evenings. Hubert and Felicia often dragged her out to lunch, attempting to raise her spirits. Jessica had recently tried to persuade Simone to come out with her and her latest boy toy for drinks, but she wasn't up to sitting in a noisy bar as a third wheel. Especially after her last conversation with Lia.

She had felt a small sense of joy when Lia called her back after CJ's death. She'd needed Lia, even if it was only through the phone. But the conversation had left her disheartened. Lia barely said a word during the entire exchange and provided only hollow words of condolence. It had hurt her that it had come to this—the relationship, once so beautiful, had now become tense and sterile.

After the call, she'd sat on her bed feeling like a fool. She'd looked down at Lia's contact page on her cell and had finally done what she should have done months before —deleted her from her cell and purged all emails between them. It had been a small victory, but it left her feeling even more alone.

As she sat with Jessica and Nolan over breakfast, laughing and talking for the better part of an hour, her mood started to lift. Her appetite also returned and she helped herself to a plate of eggs and corned beef hash. She was starting to feel a glimmer of her old self and wondered if being thirty would be a turning point in her life —that magical day when she would finally get her shit together.

"That's my cab," Jessica said when the buzzer rang. "Alright, party people, I expect you guys to be in full form when I get back."

"You got it, babe," said Nolan, kissing her.

Simone turned away. She hated her front-row experience of their love fest. Moreover, she felt out of place when she caught a glimpse of Nolan's hand sliding down the back of Jessica's jeans.

"Okay... gotta go," Jessica said, kissing him again. "Seriously, you're gonna make me miss my flight." She grabbed her purse and headed to the front door.

"Laptop," Simone yelled out.

"Shit. Thanks." She spun back, grabbed her laptop bag, then ran out the door.

"I still can't believe she got through law school," Simone deadpanned.

Nolan laughed as he started clearing off the breakfast dishes. Simone got up to help.

"What are your plans for today?" he asked her as she placed dishes in the sink.

"Nothing much. Probably going to hang out here."

"Well, why don't we do something? Anything you want."

"Really?" she said, laughing. "So you're going to be my roll dawg today?"

"Something like that." He passed her a plate to dry. "Seriously, whatever you want to do."

"Anything, huh?" she asked. "You know what? If you're down for it, I would love to go to the parade."

"That's actually a great idea," he said, smiling. "I'm down for some Caribbean action."

"Seriously? You're going to take me to Caribana?"

"Sure, why not? Let me finish up here and jump in the shower, then we can go."

"Okay, then," she said. "I'll get dressed."

Simone was excited about going to the Caribbean festival. She had only been a few times with her mother and brother, years ago, and hadn't gone since. She remembered how vibrant it was. The energy, live music, colourful risqué costumes, and thousands of people dancing in the streets to Calypso and Soca.

While Nolan was getting ready, Simone went into her closet to find an outfit to wear. She wished she had something more elaborate to put on, but settled on her dark blue overall shorts and a black triangle bikini top. As she was combing her hair into a ponytail, Nolan came in, dressed in jeans and a white tank top underneath one of his checkered work shirts.

He stopped for a moment to watch her slip on a black ball cap; he couldn't help staring. Even in the plainest outfit, she looked hot.

She turned and frowned at him. She looked him up and down.

"Nolan, are you planning to drop me off at the parade or are you actually coming with?" she asked, tying the laces of her tennis shoes. "You realize that you're going to Caribana and not one of your renos?"

"Yeah, well, I've never been," he admitted. "It's a parade, right?"

"Oh, Lord. Do you have anything other than jeans? Some shorts, maybe?"

"I have a pair of cargo shorts here."

"Good! Put them on and take off your shirt," she ordered. "You'll be fine in your tank top. It's going to be hot today, so don't forget to bring a hat."

"Yes, Ma'am." He saluted before he went off to change.

When he came back, Simone was smitten. He was dressed in black army cargo shorts that showed off his toned calves, his favourite Blue Jay cap, and a pair of aviator shades. She smiled to herself as she looked away from him.

"What?" he asked.

"Nothing," she said. "Looking good, though. Gotta make sure the girls don't try to hit on you while we're out."

"I should say the same to you," he said, looking her up and down. "Is that what Jessica calls a snatch outfit?"

"Ha!" she said smiling. "Hardly."

They headed out to the subway station, squeezing in with hundreds of other passengers heading to the parade. By the time they got to the route, everything was in full swing. They stood by the stanchions, watching crowds of dancers in colourful, sparkly headpieces and sequined costumes dancing behind the mas bands.

Nolan watched Simone dance along with the music. He hadn't seen her let loose like this since they were kids. He felt the energy of the crowd and swayed with the Calypso music, but it wasn't until a truck passed by, blasting hip-hop, that he started to really get into the scene.

He'd loved hip-hop since he was a kid and, in his early construction days, Freddy had reintroduced him to it when Biggie

Smalls and Tupac were larger than life. He had been hooked ever since.

As the truck slowly passed by, he could see a few of the parade-goers jump the gates to follow. "Come on, let's get closer," he said, grabbing Simone's hand as the DJ started to play Outkast's "The Way You Move."

When they got to an open space, he lifted her up so that she could get over the gate; then he followed behind her, holding her hand tightly, and they made their way through the dense crowd. As the DJ mixed track after track, the two of them jumped up with the crowd, rapping along with the lyrics. While they danced down the street, they saw an opening on the truck and hopped on. They spent the next hour partying there.

Simone was a little bemused by Nolan's spontaneity. She had thought he'd be a little more reserved, now that he was a recognized celebrity, but he was the complete opposite. She wasn't surprised that he was getting into the music. She had always known about his love for hip-hop. That would be Kester's lasting influence on them both. A gentle reminder that their childhood friend was still there in spirit. It was Nolan's dancing that caught her completely off guard. She couldn't believe how good a dancer he was. The smooth way he gyrated his hips, his pop-n-locks, and the way he led her were all new to her. He was enjoying himself so much—grabbing her by the waist, holding her close, *wining* right along with her—that she simply fell into it.

After a while, they were dripping with sweat and starving. They jumped off the truck when they spotted a roti stand and went over to purchase a couple of wraps. They headed up a grassy hill and picnicked next to a maple tree, watching the rest of the parade go by.

"This smells so good," he said. He bit into his wrap. "I haven't had roti in ages."

"Me, neither," she said, watching him eat. The curry juices

from his roti were drizzling out. "Careful, you're going to get it all over you."

"Thanks, but I got this," he said.

"Sure," she said, rolling her eyes. She handed him more napkins.

He watched her cut into her wrap with a plastic knife and fork and bit into his own and made a huge mess. There was no way around it so he followed suit and used his own utensils.

When they were finished eating, Nolan leaned back against the maple tree as the sun shone brightly and pulled Simone to him, sitting her between his legs. She rested her head against his chest. He wrapped his arms around her and closed his eyes. He liked this, the ease of holding her close, her hands in his, the faint scent of her perfume.

Simone felt herself falling asleep in his arms. There was a normalcy to this that made her long for more, and for a split second the man holding her wasn't her childhood friend or the man her roommate was seeing. For a brief moment, he belonged to her.

By late afternoon, fewer and fewer mas bands were driving by and they decided to call it a day. They walked back to the subway, the music fading behind them.

"Thank you for spending my birthday with me," she said. "This was an amazing day."

"Anytime," he said. "It was nice hanging out with you. I'm glad we did this."

"I'm just glad that I got to see you bust out," she laughed. "You're pretty slick with the dance moves. I'm a little surprised that I didn't know that about you."

"Come on," he said. "You already forgot about our break dancing group way back? I had a lot of moves back then."

"Yeah… the worm wasn't what I was thinking of," she said. "But you move pretty good for a white boy."

"I don't want to brag, but my dancing skills were legendary

when I lived in North Preston," he said. He moved behind her, wrapping his arms around her waist and leaning in.

"Really, huh?"

"Uh huh, and here's my best move." He slowly twirled her out and back into his arms. "That's my ladykiller move, right there."

Simone laughed as she lost her balance. She quickly grabbed onto him, trying unsuccessfully not to fall. They both laughed as he clumsily pulled her up from the pavement.

"See," he said. "Ladykiller moves."

They continued down the block and could feel a few rain-drops. Moments later, the sky opened up and it started to pour. They ran for cover with the other parade-goers and found shelter under the canopy of a closed storefront. Squeezing in with the others, they watched the sun disappear behind the dark clouds.

A cool breeze sent shivers through Simone as they waited for the rainstorm to pass. Nolan noticed her rubbing her arms and pulled her to him, using his body heat to warm her. She nestled her head against his chest, inhaled deeply, revelling in the faint smell of baby powder he wore.

"This isn't letting up," he whispered in her ear. "The train station is not that far. Let's make a run for it."

They ran hand in hand to the station, barely catching the next train. By the time they got back to the condo, they were drenched. Simone was glad they were out of the rain, but sad that their day together was ending.

"Before I forget," he said, drying his face with a towel. "I got you something for your birthday."

"Really?" She pulled out her ponytail and dried her hair.

"Stay here." He peeled off his wet tank top. "Give me a few minutes."

Simone couldn't help but notice how defined his chest and abs were. She watched him walk down the hallway. She wondered if everything else Jessica bragged about him was true.

She waited in the living room, listening to him grunt as he struggled with what seemed like a large piece of furniture.

"You okay in there?" she yelled out. "Do you need any help?"

"I'm good," he replied. "Don't come in yet."

"Okay, don't hurt yourself."

She checked her cell phone for messages and was discouraged when she didn't see one from Cynthia. She started to wonder if maybe the promotion wasn't going to happen.

Nolan came back into the living room in a dry T-shirt and track pants. She was a little disappointed that he'd got dressed so quickly. She had hoped to get another view of him.

He smiled coyly. "Come with me, but close your eyes."

She got up from the couch and closed her eyes. He put his hands on her shoulders and guided her into her bedroom and stopped. He placed his hands over her eyes. She playfully grabbed the sides of his pants.

"Ready?"

"Yes."

When he let go she saw a big grey oversized armchair. She stopped for a moment and then clasped her hands over her mouth.

"That's my chair!" she said excitedly. She ran up to it. "Nolan! That's my old chair, but I thought Jessica tossed it?"

"That was Jess's idea," he said smiling. "She thought it would be a better surprise if you thought that."

"Oh my God, Nolan! I can't believe you did this!" She sat on the chair. "It's beautiful!"

"I hope you're okay with the material," he said. "I used a heavy grey fabric instead of the leather. I thought it would go better with the rest of your bedroom furniture."

"No, I love everything about it." She got up to hug him. "Thank you so much."

"Honestly, it's a great piece of furniture. It just needed a little facelift," he said, proudly sitting on the chair. "It will probably last you fifty more years."

She glided her hand on the back of the chair feeling the woven fabric. She admired the polished wood. The chair looked so much more stylish and sleek. Simone loved her chair so much, especially now that it had come back to her from him. She sat on his lap and lightly kissed his lips.

Nolan was completely stunned by her kiss. It was sweet and tender but left him uncertain of its meaning. He gazed at her, unable to turn away, but hesitant about kissing her back.

"I'm so sorry, Nolan," she said immediately. "I didn't mean... I got carried away."

As she tried to move away he grabbed her hand. He didn't want her to leave. He wanted her. He pulled her to him and wrapped his arms around her waist as she stood in front of him. He looked up at her, searching for a sign that she might want him too.

She began to run her fingers through his hair and then straddled him. He leaned in and kissed her. They kissed slowly, taking their time with each other. Her lips were soft and moist, with a hint of mint from her lip gloss. He liked the way she tasted and began to lightly suck her bottom lip.

She wrapped her arms around his neck as she slid her tongue into his mouth. He moaned softly when their tongues met. Unable to control himself, he felt himself rise and get hard.

"Is this really happening?" he murmured, playing with the straps of her overalls. "Because I want you so much right now. Right here on this chair!"

Simone nodded.

She pulled off his T-shirt, tossed it on the floor and let her fingers trail down his tight muscular chest and he moaned again as she kissed his chest slowly up to his neck. She felt her body wake as he pushed her back and sucked the side of her neck.

Thunder echoed loudly throughout her bedroom.

While tugging at the string of her bikini top, she closed her eyes as she felt him pull it loose. She felt her heart racing as his fingers traced the sides of her breast. Tingling sensations flew up and down her spine.

Then there was a loud bang. They were startled by the loud noise and stopped for a moment.

"It's just the thunder," Nolan whispered. He caressed her slender back.

The doorbell rang. Then it rang continuously. Muffled yelling and laughter could be heard, then loud banging on the front door.

"Ignore it," he whispered, gently licking her earlobe. "Whoever it is will go away."

But the banging continued loudly and her cell phone started to ring. She glanced over to see Hubert's number flashing on the screen. She sighed, dropping her head on his shoulder.

"Give me a minute," she said. "I'll be right back."

"Promise?"

"Promise." She kissed him and re-tied her bikini top. "Don't go anywhere."

As she ran to the door, the banging grew more obnoxious. When she opened it, Hubert was there on his cell phone, with Felicia and Timothy behind him. Their hands were filled with bottles of champagne and shopping bags.

"Happy birthday, Bitch!" they sang out.

"We were two seconds from leaving," Hubert said as he put his phone away and kissed her cheek. "We come bearing gifts and booze."

"And we're here to rescue you." Felicia hugged Simone. "Jess said you were holed up here on your birthday."

Before she could say anything they all barged into her apartment. She looked towards her bedroom just as Nolan walked into the living room, buttoning up his work shirt.

"What's all this?" he said. "Looks like a party going on here."

"Not yet." Felicia was pulling out champagne glasses from the kitchen cabinet. "We're kidnapping Ms. Simone for some birthday shenanigans."

"Didn't Jessica tell you?" Simone said. "We're going out *tomorrow* night."

"That's still happening," Timothy chimed in. "This is the pre-party, honey."

"Well, I guess that's my cue to cut out," Nolan said. "I'll leave you guys to your pre-party."

Simone was disappointed. She didn't know how to send her friends away politely. It was clear they were staying regardless of what she wanted.

"Oh no, honey," Felicia said, pulling Nolan back. "We were given explicit instructions that you have to come, too. So run along and get dressed."

"Dress is casual chic, so find a nice pair of dark jeans and a muscle top," said Timothy. "Or whatever you white boys wear to the clubs. We'll have our girl ready in an hour."

"Make that two hours," Felicia said looking over at Simone, who was still dripping wet. "Girlfriend needs a little work."

Simone glanced over at Nolan as her friends made their way to her bedroom. She could tell that he was disappointed. She ran to him and whispered that she was sorry for the interruption. He held onto her tightly, pressing his forehead against hers. She smirked slightly and then kissed him deeply.

"I have to go," she moaned, before finally letting him go.

She then quickly slipped into her room with her friends and closed the bedroom door. When she turned, Timothy popped open a bottle of champagne while Felicia blasted music from her stereo.

"So what took you so long to answer the door?" Hubert said, sifting through the shopping bags. "Were we interrupting something?"

"Looks like something pretty good," Felicia said, picking up Nolan's T-shirt from the floor.

"No!" Simone said defensively. She grabbed his shirt. "He was just giving me my birthday gift."

"Oh honey, I'm sure he was," Timothy said, sitting down on her chair. "Was it big?"

"Very," Simone said dryly. "You're sitting on it, you dick!"

They all laughed as Timothy quickly got up from the chair.

"Simone, is this your chair?" Timothy yelled. "Girl, this can't be that same old nasty chair!"

"One and the same." She took off her wet overalls and slipped into her robe. "He refinished it for me."

"Well, damn! I don't know about you heifers, but it says a lot about a man who would go out of his way to fix that ratty chair," Timothy said. He pulled out a curling iron.

"Yeah, it definitely says a hell of a lot," Hubert whispered to Simone. She gave him a dirty look. "Come on people. Rome wasn't built in a day. Let's get this bitch ready."

▶

NOLAN SAT ON THE COUCH, trying to watch the Blue Jays game as the ruckus from Simone's room grew louder. It had been nearly three hours and he was dressed, ready to go, wondering if they were even going anywhere. He tried to focus on the game, but his thoughts kept going back to what had happened earlier.

He couldn't keep his mind off her lips, her breasts—her body crushed against his. He could still taste her lip gloss on his mouth. He smiled to himself; how crazy it was that the girl he'd never stopped thinking of was suddenly back in his life and reducing him to his horny fourteen-year-old self.

His mind started considering a relationship with Simone. He had only been seeing Jessica a short while and his relationship with her was maybe about to run its course. It was only because she was Simone's roommate that he'd kept hanging around her.

But the idea of coming between the two women left a sour taste in his mouth.

"I'm over-thinking this," he mumbled to himself, trying to refocus on the game.

"Over-thinking what?" Simone said. She had snuck up behind him. "Sorry we're taking so long, but we're almost ready."

"Wow," he said, turning his head to look at her. He pulled her around the couch. "Let me see you."

Her hair was softer, with long drop curls that hung down her back. She was dressed in a black and gold sequin mini-dress with an open back that plunged just above her backside. He ran his hand down her back and started to sweat. She was wearing a gold metallic G-string.

"Those fools back there are so tun up," she said, sweeping her hair up. "Can you help me with my necklace?"

"Sure," he said as she handed it to him. "You look great, by the way."

"So do you," she said as he fastened it around her neck.

He kissed the back of her neck. He wanted to pull her down on the couch and reach up her dress to feel how wet she was for him, but they quickly moved away from each other when they heard the others coming down the hallway.

"Y'all ready to go?" Felicia asked. "Cause I'm ready to cause trouble!"

"Absolutely! Let's go," Nolan said. He whispered to Simone: "The sooner we leave, the sooner we can get back!"

▶

"WHERE THE HELL ARE WE?" Felicia asked when the taxi van finally pulled up to a warehouse in Mississauga. "This place is in the middle of nowhere."

"It's a pop-up club. That's the point!" Hubert said. "But don't worry, it's gonna be the hottest party tonight."

The line-up to get into the club was two blocks long, but Hubert was a V.I.P. guest, guaranteeing them front-of-the-line access. He had designed the pop-up club for the promoter and was excited to show off his handy work.

"Jesus, Hubert," Simone gasped as they walked in. "This place looks amazing."

Music vibrated through the walls. The warehouse had cream velvet carpet throughout, with tufted walls in the lounge area. The ceiling was enhanced with mirrors and several large crystal chandeliers hung from above. At each corner was a bar serving only champagne, white wine, and vodka shots.

"Thanks, Doll! You wouldn't believe how much I got paid to design this," he said. "I'm calling it the Diamonds-and-Pearls motif."

The club had a line-up of six DJs from Toronto, Montreal, New York, Washington, DC, Paris, and Jamaica. There were three levels, with hip-hop on the top level, reggae in the middle and rave music in the basement. Hubert had scored the group a roped-off area in the top lounge. They were excited to find their table fully stocked with complimentary bottles of Patron Silver and Champagne.

"Good looking out, boo," Felicia said to Hubert as they all sat down. "This place is fire."

The music was loud and constant, with the crowd filtering in and out among the different levels. Things didn't jump off for Simone and her friends until the DJ mixed in D'Angelo's "Left and Right." Simone quickly downed a shot, grabbed Felicia's hand, and led the rest out to dance.

She started to feel herself as she strutted on the crowded dance floor. She felt sexy in the outfit Hubert had bought for her birthday and enjoyed the buzz she was feeling as they all danced together. She garnered the attention of quite a few men, who spent most of the night trying to move in on her. Only Nolan was missing, as he stayed behind nursing his beer. He had been quiet since they'd left her place. She wondered if he was regretting their brief tryst.

"What's his deal?" Hubert finally asked, gesturing to Nolan. "He's been anti-social since the moment we got here. He can't find a personality unless Jessica is around?"

"Leave him alone, Hubert," Simone said. "He doesn't know you guys very well. He'll warm up soon enough."

"Well, I'm going to help him along," he said. "He's bringing my whole damn mood down."

Hubert headed towards the bar and ordered another bottle of Patron. He went back to their table and sat beside Nolan. He poured out several shots.

"Hey, man," he said. "You alright?"

"Yeah, I'm good." Nolan was distracted by Simone talking to yet another guy.

"You know she doesn't bite," Hubert teased. "What's the deal between you guys, anyways?"

"What do you mean?"

"Between you and Simone." Hubert drank a shot. "You guys grew up together, right?"

"Yeah, we were neighbours for years. Since the second grade."

"Really?" Hubert said. "I didn't know it was that deep. So did you guys ever date? Because you seem really, really close... like real close."

"No... no," Nolan chuckled. "It was never like that. We were always just friends."

"Well then, let's toast to the benefits of friendships, but more importantly, friends with benefits," he said, clinking his glass on Nolan's bottle before downing the shot. "Whoo! That one just hit me, son! Gawddamn!"

Nolan watched Hubert drink another shot, then he looked over at Simone. The guy had his hand on her waist.

"Look, I'm dragging Timothy and Felicia to the basement," Hubert shouted over the music. "Simone hates house music with a passion, but none of my people are up here fucking with hip-hop. We'll only be gone for a minute. You think you can keep an eye on her?"

Nolan nodded. Hubert took another shot before heading back to the dance floor, where he whispered to Simone. Nolan didn't know what to do with himself as he watched her being worked on by another guy she was talking to. He felt restless, so he put aside his beer and downed the two shots Hubert had left behind.

Simone tried to walk back to the table, but the guy she was dancing with wasn't ready for her to go yet. She looked over at Nolan, hoping that he would help her out. The man was starting to motion hard for her to dance with him. It wasn't that she wasn't flattered by the attention, but, all she wanted was Nolan.

Then Nolan walked up to them. "Dance with me," he said to her. The DJ began playing Janet's "I Get Lonely". Nolan grabbed her hand and pulled her away from the guy and led her to the middle of the dance floor, where he made sure to hold her close. He wanted everyone in the club to see that she belonged to him. She slipped her arms around his neck, confirming it.

The two of them slow-danced to the song as he lightly touched the small of her back. She felt her pulse skip with the music. She could feel him get hard.

"Can we get out of here?" she whispered. "I want to go."

"Come back to my place," he said. "Spend the night with me."

She nodded.

He grabbed her hand and led her outside into a group of people waiting for taxis. He pulled her to him and started to kiss her. As their lips parted, an alarm pierced through the night. They looked around to see partygoers pouring out of the warehouse and before they knew it the area was crawling with security. The sidewalk started to fill with hundreds of people.

"Come on," Nolan said as a taxi pulled up. "I don't know what's going on, but let's get out of here before it gets crazy."

Just then, Hubert and the rest of the group came up and they all followed Nolan and Simone into the cab.

"What a ghetto-ass party," Felicia said disappointedly. "We need to get the hell out of here before more fools start acting up."

"What happened?" Simone asked. "We heard alarms."

"Some idiot, trying to act all hard, shot himself in the foot," laughed Timothy as he pushed Felicia into the back with Simone and Nolan. "Squeeze in, girl, so we can all fit."

Simone ended up on Nolan's lap, her legs towards the door, trying to adjust her dress. He slipped his arms around her waist and nuzzled against her neck.

"Where to?" the driver yelled out.

"Simone, honey, we're taking the party back to your place," Felicia said drunkenly. "I'm not fucked up enough to call it a night."

Before Simone could object, Timothy gave the driver her address.

"Gawd, that party was getting good too," he complained. He stretched his head out the window. "Look, now the Po-Po is pulling up. This joint is officially toast!"

"It's a good thing you got a cab when you did." Hubert winked at Simone.

"Yeah, thank God," Nolan added sarcastically.

Simone laid her head on Nolan's shoulder as her friends laughed about the evening's events, teasing Hubert about his friend's ghetto party, Hubert ribbing Felicia for trying to hook up with one of the DJs who showed up wearing a clear plastic outfit with bright blue neon briefs.

"But he only spoke French," she cooed. "You know I can't turn down a man who can parlez-vous my français."

Nolan laughed at their banter. He started to understand

Simone's quirky relationship with her friends. They were annoying at times, but entertaining.

He could sense that Simone was asleep on his shoulder. She was the first to go. By the time they got on the highway, everyone except the cab driver was asleep.

▶

NOLAN WOKE UP SUDDENLY. When he looked around he could see that they were close to Simone's apartment.

"Si. We're almost here."

She slowly opened her eyes, yawned and sat up. "Mmm...Okay."

"Simone, do something about them." His hand travelled up her thigh, tugging on the strap of her G-string. "I don't care where they go, just get rid of them, okay?"

She nodded as they started to make out in the back of the cab. He could feel her legs open slightly as his fingers trailed across and found what he was looking for. Just as he was about to finger her, the cabbie pulled up to the front of her building.

"Oh, God," she said, panting. "We're here."

Nolan smiled as he opened the door for her. He liked that he could get her hot.

Simone stumbled out of the cab and quickly adjusted her dress. She watched Nolan pay the taxi driver before she wandered over to the passenger's side of the taxi. She tapped Hubert's window, stirring him from his sleep.

"Hubert, I'm calling it a night," she said grinning. She could feel Nolan eagerly grab her from behind. "I'll meet up with you guys tomorrow, okay?"

"Alright, girl," Hubert said groggily. "Just keep your drawers on long enough to get inside."

Simone watched the cab take off and then turned to Nolan,

kissing him intensely. She had never wanted anyone more than she wanted him. Her whole body was on fire as they continued to make out in front of her building.

"God, I want to fuck you so bad," she moaned.

"Not as much as I do," he growled. "All I kept thinking of was how to get you alone so I could have you. If your friends didn't tag along, I would have fucked you in the cab already."

In the elevator, his hands slipped up her dress as she reached for the button for her floor. He pulled her G-string down.

"Nols, not here. The roof… I want you on the roof."

"Okay… okay," he said, trying to calm down as the elevator door opened at their floor. He grabbed her keys. "Go up and I'll meet you. I want to grab a condom."

"Bring a few," she gasped as she felt his fingers reach inside of her. "Oh, God! Please don't be long."

"Wait for me. I'll be up soon."

She got to the top floor and staggered out of the elevator onto the garden top patio, drunk and delirious, filled with nothing but thoughts of having him inside of her.

The patio had a rooftop lounge area where the tenants threw parties. It was still open and deserted. She sat on one of the lounge chairs and pulled out a compact to look at herself. She quickly fussed with her hair and reapplied her lipstick and caught herself smiling. This had been the best day of her life. She was going to be with the man she loved and nothing could ruin that for her—nothing except time and rain.

She waited nearly an hour for him to come up. As time slipped by, she constantly looked at her phone, but there wasn't a voice or text message from him. She started to feel woozy and stood up so she wouldn't pass out on the chaise. She went back to the roof door, thinking that maybe he was locked out, but then it started to rain. Holding her stilettos in her hand, she went back down to her apartment, cold and dripping wet. Inside, she found Jessica curled up on the couch with Nolan and felt humiliated and heartbroken.

"There's the birthday girl," Jessica yawned. She got up from the couch to hug her. "Si, you're soaked!"

Simone stared dumbfounded at Nolan. His eyes seemed to convey regret, but mostly he looked sheepish.

"Nolan said that he bailed after the first spot shut down," Jessica said, as she sat back down next to him. "I thought you guys were heading to another spot. What happened?"

"Plans changed," Simone said. Nolan would not look her in the eye. "When did you get back?"

"Hours ago," said Jessica. "I was trying to get a hold of you guys but no one was answering their phones."

"Yeah, bad reception all night," Nolan said.

"I'm going to bed," said Simone, abruptly.

"Okay. I guess we should too. Need my beauty sleep for later," Jessica said, yawning wearily.

Simone didn't say anything. She walked past them to her room, slamming the door behind her. She fiddled with her dress in frustration before finally yanking it off. A couple of tears slipped past but she quickly wiped them away.

She was angry that he'd left her alone for so long but angrier still that she had thrown herself at him. All she was to Nolan was an opportunity. A quick lay. A convenient piece of ass. She sat on her bed clenching her fists when she heard someone attempt to open her door, then a light knock.

"Si," Nolan whispered through the door. "I'm so sorry... I had no idea she was home and I didn't know what to say. I wanted to come for you but I never had a chance... please... just open the door."

But Simone turned on her stereo instead, blasting it as loud as she could to drown out his voice. She didn't want to hear his excuses. He had made his choice and now she was making hers.

▶

Nolan was startled awake by a door closing. Jessica was still asleep. He sprang out of bed to speak to Simone before Jessica woke up. He felt like shit for leaving her on the roof alone, waiting for him.

Last night Jessica had been in the living room, working on her case, when he'd walked in. She'd had a miserable look on her face and, before he had a moment to make an excuse to leave, she was in his arms, crying over the huge argument she'd had with one of her firm's partners. It was her fault that the case was imploding and she was scared she might lose her job if she didn't fix it.

He did his best to comfort her, to convince her to get some rest, but she said she was too upset to sleep and just wanted him to hold her. When Simone came in, drenched from the rain, he felt like a heel. He could see it in her eyes that she was furious with him, but he couldn't think of anything to say or do to make things better.

He went straight to Simone's room but it was empty. A note on her bed to Jessica said that she would meet them that night at Caché. He wanted to punch the wall when he realized that she would be gone the entire day.

"Hey babe," Jessica said sleepily as she hugged him from behind. "Where's Simone?"

"She's gone for the day," he said, passing her the note. "She's going to meet up with us later tonight."

"Well, that's not a bad thing," she said, kissing him. "It'll be nice to have the place to ourselves."

"I can't stay," he said, walking back to her room. "I promised my dad that I would help him this morning and then I need to go home and shower."

"Really?" she asked, following him. "I was hoping we could spend a little more time together this weekend."

"I know," he said, changing into his jeans and T-shirt. "But I'll see you tonight, okay?"

"I guess I can go into the office for a few hours." She sighed. "I need to figure out what to do about this case."

"Everything will work out," he said. "I'm sorry I can't stay, but if I don't leave now I'll be late."

"Okay," she said. "I'll see you later, right?"

"Absolutely." He gathered his weekend bag and pecked her cheek. "I'm sorry that I'm rushing out..."

"It's okay. Go! We'll meet up later."

Nolan tried to call Simone as soon as he left, but it went straight to voicemail. He drove over to the complex in a foul mood, cursing himself for blowing it last night. He should have gone back up to the roof.

He walked to his father's door and knocked, unsure whether Mike was still home or had already headed over to St. Augustine. Just as he was turning to leave, he heard his father's booming laughter coming from Mrs. Price's apartment. He went over and knocked lightly before opening the door. His dad was sitting at the dining table with Mrs. Price and Simone.

"Well, speak of the devil," Mike said. "We were just talking about you, Nolan."

"I was looking for you," he said to his father, glancing at Simone.

"Come in, nuh." Mrs. Price got up to give him a warm hug. "I just finish make ackee and saltfish for Simone and your fadda."

"Simone is having the birthday blues," Mike said. "We're trying to tell her that turning thirty is not the end of the world."

Simone had turned away from him. He sat down next to Mrs. Price as she and Mike prattled on about building gossip. He kept looking over at Simone, but she refused to look his way. He wanted to say something—anything—but instead kept quiet.

"This is really good, Mrs. Price," he said, looking over at Simone again. "Did Simone mention that we went to Caribana yesterday? We had some really good roti."

"Not as good as mine," Mrs. Price contended. "I remember

making fresh roti for you kids every Saturday. Mr. Mike, these kids could nyaam. I could never make enough. Chups! I make it for my grandbabies the other day and dem pickneys say dey nuh eat no yard food no more. Too many carbs!"

"If they eat at all," Mike said. "These days everyone is so wrapped up in counting calories they barely eat a thing."

"Mi don't know how deh nuh float away. Lawd Jesus!" Mrs. Price laughed, turning to Nolan.

Nolan tried to smile back but he felt distraught. Mrs. Price was looking at him and Simone with a pained expression on her face. Simone just sat there, quietly playing with her food. Mrs. Price looked questioningly at Nolan, then let out a huge sigh.

"Mr. Mike, come help me with that new air conditioner the building put in mi bedroom. Lawd, mi can't figure out how to use the blasted thing," she said. "Spare me a few minutes and show me how it work."

"Sure thing," Mike said, wiping his mouth with a napkin. "Let's take a look before I head over to St. Augie."

Mrs. Price turned towards Nolan who was now looking at Simone. "You two keep company," she said. "Soon come."

When Mike went into the back with Mrs. Price, Simone immediately got up to put her dish in the sink. Nolan followed her into the kitchen.

"Are you going to let me explain?" he said.

She brushed past him to retrieve the other dishes from the table.

"Simone! Stop and talk to me!"

"Keep your voice down!" she said, averting her eyes, still clearing the dining table. "I really don't want to talk about it right now."

"I didn't know she was home, okay? I was just as shocked to see her, I swear. I wanted to go up to you but I couldn't get away... please, Si. You know I wouldn't do that to you."

"Really, Nolan?" she said. "I mean it's not like it hasn't

happened before. You know... you make out with me, make me feel like you want me and then ditch me for another girl."

Nolan was stunned into silence. He had always wanted to apologize to her for what had happened with Sarah Jane. It was so many years ago he'd thought it was all water under the bridge. He was young and stupid back then. They both were.

"Look, Nolan, can we just drop it?" she said more calmly. "I was really drunk last night and took things too far flirting with you."

"Flirting? Is that what you call it, Simone? That's bullshit! There was definitely more than flirting going on between us. You felt it as much as I did."

"All I felt was embarrassed that I got caught up." She began stacking dishes in the sink. "Nothing more than that."

"Simone, don't do this," he said pulling her to him. "Don't push me away because of one mistake."

He kissed her.

She closed her eyes as his lips pressed against hers. She could barely breathe and felt her body go weak.

"I know you feel it," he whispered in her ear. "Don't let something like this come between us."

"Us? There's no 'us', Nolan." She opened her eyes and moved away from him. "I'm actually glad Jessica came back when she did. It stopped me from making a huge mistake."

Nolan tried to respond but his father and Mrs. Price came back into the living room.

"I have to go," Simone said, grabbing her bag.

"Simone, you're leaving so soon?" asked Mike. "We didn't get a chance to catch up."

"I'm sorry." She hugged him and then Mrs. Price. "I have to run, but I'll catch up with you soon."

"Okay, sweetheart," he said. "It was great seeing you, even if it was for a short while."

Nolan followed her down the hallway. "Simone, wait up." He

wanted to grab her and make her listen to him. He wanted her to know how sorry he was. He didn't know what to do to make things right between them. "Please let me drive you home or wherever you need to go."

"Nols, I'm fine." She gave him a tight smile as she got into the elevator and pressed for the lobby. "I'll see you later."

"Wait...Simone!"

Nolan stood there as the elevator door closed on him. Not wanting to give up, he pressed the button several times to stop the car from leaving.

Mike walked up to him, fastening his tool belt. "Are you ready to go?"

Nolan looked at the elevator and could already tell that it was making its way back to the lobby. By the time they got to the lobby, she would be long gone.

"Yeah, sure, Dad."

"I can't believe little Miss Simone is thirty," Mike said, not noticing Nolan's distress. "It wasn't that long ago when you two were running around here causing havoc. I gotta say I'm glad you two reconnected."

Riding down in the elevator with his dad, he wondered if that connection was still there. How damaged was their relationship after last night? He desperately wanted to fix things with her and hoped his chance would come later that night.

On his way home from helping Mike, he got a message from Jessica. They were all to meet at Marlow's for dinner before heading over to Caché. He took a shower to clear his mind, but all his thoughts trailed back to Simone and the mess he'd made.

At the restaurant, he found Jessica in high spirits. She'd figured out a master plan to fix the Emery case and, after heavy negotiation, she'd been able to get things back on track. She said that everyone had been sending her emails all day congratulating her on the great save.

"So nobody is getting fired today?" Nolan said. "All is good?"

"Yup," she said, beaming. "I'll have to go in on Monday for a couple of hours, to make sure all our ducks are in a row, but tonight I'm ready to put this whole mess behind me."

"I'm happy for you, Jess," he said. "I'm glad it all worked out."

There was a commotion behind them as Hubert, Felicia, Timothy, and some of Simone's other friends arrived.

"Where's Simone?" Jessica asked when they all huddled together outside the restaurant.

"I thought she would be with you guys," Felicia said. "Did anyone talk to her today?"

"She texted me an hour ago," Hubert said. He eyed Nolan. "She's running a little late."

They went to their table and ordered a round of drinks and appetizers. They were into a second round when Simone finally sauntered into the restaurant wearing a black skin-tight leather dress, with her slick straightened hair tumbling down her back.

"Whaaaat!" Timothy snapped. "You're working and working and working that dress, honey."

"Looking fierce, girl." Felicia hooted as Simone sat between her and Hubert. "Thirty and thirsty."

Nolan almost didn't recognize her. He was dazed by the sexual energy that poured out of her and couldn't keep his eyes off her voluptuous curvy body. Her makeup amped up the sexy vixen look: grey smoky eyes and glassy pink lips. He could feel himself rise and get hard just by looking at her. He wanted nothing but to take her home and fuck her, but was instantly intimidated by her icy stare. She was still angry with him.

"Woman, I hate that you ended up wearing that dress but you look sexy as hell," Jessica gushed. She ran around the table to Simone and hugged her. "Happy birthday, doll!"

"Thanks." Simone asked the waiter for a glass of champagne. "Sorry I'm late."

"Well now we know why, Miss Sex Kitten," Hubert said. "I

guess you and He-Man had a hot night. He can't keep his eyes off you."

She looked quietly around the table as the waiter poured her champagne. "I wouldn't know. You would have to ask Jessica."

"Oh… Oooohhh." Hubert stared at Nolan who was working on his third bourbon. "I guess things didn't pop off last night?"

"Nope, and can we change the subject?" she said, looking at the menu. "I really don't want to talk about him anymore. I just want to have a good time."

"I gotcha," he said patting her hand. He then stood up and tapped his knife against his champagne glass. "Okay, everyone… settle down. Now that the guest of honour has graced us with her presence, I just want to give a quick toast to the baddest bitch here.

"Simone, I know that turning thirty has been a little bitter-sweet for you. You are now officially inducted into the 'old as fuck' club. But just know that, no matter how old you are, you still remain ravishingly beautiful and one of the best friends this queen has ever had. I love you and hope that every desire you hold in your heart comes true. Happy birthday, Simone!"

"Happy birthday, Simone!" everyone sang out.

Simone shyly thanked everyone, but her smile faded when she looked over at Nolan. He wouldn't stop staring at her. She swiftly looked away. She couldn't trust herself around him.

▶

NOLAN TRIED all evening to talk to Simone, but it was only while they were swarming out to get cabs to Caché that he was able to pull her away from everyone and force her into one of the waiting cabs. He asked the cabbie to start driving.

Simone sat as far away from him as she could and stared straight ahead. He knew that look. It was the look that said her mind was made up. He had been on the receiving end of that look often enough to know that it was best to let her cool off. But he was desperate.

"Please, Simone, can we just go somewhere and talk?"

Simone pulled out her phone and began checking her text messages.

"Can you at least look at me?"

She continued to ignore him.

"Simone, why are you being so stubborn?" he said. "I'm trying to make things right and you're treating me like shit over a misunderstanding."

She looked over at him angrily. His eyes were glazed over and his face was red and puffy. It was obvious that he was drunk, and she didn't want to fight with him while he was in that state. She went back to looking straight ahead.

"So you're just going to ignore me," he said. "That's your plan? Just act like a twelve-year-old and ignore me? Grow up! We're not kids anymore!"

"You're right, we're not kids anymore and I'm done trying to figure you out, Nolan," she said. "I opened myself to you. Something I swore I would never do again, and I ended up humiliating myself letting you treat me like a fucking whore. Like some spare you pull out whenever you get bored or horny."

"How did I treat you like a whore? I have never felt that way about you. Explain exactly what I did to make you feel that way."

"Well, let's see," she said, turning to him. "You left me on the fucking roof for an hour waiting for you. You didn't call or text me to say that Jessica was back. You had me waiting there like a fucking idiot—"

"That wasn't my intention," he interjected. "I wasn't—"

"Don't interrupt me," she yelled. "You asked me to talk. Let me talk!"

"Okay! Fine. Talk!"

"While you and Jessica were all cozy on her couch, did I even cross your mind? It's the middle of the night and I'm drunk and sloppy and anyone could have come up there. All the while you were holed up with Jessica for a fucking hour, Nolan. Not once did you check on me. Not one goddamn phone call! So, yes, to answer your question, THAT made me feel like your whore... THAT made me feel like your fucking side-piece!"

"I'm sorry, Si," he said, deflated. "I never meant to make you feel that way. I never intended—"

"Look, I hate to break up your lover's quarrel back there, but are we going to drive around all night or can I get an address?" said the cabbie.

"Just give us a minute," Nolan said. "Simone, please let's go somewhere and talk alone—"

"Look, buddy, if you don't give me an address I'm going to have to ask you and your girlfriend to get out my cab," said the driver.

"For fuck's sake, man," Nolan yelled. "We're trying to figure that out... please, Simone—"

"Caché," she said to the taxi driver. "Please just drive us to Caché on Bathurst Street."

Nolan sat back in his seat. He was afraid to reach out and touch her. "Si, I never wanted to hurt you," he said after a long silence. "You know how much I care for you. You're all I've ever wanted... Jesus... Simone... you have to know that, right?"

Simone stared out the window. A small part of her wanted to let last night go but the hurt still overwhelmed her. He'd treated her like an afterthought and the humiliation still stung. She clenched her teeth trying to stop herself from crying. She hated that he still had the power to make her cry.

Moments later, the cab pulled up at the club and she quickly got out before he could see her face; when she turned around, the taxi took off with Nolan still in the back seat.

She stood by the curb as tears poured down faster than she could brush them away. She instantly regretted the argument and tried to hail another cab to go after him, but right then Jessica, Hubert, Timothy, and Felicia pulled up in their cabs.

"Let's get this party started!" Felicia whooped. "Where's Nolan... I thought he was in the cab with you."

"He just sent me a text," Jessica said. She looked at her phone. "He said that he's not feeling well and is heading home to pack for his flight to Vancouver tomorrow."

"I thought he was in town for the rest of the week?" said Felicia.

"Me too," answered Jessica. "Did he say anything to you, Si?"

"Not much," she said. She could see Hubert looking at her with concern. She quickly brushed away another tear that slipped by her.

"Well, maybe it's for the best," Hubert said. "You know... if he's not feeling well."

"Yeah... maybe it's for the best," Simone said, turning her face away.

"Come on people, let's go inside!" Felicia pulled Jessica into the club. "I'm feenin' to find my baby daddy up in here."

Hubert walked Simone to one side. "What happened, Si?"

She shook her head, letting go in his arms. "Everything is a mess."

"What's going on between the two of you?"

"I... I don't know anymore."

"Do you want me to take you home?" He handed her a tissue. "I can tell the others that you're not feeling well... tell them it was something you ate."

"No," she said adamantly. She carefully wiped her eyes. "Just give me a sec."

"Okay," he said. They slowly walked to the entrance of the club.

She took a few deep breaths. Every fibre in her body wanted to go after Nolan. Her heart ached, knowing that nothing had been resolved. She looked back at the arriving taxicabs, hoping he'd return.

"Let's get inside," Hubert said.

Simone took one final look back before letting him lead her inside.

▶

THE NEXT DAY, Simone woke up with the worst hangover she'd ever had. She remembered downing four shots of tequila the moment she walked into Caché, but not much after that. She strained to remember; had she been dancing with three ballplayers? Had she really been felt up by the Chicago rapper that was hosting the party? All she remembered was Felicia and Hubert bringing her home.

It was nearly three in the afternoon. Her head was spinning out of control. She tried to sit up. After finding her footing, she went through the apartment looking for Jessica with the hope that Nolan was there, but the condo was empty.

She checked her phone and a text and voice message were waiting for her. The text was Jessica informing her that she'd slept over at Nolan's place after finding him hugging the toilet, so drunk that she'd had to help him to bed.

But that didn't stop him from one last fuck before his flight. Girl, he was amazing. I don't even know how I'm gonna walk straight today.

Simone read the text over and over, wondering how she kept getting it so wrong. Everything in her heart told her to take that leap, to let him in, but each time all she ever felt was hurt and foolish.

She erased the text and crawled back to her bed and passed out. She woke up later that evening. The condo was still and empty. She was glad. She couldn't deal with Jessica retelling her night with Nolan. She looked at her phone and saw that she still had a voice mail message pending.

Simone, it's Cynthia, said the voice. *I'm sorry that it took so long but I have news for you. Your promotion has been approved! Let me be the first to congratulate you. You are one of the best on my team and this promotion is long overdue.*

That being said, there is a bit of a caveat. We need you in the Manhattan office. I know the plan was for you to stay on with the Toronto office, but there is a bigger need for a producer in New York. If you accept you will be expected to relocate by December 1st. There would be a $55,000 increase to your base salary and we will give you a generous amount to cover your relocation costs. I know it's not exactly what you were expecting, but it's a great opportunity, and frankly you would be crazy to pass it up. Anyways, call me when you get this.

Simone sat still on her bed. Her whole body felt numb. She looked at the clock and felt the world tilt. It was 6:00 pm. She bit her lip and hesitated. She went ahead and called Cynthia back.

"Cynthia, it's me," she said. "I'm calling about the offer. I accept."

59

Pam looked around CJ's old bedroom as she placed the final box by his bed. It had been a few months since his death. She had kept putting off collecting his belongings but, after the fifth courtesy notice, she knew she couldn't avoid it forever. Simone and Mike had offered to go with her, but she had done it alone.

She couldn't let go of CJ. Her grief travelled alongside her as she tried desperately to pull herself out. Her therapist had told her it would take time, but as the weeks passed she felt no opening of her heart—she couldn't let go.

Mike had tried in vain to be there for her. At one point, he had brought up the idea of them getting back together, but her grief got mixed up with her feelings for him and it just confused and overwhelmed her. She wasn't ready. She began avoiding him— hoping he would understand why she needed to be alone. But, as she stood in CJ's bedroom, surrounded by his belongings neatly packed away in storage boxes, she wished Mike was with her.

She sat on her son's bed, letting her fingers glide across his bedspread. He hadn't lived in the room for years but she could still feel his spirit. As she wiped away her tears, she noticed one of the storage boxes was teetering. She got up to move the box, but, as she lifted it, the bottom gave, dumping the contents on the floor. She found a roll of shipping tape and sat on the carpet to reinforce the broken box. Leaning against the bed, she placed each item back in the box: CJ's comic book collection, CDs that his sister had bought him, the Blue Jay cap that he wore everywhere. This was the hat that Mike had given him when he took CJ to his first game at the SkyDome. It was ten sizes too big and swallowed his head but he didn't care. He loved it regardless.

She picked up the photo album she'd made shortly after he was admitted to St. John's. His therapist had recommended that she create a memory book to help him with facial recognition. She flipped through the book. The first picture was of Caleb, one of a few black-and-whites Annalise had given her; along with some poorly taken Polaroids that she had taken herself, these were all she had of CJ's father.

She came across pictures she hadn't seen in years. Photos of Mike clowning around with CJ and Simone. A picture of Nolan pretending to be Hulk Hogan, lifting CJ up in the air. She remembered that moment. She and Mike had just returned from the laundry room to find CJ dangling above Nolan's head. It turned out they were mimicking a wrestling move while Simone took the picture. She'd scolded the two older ones, reminding them that he was just a baby and that they could have really hurt him.

I'm not a baby, Mommy, I'm a big boy!

"You're a big boy, huh?" she'd replied. "Well, then I want all of you, including you, big boy, to clean up this mess. Why are all my cushions on the floor?"

Each picture brought back strong memories. The birthday parties and Christmas Eves and soccer tournaments and Simone and Nolan's grade school graduation. A photo of herself covering her face as she sat smoking on the balcony with Mike. She hadn't been dressed properly and hated that Simone was taking pictures of her.

It's called action shots. You can't pose all the time. Sometimes you have to take pictures of things just happening.

She flipped to the next page and there was CJ standing next to Dex. How did that picture end up in the album? It was of CJ holding up his Most Valuable Player Award after his school's team won the district championship. She had chided Dex to get closer to CJ and Mike so that she could get all three of them in the frame, but he stubbornly stood off to the side.

She looked closely at the anger on Dex's face. He never smiled in pictures, but, in this photograph, he looked miserable. CJ also wasn't smiling as he posed for the photo. That hard look had already replaced the bright smile he'd had when he was younger.

The next picture was of CJ with Mike that CJ had insisted be taken. In this one, CJ's smile was brighter than the sun. His whole face was lit up as he stood looking up at Mike.

Pam sat amazed. How could she have missed it? How hadn't she seen what was happening right under her nose? All the signs were there. How timid CJ was any time Dex walked into the room. He was always at ease with Mike. He gravitated to Mike even if it meant hearing about it from Dex. Her eyes started to feel heavy as she stared at the picture, the moment when everything had veered off the path she had created.

"I'm sorry," she whispered to herself. "I'm so sorry. I should have paid attention. I should have known. I'm so sorry."

She then felt someone slide down next to her. She couldn't see who it was. Her eyes were blurry and the room was filled with shadows from the setting sun. All she could feel were his arms wrapped around her shoulders, her breathing slow and deep as she leaned her head on his chest.

"I'm so sorry," she repeated. "I should have known. I should have known that something was wrong. I didn't see it. I didn't want to see any of it. I'm so sorry."

Her whole body was submerged in grief. Her chest and throat started to throb and she couldn't stop and didn't want to. She needed to feel it—all of it. The pain, the guilt, the sadness, and the memories. She couldn't box it up and store it away. She didn't have the space in her heart for it anymore. She had to let go.

Afterwards, she wiped her face with a tissue from her pocket, took a deep breath and regained her sight again. She saw she was alone in the empty room, leaning against a stack of boxes, clutching the photo album. There was an overwhelming feeling of light within her. She thought she was having a panic attack, but it wasn't the feeling that usually accompanied one of her episodes. Her pulse still rushed and her heart raced, but each breath felt light and wonderful.

It was the same feeling she'd had giving birth to Simone. The joyful relief of seeing her daughter for the first time. Some moments were connected. Those times with Arley and the feeling of love that rushed through her afterwards. The way her heart expanded the first time Mike told her that he loved her. The feeling overpowered her and was fleeting. She could never quantify it or describe it. She just knew that it was beyond feeling happy. It was a calm, a peace, that would engulf her.

She sat in CJ's room and felt that light within her and cried. She cried until she heard a knock on the bedroom door. She looked up to see Mike standing there. He walked over to where she was sitting and sat next to her, wrapping his arms around her.

"I… I heard you from my apartment. I couldn't help it. I had to check… What do you have here?" he asked.

"Some old pictures," she said. "Can you stay and look at them with me?"

"Yes… yes, of course."

They sat on the floor and slowly went through the photo album. They laughed together at a photo of their children sitting on the hood of Mike's car, eating ice cream.

"If I remember correctly, that was on my day off," he said, pulling the picture out of the album. "Somehow they talked me into taking them to McDonald's for ice cream."

"Now I see what went on back then. While I was making sure they weren't tearing the whole complex down, you were bribing them with junk food. No wonder I was always the bad guy."

"And I loved you for it," he said. "To be honest, if you hadn't come into my life, Nolan would have had a steady diet of peanut butter sandwiches and gone to school looking like a vagabond his whole childhood."

Pam turned the page.

"I'm serious, Pam," he said, placing his hand on hers. "You saved my life."

Pam looked up at Mike and touched his face. His eyes looked scared as he searched for a sign, some recognition that she was okay. She didn't want him to worry. She wanted him to know that she was going to be okay. She laid her head on his shoulder and held his hand. It felt good leaning on him—even for a moment.

"I miss my baby," she said. "I miss him so much."

Silence.

"I know you do," he whispered. "I do, too."

60

Tessa sat in her living room, smoking her fifth cigarette in a row as she waited anxiously by the phone. She watched her hand shake, pouring another glass of vodka from the bottle Rowan had left behind. She looked out the kitchen window. The neighbour's dog jetted across the street, but there was no sign of Rowan or Kyle. She continued to look back and forth, out the window and at the kitchen clock.

It was almost 8:00 pm. Nolan's assistant had told her that he would be back at his trailer around 4:00 pm. It was either now or never. She didn't know how long it would be before Rowan brought Kyle back home. He was never consistent. He was either too early or never on time and it agitated him any time she complained about it.

"Shut the fuck up, Tess," he would yell. "At least I'm fucking visiting my boy. I'm sure all the other fucking dicks you sucked wouldn't even bother with him, so keep your shit to yourself."

She was used to his anger by now. Rowan had been released on parole two years ago and, when he showed up on her doorstep, it was everything she'd wanted since the moment he'd been sent away. In the beginning, it had felt like old times. Tess had her man back and they were finally a family. She'd focused on the good moments in their relationship. The long rides on his motorcycle, clinging to him as they rode up and down the seashore. Moments when they were so fired up together that endless discussions turned into passionate nights of lovemaking.

Rowan's return was everything for her son. She saw the way Kyle's face lit up the moment he met Rowan. The young boy was proud of the father he barely knew and insisted that Rowan take him to school so he could show off his tough dad to all his friends. He didn't care that he was just out of jail for killing a man.

While in prison, Rowan had made sure he was ready for the outside world. He had kept up with current events, reading any newspapers he could get his hands on, and used his extra time to get his GED. He even took a few college courses. He didn't want to be like the meatheads he rolled with, who acted like they were never getting out. He was determined to get an early release, even if it meant plastering on a phony grin for the black prison guards. But the moment he hit the pavement, it hadn't mattered that he was a model prisoner or that he'd got his GED or even that he had taken a year's worth of college courses. The moment they saw that he was an ex-con, every job opportunity immediately dried up.

"Give it time, baby," Tess would tell him. "It won't be like this forever."

Once he started drinking, he also started taking his frustrations out on her. Silly arguments grew into screaming matches that turned into full-out brawls, with Tess being thrown across their bedroom. The neighbours often called the police when the arguments became too hard to ignore, but Tess would never press charges. She was the reason he'd been in jail. She didn't want to be the reason he was sent back.

But the last straw was when she watched Kyle cower in fear after Rowan had given her a bloody nose. She never wanted to see that look on her son's face again. She immediately threw Rowan out.

She'd known something was off when she'd come home that evening to find Rowan sitting in her kitchen drinking, while Kyle was outside playing with the neighbours. She'd felt an eerie sick feeling as Rowan looked at her. He seemed angry but smug, as if all the secrets of the world had been given to him. He said he'd decided to take Kyle to a movie.

"This isn't your day."

"I'm his father, right, Tess? Kyle's father shouldn't need permission to see him," he snarled at her. "Right, Kyle?"

"Yeah, Mom," Kyle said, as he tied his shoelaces. "I never get to see Dad. Can I go, Mom? Please!"

"I have no problem with you going with your dad," she said, trying to sound calm. "It's just that I had plans for us to see *Fantastic Four*."

"Dad's taking me to see *A History of Violence*," Kyle boasted.

"I don't think that film is appropriate for a ten-year-old," Tess said to Rowan. "Why don't we all go out together to see *Fantastic Four*? Make it a family night."

"No, this is a boys' night." Rowan glowered at Tess. "Don't worry, we'll go see his *Fantastic Four* and save *A History of Violence* for when he gets older. I'm not going to get your mom mad at me."

Tess watched them walk out. Every alarm was going off. She couldn't figure out what it was that was scaring her, but she quickly found out the moment she glanced at the stack of mail sitting on the kitchen table, neatly arranged in order of size with an opened Royal Bank of Canada statement perched on top. She panicked when she picked up the statement—the monthly wire transfer that Nolan had been sending her for years was clearly visible.

She'd called Nolan but he wasn't available. His assistant had promised that he would call her the moment he finished filming, in a few hours.

When he'd left Halifax, Nolan had told her that despite Kyle not being his, he would continue to help. She had tried to refuse his money but it kept coming. At first, she stuffed the envelopes in her side drawer, promising herself that she would send it back, but after struggling to stay afloat each month, she caved and was now dependent on them.

Tess looked again at the time on her cell phone and nearly jumped out of her skin when it rang.

"Hello?"

"Tess, it's Nolan. Is everything okay? I just got your message."

"Nolan, I can't talk long. Kyle is out with Rowan and they'll be back soon," she said quickly. "I... I think he knows."

"What do you mean?"

"He keeps saying stupid shit in front of Kyle, like jokes about him not being his son."

"Tess, at some point you have to tell him," Nolan said firmly. "Despite everything, he has the right to know the truth."

"Yeah, I know. That's not what I'm worried about right now," she said, looking out the window. "He opened my bank statement. It shows the monthly wire transfers."

Nolan was silent.

◄◄

THEIR RELATIONSHIP HAD ENDED the moment Tess had finally come clean and told Nolan that he wasn't the father. For weeks she had led him to believe that he was and had even shown him the pregnancy test. When she held out the test, Nolan could barely speak. He wasn't ready for the responsibility. He was a high school dropout with no job to even help support her, but he didn't want to skip out the way he had with Sarah Jane.

The night before their arrests at the docks, he'd accepted the reality and told her that whatever it took he would be there for her and the baby. He didn't want his child growing up without him.

"Fuck, Nolan," she said, getting up from his bed to get dressed. "Why couldn't you have been a fucking prick? It wouldn't have mattered if you were a prick."

"I don't understand, Tess."

"The baby is not yours, okay!" she said. "You're off the hook."

"What do you mean? You said it was mine."

"I thought it was... I hoped it was," she said. "Last week the doctor told me that I'm not two months pregnant, I'm four months pregnant. I fucked up the dates."

"So Rowan is the father?" he said.

"I'm not sure," she replied. "I thought he was, but now I'm not sure anymore."

"Who else were you with?"

"Bryce," she said. "I was with Bryce before I was with you."

"Jesus, Tess," he said. "Did you fuck the whole crew and their fathers?"

"You're an asshole," she said. "I don't need your fucking judgment."

"Tess...Tess, I'm sorry," he said, grabbing her hand. "I didn't mean it like that. You just caught me off guard. I thought...I just thought—"

"That because we fucked it meant something?" she said, moving away from him. "You were my filler! My fucking revenge every time Rowan cheated on me. Nothing more, okay! I love Rowan. I will always love him."

Nolan sat quietly as he watched her get dressed. She pulled up her jeans, struggling to button them but they were getting too tight. She started to cry. Nolan got up and sat next to her.

"What are you going to do? Are you going to tell him that you're pregnant?"

"He already knows, Nolan. He doesn't fucking care. He said

either get rid of it or I'm on my own. You know what the kicker is? It's too late for me to even have an abortion."

"Is that what you want to do?"

"No... I don't know. I just want everything to stop being so fucking complicated."

"It's going to be okay, Tess," he whispered. "Everything will work out."

"You don't get it, Nolan!" she said, pulling away from him. "It's not okay. I can't have this baby. Not like this. I can't tell Rowan that the baby may or may not be his. He would kill me if he found out that there were others."

Nolan knew that Tess wasn't exaggerating. He had seen Rowan's temper. He was brutal when he fought on the streets and Nolan had suspected that there were times Rowan laid hands on Tess, but she would always deny it. He didn't want to see the rage that would surface if Tess admitted to him that there was a question of who the father was.

"I meant it when I said that I would be there for you, Tess. Anything you need... I'll be there for you and the baby."

The next time he saw her, after the arrests, was in a crowded courtroom as he testified against Rowan. She sat behind Rowan, her eyes dripping with hatred as the court listened to him detail the final blow that killed the homeless man.

Nolan didn't care what his testimony did to Rowan. All he cared about was Tess staying out of prison. The idea of her having the baby behind bars and possibly having to give it up made it clear—Tess couldn't do jail time.

▶▶

HE STARED at the shooting schedule pinned to the corkboard in the trailer. "Listen, Tess, if he suspects that Kyle isn't his, then it might be time," he said. "Do you want me to come up? I can protect you. I can get you out of there."

"NO! You have to promise me that you will never come out here," she yelled. "Do you hear me, Nolan? He already hates you and if he figures it's you sending us money... that's why I'm calling. You have to stop the payments. Please, Nolan. If you care anything for Kyle and me, stay out of our lives. The last thing I need is Rowan thinking that you're Kyle's father."

Nolan sat on the line quietly. He didn't want to make Tess's life any harder than it was. She wouldn't call him unless she was terrified. He wished she would get out of Nova Scotia. In the past, he had offered to move them to Vancouver, but she flat out refused, saying if there was any chance Rowan was Kyle's father, she couldn't pick up and leave. She didn't want to do that to her son.

"Okay, I will keep my distance, but you have to promise me that you will call me if you need anything."

"Nolan I have to go! Rowan is back with Kyle. Please be careful, okay?" She hung up the phone.

Nolan sat in the trailer with an uneasy feeling. He didn't want to think about what Rowan would do if he found out about the money. He picked up his cell and called his business manager.

"Derrick, it's Nolan. I need you to cancel the monthly wire... yes, the one to Tessa Baxter. I also need you to close out the account and transfer everything to a new account. I need it done by tomorrow."

61

That morning, Pam woke up feeling better than she had in years. The therapy and medication her new doctor had prescribed seemed to be working. Each day she felt stronger and, for the first time in years, she felt she had a grip on life.

Her therapist had her working on a set of goals she wanted to accomplish over the next year. Some of the things she'd listed felt silly, like eating a mushroom—she hated mushrooms—but others were clearly beneficial: learn a new language; she'd decided she would learn Spanish. And she was currently tackling her biggest challenge—to run a half-marathon by Christmas.

She didn't care for running, but oddly enough it was something she and her daughter had bonded over. Simone had become an avid runner and, when Pam told her about her goal, she got excited and insisted that she help her mother train. If someone had told Pam that she would get up every morning at 4:30 to run 13 miles, she would have certified them crazy, but she was determined. The list gave her a sense of purpose.

She checked to make sure that she had everything—the iPod Simone had bought her, her keys, scarf, hat, and gloves. She walked out into the hallway and locked her door just as Meghan was coming out of Mike's apartment. All the years that she had known Mike, she had never actually been introduced to her. She took a quick glance. Meghan was still a pretty woman. She could see why Mike was still so hung up on her.

Meghan seemed distracted as she walked briskly to the elevator. Pam held her breath, then quietly slipped back into her apartment and waited a minute before poking her head out into the hallway to make sure that she had left.

She walked to the elevator and pressed the call button. When the door opened Meghan was on her knees collecting the spilled contents of her purse. Pam felt her heart race as she bent down to help her.

"Oh just great," Meghan mumbled to herself. "Thanks, but I can manage."

"It's no problem," Pam said. She picked up a lipstick and handed it to Meghan.

Meghan's eyes were red and puffy and she turned away and stood at the other side of the elevator. Pam pressed the lobby button. She could tell that Meghan had recognized her and kept her gaze straight ahead. The last thing she wanted to do was make small talk with the woman currently sharing Mike's bed.

Pam had known it would be only a matter of time before he started dating again, but the fact that it was his ex-wife stung. She still loved him and, as she had grown stronger, she had hoped that they would find their way back to each other.

The moment the elevator reached the lobby, Pam rushed out and began her run, skipping her usual warmup stretches. She only slowed down when she was almost at the highway, where she stopped to catch her breath and cried out in pain. She held her side, the cramp nearly crippling her, and sat on the pavement, but at least the stitch was a relief from the pain she felt in her heart. She couldn't bear the thought of losing Mike for good. How could she compete with the love of his life?

After a moment, she stood up and tried to stretch out her cramp. She turned on her iPod and started with a slow jog, forcing herself to continue. By the end of the run, she felt stronger and bolder than she had ever felt before. She decided to complete another task on her list—do something stupid or out of character. She ran up the eleven flights of stairs hoping to catch Mike before he left for work.

Out of breath and heart pounding, she went right to his door and knocked. She didn't know exactly what she would say, only that she had to see him. She knocked again and looked down at her watch and realized that he wasn't home. He usually left for work by 6:00 am on Fridays.

She headed to her apartment, stripped off her clothes and rushed into the shower. She stood under the warm stream and laughed at herself until the humiliation ran down the drain along with the soapy suds.

She felt better afterwards. She quickly got dressed, with barely a moment to grab her purse before she left her apartment. As she headed down the hallway, her cell phone started to ring. She didn't recognize the number and declined the call.

At work, her body ached from her run. She reached into her purse for a pain reliever and felt her phone vibrate. She could see that the mystery caller had tried to reach her a few more times. This time there was a voice message so she dialled into her service and was stunned to hear Arley's voice. He was in town for business and hoped that she would have dinner with him that evening.

She sat back in her chair a little flustered, a little excited. The last time she'd seen him was at Annalise's funeral, which had been more than ten years after their summer encounter.

◄◄

SHE HAD INSTANTLY RECOGNIZED him when he approached her.

He was older, with salt-and-pepper hair, but his face hadn't changed much. In fact, he had gotten better with age. He was leaner and more muscular and stood tall in his tailor-fitted Italian suit. His swarthy complexion was dark and smooth as silk, but with a few more facial lines that enhanced his dapper look.

Pam sat with him for nearly an hour as he caught her up on his life. He was now the father of two girls and he commuted between Jamaica, where he worked, and South Carolina to see his children. He had taken her advice and gone back to school, then started up a small telecommunications business that had grown into a successful Internet provider company in Kingston.

"You know, I have you to thank," he said as they sat in Annalise's parlour at the repast. "If it wasn't for you I probably would still be in my Aunt Silvia's garage tinkering with her old Buick."

"I doubt I had much to do with it," Pam said.

"No, man! I'm giving credit where credit is due," he said. "If I remember exactly, you told me to go back to school and get into the IT business. At first, I thought you were crazy and had been in the Canadian cold too long, but, when I looked into it, you were right. Now, fifteen years later, I own the second largest Internet provider in the Caribbean."

Pam smiled politely. She felt her brief time with him had also changed her life. Before meeting him, she had closed herself off from the world. She'd lived for her children and work but had left little time for love. Arley had opened her up to what life could be if she let her guard down. He'd ignited a passion in her that she'd thought long extinguished. She'd never forgotten how much that summer with him had meant to her.

"I'm glad things came together for you, Arley," she said. "Tell me more about you. Did I hear right? You said you have children."

"Two girls," he said proudly, pulling out his phone to show her pictures. "The older is seven and my baby girl is turning five next week. They live with their mother in Greenville. It's hard having to commute, but Kim and I make it work."

"Kim?" she asked.

"My ex-wife." He smiled at her. "What about you? Are you married? Seeing someone?"

"Both," she said. "I mean I was married but... well, it's over now. Now I'm seeing someone. He's a wonderful man that I've been friends with for years."

Arley laughed.

"Where's the joke?" Pam asked, smiling at him.

"No, it's just funny to me that we never seem to be on the same path," he said. "When I met you, I wasn't in a good place in my life. Now, just when I seem to have everything in place, you're taken."

Pam felt her face flush as he took her hand in his.

"I've never forgotten you, Pam. I never forgot that summer we were together."

She turned away as she remembered the way it had felt. The way he touched her had brought her to her knees. All of those feelings suddenly felt fresh. The heat within her burned hot.

"Maybe one day we'll be on the same path," he said, patting her hand, extinguishing the fire. "It was wonderful seeing you again, Pam. I hope it won't be another fifteen years before I see you again."

She'd watched him walk away. When he turned and smiled at her, she'd had trouble keeping her composure.

▶▶

ALL OF THIS came back after listening to Arley's voice message. What would it mean to see him again? She gathered the courage to call him back but was relieved when she got his voice mail and hastily left a message giving him her address and a time to pick her up. She quickly hung up the phone before she changed her mind.

Pam looked at herself in the hallway mirror briefly before grabbing her clutch. She was wearing an elegant white sweater dress with a simple thin black belt around her waist. It had been a while since she'd been on an actual date. She kept telling herself that it was only dinner, but her heart pounded as she headed down to the lobby where he was waiting in his car.

"You look beautiful," he marvelled. "You haven't aged a bit since the first time we met."

"Thanks," she said as she buckled her seatbelt. She couldn't understand why he made her feel so skittish.

He turned to her when they got on the DVP. "You seem tense. Is everything okay?"

"I'm fine," she said. "It's been a long day."

"You know, Pam," he said after a while. "I had plans for us to have dinner at some *stoshous* in the city. But I have a better idea, if you're up for it."

"Sure," she said. "What do you have in mind?"

"You'll see."

He got off at the next exit and turned around, heading back on the 401 towards Scarborough. They drove another twenty minutes before he pulled up to an empty strip mall. He parked behind the mall. The parking lot was deserted. Before she could question anything, Arley opened her door, reached for her hand and led her to the side entrance of Juicy's, a small bakery Pam suddenly recognized—it had been around for years. The place was closed, but a few people remained, with an older woman sitting behind the counter. Pam started to feel at ease. She nodded to the woman before Arley led her down a long staircase to the basement. Faint music was coming from behind the walls. They walked into a tiny restaurant packed with people listening to a reggae band playing on a small stage.

The owner of the bar recognized Arley and gave him a big hug.

"Lawd, Arley! Why you never tell me you coming?" said the woman. She grinned warmly at Pam. "I could have fixed you a proper place to sit."

"Nah, man, anywhere near the stage is fine, Miss Denne," he said.

They followed the hostess to a booth off to the side of the stage.

"This is nice," said Arley.

"Good," she said. "What can I get for you both? The first round on the house."

"A gin for me." He turned to Pam. "What would you like to drink?"

Pam stuttered for a minute, not sure what to order, then she looked at Arley, who smiled at her. It was his smile that assured her that she was safe with him. That she could relax and be herself.

"A rum and coke," she said.

They sat, listening to the band play as they had their drinks. Arley asked if she was hungry. She nodded. They ordered more drinks and Miss Denne's famous jerk pork.

For years, Juicy's had been a favourite spot for many Jamaicans. Pam could see why. It wasn't a fancy restaurant, but the small, understated joint had a vibe that reminded her of the hole-in-the-wall restaurants she used to haunt when she lived in Kingston. Pam felt like she was transported back to her schoolgirl days in Jamaica.

After dinner, they sat back, listening to the band, and pretty soon Pam was tapping her feet as some of the patrons got up to dance.

"Come, let's dance," Arley said. He got up from his seat.

Pam joined him on the small dance floor. It was nice feeling his arms around her and, for a man his size, he was a pretty decent dancer. The heavy bass filled the room. Arley pulled her close to him and they slowly *wined* to the music. As more people arrived, the house DJ took over and started to play Calypso. Tables were moved to create a bigger space and soon the dance floor was packed.

They danced until the early morning. Pam felt like she was glowing, and sweat trickled down her face. "It's hot in here," she yelled out over the music, fanning herself. "Can we get some air?"

Arley pulled out a handkerchief to wipe away his own sweat. "Yes," he said. "Let's get out of here."

They walked up the long staircase, squeezed past a group of people just arriving. Outside, a gentle breeze circulated around them. They walked silently to his BMW and stood by the car as more cars pulled into the parking lot. Arley held hands with Pam while they waited for the partygoers to head inside.

When the parking lot was deserted again, he kissed her. His lips were firm but moist. His arm wrapped around her waist. They stayed like that for a moment but then timidly pulled away from each other.

"What happened?" he asked. He touched her lips. "This feels different."

Pam knew exactly what he meant. The fevered energy and passion they'd had in Jamaica, all those years ago, had been reduced to a friendly reminder of what they'd once had.

"I'm sorry," she said. "I guess too much time has passed."

"I'm sorry for that, too," he said. "Maybe we can go somewhere more private. Would that help?"

She shook her head no.

"I haven't been completely honest with you," she said, leaning against his car door. "A lot has happened to me. I'm not the same person I was in Jamaica. It's not you or where we are—I've changed."

They sat in his car as she relayed the pieces she'd held back. Her failed marriage to Dex and how he'd attacked her son and left him paralyzed. She told him about CJ's death and the guilt and depression she'd been battling for years. She told him that Mike was the love of her life but her depression had put a huge strain on their relationship and they'd ended things to give her time to refocus on herself.

"So you're the first date I've had since Mike," she said. "And I'm not sure if I'm completely over him."

Arley reached for her and kissed her again. She kissed him back, hoping she would feel something, that maybe opening her heart to him again would ignite the passion. But nothing came of it.

They drove back to her apartment in silence. He parked his car by the entrance and walked her to the front of her building. She smiled when he gave her a warm hug, slightly squeezing her before he let go.

"Pam, don't lose my number," he said. "I still care for you deeply. So keep it—in case anything changes."

She watched him get into his car and waved goodbye as he drove off. She walked into the lobby and yawned as she pressed the call button. It was almost daylight and she debated about whether she had enough strength to hike up the eleven flights or enough patience to wait for the elevator to arrive. She pressed the button again, out of boredom, to hurry the car along.

When the door opened, Mike was inside, leaning against the wall. Pam held her breath as she stood frozen outside the elevator. It was Saturday morning, which meant that he had worked his shift at McKinney's. His eyes looked weary, but when he looked up at her his mood quickly changed.

They had stood still too long and the elevator door started to close. His hand blocked it from closing and her heart raced as she walked into the elevator and into his arms. The heat between them reignited at a pitch she had not expected. He reached up her dress and tugged at her panties, pulling them off, then frantically yanked down his jeans, pressing her against the elevator wall before slowly fucking her.

Pam's pulse raced as she felt him lift her off the ground. With every thrust, she heard the elevator bell ring as they passed a floor. She gripped his shirt, holding on. She felt every inch of him inside her.

At the tenth bell, he cried out and finished, and they both were panting heavily as the eleventh bell rang out indicating their floor. Her feet touched the ground again and they looked at each other, unable to comprehend what had just happened.

The elevator door slowly opened. Mike pressed the "close door" button and pounded his fist on the emergency stop. He kissed Pam again, and then pulled her dress over her head. They tumbled to the marble floor of the elevator and made love again as the elevator car steadily rocked along with them.

62

Simone climbed into her rental car, teeth chattering, turned on the ignition and pushed up the heat to full blast. She was wearing a thin winter coat over a pink floral 1950s summer dress, along with a pair of fuchsia satin pumps. She prayed her rental would heat up faster, as she continued to shiver.

Most of her belongings were in storage or in boxes at the condo waiting for the shipping company to collect them. She had finished packing her last box that morning when she realized that she'd forgotten to pull out something to wear for Mrs. Price's 80th birthday party that evening. In a panic, she'd rushed to the vintage store down the street to find something suitable for the occasion. These were her last few weeks in Toronto, and having to pack for her move to New York, tie up loose ends at work, and help organize Mrs. Price's party left her absentminded. On top of everything, her recent conversation with Jessica had sent her mind completely elsewhere.

◀◀

AFTER THEIR ARGUMENT THAT SUMMER, Nolan had spent most of his time in Vancouver. He hadn't called her, and Simone made no effort to contact him. In the beginning, her anger kept her from reaching out to him, but as her anger subsided it was the fear that she was still in love with him that kept her from picking up the phone.

It terrified her how deeply she loved him. She had left her heart exposed to him for so long that Nolan had seized it and she couldn't figure out how to get it back, so she worked long hours and kept busy during the off hours, distracting herself. Yet, despite her efforts, she couldn't stave off the hunger she had for him.

To make matters worse, Jessica and Nolan had started to date exclusively. It began with Jessica spending weekends with Nolan at his house and then taking short trips to the West Coast when he was filming in Vancouver. When her law firm assigned her a big client based in Victoria, Jessica happily accepted and temporarily relocated to be with him.

That had been three months ago. Plenty of time for Simone to accept it and move on. More than enough time to be happy for her best friend when Jessica called all excited with the news that Nolan had proposed to her on her 30th birthday. It shouldn't have left Simone shattered or at a loss for words—but it did.

"I wasn't expecting it," Jessica gushed over the phone. "We haven't really been together that long. I mean, I knew he wanted us to get serious but not 'will you marry me' serious. I'm still floored by it all. Did he let on that he was going to propose?"

Simone leaned away from her desk at work. "No," she said, trying to ignore the tense throbbing in her throat. "He kept that all to himself."

"I just can't believe it. I wish you were here, Si," Jessica continued. "It was so beautiful. He rented out part of Stanley Park and had a table set up by the pond. It was cold as fuck but so romantic.

We had dinner right there with a bunch of geese and then, after dessert, he popped the question."

"I'm so happy for you, Jess," she said. "For both of you."

"Thank you, Si. We're thinking of having the wedding the end of August. With his busy schedule, it's the only time we can do it, so keep your calendar clear. I need my maid of honour available."

"Sure," was all Simone could muster. "Hey, Jess, I hate to run. We're having a production meeting in five minutes and I... I can't be late. Can we talk later?"

"Absolutely, hon. Oh, before I forget, did you end up finding that gold beaded purse I texted you about?"

"I haven't looked for it yet," she said. "I'll look for it tonight and let you know when I find it."

"Thanks, Si. And, if you find it, just give it to Nolan when you see him," she said. "He's going to be at Mrs. Price's birthday shindig."

"He is?" Simone asked. "I thought he couldn't make it."

"Yeah, well his dad gave him shit for trying to skip it," she said, laughing. "So now he's going, which is actually perfect because he can just grab the purse from you."

"Honestly, Jess, if I find it, I don't mind shipping it," she said. "I'm going to be so busy before I leave for New York. I doubt I'll have time to see him."

"It's not a big deal, Si," she said. "Just text him when you're in the apartment and he'll drop by. It makes more sense to give it to him than having to stand in line at the post office. Plus, I'm sure he'll want to see you before you leave."

Simone's heart had sunk farther after she hung up with Jessica. Knowing that she'd see him soon left her apprehensive. It was easy to avoid him when he was on the other end of the country, but having him at Mrs. Price's birthday party made everything so awkward and difficult.

As she parked her car by the reception hall entrance, her teeth started to chatter. The car was still freezing. She was so cold she was afraid to even open her door. She looked back to make sure the cake, floral arrangements, and centrepieces had all made it to the reception hall in one piece. She took a deep breath, opened the door, and shivered as the wind whipped through her grey wool coat.

She opened the trunk and pulled out the gold and white balloons, holding onto them as the wind threatened to tangle them together. A car pulled up behind her. She looked back to see her mother, Mike, and Nolan getting out.

"We're here just in time," Pam said. She walked up to Simone. "Give me the balloons. Nolan, don't just stand there. Mike, can you help me with these centrepieces?"

"It's okay," Simone said. "I can handle it."

"I know you can." Pam smiled at her daughter. "But now we're here to help. Come on, let's get all this stuff inside. It's freezing out here. Aren't you cold in that flimsy coat?"

◄◄

AFTER LEAVING Simone behind at the club, the day after Caribana, Nolan had gone home and sent Jessica a haphazard text telling her that he wasn't feeling well. He'd asked her to come over, telling her that he needed to see her that night. He had planned to end things with her, but wanted to explain in person.

He'd hated the way he'd left things with Simone. That night, tempers had been high between them and neither was in a good place to talk. He wanted to prove to her that he wanted her and only her.

By the time Jessica came over, he'd been throwing up in the toilet and was nearly passed out on the bathroom floor, wishing it was Simone tending to him, lifting him up, and putting him to bed.

The next morning when he found Jessica lying next to him,

fast asleep, he picked up his phone and discovered his drunk text asking her to come over and his head spun. Sunlight peered down on him and he felt like he was going to throw up again.

When he woke later, she was awake and smiling at him. He apologized for leaving the club so abruptly and told her he was glad she was there. He told her that he had been thinking a lot about them lately and figured maybe it would be best if they ended things. He said that he wasn't interested in casual hook-ups anymore and was looking for something more. He held off on telling her about his feelings for Simone. He wanted Simone to be the first to hear that he was in love with her.

Jessica seemed confused for a second. But instead of saying anything, she just kissed him. She had taken his words as an ultimatum because after the kiss she told him that she was ready to be in a committed relationship with him.

He didn't know what to do. He was still dealing with his hangover and wasn't thinking clearly and, before he had a moment to clarify what he meant, she kissed him again. She laid him back and, before he knew it, she had pulled down his underpants and was giving him a blowjob to get him hard.

She yanked his pants completely off, slipped a condom on him and eased herself on top. "I haven't had you in weeks," she said. "I've missed this so much."

She made love to him, pulling off her top and placing his hands on her breasts. It ended as quickly as it had started.

Nolan lay motionless as she slid off, leaving her leg across him.

"God, you're amazing," she said. "I'm sorry it took us this long to get here, but you're right, being casual isn't working anymore. I want what you want. I want us to be together."

Nolan didn't say anything. He wanted to be anywhere but next to her. He felt sick again and went to the bathroom. He stared at himself in the mirror and could see his haggard face and bloodshot eyes. He splashed cold water on his face.

"Babe," she called out. "I can give you a lift to the airport if you want, but we need to leave in ten minutes. I'll make some coffee."

While she was in the kitchen, Nolan packed a few items for his trip. Opening his phone to book his flight, he stumbled on the selfie he'd taken with Simone just forty-eight hours earlier. He sat down in his closet and leaned against the wall, scrolling through photos of them posing with some of the Caribana dancers, selfies of them dancing on the truck. In one, Simone was dancing for him with a smirk on her face and a slight tilt of her head. He smiled. It was the same look she had given him when they were kids—a smile reserved only for him. In another, they were on the train heading back to her condo. Simone had hated the way she looked and pleaded with him to delete it; "I look like a drowned puppy", but he'd refused, saying "You never looked more beautiful."

He wanted to call her, right that minute, even just to leave a message, but he couldn't find the words to tell her how he felt. Would apologizing just make the situation worse? He couldn't afford a repeat of the previous night. He decided that it was best to wait and figure out exactly what to do. He needed to find the perfect way to tell her that he was in love with her.

On the ride to the airport, he sat silently in the passenger seat next to Jessica, trying to keep his head from spinning. At some point, he had to tell her that it was over and get her to understand that it wasn't some ultimatum. He was about to speak, but she pulled up to the arrivals area and he lost his nerve.

"Thanks, Jess," he said, unbuckling his seatbelt. "I guess I'll talk to you later."

"I'll miss you." She reached over to kiss him.

He glanced at her when she drove away. He felt bad. There would never be a right moment to break things off. As he stood in line waiting to collect his boarding pass, he sent her a quick text saying that he needed to talk to her and it couldn't wait.

When he boarded the plane he found his seat and pulled out

his phone. Jessica had replied: she would be tied up for a few hours but he could call her when his flight landed. He sighed as he clicked off her message. He started to debate whether he should call Simone, even if it was just to say 'Hi'.

He started to dial her number as the plane taxied down the runway. The flight attendant gave him a stern look as she loudly asked all passengers to turn off all personal electronic devices. Nolan quickly obliged and turned off his phone, safely tucking it into his coat pocket.

When his plane landed in Vancouver, it was mid-evening but nearly midnight in Toronto. Once in the taxicab, he turned on his phone to get hold of Jessica before she went to bed, but was distracted by an email from Prisdel with the subject line *Simone Allen to be promoted to Series Producer*. He clicked open the email. Cynthia was announcing Simone's recent promotion and relocation to New York City, where she would help develop the International Reality Production Division.

Riding back to his West End condo, he read the email several times. He had heard that the New York office was looking to bring on a new producer but had no idea that Simone was interested in the position. He dialled Jessica's cell number.

"Did you know that Simone was planning to move to New York?" he asked.

"Well, hello to you too, Nolan," she teased. "And no, I didn't know that. Where did you hear that?"

"An email is circulating announcing her promotion," he said. "She starts in December."

"She never said a word to me, but she was asleep when I got home," Jessica said. "I heard Hubert just got promoted to Project Manager for the New York office. He found out this morning. Sounds like they both got promoted."

"Yeah, but this isn't just some promotion. She's moving to another country," he said. "I don't get why she didn't say anything to me this entire weekend."

"I don't know, hon," she said. "Maybe she just found out."

Nolan sat in silence as the taxi pulled up to his building.

"Was that the big emergency?" she asked. "Your text said that you needed to talk to me. Was this it?"

He'd forgotten about his plan to break it off with Jessica. All that seemed insignificant now. "Yeah, that was it," he said. "Look, it's getting late and I don't want to keep you up. Can we talk more tomorrow?"

"Okay," she said, yawning. "I'm going to bed. I'm exhausted."

"Okay," he said. "Good night."

"Good night," she said. "And Nolan... I love you."

He paused.

"I love you too," he said before hanging up.

▶▶︎

Now, months later, he was engaged to Jessica and back in Toronto, watching Simone unpack the rest of her car in the bitter cold. Mike and Pam had gone on ahead into the reception hall with the balloons and a few of the centrepieces. He was a little agitated, to say the least. He hadn't been around Simone in months. He watched her juggle the remaining centrepieces while trying to close her car door. He smiled as she cursed the wind that was forcing the door back open and all his anger faded away.

He walked up and grabbed one of the centrepieces from her. "Hi," he said.

She slammed the car door shut. "Hi," she replied.

They walked towards the entrance of the reception hall. Snow was falling lightly.

Simone stole a glance. Nolan was dressed in a black-lapel wool suit. He looked incredible. She averted her eyes, took a deep breath, and kept focused on the slippery ground.

"How are things?" he asked.

"Good," she replied politely.

Silence.

"I hear congratulations are in order," she continued. "Jessica told me the news."

Nolan felt a sharp sting. He tried to smile. "Thanks," he finally offered, opening the front door for her.

Silence.

"I can't believe that Mrs. Price is eighty," he said. "To me, she always seemed eighty."

Simone chuckled as they walked into the reception hall.

Nolan placed the centrepieces on one of the tables. He looked around. His father and Pam were attempting to untangle the balloons. Esma and her children were carrying in more decorations and bombonieres for the guests.

"Can I help with anything?" he asked.

"No, I think we got everything handled," Simone said. "I don't mean to run off, but I have to return my rental before they charge me an extra day."

"Why don't I come with you?" he offered. "I can follow you and give you a lift back in my car."

"No, I'm fine," she said. "I have that covered."

"Come on, Simone," he said. "How are you planning to get back?"

She stopped for a moment. She was so nervous just being alone with him that she couldn't think of a good reason why she didn't need his help.

"Okay." She looked at her watch. "But I have to come back quickly. I need to be here when Mrs. Price arrives."

"I'll have you back in no time," he said, smiling brightly.

She turned away from him. The way the corners of his eyes crinkled when he smiled always had an effect on her.

The car rental office was twenty minutes from the reception hall, but the slick roads and steady snowfall made the drive slow. When they got to the rental office, she went in to return the keys while he waited for her. She headed back across the lot through the cold heavy wind and rushed into his car, thankful for the warmth, but instantly stopped by the cold politeness between them—he was a stranger again.

"So, New York, huh?" he said as they drove back to the reception hall. "I had no idea you were planning to move to the States."

"Neither did I," she admitted. "The location move was a bit of a surprise, but I have nothing holding me here, so I went for it."

She bit her lip, instantly regretting the dig she'd made at him. She looked over, wanting to apologize, but he remained silent and kept his eyes on the road.

"Well, it sounds like a great opportunity," he said stiffly. "When do you leave?"

"Next Monday. It's American Thanksgiving, so they want me to come over after the holidays."

Silence.

"I heard that Mac's final season is pulling in great ratings," she said.

"Yeah, so far so good. We're almost done filming in Vancouver and then we'll film the rest of the season in Toronto. It's a lot of work. I'll be happy when we start the new format and just tape in one city."

"Do you have a city that you're leaning towards?"

"Most likely we'll be in Vancouver. Jessica and Jonathan have been pushing hard for us to be out west. The houses out there are incredible and the weather is beautiful... but part of me really wants to stay in Toronto. It's hard to imagine living anywhere else."

Simone nodded. She tried to smile, but hearing him talk about living so far away crushed her spirit. She watched the oncoming cars and, as they continued to drive in silence, it started to snow heavily, which brought traffic to a crawl. Nolan had to put on his windshield wipers. By the time they got back, the parking lot was packed and it took ten minutes of driving around to find a parking spot behind the building.

He turned off the engine. He wanted to tell her exactly how he felt, to tell her how beautiful she looked, that he missed her, how sorry he was for the way things had turned out between them, but he didn't know where to start. He lost his nerve once she started to unbuckle her seatbelt.

They walked slowly through the snowy parking lot. Simone, in her heels, slipped on a patch of ice and grabbed Nolan's arm.

"Thanks," she said as she regained her balance.

She kept hold of his arm until they got to the front entrance of the reception hall.

"Well, thanks for the ride. I have to go and make sure the caterers have everything they need," she said, letting him go. "I'll see you inside."

"Yeah, sounds like a plan," he said, brushing snow from her hair.

Simone froze, but quickly regained her senses and rushed inside.

The night turned out great despite the impending snow-storm. All of Mrs. Price's friends and family, from all over the city and as far away as New York and Jamaica, had arrived to help her celebrate her milestone birthday. The hall was richly decorated with beautiful flowers and balloons. Dinner, laid out in a large buffet in the back of the hall, featured all of Mrs. Price's favourite dishes and desserts. There was even a four-piece steel-drum band off to the side playing music while they ate.

After dinner, many of her family, friends, and neighbours got up to the podium to share their favourite stories of Mrs. Price. Some guests talked about growing up with her in Jamaica, others about how she had been family to them when they first moved to Canada, but the most moving stories were from Esma, who cried throughout her entire speech; she regaled them with tales of her mother's eternal patience, especially during the rockiest moments of their relationship.

Mrs. Price's grandchildren had put together a short slide show that left her crying as pictures from her youth in Jamaica splashed across the screen. Simone looked over at Nolan and they smiled at each other. Then came a picture of themselves when they were young kids. It was one of her favourites—the two of them sitting on either side of Mrs. Price, kissing her cheeks at the same time. How young they were. They were practically babies in that picture: Nolan with his mop of curly hair and Simone's crazy braids sticking up.

Simone saw Mike grab hold of Pam's hand when a picture of CJ with Mrs. Price flashed on the screen. She smiled to herself. She was glad to see her mother happy for once. She looked to see if Nolan had noticed their parents, but he was glued to the screen as photos flipped by. Pictures of Mrs. Price with her grandchildren, proudly standing next to Simone after she had graduated high school, summer picnics with the family.

Nolan couldn't take his eyes off the images. He realized once again how much he had missed being away during those years.

At the end of the slide show, Mrs. Price was brought up to say a few words.

"Lawd Jesus," she started. She looked out into the crowd with her eyes glistening. "I never thought I would see eighty but to have all of you come here to celebrate with me does this old body and soul good. Chups, you have me speechless with all dem kind words. Thank you to my wonderful grandbabies. I don't know where you get all dem blasted pictures from, Lawd Jesus! But thank you just the same. It brought back so many wonderful memories.

"I want to thank my daughter Esma and my granddaughter Simone for planning this party. When they told me that they want to have a party for me I was just thinking a little cake and ice cream. Mi never thought it would be this nice. Thanks to all of you for coming out to celebrate my birthday with me. I don't know when I may see all of you again like this but know that I appreciate all of your beautiful, smiling faces. God Bless you all."

Soon after her speech, the caterers brought in Mrs. Price's birthday cake, complete with sparkler candles that lit up the entire hall. The guests started to sing "Happy Birthday" and then went into a rousing rendition of the Jamaican birthday song.

> *Happy Birthday, Happy Birthday,*
> *Happy Birthday to you, dear Lineve!*

Nolan looked over at Simone, who was clapping and singing along with the rest of the guests. She had the brightest smile. When the song finished and everyone cheered, all of Mrs. Price's grandchildren blew out the candles to thunderous applause and, as the cake went back to the kitchen for slicing, the DJ began his set.

The music started off with old reggae and soca songs that Simone hadn't heard in years. She stood against the wall and watched the older Jamaican guests get up to dance. Nolan joined her. They chuckled at their parents dancing together.

"This is so funny and wrong at the same time," Simone said as they watched Mike and Pam glide across the dance floor, Pam laughing as she held on for dear life.

"I told you they've been practising," Nolan said.

They continued to watch until the music slowed down with some eighties R&B. When Luther Vandross' "Here and Now" came on, younger couples hit the dance floor.

"Dance with me." Nolan held out his hand.

Simone looked at his extended hand and then up at him. "I can't," she said, looking away. "It's not a good idea."

"Please, Simone. Just one dance." He took her hand anyway and led her out to the floor.

Simone felt her pulse quicken as he gently placed his arm

around her waist. She held her breath as they moved to the music. The song seemed to slow down for them. She closed her eyes and fell into the moment.

Nolan could barely keep his eyes off her. He didn't want the song to end. He felt her body relax and sway with him and when he pulled her to him, dipping his head close, he could smell the sweet jasmine vanilla perfume on her neck.

She felt the bristle of his chin against her cheek. His lips were close enough to kiss. She rested her head against his shoulder and listened to the song. Over Nolan's shoulder, she could see couples smiling as they gazed into each other's eyes. For many, this was the first song they'd danced to as husband and wife. It was their love anthem. It would always remind them of the time they'd pledged their souls to each other. She felt like a fraud dancing with Nolan, knowing that years down the line, she would never look into his eyes and see her lover, her friend, her soulmate— only what could have been.

He let go of her hand, placing both of his arms around her waist, allowing her arms to wrap around his neck as they continued to dance. He held her tightly, pressing his body against hers. As the song came to an end, he leaned in to kiss her.

She felt her body tense up when his lips brushed up against hers. She turned her head, rejecting him. "Why do you keep doing this to me?" She pulled away from him. "Is this some sick joke or do you really get off leading me on?"

"Simone, it's not like that."

"You know what? It doesn't matter," she said. "No matter how many times you hold me or kiss me or tell me that you want me, you never choose me, Nolan. It's never me."

She realized that her voice was carrying when some of the guests looked in their direction. She was even more embarrassed when she saw her mother staring at them and she started to move away from him.

He grabbed her wrist. "Wait, Si. Please. Don't walk away."

"You're hurting me, Nolan," she said, pulling away from his grip. "I can't keep doing this with you, okay! It's too much."

She rushed past her mother. Nolan stood in the middle of the dance floor alone.

Pam walked up to him and put her hand on his shoulder. "Nolan, I don't know what's been going on with you two or why things are so strained. But try to mend things before she leaves for New York. You two have been good friends for way too long to let things end sourly."

He nodded.

The mood in the hall quickly changed when the DJ started to spin hip-hop tracks. When he mixed in Kanye's "Gold Digger", the younger crowd took over the floor.

Nolan got lost in the crowd as he anxiously searched for Simone. He looked through the whole venue, but couldn't find her anywhere. He asked several people if they had seen her, but no one could tell him where she was. At last, he saw her by the exit, walking out with Mrs. Price, but, by the time he made his way through the sea of people, she was sitting with Mrs. Price in the back of a car driving away.

63

Simone sat on her bed, listening to the deafening silence between the blasts of wind. Her room felt like a cave. Only her bed, armchair, and an empty dresser were left. All of her boxes were piled in the living room, waiting for the shippers to collect them.

She scrolled aimlessly through her phone. She felt so abandoned in the empty apartment. If Hubert was still around, these last few days would have been bearable, but he had relocated to Brooklyn the month before.

Earlier that evening, she'd said goodbye to her mother. Pam had wanted to take her out for a farewell dinner, but Simone made an excuse, claiming that she had too many errands to attend to before she left. Pam was disappointed, but Simone promised her that they would have dinner together on her first visit back. Now she regretted the decision. Dinner with Pam would have kept her busy.

The reality of the move was starting to sink in. She hated how empty her room felt. The winter wind banged violently against her window and every noise bounced off the walls. It left an eerie feeling as the wind grew louder. She ended up grabbing her blanket and moved into the living room, where she was eventually able to fall asleep on the couch.

She woke when her cell phone buzzed, vibrating loudly on the coffee table, and knew exactly who was calling. He had been calling the entire week.

She picked up the phone and stared at his number on her screen. It took all her strength not to answer. She lay back on the couch and listened to yet another message pleading with her to call him back. But she was too volatile where he was concerned and couldn't risk talking to him.

A moment later the phone dinged, indicating a text message waiting for her. She looked at the message and saw Jessica's name appear on the screen.

Nolan has been trying to call you all week. Are you still in town?

I'm still here, Simone texted back. *What's up?*

Nolan wants to come over to get my purse. Are you home now?

I am but about to head out the door, she lied.

That's okay. He's not far and still has the spare key. Just leave the purse on the hall table and he'll grab it.

Simone's heart started to beat wildly.

Okay, that's fine, was all she could text back.

She quickly jotted a note on the back of a flyer, then put it and the purse on the side table. She was still wearing her pyjamas and didn't know if she would have time to get dressed and leave before he arrived, so she grabbed her blanket and cell phone and turned off all the lights before disappearing into her bedroom. She sat on her bed, waiting for him to come, feeling foolish hiding, but it had hurt too much seeing him last week at Mrs. Price's party and she didn't know if she could handle it again.

Ten minutes later, she faintly heard the front door open and Nolan's heavy boots cross the apartment. She counted his steps into the living room and back and flinched when the front door slammed shut. Tears streamed down her cheeks. She knew that he was gone for good.

Her whole body started to tremble. She could feel the onrush of a panic attack. Her breathing became erratic and she could feel her anxiety escalate. She managed to get to the bathroom and turn on the water. A shower usually calmed her down.

She got undressed and stepped under the hot water. She stood beneath the stream, but the pain was overpowering. Her whole body shook as she leaned against the shower wall and sobbed, telling herself that, if she just got through the night, everything would be fine. If she could make it to morning she would be okay. She would finally be over him.

◀◀

NOLAN STEPPED into the dark apartment and closed the front door behind him. He looked around hopefully, but could tell she was already gone. All that remained were towers of moving boxes that cluttered the living room floor. He considered waiting for her, but, after a week of unreturned calls, he knew that she didn't want to see him. He only wanted a chance to say goodbye.

He opened the front door to leave, but realized that he'd forgotten to pick up Jessica's purse. The door slammed shut. He flinched, then went back into the living room to look for the purse. He found it on the side table with a brief note from Simone to Jessica. He picked up the purse and stopped. The faint sound of rushing water was coming from the bathroom.

Over and over he had been given chances with her—more than he truly deserved. He had wasted so many moments that he couldn't leave before trying to make things right one last time.

He walked down the hallway and around the corner. A sliver of light streamed from the bottom of the bathroom door. The door was slightly ajar. He opened it a little wider to see her slip out of her clothes before stepping into the glass shower.

He stood in awe of her beauty. It was the first time he had seen her naked. He had always dreamt what she would look like, but nothing had prepared him for how stunning she was in the flesh. How fragile and powerful she looked, her hair tumbling down her back, under the cascading water.

Still holding Jessica's purse in his hand, he headed back to the front door. He paused by the entry table, then put the purse down. He slowly undressed, leaving his clothes in a pile on the floor, and returned to the bathroom. Naked, and afraid that he would lose his nerve, he stood watching her from the door.

A chill ran through his body. He quietly slipped into the steamy bathroom and felt a sharp pang when he realized that she was leaning against the shower wall, crying. He instantly regretted all the times he had pushed her away. All the times he'd taken the coward's way out instead of showing her how much she meant to him.

She barely noticed a slight breeze behind her, but was caught off guard when his fingers trailed down her back. He nuzzled against her wet hair as he gently wrapped his arms around her waist, lightly resting his hands on her stomach. He was holding her timidly, waiting for her to push him away, she knew that, but she turned around and embraced him instead. His head fell on her shoulder and they stood in the warm mist holding each other.

For a moment, she stopped breathing. She had never felt this close to him. She knew she should stop what was about to happen, but, as she felt the warmth of his body against hers, all her inhibitions washed away.

After a while Nolan reached behind her to turn off the shower, then he scooped her up and carried her out, down the hallway, back to her bedroom. She curled into his arms, shivering from the cold air. He laid her dripping body on the bed, covering her with her blanket and left the room.

She waited anxiously. She could hear him in Jessica's bedroom. When he returned he had a box of condoms in his hand. He placed the box on her dresser before closing the door.

He looked over at her and couldn't ignore her angst. She didn't need to tell him. The anguish in her eyes said it all—he would be her first.

He looked around the bare room and noticed a basket of candles on the armchair he'd refinished for her birthday. He lined up the candles on her dresser, found a book of matches at the bottom of the basket, and lit each one. The darkness yielded to the glow of flickering candles lighting their way.

She expected him to enter her right away and grew nervous as she watched him put a condom on. She pulled the blanket up to her neck and steadied herself. He gently pulled down the blanket to expose her breasts and kissed them, letting his tongue play with her nipples, drawing them out slowly.

She laughed slightly and covered her mouth with her hand. He pulled it away, kissing her fingertips. He whispered, "Do you trust me?"

She looked longingly into his eyes and nodded.

He moved down to where every intimate moment began. He wanted to start where it was familiar. Where all before him had gone. Where no one would ever enter again.

Simone's back arched when he teased her inner thigh with the warmth of his breath. She moaned when he began to trace her with the tip of his tongue, exploring every inch of her. He heard her breathing labour heavily as he languished on her clit. He liked the way she tasted.

She clamoured as shock waves rippled through her body. The intensity surging through her overwhelmed her senses. She had always stopped the others before it went this far, always pulled away before losing herself. She feebly pushed him away, begging him to stop, but he gripped her thighs and delved his tongue deeper, drawing her to her brink as an orgasm seized her.

He slowly made his way back up her body, which quivered at his slightest touch. "Do you still want me to stop?"

She shook her head no.

He drew her into a long kiss, gently pinning her arms above her head, then reached down with his fingers and continued to stroke her, sending shivers up and down her spine and, just when her body could no longer endure the intensity, he spread her legs and penetrated her.

Tears streamed down her cheeks. Overwhelming pain mixed with joy and love swept over her. She had never felt anything like it as he moved in and out of her.

"I'm going to go deeper," he whispered. "Stop me if it's too much."

She nodded.

He perched her leg on his shoulder and went deeper.

She cried out as memories of them flashed before her. Times he had held her, kissed her, the moment on the swings when she'd first realized she was in love with him. It all came flooding back.

He saw her tears and tried to slow himself down, gliding in and out; he contemplated stopping to give her a moment, but she begged him to keep going and now he was all the way inside, going faster as her cries echoed throughout the empty room.

She felt his girth continuously brush against her clit, sending her body into a rapture it had never experienced before. Nolan's heart raced as his own orgasm coursed through his body. She clung to him as their bodies moved in unison and climaxed together.

II

WHEN THEY WERE DONE, Nolan slowly pulled out, collapsing beside her. They rested next to each other, quietly catching their breath. Her body trembled. She had never cried after sex before, but she found tears streaming down her face.

He turned to her. Her face was glistening with sweat. He leaned over her and, gently cradling her face, kissed her deeply.

"Are you okay?" he asked. "Did I go too far?"

"No… I'm sorry." She wiped back her tears. "I never expected to feel this way. I'm just a little overwhelmed."

"I love you, Simone," he blurted out. "I… I love you so much."

Simone looked at him in surprise. It was the first time he had ever uttered those words to her.

"Wow," he said. "I sound really corny right now, huh?"

Simone smiled. She reached up and kissed him back.

"I love you, too," she whispered. "It just scares me how much."

"Don't be scared. We've been dancing around this for too long and I'm tired of fighting it, Simone."

She nestled in his arms in a glow of happiness and relief. It was everything she had ever wanted. But as the easy silence continued, reality slowly invaded the moment. She knew that no matter how they felt about each other, this couldn't happen again.

"We should have never let it get this far," she said. "I'm moving to New York and you're going to Vancouver… and marrying Jess."

He kissed her softly.

"I shouldn't have proposed to her," he said. "It should have been you. It was always you. Before Jessica… before Sarah Jane. If I had been honest with myself—and you —we would have been together by now."

"Or we would have been stupid, gotten pregnant too young, and they would have still shipped you off to Nova Scotia," she pointed out. "Nothing would have changed."

"Everything would have changed," he tried to tell her. "I would have never left you."

She laid her head on his chest, listening to his heart beating rapidly. She listened until it slowed its pace.

"You don't seem to get it, Si," he said. "I've been in love with you from the moment we met. I've wanted you for so long. I can't let you go."

"What are you going to do, follow me to New York?" She laughed slightly.

"Why not?"

"Nolan, you can't follow me to New York." She got up to reach for her robe. "*House Helpers* is the best thing that has ever happened to you. It's everything you've been working towards. You can't give that up."

"Then come with me to Vancouver," he said, grabbing her hand and drawing her back to bed. "Vancouver has plenty of opportunities for you. I'm still negotiating my contract. We can figure something out."

"Nolan, New York is my lifetime opportunity." She caressed his face. "Don't ask me to give it up. I... I can't give it up. I would only end up resenting it... resenting us."

"Wait... what are you saying? Are you saying that this is ending before it even gets started?"

She looked at him and nodded.

"I'm sorry, Nolan."

She watched him sit up on the other side of the bed with his back to her. He bent over and placed his head in his hands. She got out of bed and walked around to his side. Standing there, naked in front of him, she took his arms and made him hold her.

"Let's make this last as long as we can, okay? We have this empty apartment with no one to distract us for three more days. I know for a fact that there is at least one full box of cereal and a carton of milk—"

"This isn't a joke, Si." He turned away. "It's not funny."

"It's not meant to be funny, Nols," she said. She sat on his lap and wrapped her arms around his neck. "Look at me, Nolan... please."

He looked at her. Her eyes sparkled and she was smiling.

"Right now, I'm the happiest I've ever been in my life," she said. "Knowing that you love me is more than I could have ever asked for, and God knows I wish things were different, but for now all I want to do is spend what little time we have left showing you over and over how much I love you."

He sighed as she ran her fingers through his hair and he remembered the countless times she had calmed him down with this simple gesture. Her caressing fingers were like a drug.

That weekend, they spent most of their time in bed exploring each other. When they were physically exhausted they lay, bodies entwined, reminiscing about their childhood, rehashing every story, every memory, every moment they'd shared together. When they had no more words, they made love, soaking in every precious new memory they created.

The passion blazed as Nolan came to terms with Simone's decision. As much as he wanted to move mountains to be with her, it ended up being the right moment at the wrong time, with their paths firmly cemented in opposite directions. It killed him that he was going to lose her again, but deep down he knew that she was right.

Their last afternoon together was spent quietly in each other's arms as they listened to the movers coming and going with her boxes. Within a few hours, the apartment was completely empty of her belongings, except for a small suitcase she was taking with her.

"I need to go out for a bit," he said. "Please don't go anywhere. I want to take you to the airport."

"Okay," she said. "I need to lie down. You wore me out."

Nolan smiled as he watched her crash on the sofa and pull a throw over herself before falling asleep. He headed out the door and down to his truck. When he got in, he noticed that his cell phone was still plugged into the charger. He hadn't had his phone with him the whole time he was with Simone—nearly four days. Twenty messages were waiting, all from Jessica. He didn't bother to listen. He knew she would be upset that he hadn't called back.

"Nolan, where the hell have you been? I've been calling you all weekend!"

"I'm sorry. I lost my phone and just got it returned to me."

"You sound like hell," she said. "Are you okay?"

"Yeah… I spent the weekend working on a house," he lied. "I'm exhausted."

"Did you get any of my messages? I wanted to make sure you didn't forget to give Judy the deposit. The caterer, remember?"

"I didn't forget," he lied again. "I was on my way."

"But it's getting late, Nolan. Her office closes in ten minutes and Judy needs the deposit today or we won't secure the date. You were supposed to drop it off days ago."

"Christ, Jess, I get it! I'm on my way!"

He was crawling out of his skin. He didn't want to speak to her about their wedding. He wanted a moment to sit in his truck and figure out his life.

"I know you are, Nolan," she said. "I just… I'm sorry. I didn't mean to push."

"I'm sorry, Jess… can we talk later? I'm exhausted. I just want to drop off the cheque and then head home and crash."

"Okay, babe. Get some rest. I have a client dinner tonight so I won't be available for a while, but call me later. Maybe we can have phone sex. I miss that hose you call a dick."

Nolan didn't smile or even pretend to laugh. He wasn't in the mood. All he wanted to do was get to the caterer, hand over the deposit, and then head back to Simone. She only had a few hours left in Toronto and he wanted to spend as much of it with her as possible.

He drove down to the catering office, which wasn't far from the condo. When he walked in, he staggered. The receptionist's phone was ringing off the hook, his stomach was churning and he felt dizzy. He stood in the lobby of the tiny office. He hadn't eaten much that day and it was starting to take its toll.

"Can I help you?" asked the receptionist. "Who are you here to see?"

"Judy Mendoza," he said. "I'm here to drop off a cheque for the Bennett/O'Shea reception?"

"Okay, have a seat. I'll call Judy." She dialled an extension. "Can I get you something to drink? We have water, coffee or tea?"

"Yes, that would be great," he said, sitting down. "Water, please." He felt better once he'd drunk some water.

He looked at his watch. He was already missing Simone and they'd only been apart a short time. He missed the way she would curl into his arms when she slept. He missed the faint scent of jasmine in her hair. He didn't want to be in a stuffy office waiting to pass along a cheque for a wedding he didn't want, to a woman he wasn't in love with. One minute he'd been casually dating Jessica and now they were planning to wed, less than a year from today. He started to feel nauseous again and drank the rest of his water.

"You look like a man who is definitely getting married," smiled a small Filipino woman standing in front of him. "You're sweating like you're about to walk down the aisle."

"Oh no," he said. "I'm just under the weather."

"Okay, then," she said. "I'm Judy Mendoza. Are you Jessica's fiancé?"

"Yes. Nolan O'Shea." He stood up to shake her hand. "She asked me to drop off the deposit."

"Good. Has anyone offered you any water? You look absolutely ill."

"I'm fine." He held up his water bottle. "Your receptionist took care of me."

"Alright, well I won't keep you," she said. "I just need the cheque for $10,000 written out to Capri Group Caterers."

"Excuse me, Judy, it's the Kelley party," the receptionist interrupted. "They're on hold wanting to talk to you about switching the starter."

"Seriously?" she said. "It's a week before the reception. I'm sorry, Nolan, but would you mind giving the deposit to my receptionist, Becky? I have to take this call."

"Sure." He pulled out his cheque-book.

He started to write out the cheque, but stalled when he had to sign his name. Signing meant accepting his life without Simone. It meant moving on from the only woman he had ever loved. He wasn't ready to do that.

"You know, you look so familiar," said Becky, breaking his train of thought. "Aren't you that guy from *House Helpers*? Nolan… Nolan O'Shea, right?"

He tried to smile.

"Oh my God," she cried out. "I can't believe that you're him. I mean… you've been here all this time and it's only now… I can't believe I didn't recognize you. Oh my God! My mom and I watch your show all the time. You look so different in person."

"Thanks." He handed her the cheque. "I hear that a lot."

"My mom is not going to believe this," she rambled on happily. "Do you think you could sign an autograph for me?"

"Sure," he said. His spirits started to lift.

By the time he'd signed her autograph, a gaggle of employees was swarming him for autographs and pictures with him. He spoke with them for another ten minutes before heading back to the apartment.

When he walked in, Simone was still fast asleep on the sectional, snoring slightly, her mass of curls all out in a heaping mess. He smiled to himself and wished he had a few more days to watch her sleep. He wished they could have a few more lifetimes instead of the few hours before he had to drop her off at the airport.

He sat on the edge of the sofa, trying not to wake her. Her throw slid to the floor. She was dressed in her grey off-the-shoulder sweat top and panties. One of her legs dangled off the sofa and he caught a glimpse of her light blue boy shorts. He was instantly hard.

He reached and gently pulled aside the crotch of her shorts and kissed her clit. He slowly licked her out and she moaned, drowsily opening her eyes.

"Hmmmm. You really know how to wake a girl."

Her smile faded when she looked into his eyes and saw the urgency. Her heart pounded as he pulled her on top of him. She hauled off his T-shirt and worked to unbuckle his pants and he quickly pulled his jeans and briefs down to his feet, kicking them to the side. He pulled off her top and ripped her panties, trying to make room to enter her. She was hungry for him, desperate for one last memory. One last time he was all hers. She started to breathe heavily, her vagina pulsating as she felt his tip enter her. She suddenly pulled away.

"Condom," she said breathlessly. "We used the last one last night."

He couldn't believe that he hadn't thought to get more while he was out, but his impulse to be with her overrode any common sense. All he wanted was her—the woman he wanted to marry, the woman he wanted to spend the rest of his life with.

"I can't wait," he said, grabbing her rear and pulling her back on top of him. "I need you right now."

She felt his raw shaft plunge inside her. It was more electric than anything she had ever felt and ignited a fire in her. The feeling of his big raw penis inside her made her cum hard. She caught her breath and slowed her pace, hoping to prolong it. He took her cue, steadied his breathing and let her grind slowly; but, no matter how hard she tried, she couldn't stop the intense orgasm coursing through her.

Knowing that she would be leaving in a short while, he turned her onto her back and thrust himself roughly inside her. He was angry that he was letting her go. Angry that he hadn't fought harder for her. Angry that he didn't have the courage to give it all up for her. As he fucked harder she cried out, begging him to go deeper.

The final thrust came and the little he had left in him exploded inside her. He lay paralyzed inside her, still releasing, as she hungrily licked and then bit his chest. He finally relaxed, pulled out and collapsed on her, breathing heavily.

They clung to each other as the sun slowly dipped below the horizon, casting large shadows into the apartment. She wrapped her legs around him, running her fingers through his hair. She could feel her chest get wet as his tears fell. She held him tightly, kissing the top of his head, desperately trying to keep it together. It took everything in her to keep from breaking down. She didn't want to leave him. She wanted a life with him, but felt lost and unsure.

"It's getting late," he whispered. "We should probably get going or you'll miss your flight."

"Okay." She hesitated. "Okay."

▶

THEY DROVE to the airport with their hands interlocked. She looked out her window at the highway lights passing and could feel her heart breaking piece by piece.

He pulled up to Pearson's departure area, parked, and put his emergency lights on. He got out to help her with her bag, barely able to look at her.

"Nolan," she said quietly. "I love—"

"Don't say it. If you say it, I won't be able to walk away from you."

She nodded.

He wrapped his winter coat around her, creating a cocoon, then looked into her eyes, and pressed his forehead against hers and cried. No one outside of them would see her use her thumbs to wipe away his tears. No one outside of them would see them silently tell each other *I love you.*

"I have to go," she whispered. She kissed him one last time.

He gave her the bag and she walked away from him. He stood

by his truck and watched her go inside with other passengers. He stood there for a little while longer before his cell phone rang.

"Nolan? Babe, you there?"

"Yeah," he said. "What's up?"

"You sound even worse than earlier," Jessica said over loud music in the background. "Judy just called me. You gave her the cheque but you forgot to sign it. She said you seemed really sick and probably didn't realize it. Are you okay?"

"Not really," he said. "I'll go over tomorrow and sign the cheque."

"Thank you, my love," she said. "Go and get some rest."

"Okay."

"Oh... oh, Nolan!"

"Yeah."

"Did you get the purse from Simone?"

He had completely forgotten about the purse. It probably ended up getting packed with the side table when the movers came by for her stuff.

"No," he said. "I wasn't able to find it."

"Oh, shoot. No matter, I'll figure something out. You just get some rest and I'll talk to you in the morning, okay?"

"Yeah, okay. Good night."

He quickly threw the phone onto the passenger seat. He looked through the glass doors, hoping to see Simone, but she was lost in a sea of travellers, right along with his heart. He closed his eyes, unable to manage the emptiness he felt. He took a deep breath and started his truck. As he drove back to his house, he tried to figure how he was going to live the rest of his life pretending he was better off without her.

PART VI

64

Dana sat in her kitchen with her mother and Nolan. She'd made a huge brunch, expecting a crowd, but Freddy had cancelled at the last minute. Two of his kids were home, sick with the flu, and Amaya was working a double shift at the hospital.

Her dining table was a sorry state; nearly a pound of cooked bacon and a carton's worth of scrambled eggs were getting cold. Her brother and mother were quietly eating. Neither of them had been talkative since they'd sat down. They were to drive Meghan to the airport after brunch.

She knew why her mother was distant. She had been travelling back and forth between here and Halifax the last two months, trying to rekindle a relationship with their father. She had even looked into relocating to Toronto permanently, hoping they could make a fresh new start, but it had become clear that he was still hung up on "the beauty queen" next door. Dana felt bad for her mother. Mike was still in love with Pam and, no matter how much Meghan tried, competing for his affections had become a lost cause.

Dana was more worried about her brother. He had come over

G. BARTON-SINKIA

without Jessica and had spent most of brunch keeping a silent vigil over his cell phone. He had made the excuse that his fiancée had to cancel due to a last-minute client meeting, but Dana knew that wasn't the case.

Jessica had called her the evening before, angry and in tears after a heated argument with Nolan, wanting her future sister-in-law to help her figure him out. She said she had thought it was the strain of them being in different cities most of the time, so she'd persuaded the partners to give her the flexibility to work from either the Toronto or the Vancouver office, but spending more time together seemed to make matters worse.

"Please talk to him," Jessica had pleaded. "I don't know what's got into him, but everything I say or do seems to start an argument. Half the time, I don't even know what I've said to upset him."

Dana didn't like getting involved in her brother's love life, but she had noticed his moody behaviour. He kept to himself and seemed irritable; it echoed the Nolan she remembered from right before he was sent to prison. The brother who bottled up his anger to the point of self-destruction.

"Everything okay with you and Jessica?" she asked him after they'd dropped their mother off at the airport.

"Yeah, we're fine."

"So then why is she calling me in tears? She called last night after your fight. She says that you want to postpone the wedding."

"Yeah, so what of it?" he said, looking over at his phone as he drove onto the highway. "I mean, Jesus... I have enough on my plate already. I don't understand the rush! Why can't she wait a year or two?"

"The same reason you couldn't wait a year or two to propose to her," Dana reminded him. "Are you thinking of calling off the wedding?"

"Yes... no, I mean, I don't know..." he stumbled. "I'm just

stressed right now. I've been filming all week and the schedule isn't letting up anytime soon."

"Then tell her that."

"You don't think I haven't?" He glanced at his phone when it dinged. "That's the reason why we had this argument in the first place. She sent out the fucking invitations last week without telling me, so now it's too late."

"Nols, it's only too late if you get married," she said. "If you are not ready, no one is going to fault you for wanting to slow things down."

Nolan didn't respond.

"Nolan, do you love Jessica?"

Silence.

"Yes, of course I do."

"Why?"

"What do you mean why?"

"Why do you love her?" she pressed. "This is the woman you're planning to spend the rest of your life with. The future mother of your children. Tell me why you love her."

Dana studied her brother. He seemed perplexed by the question.

"Nolan, if you don't love Jessica, then don't go through with it. You deserve to be happy, but she deserves to be with someone who wants her for the right reasons."

He picked up his cell phone but then put it back down again.

"I know," he said. "I do love her, Dana. I do. I'm just stressed with work, but I'll be better. I promise. She doesn't have to worry about me anymore."

"Then talk to her, Nols. Tell her that everything is going to be okay."

"I will," he said. "I'll talk to her tonight and make things right."

▶

NOLAN *WAS* OVERWHELMED with all of the wedding plans. He had already sunk almost $200,000 and they had more expenses to deal with. But it wasn't his wedding or even the cost that was ruining his mood. He was miserable without Simone.

Even though she had moved to New York months ago, he hadn't expected to be cut out of her life entirely. He had hoped they would, at least, remain friends, but all of his attempts to contact her were met by a wall of silence. Every phone call went straight to voicemail and every text message went unanswered. He stubbornly continued leaving messages despite the anguish her silence created and, after a while, it started to feel therapeutic talking to her voicemail. He talked to it as if she was right there listening to him sharing his day with her. He always ended each message telling her that he loved and needed her.

He had sent his final message to her that morning after his argument with Jessica, right after they'd received Simone's RSVP reply stating that she would not be attending the wedding. It was a long emotional message and he'd poured out his soul, telling her she was the best thing that had ever happened to him but if he'd known it would come to this he would have never slept with her. He would have rather remained friends if it meant keeping her in his life. He hit send, hoping it would compel her to respond, but, after hours of waiting, he'd given up.

He should have been able to tell his sister that he loved Jessica because she was perfect for him, a sweet, funny, beautiful woman who patiently put up with him even though he was hard to be around. That he loved her kindness. Her heart. Her spirit. But he couldn't say this to his sister because, despite every box he checked off, the one thing that stopped him from truly loving Jessica was that she wasn't Simone.

65

Rowan had been working as the bar-back of Blood Hounds, a biker bar just outside of Hamilton, for a few months. Blood Hounds was notorious and, when he showed up in Hamilton looking for work, his old cellmate Spider Jones got him a meeting with Old Phil, who ran the joint, as well as much of Southern Ontario's crime syndicate. No one made a move on Hamilton streets without his say-so. Rowan was grateful to Spider for vouching for him. This was the first steady job he'd been able to get since being paroled.

After his release, he'd gone back to Halifax to stay with his father, but Ray had re-married while he'd been in prison and his Mi'kmaq-French stepmother didn't want Rowan anywhere near her or her children. She wouldn't even let him inside when he came by to see his father. They had to sit on the front porch of the house.

"So you're going to let that squaw bitch fucking run me off?" Rowan said. "I don't fucking care about her or her cherry nigger bastards. I'm your son."

"Yeah, well, her name is on the lease." Ray spat on the ground. "You want the both of us on the streets?"

"You're pathetic," Rowan said.

"Who, me?" Ray laughed. "I'm not the one who spent a dime at Renous and, the last time I checked, I can account for all of my children. Can you?"

"You're a fucking sellout," Rowan said. "What happened to you, man?"

"Nothing happened to me." His father got up from the porch steps. "Figure out what happened to you and, in the meantime, go back to the halfway house and get a job. Or, better yet, find your mother. I'm sure she has room for you."

Rowan watched his father vanish into the house, slamming the front door. He had always hated him. Ever since Ray left him and his mother when he was five years old. Ten years later his mother had been sent to rehab for alcohol abuse. He had always blamed his father for his mother's downward spiral, years going in and out of rehab, unable to get straight.

Rowan spent months stuck in the halfway house. His room was dirtier than the prison cell he'd lived in and there were just as many restrictions. When he couldn't put up with it a minute longer, he talked his parole officer into letting him live with Tess and his son, bullshitting that a steady home life and strong ties with his son would keep him out of trouble.

For a while, it worked. Living with Tess and Kyle gave him purpose and he figured he could start a new life. A quieter life, without the drama that had swallowed him whole for eight years. But no matter how much he tried to reinstate himself in the community, all anyone ever saw was a felon.

Tess had suggested that he lighten up his look. She bought him a suit for interviews and helped him cover some of his tattoos, but employers would look at his application and quickly dismiss him because of his criminal record.

It frustrated him that he had to rely on Tess. He didn't feel like a man, having to depend on her for everything. She gave him pocket money and took care of all the bills, while he just sat around the empty house, waiting for Kyle to come home from school. He hated being stuck in the house, so he'd sit on the front porch watching the neighbours.

"Hey baby," Tess said, home from work. "How was your day?"

"The same as usual." He glared at the group of teenagers sitting on their front stoop, staring back at him. "What do you know about those jigaboos across the street?"

"Don't call them that, Rowan," she said. "They're good people. Plus Kyle plays with their brother Donnie."

"You're slipping, Tessa," he said. "What happened to the girl I knew who would rather spit in their faces than acknowledge their existence?"

"That girl grew up and appreciates when someone is kind enough to watch Kyle while she has to work," she said firmly. "Do you think it's been easy having to do everything on my own?"

"You don't think I've been trying to find a job? It's not for the lack of trying. I wish you would stop making me feel like it is."

"I'm sorry, baby," she said. "I didn't mean it that way. I'm just saying that, when you were gone, it was hard and they helped me when I needed it. I know that if you were here I wouldn't even have looked in their direction."

"Well, now that I'm back, I don't want you dealing with them anymore. And I don't want Kyle hanging out with them either. I think they're dealers."

Tess laughed at him. "Rowan, you can't be serious. Mrs. Oliver is sixty years old and she lives with her three grandsons."

"You see that little punk that wears orange all the time? He comes from school with his crew and they sit on the porch all afternoon. People come up to him passing shit across."

"Don't worry about it, Ro," she said, lowering her voice. Her face had turned a slight shade of pink. "You're home now and that's all that matters to me and Kyle. Especially Kyle!"

Kyle was the main reason he struggled to keep going. He spent afternoons teaching him how to throw a curveball and helping him with his homework, but it wasn't enough. His son idolized him. He wanted to be more to Kyle than an ex-con who couldn't find work.

He had hoped his luck had turned when he was given a job lead by his probation officer. The city was looking for a landscaper for the local parks. It was the one job he'd come across that didn't require any skill and paid well. He was told it was a sure thing and that, as long as he did well in the interview, there would be work for him. The meeting was a disaster. The black female supervisor was an old high school classmate. She took one look at him, recognized him, and told him she didn't think he would be a good fit. He tried to convince her that he was perfect for the job, he was reliable and good with people.

"I know exactly how you are with people," she said, with her hand on her desk phone. "I'm sorry, but no." She refused to even look at his resume.

He was so angry that he stormed out of her office, kicking over her trash bin. He went to a bar and spent the rest of the evening drinking. He didn't have enough to cover his tab and had to call Tess to come down or the cops would throw him in jail. Tess quickly came.

"How is it that I can't fucking rub two dimes together and you have a brand-new Honda?" he said the moment they got into her car. "I never get it, Tess. You're a fucking waitress. The most white trash cliché job you can get and you're not even full time. You're fucking part time! Yet you have a new Honda Accord. How is that, Tess?"

"I work hard, Rowan," she said.

"Oh there you go again with that whole work hard bit," he said, slurring his words. "You work hard on your back. Is that what it is? You're spending your time servicing local johns?"

"Fuck off, Rowan."

"No, you fuck off. You seem to have all the cash in the world coming out of your pussy."

"You know what," she said, stopping the car, "you're a fucking bastard. You call me in the middle of the night, I have to take Kyle to the neighbours so I can come and get you, and this is how you act?"

"Oh, so that's it," he said, smiling at her. "You're dealing. Just like those monkey boys across the street. I fucking told you that I don't want Kyle hanging out with those assholes."

"Fuck you."

"No, fuck you!"

He slapped her and then pounded her with his fist. She started to cry when one punch gave her a bloody lip.

She kicked him back, hard and often. He got the door open and fell out of the car. She sped off, leaving him in the middle of the empty intersection.

He could feel blood trickling down the side of his face. He struggled to get up, but the last kick to his temple had left his vision blurry. He heard a siren chirp and shuffled to a nearby bus bench. Once the patrol car had slowly driven past, he got up and walked the rest of the way home. He pounded loudly on Tess's front door and waited for her to let him in. Instead, the deadbolt slid shut and the porch lights turned off.

The next morning, he opened his eyes to blinding sunlight and Kyle peering over him asking his mother what was wrong with him.

"Kyle, go catch your bus," she told him. "Quick before you miss it."

"Is Dad okay?"

"He's fine. Go on so I can bring him inside."

She struggled to help Rowan up. He shrugged her away and got up and walked into the house. She followed him to the bathroom and began tending to the gash on his left eye and cheek. He squinted when she applied the alcohol rub, but kept still.

He gently touched her cuts. She flinched.

"I'm sorry, Tess…"

"Just stop," she said pushing his hand away.

"I'm sorry, Tess," he said. "I'm so fucking sorry. I never would have… I promise I will never lay a hand on you again."

She stared at him for a moment and then nodded. He reached for the back of her head, pulled her to him and kissed her. He felt her respond and picked her up and took her to their bedroom, where he took out the rest of his aggression on her.

As the weeks went by, their arguments started up again, along with Rowan's heavy drinking. Anything she said set him off. The biggest puzzle was her finances. He kept demanding that she tell him where her money was coming from and she kept sidetracking him.

It got so heated with him badgering her that she finally told him the money was from her grandmother after she died. But that made no sense. Her family was as trailer-trash as they come. When he first met her, she'd been living on her aunt's couch after her mother got evicted. None of her family could possibly have the kind of money she was showing off. That's when he figured it out. She was stepping out on him.

His accusations led to a huge fight in front of Kyle. He pulled her down by her hair and then flung her across the room. Kyle screamed at him to stop and tried to come between them. Rowan stopped. He couldn't think straight. Tess then screamed at him to get out, threatening to call his parole officer.

"I'm going, but I'm coming back to see my son!"

She stuffed all his clothes and belongings in his duffle bag. "Stay the fuck away from us." She hurled his bag on the front lawn. "I don't want you anywhere near us. Do you hear me, Rowan? Stay the fuck away!"

"I know my fucking rights, Tessa. I know the inside of a court-room and can get visitation. He's my son."

Tess froze.

He could see the fear in her eyes and realized that he had hit a nerve. He didn't know what it was, but knew that there was something that scared her.

The entire neighbourhood seemed to be in their driveways watching the early-morning commotion. Across the street, the old woman, her hair still in curlers, was shaking her head, and her grandsons on their stoop were snickering. He spat in their direction, then grabbed his duffle bag and walked off.

The next few days, he bounced from house to house, but, by the end of the week, he was staying in a friend's garage and looking for a permanent address. When he'd cooled off, he went back to Tess's house.

"What are you doing here?" she said through the screen door.

"I'm here to see Kyle," he said. "Unless you forgot, he's my fucking kid too." He watched her back up. He smiled slightly. "Look, I'm not here for any trouble. I just want to spend time with him."

He could see Kyle behind his mother and smiled widely. Kyle smiled back. Tess turned to her son and sighed.

"If you want, we can get lawyers involved," he offered.

"No!" she said. "Look, I work double shifts on Tuesday and Thursdays. You can pick him up after school. Those are my terms."

"Fine," he said. "It's not Tuesday, but can I at least spend an hour with him?"

Tess nodded. Kyle ran past her and hugged him. Rowan put him in a playful headlock. The two played catch in the front yard until the street lights came on.

That night, Rowan sat on his cot and pulled out pictures of Kyle that Tess had sent him over the years in prison. He carefully examined every line on Kyle's face, the shape of his nose, the way his ears stuck out, the shade of his hair. He looked a lot like Tess— too much like her. There was hardly a feature that resembled him. The next day he took the photos to his father at work, asking him who Kyle looked like.

"I don't know," Ray said. He was under the rear of a car in the service bay. He held up one photo and then handed them all back to Rowan. "He looks a little like your Gramps or maybe your Uncle Joey." He tightened a donut on the exhaust of the car. "Why are you asking?"

"No reason."

"Well, if you're so concerned, check in with the mailman! Maybe he looks like him." Ray laughed. "Relax, Rowan! It's a joke. If you're so worried that Kyle might not be your kid, then ask his mother or go on that Maury Povich show. That kike has been sorting out nigger babies for years. I'm sure he'll be able to help your sorry ass."

Ray was still laughing as Rowan stalked off. He hated that his father was right. He either had to ask Tess or find the cash to test Kyle himself. He decided it was cheaper to go the former route.

On nights he picked up Kyle, he was cordial with Tess, but made off-hand remarks to test the waters. He would tell her that they were going to his friend Maury Povich's house and watch her reaction. Or ask Kyle if he could borrow his hairbrush, he wanted to straighten up his hair before they went out.

"Dad, you're such a goof. You're bald as a cue ball."

"Really? I hadn't noticed," he said, smiling at Tess. "I guess I forgot. Maybe I can borrow some of your hair. Test it out and see if it's as good as mine."

He loved to see Tess squirm. And she squirmed any time he alluded to Kyle's paternity. She knew exactly what he was inferring. There was something there, but he needed a lead to guide him to the truth.

One night, he was in high spirits because he'd heard about a very promising job. He wanted to celebrate and scraped up enough money to take Kyle out for a burger. He sat with Kyle and watched him devour his burger. They spoke about school, his classes, and Kyle confided in him about bullies and wanted his father's advice on how to deal with them.

"I'd rather have a son with a bloody lip than one who runs away from a fight," he said. "Being a man, Kyle, is standing on your own two feet. Once you come out from behind your mother's skirt, that's when you become a man I can be proud of."

"I'm a man," Kyle said proudly.

"Oh yeah?" he said, playfully punching his shoulder. "Show me your stuff."

Kyle landed a powerful punch on Rowan's shoulder.

"Alright, got me a fighter," he said, pretending to spar. "Maybe when I get things together, I can take you to the gym. Get you in fighting condition."

"Really, Dad? I really want you to show me some moves."

"When you're older," he said.

"I'm old enough," Kyle said. "Old enough that I don't have to go to Mrs. Oliver's house after school. Mom said I can stay home by myself now."

"Really? When did that start happening?"

"Not that long ago." He sucked up the rest of his chocolate shake. "Mom says it's a waste of money especially since all I do is just play with Donnie most of the time."

The next afternoon he called Tess's and Kyle answered.

"She's doing a double shift today. She won't be home until five."

"Then let's go to the movies," he said. "Any movie you want."

"Mom doesn't like me going anywhere on a school night."

"Well, call her cell and ask her."

"I think her phone is dead," he said. "I tried to call earlier. I wish I could go, Dad, but she'll kill me if I go off and not tell her."

"I hear you, buddy. Then I'll come over and hang out until she comes home. That way we'll ask her before heading out."

"I don't know, Dad. She doesn't like anyone in the house while she's out."

"People like your friends, and girls," Rowan said, laughing. "I don't think she means me and, if she has a problem with that, I'll talk to her, okay?"

"Okay, Dad," Kyle said.

Twenty minutes later, Rowan was in Tess's house, rifling through her drawers as Kyle played outside with Donnie. He searched the entire house. He went through her bedroom, the kitchen, and even the boxes in the basement. It was only when the mailman came by that he found something.

Rowan curtly thanked him as he handed him the stack of mail. Rowan smirked to himself. The mailman could be ruled out as a potential baby daddy. The carrier was an elderly black man who should have retired ten years ago.

"Fucking niggers can't let go of a job," he mumbled as he looked through the flyers and utility bills. He flipped through the rest of the mail and stopped when he came across a bank statement. He opened the envelope. It was a joint account between Tess and Griffith Management. He couldn't figure out what that meant.

It showed $2500 deposited into the account at the beginning and in the middle of the month. The funds had been withdrawn the day after the deposits were made. She was getting $5,000 a month from some mystery management company. Jesus.

He didn't know what to make of it, but he knew that, if he questioned her, she would feed him some lie. He looked at the account number but only the last four digits were visible. He put the mail in a neat pile when Kyle came into the kitchen for a drink of water. He left the bank statement open on top of the stack.

The next day he walked into a Royal Bank of Canada branch and asked about the account. The teller looked at him suspiciously and told him it was against the law to give out any information unless he was the account holder. He tried to look up Griffith Management in the white pages and called any businesses that had the name Griffith but wasted an hour getting nowhere. The only way was to deal with Tess directly.

He went to her house the next evening, but she wasn't home and neither was Kyle. He went back the next day and again she was gone. He showed up at her job but the restaurant manager said that she'd quit without any warning. He called her cell phone and left several angry messages. She didn't return his calls and, by the end of the week, he was served with a restraining order barring him from coming within 100 feet of her or Kyle.

He was boiling hot and it was clear that he was onto something regarding Kyle's paternity. He went to legal aid. They took down his story and set up a follow-up appointment.

"Mr. Douglas, there wasn't much I could uncover," said his lawyer two days later. "A lot of it is sealed and all I can gather is that the restraining order expires in a year, at which time it will be reviewed for renewal. According to court transcripts, Ms. Baxter stated there had been, quote 'several incidents of abuse and many threats'; that is why the order of protection was made."

"That's bullshit!" he yelled. "And don't I have rights? She can't keep me away from my son."

"According to the documents, the minor is not listed as your son," she said. "His father is listed on his birth certificate as unknown. She claims that he was a product of rape—"

"Rape! Is she fucking out of her mind? She's a fucking whore who slept with any dick that could stand straight."

"Please lower your voice, Mr. Douglas," she said. "Please, sit down." She went on to explain that it was common for women to do that when unsure of who the father was.

"It bars potential fathers from demanding custody or visitation. The only thing I can tell you is that, if you want to challenge this, we can initiate an order for her to produce a paternity test."

"Fine," he said. "Where is she and I'll make her test Kyle?"

"I'm sorry, Mr. Douglas, but that's not possible," she said. "Do you know what a restraining order is? Her whereabouts are sealed for her protection. There is no going around that. All I have is a signed affidavit stating that you are not the father."

"What the fuck does that mean?" he asked. "Does it say who Kyle's father is?"

"Yes, according to what I can see she does name the father but that information has also been sealed."

"How do they know it isn't me? She could be lying."

"Because the real father was probably tested," she said. "Or the court took her word. There is no record of you supporting the minor, is there?"

"No, I haven't had steady work since getting out of prison."

"Did you establish a visitation schedule with the minor?"

"Yeah, it started off every Tuesday and Thursday," he said, "but usually I would call her and figure out when I could take him to the movies or the park."

"That's not enough, Mr. Douglas," she said. "Was there a written arrangement or something organized by the courts? Anything to establish that you are the father?"

"No, why the fuck would I need to do that? He's my fucking son. I don't need to get permission to see him."

"Yes, I understand that, Mr. Douglas, but her letting you take the minor to the movies doesn't establish that you're the father."

"Can you stop calling him the minor?" Rowan said. "He's my fucking kid!"

"I don't know what to tell you, Mr. Douglas."

Just then, two security officers arrived. Rowan looked at them and then at her. Nothing would come out of this meeting. He got up from his seat and pushed past the guards and out of the office.

He went back to Tess's house and crossed the lawn and looked through her front window. The living room had been cleared out. There was a "For Rent" sign on the lawn. He kicked the sign down.

He left Halifax shortly afterward. It violated the conditions of his parole, but he didn't care. He couldn't get a decent job in Nova Scotia and figured living under the radar was what he needed to get his life back. When he arrived in Hamilton, he looked up his buddy Spider and, after four rounds of drinks, Spider promised to set up a meeting between him and Old Phil.

"Anything you can get me, man," Rowan said to his friend.

"I got you, brother," Spider said. The old cellmates clasped hands. "You're home now. Old Phil takes good care of his own."

"As it should be," Rowan said, stiff-hugging Spider.

S imone grasped the sheets of her bed, unable to move. Her eyes watered as she tried to exhale slowly through her nostrils. She had called in sick three days in a row and didn't know if she could get away with calling in sick another day. She had too much to do and deadlines were quickly approaching, but she couldn't budge.

She shifted her body slightly and could feel it climbing up her throat, leaving her little time to grab the wastebasket. This bout was more violent than the last. There was nothing left in her stomach to bring up, so all that surfaced was green bile that burned the lining of her throat.

She collapsed back on the bed, wishing for death, knowing it was life that was making her so sick. The life she and Nolan had created that for weeks she had mistaken for the stomach flu. Dizziness and fatigue started it all; then she got nauseous every time a co-worker cooked eggs in the staff kitchen. Then came the strange metallic taste that made her spit out her chewing gum and order her assistant to go out and buy four different flavours of gum. She swore to Hubert it was either the flu or stomach cancer.

When she finally went to the doctor, the doctor smiled and told her she was pregnant.

"I...I can't be pregnant! It has to be something else!"

"Are those tears of joy?"

She shook her head in disbelief. "Oh God, what the hell am I going to do?"

She'd spent the past three days in bed contemplating that question. She was terrified. She had given Nolan space and time to move on. Now all she wanted was for him to tell her that everything would be okay and that they were in this together.

When she'd left him to come to New York, the magical glow of their weekend had faded into a heavy guilt. Jessica had been her best friend for almost ten years and had been there through everything. Sleeping with Nolan was the ultimate betrayal of that friendship. She hoped that avoiding him would atone for her mistakes and give her some peace so that she would be able to face Jessica again.

But he hadn't left her alone. Every night she'd cry herself to sleep, listening to his voice messages and reading his text messages, words of love telling her that he was finding it difficult to move on. The deep richness of his voice stirred a craving in her that longed to have him inside her again. He called and called, acting as if nothing had ended between them. As if their only problem was the distance that kept them apart.

Mrs. Price is pissed that you haven't called her. I told her that I was having the same problem.

He would end each call saying that he loved and missed her and each day it rejuvenated her, knowing that. It took everything in her not to call him back. She wanted them to be together, but couldn't rid herself of the guilt. And now she was pregnant with his child and would be saddled with the shame for the rest of her life.

She sent a text to her assistant telling her to reschedule everything for tomorrow, she was still too sick to come into work.

In the afternoon Hubert came over.

"Hey faker, I have some of your mail," he said. "Cynthia ordered me to check up on you but if you're contagious then I'm sitting far away from your ass."

Simone sat on her couch with a blanket on her lap, unable to smile or respond. "It's not contagious."

Hubert threw himself down next to her and took his share of the blanket. He leaned his head on her shoulder.

"Si, all kidding aside… is everything okay? Because you look like shit."

"I'm pregnant," she said quietly. "I found out a few days ago."

"Holy shit," he said sitting up straight. "Si, are you serious?"

She stared out her living room window. They sat silently for a while.

"Simone, tell me to fuck off if I'm getting too personal, but is Nolan the father?"

She trembled. Tears sprang from her eyes. She told him about her weekend with Nolan and how guilty she felt, but, now that a baby was involved, she didn't know what to do.

"Sleeping with Jessica's man was clearly not the best decision," he said. "But right now it's not about you or him, or even Jessica's feelings. You need to do what's right for your baby."

Simone nodded. She wiped back the tears. It felt good finally being able to tell someone. The pregnancy and all the emotional complications had been eating at her and now it was out.

"Do you love him?" Hubert asked.

"Yes," she said. "I always have."

"Then you know what you have to do, Si. Nothing worth fighting for is ever easy." She continued to look out the window at the cars zooming by. "You know what we need? A bottle of vodka and two very large glasses, but would you settle for some tea?"

"That would be great," she said.

"Okay, you relax and I'll be back."

Simone stretched her arms. Her back felt stiff from sitting on the couch for so long. She got up and picked up the stack of mail from the coffee table. As she went through them, she came across a heavy pearl-coloured envelope with gold lettering and opened it. Gold specs of confetti spilled onto her rug. She poured the rest of the confetti onto the coffee table, then pulled out the invitation.

Mr. Alexander and Mrs. Trudy Bennett
Together with
Mr. Michael O'Shea and Ms. Meghan Donner
Request the Pleasure of
Simone Allen
At the wedding of their daughter and son
Jessica & Nolan

The pit of her stomach rumbled and she ran into the bathroom and threw up. Hubert appeared at the bathroom door to see if she was okay, but she slammed it, begging him for some privacy.

When she went back to the living room, he was reading the invitation. She shrugged her shoulders in defeat.

"Oh, Simone," he said. "Hon, you need to call him, right now. You need to tell him about the baby. The sooner he knows, the better. They can cancel the wedding, right?"

"I can't, Hubert. It's too late."

"You said you loved him."

"Hubert, you don't get it. He's chosen her and is moving on. I can't just turn around and tell him now. It's not fair to him…to the both of them."

"Si, this is your hormones taking over." He took her hand. "You're not giving him the chance to choose you."

"I'm making it easier for him, so he doesn't have to." She picked up the reply card. "I have to let him go."

The next day Simone woke up and made it to the toilet just in time to heave the few crackers she'd eaten that morning. She dragged herself into the shower and turned on the hot water. She stood under the stream with her hand on her stomach.

"I've lost him, but I have you," she said. "It will be okay. No matter what happens, we'll be okay."

After her shower, she got dressed. She felt stronger. She put on a pair of black slacks and a peach blouse, picked up her briefcase and grabbed her keys and the reply card to Nolan's wedding. At the subway entrance, she stopped by the mailbox, listening to the train rumble across the tracks. She opened her purse, pulled out the pearl reply card and dropped it into the mailbox. She could feel the pressure release and the train's wind billowing through the tunnel as she rushed down the staircase.

▶▶

"IF SHE DONE STOP SPENDING all her money on foolishness like shoes and clothes, she would have plenty money for dem damn pickneys' schooling," Mrs. Price bellowed. "All that money she waste on foolishness is coming back to bite her in the behind."

"Hush, Mrs. Price," Pam said. "That's for her business. The last thing she needs is for you to remind her every time."

"Chups," she said, kissing her teeth. "If I had said it more, her house wouldn't have been foreclosed on. You and Mike were smart, nuh! You both stayed put like me, and I don't see none of you going broke over foolishness."

Pam shook her head. She was helping her old neighbour clean out her closet. Esma had promised to help, but had to work that weekend. She and her husband were feeling the effects of having to put three kids through university.

On her good days, Mrs. Price was as sharp as a knife, which made it hard for them to accept that something was wrong with her. She had stopped sitting for kids years ago. Right now she only sat occasionally for her youngest grandchild, Andre.

Several times, she had left a pot of rice to burn on the stove while she wandered the hallways, looking for children she'd sat for years before. The neighbours had complained of her wailing late in the night. The property management team threatened to evict her. When Mike said he'd quit doing odd jobs for the building if Mrs. Price was evicted, they backed off, insisting that a doctor look into her "episodes."

Her doctor diagnosed her with Alzheimer's disease. At times she seemed aware of everything and everyone around her, but the symptoms were getting worse. Pam had seen confusion and delirium, and recently the old lady was not able to recognize her daughter without being reminded.

The doctor ordered an evening nurse to stay with Mrs. Price until Esma was able to secure a bed in a facility. In the meantime, she and Pam were sorting through nearly forty years of belongings. It saddened Pam that her neighbour wouldn't be across the hall from her much longer.

"Esma, see this picture? This is you and your brother right before I left for Canada." She passed Pam an old black-and-white picture of herself from the 1930s. "What a maaga pickney! Lawd Jesus."

Pam smiled at the picture. She had stopped correcting Mrs. Price every time she got mixed up—correcting her was fruitless. She never remembered what she had said and it really didn't matter who the little girl in the picture was, or that Pam wasn't Esma.

"Pretty girl," Pam said as she handed the picture back.

"Yes, very pretty girl," Mrs. Price repeated.

In the middle of the afternoon, Esma arrived with a stack of boxes. The three women sorted steadily through pictures and keepsakes. They filled nearly three boxes with just photos.

"Mama, you are the original pack rat," Esma teased. "I have no idea what to do with all this junk."

"It's not junk." Mrs. Price said. "All of these pictures and things are my life. My life wasn't junk."

"I know, Mama." Esma seemed exhausted. She patted her mother's hand. "I didn't mean it that way. It's just a lot to sort through and you can't take it all with you."

Silence.

"Esma," said Pam, "you remember the last time your mother conned us into helping her with her spring cleaning?"

Esma brightened a little. "We had to bring her trunk from the storage unit in the basement. It took me, you, and Mike nearly half the day to find, lift, and haul that blasted trunk up here."

"We spent the other half cleaning all those old dusty blankets and bed sheets," Pam said, kissing her teeth.

"Only to have us fold them all up and put them back in the trunk," Esma said, laughing.

"Lawd Jesus, she had us put the trunk right back in her locker," Pam burst out laughing. "Mi mad, mi mad! Lawd, mi never see Mike cuss so."

"Ah who do such a ting?" Mrs. Price said.

Silence.

The two women fell on the floor laughing. Tears streamed down their cheeks.

Mrs. Price looked confused, but then she started to laugh as well.

"We still have dem sheets?" she asked innocently.

By the end of the day, Esma and Pam had cleaned out most of her bedroom and Mike came over with Nolan's truck to transport the boxes. Most were being sent to charities for donation, but Esma said she wanted to take home all the photographs so she could organize them into albums for her mother.

The women sat in the kitchen, enjoying coffee and Easter Bun, while Mike came and went with the boxes. He lightly touched Pam's hand before he picked up the final box. When he did, Pam reached over and pulled down his winter scarf and kissed him.

"Mmm hmmm," Esma said to her after he left. "You two at it again? Do I even need to ask?"

"Nope," Pam said smiling as she sat back down. "Not one word."

The ladies started to laugh when they heard a light knock on the door. Pam looked over, thinking that it was Mike coming back, but couldn't stop smiling when she saw Simone. The two talked daily but Simone had never mentioned a visit.

"Simone, what are you doing home?" she said.

"What a surprise," Esma said. "Look Mama... Simone is here."

"Lawd Jesus," Mrs. Price said, giving Simone the once over. "Girl, yuh look fat!"

"Mama!" Esma said. "Ignore her, Simone. She's getting mean in her old age."

Simone gave Mrs. Price a side hug.

"When did you get in?" Pam said, also hugging Simone. She quickly recoiled when she felt Simone's stomach pressed against her.

Simone looked nervous and weary. "Mummy, I need you," she whispered. "Can we talk in private?"

Pam made an excuse to Esma and Mrs. Price and took Simone to her apartment. They went into her bedroom and closed the door. She sent Mike a text to cancel their evening plans. She would explain later.

"How far along are you?" she asked anxiously.

"Almost five months." Simone took off her winter coat and sat on her mother's bed. "I'm due at the end of the summer."

"My God, Simone! Why didn't you say something? All those times on the phone... you didn't say a word!"

"Please don't yell at me."

"I'm sorry... I'm sorry, I'm just.... Are you okay?"

"I am," she said, breathing deeply. "I get tired a lot but I'm good."

"Oh, Simone," Pam sat down next to her daughter. "Please tell me that you're not doing this alone. Please tell me that you're at least with someone."

"It'll be okay," Simone said. "You did it alone with two kids and we didn't come out so bad."

"Simone, it's not about how the kids will come out, it's how you will come out. Being a single mother is hard. Forget hard, it's damn near impossible most of the time, and it's heartbreaking and lonely the rest of the time. Are you planning to come back to Toronto at least?"

"I can't," she said. "My job is in New York. I can't leave it."

"But your family is here, Simone. We're here and can help you. You have no idea how difficult it will be having a baby without any support. What about the father and his people? Are they in the picture at least?"

Simone shook her head no.

"Who is he?" she asked. "Someone you met in New York? Or that Hubert fellow?"

"No, Mummy, Hubert is gay." Simone gave a tight smile.

"Then who is it?"

"Please don't ask. He's not a factor anymore, okay? He doesn't know, and I plan to keep it that way."

"Why would you do that!?" Pam said. "He lay down with you. He's just as responsible."

"It's not that simple, Mummy. Can we just drop it?"

"You are delivering the same fate to your child that was given to you," Pam said. "You, of all people, should know what it's like growing up not knowing your father. I'm not even talking about having him in your life, but just letting us—and the baby—know who he is."

"Careful, Ms. Pam!" Simone snipped at her mother. "Your hypocrisy is showing."

"And you don't think that I regret keeping the truth from you?" Pam said. "I regret it every day! You spent most of your life hating me because I refused to face what happened to me. Everyone deserves the truth, no matter the price. I know that now."

Simone sat quietly on the bed.

"Do you know the reason why I kept it from you?" Pam said. "I couldn't stomach having to tell a seven-year-old that she was born because four masked men brutally raped me. How do you explain to a seven-year-old or a fifteen-year-old or even a thirty-year-old that you can't tell them who their father is because you don't even know yourself? How do you tell someone you love that they exist because of something so horrible?"

"So how do I tell my own child?" Simone said. "If I tell the father, my baby is going to grow up knowing that it was a mistake. It's the same thing."

"It isn't, Simone," her mother said. "Did you love this man?"

"Yes, I did."

"Then tell him. Then later tell the child who he is. That way the child will always know that he or she was brought into this world in love. That will be enough."

"You don't get it," Simone said. "I can't tell him—"

"You can't, or you won't? All I see is that you're trying to save face. No matter what you tell yourself, it won't give you peace. You hear me, Simone! Whether you like it or not, in the end, everything comes out in the wash."

W ednesday luncheon with his father had been a
tradition since Nolan had moved back from Halifax.
And, when he started to make good money, the
quick bite at Johnny's Hamburgers was replaced with lunches at
The Keg.

He had been in town almost four months now, ever since
filming in Vancouver had wrapped up. With the show's popularity
in full swing, his schedule in both cities had become completely
gruelling, and, by the time he got to Toronto, he wasn't in the
mood to do much of anything except work and sleep. His
standing lunch date with his father was the only thing he made
time for.

Jessica had been pressing him to put together his list of
groomsmen. Other than Freddy, he didn't really have many close
friends, but she was adamant about including all of her girlfriends
and needed him to have at least four groomsmen. He had no idea
who to add, but he definitely knew that he wanted his father to be
his best man.

"I don't know what to say, Nols," Mike said, smiling ear to ear.

"Are you sure that Jessica is okay with me as your best man? Not one of your other friends?"

"I don't think there could be a better person," Nolan said. "I've asked Freddy to be one of my groomsmen, but I want you as my best man."

"Well, it means a lot," Mike said, sipping his beer. "You seem pretty calm for a guy who is getting married in a few months. No jitters yet?"

"To be honest, the sooner we can get this over with, the better," Nolan said. "It's more Jess's day than mine."

"It usually is." Mike chuckled. "Speaking of which, Jessica has been hounding me on whether I'm bringing a date."

"Yeah, she has an aunt who just got a divorce." Nolan rolled his eyes. "She's dying to introduce you guys."

"Oh, Jesus," Mike said. "Tell her thanks, but I already have a date for the wedding."

"Really? Who's the lucky lady?"

"Pam," Mike said, beaming. "So be sure that Jessica doesn't sit us with Maureen. I haven't told Maureen that I'm taking her and I really don't want to hear her bitch about it."

"Pam, huh?" Nolan said. "Well, at least one of the Allen women will be attending. Simone isn't coming."

"Well, what did you expect?" Mike said. "I doubt her doctor would give her permission to travel. Come to think of it, she'll probably have the baby by then."

"Wait! What baby?"

"What do you mean, what baby, Nolan? The same baby she's been pregnant with for the last six months."

"I...I didn't know she was pregnant. I had no idea."

The waitress came by with their steaks.

"I thought you guys talked all the time?" Mike said, digging his knife into the meat. "I just assumed that you knew. Then again, Pam and I only found out last month. Other than her due date,

Simone has been a little light on the details. It's caused a huge stink between her and her mother."

Nolan felt his stomach twist in knots. What was going on? Simone had told Jessica that she'd be working on location on the wedding date and couldn't get the schedule changed. Why wouldn't she mention that she was pregnant?

"Keep this to yourself," Mike continued. "But I found out from Mrs. Price that Simone got involved with a married man. Some one-night stand. She hasn't even told the guy. Afraid it would break up his marriage. Honestly, I think she's just embarrassed that she let herself get into this situation."

Nolan thought back to their weekend. The week of American Thanksgiving. He remembered how crowded the airport had been when he dropped her off. The weekend before she moved to New York City—six months ago.

"I'm just shocked by it all," Mike said, shaking his head. "Isn't she a lesbian? Well, I guess now she's bi-sexual or transsexual. I can't keep up with what everyone calls it... Nolan, aren't you going to eat?"

"Yeah, I just need another drink." He waved the bartender over. "Can I get another beer... actually, can I get an old fashioned?"

"A little early for an old fashioned," Mike said raising his eyebrows. "So, did you know the guy?"

"The guy?" Nolan replied, distracted. "What guy?"

"The one that knocked her up," he said. "Maybe you know him? Do you know who he might be?"

"Yeah... I know who he is."

"She's a smart girl," Mike sighed. "Why would she let herself get pregnant, let alone involved with a married man? I mean she had to have known that he was married."

"He isn't married," Nolan said. "He's engaged."

The bartender brought him his drink and he downed it. Mike looked up at him. His father was staring at him. He lowered his head and played with his ice cube.

"Look at me, Nolan," Mike said. "It's you, isn't it?"

Nolan hailed the bartender and ordered another drink. He told his father everything. How he'd fallen back in love with her when they reconnected last year. That she probably got pregnant the one time they didn't use a condom, right before she went to New York.

Mike looked stunned.

Nolan told him that he'd been a mess ever since. He'd called her daily for two months, but she never returned a single call. He'd given up when she sent back the RSVP to say she wouldn't be attending the wedding. And now he was finally resigned to the fact that it was over.

"My God, Nolan! What the hell were you thinking?" Mike pushed his plate away. "Does Jessica know?"

"No. When Simone made it clear that it was over, I didn't...I just kept it to myself."

"This is a fucking mess! Well, maybe it's for the best that she kept the pregnancy from you," Mike said. "Nolan, you are about to start a life with Jessica. Having another woman's baby in the picture will kill your marriage before it even has a chance to start. Is that what you want?"

"Lay off, Dad," he said sharply.

"I know you don't want to hear this, but you're a goddamn fool if you think otherwise."

"You're right, Dad," he shouted. "I don't want to fucking hear this."

"Well, you need to," Mike said. "I thought you were over this bloody crush you've had on Simone!"

"Do you think I haven't tried? I've tried forgetting her. I've tried avoiding her. I've tried hating her and you know what? I always end up miserable without her."

"So now what?"

"I need to find out what the fuck is going on." He got up from the table, pulling money from his wallet. "I need to talk to her, because right now nothing makes any sense."

▶

ON HIS WAY back to his apartment, he called the airline. The earliest flight to New York was a stand-by later that afternoon. He was supposed to be in Toronto the next day for a meeting with Prisdel executives to sign a new contract. He called his agent to change the meeting to Friday afternoon in their New York office.

When he got home, Jessica was sitting in the dining room on a conference call. She mouthed that she would only be a few more minutes. Nolan nodded. He headed to the bedroom to pack.

He was almost finished when Jessica came in sipping a glass of wine. He had thrown clothes all over the place, frantically searching his dresser drawers for his passport.

"Babe, did you see your Dad... what's going on here? What are you looking for?"

"My passport," he said. "I had it a few weeks ago."

"It's in the lockbox, babe. Why do you need your passport?"

"I'm going to New York," he said. "My flight leaves in a few hours."

"You're not scheduled to be in New York. Don't you have your meeting with Prisdel tomorrow?"

"It's switched to Friday in New York," he said, rummaging through the lockbox. "Where the fuck is my passport?"

"Okay, but what's the rush? You don't have to leave right away."

"There's something I need to take care of before the meeting," he said. "Seriously, it's not in the lockbox."

"Babe... babe, it's right here." She pulled the passport from the bottom of the box. "Here."

"Thanks," he said. He put the passport in his carry-on bag.

"So you're heading out right now?"

"Yup."

"To see her?" she said calmly. "That's the only reason I can imagine why you're rushing out to New York."

Nolan stopped still and looked at Jessica. She was trembling, the glass tilted in her hand. He didn't want to have this conversation with her now.

"Were you ever going to tell me that you slept with her, Nolan?" she said. "Was that ever going to come up before we got married?"

Her eyes were glassy with tears, but her voice was strong.

"I'm sorry, Jessica," was all he could muster. He sat on the side of the bed. "I don't know what to say."

"You can tell me why you're rushing to see her," she said. "Why you're dropping everything just to be with her."

"Simone's pregnant," he said. "I just found out."

"Well, I knew all about it." She laughed angrily. "She's six months and due the end of the summer. Do you want to know how I know, Nolan? I know because I'm not stupid!"

"I never thought you were," he said quietly.

"Well, you must have thought I was too dim to notice that you were M.I.A. that entire weekend before she left for New York," she said, raising her voice. "And too stupid to notice how quiet and moody you were after she left. Or maybe you thought that you'd covered your tracks when you replaced the box of condoms in my closet. Maybe you thought I would be too fucking stupid to notice."

Nolan could feel the room closing in. He felt foolish. Jessica had known about his weekend with Simone all along.

"You know... I wish I didn't know," she said. "I wish I was that fucking clueless."

"Jessica, I've tried to forget her," he said. "But I can't shut off my feelings."

"Try harder," she screamed. "Everything is on the table now!

Your secret is out. I fucking hate you for sleeping with her, but I will get over it, the same way you will eventually get over her!"

"Jess, it's not that simple," he said feebly. "I can't just pretend that she's not having my baby."

"Yes, you can!" she cried out. "Do you know how easy it would have been for her to tell you she was pregnant? She chose not to. She doesn't want you in her life, Nolan, and, if you can get it through your thick skull, you will know that I'm right."

Nolan wanted to argue, tell her that she was wrong, but, in the back of his mind, he couldn't understand it either. Why hadn't Simone told him the moment she'd found out? Had she erased him? Had she ever loved him at all? He needed to find out. He needed her to tell him to his face.

"I have to go, Jessica," he said. "I need to talk to her." He stood and picked up his bags.

"If you go to her, then we're through," she said. "Do you under-stand me, Nolan? If you do this, don't come back when she fucking rejects you."

Nolan walked out the bedroom. He flinched slightly as he felt her wine glass shatter against the wall, but he didn't turn around. He continued out the front door.

6 8

Simone sat at her desk, unable to concentrate. She hadn't felt like herself the entire day. She wished that she had stayed home and rested. Her doctor had warned her that her last test was troubling. Her blood pressure was higher than it should have been and she had been told to take it easy.

But she hated idling at home. She needed the noise of the office. The chatter. The phones ringing off the hook. She needed her mind focused on anything but her pregnancy and Nolan.

"Simone, I'm grabbing drinks with Nate," Hubert said, popping his head in her office. "Come with us. I need a buffer so I don't say something stupid."

"Hubert, stop acting like a pussy and just ask him out already," she teased. "It's getting embarrassing."

"Easy for you," he said. "Not all of us have that baby bump working for us. I'm sure every man and woman is lusting after your ass with that killer body you're rocking. Me, on the other hand, gots to work hard on my game."

"You're an idiot. Give me ten minutes and I'll meet you in the lobby."

When Hubert left, she quickly looked over her schedule for the next day. As she started to put away her paperwork she felt a sharp pain in her lower back. She closed her eyes and took a deep breath, waiting for it to ease off.

"It's nothing," she whispered to herself. "Just stress. I'm overdoing it."

She went into her purse and pulled out her compact. She frowned at her reflection. She was paler than usual. She pulled at the bags under her eyes that made her look haggard. No amount of makeup could conceal the lack of sleep she was getting.

Over the last few weeks, her panic attacks had come back with a vengeance. Her go-to remedy had always been a long hot shower, followed by a shot of vodka to ease the tension. In the past, Jessica had tried to persuade her to talk to someone, but she always laughed it off, saying that black people don't do therapy. But now, with the baby, she felt helpless as she suffered through her anxiety alone.

She took one last look at herself, reapplied her lip gloss, and tightened her ponytail. She was about to add some blush when Hubert came rushing into her office.

"Simone, he's here! And he's either really pissed, really drunk, or both. Either way, he's on the warpath."

"What are you talking about? Who's here?"

"Your baby daddy," he said, just as she spotted Nolan heading towards her office. "I keep forgetting how massive he is. They make him look so puny on the screen. We really need to fire his camera crew."

She'd known that it would be only a matter of time before he found out, but she had hoped it would be after the wedding. The last thing she wanted was to cause any further damage to his relationship with Jessica.

"Nolan," she said when he walked into her office. "What are you doing here?"

"What do you think?" he said. He looked around and saw

Hubert glaring at him. "Hubert, can I talk to Simone in private, please?"

"I don't know, partner, you seem a little hot right now," Hubert said. "Maybe I should stay."

"It's okay, Hubert," she said. "I'll be okay. You go ahead with Nate and I'll catch up with you both later." Hubert slowly passed behind Nolan, gesturing her to call him.

Simone continued packing her briefcase as if Nolan wasn't there. Nolan looked at her. He was startled at how small she appeared. She looked very pale and frail. If he hadn't known, he would never have guessed she was pregnant.

"Why did I have to figure it out myself?" he said, after a long silence. "Why couldn't you just come out and tell me?"

"And what would you have me do, Nolan?" she said. "Call you over the phone and say, 'Hey, Nolan remember that weekend we fucked… you know, the weekend when I screwed my best friend's fiancé? Well, guess what? When you walk down the aisle I'll probably be in labour with your baby'."

"Yes!" he yelled. "In fact, it would have been nice if you had told me the moment you found out instead of leaving me in the fucking dark. Is that really a hard concept to grasp?"

"Well, it wasn't easy for me," she said, trying to keep her voice down. "You have no idea how many times I wanted to tell you! It killed me that I couldn't."

"You could have fooled me," he said. "Because for nearly two months I called every day, leaving you messages, telling you how much I love you, how miserable I've been without you—and you never bothered to fucking call me!"

"Because we were done, Nolan!" she said, choking back tears. "We were done when we said goodbye. We were done when I left Toronto. We were done when I got your wedding invitation in the mail."

"Oh, so that's it! You're mad that I'm still marrying Jess!"

"No! That's not it!"

"No, I think that's exactly why you kept it from me. You end things and tell me to move on and, the moment I do, you punish me for it."

"That's not true, Nolan," she said, squinting as she suffered through another cramp. "I wasn't trying to punish you, okay! I was afraid to tell you. I was scared how you would react."

"You know damn well that I would have dropped everything to be with you." His voice echoed loudly. "The problem is that you had me thinking that you loved me, but you never fucking loved me. It was all bullshit."

"Don't say that!" she cried out as another cramp pierced through her abdomen. "All I've ever done was love you. I've loved you my whole life! All the times I waited by the sidelines, I've loved you. I gave myself to you and lost my best friend in the process, all because I loved you! So don't you dare question..." She stood up, shaking, unable to finish. A panic attack was coming on. She tried to slow her breathing, but then a sharp pain sliced through her.

"What's wrong?" he said. He noticed her clutching the side of her desk.

"It's nothing. I'm fine," she said, then cried out in agony.

"Jesus, Simone!" he said as he rushed to her. "What's wrong?"

"Oh, God." She clutched her stomach, trying to breathe. "Something doesn't feel right."

He walked her to her office couch. "Sit here. I'm going to get help."

He went to her desk phone to call the receptionist, but Simone screamed out in pain and he dropped the phone and grabbed her before she slid to the floor.

"I need some help!" he yelled. "Someone call an ambulance."

Simone's assistant rushed in with Hubert behind her.

"Call an ambulance," Nolan said. He held her head up. "Something's wrong."

Simone lay curled up on the floor, crying in pain. She was

scared. She could see Nolan was, too. He didn't know what to do for her. He just sat there, cradling her head in his lap until the paramedics finally arrived.

"Can you tell us what's wrong, Miss?" said one.

"I don't know," she said. "I had sharp pains earlier this morning but it started to get worse. Oh God... it hurts so much."

"What's your name, honey?"

Simone tried to speak, but the pain surged again.

"Her name is Simone Allen," Nolan said.

"What a pretty name," she said. "Are you expecting?"

She nodded.

"Can you tell us how many weeks?"

"Twenty-six weeks," she said, groaning. Her eyes started to close.

"No, no, honey," said the paramedic. "Stay with us now. Keep talking, sweetie."

"It hurts so much," she said. She cracked open her eyes. "Please help me."

"We will," said the male paramedic. "Okay, let's get you to Mount Sinai and have them look at you."

After checking her vitals, the paramedics placed her on the gurney and wheeled her out.

Nolan followed closely behind to the elevator bank.

"I'm sorry, sir, but you have to step out," said the male paramedic as Nolan tried to get into the elevator with them. "There isn't enough room."

Simone cried in agony and tried to pull her oxygen mask off, but, before she could say anything, the paramedic held the mask to her face.

"I need to be with her," Nolan said. He tried to get in the elevator.

"Sir, I'm not going to tell you again," yelled the paramedic. "Get out of our way!"

"He's the father," Nolan could hear from behind him. "Can't you let him ride in the ambulance with her?"

Nolan looked behind to see Hubert holding up Simone's purse and briefcase.

"I'm sorry, but there isn't room for us and him," said the female paramedic. "We're heading to Mount Sinai. You can meet us there. That's the best we can do."

"Nolan!" Simone cried out.

"It's okay, Simone," said the female paramedic. "He's going to follow us, okay, honey? Come on, let's go."

"Simone, I'll take him to the hospital," said Hubert. "We'll be right behind you."

▶

AS THE ELEVATOR CLOSED, Nolan could see that she was passing out in pain and his heart sank as he realized that there was something terribly wrong with her.

He and Hubert took the next elevator down and hailed a cab. When they arrived at the emergency room, they were told that she had been sent up to the maternity ward for observation. Nolan rushed up to maternity, where he saw an orderly wheel her into a room. He bypassed the nurses' station and went into the room with her.

"Simone, are you okay?"

"I don't know," she said. "It hurts so much, Nolan. I'm scared something is wrong with her."

"It's okay, Si," he said, a little stunned to find out that they were having a girl. "She's going to be okay. I promise. She's strong like you and determined like me."

Simone looked up at him with glassy eyes and nodded.

"Sir, this area is for patients only," said a small Jamaican nurse. "We're going to have to ask you to step out."

"Like hell I am," he said. "This is the mother of my baby. I'm not going anywhere."

"Nolan, don't leave," Simone said. "I'm scared that I'm losing her. Please let him stay... ugh..."

"Okay... okay," said the nurse. "He can stay until the doctor arrives, but you'll have to go to the waiting room when we do a full exam."

She stepped out and a few moments later came back and started strapping pads to Simone's stomach. She explained to them that the machine was going to monitor the baby's heart rate for an hour.

"Okay, Mama," said the nurse in her thick accent. "Hold tight until Dr. Neuberger arrives and don't worry yourself too much. He's the best in the city. He brought my own into the world and they're all healthy and strong."

"It hurts so much." She grasped Nolan's hand.

"I know, honey," said the nurse, taking her temperature. "Just sit tight."

Simone lay back, trying to breathe. Tears streamed down the sides of her face. Nolan felt helpless. He didn't know what to say or do. He worried that their argument had triggered this setback.

"Simone, concentrate on me for a minute." He began stroking her hair while whispering in a hushed tone. "Remember when we were little and climbed that tree by the swings? The one with the huge trunk? We were going to build a secret tree house at the very top. Do you remember? We tried to climb to the top but chickened out halfway, so we decided to build our secret club-house right there out of some old boxes we found in the dumpster. We ended up with tick bites all over our bodies. Do you remember?"

Simone laughed a little as she nodded. He could see her breathing slow down as she powered through the pain. He kissed her forehead. He described the playground and all their secret hiding places. How they ran around all day and played tag on the

G. BARTON-SINKIA

roof. She groaned softly as he continued to whisper to her. She was almost asleep when the doctor arrived.

"Who do we have here?" Dr. Neuberger picked up Simone's chart. "Hello, Ms. Allen. Can I call you Simone?"

Simone nodded.

"And who else do we have here?" He turned to Nolan.

"Nolan," he said. "Nolan O'Shea... I'm the father."

"Oh yes," he said. "My wife and I watched your program when we were in Canada. Good show. Too many commercials."

He continued to look at her chart, then went to the fetal monitor and read the findings.

"Well, my dear, it shows on my chart that you're about twenty-six weeks," he said. "Are you experiencing any spotting?"

She shook her head no.

"Good. That's always a good thing. Can you tell me where it hurts?"

"It hurts around the lower part of my stomach and my lower ugh... oh God... my lower back," she said. "Am I going into labour?"

"That's what we're here to check out." He glanced at her chart again. "First thing we're going to do is order an ultrasound. The fetal monitor shows that your baby's heart rate is strong and there doesn't seem to be any significant contractions, but we need to see what's causing the pain. For now, lie back and try to relax. Once we know more, I'll be able to give you something for the pain. Okay?"

She nodded, then gritted her teeth when the pain surged again.

"Okay, then," said the doctor. "I'll be back."

Simone continued to breathe steadily while she looked up at the fluorescent lights above her. She turned towards Nolan. He was white as a ghost.

"I'm so sorry, Nolan," she said. "I'm sorry that I didn't tell you. I... I should have told you. I wanted to, so many times," she said, trying to sit up. "I was scared that you would hate me or think that I was trying to ruin things for you."

"It's okay, Si. Lie still and relax," he said, easing her back down. "I just want you to concentrate on our baby girl, okay? That's the only thing that matters."

Moments later the doctor was back with the sonogram equipment. He placed a heaping amount of gel on her stomach. Simone's stomach curved like a golden globe. Nolan was in awe. His child was in there. He wanted to reach out and touch her stomach, but he held off and squeezed her hand instead.

When they began, Nolan couldn't tell what he was looking at.

"Is this your first sonogram?" the doctor asked.

Nolan nodded.

"Well let me give you a crash course. This top part here is your daughter's head, that over there is her stomach. Did you see that? She just turned around and mooned you. I can tell this one is going to give you trouble."

Nolan laughed out loud as he watched his daughter slowly moving around. He recognized her eyes and nose and her little feet and hands.

"That's her," he whispered to Simone. "That's ours."

Simone nodded. She smiled through the pain.

"And there's the culprit," said the doctor. "Do you see that bubble on the screen? It doesn't look like much, but it's about the size of a lemon."

Simone and Nolan both nodded.

"Well, that is a fibroid and a pretty sizeable one," he said. "The pain you are feeling is the baby pushing up against it. Your little girl is cutting off the fibroid's oxygen and blood supply. It's called degeneration. Essentially the fibroid is dying, which is why you are experiencing pain."

"Will the fibroid hurt her?" Simone asked. "Is it serious?"

"Where it is positioned, it doesn't pose a threat and she doesn't feel a thing," he said. "But I want to keep you a little while longer, maybe overnight, to monitor you. Nothing to be alarmed about, but your blood pressure is a little high. I want to check on it, just as a precaution."

The nurse came back with some mild pain meds. By the time they wheeled her to a bigger hospital room, Simone had fallen asleep.

Nolan went to the lobby, where Hubert was still waiting with Nate, who had come by when he found out that Simone was in the hospital.

"How's she doing?" Hubert asked. "She gave us a huge scare."

"She's sleeping right now," Nolan said. "They're running more tests, but I think she and the baby are going to be okay."

"Well, thank God," Hubert said. "Maggie, our receptionist called. You left your stuff behind at the office. They don't know which hotel you're staying at."

"I didn't book one yet," he said. "I kind of flew here as soon as I heard... that she... I just found out that she was pregnant."

"Oh, wow," Nate said. "And you just jumped on a plane?"

"Something like that," he said.

"Well, it's about time you were in the picture," Hubert said. "This pregnancy has been a total bitch for her."

"That bad?" Nolan asked.

"This is probably the cherry on top," Hubert said. "It's been rough on her from the very beginning. Constant morning sickness, mood swings, and being worried about you. I hope you don't mind, but she told me what happened between you two."

"I wish she'd told me sooner," he said. "I honestly had no idea what's been happening. She never returned any of my calls."

"Well, you know her better than anyone," Hubert said. "When she gets a notion in her head, she's like a Rottweiler with an old shoe. She was convinced you were better off not knowing. Look, it's too late to find a hotel. I'm assuming you're going to make sure she gets home?"

"Absolutely," Nolan said. "I'm not going anywhere."

"Good! We'll grab your stuff." Hubert fished through Simone's purse for her house keys. "I'll drop your bags off at her place and you take these lovely hospital papers and start filling them out. These bitches are fucking Nazis about their paperwork."

"Sure thing." Nolan took the paperwork and Simone's belongings. "And thanks, Hubert, for your help. I really appreciate everything."

"Anything for my girl," he said. "Oh, I'll leave the keys under the mat." He and Nate walked into the hospital elevator. "Tell her to relax and that I'll call her in the morning."

▶

NOLAN WAS asleep in the chair next to her hospital bed when Simone woke up, a little bewildered. It took her a moment to figure out that she was in the hospital and why Nolan was sitting there fast asleep with his head lagging back. After a while, he woke up and smiled.

"Hey," he said. "You're awake. How do you feel?"

"Better," she said, trying to sit up. "It's not as bad as it was earlier. I think the meds are working."

Nolan got up quickly and used the bed's remote to adjust her position.

"There," he said. "Doctor said that you shouldn't be sitting up too much. They're still monitoring her."

"I'm so sorry, Nolan," she said, grabbing his hand. "I'm so sorry that I didn't tell you from the very beginning. I didn't want this coming between you and Jess—"

"Simone, it's over between Jessica and I," he said. "It's been over for a while, I just didn't have the guts to admit it."

Simone wanted to say something, but the doctor had walked into the room.

"Alright kids, the good news is that the tests show your blood pressure stabilizing," he said. "It looks like the fibroid is the only issue. Unfortunately, you'll have to ride out the pain until the blood flow stops entirely. The better news is that you can go home. I have a prescription for you, in case you experience any more severe pain in the next day or so, but other than that, follow up with your regular OB-GYN tomorrow. She'll want to check you over."

"Thank you," Simone said. "You don't know how happy I am to hear that."

"My pleasure," he said. "Just take it easy. Nothing too strenuous. Just lots of fluids and rest for the next few days."

"I'll make sure of it," said Nolan. "Thank you, Dr. Neuberger."

They caught a cab from the hospital to her apartment in Brooklyn. She sat in the back, leaning her head on his shoulder. They rode in silence. When they got to her brownstone, Nolan retrieved the key from under the welcome mat and unlocked the door.

His bags were sitting in the middle of the living room. She turned to him and buried her head in his chest and wept. She didn't know if it was fatigue or hormones, but she couldn't stop the emotions when she saw his suitcases.

"Come on," he said, kissing the top of her head. "Go lie down and I'll get you something to eat."

She went to her room and slipped out of her clothes and into an old T-shirt before crawling into bed. She could hear Nolan rummaging through her kitchen. If she wasn't so weak, she would have gone and helped him find everything, but she could barely keep her eyes open.

Nolan came into her room with a few slices of toast and a cup of tea. He helped her sit up and plumped her pillows. She sat in bed and ate while he went and took a shower. By the time he got out of the shower she was fast asleep.

He contemplated sleeping on the couch. He wasn't sure where he stood with her and the last thing he wanted to do was add any more stress by being presumptuous. So he grabbed one of her pillows and went to sleep in the living room.

In the middle of the night, she woke and Nolan was gone. She started to panic and got out of bed and went into the living room where she found him asleep on the couch and her heart broke. He'd chosen to sleep on the couch instead of next to her. She started to see how much she had hurt him. She got one of her blankets and laid it on him before going back to bed.

"What's wrong?" he mumbled. "Is the baby okay?"

"She's fine... it's okay... I just thought you left. I didn't mean to wake you. Go back to sleep."

He reached for her hand and gently pulled her back. "Si, do you want me to go? I will go if that's what you want."

"No... no. That's not what I want."

"Then tell me what you want," he said, sitting up. "Tell me what you want and I'll do it. I'll do anything to make you happy."

"I... I just want you," she said as tears quickly slipped down her cheek. "I don't want to spend another night without you."

Nolan kissed her.

"Come back to bed with me." She tugged his hand. "I don't want to be alone."

The two of them went back to her bedroom. They crawled into bed and quickly fell asleep in each other's arms.

▶

SIMONE WAS the first to wake. The sun was shining through the curtains, making her bedroom sparkle. She smiled at Nolan asleep next to her. She reached out and ran her fingers through his hair, praying that this wasn't a dream she would wake up from. When he felt her touch he woke up and smiled.

"Hi."

"Hi," she responded.

He pushed the strands of curls from her face. He pulled up her shirt and gently stroked her stomach. His heart skipped when he felt the baby move.

"Oh, wow," he said. "Is she moving right now?"

"Uh huh." Simone winced a little. "A lot right now."

They lay there while he felt his daughter move around. He gently rubbed her stomach, hoping she could feel him and know that he was there. He wanted her to know that he would always be there. His smile widened when he felt her move again.

"Thank you," he said. "Thank you for her."

Simone looked at him and felt a love from him that felt different. He didn't look at her with anger, or in lust, or as a boy with a crush; this was a man gazing at her, finally at peace.

"Simone," he said.

"Yes?"

"Marry me." He lightly kissed her lips. "Marry me."

PART VII

69

Rowan stood behind the bar, waiting for the next drop. He hated when Pinkie was late. She was always late. At times a few hours, but often days, sometimes weeks late with her pull. If she wasn't Old Phil's niece, he would have strong-armed her months ago, but she was untouchable. You mess with Pinkie, then you mess with Old Phil, and Rowan wasn't looking to start a war.

He hated his life at Blood Hounds, working for peanuts. Although the bar was a hotbed for drug trafficking and headquarters for a profitable prostitution ring, he was left out of the action. He couldn't prove himself to Old Phil because he'd jumped parole and couldn't risk doing anything that would send him back to prison.

Old Phil and his cohorts found it amusing that, for all his big talk, Rowan was too scared to even get his motorcycle license. They nicknamed him Ghost because he was pretty much dead to the world. Rowan hated that nickname as well as this bunch of old-timers who continuously had his balls in a vice. Even after getting a fake ID, he couldn't shake the name or the feeling he'd never again be his own man. The stranglehold of feeling beholden to anyone or anything was a slow churning suffocation.

In the past, he'd been a kingpin. Everyone had feared and revered him. In prison, he'd felt powerful and, during those years, he'd dreamt that the outside world would recognize his quality and be his salvation. But, despite the scraps Old Phil threw his way, he couldn't get his life together.

One of the scraps was being point man for Old Phil's runners. Big deal. This was not the start he needed to rise in the ranks. He wanted to be in the backroom with Old Phil and the lieutenants and be a part of the real action, not pulling draft beer and waiting for Pinkie to arrive with the receipts.

The Red Sox game had just finished and the Leafs game was about to start. The bar was empty except for a few layabouts who hung around to catch the games. Old Phil had finally installed cable, which made the regulars happy.

As he flipped through the channels, he came across HGTV. He stopped for a moment to watch a young married couple try to tell some builder-host guy how they wanted their kitchen to look. He sat down behind the bar, glued to the show, trying to figure out where he had seen the guy. The way he smiled looked so familiar, saying how he was going to maximize their space. The home-owners seemed unconvinced.

Okay, Nolan. But seriously, if this doesn't work, I'm holding you responsible.

The young woman was cute.

Carol, you are not going to be disappointed. I guarantee it.

He suddenly realized this guy looked like Nolan from back in Halifax. Nolan, who had sold him out. Nolan, who cost him eight years of his life.

"Ghost, why the fuck are we watching this crap?" Cheetos yelled at him. "The Leafs game started five minutes ago."

"Hold on," Rowan said, ignoring the grumblings. The segment

was coming to an end and he wanted to catch the name of the program. He was convinced that it was the same Nolan.

"For Christ sakes, Ghost." Old Phil grabbed the remote. "No one here wants to see this shit."

The name of the show flashed on the screen just as Old Phil changed the channel to the Leafs game, then shook his head and headed down to the basement to do inventory.

"House Helpers," Rowan said to himself.

"House Helpers?" a voice said. "You're getting soft, Ghost. I didn't know you were into that crap."

Rowan looked round to see Pinkie slide into a seat by the bar. She was a slight woman with a blonde pixie cut, barely five-two.

"You're three hours late," he said, glaring. "Your Uncle has been up my ass all morning. Do you have the receipts?"

"I need a few more days," she said.

"No way, Pinkie," he said, wiping down the bar top. "He fucking told me that he expects all the receipts in today. No exceptions."

"Come on, man. I need a couple more days. You know that I'm good for it. Come on, Rowan."

He looked at her. It meant spotting her half of his savings until she paid him back, but when it came to Pinkie you didn't have a choice.

"You still messing with that bail agent?" he asked her.

"Why? You want to take me out on a date?" she teased.

"Fuck that," he said. "I'm doing you a favour, so do me one. I'm trying to find someone. Can he help me?"

"Sure he can. Give me the two days and I'll give you his number." She smiled sweetly.

"Fine," he said, pouring her a beer.

She wrote down the number. "This is Trevor's cell. Tell him Tracey sent you."

"Your name is Tracey?" he said, laughing.

"Fuck off, Rowan." She drank her draft. "I gotta go. Don't tell my uncle that you saw me."

"Two days!" he yelled as she ran out the door.

He picked up the bar phone, called Trevor, and left a message saying he was a friend of Tracey's and was looking for a guy from Halifax called Nolan O'Shea. The next day Trevor called him back at the bar.

"That was quick," Rowan said.

"It wasn't much of a challenge," Trevor said. "He's a celebrity. Do you know the guy?"

"Yup. We use to roll together back in the day. Lost touch with him."

"Well, his private number and address are not listed," Trevor said. "The only information I could find was an address and phone number for Griffith Management."

"Griffith Management?" Rowan said. "I know that name. What is it?"

"Not entirely sure. It looks like it's his business manager's contact information."

Rowan gritted his teeth. It all started to make sense. The celebrity dad, the big monthly payments. Nolan was Kyle's father.

"The only other thing I have is an address in New York City under his wife's name," Trevor said. "Do you want it?"

"Yeah." He grabbed a piece of paper. "I'm ready."

Rowan jotted down the information and quickly hung up. He leaned against the bar, glaring at the piece of paper.

"What the fuck!"

Nolan was a success and lived like a fucking prince while he was stuck in this dump, grasping at straws. Nolan was a punk for testifying against him, but Kyle's father? That cut extra deep.

Rowan called Old Phil and told him that his mother was sick and he needed a few days to get her straight. After his shift, he borrowed Spider's bike and took off to New York City.

He gunned it down the highway, his anger festering. All those years in prison, he had hated Nolan, but, since getting out, he hadn't given him a thought. Seeing him on camera, smiling as if he didn't have a care in the world, cast everything in a different light. And especially knowing that he was Kyle's father. Jesus Christ. He had suspected that Nolan was sleeping with Tess, but then he suspected everyone of sleeping with Tess.

As he approached the border, it all became clear as day. Nolan didn't take the deal to get a shorter sentence, he did it to protect Tess—the mother of his kid.

"Welcome to the United States!" said a young black woman from her booth. "Please provide your passport and the purpose of your visit."

Rowan handed over his driver's license. The border protection officer looked him up and down. She took in his tats, his leather coat with the Blood Hounds logo, and then the shirt that said *white power-white pride*. She looked at his license and handed it back to him.

"Sir, I need your passport."

"My passport? Since when did I need to show a passport? I never had to use one before!"

"Sir, as of June 1st, Homeland Security requires a valid passport for all border crossings," she said. "That means your driver's license will not help you."

"That's bullshit! I want to speak to your boss."

"That's fine, sir." She smirked at him. "You can pull up to our offices. They will talk to you about our policies and procedures."

"Forget it," he said, starting up his bike. "I'll turn around."

"I'm sorry, sir, but you can't just turn around," she said. "You will need to go to our offices. They will inform you on how to get back to Canada."

Rowan killed his hard stare quickly when he realized that he was being pulled over. Not only was he trying to cross the border using a fake ID, but he had a gun hidden in the pannier. He couldn't afford border agents finding his piece.

He waited in the office for almost two hours before they got to him. He tried to appear calm, but he was sweating profusely underneath his jacket as the old white officer looked him over and then shook his head, giving him a stern warning about entering the country without proper identification. He was then sent on his way.

He headed back to Hamilton, trying not to speed. He didn't want to face any more law enforcers.

"Back so soon?" Old Phil said. "How's your old lady?"

"She's fine," he said. "False alarm."

"Hmmm," Old Phil said. He pulled out the receipts for the previous night. "Well, that was a waste of time."

"Yeah," Rowan said. "A fucking waste of time."

70

S he stood by the doorway in her white paisley nightgown, watching them sleep. She looked down the dark hallway, too scared to go back to her room. She could hear them breathing and wanted to call out to them, but they hadn't heard her when she'd called from her room. She didn't know if they would hear her now.

"Mama," she called out. She carefully crept in. "Mama... Mama."

Everything was new and it scared her. She didn't know where she was, only that nothing looked the same. She started to tremble. She called out again. "Mama?"

Simone jolted awake. The shadowy figure of her daughter was standing by her bed.

"Malia," she said. "Baby, what are you doing out of bed?"

Simone turned on the nightstand lamp. Her two-year-old was clutching the stuffed bunny she slept with each night. Her nose was runny, her eyes red and wet from crying.

"Mama," she said again, raising her arms in the air. "Up, Mama, up!"

Simone got up and picked up her daughter. She grabbed a

tissue and wiped Malia's eyes and runny nose, trying to comfort her, whispering that she should go right back to sleep. "Hush now, you're going to wake daddy." But Nolan had already heard Malia's little voice. He turned over to see what was going on.

"She climbed out of her crib again," Simone whispered. "She needs a toddler bed."

"I know." He yawned, stretching his legs. "Tomorrow, I promise."

She lay back in bed, placing Malia next to her. Malia continued to fuss. Simone pushed aside the mound of curls that fell onto her tiny face, then she pulled down her tank top and fed her. Five minutes later the little girl was fast asleep.

Nolan got up, took her back to her bedroom, and laid her in her crib, making sure her side rail was locked properly. He noticed that the crib was too close to the changing table and lifted the table up, placing it on the other side of the room.

"She's using the changing table to climb out of her crib," he whispered to Simone, chuckling, as he climbed back into bed. "She's a crafty one."

"I wonder where she gets that from?" Simone turned to him. "I'm not naming any names, but I can send you a short list."

Nolan bit her neck gently. Simone laughed out loud.

"Shhh," he said, kissing the spot. "If you wake boss lady I'm letting you fend for yourself."

He pulled her to him and moaned when she slipped her hand into his pants and stroked him. It didn't take much to get him off. Just feeling her body next to him each night was enough to get him going. He kissed her hungrily and could feel her hands grab his ass while sliding his pyjama bottoms off.

He kissed her neck before eagerly pulling her top off, moving down to her breasts, sucking gently. He lightly touched her stomach. She was only four months along with their second child, still small enough for him to crawl on top of her.

"Can you handle me without making too much noise?" he teased.

"Hey, I'm not the one who woke her up the last time," she said, lightly caressing his back.

He reached over her to turn off the light, then went under the covers to pull off her panties. Simone leaned up to kiss him as she opened her legs. She was wet and ready when they heard Malia's shrill cry. Simone fell back as the calls for her grew loud and steady.

"Your daughter is the perpetual cock-blocker." Nolan rolled off her. "Do you want me to put her back to sleep?"

"It wouldn't make a difference. She's not used to her new room. Just let her sleep with us."

"You're spoiling her," he sighed, getting up. "You know she can't sleep with us forever."

"Yeah, but she can't scream her head off all night, either. I don't think our neighbours down the hall would appreciate it."

"You make a good point," he said, heading to Malia's room. "I'll be back."

"Nolan!" Simone called out laughing. "You're forgetting something?"

He looked back.

She threw him his pyjama pants. He grabbed them and bent over while pulling them up over his muscular legs. As she watched him slip the seat over his tight ass, she groaned, wishing Malia had stayed asleep a little while longer.

By the time he came back, Malia was fast asleep in his arms. He passed her to Simone, who laid the little girl on their bed before curling up next to her. Nolan turned off the lights and wrapped his arms around both of them.

Simone woke the next morning and yawned drowsily. It was already 10:00 am. She had barely slept, with the child tossing and turning all night.

She could hear Malia squealing as Nolan chased her up and

down the hallway. She turned over and felt her stomach flutter. She gently caressed it. She hoped it would be a boy this time. A little brother for Malia to play with.

She slowly got out of bed and stretched before putting on her robe and slippers. It was her last day of vacation and she hated how cluttered the loft looked, with boxes still scattered throughout, waiting to be unpacked.

◄◄

THEY HAD SPENT NEARLY two and a half years in New York, moving back to Toronto a week ago. Two months before that, Cynthia had called to say that she was leaving Prisdel to direct documentaries and wanted Simone to take over her position.

They'd spoken late into the evening.

"I don't know what to say," Simone said. "It's everything I've ever wanted. There's got to be a catch somewhere. Do I have to move to Timbuktu or sell my next child?"

"Nothing like that," Cynthia laughed. "I'm seriously stepping down and you're seriously being asked to run things. I'll still be around if you need me, but it will be yours to grow. You and Nolan would have to return to Toronto, though."

"It sounds like a wonderful opportunity, but I need to discuss it with Nolan. Can you give me a few days before I give you my decision?"

"Of course! You and Nolan take the time you need and call me when you decide."

Simone had no doubt that it was something Nolan wanted. This would be the answer to their prayers. He had been yearning to return to Toronto ever since he moved to New York.

◄◄

WHEN THEY RELOCATED *HOUSE HELPERS*, everyone had been surprised by the decision. Almost no one knew that the reason was solely because of their new family. Neither Vancouver nor Toronto was an option. Some had thought it was crazy to change the *House Helpers* format and many fans revolted when the news broke that their beloved show was going to be Americanized. It was a Canadian staple and moving it to the United States was the equivalent of selling Tim Hortons to McDonald's.

But Nolan had been adamant—either move the show to New York or find another host. Cynthia and Jonathan had tried to talk him out of it, but his mind was made up and, unless they could offer him a daily thirty-minute commute from Vancouver, he wasn't budging.

"Hold on, Nolan! Don't get ahead of yourself," Jonathan had said when they all met to sign his new contract. "I don't get why you're doing this. The terms of your contract are all set and it is a pretty brilliant deal. Now you're asking us to tear it apart and redo everything?"

"Things have changed in my life," he told them. "I'm going to be a new father and, in a few weeks, I'll be married. I need to be where my wife is and if that doesn't work for you then we'll have to part ways. I'm sorry, Jon, but I need New York or I don't sign."

"But when did Jessica move to New York?" Jonathan asked.

"Jessica didn't." Cynthia looked directly at Nolan. "Simone Allen did—am I right?"

"Yes," Nolan said.

"I don't know why I didn't see it sooner," she said, smiling at him.

"See what?" Jonathan asked. "And what does Simone Allen have to do with this?"

"Jonathan," Cynthia said, gathering up her notebook, "we're moving *House Helpers* to New York. Nolan, we'll talk it over with the other executive producers and try to work something out. I can't promise you anything, but I'll do my best to make it happen."

"Wait... would someone please tell me what just happened?" Jonathan asked.

"Oh, for God sakes, Jon," Cynthia said. "Nolan and Simone are having a baby and getting married. That's what's going on!"

"Wait. Simone is pregnant?" Jonathan asked.

Nolan laughed, patting Jonathan on the back.

"Thank you, Cynthia," he said, hugging her. "I appreciate anything you can do for me... for us."

Nolan went back to Simone's apartment, where she was resting. He climbed into her bed and kissed her awake, then told her about his meeting. Simone started to panic, scared that the rest of Prisdel's executive board wouldn't approve moving the show to New York, and for three days they sat on pins and needles waiting to hear back from Jonathan.

Trying to be optimistic, Nolan, Cynthia, and Simone spent the evenings coming up with a new format that they hoped would keep their Canadian fan base going and capture the coveted American market. The new concept would feature Canadians moving to New York City and surrounding boroughs. The focus would be on families adjusting to a new country and rebuilding their lives and homes with the helpful Nolan O'Shea leading the way.

The Prisdel executives could not agree on the new format; the decision was split. Jonathan had the deciding vote.

"Whether we lose Nolan or change the format, we're fucked regardless," he said, before casting his vote in favour of the new format.

Simone and Nolan worked tirelessly to make the new concept work logistically. Nolan worried about Simone working so much with the baby arriving soon, but she insisted on being involved.

"Nols, I'm not doing this just for you," she said. "This is for us —the future of our family."

They went to bed at three each morning right into the first week of pre-production, which ended up being an ultimate disaster. Their premiere family pulled out at the last minute, leaving Simone and her team scrambling. She tried to arrange for another family to start earlier, but the schedule was so tight she was forced to find a brand-new family. It turned out she was able to call on their old elementary friend, Ilene Cheng.

Ilene was married to a neurosurgeon who was starting his residency at NYU Langone Medical Center in Manhattan; they had just bought a house in Queens and Ilene hated everything about it. She hated the area, her neighbourhood, and even the way the tree in her front yard sloped. It didn't help that she was miserably pregnant with twin boys.

"I hate this city," she told Simone over the phone. "But if doing this show means fixing this dump then you can count us in."

A rewrite to the episode introduced Ilene as Nolan's childhood friend. The production team had dug up pictures of them at St. Augustine, one being Nolan's seventh-grade white Gumby school picture.

The first week of filming was difficult. Ilene took her role on the show very seriously, giving Nolan a hard time on how she wanted her "dream dump" to look. She fought him on every idea he had and, when the cameras were rolling, she was exceptionally bitchy.

Nolan tried his charm on her, amping up his flirtation to win her over, but she was impossible to please. No matter the effort, Ilene was never happy. All she did was grumble about how much she hated the house. By the end of the second week of filming, Nolan started to despise the house as well.

Each night, he complained to Simone about working with Ilene, but, each day, when Simone saw the dailies, she grew excited. The episode was progressing through a series of heated dramatic arguments. At one point, they got Ilene crying on camera. She was exhausted, pregnant with twins, and she broke down when Nolan told her that the nursery wouldn't be ready in time for her C-Section.

It was great television—a tender moment between two former classmates: Nolan sitting with Ilene listening to her express how scared she was living in Queens. All her family was back in Canada and she didn't know a soul in her new city.

"You know me," he reminded her. "I'm here."

"I know," she said, smiling at him, wiping her tears aside. "It's just not easy to pick up your whole world and just drop it anywhere. It's a lot of change."

"Trust me, I know how you feel," he said. "But remember that it's a good change. Roger is working at the best hospital in the country and you're going to have two beautiful babies to keep you busy. By the time you're ready to take on Queens, you'll have a dream house and the lay of the land. I promise."

"I'm going to hold you to it," she said.

"Are you kidding?" he said. "Now that we live so close I'm expecting a permanent invite to Sunday dinners."

"You got it." She hugged Nolan.

Cue the theme music. Cue commercials.

It was one of the show's most authentic moments. Not only did Nolan do an amazing job of transforming Ilene's home, but the emotional scenes really proved the success of the premise. Simone was so proud that she showed the executive team a raw cut of the premiere episode. The entire room stood up and applauded.

Billed as *House Helpers Take New York*, the show's new format was a big hit in Canada. When it premiered in America, the producers received hundreds of applications from families around the world wanting to be featured on the program.

House Helpers was nominated for an Emmy for the first time in its history. Simone was proud that Ilene's episode had landed them the nomination and equally excited that her husband got a nomination for best reality series host. Neither the show nor the host won in their categories, but the publicity generated from the nominations catapulted *House Helpers* to "Must See" status and viewership increased weekly. By the end of the season, Nolan was a household name in America. He couldn't walk down a street in New York without someone honking or yelling his name.

Nolan was smitten by the sudden fame. His friends and family called, tickled to see him on different talk shows, promoting the show. His life seemed, at last, to be falling into place. His career was where it needed to be; his wife and child were by his side.

But everything shifted the afternoon Simone came home with news that she was pregnant again.

"Si, I don't want to raise our family in New York," he said, after putting Malia down for her nap. "It's not what I imagined for us."

"I get it," she said. "You miss home."

He sat next to her on the couch. "It's more than being homesick," he said. "New York was temporary, but, with another baby on the way, it's starting to feel permanent. Doesn't it bother you that Malia doesn't know her own family? I mean, the last time Dad and Pam came down, she spent the entire time hiding behind your skirt. She cried every time they picked her up."

"She's young, Nols," Simone said. "To her, everyone is a stranger."

"But that's my point," he said. "The only time our parents get to see her are a few days here and there or when we post pictures of her on Facebook. She's closer to the nanny than she is to her own grandparents. That's not right. That's not how we grew up."

"You mean Mrs. Price?" Simone said. "Neither of us are related to her. Our parents raised us like one big extended family."

"But that was different," he said. "Phyllis is one of three nannies we've had since Malia was born. To them, this is a job. For Mrs. Price and our folks, it *was* family. We looked out for each other. I don't feel like we have that same kind of unit here."

Simone didn't know what to say. She wanted nothing more than for them to go home, but their professional lives were tied to New York. Their careers were thriving and leaving would mean giving up everything they'd worked so hard for.

"I'm not trying to sound ungrateful, Si," he said, pulling her closer to him. "And I don't want you to think that I'm not happy, because I am. You, Malia, and this baby are my whole world. I just want us to be closer to our family and not exiled in New York because of our careers."

"I get it," she said. "So what do you want to do?"

"Honestly?"

"Yes. Honestly."

"I want to move back to Toronto before the baby is born."

He didn't know how Simone would react. He hated asking her to give up New York. He wasn't sure what it would mean for their careers. He just knew that Toronto was home and he wanted to go home.

"Okay," she said, taking a deep breath. "Okay... we'll do it. When your contract is up we'll find a way to move back home."

"Are you sure? I know how much being here means to you."

"Nolan, the only thing that matters to me is us... our family." She kissed him. "Where you go, I go."

Simone couldn't believe their luck when Cynthia called a few weeks later announcing her new plans. Her departure couldn't have come at a better time. The executives at Prisdel not only approved Simone taking over Cynthia's position, they also approved moving *House Helpers* back to Toronto, using the NYC format with Toronto as the destination city.

▶▶|

SIMONE SMILED to herself at Malia's infectious giggles echoing through the hallway. She opened the bedroom door to find the little girl squealing with laughter and Nolan tickling her. Simone slowly rubbed her stomach as she watched the loves of her life playing on the floor of their new Toronto loft.

Her daughter's eyes lit up. Her mother was finally awake. She wiggled out of her father's grip and ran full tilt, jumping into Simone's arms.

"Careful, baby," Simone said, holding her tight. "You can't jump on Mama anymore."

"Did you get enough rest?" Nolan asked her.

"As much as I can get," she said, planting kisses all over Malia's chubby face. "Thanks for letting me sleep in."

Malia then jumped out of her mother's arms and back into her father's arms. Nolan barely caught her as she tried to tickle his prickly chin. He scratched her face playfully with his beard. Malia laughed and tried to push his face away.

"Someone needs to shave, huh, MalMal?" Nolan yawned. "Okay, baby, Mama is up and Daddy is falling apart. I'm going back to sleep."

He handed her back to her mother and kissed Simone. Then he headed to their bedroom.

"Daddy!" Malia called out as he walked down the hallway.

"Yes, Pooh Bear?" He walked back to her.

"Bye, Daddy! See you later!" she said carefully and proudly.

Nolan blinked at her, gave her a huge grin, then turned to Simone, who smiled at hearing her daughter string together a proper sentence.

"Good job, smart girl!" he said, lifting her up in the air. "See you later, MalMal."

"I don't get it, Dad," Dana said. She and Mike were sitting at her kitchen island. Pam and Freddy were hunched in the breakfast nook, trying to stay clear of the heated argument. "You complain about your job... no, excuse me, your jobs. You constantly tell us how tiring it is to work this much and how you want a life—and I give it to you on a silver platter and you say no?"

It was the first warm day of spring and Dana had invited everyone over for a barbecue to announce that she and Freddy had finalized the paperwork and were now officially owners of a small property management company. It was the latest trend their business was following: purchasing commercial residential property to renovate and manage.

Dana had just asked her dad to manage the properties for her and was anxious to have him take the reins as soon as possible.

"I didn't say no," Mike said. "I just don't think I would be a good fit."

"Why? You're a supervisor at Ryerson. What's the difference?"

"That's a team of janitors," he said. "You're asking me to

manage nearly fifty people. You and Pam are built for jobs like this. I can barely figure out how to use the bloody computer."

"So you'll learn, Dad," she said. "I'll show you. Pam can help you! Don't you want to be your own boss, for once, instead of having to answer to someone else?"

"Sweetheart, that's your dream," he said. "I'm not cut out for this. You and Freddy should find someone more qualified."

"Dad, we acquired this with you in mind!" she said. "How can you just say no?"

"Honey, I never asked you—"

"You know what? Forget it!" she said, interrupting him as Nolan and Simone walked into the kitchen with Malia. "You spend your entire life complaining that everyone gets a free ride and that you never catch a break, but really it's you. Mom was right! You have no fucking ambition."

"Dana!" Pam called out. "That's enough!"

"Stay out of it, Pam," she said. "This is family business between me and my father. It doesn't concern you!"

"Watch yourself, little girl," Mike said.

"I'm sorry, Dad, but this is a great opportunity for you. Don't you want something better for yourself? Don't you want to move ahead? It's like you're stuck in neutral. I don't get it!"

"Dana, I'm not the person you call to manage budgets and hound people for their rent," he said. "That's not me."

"It can be, Dad!" she said. "If you give it a chance and don't be so bloody afraid of change… Pam, you know Dad can do this! He's capable of doing something more than replacing light bulbs and slinging drinks to drunk sorority girls."

"Dana, your father is a grown man capable of deciding for himself what makes him happy," Pam said. "You need to respect that."

The four sat silently in the awkward moment.

Dana looked over at her father. She could see how humiliated he was. She hadn't meant to belittle him in front of everyone, but she couldn't understand why he was being so stubborn. Her brother and Freddy had invested heavily in the purchase and she had finally convinced Freddy that her father would be the best person for the job. Now Mike wouldn't step up to the plate.

"Dana, why don't we take a breather?" Freddy said. "Everyone is a little fired up right now."

"What's the point! He's so goddamn stubborn," she said, walking past her brother. "You talk to him. I'm through trying to make sense of his bullshit."

▶

SIMONE GLANCED AT NOLAN, who seemed just as confused as she was. She watched Dana walk out to the backyard and light up a cigarette. Her mother had got up and was now standing next to Mike, rubbing his back.

"Let me find out what's going on," Nolan said. He followed his sister out.

Simone had been looking forward to this family get-together, but the only ones who seemed like they were having any kind of fun were Freddy's kids, who were running around the yard like crazy, yelling and screaming, almost knocking over Nolan and Dana.

"You kids are giving me a goddamn headache," Freddy yelled out at them. "Jayla, I asked you to keep your brothers in line and keep their behinds quiet!"

"Sorry, Daddy," said the ten-year-old, poking her head in. "Hi, Auntie Simone. Hi, Malia!"

"Hi, sweetie!" Simone said, crouching to hug Jayla. "Can you please take Malia outside with you?"

Jayla grabbed Malia's hand and ran outside. Malia was so excited when she saw all the others playing that the hysterics and chasing and screaming started up again.

Simone turned to the others in the kitchen. "What did we just walk into?"

Mike got up and walked out of the kitchen into the sunroom.

"Dana is upset with her father," Pam explained. "Mike is backing out of working with her and Freddy. He's not sure if he can do it."

"Of course he can," Simone said, taking a banana from the fruit bowl. "He's perfectly capable of running it."

"But he doesn't feel that way," Pam said. "He's turning fifty-seven this year and the idea of starting over scares him."

Pam left the kitchen to sit with Mike.

Simone looked out to see Nolan sitting on a deck chair next to his sister, probably listening to her ramble on about their father's decision.

"Where's Amaya?" Simone asked, turning to Freddy.

"She's home with a migraine," he said. "At this point, I might be joining her... damn it, Christian!" he shouted out the open door. "Get down from the picnic table. This fool is going to give me a fucking stroke."

He ran outside. Moments later, all the kids were chasing and tackling him. Eventually, he was on the ground and Malia was sitting on top of his head, screaming like she was possessed.

Simone went to the kitchen door and leaned on the jamb. She surveyed the yard and shook her head; now Nolan and Dana were in a heated argument. As the kids ran towards the side of the house, she could faintly hear her husband chastising his sister for bullying their father.

▶

PAM SAT next to Mike on Dana's porch swing in the sunroom. "You know she's right. You can do this."

"I like my life the way it is, okay?" Mike said stiffly.

"So you like working like a dog? Tell me, Michael O'Shea, what exactly has you running scared? The Mike I know never runs scared from a challenge."

"I'm not a suit, Pam. I'm not that guy! You and Dana went to school for this. I've spent my whole life working with my hands. I can't run a business."

"That's the same excuse you gave when you turned down the managerial position Ryerson offered you five years ago and now you're hiding behind that same excuse again?"

"And what if I screw up Dana's business? I couldn't forgive myself."

"Mike, they're not setting you up to fail," she said. "You'll have an experienced staff and everyone believes in you. You're the only one that needs convincing." She kissed his stubbly cheek before easing out of the seat. "Whatever you decide, I'm going to support you. But don't sell yourself short. You're better than that."

Pam walked back into the kitchen, where she found Dana at the kitchen sink, furiously scrubbing a frying pan, her eyes red and puffy from crying. Nolan was sitting with Simone, nursing a beer, as she held his hand and whispered in his ear. The atmosphere was so tense. Pam took the frying pan from Dana before she could scrub off all the Teflon, then put her arms around Dana's waist and gave her a little squeeze before rinsing the pan.

"I didn't mean to make him feel like shit," Dana said, putting down the dishcloth, wiping back her tears. "I really want this for him."

"I know," Pam said. "Just give him some time, okay? Let him think it over some more."

Dana nodded. She wiped her eyes with the dishtowel. "I'm sorry I snapped at you. I lost my temper and—"

"It's okay... we're okay." Pam smiled at her before she turned to everyone in the kitchen. "Okay, people! This barbecue is not going to start itself." She handed the platter of steaks to Dana and then took the cucumber salad from the fridge and passed it to Simone. "Dana, where's the lighter fluid?"

"It's in the top drawer by the sink." Dana headed over to get it.

Freddy was screaming at his kids again.

"Nolan, go back out there and help Freddy with those kids," Pam said. "They're going to tear him apart."

"Yes, Ma'am!" Nolan said, putting down his beer before going outside.

Once the children saw Nolan they all started screaming as they ran towards him, tackling him to the ground in one swoop. Freddy then joined them, taking Malia up and mimicking a wrestling move on her father.

Dana laughed as she stopped to watch the rowdy kids split up and turn on both men. She suddenly felt a strong hand on her shoulder. She turned to see her father. She smiled weakly at him. He hugged her tightly.

"Come on," he said, motioning Dana to the backyard. They walked over to Pam. Mike grabbed the platter of steaks from her and kissed her before he took his place at the grill.

72

S

imone sat in front of her laptop in her new twelfth-floor office at Prisdel, debating whether or not to send the email. She had read it repeatedly. Each time she felt as if her heart was going to leap out of her chest. She wondered if contacting her would even make a difference in either of their lives.

But they were now in the same city, practically living in the same area. The downtown core was like a little village. She'd known it would only be a matter of time before she would bump into Jessica. She just hadn't expected it to be a few weeks after moving back to Toronto.

She and Malia had been exploring their neighbourhood and had stumbled on a weekly farmer's market at Trinity Bellwoods Park. It was smaller than the ones she had frequented in Brooklyn, but had a better selection of fruits and vegetables than the corner grocery store. She was sifting through a basket of guineps when she noticed Jessica on her cell phone in the next aisle.

Jessica had changed. She had cut her hair short in a sophisticated layered bob and was wearing an expensive Alexander McQueen suit. Simone overheard her reprimand a caller for not sending out a brief on time. Her cell conversation sounded heated and Simone didn't want to be in Jessica's line of fire, especially while Malia was with her. She attempted to hurry away without being noticed, but, in the rush, Malia fell on the concrete and scraped her knee.

The little girl howled as Simone scrambled to help her up. "Ouch, Mama!" A trickle of blood surfaced. "Ow ow... ouchy!"

Simone pulled out a tissue to wipe away the blood. When she looked up, Jessica was ten feet away. They made eye contact. Jessica looked down at Malia and went pale. Simone barely had a moment to call out her name before Jessica turned and rushed away. She stood up to see Jessica run into a waiting taxi. The taxi took off and turned the corner, disappearing from view. Malia continued to whimper, pulling on her skirt.

"Mama, it broken."

"Oh no, baby, it's not broken. It's just a little blood," she said, bending back down to kiss the scraped knee. "Mommy's kisses will make MalMal feel all better, okay?"

She pushed back her daughter's curly copper hair and kissed the top of her forehead until Malia looked up and smiled at her.

"Okay, Mama. All better. It not hurt now." The little girl grabbed her mother's hand. "Ice cream, Mama?" Simone nodded and looked once around to where Jessica had been standing before leading Malia out of the park.

Now, a day later, she read the email again. It wasn't a long message. She had made sure to keep it concise and honest. Long enough to tell her how she felt, but short enough for Jessica to read in its entirety before clicking the delete button.

She hovered over the send button. It wasn't the content or length of her email that made her stall. She was about to break a promise to Nolan and wasn't entirely sure if reaching out to Jessica was worth the strain it would put on her marriage.

The last time she'd heard from Jessica was a few months after she'd married Nolan. It hadn't been much of an affair. They had gone back to Toronto and to City Hall for the ceremony. Mike had surprised them with a small private reception at McKinney's with only close friends and family, then they'd slipped back to New York.

Towards the end of her pregnancy, her blood pressure was so high that her doctor had put her on permanent bed rest until the baby was born. She'd been ordered to stay off her feet, away from work and any undue stress.

Nolan had come home in a lousy mood after another stressful day working on Ilene's Queens homestead while she was sorting through half a dozen voice messages from Jessica, each more abusive and indignant than the last. She'd been so preoccupied, listening and deleting, that she hadn't heard Nolan come into the bedroom.

You were supposed to be my friend, you fucking cunt! Jessica's words came slurred through tears. *He was mine from the start and you took him from me! You fucking took him!*

Delete.

I hope you both get what you deserve. Better yet! I hope your fucking spawn comes out stillborn, then the both of you will know exactly how I feel right now!

Nolan swiftly grabbed the phone, startling her. He found and scrolled through a slew of text messages Jessica had left.

"She doesn't mean it," Simone said. "She's drunk and…"

"How long has she been doing this?" he asked.

"A few days," Simone said, trying to sit up.

"We don't fucking need this," he mumbled, storming out of the bedroom.

Simone slowly got out of bed. By the time she was on her feet, she could hear Nolan in the bathroom on the phone, hollering at Jessica that she was a pathetic bitch.

She hobbled to the bathroom and banged on the locked door. "Nolan, what are you doing? Nolan, don't do this! You're making things worse!"

She leaned on the door and listened to him lay into Jessica, telling her he had never loved her and leaving her for Simone was the best decision he had ever made and his only regret was that he even fucked with her in the first place and he would get a fucking restraining order against her if she ever called or came near them again. She was shaking when he emerged from the bathroom.

"Not a fucking word, Simone," he snarled. "Not one fucking word!"

She followed him back to their bedroom. "She didn't deserve that. We did this. We created this mess."

"I don't care how upset she is," he yelled. "You don't fucking go after someone's kid!"

"But did you have to cut so deep?" she yelled back. "She's just angry—"

"I'm fucking angry, okay?" he screamed. "When I went back to the condo to get my stuff, she destroyed everything! EVERY-THING! She poured bleach on my clothes and papers and fucking smashed my laptop to bits and threw my tools in the dumpster—and even then I gave her a fucking pass!

"When she threatened to sue me, I could have fought it but I kept my mouth shut and just settled. I let her keep almost $200,000 in deposits for the wedding. That doesn't even count the fucking money I spent on her ring! But I draw the line when she drags our baby into her fucking tantrums."

"Okay, I get it," Simone said.

"No, I don't think you do get it!" he said. "I'm done fucking with her! I don't want you in contact with that bitch ever again! Do you hear me? I don't want her anywhere near you or our baby. Not now! Not ever!"

Simone had never seen him that enraged and his anger terri-fied her.

"Oh God," he said when she started to cry. "Jesus… please don't cry, Si. I'm angry with Jessica, not you, okay?"

She nodded.

"Baby, I know that she was your best friend and that you want to fix this," he said more softly. "But at this point, it's beyond fixing."

"I hate that we did this to her," she said.

"I don't," he said, looking at her. "I finally did what was right for us. You and our little girl are my life. I don't regret any of it. Do you regret it? Do you regret us?"

"No, I don't regret us—"

"Then you have to let Jessica go," he said firmly. "Look, I get it! We hurt her badly and it wasn't right, but it's either live in this guilt until Jessica gets over it or accept that she may never forgive us and be okay with that."

Simone had known deep down that he was right, but it hadn't hurt any less losing her best friend. She had promised him that she would respect his wishes and they'd both changed their telephone numbers and email addresses the next day. Eventually, the guilt she had felt started to fade.

But now, after seeing Jessica again, the guilt resurfaced. She couldn't push Jessica's reaction out of her mind. The look of contempt for her and Malia had left her feeling hollow and suddenly the loss of their friendship felt as fresh and raw as if it had just happened.

She passed her mouse over the send icon but stopped and re-read her email. It looked so cold and impersonal. She deleted it, opened her desk drawer and pulled out a sheet of personal stationery. She spent the next hour thinking and then poured her heart out in three short paragraphs. The letter left her in tears, but it felt cathartic. She folded the note and sealed it in an envelope, then picked up the phone and dialled out.

"Hey, girl. You have time for lunch today?"

"Simone, is that you?" Felicia said loudly. "Heffa, it took you long enough to call. I was starting to wonder when your stush ass was going to hit me up."

"It's been crazy the last few weeks. I'm still unpacking. How about meeting at Canoe in an hour?"

"Canoe, huh? Girl, you know I'm never going to pass up lunch at Canoe. Consider me there."

▶

SIMONE SAT with Felicia at the popular restaurant and was happy to see her old friend again. Shortly after her move to New York, Felicia had accepted a position as an editor for CTV's *Nightly News*. They had lost touch with each other over the years, but, at the restaurant, they picked up as if no time had passed.

Felicia was now engaged to a man she had been seeing on and off for years. He had finally proposed to her and she was excitedly telling Simone about her upcoming wedding.

"I'm so happy for you," Simone said. "When's the big day?"

"Next month," she said. "I'm sorry that I didn't invite you but... you know... Jessica is my maid of honour and everything. I didn't think it would be a good idea having you both in the same space."

"Yeah, I get it," Simone said. "How is Jessica?"

"She's good. Real good. After everything with Nolan... well, she took it real hard. The stress of everything took a huge toll on her. Did you know she ended up quitting her law firm?"

"Oh, no," Simone said, her guilt bubbling up. "She worked so hard. She wanted to make partner."

"Trust me, it was a good thing," Felicia said. "She was burnt out trying to please everyone. She ended up starting her own practice."

"Really!"

"Yup! She's a divorce lawyer now," Felicia said, grinning. "And, boy, is she good at it. She set up my pre-nup with Brian. Not that either of us have any assets worth protecting, but I let her do it to make her happy."

"Is she happy?" Simone asked. "Because I need to know that she's happy again. I need to apologize to her."

"Simone, apologize for what?" Felicia asked. "For falling for Nolan or sleeping with him? Or are you going to apologize for stealing him away? Girl, do us all a favour and quit bullshitting yourself. You and Nolan have a good thing going and it sucks that you lost Jessica as a result, but nothing in life is fair."

"That's what Nolan said." She twisted her napkin around her finger. "But she was my best friend and what I did to her—"

"Simone, if we're going to be real about all of this, then you should know that she knew about you two from the get-go," Felicia said. "Do you honestly think that she had no clue that you and Nolan were together?"

"I... I don't understand... what do you mean?"

"Si, Jessica caught a whiff the moment y'all met up at the airport. She told me as much," she said as she dug into her salad. "She called me daily, complaining about how close you guys were, especially after your brother died. She tried to pretend that it didn't piss her off seeing him holding your hand and being all attentive and shit, but it bugged her—a lot. I mean, we all saw it. It was pretty fucking obvious how much he loved you. She brushed it off when Nolan proposed. She figured he was over you. But, when she found out that you were pregnant, well... you know the rest of the story."

Simone looked away from Felicia, out the restaurant window at the city skyline. "I should have realized from the start that she was in love with him."

"Girl, she never really loved Nolan. Don't get me wrong, she loved fucking him; but I think what she really loved was knowing that she had him and you didn't. Look, I know that Jess was your best friend and everything, but, when Nolan came into the picture, you stopped being her friend and started being her competition."

Simone looked down at her salad. She could feel her eyes fill with tears. Felicia reached out to squeeze her hand.

"Simone, move on with your life." She looked back up at Felicia who smiled at her. "Simone, I'm absolving you of your guilt," she said making the sign of the cross. "I hereby give you permission to quit beating yourself up over this. Jessica is doing great! She's happy. I promise. She's seeing a new guy and he's really nice. Just be happy for her and let it go."

"I saw her yesterday," she admitted. "We bumped into each other at Trinity Park."

"Really! And what happened?"

"Nothing. She ran off before I had a chance to say hello."

She reached into her purse and pulled out the envelope with Jessica's name on it and handed it to Felicia.

"Nuh-uh," Felicia said, pushing the envelope back to her. "I'm trying hard to stay out of y'all's mess."

"Please, Felicia," she said. "I'm not asking you to broker a peace treaty between us and I'm not even expecting her to respond. I just want her to know… please just give it to her. Everything that needs to be said is there. Please. It would mean a lot to me."

Felicia looked at the envelope and gave her a side-eye glance before finally placing the letter in her handbag. "You owe me, girl," she said. "And you better name that next baby after me!"

"We think it's going to be a boy," Simone said laughing.

"Then name him Felicio," she said. "Felicio O'Shea has a nice ring to it."

73

M ike sat at his new desk, baffled by the error code that flashed in front of him. He had tried to input his receptionist's time sheet but he couldn't figure out how to enter in her vacation hours properly. He tossed his glasses on the desk and rubbed his eyes.

He hated the new program. It was much more confusing than the system he'd used at Ryerson, but Dana was adamant. She'd promised him that, once he got used to it, he would see how efficient it was.

He picked up the phone and dialled Maureen's extension. She had also stayed late to write up her staff reviews.

"Maureen, I can't deal with this shitty program," he said. "You think you can give me a hand over here?"

"What's the problem?"

"Vivian's hours are not adding up properly," he said. "Every time I put in her vacation it comes up with an error message."

"Did you put in her vacation hours on the main page or under the supplement hours page?"

"Oh, for fuck's sake," he said. "I hate this bloody program."

"You'll get the hang of it," she said, laughing. "In five to ten years."

Maureen had joined Courtyard Properties right along with Mike. It was the only condition he had insisted on. He told his daughter that if he was going to run a management company, he needed someone he could trust to help him. He wanted a second-in-command, in case he dropped the ball, and he believed Maureen would be the perfect fit.

"She's family," he said. "And she knows a hell of a lot more about these programs than I do."

"But she's a mess, Dad!" Dana complained. "Don't get me wrong... I love Maureen, but she's loud and opinionated and thinks that she knows everything. I'm surprised that Pam lasted this long with her."

"I know she's all of that and more, but Maureen has always looked out for me," he said. "I trust her. I know she won't let me down."

Mike's hunch was right. The moment Maureen came on board, she took to her job as Operations Manager like a firecracker, organizing the hell out of the entire staff. She told him she loved working with him and felt invested in the company as if it was her own. Dana, too, was pleasantly surprised at Maureen's enthusiasm and the ideas she brought to the table. And Pam was overjoyed that Maureen had left the hospital to work with Mike and thanked him nightly for it, although she was always tactful around Maureen. Over the years, the two women had learned to be civil to each other, especially after Maureen finally learned that he and Pam were together. Mike leaned back in his chair and put his hands behind his head. He smiled to himself as he recalled the conversation he'd had with Maureen at McKinney's shortly before Simone and Nolan's wedding.

"I don't know why you had to keep it a bloody secret," Maureen had said.

"Really, Maureen? You spent the last eighteen years belly-aching about her. Do you really think I was going to tell you that she was my girlfriend?"

"Girlfriend, huh?" Maureen said. "And here I was thinking that you were just dating her. She's your girlfriend now, huh!"

"Maureen, Pam and I have been together for almost a decade," he said. "She's not some woman I take out for a good time. She's the woman I plan to spend the rest of my life with."

Maureen had looked totally befuddled. He'd been fully sober and serious. Then he winked at her, and she smiled at him before she burst into a hearty laugh.

"Well, then," she said, sipping her beer. "I guess there's no getting rid of her."

"Nope," he said and downed his.

"Even on the holidays?" she asked.

"Especially on the holidays," he told her. "And family vacations too, so you better get on board. I'm planning to take her somewhere nice this summer. I'm thinking Mexico. I've always wanted to go."

"Do I really need to hear this?" Maureen groaned. "This lovely-dovey side of you is making me want to hurl."

Mike had laughed as he watched Maureen cover her ears.

▶

"You know, I've changed diapers before," Pam said as Simone rushed to change Malia. "You don't need to worry so much."

Simone ignored her mother. She put Malia in her pyjamas. It was the third evening in a row that she and Nolan were leaving Malia for a work-related event. She hated having to miss another bedtime routine. And, with the baby due in weeks, she felt big and slow.

"There!" she said, satisfied that Malia was all clean. "Can you make sure she brushes her teeth before bedtime?"

"Yes, Simone." Pam picked up her granddaughter. "We will brush her teeth, read her a story, and make sure she has her bottle. You and Nolan are going to be late if you don't head down to the stadium."

"Okay." Simone shut her eyes for a moment and went through her mental to-do list before they headed out. "I think that's everything."

Nolan looked in anxiously as she ran around completing a few more tasks on the never-ending list. When she was pulling out a frozen chicken to roast the next day, he stepped in.

"Si, baby... we have to go or I'm going to miss my call time." He took the chicken from her and placed it in the sink. "The driver has been waiting for nearly ten minutes. Can we please get going?"

"Okay... okay... I'm good." She smiled at Malia, who looked so sad. "Oh, don't give me that look, Malia! Grandma and Grandpa are here. Mommy and Daddy won't be long."

"Si!" Nolan said.

"Okay! Okay!" She finally slipped her flats on. "Make sure you guys show Malia the opening pitch, so she can see her Daddy... oh, and please call my cell before she goes to bed so I can say goodnight."

"We got it, Splimoney," Mike said, gently pushing her towards the door. "Go!"

"Okay!" Simone kissed her mother and then Mike goodbye before she covered her daughter with kisses. "I'm ready."

"Bye, MalMal," Nolan said as he pulled her into the hallway before she could find another excuse to stay longer.

Once in the car, Simone could not get comfortable in her seat. Nolan laughed at her squirming. She hit his arm. She was bigger this time around. The doctor suspected that their son would probably be over nine pounds at birth.

After the baby was born, they were going to hold off for at least five years before trying for more. She'd made Nolan promise that. She felt so worn down that she wasn't even sure how she was going to deliver this one.

Nolan grabbed her hand and kissed it. He loved her more than he ever had. The way she took care of them and how she carried the pregnancy—Pam had told them that she was having severe back pains because she was all belly, but Simone almost never complained outright. He knew that he was lucky to have her.

"Last one, I promise," he said to her, when she finally settled in her seat. "After this, you'll have me at your beck and call."

"You better keep your promise," she said, giving him that look he knew so well. "No more last-minute events or meet-and-greets."

"I promise," he said, kissing her neck. "Nothing but sleeping in and me pampering you until the baby is born."

"And after," she said, smirking.

"And after," he said.

The driver pulled up to the stadium entrance, where a Rogers Centre rep stood waiting for them. They were escorted into the stadium and to their reserved box seats behind the plate. Simone sighed as she tried to get comfortable all over again. She was happy her husband would be throwing out the first pitch, that was a real honour, but she was exhausted by the time they took their seats.

"After I throw out the pitch, I have to pose for a few photos," he told her. "After that, we can leave, okay?" He could see the strain on her face. He knew that she wouldn't last more than an hour.

"Are you sure?" she asked. "I hate pulling you away from the game."

"No, it's okay," he said. "We can watch the rest of the game from home."

Simone smiled and nodded.

A few minutes later, Nolan was whisked away to begin his promotional duties. He goofed around for a commercial spot at home plate before the game started, and posed for pictures with some of the players for a charity that *House Helpers* was co-sponsoring with the Blue Jays.

An hour later, he threw out the first pitch. By the time they'd finished taking promotional pictures and he'd spoken with the general manager, Simone was nodding off to sleep in her seat.

He woke her gently. "Are you ready to go?"

"I need to pee first," she said.

"Okay, there's a washroom on our way out."

He helped her to her feet and they walked hand in hand to the women's restroom. People began to surround them, asking Nolan for his autograph. She was used to it, especially since their return home, but she was too tired to stop and watch him talk to his fans.

"Nols, meet me by the washroom," she said. "I'm dying to pee."

"I'm sorry, baby," he said, turning from a young boy waiting patiently for him to sign his program. "We'll leave the moment you come out, okay?"

The crowd had swollen to a point where the emergency exits were blocked. The stadium's security team was ushering people back to their seats as she went into the ladies room. Many disappointed fans were calling out to Nolan to sign more autographs.

▶

HE HADN'T SEEN the first pitch, so he had no idea who had thrown it. He was pissed off because some fan had shoved him and spilled beer all over his janitorial uniform. The large crowd surrounded some celebrity. He was too busy mopping up the spill to care what the commotion was all about. There was always some celebrity that the fans flocked to, but then he heard Nolan's name being called out and the hairs on the back of his neck stood right up.

He couldn't believe how close he was. He looked taller than he remembered. He had grown his hair back, but he still had that cocky smile on his face. He wondered if he still had his 14/88 tattoo. It would matter if he did. If the tattoo was still there, then Nolan was the same guy, would still feel the same way, still believe the same stuff, and then he could let his hatred go. He could move on. He could move on and let it all go.

He watched Nolan standing against the wall checking his cell phone. He watched a pregnant black woman walk up to him, some fan asking for his autograph. But then he saw him take her hand. He looked on with disgust.

He blazed when he noticed their matching wedding rings. He had known that Nolan was married, but he couldn't believe that he'd married one of them. One of their filthy women, tampering with the white man's future by producing some mutant coon.

He observed coolly the way he held her and even kissed her in public. He hoped that they would be heading back to their seats to give him time to think, but it was clear that they were leaving. He followed them to the exit. He didn't know what he would say; he only knew that he had to keep close to them. He followed them as far as the front of the stadium.

"The car service wasn't expecting us to leave so soon," he heard Nolan say to his wife. "Do you want to wait for a taxi or should we take the train?"

"The train is faster," she said.

He leaned on his broom and watched them walk away. He still had his shift to finish. This SkyDome gig was the first decent job he'd had since relocating to Toronto. He was trying to start over. He didn't know if he wanted to risk losing his job over Nolan O'Shea and his black whore, but he knew that, if he didn't do something to find out the truth, he would probably lose the only opportunity he might ever have.

He followed them onto the subway, staying back a bit to jump the stall. He could hear the TTC ticket agent calling after him, but the train had arrived and he leapt after them onto the car and sat close by, keeping his eyes straight ahead.

"Pam's going to think you don't trust her if we go home so soon," he heard Nolan say.

"Probably," he heard the woman reply. "I don't care. I haven't put Malia to bed all week. I'm glad we're heading home."

He looked over slightly to see Nolan's arm around her through the fifteen-minute ride. They all got off at Bathurst Station. He followed as close as he could without being seen until they got out of the station.

Nolan hailed a cab.

"902 Queen Street West," he called out to the driver as he helped the black woman into the back of the cab.

Rowan said the address to himself over and over as he watched them drive off.

◄◄

PAM ARRANGED Malia on the couch between her and Mike to watch Nolan throw out the first pitch.

"Look, Malia! Daddy is on TV!" she said, but her granddaughter was fast asleep.

Mike eased off the couch, picked Malia up, and carried her to her room. He put her in her bed and kissed her forehead before tucking her in. When he came out, Pam was on her cell phone texting Simone that Malia had fallen asleep and wishing them a good night.

Mike sat on the couch next to Pam and lifted her hand. He looked at the engagement ring that she had only worn for a month. It was as shiny and bright as the day he'd purchased it. He kissed her cheek and she nestled in his arms.

It had been a long time coming, but, in a few months, they would finally tie the knot. They had agreed to wait until after their grandson was born—Pam wanted to help Simone with the baby the first month—but then they would get married and head out for their month-long honeymoon in Mexico.

Mike kissed Pam. As she tried to watch the game, he pulled off her cardigan, then reached up her pale yellow sundress.

"The baby is in the other room," she said, pushing him away. "Not here."

"Why not?" He playfully tugged her straps down. "Malia is asleep and Nolan and Simone won't be home for hours."

He kissed her chest before unzipping the back of her dress. She kissed him passionately as he firmly squeezed her smooth thighs. That was his favourite thing, the way her thighs felt in his hands.

She giggled.

But, before they could go any further, they heard the locks on the front door click and they scrambled to their feet as Simone and Nolan walked into the loft.

Mike expertly zipped up the back of Pam's dress before their children walked into the living room.

"What are you both doing home so soon?" Mike said. "The ball game is still going."

"Simone wasn't feeling well," Nolan said.

Mike quickly realized that his fly was open and zipped it up.

"What have you kids been up to?" Nolan said, smirking as he looked from his father to Pam.

"Nothing much," Pam said, clearly embarrassed at the smile Nolan was giving them. "Just watching the game. Saw your pitch."

"Sure you did." Nolan walked over to the fridge. "Want a beer, Mike?"

"No, thanks."

Simone went to check on Malia.

"All okay?" asked Nolan when she came out.

"Fast asleep."

Mike got his and Pam's shoes from the hallway closet.

"Are you guys leaving already?" Simone asked as Pam picked up her purse. "I was going to make some tea."

"Another time," Mike said. He kissed Simone on the forehead. "I want to head home before rush hour traffic. "Give that baby girl a kiss for us."

"Will do," Nolan said.

"Bye, you two," said Pam.

Nolan laughed as he closed the door behind them. He always got a kick out of seeing his father with Pam. Neither of them were experts at public displays of affection. They still had a hard time letting people know that they were together. When they announced that they were getting married, Nolan and Simone had teased them relentlessly.

"I'm just glad you both are finally out in the open," Nolan had told his father. "It was getting pretty lame watching you both pretend that you haven't been living together for years."

Nolan walked back into the kitchen still chuckling to himself. "I think our parents were about to smash on our couch before we came in," he said.

Simone squinched up her eyes in disgust. "Oh God! I don't want to even picture that ever."

As they both broke down into exhausted laughter, they heard Malia cry out.

"I'll put her back to sleep," Nolan said, "while you think about our parents doing it in our house. On our couch. Where we sit."

"That is so wrong!" he heard her say as he walked into Malia's bedroom. "Oh my God, she left her cardigan, too!"

Nolan picked up Malia. She smiled at him when he sat down in the rocking chair by her bed. She snuggled into his arms as he rocked her. He heard a knock on the front door.

"I bet it's my mother," Simone yelled out. "She's probably back for her sweater."

He looked down at Malia and stroked her hair. She looked up at him with such pure love. She tilted her head slightly, waiting for him to sing to her. He wasn't much of a singer and mostly knew only rap songs by heart.

The one song he knew well enough to sing was The Beatles' "Here, There and Everywhere." His mother had sung it to him often when he was a boy. It was the song he and Simone first danced to as husband and wife, the song he softly sang to Malia after her delivery, while Simone slept. "Here, There and Everywhere" was the only song Malia would fall asleep to if she was having a restless night. He sang to her now and, by the chorus, her eyelids were heavy. Before she finally passed out in his arms, he took a deep breath and gently kissed the top of her head.

"You smell like heaven, MalMal," he whispered.

He got up slowly and tucked her back in her bed.

He walked out into the living room and saw Simone sitting at their dining room table with a man who was dressed like a janitor. He was boisterously talking to her while drinking from her favourite mug. He recognized the voice from somewhere but wasn't sure what was happening or what he was walking into. Simone sat still with her head down. As Nolan got closer, he could see the 14/88 tattoo on the back of the man's neck and felt a cold chill. He knew that rusty voice. He knew who the man was.

Rowan turned. Nolan saw the gun pressed against the side of Simone's stomach.

"There he is," Rowan said with a sinister smile. "We were wondering when you were going to come out."

Nolan had never seen Simone so petrified. Her eyes pleaded with him to do something. He felt his stomach twist as he watched her look down at the gun. He stood in the middle of the living room unable to react.

"Rowan," he finally said. "What are you doing?"

"Nothing," Rowan said smiling. "Just having a lovely conversation with your wife. Telling her about the times when we use to roll together? Had to catch her up on what her hubby was like in Halifax. Did you ever tell your wife about the good old days?"

Nolan kept his expression stony as he tried to figure out what to do. His cell phone was still on the counter by Simone's purse. He didn't know if he could reach it without Rowan hurting her or the baby. He couldn't risk it.

"Sit down, Nolan," Rowan said bluntly. "Join us. Tell your wife... what's your name, darling?" He jabbed the gun into her stomach.

"Simone," she whispered.

"Ah, Simone. Sounds a little ghetto for such a pretty thing like you." He used the gun to caress her face. "I used to know a Simone back home. She was a nigger whore that used to suck my dick for a five-piece. Do you suck dick, Simone?"

Simone shrank away from him in disgust.

Nolan wanted to smash his face in, but Rowan stuck the gun back into her stomach and laughed.

"Nolan, you never told me that you were into black chicks. I mean, had I known that you were a nigger-lover all that time, I would have beaten the shit out of you and we wouldn't be sitting here having this friendly conversation."

"What the fuck do you want from us?" Nolan said.

"Nothing," he said smiling. "Not a damn thing. Just here chatting with your wife. Telling her about all the shit we used to get into. Remember that nigger faggot we beat up? Whoo! The way you swung that bat. That shit was fucking beautiful!"

Nolan could feel his heart pounding in his ears.

"Did he ever tell you about that, sweetheart?" he said to Simone. Long tears spilled from her eyes. "Did he tell you that back in the day he ran alongside me and my crew? Nolan was a fucking beast! And the shit he would say—"

"It's all shit," she spoke up.

"What's that, honey?" he said jabbing her again with the gun.

"You heard me, you piece of shit," she said. There was venom in her eyes. "What! Did you think I didn't know about Nolan's past? Did you think that I lived under a fucking rock? I read every news article. I even pulled up the court transcripts when you beat and killed that homeless guy. So nothing you plan to tell me is anything new."

Nolan looked at Simone in shock.

She was sneering at Rowan as if she wanted to claw his eyes out, but she kept her composure. "I knew my husband long before you ever met him," she said calmly. "I had him before you even laid an eye on him. The Nolan you knew was not the Nolan I've known all my life and not the person sitting here. So whatever you have to say to me is as much a waste of time as you are a waste of space."

She then looked at Nolan and he could see the fear in her eyes. He knew that she was really terrified by the whole situation.

"Wow!" Rowan said. "You got yourself a 'ride-or-die' bitch! I can see why you decided to roll in the dirt with this mulatto cunt."

"Shut the fuck up, Rowan."

"Oh no… is the Nolan I know bubbling up?" he mimicked, laughing. He waved his gun in the air. "You know… maybe if I got a taste of your little piece of action here, I'll see the light too."

Nolan swiftly moved towards him but Rowan slammed Simone's head on the table. She yelped in pain when he grabbed her by the hair, pulling her head up.

Nolan could see blood trickling from the side of her head. "Don't hurt her," he screamed. "Your beef is with me, not her. Just leave her alone."

"The way you left Tess alone?" he said, smiling. "Did you leave Tess alone, Nolan? I told you to sit down."

Nolan sat down on the chair by the wall. He finally realized what this was all about.

"I'm not Kyle's father," he said steadily.

"Bullshit!" Rowan yelled. "All those cheques from Griffith Management! Tess and Kyle was the reason you turned on me! You think I'm a fucking idiot? I know everything now!"

"You know nothing, Rowan," Nolan said. "Yes, I sent money to

Tess over the years because she had no one to help her. I testified against you because it was the right thing to do. You fucking killed the guy! Even when I tried to pull you off him you beat him to death. You were out of control and, if I hadn't taken the deal, Tess would have been sent up right along with us.

"And yes, I was with Tess, but I'm not Kyle's father. She got pregnant before we got together. For a while, I thought Kyle was mine. That's what she told me... but the night before we got arrested... before all that shit went down at the dock... she told me the truth. She didn't know if Kyle was yours or Bryce's—"

"Bryce!" Rowan said loudly. "Get the fuck out of here with that. Bryce could barely tie my shoelaces without shitting himself. There's no way she was fucking with Bryce."

"I don't know what to tell you," Nolan said. "It's the truth."

Rowan put his face in his hands.

Simone was coming to. She lifted her head up. She almost fell off the chair.

"Simone... Si," Nolan said, rushing to her.

He grabbed her and they both fell to the ground. He held her tightly as she trembled and started to sob. She began to hyperventilate.

"Rowan, I need to take her to the hospital. Just let us go...Please!"

Rowan looked down at Simone curled up in the fetal position and nodded. Nolan slowly helped Simone to her feet.

"Where's Tess?" Rowan asked him. "That's all I need. Just tell me where she is."

Nolan knew exactly where Tess was. He had helped her with her deposit. He'd set her up in Vancouver. She was doing well. Kyle was doing well. She had a job and they had a new life and he didn't want to take that away from them. He couldn't do that to Tess.

"I don't know where she is," he lied. "I haven't spoken to her in years."

"You were never a good liar." Rowan pointed the gun at Simone. He shot her twice in the back.

Simone tumbled to the ground.

Rowan walked towards Nolan and shot him once in his chest.

Nolan stumbled before falling next to her.

▶

SIMONE GASPED FOR AIR. She could feel the baby twisting and turning. She felt pinned to the ground. She barely had enough strength to turn her head to Nolan. She started muttering to herself. Her eyes twitched frantically until they slowly closed.

Nolan dragged himself closer to her. He grabbed Simone's hand. "Not yet."

He couldn't feel anything. All he could hear was his pounding heart slowing down. He wanted to call out to her, but, every time he opened his mouth, blood seeped into his throat. Instead, he lay quietly and watched her sleep.

It was what he did anytime she slept: He would lie next to her and count the breaths she took, study her face and the way her hair curled over her left eye. She was the most beautiful when she slept. He lay watching her until all he could do was stare.

▶

ROWAN STOOD over them until they were still. He could faintly hear sirens. He was about to leave when a little girl walked quietly into the living room. She was dressed in a white paisley night-gown and looked curiously at him. She held a stuffed bunny in her hand.

"Hi," she said brightly.

She rubbed her eyes. She stood against the large windowpane

with the moon illuminating her. She looked up at him and smiled, her curly copper-brown ringlets covering her eyes. He watched the little girl look down at her parents. She sat between them like she did most mornings when she crawled into their bed.

"Time for bed, Mama?" she asked.

Her mother didn't answer.

She looked over at her father. His eyes wide open. "Time for bed, Daddy?"

She then nestled between them; their warm blood pooled around her.

Rowan started to shake as he watched her shut her eyes. He quickly stepped back and threw up.

She sat up and smiled at him again. "All done?" she asked him. It was what her mother would say anytime she ate too much and got sick. "Sleepy time now."

He watched her lie back down as the sirens grew louder and louder. He dropped the gun in his panic and stumbled back out the door, into the hallway. He wanted to get away from her. Her ghostly pale face smiled up at him.

As he turned, he saw the neighbour peek through the crack of her door. It was the same woman he'd seen earlier, before he'd pushed into Nolan's apartment. He heard the woman cry out in Mandarin before slamming the door. He headed to the elevator, but could hear the police walkie-talkies down through the elevator shaft, so he backed up and ran to the stairwell and headed down the flight of stairs. At the second floor, he looked up. The police were chasing after him from above. By the time he got to the ground floor he was surrounded.

He was quickly apprehended and arrested.

As he sat on the curb, being read his rights, he watched a female officer hold the little girl in her arms. Her eyes were red and puffy. She was crying out for her parents. The shrill scream of the little girl pierced his ears. The officer was given a blanket to cover the blood-soaked nightgown. He watched the officer comfort the little girl. She still sniffled as she wearily laid her head on the officer's shoulder, but perked up when she spotted him. She lifted her head and rubbed her eyes. She smiled slightly at him.

"Bye-bye," she said, waving to him. "See you later."

74

She cried when she heard about their deaths on the radio, but she didn't go to the funeral. She couldn't bear it. The tears. The chatter of tragedy and the prayers, and how they hoped the murderer rotted in hell. All she could do was sit by the living room window and watch the rain pour down.

She had hated them for so long, but, when she finally gave way to her grief, she was left confused as to why it hurt so much.

"It's because you really loved them," Felicia had told her an hour ago, when they came together to mourn privately. "Despite all that happened, you loved them both."

Felicia picked up the letter from the coffee table and handed it to her.

"Read it," she told her. "I think it's time you did. She wanted you to read it."

"I don't know if I can."

"I think you should."

Jessica opened it and pulled out the letter. She looked down at Simone's handwriting, which brought on more tears. She couldn't bear to read it, but knew that she had to. She needed to hear from her best friend one last time.

Jessica,

I can't apologize for loving him. I just can't. I've loved him all my life. He's been my life force since the moment we met and when he went away it tore me apart and broke my heart. Without him I was just a shell of myself. I was going through the motions but I was empty inside.

When I saw him again my heart started beating again. Each day started to mean something. When he came back to me I couldn't say no to him. I couldn't say no to loving him. Despite everything I know about him and the mistakes he has made. The mistakes I've made. I couldn't see my life without him.

The only apology I can give you is how sorry I am for hurting you. I will have to live with that for the rest of my life and I know it might not mean anything to you but please know that I love you. We both do.

Si

Jessica quietly folded the note and held it. She started to cry. She looked out the window and felt her heart break. She wondered if it would ever be the same now that they were gone. She thought of the daughter they'd left behind. The baby that was gone. And for a moment her world stopped. All time stopped.

EPILOGUE

Mike sat in the empty apartment, looking around. For the third time in four years, he was packing up a home. First, the apartment that he'd given up when he and Pam married, then Nolan and Simone's loft after they sold the place, and now their apartment. He was finally saying goodbye to the complex, the place he'd called home for thirty years.

His back ached. He sat on the last remaining box, but he knew this was it, this would be the last memory left. He looked around the apartment and heard their laughter echoing along the empty hallway to the bedrooms. He looked over, thinking that it was them—that it was their spirit he was hearing, but it wasn't. It was Malia running back into the living room.

"Grandpa, are you ready to go?" she asked him. "We just have this one last box, right?"

"Yes, baby," he said, smiling at her. "Where's your grandmother?"

"She's saying goodbye to Mrs. Wang. She told us that she'll meet us by the elevator."

"Okay," he said picking up the last box. It was lighter than he thought it would be.

When he got to the elevator he watched Pam hug Mrs. Wang goodbye. She was the last tenant left from the old days. All the old neighbours were long gone. Pam walked quickly to them past their old apartments. She looked at Mike and smiled, tears brimming.

"Let's go," she said when the elevator door opened up. "Did you check to make sure nothing was left behind?"

"Yup." He pressed the button for the lobby. "This is the last of it."

When they got to the car, Malia crawled into the back seat and Mike put the box next to her. He looked at her and smiled. With a tilt of her head, she smirked at him. She looked so much like Nolan but was everything like her mother.

He took a deep breath. He didn't want to get emotional. Malia always hated it any time he cried. She said that, every time he cried, she felt like crying and she had nothing to cry about.

He closed the door and got into the driver's seat and gently took his wife's hand before starting up the car and driving down the driveway.

Malia looked back at the buildings. She was going to miss them. They had been her home for over four years. But Grandpa promised that they weren't going far. She would still see her friends when she went back to school in the fall.

She turned around and started to rifle through her messenger bag, which was stuffed with old music cassette tapes that had belonged to her mother. Her grandmother had given them to her a year ago, when she turned six. She had been elated to see something that belonged to her mother. While she had videotapes of her father to watch, she didn't have much from her mother. Only a few photos of her as a child, a few pictures of them after they got married, and her music tapes.

She hunted through her cassette collection until she found the one she liked best. It was called a mix tape, her grandmother had told her, and it had songs her mother had taped from the radio. It had *RMofH* scratched on the label. She had asked her grandparents what *RMofH* meant but they were just as clueless. She wished her mother was there to tell her what it meant.

She rewound the tape to the beginning and then put in her earbuds and pressed the play button. She listened to the song she had taped from the radio yesterday. It was her new favourite. She hummed along before singing loudly to Justin Bieber's "Baby." The car continued past the houses as she sang at the top of her lungs.

They took the shortcut through Truman Road down Bannatyne Drive. It wasn't a long drive but had lots of twists and turns. Mike finally slowed the car down and they parked in front of their new home—a small bungalow at the corner of the street.

Malia stopped singing and watched Mike smile at Pam before he reached over to kiss her. She stuck out her tongue and made a face at them. She hated every time they kissed. Kissing was gross.

Instead, she kept singing until the song ended. By the next pause, the song repeated and repeated and repeated. She had filled the entire tape with the same song. She continued to sing until the tape stopped. Malia looked at the faded red battery light on the side of her Walkman and then sighed.

She looked up and out the passenger window to see the new house. It looked bigger than the pictures on Aunt Dana's computer. The thick hedges that lined the front yard and the big red maple tree that stood beside the driveway were a little scary. She held her breath for a moment. The leaves danced gently in the summer breeze.

"Grandma, will they be here with us?" she asked. "What if they don't know that we're gone? They'll be able to find us, right?"

Pam looked across at Mike, who continued to hold her hand, then turned towards her granddaughter and nodded swiftly. "Yes, baby," Pam said. "Wherever you go, they'll be there."

"Okay," she said taking a deep breath before she opened the passenger door. "I'm ready to go inside now."

She got out of the car and ran to the tree to get a closer look. As she touched the trunk and looked up, the leaves stood still for a moment. She lay down beneath the tree in the tall grass, looking up. The wind picked up again, the leaves swayed back and forth again.

Feeling the warmth of the sun on her face, she closed her eyes and began mimicking a snow angel as the sunlight beamed down on her.

■

ACKNOWLEDGMENTS

Writing *By The Next Pause* has been an incredible journey. My motto throughout the entire process has been, *"Fashion characters without asking permission. Construct universes without a manual. Create a story worth telling."* It has carried me through so many peaks and valleys while writing this novel.

Simone, Nolan, Pam, and Mike have been characters in my mind for years. I have tried countless times to construct their universe but had never found the right way. Five years ago, I realized that unless I take that leap and fully commit to this experience, I would never be able to write this novel. It's a decision that I have never regretted and an absolute dream come true, being able to bring these characters to life.

I don't think I could have done any of this without God's grace and strength. He has kept me focused and determined to push through the noise and to tell this story. I am forever thankful.

I also couldn't have gotten through countless hours of writing, editing, and all the highs and lows of creating this book without my husband Anthony Farrell. He gave me the confidence and means to follow my dreams. None of it could have manifested without his continued love and support. Thank you, my love!

Thank you to my children, Avery and London, who empowered me to follow this path. Thank you for being my biggest cheerleaders. I hope you will be proud of my novel when you're finally old enough to read it.

A special thank you to my editor Michael Kenyon who worked with me to shape this novel. Michael, you are the Harold Latham to my Margaret Mitchell. You took a chance on me and I am eternally grateful for all the time, knowledge and expertise you brought to *By The Next Pause*. I couldn't have done it without you.

I'm especially grateful and thankful to Ingrid Paulson for designing the beautiful and thoughtful cover for *By The Next Pause*. In one swoop, you've created a cover that completely conveys everything this book is. You are an absolute genius!

I would like to send out a special thank you to Prof. Franz J. Vesely and the Estate of Viktor Frankl for permission to use *Man's Search for Meaning* and Lauryn Hill and Hal Leonard Corporation for the use of "Nothing Even Matters". Your words inspired me while writing this novel and being able to use them is deeply humbling and much appreciated. Thank you!

To my lit squad – Tracy Stapleton, Jaime Hedges, Dana Pupkin Sebastian, Marion Smith, Salpi Tintle, and Jennifer Hatvani. You all had the difficult task of reading this monster of a book, in its earliest stages. Through this process, you saw my vision and provided me with immeasurable insights that helped shape *By The Next Pause* into the book it is today. Thank you for all of your help and support.

A special shout out to Marion Smith: You went beyond the call of duty for me and I cannot express in words how much I love you for all the help and advice you gave me throughout my entire process. Thank you so much for all the late night chats, when I doubted myself, and all the help with my manuscript towards the end. I am forever grateful!

To my mother, Laverne Sinkia, for making sure my patois was on point and my father, Robert Sinkia, for all of his advice.

Thank you both for listening to me ramble when I doubted my ability to make it to the finish line. Most importantly, for always believing in me. You always told me that I was a writer. It took me a long time to believe you but I'm glad that I finally did.

Thank you to Aimée Sloggett, Brenda Myers, Kim Collier, Dee J. Adams, Desiree Thomas, Antoinette Julien, Katherine Torrez, Sandra Barton, Julie Cupp and her incredible team at Formatting Fairies, Jennifer Radford, Sheree Guitar, Marco Timpano and Anna De Angelis for all of your assistance and advice.

Last but definitely not least; I would like to thank all of my friends and family who have supported me from the beginning. Your notes of encouragement and words of wisdom gave me life! I am truly ecstatic that you're finally able to read *By The Next Pause*. I hope I make you proud.

One final note to my readers; thank you for actually reading *By The Next Pause*. The fact that you've chosen to take this journey means the world to me. My only wish is that after reading, the story and its characters have galvanized your hearts the same way it has mine.

For more information about this book and upcoming releases, please visit www.gbartonsinkia.ca.

AUTHOR BIO

G. Barton-Sinkia was born and raised in Toronto, Ontario. She went on to earn a Bachelor of Arts degree at Carleton University's School of Journalism before moving to Atlanta, Georgia. Prior to her return to Canada, she was a Vice President at a major California bank before finally venturing out to become an author. Outside of writing, she enjoys learning to play the guitar, making wicked awesome playlists and dabbles in cooking Caribbean cuisine. She and her husband share a home in Toronto with their two rambunctious children and their dog Moose.

Visit her at www.gbartonsinkia.ca.